BEASTSLAYER:
Rise of the Rgnadon

and other tales

CHRIS TURNER

This is a work of fiction. All the characters and events portrayed in these stories are either fictitious or are used fictitiously.

Cover Art: Nele Diel

Published by Innersky Books
www.innersky.ca

Copyright © 2017 Chris Turner

All rights reserved.

ISBN-13: 978-1-927117-96-5

CONTENTS

1 : The Dragon of Skar   5

2 : Dragon Lords   55

3 : The Huntress of Caerlin   213

4 : Enchantress of Rurne   321

5 : Ahrion's Minions   351

6 : Beastslayer: Rise of the   383
Rgnadon

7 : Curse of the Kraken   699

THE DRAGON OF SKAR

Know, oh prince, that between the years when the oceans drank Atlantis and the gleaming cities, and the years of the rise of the Sons of Aryas, there was an Age undreamed of, when shining kingdoms lay spread across the world like blue mantles beneath the stars. Hither came Conan the Cimmerian, black-haired, sullen-eyed, sword in hand, a thief, a reaver, a slayer, with gigantic melancholies and gigantic mirth, to tread the jeweled thrones of the Earth under his sandaled feet.

— *Robert E. Howard*

Conan, seized with a sense of homesickness for his native Cimmeria, makes his way back from Asgalun with the bowman Subotai after dealing with the wicked cult leader Thulsa Doom. Seven days ago, they left the wizard Kilka in his valley, he who had also given them considerable aid against Thulsa Doom. Even though they had asked him, he would not leave his place of heritage, for as he had been born there, he vowed to die there. Having dodged unpredictable Argossean hill tribes and feral predators, the two heroes carve a path more or less due north to Corinthia.

Two day's march out of the city of Korshemish, they find themselves less than a league away from the remote Ophirean border in the high mountains of Mirdash. Here, safe trails are few and inhabitants are even fewer. The territory is unknown to the Cimmerian; he and his companion are eager to quit this bleak region and seek the relative comfort of the Ophirean steppes . . .

CHRIS TURNER

I : The Mountain of Skar

It was a cruel march for Conan and Subotai that day. They had set a monstrous pace for themselves and now they had covered long leagues through the bleak hill tundra of the Ashikar region. Twilight was almost upon them. The weather had taken a turn for the worse; a savage wind gusted and plied sheets of icy rain against their faces, which felt no less biting than pinpricks of hail. Fog-wisps obscured the landscape and despite the lashing rain, they could barely see ten feet ahead of them. The rocky path was thin, unrelenting and twisted. One false step and a wayfarer could find himself tumbling down a steep defile or a bottomless pit. Jagged mountains reared around them like shark fins. But they could barely see these, being shrouded in wispy clouds. Above the timber line, barely any vegetation grew to offer the two shelter from the biting rain.

The sky grew darker by the minute; now they knew they would have to seek shelter soon or be prey to roving beasts.

Conan guessed before they tackled that mountain that it was not in their best interests to engage heights so late in the day, but youthful overconfidence shrouded his wisdom. It was not less than an hour ago that Subotai had agreed to plod onward, despite his qualms. Conan had seen the doubt in his companion's eyes—indecision as this went against the easterner's better judgment. The Hyrkanian's trust in him was high enough that he would follow him to the grave. This was Subotai—thief and archer, lynxish renegade from faraway Hyrkania. The agile bowman carried a silver scimitar at his side, a deadly bow on his back and was the best archer this side of Zamora. Nigh a moon ago, he and Conan had together raided an accursed temple of Set, one of Thulsa Doom's headquarters, right before the evil overlord Rexor's astonished eyes.

It had been a grand adventure. And disastrous . . . culminating in the death of Valeria, Conan's beloved mate.

The Cimmerian was proud to have Subotai as a traveling companion and would often look with approval out of the corner of his eye at his perfect practice shots. Subotai was not one to bandy words; he was quick and cunning, an intelligent tactician and fearless hunter. There was something unspoken that hovered about him, like a voice whispering of a darker past, as if the warrior within guarded a secret that was both dark and mysterious. Conan made shrewd guesses that perhaps at one time, in another life, Subotai was not a thief, but a noble warrior plunged into the chaotic, cruel Hyborian world, grown up with the inflexible tenets of caste imposed on him and wounds that would never heal. An awareness withal that his current profession as thief and renegade was made to cover up his identity, an odd path to have taken, to say the least.

Conan himself stood two heads taller than the sleek, mustached Subotai. Even after such a brutish march, his blue eyes blazed opal-fire and the dark mantle of his hair ran wet with water. There was an aura of power about his figure; chiseled into his harsh features was not cruelty, but the grim memoirs of the goreish frenzy of a thousand battles. Clothed in high boots, tough leather trousers and a leather jerkin, Conan had discarded his helm long ago after the last battle with Thulsa Doom and his thugs. By his vengeful hand, Thror and Rexor had both perished in pools of blood. As they deserved. Thror, impaled by a Cimmerian-made trap, Rexor by the gleaming blade of the barbarian's own bloody sword.

The rain poured down heavily and Conan's jerkin was drenched. His boots squished at every stride. Both warriors fought to slosh through deep puddles and muddy streams that were quick to be fed by the moody storms. It made the going treacherous. With hair flattened to their skulls, the two together looked like a pair of drowned rats hobbling on a cow path.

The Mirdash range was where they trudged, particularly, the shins of *Skar* mountain. Had the Cimmerian known his geography better he could have turned east to better mountain passes. Nor did his Hyrkanian comrade guard such knowledge, for his experience with these far westlands was slim.

"By Crom!" muttered Conan. "We should have left this grizzly

8

mountain behind long ago."

Subotai gave a sour grunt.

Conan pondered his sudden whim to trek to such remote backward country when he could just as easily waste himself in the decadence and opulence of Shadizar and cities like Asgalun.

The hill barbarian grimaced wryly. He had given up the thought long ago . . . the life of pampered civilization was not his calling.

It was then that they spied a strange if not disquieting sight: a long stake driven into the center of the path. It teetered in the wind and held various ghastly cargo. From top to bottom dangled a grotesque array of skulls—human—corded with their own dry-rotted flesh. The skulls all chimed against one another as the wind lashed them. Not fresh were these but still sickening-sweet, at least within any perception of reason.

For a long moment, Conan brooded idly. The sight was not pleasant, or altogether unfamiliar; indeed it brought up ghastly memories of a place far away—long moons ago . . . *fleeing for his life, lost in the stifling, heat-drenched jungles of faraway Kush. A poison arrow spiked in his thigh, and his body burning in fever. Delirium and despair were but two parallel states he moved between like sleep and waking. He had managed to escape his pursuers but for how much longer? The barbaric rhythms beating in the fetid air nauseated him; the inhuman chanting sickened his soul. He could see the ghastly spears of tribesmen, the freshly carved animal and human heads bobbing on pikes, rearing grotesquely above the mist . . . he could hear the slither of serpents all around him. The pad of stealthy feet as the long-lost jungle-tribe stalked him. Headhunters...cannibals!*—Conan snapped himself back to reality—no less eloquently were these heads garnished on sticks than the gory pumpkins that gazed back at him then.

He tore himself away from the sight with a shudder.

"What do you suppose it means?" he asked Subotai.

The archer, who had been studying the display, merely shrugged. His only response was a grim croak. "A grisly warning—an omen to all who would pass here."

"You think?" growled Conan. "Adequate sign for us to stop where we are for the evening and seek shelter?"

"In this?" Subotai peered up, grimacing. "Without shelter? We'd die of exposure."

"Then, let's keep on!"

The two took up their cheerless march...the path wound ever onward and upwards through the ominous peaks.

It was not long after, beyond a sharp bend, that they discovered a dark cleft in the mountainside. The gap would allow a single man entry, which at least looked dry, but was blacker than night. It cast an unearthly shudder up Conan's spine. This was not any hole he would enter by choice. Drenched and dispirited, he agreed, however, that it was worth a try; perhaps it was their only choice this side of the pass for shelter, if such existed on this lonely, forsaken road.

Conan set a foot into the crevice. His broadsword clutched in bare fist, naked steel bared on the possibility that it was inhabited by some horror or other. A risky step, considering they had no light or torch to guide them, yet Conan had stuck his nose into many a dark hole in his day.

Long moments ticked away. Subotai poked his head inside the gap, his ears perking at an appraising grunt from inside. The Cimmerian motioned him in with a wave of his fist. A musky odor permeated this cavernous space. But more importantly, Conan tested with his feet and found the floor dry and not befouled with fetid pools. He began clearing a spot in the middle of the cave with his boot heels while Subotai worked to spark up a small fire, scratching on pebbles a piece of flint he kept in his waist belt. In good time, he had some dry leaves crackling to life, gathered from a corner. He ripped some dry branches off a ragged tree that had sprouted out near the doorway, and made two small torches. Stabbing them into the ground, he and Conan piled stones around the bases to keep them from falling.

In the grim, ruddy glare, the adventurers sat and brooded. They found the cave cozy enough, though small and roughly circular with rubble strewn along the sides. Best yet, the cave was dry. The flames cast eerie, phantom shadows on the walls around them. On the facing wall, primitive drawings, ancient beyond belief, gaped at them. They were carved with some manner of crude tool. An ancient image depicted a cave bear chasing an antelope; another a huge pterodactyl locked in flight for prey of its own. Glyphs of some lost language were scrawled underneath the creature and aside the depictions. A set of small animal bones, ribs and a battered skull, were strewn in a shadowy corner, parched and brittled with age. The Cimmerian's boot heel made short work of them. Aside from these somber tokens, the cave appeared unoccupied, or at least of man or beast, much to their satisfaction.

A dark passage wound to the left; yet neither of them felt much inclined to explore its mysteries at this late hour.

They had only some bread and mutton on their persons, which they skewered on sticks and roasted over the torches. Their hunger was savage enough that they forgot their bedraggled plight and ate like ravenous wolves. They washed down their meal with bitter Kothian ale leftover from their canteens. Of this, they drank sparingly, for neither knew when they would find fresh water again—especially if the storm continued in this miserable fashion, churning the streams to mud along the way.

They finished their meager meal in good time and sat back on their haunches, watching the storm rage outside. The night deepened. To dispel the gloom they traded stories, but the attempts at cheer were half-hearted, especially for Conan, who still pined for his lost mate Valeria, fallen to one of Thulsa Doom's enchanted arrows. Even the Hyrkanian's mirthful banter could not brighten Conan. Their conversation dwindled and they curled up not far from the wall and went to sleep.

The elements would argue otherwise. Outside the wind howled and the rain beat down in relentless torrents while shafts of lightning arced across the sky and sprayed light through the gap. In the absence of moon and stars, the cave remained wholly dark.

Conan slept in fits and starts. In his dreams, he heard inhuman chanting fill the spaces, accompanied by dreadful, prosaic drumbeats. The sound clutched at his sanity like claws scraping against a marble pillar. On a mind-numbing mission it droned without avail, and there were screams—hideous, bloodcurdling wails that clawed at the background. Was it the souls of the dying who had suffered on the stakes outside? How could such be a dream if he were awake and he was still hearing the nightmarish symphony?

He jerked himself upright. Snatching up his sword, he trained his keen Cimmerian eyes on the gloom. But there was nothing to be seen or heard. Only the eerie patter of the rain. He shrugged off the experience as simple imagination. But such was not easy to do—for there was that horrible drum again, beating, thrumming, and the ghastly voices with it, distant yet human.

A slimy shiver crawled up Conan's spine. He shook his comrade awake. A quick signal from the barbarian brought Subotai to silence. The Hyrkanian perked up his ears, scowling. He too thought to hear the sounds, but could not be sure. He motioned Conan toward the back exit. Instantly, he leapt to his feet, crouching on the balls of his feet. Conan, no less wary, hauled himself to the far wall. He grabbed one of the torches. The punky wood still had a tip of glowing embers, with which he lit another and passed it to his comrade.

Subotai's razor senses were keyed; he pressed an ear against the cave wall. Conan guessed he heard his own heartbeat, distorted and amplified many times, but it was the accursed drumbeat that came as the most disturbing.

Conan did not like the look of bewilderment in his friend's eyes. He had seen that look before, when they were knee-deep in terror in the temple of Set filled with dreams of plunder. His comrade had looked upon the visage of the guardian serpent; in that blink of an eye, he comprehended the fullest horror of its existence. There were drums in that incense-filled chamber as well, throbbing, pulsing, echoing with the beat of madness of Thulsa Doom's sinister snake cult.

With an unpleasant scowl, the Cimmerian beckoned Subotai follow him through the crevice on the other side of the cavern. He disappeared through the unexplored passage. The Hyrkanian grabbed a torch of his own, ducked, and hesitated before stepping tentatively through.

The passage was narrow and Conan could feel cool drafts whisk against his face. It had a peculiar odor; a foul, fetid smell of deep unexplored subterranean passages. There was something foreign there too: like a tinge of smoke or traces of salts or minerals...or some kind of offensive incense.

Conan grimaced. The drums grew louder. He and Subotai skulked along the narrow shaft like ghosts. They saw a pale glow cast ahead on the wall at waist height.

Approaching stealthily, the two drew their weapons. They found the source of the light dimly revealed: a gleaming, tawny trail cut through a thin slit in the cave wall. No wider than a man's fist. Taking turns, they crouched and glared through.

A dire scene presented itself.

Far below in that great torchlit cavern, a horde of hideous, ghoulish figures cavorted around a chained monster—a mammoth, scaly, dragon with huge wings. It had great taloned paws and long, sinuous tail. Dwarfed by the gigantic creature lying at the cavern's far end, the ghoul-like creatures were mere ants in comparison. These were mountain gnomes. Fortunate for them, this monster was chained, otherwise the cave-denizens would surely have become a quick, grisly meal.

Someone or something had succeeded in coiling heavy chains around the beast's forepaws and cemented the end of each link solidly into pure stone. The fact that these chains were huge was awe-inspiring—chains beyond imagining, even at this distant vantage. Who or what could have manufactured such things, was beyond doubt a miracle worker indeed.

The mighty dragon lay on a great basaltic mantle, surrounded by hot, sulfurous springs on three sides. This explained the pungent smell in the air. Islands of rock made risky stepping stones amid the death-dealing pools. The fumes were ill to the lungs and Conan guessed the merest touch could sear flesh.

He could see the unholy guardian; it had eyes of a lobster, antlers of a deer, the body of a snake. The creature was wedged back tight against an almost sheer rock face carved with a smattering of macabre idols and totems. Winged beasts depicted demons poised in flight; sylphs and trunked gods and fanged creatures filled the spaces in unnatural poses. Some were red-smeared, tapestrying the wall with visages to grin down upon the captive dragon. Ancient script, beyond the intelligence of Conan, riddled the pagan pantheon. Probably, at one time or other this cavern had been the hell-cult of some accursed race; the gnomes had rediscovered it after the previous civilization had long since vanished upon the falling of Atlantis.

The gnomes themselves were no less ghoulish in appearance. Their malformed skull bones shone through a thin sheen of pale-bluish skin. Each had a bald pate and a single hoary eye near the top of its brow. Though only four feet high, the things sported long greenish wisps of straw-hair that dangled past their humped shoulders like untamed weeds, giving them the appearance of carnival zombies. Conan could not repress a shiver. Ape-like, gangly arms stretched near to knee height. On these, they wore armlets of wood and were near naked except for the odd ragged loincloth or two. Some of them wielded clubs, yet most of this brood clutched dire pikes fashioned of crude sticks on which was thonged a single, sharpened stone.

This was not all the nightmare afforded. A ring of closely-knit stakes penned in a group of humans, dirty, unkempt dispirited souls, wrapped in tattered, blood-smeared rags. They appeared to be hill folk, once fierce, proud tribespeople, now reduced to wretches, judging from the dull look in their eyes and the raw-boned features that stared back. But now they had lost even that and most of their hardened edge, also the suggestion of strong thews: No . . . more a pitiful band of slaves waiting to die, grown hollow and emaciated with despair. They moaned and whined and thrust their heads in their hands and struggled to stay as far away from the gnomes as possible. Especially certain guards who came by at times to taunt and poke at them with long, sharpened stakes. The fiends would caper away in a depraved swagger, cavorting and waving gangly arms, as if drugged with the sap of the unholy lotus plant. A barbaric kingly shape squatted on a dais, staff in hand, flinging orders to the others in a rude tongue.

Conan recoiled, appalled. The cavern's floor was littered with boulders. They leaned on drunken angles, as if they had tumbled down from upon high long ago. Only a broad avenue of smooth stone was paved through the center. On all the cavern's sides, rude pathways had been etched, winding up to numerous dark passageways, from which occasionally the glinting of a guttering torch cut the shadows. From here, more gnomes came and went.

A team of a dozen worker-gnomes busied themselves constructing what looked like another slave pen. It seemed that their god, or master, whatever it may be, desired more blood. The Cimmerian could feel only black rage. Primitive saws made rude work of a pile of hewn trees: the result being a series of sturdy stakes that stood just over man-height. The brutes hammered these stakes into the ground with their stone-thonged cudgels with wooden handles; others bound the stakes together with thick cords. Conan and Subotai watched the construction with angry dismay. Indeed Conan could read the hopelessness drifting through the captives' brains; souls who hungered to be spitted on those freshly sharpened pikes rather than endure the outrages of the gnomes, or fall prey to the ultimate horror that lay before them.

Subotai jerked his head back from the scene, his face was a pale mask of confusion. He spoke words like a ghost, "From where did these one-eyed devils come?"

"The question is more, *when*, my friend," answered Conan dismally. "I think they are stone gnomes." A faint recollection tugged at the back of his memory.

"The stone gnomes of Skar—" he murmured, "spawned from a foul race before the dawn of man. 'Tis said they were created from the joining of ape and demon when such things ran free in the world. Listen, Subotai! I will tell you a tale, one of horror that an Argossean mercenary told me when I sailed the *Karkissian*. His name was Grondel, and he had heard many strange tales from lands faraway...a man learned in the lore of myth of the westlands. I knew him one not to lie. We fled together on horseback from the persecutions of emperor Zrom's horsemen after we landed. On the last night that we were together, we sat round a campfire in the Belendrian woodlands and shared our last meal. He died the next day in an assault by arrows. He told me of the *stone gnomes*—aye, and of their cursed dragon-god!"

He paused to recollect the mercenary's words. "I wouldn't have believed the tale then had he not told me that when he was a young boy, his own brother had been carried away by the fiends, snatched from their home village of Baskalon and sacrificed—or worse—if there was ever a worse—and I could only see by the look of terror in his eyes that he spoke the truth! Subotai, you and I have only snatched glimpses of the terrors of this world." With a bunched fist, Conan launched into the story spoken by Grondel:

"He said a dragon was known to haunt the Ashikarian mountains long before the time of men. A lone survivor of the pre-cataclysmic days, who had subdued the gnome fiends spawned from the earth below. She feasted on them and when they came up from their worm-holes to gather wood or hunt for warm-blooded prey, she would snap them up, for they grew bold, tired of the slugs and worms they were used to feed on below. Hidden in her high eyrie, she would swoop down upon them, catch them unawares. She hated the sight of these dark ghoulish grotesques for they were evil and hardly more than worm-like bottom feeders to her. For an age she routed them out and rid the region of what would be an evident menace, lest they run rampant and terrorize the Upper World and hobble down to the civilizations of the south to feed. Then one day, a crafty wizard, bedizened with silk and hobbling on a knobbly cane, crossed paths with a gang of the gnomes and whispered in their ears. They sought to hew him at first and feed on his warm meat, but he was protected by potent spells and they could not get close enough to him to inflict their ghoulishness.

"'Listen, fiends!' he told them. 'Do not try to eat me! I have a proposition for you all. I will catch and subdue your dragon which haunts your lives. In return, a hundred of your strongest will mine gold

16

for me, for ten years. My witching rod says that there is a precious hoard hidden deep in your foul dens!'

"Of course the gnomes agreed to the wizard's price, so harried by the menace they were. The wizard told a band of their bravest to come out on the night of the new moon when the sky was darkest and the dragon could not see them, and they could hide in the valley of Trembling Shades: 'twas a haunted vale narrowing to a mere few yards. The gnomes did as they were told, and come morning, the peril was on them. From the safety of an eyrie above, the wizard cried out a spell while he urged them to goad the dragon. They did, and many of them perished in the wake of the monster's jaws, but the wizard cared not, for his plan had succeeded. In her fury, the dragon swooped too low and now lay pinned between the parallel cliffs. She struggled hard and long, though the creature could not free herself. The wizard descended, staying well clear of the dragon's breath, and he lit a fire and began brewing a potion in a great cauldron; this conniver was well-versed in the Black Arts. He spilled the elixir at the dragon's feet; quickly he fled to avoid being consumed by his own craft. The dragon, so pinned, was forced to inhale its powerful fumes. She was soon beguiled and slept.

"The wizard had strong ropes tied round the beast's torso. With the help of five-hundred gnomes, they formed a strong chain and dragged her free. Still enchanted, on the wizard's command, the dragon came awake, rising into the sky. She poised overtop a high mountain, the mountain of Skar, the very mountain where we are sheltered, and blasted a great hole with its fierce breath. Weakened, she sank down into the hole, into a domed cavern and lay down as if in trance.

"From the strong ores under the mountain, the wizard forged thick chains and commanded the hundred gnomes he had won to drag the chains overtop the beast and loop them round her massive paws while she sat stunned like a zombie. They melted ingots onto the stone and there the beast lay. The wizard oversaw the construction of a great replacement dome overtop the crater and with the help of arcane magic, sealed it forever, ensnaring the dragon-beast in her tomb under the mountain. They named her a god; they called her *Skar*—Skar of the mountain!

"True to their promise, the gnomes hauled baskets of raw gold from the nether-depths. Now the wizard watched on with gratification, wringing his wrists with glee as he counted his treasure trove. Time passed. He grew careless, foolishly believing the dim-witted lummoxes had not the intelligence to usurp him. One dark day whilst he slept, they crept up behind him in hordes and managed to elude his magical protection. They slew him with their clubs and that night feasted on his flesh, gnawing his bones and spine to white sticks. Then drinking and reveling all through the night, boasting of how they had rid themselves of a greedy wizard and a troublesome dragon. No more must the stone gnomes of Skar slave away for the purpose of the cursed, yellow gold of men that they had no love for! So did Zulkelera, the great dragon, disappear from the earth, along with the mysterious mage and his dark secrets.

"That was when the terror began, by Crom!" Conan rasped. "It all comes back to me. Free to wander under the glare of the moon, the gnomes crept down in the dark hours of the night and raided villages, sometimes journeying for leagues to find their prey. But always they did—by Crom, so Grondel told me—a villager or two scooped up here or a bondsman there from their happy homes. Who would miss them? Only a grisly trace was left—four-toed prints in the mud outside a window, sinister scratches on a broken door, creaking on its hinges, as it wagged in the wind.

"To this day, Subotai, the gnomes worship their God as a demon, offering human sacrifice only to keep it alive and to gloat over its downfall.

"'Tis a fell tale," Subotai hissed.

"That is the tale he told me, by Crom, and I'll not sit by and watch my fellow men suffer gruesome torture at the hand of these inhuman devils!" Conan whipped out his sword and gripped it until his knuckles were white.

Subotai, visibly moved, rose from his crouch. He unsheathed his own weapon. "But what can we do from this height?"

Conan uttered a rancorous grunt. "Nothing. We can follow this passage and see if it leads to a way down there and maybe catch the fiends by surprise."

"It's as good an idea as any. But I don't like it. Suppose we find a way down into the cavern. What then? We're just two against the mass of a hundred, if not more of these goblins, even while holding the element of surprise."

The barbarian would not listen. On long steel-thewed legs, he loped off down the tunnel. The Hyrkanian either must join him in his bold quest or wait in the gloom and watch the final confrontation below.

In the end, the two crept along the passage like bloodhounds, exploring the tunnel together. But after fifty yards the passage petered out to a crawlspace little more than a foot square. Forced to retrace his steps, Conan was reluctant to give up.

With grumbles, he arrived with Subotai back at the slit in the wall. Both paced back and forth, only to witness further atrocities. Several gnomes had dragged five humans before the dragon-god's talons where bubbled three brackish pools. The human sacrifices were stripped of clothing, scrubbed, and oiled with a white cream. Long-fingered, gnomish hands held them, deaf to their cries. They were being prepared for some ghastly rite.

In terror, one of the prisoners wrenched free of his captors. He catapulted sideways, only to fall headlong into a steaming pool. He came up bobbing to the surface, screaming as the boiling green froth burst his eyes and flesh. Soon his body was no more than a mass of stringy pulp. The tumult stirred the dragon. A dim, groggy eyelid creaked open.

The gnomes, seemingly used to this pattern, fled in panic and exultation as two women were snapped up in the monster's jaws and crushed to oblivion. The remaining two, knowing that they had no chance against the creature, raced toward the steaming pools, glad to dive to ready-made doom.

One made it and was scalded instantly, the other was scooped up in the dragon's jaw and the terrible jaws clacked again and did their grisly work. The sickening crunch of snapping bones and the tearing of flesh was not unheard from Conan's and Subotai's lofty perch.

Subotai's face grew white. Conan's liver lurched and he paced the passage like a tiger. The depravity of the creatures of this earth never ceased to amaze him. For brief seconds his mind flickered on a more primitive sense of himself. Risen through the ages of slime, was he once a spawn like these ghoulish vermin? He shook off the chilling thought.

"We must stop this madness," Conan muttered.

"But how?"

"There must be a way."

"Like we should have slept in a different cave?" said Subotai.

"Very funny, thief. We can't just leave them here to perish."

Subotai did not answer. He knew his friend well enough: he was the most feral warrior he had ever met. He would fight single-handedly to the death to save those doomed people, even if it meant his own demise—and even if he only thought there existed remotely a chance. Conan too had one time been a slave—the horrific memories still burned in his soul, and the sight below inspired a volcanic rage in him that Subotai had rarely seen. Subotai had never known a nobler man—and never would.

But the quality of nobleness had its limits—and the grisly situation below was proof.

They heard a clattering of pikes, then a dreadful shambling: of flat paw-feet on stone, padding their way toward them. They wheeled to behold pikes flashing in the gloom. Clubs waved in the shadows. Scores of warriors and scouts bearing torches and weapons leaped out at them from the back of the passageway. The things must have smelt their human sweat—and they snuck up on them from behind, like cannibal pygmies.

With two mighty slashes, Conan laid two of the creatures down in bluish pools of their own blood.

Four more lunged out with snarls on their fish-like mouths. Subotai's scimitar described terrible arcs of agony. Three fell with maimed limbs. Others tripped over the sacrifices and were trampled mercilessly in the oncoming stampede.

Conan and he fought back to back—as valiantly as ever two warriors could.

Yet it was a one-sided battle. No room to maneuver. The tunnel was too crowded. Under a crushing wall of enemy flesh, they were pinned. Weapons were snatched out of their grips; many strong and hairy gnomish hands laid hold of them and tossed them up in the air. Conan's skin crawled at the very touch of these half-men. Carried on high by dozens of arms outside into the rain, they were lashed, hands and feet, to two huge stakes and carted away like pigs up the mountain trail presumably by some secret path to the cavern below. In such pitiless condition, Conan and Subotai entertained no doubts that they too would suffer the same ghastly fate as the sacrifices below.

A hundred yards or so up the path, the two were thrust down into a gaping hole, much larger than the last, and carried into the bowels of the mountain. The fiends had begun to chant, a haunting melody that sickened their souls. All the while the unearthly chanting droned on, and they could hear the fey toll of drums.

Conan twisted his neck round. He gazed back upon a trio of grinning drummers, whose gnarly hands pounded those crude, wooden kegs of drums in unison.

No longer could he see Subotai. They'd taken him down some unnameable passageway—to greet whatever doom the barbarian dared not imagine.

The nightmare continued. Conan only remembered being dragged down corridor after corridor, snaking down, down, ever down stench-ridden tunnels, lit by evil torches, before he was forced to drink a vile liquid. He gagged on the witchwater. It struck his tongue and he tried to spit it out, but they held open his mouth and stuck their foul fingers down his throat and worked his jaws until he was forced to swallow it. Gasping and choking, he shook convulsively. His eyes puffed up like shells. Hideous gnomish faces leered about him from all angles, taunting him with baboon-like sneers. The faces grew larger and larger until his panorama was filled with a loathsome wall of them. He tried to lash out, to claw his way free, but his limbs were like dead weights under their crush, and his power was gone.

The phantom figures blurred in a cloud of nightmare. Apish arms carried him away into the darkness. In one final drunken wheel, the world tottered and Conan plunged into unconsciousness.

II : Games of Skar

Conan awoke in a crumpled heap in a fetid pit. The stench was so bad that he gagged up the meat and ale he had last eaten and felt none the better. Rats and other beastly things crawled among the foul straw piled around him.

The Cimmerian's brain roiled. What manner of nightmare was he in?

The gnomes and the dragon beast seemed now all like phantom figures of a faraway dream. Where was Subotai? Last he remembered the Hyrkanian was hoisted on the shoulders of the gnomes and carried down screaming in the pit. What of the forsaken humans? Doubtless hours dead. How they would all pay! While he still lived, he would see these mongrels drown in pools of their own blood. But grasping the tendrils of hope that tugged at his will, he found the task difficult. Not only the urge to plunge into hopelessness and let the nightmare claim him, but the sense of impossibility of it. Was it not easier to curl up and die?

His hill barbarian's sense of survival would not allow such a cowardly end. The grim situation only fueled him with unheard of rage. A savage lust for survival bloomed in his breast and a cry erupted from his parched lips. He forced himself to stagger forth. He clawed the numbing madness out of his brain and reeled forward toward what looked to be a stone wall in the semi-dark.

The hell-den was large. A massive portal blocked the way out of the pit. A small barred window showed in the door.

Peering through, he saw many gnomes squinting at him, pointing and laughing as if he were some animal on display. In a flood of rancor, the Cimmerian hurtled a fist through the bars and smote one of the fiends square in the face.

Bone crunched and there came a shriek of pain. The barbarian pulled back his bloodied fist. The portal groaned open and an angry gnome with a bloody mashed nose stumbled in, pike in hand: the creature eager to extract revenge on the heathen who had caused him such hurts.

The impulse proved a mistake. Conan was not in the best of moods and he grabbed the near sightless creature, half-blinded in its own blood, and hoisted it over his head and brought it down hard on the crest of his knee, snapping its back. He tossed the corpse away and there it lay face down in the filth of its own fluids with the rats. The vermin came skittering to feed on the fresh meat.

Breath heaving, Conan again felt like retching.

Dismayed at the death of their peer, a score of gnomes plowed their way in past the threshold and lunged at the barbarian. Ripped and torn by their frenzy, Conan battled on without weapon, the air filled with guttural gibbering in an abominable tongue. He heaved gnomes right and left like sacks of grain with his bare hands, heedless of the sharp jabs of their pikes that fell upon him. He dealt them all murderous blows. In the end, twelve lay dead or mortally wounded on the floor, stained in their own blood amid the ordure, and another was on the way before Conan was finally pulled down and his wrists lashed with tight cord. For the life of him, he could not figure out why the creatures did not kill him. Did he not earn the right to die like the others?

He grunted and pondered the question. It was a trivial point at this time.

He was frogmarched through dim torch-lit corridors and soon lost count of the earthen flights of stairs he was forced to climb and descend. What still burned in his brain was the taunting voices of the fiends all around him, driving him on like a brute-beast. They were like locusts, joining up at every turn, until there was a great gibbering mass of them gathered for as far as his eye could see. Even in the madness of the procession, he struck out at them with his roped fists, kicked them with bloodied shins. At the first hint of slack he was ready to tear free and send more of them to hell . . .

But no such event was to occur. Interminable moments later, Conan was shoved into a tight, semi-circular cell. A wooden door thudded behind him. He leaped up to struggle with it, but before he could react, a chain was pulled from the outside and a trap grille opened up underneath him. He plunged down, down through an angled shaft, rolling and bashing, finally to tumble onto a sandy floor, punished with great contusions.

Head spinning, disoriented, he clambered to his feet. Massaging his aching wounds, he groaned. There, nigh a stone's throw above, gnomish cries greeted his ears with great amazement.

He had plunged into another large pit, somewhat of a huge oval-shaped auditorium. The floor was clean and at least had sand in the bottom. Though he was bathed in a sullen reddish glow. Overhead burned great torches set in vats of oil, hung from the cavern's ceiling on stout chains. He struggled to focus on the many hideous gnomish faces that peered down at him from stone tiers high above and off to the sides. Flags and banners rose; the gnomes, perhaps about a hundred and fifty of them, cheered on in their guttural voices. What was it all about? Dismay hit him like mortar.

At the nearest end of the auditorium sat a somber gnome on a high carven stool. He had the look of a monarch about him, with his many colorful baubles strung round his neck and surrounded by ten, hard-faced gnomish guards each bearing club and pike. Conan noted a fiendish-looking sentry with buck teeth-fangs at the gnome's side. The leader appeared important enough, garbed in his fine reed-spun suit, and a plumed, jeweled crown. If only Conan knew, this was Madzgul, the chief lord and dictator of the gnomes. He sat on his dais and glared down with contempt upon the barbarian. He raised a set of gnarly hands in profound gesture; immediately he called for silence. Speaking in a flurry of gutturals, he roared and Conan was glad he couldn't understand the foul language. The dictator told the people of how the gods shone on their kind and how they had been granted the 'gift' of two robust foreign sacrifices. One was to satiate the lusts of Skar, the other to delight and amaze them in their great arena.

The crowd burst into an explosion of applause. Madzgul cast his paw-hands on a gong and a grim trumpet sounded. The mob's howls grew to a thunderous roar.

The games had begun.

By the mercy of a spectator alone, a weapon was thrown into the pit for the human. Conan lunged for it. It was a small, black-hilted dagger caked with dark blood of ages and Conan stroked gratefully its still keen edge. He knew in the depths of his heart that some dire outcome was about to take place.

Not a single horror this day, but a flurry. Conan spat curses. In a split of a second he knew for what awful purpose he had been spared.

The half mangled ghoulish hand that stuck out of the sand should have given him a clue. The grim trails of blood that he now spied turned over in the sand.

Conan looked above and discerned crude, banner-like depictions of a chained dragon bellowing fire set upon a dais. Other gnomes waved banners of grim-eyed carrion fowl. These were betting teams. The Cimmerian heard crude stone coins clink to the change of hands. The wagers were sizable and activity was brisk in the lower seats. He was to participate in gladiatorial battle. To perish here in this grim theater was his destiny.

The Cimmerian did not give in to despair. Nor would he be gutted like some fish freshly hooked. He was Conan—reaver and slayer of demons! If anything, he would deal these vermin such agony they would not forget before they pulled him down to Crom!

The muffled sound of chains rattled from the far end of the pit. He whirled to behold a mammoth iron portcullis being raised by four iron-thewed gatekeepers. What the—?

The rusted bars shook as something tried to tear its way out. Conan saw that some horrid beast was to be his first foe.

But no! It was only a show to scare him. The portcullis sank down in the dirt again. From a nearby gate, another presence emerged. A giant, taller than himself. An ugly brute if there ever was one who sported a face like a mongoose, scarred and gray-pink with years of abuse. A cyclopean eye lay gilded in a shiny ring-laurel. Shin-mail, greaves and copper breastplate draped the muscled body. He held a black, blood-crusted, half pike strapped to his forearm. The weapon seemed an extension of his limb, spiked with crazy fish-hooks.

Conan's lips parted in a feral snarl. The warrior looked very much like the monarch king himself. The Cimmerian frowned. Yes, the resemblance was uncanny—a brother, perhaps? Cousin?

Conan had no time to speculate. The pit fighter strode on log-like legs to face him in the center of the arena. The two glared at each other before the gnome crouched in a fighter's stance. Conan felt a thrill of anticipation ripple through his body. The king Madzgul gave the signal: a gnarled fist, pointed down.

The gnome gurgled, dipped his head, and somewhere a trumpet blared. The creature charged, ramming egg-like skull full into Conan's gut. Taken by surprise, Conan was hurled backward, eyes never leaving the menacing pike. He recovered. He was on his feet before the enemy's wicked fishhook could slice off his outstretched arm.

Conan moved out of reach. The two circled each other like wolverines. Conan showed no emotion, as hopelessly outmatched as he seemed. His puny blade bared in comparison to the gleaming shaft of his adversary seemed a mockery. Nor did Conan show any fear, for he was born and bred in the harsh hills of Cimmeria for combat, his body hardened by years of toil as in his youth, a slave in the mines, wrested from his parents slain by Thulsa Doom's raiders so long ago.

Encouraged by the rich cheers of his fellows, the gnome warrior charged again, becoming impatient with all the dancing about and the circling. Conan felt a familiar whoosh of breath knocked out of his lungs. Again he was astounded at the speed of the fighter. He could not avoid being grabbed by its thick monkey arms encircling him in a bear's hug. Conan managed to gore its sides with a few brief knife hacks, but not enough to do anything of damage.

The gnome, grinning and gnashing, rammed his eye ring on Conan's skull. Conan blinked back stars. Only by some inner intuition did he shake the daze out of his skull and force himself to go slack, wriggling out of the beast's strangling embrace. A moment later he was lifting his weight in a pantherish lunge. An instant was all he needed . . .

He slashed at the thing's eye. The creature's world went black. Conan bent back the weapon-wielding arm, heard bone snap and a gurgle of pain erupt as he jammed the hideous blade up into the exposed lower chin. The steel slid through the creature's mouth and up out the top of its skull. The gnome did a strange saltarello, then fell face first before Conan's feet.

Breath rasping, Conan gripped his blade as if waiting for the thing to rise again. But it did not. There was an unholy pause in the auditorium and the crowd became deathly quiet. Madzgul stared aghast at the broken form of his kinsman. His lower lip trembled, then his crooked teeth showed a baleful blaze of hate and rage. In a single sweep, he raised a jeweled fist to the ceiling, bellowed at the top of his lungs.

The cue was evident: a quick sign for the guards in the dugout to raise the nearby portcullis. A rattling of chains jangled and Conan's eyes grew wide in horror.

Out burst the caged creature, snorting and frothing from the mouth—a beast horrible to behold, uncomfortably similar to the ferocious mountain sloth of the Kothian highlands.

The creature's mouth was split with fangs; a set of horrid spikes bristled on its back like shark fins. Eyes were black and ferret rivets and more like evil gimlets than organs. Its long snout undulated like an anteater's; its bulky torso swiveled like a weasel as it snuffed around hunting for blood. The thing sucked in great lungfuls of air while it pawed the sand in challenge. Without warning, it rushed him at a terrific pace.

Conan thought fast, but there was nowhere to run. He tried to wrest the blade from his fallen foe, but it was absurdly fastened, almost inbred in the very flesh. He cursed with disgust, took long strides toward the wall. The sloth's long shaggy hair trailed and dragged on the sand, leaving terrible brush-like lines in the sand. In a heartbeat it was on him and Conan was almost trampled to death before he could raise his small weapon. Like the steely-nerved hill panther he was, he dove out of the way.

The sloth monster slowed its rush and charged again. The gnome king gave a grunt of satisfaction. Conan caught his breath. He leapt to the side within a hair's breadth of its cruel paws. The snout lashed out and Conan was caught in the shins and somersaulted in the air. He cried out, arched his back and landed unsteadily on his feet.

The crowd whooped in delight. Despite the ghoulish look on Madzgul's face, they were entertained. Never before had they witnessed such acrobatics—or had any of their sacrifices survived the charge of the sloth!

Conan made a savage leap. With a desperate cry he clawed his way onto the sloth's back. Clinging from its fins for dear life, he tried to jam his dagger into its leathery hide as the thing roved round in circles searching for him.

To no avail. He pulled himself along the spikes until he sat astride its neck. He lifted the dagger again and again and dealt the thing a series of vicious jabs. Little did such blows do to its tough hide—he would be lucky if the blade would even penetrate flesh, rather than turn on its shaft and snap off.

Conan's position was precarious. He was moments from being bucked off and gored. He caught a vivid flash of himself in the distance, looking the utter fool, trying to tame a savage beast with a toy dagger. The crowd, absolutely absorbed in their primitive savagery, howled in pleasure at the outlanders' performance.

The beast was too dimwitted to halt and roll over and crush its opponent. Conan was grateful for the fact. True, the sloth was strong ferociously strong—and it finally wrenched its neck to and fro like a rabid dog, flinging the barbarian high into the air.

Conan soared like a rag-doll only to crash headlong into the first tier of spectators, crushing two as he fell. He was instantly catlike on his feet, prepared to fight.

"Time to die, fiends!" he snarled. He brandished his dagger and rained deathly blows among those in the crowd who rose in fright. Those foolish enough to block his path were cut down. For a second, Conan thought to carve a crimson path right to the leader, but he knew he would be quickly cut down. Too many of the king's bodyguard. They were huddled all around him. Even now, Madzgul's guards were leaping down after him with murderous efficiency. Yet killing the chief might bring the regime of his accursed reign crashing down . . .

He chose a safer route, turned, raced below down a long flight of steps, confusing the horde. He bounded out of the auditorium, up another crooked stair. He emerged into a dank tunnel. Behind him, he could still hear the clamor of chaos and confusion, the grunting and snarling of spectators. He laughed in triumph. His voice sounded hollow to his ears. Hardly did he dare to catch his breath, even spare a look back, for he knew the fiends would be quick on his tail for every second he squandered.

A frenzied crew were out for his blood, and there would be no quarter given. Especially after despatching the lord's champion.

Where in blazes was he to flee? These worm holes ran everywhere under this cursed mountain. His only hope was to get out of these sinister tunnels and back up to the surface, to the world he knew. But how? He knew not these frightful burrows. A wave of frustration swept over him. Trusting his Cimmerian sense, he closed his eyes, received the inspiration 'always up'. First right, then left, but he always clambered up.

The choice was wise.

Behind him, he could hear the echoes of footfall of untold pursuers. There were too many tunnels and enemies for him to have any margin of safety. The obvious disadvantage was that these creatures knew the tunnels better than he did. Being shorter and more dexterous, they could navigate the twists and turns with greater ease. He was always slipping on muck or grazing his elbows and fingers on the rough rock, while their clawed toes dug into the earth like wolves and gave them extra spring. He had to duck in low places because of his superior height while they, smaller and squatter, forged on without worry of cracking their skulls or taking out an eye. In these moments, Conan wondered how he had survived all these years in these savage lands. In minutes they would be on him, pulling him down, ripping him to shreds. Having a sudden insight, the Cimmerian ducked into a narrow passage. He flung himself flush to the ground, ignoring the molder and decay. Clutching the dagger to his breast, he searched for a plan, hardly daring to breathe. A flood of footfall passed mere feet from his face.

Eleven foes as he counted them whisked by.

Fools! He breathed a sigh of relief. The maneuver was too easy. Something ominous was waiting to spring. He could sense it. Nevertheless, he knew he must retrace his steps and follow these fiends. They would lead him out of this foul maze.

The Cimmerian was not far off in this guess. He tracked them like a hunter, trailing close enough not to lose them, but far enough away to escape if need be. He had no doubt that as ghoulish a lot as they were, they could smell the scent of human blood from an easy distance.

He passed arched junctions and had to duck wooden beams and dodge posts that held up the roof of rock. His jangled nerves tingled with adrenaline. Occasionally he would wrench his head around at the sound of a sinister squeak or an unwholesome growl. Rats haunted these corridors. He could see their beady eyes gleaming back at him in interest as he raced on.

The gnomes thudded on. The barbarian felt himself lost. Without the sun and wind to guide him, how could he navigate these loathsome tunnels? He might as well be in the dragon-god's stomach now...spare everyone the hassle! He bit his lip, tasting blood.

The troop realized they had lost their quarry. They let up their pace. Conan paused, breath held, before a bend in the tunnel. He could hear them arguing among themselves. Growls, snarls, and whines. There was a thump then a bang. Another cry—a painful one. The Cimmerian grinned, wincing, guessing that the discussion had gone sourly for the one who had spoken out of turn.

Voices drew nearer. The party had split up. Conan stifled a curse. More foes to track, he thought. Quickly, he shot back into the adjacent side passage and crouched in the murk. He scooped dirt over himself to mask his human scent.

Just in time. Six pairs of shambling feet passed by, their jowls snuffling and chanting a war cry. When the way was safe, he crept back to the main corridor. He took pursuit of the remaining party and thanked Crom that they had not decided to explore the passage he lay in . . .

Conan's prayer was perhaps given a little too prematurely . . .

One of the gnomes smelled his man-sweat and deserted the pack to slink up on quiet feet. Catching sight of barbarian's hunching form, he pounced on him with a scream. He brought up his pike, ready to spit the Cimmerian and claim the chief's reward.

The weapon whistled close to the Cimmerian's ear. But Conan had ducked, avoiding the inevitable blow. The thing was slow on the defense, grasping him with great gangly arms and chewing on his neck. Conan cried out. Fangs dug deep into his neck, drawing blood like a vampire. The Cimmerian howled in anguish. He ground his teeth, fighting the urge to gurgle in pain, for it would alert the other hunters. It took every ounce of his strength to throw the thing off, but still it came back, gibbering and gnashing, grinning with outstretched arms and blood dripping from its foul gray mouth full of yellowed teeth. The Cimmerian sidestepped its charge. He countered, stabbed his knife into the apish thing. Now it was off balance and swung on its heels. One blow caught it square in the jaw, a blow which ripped upward to take out the thing's only eye. It hobbled around like an epileptic marionette, holding its maimed organ, seeking to rid itself of the searing pain.

It could not. Conan found it easy to put the creature out of its misery. He leaped onto its hairy back and slit its throat. The thing rolled over, blood spilling from its cloven neck.

Conan's lungs heaved. He was only hopeful that its squeaking tumult had not alerted his ghoulish friends.

No sign of movement in the tunnel. No sound of tramping feet.

Conan ripped off part of his underclothing and bound his ravaged neck. After much anguish, he succeeded in assuaging the blood flow somewhat crudely but not entirely. The initial blood loss had left him nauseous and woozy. Still, he resumed his grisly trek, with teeth-gritted in determination; doubtless others would soon miss their comrade and come investigate. Another roving band finding the battered corpse...they would take up his trail and rout him out. With these grim musings, he loped off in a stumbling shamble, trailing blood, hoping to catch up with the other band before they doubled back.

He did catch up to them. Keeping to the main pathway, the Cimmerian could hear their feverish tramp sloshing through muck and clay. The going was much harder. The corridors were fouled with stench-ridden pools. Conan had to dodge the puddles for fear of being heard, but he tempered his pace and loped on with vengeance . . .

III : A God is Reborn!

A lurid glow penetrated the unholy dark. The pad of gnome feet had faded. Conan crouched down at the threshold and watched through glowering eyes as the troop marched down a rocky path hedged with scattered boulders into the great pit that housed the dragon. At last! His threadbare hope was coming to fruition. He looked upon a familiar sight. They had reached the end of the cavern of the dragon-goddess—as he had hoped. Grimacing, Conan realized that his efforts were bearing fruits, for he knew from here that he could make his way to the surface.

But where was Subotai?

On the cavern's farthest side, zigzagging stone steps climbed to dark passageways. A bowshot away milled more gnomes, coming and going, wielding pikes. The cavern looked even more boundless than what he had remembered.

Conan peered in mingled contempt and wonderment. Ropes and chains hung from a vaulted ceiling in tangled masses. For what purpose he could not guess.

Below, the leader of the descending troop spoke momentarily to some underlings gathered in a tight huddle. He pointed back to the way they had come.

Conan quickly ducked out of sight. After a brief discussion, the troop made their way up the stair to another passage, while another team gathered to tackle the search in other corridors. Conan reflected, tugging at his chin. Fortunately he was not blessed with a surprise party. The act gave him time to consider his options rather than face a one-sided battle. Everything pointed to the fact he must rethink a plan of attack.

With contempt, he looked down into the noisome pit. The dragon appeared to be given to apathy, or perhaps slumber, drugged by the gnome's foul witchwater. Either way it was not his concern, as long as the thing continued to sleep, for it was a fearsome juggernaut, one with which he did not want to cross paths.

The human slave-pen was as before. But now Conan looked upon only half of the crew remaining—a testament that those who did not look dead already were sprawled in grime and filth. They half-clasped each other in despaired huddles. To his relief he spied Subotai among the survivors. A surge of gladness smote his heart. From what he could see of his friend, he was a scraped and bloody mess, arms hanging loosely at his sides. His leathers were blood-tattered and his face looked haggard and pale. But he was still alive and it gave Conan a glimmer of hope—and a sudden impulsive plan.

Gritting his teeth, he contemplated his rescue of the Hyrkanian and perhaps even liberating the other captives in the pen. At least they would have a fighting chance, especially now that the gnomes' forces were divided in a search mission for him. He had first to alert Subotai. But how? He must not alert the guards.

A sudden idea hit him. He scooped up a handful of pebbles and tossed one first, then another toward the slave pen.

His aim was better than good. A quick turn of a monitor's beetle-eye and Conan launched another in another direction. Although battered, Subotai was still alert, and upon the first thwack of the pebble against a post, the Hyrkanian's face crinkled in mirth. His swollen eye opened and he raked in the whole of the upper chamber. He saw, with a cat's eye gleam, his friend crouched in a gloomed passage.

Conan tugged at his left ear. Long ago, they had rehearsed such cues, just for such dire occasions as now, as they had when they fought Thulsa Doom and his minions in the snake temples. Subotai understood that he must divert the guards as best he could, and generally raise hell at the Cimmerian's next signal.

Conan crept from his place of safety: a weaselly, stealthy muscle-bound shape. He slunk down in the pit, staying hidden in the shadows. Anything could go wrong—and likely would. There was little boulder protection here and he hugged the ground, squirming along like a serpent, yet sneaking behind rocks as often as he could to shield his passage. He was almost within a stone's toss of the stockade when he breathed a sigh and steeled his legs for a burst of speed. His success lay in the hands of Crom! A guard was about to turn when Conan burst from his place of concealment. But the Hyrkanian gave a diversionary yell. The gnome started, for he did not tolerate prisoners' outbursts or delinquencies as Subotai did now by grabbing one of his fellow captives and threatening to beat him. Single eye blazing, the guard raced over to club the archer with his pike. The act gave Conan the opportunity to fall upon the creature and deal him blows he would not forget. Digging first fingers into its eye, he pulled, and nearly tore the thing's skull apart. The creature screamed, hobbling about for several electrified seconds before crumpling. Others leapt upon Conan. He pinwheeled, gave them gutfuls of dagger points while parrying pike thrusts. Those he wounded, he hacked and stomped to oblivion; those who craftily dove on his back, he wrenched off with quick twists and shakes and sent them hurtling over his back to their scalding deaths in the smoking pools. He suffered enough pike jabs to seriously undermine any ordinary fighter, but his fury was doubled, despite his not insignificant neck wound. The adrenaline rush helped pull his body tight like a shield to accept the thrusts that fell like pin pricks against a bull's hide. The mountain peoples had never seen such a ferocious fighter or wild display of butchery, and they wondered if this man were another fiend risen from the depths of hell to punish them before the dragon-goddess.

The last of twelve was down and Conan turned his attention to the slave pen. Already shouts and curses had him grinning with expectation. The tramp of bare feet from the upper walkways indicated reinforcements were on their way. Conan wasted no time in dealing with the pen. He jammed three pikes together and started prying apart the stakes. His corded thews bulged. The captives howled, mad with the prospect that they would soon be free.

"Get out! While you can!" Conan bellowed. "All of you!"

Some could not run and they stumbled on shaky legs; others were too weak to escape and fell back in torpor. Subotai pushed past the throng and clasped Conan's forearm. "Cimmerian. You came!" He respectfully wiped the grime from his ashen face.

"As you did once for me, friend," Conan murmured. "I recall hanging from a certain tree in a remote place on a blistering day—a piece of desert meat for crows . . . and from a dim dream came a nimble archer to cut me free."

Subotai gave a haggard grin. "No time to reminisce, Conan. Let's flee this warren and take down as many as we can!"

"I could not have a better idea." Conan turned, snarling. "They stream out upon us like ants!"

Droves of the brutes came on now in crushing numbers, their shambling flesh like scuttlings from the underworld. Gangling arms flapped like reeds in the wind. Inhuman gibbers filled the chamber. Pikes clashed and feet tramped. Death was all around them!

The human captives howled. Some of them fell back into the steaming pools, weakened by excesses of the witchwater. Conan had little hope for these wretches. Others were pitted on pikes. While others cringed back, sinking down in the pen, accepting their defeat and doom.

"Hurry!" spat Conan. "There's no time to waste on this wretched lot. We'll take a last stand before the dragon-god kills us. Let's see how she likes being wakened by the goblin's howling. In the meantime, let's hope these spooks enjoy hot baths!"

"Your sword, Conan!" Subotai snatched up the lost blade strewn in the rags aside the pen and tossed it at him. "I heard them jabbering at the runes carved on its tang and they saved it, thinking it was some magic item, or some kind of talisman."

"It is, Subotai. A gift from Crom. And for you—" Conan tossed him the bloody dagger he'd acquired from the games. The Hyrkanian caught the blade in a fist. "I was graced with this by a loyal fan. Make use of it while you can!"

"The dragon wakes!"

Conan peered about in wonder. The awakening beast's shadow cast a dark drape over the pen and its hunched occupants. The scaled crocodile head and lizard neck towered over them, bobbing like a cobra. Weathered wings crackled like old leather rippling as the chains binding its webbed feet clanked like a rattle of grim castanets. Tumult strained the very stone the massive paws were shackled to. A foul smoke poured from the dragon's fang-filled maw. "Follow me!" Conan bawled. "The guards may still be our last chance! I'll send those swine to hell before I die at the hands of this monster!"

The Cimmerian leaped like a tiger, stretched massive legs in huge bounds. From island to island he hopped amid the frothing pools.

The massive creature was momentarily taken in confusion. Conan strode to its tail, bent down, groping for rocks. The dragon turned full round, rattling chains and cast him a basilisk's glare. Opening its maw to belch fire, it could only emit a cloud of noxious charcoaly vapor. Even that half choked the Cimmerian. The witchwater had seen to the dragon's impotence.

"No, you fool of a dragon! Suffocate your enemies, not me!"

The attacking gnomes thought the overworlder gone mad, talking to the dragon and venturing so close. They uttered low gibberings, if such were a proper word. Their mirth was short-lived. Their gibbers quickly turned to wails. They saw what the Cimmerian planned. He had grabbed a huge rock and lifting it high, smote it down hard on the chain binding the dragon's left talon.

The blow left a gash in the metal, but was nowhere near yielding. Another smash, and yet another, and the link began to show signs of splintering. With a savage roar, the dragon ripped its limb free.

Madzgul, the gnomes' leader, had arrived and gathered his troops. Seeing the barbarian's handiwork, he gave a howl of dismay and issued sharp orders. In obeisance, a score of pike-wielding gnomes rushed to impale Conan. They hopscotched forward, following the madness of the Cimmerian's island-hopping, though with considerably less grace. They hesitated, standing at a position abreast the dragon, confused by the grim look of their age-old enemy. Urged on by Madzgul's rumbling curses, they rushed the Cimmerian, howling in wrath.

Conan was not to be daunted by such freaks. He grabbed fist-sized stones and hurled them at the oncoming mob. Subotai took up stones of his own. Three caught their mark and left gaping skull wounds on the incomers. Moaning, holding gored crowns, many from the throng toppled into the scorching sulfur pools. Others the dragon's jaws claimed, for the creature recognized its oppressors, and its friends.

Many of the enemy swarmed before Conan. They were much too close. Conan was forced to fight them in close quarters with slashes and kicks. Reining supreme, his broadsword sang bloody hymns in the fray. With bloody relish, he hacked out mighty swaths of death. How many of these fools must die by his blade before they learned to stay back?!

"Back, I say! Back!" he roared.

Subotai was backed to a wall, within fire-breath distance from Conan. The way to freedom was separated by a strait of sulfurous water. Sweating and cursing, the Hyrkanian fought valiantly by jabbing with pike in one hand while stabbing with dagger in the other. There were six of them on him at the moment and it would have gone bad for the archer had not a screaming order from Madzgul brought his foes to a screeching halt. They branched off in pursuit, island-hopping in the direction of the dragon-goddess Zulkelera. Subotai wheezed out a puzzled grunt. He gathered his wits and understood that Madzgul had ordered a concentrated siege on Conan—the bigger threat! Cursing the chief's cunning, Subotai chased after them, eager to assist his friend in any way he could.

By strange fate the vanguard had either been gored or killed by the combination of the Cimmerian's hacks and the dragon's jaws. Conan had reached the farthest flank of the dragon and with gigantic leaps crested its huge tail to leap down on the other side. The dragon was not oblivious to this strategy and designed that this savage, brawny-thewed warrior was her savior, not her enemy. She did not crush him with an easy sweep of her tail as she could; rather she turned on the foolish gnomes that drew too close and snatched them in her jaws or spewed them with her breath which was regaining power.

Conan sought another boulder in a desperate crawl. He hadn't much time—he saw his foes circling his new protector, giving wide berth to her breath as they paused to regroup for another attack.

"The cowards will not brave the monster's tail," Conan muttered to himself.

He let tumble another great boulder on the chain. It was forged well, stout and heavy, and only on the third smash did a link give way. Both of the creature's hind legs were free and Conan's foes were almost on top of him—at least those that survived the dragon's jaws and her awakening fire.

"Now, I give you half your freedom, doomgiver!" Conan cried with vindication above the din. "Take the other half and wreak your revenge!"

As if divining the Cimmerian's challenge, the dragon-goddess opened her sharp-fanged maw and uttered a fear-inspiring bellow. The very rock shook to the core and the boulders tumbled down from above, smashing hapless gnomes by the dozens. Conan momentarily caught a glimpse of the night sky. The dragon, using the back wall for support, wedged her hind legs up and heaved with all her strength.

The chains groaned—a baleful creaking tore at the air and iron buckled under the strain.

The chains binding her forepaws slowly began to give. Conan watched in dumbfounded wonder. For the first time on this terrible night he knew triumph. First one link snapped, then another, then the monster's other paw pulled the chain right out of the steaming stone! The beast toppled, searing its snout by its own momentum in the boiling waters. But she felt no pain for her anger at this time was greater than any hurt and her fiery breath superseded the heat coming from the steaming water.

When the beast emerged from the boiling froth, the gnomes stood rapt, for the dragon had sniffed them out and drunk deep of the hot sulfurous fumes. It had the distinct side effect of fully restoring her fiery breath. Now as Zulkelera stumbled on her disused legs, she blew gusts of lethal flame into their midst, blackening boulders and sizzling pools, scorching flesh. The dragon-fire was rekindling! The beast remembered of old her glory and how she had been goddess of the skies, mistress of the roaring winds. Bewitched long ago she had been tricked by an overweening wizard, chained at the hands of these filthy goblins. Her memory ran deep. Though she had lain dormant for an age, the images flashed through her ancient mind in a series of angry pulses.

The gnomes drew back in horror. The sight of the dragon-goddess in all her majesty sent them spinning away aghast. They threw up their hands and scattered in all directions. Some gibbered and howled in their primitive tongue. Others, berserk with terror, clawed past each another, trampling their peers in a mad dash for safety as the dragon rumbled forth with vengeance. Few escaped her wrath, dragging themselves like rats into gloomy corridors. Most were either trampled or scorched into oblivion by her belching fire. Some were even unfortunate enough to personally met her grinning jaws—a swift and terrible end. Either scorched or devoured, each style of doom as hideous as the other.

The cavern was filled with fire—and blood and gore. Charred stone lay blackened under the dragon-fire. No more did the gnomes' witch-water cast a spell over Zulkelera. All the injustice of ages she had suffered for these long years, was now to be repaid. She would know revenge—and the gnomes, her age-old oppressors, would pay dearly for their sacrilege! The dragon-goddess of Skar, once known as Zulkelera, basked in her revenge—as was written in the Khemish scripts of old. The monster's tail slashed, crushing gnomes and the enslaved human captives between swaths of broken stone. Between her mighty swings and stone-scraping talons, the gnomes knew slaughter, as they were forced to plunge headlong into scorching pools.

Conan and Subotai scrambled up the cavern's side, clawing their way up the loose gravel. Each hoped for an escape. They ran headlong into the first passage they found, disoriented for a brief moment, searching for some shelter. But behind they could hear the dragon's path of destruction. The crash of rock, the sear of flames, the cries of the dying. A fork in the tunnel brought them to a sudden halt.

"Subotai!—which, way right or left? Quick! Both look wrong."

The Hyrkanian motioned. "To the left, Conan. Always to the left. In our land, left is lucky."

The Cimmerian gave a sour grunt. "In ours, left always leads to doom."

The Hyrkanian shrugged. "Can't always have it your way. Choose!—tried eastern wisdom or western myth and dogma."

Conan cursed. "To hell with it! As my luck has been terrible, I think I'll trust yours."

They sped on up the left branch. They met more gnomes fleeing through the tunnels. The brutes, being filled with terror, only delayed them for an instant, for such was the barbarian's bloody wrath after a night full of abominations that he cleaved skulls and severed limbs as if they were no more than pesky mice.

The torches had burned down to dim cones and so Subotai acted as scout, leading the way down the tunnel. His eyes, better in this gloom, gleamed like an eagle's. A gaunt-faced Conan took up the rear. Whenever Conan spied gnomes up ahead, Subotai would run back, and together they would hew them down in arcs of crimson, leaving a bloody mash of corpses in their wake. Rats and vermin and other dark things feasted in lavish accord that night.

The passage rose and as they drew farther away, the sounds of the dragon's roars faded. The Hyrkanian uttered a glad cry. Ahead burned a wan glow. The refugees had at last reached the topside. Out of the dank tunnels they crawled. The air was like the sweetest nectar to their lungs. The rain storm had abated. Now a cool wind pulled tattered cloud across a wan yellow sky. A crescent moon was sinking in the western horizon.

Conan felt a sinking sensation. Although they had escaped the gnome kingdom, all was not well, for he felt as if a sinister presence was lurking around the corner. Though he could not hear the patter of footfall, he felt the scores of shambling feet thudding beneath them, hurrying, scrambling forth on some frightful mission.

The ground trembled; he heard the pounding of the dragon-goddess, doubtless fighting for her freedom from her age-old prison.

In the cavern's depths the ghastly beat of drums persisted. The booms were the same as heard at the onset of this nightmare so long ago: *thum, thum,* low, bleak and monotonous. Shivering, Conan and

Subotai looked at each other. Masses of shadowy mountains loomed ahead like rotten teeth in the morning gloom; these were the final passes to the Ophirean marches. In this direction was it the only way they could go?

What was that—drums? Again?

They pushed on along a narrow path. Twisting and winding the two followed its course along some unforgivable ravine, stumbling along the rutted passage with little hope. Their hearts felt heavy. The slow progress brought cause for alarm should the surviving gnomes appear and ambush them, or the dragon win free and have a sudden change of mind. Having deviated from the main path, Conan saw that they were merely treading in circles.

His hackles raised. Trouble was brewing, he knew it. Its ugly face shimmered in the air. His barbaric instinct was a source of never failing insight. The sound of drums grew louder and stirred primitive fears in Conan; a faint keening wind moaned. Presently they came upon three stakes of grisly pikes upon which dangled the remaining mountain people's heads, faces still glaring in ignominious death.

Conan and Subotai stared in horror. The heads were freshly harvested!. So, there were survivors! Dead now. The heads rattled in the breeze, tied with stout cord, making dull thumping noises as they knocked together. A ghoulish decoration to stumble upon on a dark night. It appeared as if, despite the terror of the dragon-goddess, several of the blood-thirsty gnomes still had the time to sacrifice the helpless humans!

Conan balled his fists. When does a man call himself a man? When he has slain so many foul creatures of the earth that his hands run red with blood and his mind spins in lunacy? Was there a god like Crom, who counted the chips a man collects to win his liberation in the final hour? The Cimmerian thrust aside such rogue thoughts. The idle musings of fools!

The drums grew louder. They sounded as if they were right behind them now. He and Subotai wheeled round in disgust. By some horrible piece of luck, a gang of gnomes had sniffed them out, and now they charged them with a mixture of hatred and contempt.

Conan roared a savage oath. He drew his sword and Subotai, grabbed his arm and hissed, "Better to flee these demons, Cimmerian."

Conan did not argue. They scrambled for their lives through the mountain pass, although all seemed lost, for there was little chance that they could outrun a frenzied mob of this size. The going was far more treacherous than at first glance after the night rains. They slipped and fell in the mud, cursing, as the gnomes gained ground on them, and hurled spear-pikes. One grazingly caught the back of Conan's leg and he cried out, stumbling, grunting in anguish. Enraged he pulled the shaft out and ran, half-limping onward. What was one more bleeding wound?

They came to a thin strait of rock traversing a deep gulch. In the misty hollows they could hear the sound of gushing water below. Subotai ran across the threshold and peered back. To his surprise he saw that Conan had halted in mid-step and turned snarling like a wolf, with his bare steel raised.

"What are you doing, you fool?" Subotai cried. "There're too many of them."

"Let the gates of hell swing loose with the devils!" Conan cried. "I care not any more, Subotai. I swear by Crom that while I live, these swamp filth will feel pain! Fly, Subotai, fly—escape while you can!"

But the Hyrkanian did not flee. He knelt there, taking firm stance with his pike, ready to hurl the weapon should his friend need support. The horde came charging on, gnashing like locusts. Conan swung cold steel. Through grime-streaked eyes Subotai watched the slaughter and admired the terrible gleaming sinews sprung tautly in heroic battle. He only rued the day that the fiends had taken and destroyed his bow in the murky depths. How he would drop these scum like flies!

Conan held the bridge with his feet squared at midpoint. There was no better time to feel the weight of good steel in his right hand. His bloody sword hacked and hewed; body members flew, gaping wounds fountained blue ichor. The gnomes did not let up. Dying shrieks emptied from their maws as he swiped them off the bridge. Conan himself was full of cuts and gashes from the gnomes' pikes, but he heeded this not and fought on with savage tenacity. Eventually the bloodied Cimmerian had to give ground; the flood of them was too much.

Scores of them leapt at him and howled, close enough to gnash his shins with their terrible teeth.

"Run, Subotai, run! I can't hold them any longer."

Stumbling across the strait, Conan fell back. He would have died there if Subotai had not thrust the pike at a fleet-footed enemy who had crept up behind him and was ready to drag him down. Conan, scrambled and cursed in the muck and blood, and was lucky to escape with his life.

Together the two fled and rounded a bend. All the way was an uphill climb. Their hearts beat with battle lust. What path of safety could lead up? True enough, the path petered out to a dark gaping passageway. What to do now? Surely they would fall prey to some horror in the gloom-haunted tunnels. They had not time to scale the wall.

"Quick! Into the passage!" Conan took up the lead.

To his surprise, he found it was not a passageway at all but a great cave. Before he knew it, he had tripped over a bulky thing. A chilling shiver ran up his spine. He sensed fur brush his leg and lumps of iron muscle underneath. A great roar brought the Cimmerian scrambling to his feet and freezing in icy terror at that which had every hair standing on the back of his neck. In the inky gloom, he could feel the awful presence of what it was he had tripped over. He had stumbled into the lair of an elder beast—one of those mythic creatures better left to stories sung around campfires. The merest glimmers of bestial rage pricked its primitive brain. Hardly was it pleased to have been so rudely awakened from its slumber. Though spring was almost upon them, the fact was irrelevant. Nothing roused the great cave bear from its dreams without paying penalties—severe ones—and it crouched in the darkness, a thing of older menace, contemplating the obnoxious man-thing who dared disturb it, before raising a fierce snarl and charging without thought.

Scrambling back on all fours, Conan raced back for the exit, pulling his comrade along with him.

"Quick, Hyrkanian—if you value your life!"

Aye, better to face the grim horde than get ripped to shreds by this beast. And meet them they did—a bloodthirsty, frenzied, gibbering, pike-slashing mob.

Sandwiched between two foes, hope seemed nonexistent.

The bear tore out mere yards behind them, and despite the tight manacle of foes, Conan and Subotai were sensible enough to take to scaling the wall not far from the cave's flank. Thus spared from a charging doom.

The gnomes were not so fortunate. Barely had Madzgul and his guard screeched to a halt, open-mouthed, before the wall of snarling fury stampeded into their midst like a furred gale.

It tore and gored.

In the light of day, the cave bear was a black-maned horror, snorting death as twin sets of tusks reared on the end of an ugly snout. As a result of some hideous mutation, the beast bore tusks—as did many of its kind in these forsaken mountains—and so did many a gnome fall in tattered ruin as the hungry terror vented its wrath on anything and everything living that moved.

Several gnomes tried to slip away and spit the humans while the bear gnawed their fellows, but the beast would have nothing of it. Roaring challenges, it swatted them like flies, dragged them down like dolls, mauling them. More gnomes fell to its brutal assaults, its fangs and claws, while Conan and Subotai escaped, clawing their way up the cliff like petrified lemmings.

They gained the top of the scarp. Looking down, they caught a grisly view of the carnage. The bear had suffered murderous pike stabs, some of them bordering on fatal, before in a final defiance, it made a last insane charge. Swatting its persecutors like flies off the ledge or chewing their heads off with its grisly jaws, it pushed on with savage force. Pikes snapped like twigs: curses, screams, and death echoed off the rocks like cacophonous laments. Bestial roars made the mountain tremble. The thin ledge was a smear of gnome gore. Mangled and half chewed bodies littered the main path—and now snow-flakes began to fall to freeze the swards of blood-drenched rock.

The great cave bear began to totter, riddled with pikes and weakened from loss of blood. It knew it was floundering and uttered a cry, a kind of forlorn, wind-like moaning. His siblings heard the wail and out of their lotus dreams they came awake, charging; three monsters come to finish the slaughter. Seeing the howling gnomes spitting their brother in glee, their rage became all the greater.

Conan and Subotai turned, their backs caked with blood and grime. They hobbled far away from that grisly ledge, trying without success to keep the dreadful images of bloody carnage out of their brains.

By Crom's mercy, they had escaped where others had perished.

Yet not all the gnomes had fallen afoul of the bears' onslaught . . .

A handful had escaped—among them Madzgul and his trusted bodyguard. They knew these pathways like the back of their hands. Many back nooks and crannies were there for the taking. Running far away from the cave bears' clutches, five had found an escape route, and now they had re-entered the mountain from a secret entrance. Like thieves they navigated the dark relentless tunnels and came up on the other side of the mountain, urging their feet on by the lusty goads of Madzgul who promised golden revenge.

They continued their merciless pilgrimage, using skills that only their ghoul-spawned eyes could master, tracking their quarry under the sallowing sun. It was Madzgul who crouched low, a snarl juddering from his unpleasant maw. His right-hand gnome captain slunk on his heels, along with three other grim, competent warriors.

Conan and Subotai had gained higher ground. They could spy the sinuous track they had switch-backed up since the last encounter with the bear. As they loped along like wounded animals, the Hyrkanian caught a flash of movement in the brush. Stifling a cry, he pulled Conan back. Madzgul and his crew were scrambling up the steep slope straight at them, heedless of the loose rock and shale. They clawed at the scree like ragged fiends. Conan knew that if he didn't think of something, they would be on them in minutes. Without arrows and in their weakened state, they were sitting ducks for this elite guard. However, Conan was a ruthless enemy—and a survivor. He knew that there was always a way to win a war—and without ingenuity he wouldn't have lasted to this day. A keen wolf-fire blazed in his eyes that scanned the surroundings, looking for something that might save them.

A boulder poised high on the brink of scarp gave him a devilish plan. Painfully he groped his way up and began to test its balance. The stone was locked solid, apparently immovable, but he heaved nonetheless. It gave but an inch. Subotai scrambled up to help him. Heaving again and again, their combined thews bulging with a thin sweat managed to rock it like a pendulum. The boulder gained momentum. The barbarian, thinking that his arms were about to rip off, gave a gurgling gasp. The boulder toppled off the edge. The beginnings of a landslide came soon after, enough for the gnomes to halt in dismay and gape up with stunned wonder. A hail of rock, ice and dust followed the boulder, swallowing the snaking pathway below. The stricken gnomes clawed their way down the path. All except Madzgul, who with a grim face, thrust himself over the ledge by the path and at the last minute, clung there desperately to a shrub growing out of the rock face. So great was the force of the rock and debris smashing over his head he was spared instant death and not carried far down into the valley below like his fellows. The rumble of death caused the fleeing gnomes a last wave of despairing nausea before they knew death. It came quickly enough. They were crushed under tons of rock—all except Madzgul who in some freakish conjunction, had the foresight not to panic. As the last tumbling boulders fell, Conan and Subotai watched the mutant, ape-like creature claw his way up the battered shrub and back up the cliff, with all the evil, glaring eyes of a wraith, and make his way steadfast up toward them.

"Will the devil never die?" croaked Subotai.

"Crom's teeth! Must I keep hewing him down for the rest of my days?"

"It seems you must, Conan," Subotai rasped. "He's your nemesis, mine no less. But what is that he is clutching? It looks like a scepter."

Conan stared with disbelief. "Vain 'til the end of his evil reign. Well, little goblin—little good it will do against the bite of my steel." He slashed the air with his blade. "Let the brute come, Subotai. Let him receive the reward he deserves!"

Conan perhaps underestimated the gnome king. For in his bloody paw, Madzgul wielded something that the wizard Beleme had once coveted—an object spirited away after his carving up, passed down as a trophy among the chieftains over the eons. Unlike his dimwitted ancestors, Madzgul had discovered, in his cunning, some partial secrets of its magic, and used it when he needed for his own macabre purposes. The scepter was a gnarled willow stick. On its end bobbed a luminous violet bauble—an amethyst of unknown origin.

Conan saw for the first time a lurid amber glow shining from its tip. A cord of thong wrapped the talisman to the gnome's wrist.

Soon a panting, grimy wretch groped its way to the scarp. Now, struggling to its feet, it showed a mangled puffed cheek throbbing, a single saffron eye glaring like a sinister signpost and loose limbs dripping bluish blood.

The thing held forth its treasure, the Skelar of Horn: the talisman of lost Helos. Naked steel bared, Conan rushed to lop off his head. But the gnome twirled the amulet while uttering a spate of hideous laughs. Whipping against the air in tight loops, the stick created an odd whistling sound. It was like a drove of sandpipers crying off-key.

The Cimmerian frowned. What was the fool doing? He struck, but the gnome jerked its wrist, throwing the scepter out of its orbit and caught the Cimmerian's blade like a magnet. Stunned, Conan felt his power drained. He could not swing.

Caught such in the amulet's embrace, his blade began to glow a dull red and Conan flung it aside, lest his hand be singed. He watched in dismay what was left of his treasured blade hiss and bubble to liquid goop and finally melt into the earth.

"Crom!" he hissed. "Damn sorcery!"

With surprising speed and agility Madzgul leapt on him before he could react. The gnome was surprisingly strong for his size. He managed to grapple Conan to the ground. Subotai was too far away to do anything useful. The chief's grip was like iron and he sprayed foaming froth from his stinking maw on the Cimmerian's neck as he readied to chew.

Recoiling from the foul stench, Conan twisted. He rolled and tried to fling the gnome off him, but its ape-like limbs only gripped him tighter. The embrace was crushing the life out of him. The fiend's arms were wrapped around Conan's midsection, and from his back he tried to lay a mortal magic touch of his amulet to Conan's temple. With animal swiftness, Conan reached around and caught the hairy arm that housed the talisman and squeezed.

Bone gave in Conan's vice-like grip and the gnome almost dropped the thing. With a wrist crushed and paralyzed beyond repair, the gnome king leered. Yet the hurt did not deter the ghoul, which had once fought his way from the gladiatorial games under the mountain to the rank of chieftain of the stone gnomes. Quick as a serpent, it had its monkeyish arms hooked again around Conan's back, and pulled the damaged hand with the good one to squeeze the breath out of him with renewed strength.

Subotai was helpless to engage in the battle, fearing to gore Conan. But in one hand he clutched his dagger, and in the other a rock, and as they rolled, he rushed after them. He tried to stab and bash the gnome, but such efforts proved useless. Instead, he dropped his weapons and grabbed the scepter as it dragged on the ground and tried to yank it from Madzgul's dangling wrist. The thing screamed—not from the pain—but in sullen rage at the thought of losing its precious talisman.

The gnome king relaxed his grip which gave the Cimmerian the split second he needed.

Before burying lethal incisors into the Cimmerian's neck for a last time, he vented a cry of undisguised glee. But Conan was wise to the trick and he forced his corded arms in between their bodies. The glimmer of hate in the egg-like eye was terrible to behold as the brain behind recalled Conan's killing of his blood brother in the games.

Conan paid no heed. Grabbing the thing's head, he beat it against his own. Again and again he cracked his skull against the other's, squinting his eyes, ignoring his own pain, until its one eye was a mass of bloodied pulp, pasted against his forehead.

A horrific explosion rent the air. Behind them a mountain burst in ruin. A gush of rock fountained upward like a geyser. Out of the smoking peak streamed Skar, the dragon-goddess. She was a triumphant hellion in her freedom. Horrible to behold. And yet, victorious. Wings spread in ghastly majesty, her talons raked the air, her huge snout breathing smoke and brimstone. A long familiar cry filled the vale: of wrath turned to triumph. Conan felt his gnashing enemy's muscles go slack. It knew that sound—this time it was not a meek and drugged sound, but the blare of a nightmarish vengeance, and it drew nearer as if smelling the foul scent of its mortal enemy. Despite the danger, the gnome clawed its way away from the Cimmerian. Madzgul fled, stumbling, dragging its talisman in the dirt. But to Skar, this was a laughable enterprise. Down the dragon swooped—like a she-basilisk, breathing fire, and her claws outstretched.

Conan and Subotai watched spellbound as the dragon hurtled toward them. They crouched side by side, preparing for their doom, fearing to be burnt to crisps or rent by her iron-hewn teeth. But at closer range Zulkelera knew them as friends, not of the race of her hated enemy. She flapped over them, wings beating up a gale, and headed straight for Madzgul. The panicked gnome wheeled in fright as if the hot reek of her breath were on his back. Through bleary clouds of blood and mental mist, the gnome felt the presence of the hulk that quickly crowded his horizon. With his sole eye mashed beyond repair, he was blind to her assaults. In a last attempt at salvation, he tried to twirl the talisman in its pattern of doom. But his mangled wrist would allow no such movement; the scepter flailed about in a jigsaw orbit to the only advantage of cracking the doomed ghoul on his own skull.

In one fell motion Skar swooped and snatched up Madzgul in its teeth. There was no horrible crunching of jaws or scorching of flesh—

only a leathery grasping of scaly forepaws on ghoulish hide as the winged beast carried him away. There Madzgul dangled like a doll in the sky, feet-paws splayed upwards and kicking, and magic scepter trailing uselessly in his grip. The dragon lifted him high in the sky and his final screams quavered and died in the chill wind. Away the wretched king was carried; to what foul den or murky doom Conan could not say, only to suffer what tortures or horrors, the two could only shudder at.

So the last of the gnomish rulers perished along with their ken— and so perished the race of Zulkelera's oppressors. As was deserved, for who could deny the atrocities the gnomes had inflicted upon the dragon, or count the hordes of innocent humans who had been dragged from their homes and sacrificed at the gnomes' ghastly hands. And now that they had been avenged, Conan and Subotai fell to their weary knees. Weaponless and without mail, they lay there for a time before they trudged on with gloomy reflection. Conan's face was carved in an inscrutable mask, his massive torso grime-stained, his bloody hands dangling at his sides: a man who had survived a last defiant attack, battered and cut. The two comrades took comfort in their own company as they limped away, but neither felt cheer in any of their deeds—nay, only a faint registration of sadness at the toll of death, but gladness at still being alive to breathe the fresh mountain air.

Conan peered up at the sky, looking for the image of a mirthless Crom set among the tattered masses of cloud: Crom who judged men and laughed at the puny machinations of mortals. "So much for your justice, Crom," Conan croaked, shaking his fist at the sky "—and so much for magic, eh, Subotai? Let us begone from these cursed hills!" The Cimmerian spat blood. "Let us have no more of these hell-games today!"

And so in the days after the oceans drank Atlantis, Conan and Subotai had survived another battle.

They climbed down from the scarp and weaved their way among the tapestry of giant boulders. Thorny shrubs and stunted trees grew in their path. But they weaved around them in a trance, too tired to lift their heads. Half way down the valley, they spied a sodden trail which led around the ice-smeared mountain. They set an angled course to intercept it. In time they did. Side by side, they stumbled past the bleak peak and plodded on with no sign of gnomes or the grisly, head-hung pikes . . . only the mournful wail of the wind and the occasional croak of a black-mantled raven atop a dead twisted tree.

Not long afterward, they heard the rusty creak of wings, though distant. Each craned his neck and spied the behemoth, appearing from a rent in the clouds. As she drew closer, they watched in awe—for the effortless cadence of her wings, the sleek majestic power of her body amazed them. The dragon circled high overhead then breathed a gust of fire. Making a final pass, she banked, her breast gleaming reddish-gold in the morning sun, before disappearing behind a mass of cloud-wreathed peaks. She was gone in a memory, as if she had never been.

Only for a moment were Conan and Subotai awed and curious of the dragon's reappearance. The winged guardian would keep watchful eye over these lonely passes for some time to come. It would be a cold day in hell before enemies would ever haunt the pass . . .

With a youthful grin, Subotai laid his hand on his friend's shoulder and together they stumbled down the path. Midmorning was among them. Sunshine glinted through cloud holes and brought them cheer, more than the dark crown of peaks cast on either side of them. The Ophirean pass was a few leagues distant: perhaps a few hours' hike away, yet they still had many leagues to travel before they reached the rolling plains of Ophir.

Little did they know that their adventure had only begun . . .

DRAGON LORDS

I: Dragonskull

Vetravincus, wandering mercenary, was on a mission to fence a jewel. He found himself jostling shoulders among the crowd in the central market of Dragonskull, a lawless oasis in the arid wastes, also famous for dragon bones scattered among the dunes. Less than two generations had passed since a slave caravan of brigands, deviants and cutthroats, bound for King Juna's prison mines, broke their chains and took control of the town. Often a man was beaten for some minor offense, or his throat cut or his valuables seized; worse was done to women.

Of foul play, Vetra was little worried. His broadsword was forged with crucible steel, sharp enough to cut through bone, and hung from his armored back in a shagreen scabbard. His hard features, broad shoulders, sure step and reinforced ringmail were enough to give pause to the most impulsive footpads.

Vetra heard someone cry out and he grasped the pommel of his sword. A boy struggled in the hairy arms of a red-faced merchant. A yam and a cuchri fruit lay mashed at their feet. A flash of steel glinted in the noonday sun; the merchant raised a cleaver to the gaunt-faced boy. Vetra lunged and pulled the boy away.

"What're you doing?" the merchant screamed, his cleaver missing the youthful hand and sticking deep into a wooden table. "He stole—"

Vetra smashed the pommel of his broadsword into the merchant's mouth. Blood, broken teeth, and curses filled the air. Vetra grabbed the man by his scraggly beard and pulled him close.

He could smell the fruit merchant's fear; piss ran down the vendor's leg and rancid meat wafted from his agonized face.

Vetra put his blade to the merchant's throat. "Have you ever swiped a grape? Have you ever been that hungry?"

The merchant opened his bleeding mouth to say something but stopped. His eyes flicked to the side.

Vetra turned and saw a large man approaching. Dragon tattoos rippled on bare, muscled arms, and a dirty blond beard curled low under a pointed chin.

The big man snarled. "Who are you to impose law on us, outlander?"

Vetra sheathed his weapon. "I meant no imposition to your laws." He glanced down at the child and mouthed the word 'Run.'

The boy jumped to his feet and tore off through the crowd, panic-stricken. He squeezed his way through moving carts, tables and milling bodies, eluding the grasping hands of bystanders.

"Stop that weasel!" the big man yelled to the crowd. He put his hand out to Vetra. "Out of my way! I'll not kill the thieving brat. Just put him to work in Berit's smithy, or chain him to a post in the tannery."

Vetra chuckled and stepped aside. "You'll never catch him. His feet are faster than a rabbit's." He shook his head and sauntered up the monger's lane, merging with the crowd. He peered left and right, his dark eyes on the alert for trouble. At least he had saved a young urchin from mutilation, no doubt a better deed than anybody in that motley crowd had done that day.

The aisle merged into a common square packed with bustling traffic. Carts jolted past without heed for people safety; noise and dust were like layers of froth off a devil's brew. A camel came bearing down on him and he stepped aside from the grunting beast, whose rider shook a fist at him. The diversity of the throng fascinated him. Lean Guirites from Amashra swarmed the streets with keen, curved, gold-chased swords belted at their hips. Thrules, four to five feet tall, wore loose, purple robes to the ankle, whispering among themselves with hoods drawn tight, concealing all but their cat-like eyes. Wood traders from Kamuchaya trundled in by cart; silk merchants from Asban on their desert ponies, whipping their dust-ridden beasts through the throng. Behundrians dominated the scene, swarthy, stocky residents with tempers and arrogance to match, who imposed their law, which was cruel at best.

Spices, jewels, and fruit, along with silk and ivory flowed from the east while fish, wheat, timber, and steel came from the west. The odd caravan of gold came from the south, with armed escort, from as far as Pakshar and then by way of Senesch on the coast. The Kirns of the South, the Mosetes of the North, the Guirites of the East, all plied the common route, some friends, some foes. They traveled the same dusty streets, rubbing shoulders with each other on foot or donkey or camel, drank by each other's side in the seedy ale holes and saloons or rolled dice in the gambling houses that graced the town.

Vetra ducked under awnings and pushed his way through the back curtain of a fabric shop. He gave not a glance at the fine silks and Damir linens, but took a shadowy route through a narrow alley with wet clothes strung up from the railings of the overhead apartments. A particular dealer resided here who could fence these emeralds of his. Pity he had to come all the way to this remote outpost for this. He had learned upon arrival that a recent entry permit was imposed on non-Behundrians. Persons in transit were exempt, but to be caught without one while even entering the bazaar was considered an offense—a hefty ten talon fine, or time done in the stockade. Nothing more than a local collection tax, he thought. Two silver talons, one permit.

He pushed down his disgust and wiped the back of his shiny black hair. He was sweating like a stallion.

The three small emeralds were uncut, likely stolen, and payment for his last job. Easier to fence it here in out-of-the-way Dragonskull than be caught in Lausern, pegged as a smuggler by the Vizier's street watch. He had to find the dealer who would move it first, otherwise his trip was a waste of time. As for the permit, well, he was willing to take a chance...

The alley reeked of sour cabbage and spoiled wine. Trickles of noisome gray water ran in gutters. Vetra turned. A man's cry? A scream of pain? His lips parted in a scowl. Best to keep walking. But he knew he would not.

Down the narrow, littered alley he stole like a thief, his *garbandia* knife clutched in one hand, his other on the pommel of his sword in its worn scabbard. He thought he heard a sound behind him, a stalker, crouching hidden behind refuse heap and crumbled wall. He paused.

Nothing.

A large rat skittered out and down a dark hole.

Angry shouts drifted through a canvas-covered gap in a plastered wall. The sounds rose in pitch, the wheezing gasp of a pleading man, grunts and blows, then various chuckles and throaty murmurs. Hackles raised, Vetra bent his head, unable to overcome his curiosity. He pulled back the canvas flap and peered into a windowless chamber dimly lit by oil lamps. A man was gibbering, spreadeagled on a low table. A dozen figures surrounded the victim, and taunted him with cruel knives and wicked bits of sharp, rusted iron.

"I tell you, Rafa, I don't know where the map is." The prisoner was lashed hand and foot in stout cord and struggled helplessly as he wailed.

"Liar!" cried Rafa. "I saw you chewing the parchment and swallowing it. Only a knave or fool would do that before looking at the map. Nestor! Jangir! Put the tong to him. This rogue deceives us."

Nestor nodded, a brawny ape of a man, with a ragged overcloak, iron wristbands and yellow front teeth.

The sound of sizzling flesh came to Vetra's ears. He clenched his jaw.

Predatory laughs added to the tortured man's howls.

Vetra, for the life of him, could not stand by and witness a defenseless man tortured and killed, even if he were possibly a villain.

He ripped a hole through the canvas and leaped in, sword gripped. He saw they had branded the victim's right calf with a lurid mark: a long knife piercing a dragon skull. The victim was a short man, no more than five feet tall. He looked Thrule, but for his wincing features, thin Behundrian nose and more strongly defined jaw. It was hard to see past his shaggy mop of sweat-matted brown hair.

The victim was struggling anew now, and in a fierce display of strength had to be restrained with force despite the strong cords binding his limbs.

Vetra barreled straight for the man with the tongs. The best attack was a surprise one. Without preamble, Vetra pounced, cleaving skull and jawbone in a spray of blood and brains. The villains around him fell back with cries of horror. Leaning in, Vetra slashed more throats and limbs.

They circled closer, having wits to stay out of reach of his hissing blade. Now they came rounding in, and he was penned like a boar among huntsmen.

A bold young voice called out from the shadows. "Oi! Ugly face!"

The rogues quickly faced the unknown voice, and Vetra took the opportunity to slice the next nearest man's throat. The man staggered into his fellow villains, gurgling blood, a ghastly expression on his face.

Vetra ducked a whooshing blade. Darting sideways, he crouched as another sword edge thumped off his padded leather undershirt, ripping white desert robe. In the same motion, he slashed the victim's cords that bound legs and arms. The prisoner rolled off the table and crawled across the floor out of reach of the scrabbling men. He snatched up the tong while Vetra held off the attackers then hurled it into the face of his captors, eliciting a cry of anguish.

"Get her!" the leader cried.

A flat-faced thug broke from the pack and turned on the intruder who had voiced the taunt, a young woman with cinnamon hair trailing down her slender shoulders. A gleaming knife was gripped in her hand, a dangling scourge clasped in the other.

The aggressor towered a foot over her, sword hanging loosely at his side, sizing her up, as a bull eyes a ripe cow. His leering face bobbed closer to inspect her with more care. He reached a hand out like a snake to grab her wrist.

Her blade flashed and slashed a crimson line across the back of the hand. He grunted in surprise. A knee to the groin doubled him over. Her lithe body then spun with a long leg arching up to crack the side of his head. The man crunched to the floor. The smack of leather on flesh resounded throughout the room. Two more leering figures broke away and came leaping after her, their hoods rustling and white desert garb trailing to their ankles. She sprang forth, whip whirling behind her head. She moved in sync with the rhythm of her foes as they came at her, cursing and grunting.

"A girl? Really, swordster?" Rafa sneered. "You are quite the hero, bringing an entourage from the local bordello!"

Vetra grunted, ignoring the taunts. He twisted to avoid the rake of the grinning man's two-foot *Shamari* blade. He was in the thick of the fray, besieged by foes. Parrying left and right, he swore and swiveled left, evading a one-eared attacker who lunged for his vitals. Blood ran down the hilt of Vetra's naked blade as he cut down hard. A high squeal erupted from a man bowed over in agony.

Meanwhile, the freed victim rolled underfoot. Despite his pitiful state, he hobbled to his feet and grabbed a weapon from the hand of the felled torturer then met an upraised sword aimed for his skull. Vetra laughed, cutting down a man to edge closer to the ginger-haired girl who had saved his neck.

Vetra saw her scourge rising and falling in sprays of red. A wicked weapon of leather strips and rusted nails, meting out an unforgiving punishment. She disarmed the first attacker, lashing out with a shrill cry, to leave a gaping gash on the man's arm.

Rafa came striding in with a howl of disgust, keen on despatching the hellcat. But in his anger he underestimated his opponent, driving in too close too fast. A quick lash took out his eye. His lips gave rise to a screech of a pain. Hand thrust to his bloody socket, the man reeled, trying to stop the jet of blood gushing from between his fingers.

Vetra, summoning a savage fire from deep in his warrior's heart, gave a berserker's yell and launched full on the last four villains who faced him. Sword swung like a mallet, dismembering jaws and bursting brains. But more foes came pouring out from the shadows of a hidden entrance. Many more.

He shook the blood and sweat out of his eyes and edged back, his sword dripping in a white-fisted hand, snarling like a panther. "Quick! If you value your lives!"

The young woman and the freed man wasted no time: together the three of them cleared a path to the back flap.

Vetra squinted under the daytime glare to examine his mysterious aide in better light now. She was lighter skinned and wore a sleeveless vest, short leather breeches, brown belt and soft leather boots. Her shins were bare, and small ornamental bracelets and cheap rings decorated her ankles and fingers. She was in fit shape, with green eyes, provocative curves, and was scarcely winded.

The three staggered out of the shadows, scuttling to the end of the alley.

"What's your name, girl?" demanded Vetra as they ran.

"Jhara. And yours?"

"Vetra. Why did you help me back there?"

"You saved my brother. I was curious about your business in Dragonskull. Not often does a stranger risk his neck for a nameless urchin." Her breath caught in her throat as she kept abreast the mercenary while the rescued man was struggling to keep up, wheezing up a storm.

Vetra laughed, a snort of contempt.

"You seem to have a knack for getting yourself in trouble," she said. "That's Rafa's lair, don't you know? His thugs pay allegiance to Cthan, the sheriff. Are you a daft brute or just a simpleton, going in there and taking on the whole crew?"

Vetra made a brusque motion. "Where did you learn to fight like that?" He halted, peering back down the alley. The Thrule held his branded leg, wincing with every step. Only three of the dozen pursued and they strode with leisure, as if they had all the time in the world. Vetra frowned. Confident swine they were, to saunter with such laziness, as if they had the luxury of kings to ferret out a cocky outlander and a few rebels.

"My father... He never let me use a sword." The girl offered a wry, white-toothed grin, though there was pain in that smile. "Said I would kill somebody."

Vetra shook his head with bemusement. The whip she used earlier was sewn with hooked, rusted nails and ended with a blood-stained wooden handle. "In that I have no doubt."

He glanced at the hectic market scene. Folk and mongers moved about their business, oblivious to the violence that had just taken place. His puzzled curl of lip returned upon remembering the girl's performance.

"One learns to think fast on her feet," she added, seeing his appraising look, "especially a woman, growing up on the streets."

"My advice is get a proper sword," he muttered. "And you, Thrule, what's your story?" He peered at the man that they rescued.

"I am not a Thrule," he gasped, stumbling up, his chest heaving. "I am a half Thrule. Lehundr. Snatched by those thugs but an hour ago." A flicker of doubt passed his eyes as he debated whether or not he could trust the swordsman who hulked before him. "I have desert ponies waiting in the stables of the Prospector's Inn. My uncle runs the place. Not the fastest steeds, but sturdy ones and reliable. We can be out of here in short order."

Vetra considered the prospect while rubbing his jaw. Recent events had gone awry and suggested it was time to quit Dragonskull. His gems would have to wait till another day. They were not worth his life. Though he liked not the prospect of delay.

"The fools, they thought I was eating a map," Lehundr continued, croaking out a harsh laugh. Again, a doubtful hesitation, but he continued. "It was but a decoy. The real one is weaved into my caftan here." He lifted his torn cloak for an instant and Vetra caught a fleeting glimpse of two dragon heads facing each other—a mystical and sinister sign if he ever saw one—the beasts poised as if a cleverly woven part of the fabric, evoking mystic terror in any who saw it. The fabric was ancient and the pigments dyeing the wool were dulled and faded by years of sun.

"They wanted the map and were ready to kill for it," he explained. "The rest you can guess."

Vetra grunted. "Those killers are not going to give up their hunt to lynch a few ornery trespassers. We got lucky. And I don't know why they haven't pinned us down and gutted us already."

Almost as if in answer, his keen eyes detected five grim figures on the other side of the market, blood trailing from their cheeks and arms.

A quick glance over his shoulder showed four more stumbling out of the adjoining alleyway.

Vetra pulled the two into a nearby back alley. "Quick, girl! Make yourself scarce. You, Thrule—or half Thrule, whatever you are—follow me!"

"What about the treasure?" Jhara demanded. "I heard about the map. We're all going to be rich!"

"Are we now?" grunted Vetra. "Recall, we just narrowly escaped getting our throats cut. Look yonder, what do you see?"

"A market and a bunch of bustling fools."

"No, death. Go take care of your brother. Begone, this is my last warning."

"That's not how this is going to play out—" She gave lip to a rush of words, but seeing the mercenary's inflexible face, her mouth curled in a sullen scowl and she turned and dashed off. She disappeared down the alley in a flash of gleaming brown leather and bouncing hair.

Vetra shook his head with perplexity. Her appearance was certainly one of the more bizarre things he had seen in a long time.

He had a hunch yet more bizarre things were to follow.

Lehundr stared in awkward fashion, wiping his bloody blade on his torn garment.

"Where did you get that map?" Vetra demanded as he forged his way through the market crowd.

"Off a wandering Guirite, who knew not what he had. He was selling knickknacks and memorabilia from his market stand and I happened to notice it hanging there, pinned to a hide, as an emblem or decoration. He said it was a good luck charm. I recognized it for what it was—the mark of the Dragon Keeper. My father had schooled me well in the legends of the Dragon Lords. He said their treasure was an ancient secret woven into a map."

"Well, you paid a hefty price for that bit of fabric." He motioned to Lehundr's quivering leg.

"Help me get to the Thrule district. I have healing ointments there."

"I doubt any salve is going to fix that burn too quickly."

"You don't know Thrule medicine."

Vetra's eyes darted about. What to do about this Thrule? He was in bad shape and likely would not survive another assault if the band of ruffians caught him again.

Almost as if in answer he saw a garish sign to the trader's post looming like a sore thumb: a wooden slab with carved-out pickaxes and shovels crossed together.

Another reckless camel came veering in, the scowling man cursing from its saddle. Vetra was deafened by the animal's grunt in his ear. He stumbled into a wizened merchant, carrying a load of silk bales, who rang out some Moscte words at him for being in his way.

"Quick, in here!" Vetra growled, annoyed with the overloaded street. The oppressive heat was getting to him. He pushed the Thrule on through.

They plunged past the swinging wooden door. A wall of noise, confusion and impatient voices assailed them.

Figures moved every which way in a bright-lit open pavilion.

Sunlight streamed from the long windows that ran along the upper gallery below an arched, bricked ceiling.

Weigh scales lined the nearby wall, men measuring vials of silver dust, gold nuggets and ore chips, others wielding heavy sacks of precious metals. A few gripped freshly signed deeds and land rights. The depot was a central hub where all the traders secured their commerce, signed trade deals, filed mineral claims, and lodged complaints.

An open area at the back of the depot fronted a sprawling cobbled courtyard rich with milling folk who toted sacks of grains and other goods to the weigh stations—barrels of precious water, crates of Thorian metal, rolls of silk, or linen, baskets of dates and coconuts, raw leather, rugs, amphorae of wine. The heaving, jostling men swarmed about like ants. Vetra stared past the figures and tethered horses at the temple of Dergath and its forked spires and shiny jade dome rising into the white-washed sky. To its side rose the great curving bulk of the stone reservoir of water that kept the town alive.

Shaking his head at the chaos, Vetra strode to the central area. Straightaway he was accosted by a uniformed man selling trading permits at an alleged discount. The man rattled clay tokens in his fingers with confident ease and pushed one in Vetra's hands. Vetra squinted at the disk with skepticism, then, seeing it bore a true Dragonskull seal, flipped a silver coin at him, thinking it could come in handy if they were accosted by the town watch. The hyena like cackles of men came from behind and he turned upon the three grubby traders who stared at him with obvious amusement.

A sudden suspicion dawned on Vetra and he stared at Lehundr who straggled behind in a daze, in no shape to call out a warning. Leaning back, Vetra shifted, realizing he had been duped and reached out to grab the vendor. But the smiley-faced con was gone.

He herded Lehundr up ahead and they inserted themselves in a line leading to a main counter, trying to appear as unobtrusive as possible. Lehundr's darting eyes and burn on his leg marked him out.

The trade-clerk of the depot shouted across the nearby counter over the din of voices. "You'll get your blasted silver dust, you damned rogue!"

The fuming, red-eared figure on the other side of the wicket glared. "I doubt that! Give me back my coins, you jackal. All five hundred. Shipment was due a week ago, and it still hasn't arrived out of Dalispar. I've been swilling Jirrir's sour ale and eating stringy mutton with my bully-boys for the last week, itching to carve out someone's liver."

The trade-clerk snarled. "Hire yourselves some trollops then, down Smeldra's way. Amuse yourself for a few more days. Your silver'll come, by Dron, or I'll cut off my beard and eat it."

"Well, you'd better get a knife because—"

A loud shout pierced the air. Then a thud and clash of arms as a dispute over a transaction gained momentum.

Wood flashed in a fist and a brute cracked his club over the head of a lean desert man with a rat-face. "That'll teach you to backbite, you lily-livered Kirn."

The brute's aide grumbled, "Well, Onast, any more of your bullies got a beef with us?"

"Ah," the tradepost-clerk grunted. "This place is a barn." He turned to Vetra, who had thrust himself next in line while a long line of men were distracted. "Well, what's your complaint, outlander?" The clerk glared at Vetra, and the mercenary casually loosened his outer garment to better disguise his rugged physique.

"No complaint," Vetra remarked. "I came to get a trader's permit."

"Trader's permit? That's that office down the hall," he barked, jerking a thumb. "Why waste my time here?"

"I was ripped off by your so-called assistant who carries no more than a few trinkets of pretty clay."

"Say what?"

Vetra gritted his teeth, his anger not allowing him to let it go. "I said, the impostor claims he was the one I should pay money for a permit." He held up a faked token stained with yellow and red.

The clerked grinned. "Well, if you were fool enough to give honest coins to that good-for-nothing—"

"You!" burst out a voice. Vetra whirled to recognize an oily-skinned man wearing a turban from back at the market "—you were the rascal who Vilivet was talking about, some foreigner who thought to flout our market law."

A rustle came from behind the clerk. A tall, broad-chested man came out of the back office, his ears pricked. "What's this I hear about Vilivet?" There was a dangerous glitter in the man's eyes, as a lizard eyes a cringing mouse. "Is there a problem here?"

"No problem, Cthan," mumbled the trade-clerk.

"Aye, no problem," grunted Vetra. "I just suggest you teach your clerk better manners." He recalled the name 'Cthan' dropped by Jhara and noticed that Lehundr seemed to shrink in the presence of the hulking lawbringer of Dragonskull.

The oily-skinned man piped up in anger: "The outlander's a sword-trickster. Took a thieving urchin from under our thumbs and stared down Vilivet."

Cthan snorted. "What do I care of your little squabbles? If Vilivet can't handle one grubby foreigner, then he deserves his hide whipped. Serve the man and be done, Sabias, before I wallop you. I get enough complaints about your surliness as it is."

"As you like." Sabias growled. "And you, Thrule," he grunted down at Lehundr, "what are you looking at? I should have you thrown out and whipped. Thrules go in the other line!" He clutched his writing stick in a white-knuckled fist.

Lehundr had been staring in fascination, still dazed from his near encounter with death. A line of drool slithered down from the corner of his mouth, a detail which had likely triggered the clerk's dislike.

Lehundr, whose natural habit seemed to be to look down, let the flap of his torn hood hide his face. His noiseless movement of upraised hand with open palm seemed a gesture of implicit subservience. Yet Vetra could see by his resentful shrug he was not pleased to be insulted.

"Leave him out of this," Vetra rumbled with impatience. "The half Thrule's with me."

"And what's your claim in this affair?"

"First of all he's a half Thrule, not a Thrule, and he's got your blood in him too," reiterated Vetra, "and if there's any thrashing or bullying to do, it'll be done by me. He glared down at the clerk who was starting to irk him.

The trade-clerk bristled at the outlander's insolence. Seeing the merciless fire in Vetra's eyes and the glint of steel rising out of his scabbard, he grumbled an oath and crashed a fist on the table. "Your door's down there, big man. Take your Thrule with you."

Vetra marched away like a lazy cat, earning the appreciation of several onlookers. He and Lehundr pushed past several grumbling and jeering men, tired of waiting in line.

Vetra motioned to the Thrule. "Don't like you, do they?" He stared down at his companion's five-foot height.

"They don't like anyone here," muttered the shorter man. "The Behundrians, I mean. A word of advice, friend, not that I don't appreciate your grit in sticking up for me, but watch your step. One man and a sword isn't going to take on a whole gang of villains. You don't know them like I do."

Vetra gave a sinister laugh. He pushed his gleaming blade back in his scabbard and sauntered through the throng. "I see you are eager to be gone, and for that I don't blame you. Best be on your way, Thrule, before those bullies target you again."

At that moment two riders thundered up to the depot's back station, kicking up a dust storm. Their mounts were lathered with sweat and looked to have seen some heavy riding. One cried out in a hoarse voice, "The main water pipe is down again. No breaches for a league or so, we checked. But 'tis the Thrules! They've taken the pipe somewhere further up the line. Rebels from the north—the Thorian mines have been hit too."

The booming voice of the sheriff rolled over the general noise.

"Damn those nomads! They've likely sabotaged the main water head at Sunswatch. Outback rebels, I wager. Round up your swords, men—and your camels. We've a rebellion to quash."

A chorus of vengeful shouts and murmurs rose from the gathered men.

Vetra frowned. That the Thorian mines were compromised meant there would be a major movement of militia eastward. Large coin was at stake. The rare mineral Thorian, the magical element from which the wizard Slune had figured out how to manufacture the finest steel, was a lifeline of the Sahir trade. The Dragonskull constabulary, as their purpose demanded, would have to protect the common interest.

Cthan swore, grimaced at an arguing deputy, fit to be tied. "I'll send word to Thraxen's force at Menihem. We'll meet them and rout out the vermin and put an end to this little rebellion once and for all. A round of stiff arrack for the lads."

Vetra forewent his trader's permit. He slipped out the back of the station with Lehundr close on his heels. This place was too conspicuous. While a hubbub of desert mounts being saddled and packed for war reigned there was no better time to escape unnoticed. Even so, Vetra paused. The excited jabber of men's voices aside, he had not liked the suspicious retreat of a particular squint-eyed, curly-haired man upon mention of 'outlander' earlier. He had no doubt there were more of Rafa's spies about.

* * *

The mid afternoon sun blazed down like an angry furnace. Vetra and Lehundr crouched outside the stables at the back of Lehundr's uncle's Inn, for fear of being seen. The smell of dung lay thick in their noses. Three sturdy ponies swished tails at the pesky flies in the shade of the alley behind the stables. The inn rose several feet over the horse stalls: a two-storey clay and stone dwelling with arched doors and painted gumwood typical of the region's desert dwellings. Few folk were about these quarters. The air was hot and heavy and would not be cooling down for some hours. Not fast enough for

Vetra's tastes.

"We should be traveling by night," Vetra murmured, "for reasons of stealth and coolness." He poked about in the dusty shadows and gathered what extra supplies from the stable he thought they needed: lantern, rope, extra wicks, a pickaxe.

Lehundr gave his head a decided shake. He fingered the salve he had acquired from the stable. "Rafa will learn that we were at the depot and come hunting for us. So we can't wait until nightfall. In fact, they will be coming here before long." To his burn wound he applied more of the ointment, a mixture of cactus and eucalyptus leaf.

"Nothing we can do about that," mused Vetra. "Better pack up and go."

"Come with me, Vetra!" the Thrule urged. "I need a good man on this job. A fighter! A swordsman. You're a man of mettle. We'll split the spoils. The map is genuine, I know it!" He lifted his outer robe again in excitement.

Vetra stared critically at the folds of fabric which showed the dragons and some crude, cryptic sketch of valleys and temples and skulls. It seemed to point to a hidden tomb, delineated by a dragon rune stone, north of the place where the pipeline snaked, if his bearings were right. "It follows the line of the pipe."

"So—we'll give the invading rebel Thrules wide berth."

"Meaning, you think I'm going to hunt down this will-o-the-wisp of yours? Get knifed, and die with gold in my hands? No, we'll get out of town, hide our heads for a while, but that's all I can guarantee. This treasure seems too much of a longshot."

"Why, though? The girl was not stupid she could smell the promise of riches."

Vetra ignored the remark and noticed the short, gleaming falchion Lehundr had tucked at his waist. "I see you favor the shorter blade."

"Yes, it's lighter, quicker and more versatile in battle."

"The reach is shorter and you could get yourself gutted by a better fighter with a longer blade, especially on horseback."

"You would know."

Vetra chuckled. "Well, I hope you know how to use it. My experience with treasure is that plenty of blood flows alongside it."

Lehundr gave a furtive grin. He draped the soft woolen scarf about his neck to ward off the daytime flies. Adjusting his coiled turban, he chuckled. Vetra thought he looked less like a Thrule, and more like a Behundrian.

"Daytime could be dangerous," Vetra commented. "The deserts are populated with nomads, like tics on a dog's hide. I don't know what tribes are out there but their allegiance may not be to our favor, nor their temperaments. The region is unfamiliar to me, but I've heard many a tale of wayfarers and traders alike, pulled down by grasping hands, ambushed by desperadoes."

Lehundr clicked his tongue. "Relax, I know the terrain. I can guide us."

Even in daylight hours the sounds of men's shouts and laughter drifted from a nearby canteen. Vetra heard loud coarse music, the odd bray of a donkey or the whinny of a horse. Not even he noticed the slim, covert form who had snuck up alongside Lehundr's extra packbeast while the men stood conversing in the heat, downing some cheap ale at the stable's gate before their jaunt into the scrublands.

Vetra winced and shook his head. "Bah, this tastes like tar."

"Only the best Thrule stock," scoffed Lehundr. "What, don't like my uncle's mix? Drink up, friend. It may be all you'll get for a long time."

Vetra peered around, the smells and sights registering only as blips on his consciousness. The day had unfolded in unexpected fashion and now his senses prickled with a sense of danger. He upended the tankard on the sand by the stable. "I think I'd rather die and go to Dergath than take this swill."

The mercenary loosened his caftan, itching with the sweat that soaked the soft wool and made it stick to the back of his neck. The sour ale sloshing in his stomach did him little favors. He scratched at his stubbled cheeks, brushing back his shiny black hair under the coiled desert cap that he had chosen to stave off the desert heat. He was glad he had decided to 'go local', wearing lighter, airier garb, to downplay his real status as a mercenary. No small number of enemies had he made in his line of work, even as far as Dragonskull. Eyes and ears and noses were no less sharp in this town. Under his flowing white caftan, the boiled hide and ring mail protected his chest and vitals. One could never be too careful, even while not on the job. Time for him to skip town.

Vetra's eyes widened at the size of the half Thrule's saddlebag. Lehundr was now adding a sieve and trowel. "What? I thought you were talking about a few day's trip, not a five-year hunting mission? Lighten your load. And what's with all the cooking utensils and mineral-hunting gear?"

"One can never be too careful," the half Thrule argued. "The desert is a dangerous place. Besides, we need some story, some alibi. There are many prying eyes about."

Vetra shrugged. He saw that his companion's stride had greatly improved.

Lehundr, catching his expression, showed a wide grin. "We Thrules know something of healing."

"You're a half Thrule," Vetra reminded him.

"Does it matter? I still have a nomadic heritage."

"You seem proud of it—also ashamed."

Lehundr looked away. It seemed the Thrule kept more than one dark secret.

A disturbance gripped the nearby inn—cries, broken glass, the distant thuds of fists and crashing furniture. Vetra tensed, gripped his blade, while Lehundr's troubled hiss rasped between his teeth. He tightened fingers on Vetra's arm. From the open window drifted hoarse demands, whimperings of pain, and the screams of tavern wenches.

Four turbaned figures in dirty caftans burst out of the inn's back alleyway, dragging Lehundr's uncle by the ears. They thrust him out into the yard and kneed him down. His face was a bloody mess, his lip cut, eyes wild and puffed, cheeks dripping with blood.

Vetra drew his blade. He strode to meet them. The ponies started at the clamor, nostrils flared at the smell of blood; they yanked at their tethers.

The foremost man flourished a long scimitar at Lehundr. "Both of you are liars—" he thundered, referring with disgust to Lehundr's uncle. "Who's this then? Your map-bearing rat?"

They kicked the old man rolling in the dust. He clawed at his torturer's feet, hooking fingers into the baggy folds draping their shins.

"The map, or your life, Thrule," threatened the lead thug. He ignored Vetra and pointed his curved blade at the map bearer.

Vetra brought his sword high and gleaming steel crashed toward the man who was pressing his foot on the innkeeper's neck.

The thug swung a silver falchion and nearly chopped the innkeeper in two, but Vetra's stroke caught the blade. A rasp of metal and Vetra's weapon shimmered in a blinding arc. The sweaty grin froze on the swarthy face as three feet of glittering steel plowed through his chest and up out his back. He crumpled in a bloody heap.

His colleagues gaped at the sudden violence of the attack and scrambled back in horror. Two circled in to lay swords to their new enemy.

Vetra dodged his foes, parrying strikes which would have impaled him like a hog. He stepped over the body—then smote with savage strength. He followed up with a lightning-fast riposte, a bellowing roar on his lips.

The half Thrule scurried out of the fray to help his uncle, but was drawn into a vicious sword fight with the fourth man. They circled and shuffled around like barbarians, grunting, clashing, muscles bunched and triceps straining, while Vetra contended with his two foes.

Vetra's temper grew. The heat burned down on his head, tapping wounds of raw rage and frustration. He hewed and smote like a wild man. His temples throbbed; every muscle in his body rippled and stood out like lumps of iron. Ever since he had come to this wretched hub, men had been trying to kill him, and it made his blood boil. He grunted and whirled about, ducking, stabbed steel at the figures. They grew warier, their eyes widening at the efficient skill of the enemy they faced. His closest attacker feinted, a crafty, drawn out lunge. The man was a lean, hawk-faced fighter, and pretended to fall while his comrade came in leering with upraised blade.

Vetra saw the plan in an instant. He crouched low—and before his head went rolling across the sand, he twisted, surprise registering on their faces. He jammed an elbow in the kidneys of the jeering man that Lehundr now faced.

The half Thrule ripped blade across his attacker's throat.

Two down.

Vetra was bowled over in the rush by the two others in the brief moment it took him to make that rippling thrust. He staggered across the dirt, narrowly avoiding a mortal jab and follow-up boot heel in his face. A grisly vision of death swept across his mind as a desert rogue's blade slipped past his guard. But Lehundr came in grunting with weapon raised and swinging two-handed over his shoulder. The blade met the assailant's and the gleaming steel only glanced off Vetra's arm, slicing his forearm. The mercenary winced, but he shot his blade out to meet the man's desperate counterstrike even as he felt the throb of the wound up to his elbow.

Vetra's blade rang without mercy, a flurry of cuts that were too fast for his foe to follow. The groaning man fell to his knees, choking on his own blood. Vetra put his boot on the dying figure, pulled his blade free and used his left heel to mangle the man's face.

While the other bled out on the sand, the remaining rogue fled wheezing and grunting up the alley, holding his flayed ribs.

"Coward!"

Lehundr sought to chase after him but Vetra pulled him back. "Forget that scum, we have to leave!"

"But he'll blab to Rafa—"

"Forget Rafa! Dergath weeps, but warm blood runs everywhere your cursed map goes!"

The half Thrule grimaced, acknowledging the truth of it. He stumbled over to his crawling uncle.

"Go," his uncle croaked at him, pushing him away. "These swine will bring more with them. Better for you to be far away from here. I'll close the cursed hostel and hide away in Cyr-Down."

Lehundr hung his head. Vetra gathered the ponies and barked at Lehundr to get a move on.

The half Thrule struggled up onto his mount, blinking, squinting back his rage and frustration, muttering at the ill choices he had made.

Vetra sat his pony, a figure of silent wrath. He bandaged his arm, wrapping the sleeve of his caftan in a rude sash around his bloody wound.

Lehundr and he cantered back out the alley with the packbeast in tow. The great eastern road, now a ribbon of white satin shimmered in the drowsy heat through the gaps between the plaster homes. They left the rowdy sounds of Dragonskull behind.

II: The Ring of Pain

Their progress was stalled by the presence of a bearded rogue watching the eastern gateway: two flanking walls of loose sandstone blocks piled one on another, crossed by a wooden gate. Not much of a barrier, Vetra thought, but it was what Dragonskull had to offer. The man leaned on a spear, fingering a long blade clutched in a brown fist. His eyes were trained on the horizon. Vetra recognized the thug from the alley, so he signaled Lehundr to a halt.

Quicker to split the man's skull and be done with it, Vetra mused. But that would leave a clear signal to Rafa and his gang where they were headed. No, better to double back through town and dispose of the spy who was predictably stationed at the western entrance, thus throwing off the scent. But he rejected the plan: too risky. It entailed a complex detour and chance for a run-in. Easier to make a roundabout route and escape by stealth, winding around Dragonskull.

He and Lehundr ducked low in their saddles, and threaded their way back through narrow alleys and deserted service yards, leaving by another unguarded exit that Lehundr knew of. On the way they passed the stone water reservoir and its snaking pipe which swung out over its wide, glaring lip.

Vetra recalled that Dragonskull had once been a thriving mining community named New Thoria after the famed metal Thorian. The mines had dwindled since and Dragonskull would have become a ghost town, had it not been for the trade route, and ultimately the discovery of a water source.

Where water would normally gurgle from the pipe to fill the reservoir's basin, the spout was dry as desert bones. Vetra saw men clustered at the reservoir's base trying to sort out matters about the stopped flow, arguing and gesticulating, and the local constabulary was having a tough time trying to stop panicked locals from climbing the rungs up the vessel to fill bucket and barrel and drain what was now a scarce resource. Not a trickle came from its stony mouth; the work of the rebel Thrules, if the informers were to be believed. How they pumped water that distance was beyond Vetra. He shook his head, figuring it must by sorcery or some esoteric science.

Breaking through a rickety fence and a stand of eucalyptus swaying in the afternoon breeze, they took a goat path north and east that crossed the dusty highway, not two bowshots away.

Past the edge of town, the well-worn track led to the Great Highway, a twin rutted path that snaked in a straight, lonely line for leagues to come—as far as Dalispar in distant Mekutomia.

The oasis that graced this ore-rich area had dried up, much to the disappointment of the early prospectors who pumped water from the nearest water source—a massive oasis some five leagues out. It was here where Vetra and Lehundr fled, and turned their treasure-seeking eyes.

They passed wagons, driven by camels, sometimes teams of desert bullock, many a mean-eyed blue-black ruminant with huge horns and flaring, flat-faced snouts. They snorted and bawled, swinging heads back and forth in their yokes, nursing bellows deep in wattled throats.

They were no more past these when the white tips of bones appeared, peeking up from the sand. A gigantic dragon skull lay on its side, twisted askew. Eye sockets gaped like empty pools.

From where the creature had come, Vetra could hardly guess. He only knew that the beast was one of the great winged fliers that came from an age well in the past when dragons ruled the skies. This parched region had been a dragon haunt.

But now the ignorant Behundrians had affixed wooden signs and crude placards on the magnificent beast's brow. Carven characters were etched on its gleaming white skull: "*Dragonskull. Now entering the golden settlement: Dragonnook, of old.*"

"Why'd they scribe the old skull? Nobody around here can read."

Lehundr shook his head, muttering his distaste for the lurid script. "The old ones would roll in their graves if they were to witness such sacrilege."

Vetra's brows rose, wondering what attracted the half Thrule to dragons.

He saw only a few of the larger vertebrae of the dragon peeking through the sand, indicating the creature's massive girth. The rest of the bones he assumed were scavenged long ago by the locals to be made into souvenirs.

He could not help but marvel at this awesome creature that spanned twenty wagons' lengths.

"It's the largest in all of Behundria and Sahir," remarked Lehundr. "So was the town named, *Dragonskull*. Whether they could fly is not known. What is left of their wing bones are shrunken parodies for beasts of their size."

Vetra rubbed his sweaty brow.

"It was said their empire stretched as far as Lausern in Lvendar to Mekutomia in the far east. That their lords were half human, half dragon with bodies of men and feet, head and necks of dragons."

"I am glad to live in this age, rather than theirs," muttered Vetra.

"Are you sure?" challenged Lehundr. "What makes you think this age so much better?"

Any argument he realized would not alter the Thrule's opinion. What did he really know about the dragons anyway? Their lords, half man, half dragon? He was about to snort out a response when Lehundr added:

"'Twas their half human-dragon lords that held a reign that lasted a thousand years. Legend says they came from a faraway world. I don't personally believe it. There are as many tales of their existence as there are grains of sand in this desert. A certain chilling legend speaks of a time when dragons flew to earth from a distant world beyond the moon. Others say a band of wizards created the lords and morphed with the dragons themselves through wizardly agencies to become the hybrids we see in the crumbled statues poised before us."

"If the old dragons were so masterful, why did they die? Why would a dead race have treasure?"

Lehundr gave a sullen shrug. "Their empire was vast. Their riches as lavish. Dwelling on earth so long, they lost their powers, 'tis said, and the dragon-men came to lord over them in their weakened state, and thus become their masters. The new dragon-lords were fortunately somewhat of a benign force, as far as lords go."

Vetra struggled to control his contempt at such a concept. "Men masquerading as dragons. Putting on headdresses and dancing around a fire in the dead of night. I've seen it from tribe to tribe, temple to temple. Men or dragons, if either had such treasure, they would have kept it well hidden."

"Perhaps, but as to which age is better, if you live long enough here," said Lehundr, "you come to believe otherwise."

The miles passed, the sun a beating scourge, and the clop of ponies' hooves a monotonous beat on the packed sand. The old dragon ruins jutted more frequently out of the scrub, and the dunes took on a shimmering quality—sheltering half-fallen fanes, monuments and temples carved in crumbling stone: eerie statues of dragon men, or weathered full dragon, carved with uncanny skill.

A rambling cart with rickety wheels carrying silks and olives from the east came trundling in a cloud of dust: turbaned Guirites driving a team of desert horse. The outriders stood in their high, leather-padded saddles and colored caftans, with crossbows raised. Vetra lifted his hand in greeting.

Seeing no threat from two lone wayfarers dawdling along the road on their ponies, the caravan men lowered their weapons. "Akzam San!" they chorused in a lively shout, meaning "Peace go with you."

Vetra and Lehundr tipped heads in respect and moved off the road to let them pass.

They drove their ponies in a leisurely trot, squinting into the bright glare off the sand, a hot dry breeze in their face bringing sand flies and dust into their eyes. Alongside the road and twisting through the desert came the stone pipeline that carried the lifeblood water to

Dragonskull. Vetra stared at it, shaking his head in curious wonder. He marveled at the human engineering and ingenuity that could create something of this magnitude.

They encountered various traffic, from single caravans, to long trains of covered wagons and bulls with camp-following doxies and footmen wielding pikes. But never solo travelers or even packs of two. Two lone wayfarers with their light packs and blood-stained garments and blithe salutes caused many a suspicious look—and interest.

A painted harlot approached Vetra who had paused to rest his pony, her hips swinging, and cheap bangles tinkling on ankles and wrists.

Vetra scanned her long bare legs and her inviting, full lips and quickly declined the unsaid offer. "Business over pleasure, princess. I'm sure you'll find many a dog in Dragonskull that'll lap at your well-mounted behind."

"Not nearly as manly as you."

"Perhaps."

"What about your little friend?" the trollop followed up with a suggestive wink, her smirk hardened around the edges. "Half price for him."

Vetra laughed. So did the trollop. But Lehundr did not laugh, miffed as he was at being compared with such harshness to the mercenary.

Vetra reached over and slapped Lehundr playfully on the back. "Don't take it so hard, Thrule. These sluts are ignorant." He gazed in amusement as another of the doxy's painted friends slunk by. "I know better wares in Lausern who would practically give it to you for mug of mead."

A ghost of a grin touched Lehundr's dry lips, and he shrugged off his sudden resentment.

They made progress east with their sweating hides and panting mounts with the sun glaring at their backs.

No sign of Rafa or any headstrong, galloping host of his. It was a bare, desolate place, these outlands. Sand-scorched and dust-swept, as wild as the wind, with animal tracks zigzagging every which way across the parched landscape. The moan of the wind around carven rocks or twisted gumtrees caused Vetra a lonely shiver. His keen eyes saw the odd footpath of nomads, a distant low ridge strewn with boulders and dotted with the spiky azenia shrub, brown and faded green, and some faint yellow desert flowers.

Not a bowshot off the roadside, the remains of a stone dragon's tail curled around a huge sandstone man-shaped god with bicorn crown and hooked stave. The symbolism implied some form of an alliance perhaps—denoting a period when men and dragons had been at peace. Flanking the other side of the thoroughfare teetered a gigantic toppled statue with a dragonish head and tail, fangs and detailed scales, but the legs and torso of a man holding a trident.

It brought an eerie chill down Vetra's back, for reasons he could not name. Lehundr and he rode past the monument in solemn silence, the Thrule bowing his head in honor of the old lords of the desert.

Vetra frowned. "Why do you bow?"

"Why not? I pay obeisance to the ancient ones, like all the Thrules do."

"The Thrules—a people without a leader, beaten down and treated like curs by the Behundrians."

Lehundr grunted, "I could say the same for a dozen races across the lands."

Vetra shrugged. He rubbed his eyes while Lehundr rode on in silence.

They stopped an hour or so later off the beaten caravan trail to rest the ponies. Both were tasked by the late afternoon heat and vigorous ride.

Dismounting to stretch his legs, Vetra gazed around warily at the desolate surroundings. "I almost feel as if ears are listening to our every conversation. Though we are nowhere near that hive of Dragonskull. Are there sprites hiding behind each cactus waiting for their chance?"

Lehundr gave a chuckle. He leaned elbows on thighs as he crouched. "You have a tall imagination for a fighter of your standing, Vetra. Still, it pays to be vigilant." The Thrule darted his own wary glance over his shoulder.

The heat waves shimmered with a wanton fury. Cactus and low, spiked shrubs merged to the eye on the horizon to dance with the rhythms of the hot, dry wind. The land of the ancient dragons was a harsh environment, thought Vetra.

He gained his mount and heeled his pony on, taking only a sparing draft of water from his canteen. He was grateful that Lehundr had packed extra water bladders on the packbeast.

A band of five horsemen riding hard for Dragonskull, slowed and on a signal from their leader, reigned in and surrounded the two men.

The leader squinted with curiosity at the mercenary and Thrule. "Afternoon, outlander. Mighty hot for a pilgrimage. You bound for Sunswatch?"

Vetra said nothing, sizing up his questioner, sitting his mount in easy, carefree manner. Lehundr stared hard at the men: cruel, sardonic bullies with iron at their hips, whips in their hand, axes and water bladders strapped at their mount's sides. The Thrule's pony backed up a few steps.

"The desert's a dangerous place," the tall Mosete continued in an easy drawl. His finger twirled his sandy-colored mustache. "Man can get his valuables robbed, his throat cut. What do you say? Me and my deputy Needs here can protect you—for a fee, of course."

Vetra gazed on in amusement. "Funny, I was just going to extend the same offer to you. The oafs we killed back in Dragonskull were slow in accepting our token of friendship."

The man's scarred face went hard. "Really? How many?"

"A dozen, I reckon."

The rider snorted. "Well, I think you're a liar." On a signal of his leader, his deputy Needs came charging in, blade swinging.

Vetra leaned back in his saddle. A vicious sweep, too fast for the eye, slashed into the rider's shoulder, slitting flesh from neck to ribs.

A ghastly spray of blood wetted the sand, and the man toppled off his brown bay, writhing in blood.

With a malicious roar, another rider came reeling in. Lehundr pulled away, his falchion gleaming, but Vetra was faster, and his blade hissed out, parrying sword, and Vetra's left fist crashed into the man's jaw, breaking teeth and bone.

The man slumped in his saddle. Vetra turned hard and drove steel through the man's chest. The bandit's horse fled off into the desert, dragging the dead man by the heel, whose foot had caught in his stirrup.

The leader took off his cap and wiped down his brow. "Well, that's an unexpected turn of events. What to do, what to do..." With an ugly scowl, the expectant looks of his men hot on his back, he urged his mount forward, hand reaching for his hilt.

Vetra glanced sideways, as if the lizard at his horse's hooves was of more interest than the man's approach. Their eyes locked, but the attacker seemed fazed by the mercenary's unflinching gaze. A sudden perturbation crept over his face, like a shadow fleeting by under a passing cloud.

Vetra had stared down men like this before, and he knew the man for the bully he was: a callous, condescending brute who had won perhaps too many well-picked fights and had a knack for preying on weaklings which by uncanny luck had boosted his confidence. He had judged his marks by the size of their ponies. But for all his cowardice, the man was not completely daft, for when a cloud of dust rose up the trail, he reined aside.

"You've just been saved, outlander, by luck."

Vetra laughed. "Sure, keep on believing that."

The leader snarled and the survivors rode off in a cloud of dust, mouths full of foul oaths.

"Cowards," spat Vetra. "Is all this backhill country full of villains?"

Lehundr shrugged, dabbing at his brow. "No shortage of ruffians and bullies here, I'm afraid. It gets worse."

Vetra shook his head. "Well, it's good that I am a tolerant man, Lehundr. Have a care, Thrule, and don't sweat so much."

They slowed their own ponies, to let the oncoming riders and their guarded caravan pass. Even as he stopped to check the jewels were still there, Vetra frowned at Lehundr's packbeast's cargo bag which seemed heavily laden and bulkier than normal. Something didn't seem quite right about it and Vetra stared at it for a long time, as if it had moved in the shimmering heat. Finally he shook his head and muttered some words about the desert heat getting to him.

The miles passed in a blur of dust and heat. The soil tended to a slightly reddish hue, and sometimes white sand would form dunes, caked with twitch-weeds and low shrubs like juniper. Always the tall, smooth-boled gumtrees dotted the landscape, arching their pale gray and green limbs skyward. Such giants offered welcome shade when they passed by. The only creature that dared the daytime sun were the tiny lizards that darted around the trees' trunks.

Lehundr lifted a hand in warning before long. "The great oasis is fast approaching. See how the pipe runs up the hill alongside the road? We should be on guard for hostility."

They moved with more caution now, well off the dusty track. But not as far as Vetra would have liked for he saw a ravine drop sharply to their left.

The sun pushed its somnolent face lower in the sky, turning a slightly more jaundiced hue. The wind had died, and Vetra brought his pony around to climb a low hill, north of the one where the pipe ran.

Commotion echoed from the valley below. Vetra pulled his mount out of sight, before crouching in the warm sand atop the high dune. He hissed at Lehundr to do the same.

Vultures circled above. He smelled the strong scent of carrion. A battle had raged here recently, for he could see the dark sand below was stained blood red and bodies lay strewn everywhere, both Thrule and Behundrian.

A cluster of Thrules in wine-colored robes and loose hoods milled about a strange wheel, or some gigantic gumwood ring. The wheel lay flat on the sand, fifty feet in diameter and turned slowly under the desert heat. Its movement was aided by eight heaving bullocks with upturned horns, yoked to the ring's perimeter. The mechanism powered a conveyor system up the slope, consisting of large buckets attached to chain and pulley. The conveyor drew water from the nearby oasis up the hill into the great pipe which ran from the summit down the hill's opposite side and alongside the eastern road. Now the pipe lay broken at a lower point, pierced by pickaxe and hammer, and Thrules collected the spouting water into barrels and water bladders of their own, which they hauled with their packbeasts to a roped-off area.

The oasis was surrounded by giant gum trees and billowing palm with branches laden with ripe dates. A line of ruined stone columns reared up at its center. The site was ancient, Vetra recognized. Flanking it were two stone, gaunt dragon-men, the lords of the time, holding wine cups up to the air as if to catch the rain.

At least a hundred Thrules swarmed the area. A central leader, waving falchion, gesticulated at the others. A red shawl flared around his shoulders. A score of hooded figures scouted the dead, scavenging the bodies for supplies and weapons. Vultures continued to wheel and to drop down with hungry cries to examine and plunder the corpses with parted beaks thick with flesh. Vetra saw some animals had been killed too. Bloated bellies of bullocks lay upturned, exposed to the sun, their hides teeming with flies, and an awful stench. Whether they had died from sickness, or purposeful violence was not evident. Around the wheel, some of the brute beasts' places had been supplanted by Thrules who were chained at the leg to do the task normally done by bulls. They were being unshackled with growls of disgust and anger.

Vetra's lip twisted in contempt. Likely the Thrules had taken revenge, had come to liberate their kin.

"The Ring of Pain," muttered Lehundr. "The symbol of our

brothers' bondage. This time they have not been idle."

"A pump?"

"That wheel down there is where our people have been enslaved ever since I can remember, to draw water for the precious Behundrians. Look at the chained oxen which drive the capstan. It pumps water to the Dragonskull traders' post. Sometimes when the bulls die, 'tis only Thrules who drive it. Their oasis at Dragonskull dried up long ago, and some engineer had the clever idea to pump water from this oasis, which is as you see."

Vetra rubbed his jaw, frowning in reflection. Like the spokes of a radiating wheel had the oxen been stationed. Where one of the yokes was empty, a great plank of wood had been strapped to outfit what looked ten Thrules to take the brute beast's place. He saw the Thrules had taken axes to the chained shackles that held their remaining brothers.

He shook his head in marvel. His lip pressed in a grim line.

Some of the mystery of the water's propulsion was dissipated in the course of his scrutiny. Gravity more or less pulled the water down the stone pipe toward Dragonskull. It was just a matter of getting the flow started, which the great pump with the wheel powered by the bullocks, provided.

Vetra caught the glint of vats and screens by the oasis shore. A thin tributary pipe drew water from the sparkling waters. The pump also served a parallel purpose: to draw out emerald-speckled water which when dried, left a precious Thorian residue. Shne the wizard-alchemist had long ago discovered such sediments could manufacture the hardest steel.

Vetra and Lehundr crouched, studying the proceedings below from the nearby hill, squinting against the glare of the sinking sun. "The way I see it, we have to get by this pump site to get to your tomb or dragon fort, but this ravine below us makes it treacherous. If we can skirt its edge maybe, slip by them without—"

A sudden sound of a rock tumbling down the hill had him whirling toward the bushes behind him. Five dark-robed Thrules scrambled out of the cacti grove, training crossbows at them.

"Down!" One motioned with his weapon to Vetra and Lehundr. "Now! Move—down the slope! No tricks!"

Vetra glared. The offender was a young bowman, of more than average height who he sized up in a glance. His swarthy features and thin hooked nose lay shadowed behind a hood. Fingers twitched on a mechanical trigger bar.

Vetra knew they would riddle him full of bolts before he could take two steps to cut them down. With a rumbling curse, he jerked about and made his way down the crumbling slope. White-knuckled, he gripped his sword. That they had let him keep it was a sign of inexperience. Lehundr scrambled behind. The other Thrules snatched up the reins of their ponies and led them down toward the encampment, prodding them with the ends of their bows. One nudged Vetra a little too forcefully and Vetra turned about snarling, swatting the crossbow aside with a sputter of rage. The bolt flew wide. The other Thrules came running, sending Lehundr sprawling forward.

"Down!" they cried. The lead Thrule, sweating and quivering in rancor at Vetra's truculent manner, pushed and prodded him on, while two others stepped in beside him, bows trained at his midsection. One Thrule tried to tear the sword from Vetra's iron grip, but the mercenary laughed at his pathetic attempt. That they hadn't riddled him full of bolts meant they wanted to keep the prisoners alive, probably because Lehundr himself was half Thrule. He pegged his young captor as an unschooled and unseasoned pup, a new recruit whose heart was probably hammering in his chest.

Vetra let itchy fingers play on the hilt of his sword. The chance that he could gain advantage in this situation was slim; with reluctance he forewent a quick skirmish. Not the right moment...

Surprised shouts came drifting from below. The captain of the troop came marching up, curses thick on his lips at the intruders who dared approach the wheel. The lead bowman ordered the five who held Vetra captive to a halt.

Vetra saw some gripped falchions in their hands, others short curved blades with ends wider than their middles. No taller than chest-height, these Thrules had polished gumwood boomerangs strapped in small packs on their backs. Their loose hoods showed only their eyes and mouths; their bare hands, browned by desert sun. Plump ponies laden with supplies stood a pebble's toss away near the bullock ring, swishing tails to keep away the flies.

Vetra thought hard how he was going to outwit these offenders. Lehundr, rigid as a board, uttered no word, but his black eyes darted wildly about and passed over Vetra with meaningful fervor. He and Lehundr exchanged glances.

As the leader approached, a great cry went up among the Thrules. Vetra could only assume they thought that more of the enemy Behundrians had been caught spying.

He noticed the relaxed stance of the bowmen, and the weapons slackened in their hands. At the moment of the first cry, he struck with instinctive ferocity. Fists and hilt flew out, then he ducked in a protective crouch. The Thrule next to him dropped like a stone.

Bows came up. His Thrule captor gave a choked cry.

Vetra pulled the body of the nearest bowman toward his own. The struggling Thrule took the other's bolt square in the chest.

Vetra threw the body aside while Lehundr stumbled in a limping dash toward his pony. He seized the animal's reins as the bolt of a Thrule whizzed mere inches from his ear.

Vetra grunted. He sprinted to take out the next man between him and his horse. Blades came up to lock in feverish clangor with a competent Thrule, dancing on his sandaled feet. The robed man swirled close to his back, ready to arc a murderous backhand sweep across Vetra's throat. Vetra twisted around him and lifted a knee to plunge his boot in the small of his back. He pushed him savagely to send him rolling down the slope. Vetra threw himself to the ground, while bolts sped overhead to smash into the foliage.

"Stop this madness!" a booming voice rang over the clangor and thunk of bolts. The commanding figure pushed aside one of the aggressors while wrenching the weapon out of the young Thrule's hand pointed at Vetra. He rounded fiercely upon the mercenary. "You look like no friends of Behundrians."

Vetra grunted. "You think? Maybe we're dragons? Out to spit fire at you and burn up your water—an ugly sod of an outlander and a half Thrule? Dergath weeps. Muzzle your dogs!"

Something in Vetra's sarcasm caused the other to pause and break out in a scowl. "Who are you then?"

"I'm Vetravincus. This is Lehundr. I'm a trader and a sometimes mercenary."

"Well, what do you do here? This is sacred land. Don't you know it is a time of war?" He gazed with rising anger at his dead kinsman.

"That we know. We heard it all the way back in Dragonskull." He spat out a gob of phlegm. "We came in search of—"

"What he means to say," interrupted Lehundr quickly, "is that we're prospectors—in search of new lodes of silver and iron. You'll see our tools on my pony, picks and screens, and more strapped to our packbeast."

"Is that so? Then I expect if I search your belongings, I'll find more of these gold-hunters's wares?" The man strode over toward the mounts. "Zren, Yuel, Munan, go search—" he jerked his head.

The surly youth who had escorted Vetra down the hill pushed past the two other Thrules, thumbing his thin, hooked nose to rifle through the packs strapped on the packbeast. One quivered under his touch and he cursed it, but he jerked back with a sharp cry as a lithe form came springing out of the large bag, bowling him over. The figure sprang back, her hair matted with sweat, wielding a crude knife and a strange knout, with wicked metal barbs.

The Thrule's cry rang with choked surprise as steel gleamed in her hands.

Others poised ready to attack. Jhara stood with her legs braced, blinking in the sun, eyeing the three hooded foes who circled her with curled lips. Her face creased in wary appraisal, then amusement, crouching on the balls of her feet like a she-cat.

The younger Thrule came at her, underestimating her puny weaponry. "Come to me, birdie!" She round-house kicked him in the head. He fell with a crunch, clutching at his head, moaning.

The other came in, swinging a curved blade high.

She grunted and ducked, elbows out, fists clenched and landed a fierce punch. Springing up from her crouch, she was ready to lash into flesh. The young Thrule was rising to his feet, shaking his head and groaning.

"Is that all you got?" she taunted. One hand clutched tightly on her curled dagger that gleamed in the noonday sun. The dangling whip in the other traced shimmering circles and drew blood and bits of skin. Already it had snagged black cloth and blood was flowing from it.

Vetra could not hold back a strange surge of admiration for this spunky girl, in spite of his surprise.

"Stealing young girls now, are you?" grunted the Thrule leader, disgust clear on his face.

"I had no knowledge of her," Vetra growled, miffed at the chief's quizzical, cold stare.

Creeping like cats, many Thrules moved to surround Vetra. Others blocked the girl's path and Lehundr's prancing feet found no avenue of escape. Vetra drew his blade. Snarling through his teeth, he stood bent-kneed and dared any to take him.

Lehundr gibbered attestations in Vetra's defense, but to no avail. "He speaks truth. I came with him from Dragonskull, escaping the persecutions of Behundrian thugs."

"Do not listen to them, Zaln," hissed the young Thrule guard who had prodded Vetra down the hill. "Ulra lies dead with a bolt through his chest because of these pigs' aggression."

"No thanks to your stupidity in holding us under crossbow threat," growled Vetra.

Zaln, the leader, paused, nodding silently to his scout. He turned to Lehundr. "And we should listen to you, why? Because you lied to us earlier? Coming from a half Thrule, this means nothing. Take them!"

"Peace!" uttered the girl. "They speak the truth. I emptied out their cargo bag and stowed away when they were swilling ale at the stables. They had nothing to do with me and are not 'women stealers'. I merely wanted to follow them—this rogue in particular." She waved her bloody whip at Vetra.

The leader frowned with wonder. "And why should you do that?"

"Because this big ox helped save my brother—and because of the map."

"Map? What map?" Zaln growled.

"Stupid girl!" shouted Lehundr. "Shut your mouth or I'll—"

"No, you'll do nothing—so hold your tongue, half Thrule!" Zaln ordered his men to keep the half Thrule constrained, who had rushed over to the girl's mount.

"I ask you again, what do you do here at the Ring of Pain?"

"It is as we have said," muttered Lehundr stubbornly. "Prospectors."

The leader sneered an explosive sound. "A girl who fights with knives and scourge, and a limping, lying half Thrule and a sullen mercenary? I doubt it. I hardly think the word 'prospectors' applies to you. What's your game?"

"Let it go, Lehundr," sighed Vetra. "Sometimes it's better to tell the truth."

"But—"

Vetra waved him off. He pushed past the scowling Thrules, and ignored the wicked crossbows trained at him. He pulled up Lehundr's caftan and exposed the vest beneath. "Because of this, we are here: an ancient roadmap. It shows where the secret hoard of the Dragon-lords is." There was a leaden pause as dull murmurs passed through the awed group. "It could mean immense riches. Not that we're expecting anything," Vetra added with a cryptic grin. "The reality is there's no way we're getting past armed men, or your own patrols and camps. That's why we were skulking so close, and that ravine is not helping. It'll be seething here by sundown with avengers from Dragonskull. Either you help us, or let us go."

"How be we just kill you?" piped up Zren like a surly badger. "Like we did these Behundrians, and take the map for our own?"

"What? And be just as treacherous and base as your enemies?" said Vetra with comic irony. "That's exactly what the Behundrians tried to do."

"Cool your head, Zren. You're much too hot under the hood. I'm in charge here," murmured Zaln. "Nothing is decided yet."

"Perhaps you could help us?" suggested Vetra, half sarcastically to the young Thrule. "Unless you're all just as shifty and treacherous as that blackguard Cthan and his Behundrian scum at the outpost? I don't think you're as cold-blooded as that lizard and his cronies like Rafa, otherwise your whole rebellion is just a sham, a web of hypocrisy."

"You do not know all," said Zaln through clenched teeth. "We defend what is ours."

"You broke the pipe they made," argued Vetra. "You incited their wrath. How can you not expect retaliation?" he growled.

The leader turned on him, his brows bristling. "They kidnap our women. They sell us and use us as slaves. They breed us for more slaves to work for the cruel lords of the east—Eustan, Daranthia, Gattrland and other parts. You do not know all, outlander. So, do not judge us through the eyes of your own biases."

Vetra frowned, licking his lips. "It seems Cthan has severely misrepresented your cause."

The leader spat out a contemptible wad of phlegm. "Cthan is no more than a lying desert snake and double-talking torturer. He promised us our lands back under the last treaty—that we may pasture our goats and llamas upon the lush oases. He waves instead a charter of forged signatures in front of our noses, saying that we agree to forfeit our lands to his prospectors and overlords."

The Thrule chief's eyes flickered with fury, but then he pulled back his hood to reveal wisps of long steely gray hair. His eyes softened into wide pools as he crept closer to examine Lehundr's map. "Maybe. Can it be...? Yes. It must." He traced his gnarled fingers across the ancient fabric. "This looks more like the inner sanctum of the old temple, that of the ancient Dhraken. A tomb of exotic mystery."

"It is," assured Lehundr with triumph.

"There—" Zaln stabbed a finger "—the key in the tomb." His eyes glazed, passed swiftly over the ancient dragon script, as if he knew the gist of that ancient dead language. "A key that would open the great fortress, Dragon Forge?—one closed for an age."

Lehundr wagged his head; a hushed whisper was on his lips.

"I don't know if anyone's been up to the fortress for years. 'Tis hallowed ground—"

"Some say it is cursed, but 'tisn't," Lehundr cut in. "The dragon-lords were wise; they hid their treasure from the likes of greedy, ambitious overlords."

Zaln wasted no time in arguing. "Take captain Dunon and Gefzad along and five others. Assemble packbeasts with water bladders to head north. The rest will stay here to defend the Ring of Pain and the Oasis from our foes."

Dunon motioned around the scattered bodies and still burning wreckage. "Are you sure we should split our forces at this time? The Behundrians will be on the move soon enough."

Zren shook his head like a wild dog. "Aye, I say we slay this rabble, take the map, and search for the treasure at a later time."

The chief laughed sharply. "There's enough death here today. I'm sure you can see that."

Vetra shrugged, casting a sad look around him. As much as he despised the pesky Thrule, he had to agree with him on one point. They had enough on their plate without watering down their forces. Somewhere he had a bad feeling that these resistance fighters were living on borrowed time.

On cue, the attack came sooner than expected.

No sooner had Gefzad organized the team when the hoofs of

enemy horse and camel came raising clods of dirt and the chorus of vindictive wails of men came howling like wolves. A team of camels came pouring over the rise; men were pointing and gesticulating and sabers swinging in their hands. Others loped on foot, wielding crossbows and maces.

The Thrules jolted to attention, raising weapons and forming ranks.

Vetra swore. "Down!"

Bolts came whizzing by. Crossbow men from the attackers were kneeling in the sand, ready to arm and shoot again. A volley of lethal iron whooshed by and thudded into date palms and Thrule flesh like the swarm of many bees.

Camels burst out of the dunes with snarls on their lips. Men atop the beasts hacked down on the surprised Thrules.

The little robed figures scrabbled on their knees, ducking strikes and stabs and hacking at the legs of the cantering camels. Thrules died under those hoofs, but three of the ornery beasts fell hamstrung, spilling their riders to the sand where they were quickly despatched with glinting, gore-flecked Thrule knives.

"Stay back! And follow my lead," Vetra roared at Jhara.

"Fall back!" Dunon cried. "Take cover in the scrub, damn you. Use the cacti as shields! Rake them with bolts!"

In the melee Vetra recognized such rogues as Rafa and Vilivet and several other rough-looking characters from the depot—the bullies and cutthroats who ran the town.

Vilivet snarled, spittle flecking from his fleshy lips: "It's that damn bitch from the market," he cried, "the same whose brother has been stealing from our honest merchants. Get her! She carved up a bunch of Rafa's men."

Cthan and his men gave gusty curses, made the quick leap that Vetra and the girl had joined ranks with the rebels, seeing him rubbing shoulders with Zaln and Lehundr.

A cry came from a sandy-haired ruffian waving a broadsword with leather helm flapping down his cheeks. "Aye, and it's that meddlesome outlander. Take him alive! I want him alive."

Vetra gave back an insulting roar. "Only in hell's last inferno will you take me alive."

They charged into the Thrule huddle. Vetra and the others scattered. Jhara scrambled forward to grab a saber from a fallen camel rider. Cthan rose in his stirrups and looped back with a snarl, smashing down blade to send a Thrule running alongside to oblivion. "First the Thrule leader, you jackleg fools," he bellowed. "The girl'll be spreadeagled on a mattress before long." He arched out a swinging strike and ran a Thrule through the mouth who scrambled beside his camel. "We're here to slay the oasis robbers, not some ragbag trio of thieves."

Cthan pushed his camel through the defenders. The Thrule charge had lost its momentum and the sheriff mowed down Thrules like wheat. His sword raged up and down taking cuts and parries, hewing crimson bodies with it. Bolts whipped around him. Two of his henchmen fell from their beasts pierced through the hearts, but not him. Rafa at his side rode one-eyed with a patch over his left eye. His sleek roan bucked and snorted in battle lust. The sands bloomed red. Footmen of the oncoming host chopped and stabbed down at bodies that lay twitching and bleeding.

Jhara wielded the two-foot saber two-handed. She blocked a cut, ducked, and a Behundrian's whistling blade glanced off her forearm, drawing a thin line of blood. She wailed, and shrank back.

"That young slut with him is an accomplice. Take her! She's a dervish with knives."

Vetra, fighting whistling cuts of his own, smote alongside her, shouldered his weight in to block the slash that would have taken off her head. He jerked a hard, disemboweling thrust that lay the Behundrian attacker howling in his own blood and entrails.

Lehundr gasped and flailed with awkward mobility. He stumbled on his branded left leg. He struggled in an arm lock with a Dragonskull guard who tried to twist the short blade from his hand. Thrules came clambering up and plunged their knives into the aggressor's back. Lehundr rolled free.

Vetra winced as a glancing blow from the flat end of a Behundrian's sword laid open a gash in his scalp. He shook the blood out of his eyes. He and his allies were hopelessly outnumbered and it looked as if they were all dead men. Like it or not, he was caught in a war which he wished no part of. In his dim vision, he caught a glimpse of the unmoving Ring of Pain and the raging beasts trying to escape, terrorized by the stench of blood.

It gave him an idea, albeit a risky one. He staggered to the ring, spurred by a sudden inspiration. The bulls were pawing at the dirt, snorting, ready to tear the whole harness and hitch off their heads if they must. With vicious hacks of his blade Vetra loosed the first yoke and the bulls stormed out, razor-curled horns lowered in offense. They shook their heads and bellowed while Vetra hewed the yokes off two more of them.

These were wild bulls, chosen for their powerful pulling ability and their dogged endurance to withstand the extreme heat of the Behundrian wastes. The dreaded bullocks were mean creatures in their own right with eight-inch horns and powerful hindquarters. They went mad, kicking hind legs and rearing with foam on their muzzles, drunk with the delight of freedom.

Four more Vetra freed, and he leapt aside to avoid their goring horns and trampling hooves. He roared at Jhara to get down. She narrowly jerked aside in time, as a raging, bucking beast fled by and aimed straight for the warring Behundrians. Four more beasts were stampeding their way into the Behundrian fray, mowing down Thrules who could not get out of the way fast enough. In a bloodlust frenzy, the bulls' natural instincts to gore and trample was whetted.

Smashing horns into camels, the beasts plowed on like battering rams, toppling anything in sight. They were unstoppable. Men fell shrieking, dying, gored and bowled over only to be trampled by the hoofs or the wild rush of the camels.

Bolts flew and felled two of the monsters. But not before other bulls had broken through and done significant damage. A dozen camels had been gored or lay groaning in streaming, blood-drenched heaps.

Two younger bulls fled into the scrub, bloodied and rearing with wrath, while the remaining three beasts, still caught in the fray, kept heads down and charged anything in their path.

Cthan's camel, impaled by horns, lay in a twitching heap, bleeding out in the sand, while both human and bullock trampled over its belly and the other corpses littering the sandy plain.

Vetra's steel split the skull of a charging Behundrian. He turned in time to clash swords with Cthan who came charging at him like a bull. The sheriff's strength was phenomenal, uncanny in the suffocating heat and the stench of blood as the fighters struggled in a death dance. Their leg muscles knotted, swords quivering in deadlock over their heads. Cthan, the near bald giant, heaved Vetra back and he staggered away from the broken length of pipe. Vetra looked up as in a dream, dwarfed under the shadow of the dragon-lord statue tipping his cup in mocking salute. He shook the haze from his head and parried Cthan's strikes as his obstinate enemy came in again, roaring a curse. The strident clang of their swords resounded but was lost in the noise of the jostling bodies and dying shrieks of men who slashed and hewed, oblivious to the baying and bleating of brute beasts and the roar of battle and thunk of their horns as they found flesh.

In a sudden burst of volcanic strength, Vetra plunged forth and forced back Cthan's advance. A surprised grimace fled over the rogue's face. Wide-eyed, he careened back, but with a grotesque laugh. He was actually enjoying this, wallowing in blood! Vetra thought with amazement.

"So, you have some fight in you after all, outland scum. Thank the gods! I thought you were just a spineless imp like these Thrules."

"Come and find out," spat Vetra. He twisted sideways and lashed out, kicked the sheriff and sent him reeling backward into a ghastly pile of dead bodies. The sheriff sprang to his feet and Vetra lunged in to run the lawman through, put steel through his gullet. But one of

Cthan's men edged in, brushing aside the mercenary's stroke and raised steel for his own mortal strike. Denied vengeance on the sheriff, Vetra bellowed. He wormed forward, breaking half the protector's teeth with a jabbing elbow before running him through to the heart, blade standing out of the back of his chest like a spike. The glaze-eyed figure fell and Vetra pulled the dripping steel free with a snarl. He kicked the corpse away, blocking in time to parry Cthan's follow-up thrust.

Two Thrules came smashing in to send Cthan staggering. A group of Behundrians joined the fray. A seethe and roil of bodies made it difficult to make sense of who was friend and who was foe, as the fighters were swept away in a tide as a dying camel crashed headlong into the attackers. Vetra plunged his blade into a man's back, wrenching his sword free in a gush of blood. Taking deep breaths, he crouched, looking about. Nearby Lehundr defended against Rafa's whirlwind of blades, beaten back mercilessly like a scarecrow.

The Dragonskull thug yelled, "I'll see you in hell, half Thrule! You'll give me that cursed map now, or I'll peel each layer of skin from your sorry hide and stuff them down your throat! You'll beg me for mercy to kill you."

Despite his loss of an eye, the gang leader was about to carve Lehundr to pieces, when silent and deadly as a viper, a thong laid into his side and he jerked around with a gasp. Jhara pulled the weapon free with its flap of flesh. Holding his ribs, Rafa screeched and doubled over and Lehundr kicked him away, his sword barely moving up in time to block the thrust of another bloody shaft as one of Rafa's bravos came chopping down at him in blind fury.

It was a fierce free-for-all in every sense of the word, where only the rules of the wasteland prevailed. The Thrules, disorganized and disheartened and weaving in and out of the chaotic skirmish like rabbits, were fading fast. The wreckage and slumped bodies were appalling, and without any leadership or direction, the defenders fled in terror.

"Retreat! Into the brush," shouted Vetra over the mad slaughter. "There are too many of them."

Some heeded his advice while others kept on fighting. Those who backed their chief Zaln, parried and blocked saber blows, but were quickly surrounded by howling enemy and put to the sword.

"Fools! They'll die in vain," grunted Vetra. "Why don't they pull back, hack their way through?" Rage and frustration soured his blood lust. "All for some water, and futile moments of holding a doomed position?"

Gefzad cried through his teeth, "We gain victory over an age-old enemy!"

"You die in your glory. Quick!" he pulled at Jhara and shouldered Lehundr back toward the hill. "We must get to cover. We will fight them in the scrublands—on our own terms!" They cut their way through Cthan's scattered flanks.

Up the hill they scrambled—the same from whence they came. The crash of camels thundered after them.

Dunon saw the practicality of the mercenary's plan and hurried after, though he was torn by the image of his chief who fought a valiant fight, a last stand, but for a lost cause. With a bolt shivering close to his ear, he put a hand to a jagged cut on his forehead and clambered after Vetra, Jhara and the others, dodging missiles while Gefzad and his kinsmen stumbled at his heels.

What others of the miserable Thrule band scrambled after, Vetra did not know, for he was clearing a path up the hill through bush and stump. But a band of blood-dripping Behundrians joined in pursuit.

III: Road to Nowhere

The whine of bolts and savage cries rang long after their headlong escape. Vetra and company weaved their way through stump and scrub bush, in an attempt to lose their pursuers.

Vetra pushed on, panting in ragged gusts, blazing a trail for his allies along the thicketed ridge, hacking spiky fronds and low desert thorn. How he hated to be chased like a wounded animal, but this was the reality of the day. They had been heavily outnumbered. The fact that any of them were still alive was testament to their combined skill. The sounds of pursuit faded. He moved among the company, taking a head count and scanning for injuries.

Lehundr was cut and scratched; his limp had gotten worse. Jhara looked battered and sore, flexing the fingers of her left hand whose wrist bore a raw wound, but she held her head high, her fierce pride shining through. The ragtag of Thrule infantry were in no better shape, scrabbling and gasping with wounds, cuts and injured pride. One warrior's arm was broken, others were torn, disheveled, bleeding and dehydrated from battle and the harrowing escape. Twenty-eight of them stood sullen and bedraggled amid the foliage, dragging two packbeasts laden with gear. Zren the truculent bowman, scowled and cursed, whipping his sword about, shredding cacti. Dunon and Besu conversed in heated tones, spittle dribbling from their lips. Aus, a squad leader and his aide Gefzad kept eyes trained on the hillside, while the magician-priest, who Vetra learned was Samos, twirled his stave and muttered chants to his amulets. Vetra reflected that his magic had done little to protect the beleaguered rebels. Among the dust-bitten Thrules, there were maybe a dozen bowmen, all armed with swords or knives.

From his cacti-strewn dune, Vetra and the others crouched on their hands and knees. They gazed through a screen of juniper at the corpse-littered battle plain below. The party of Behundrians that had been sent out to kill them returned and gesticulated to their leader, the bald-headed Cthan and the sword-wielding Dragonskull constabulary. The Behundrians, washed in blood and grime, assessed the gushing rent in the pipe, and knelt to repair it with what tools they had brought with them.

"They don't know where we are," whispered Dunon with gratification.

"They will soon," grunted Vetra. "Look."

"Zaln!" cursed Aus.

They had stripped and beaten the Thrule leader. Those on the hill recognized him only by his ragged wisps of gray hair.

"They'll torture your leader before long," said Vetra. "He'll tell them of your strategies, secrets and hidden lairs."

"He will not talk," asserted Gefzad stubbornly.

Aus, whose hood had been torn off, gave fierce acknowledgment of his comrade's assertion. His hair was matted with blood and Vetra could see his teeth gleaming white in the sun.

"They'll make him," assured Vetra.

Dunon looked away. He was a man grown old and weary from these desert feuds.

"We'll travel together toward the canyons of shadows, in the vale of Zabenzar," he said in sober voice. "Let me see this map again." He lifted Lehundr's desert robe. "Aye, see the eagle's croft on this left tear above the dragon head? Only on the bluffs could be where tombs lie. They must have been looted or destroyed by tomb robbers by now."

"We'll travel as a group and hope they're intact," agreed Besu. He was one of the taller, leaner members of the Thrule company. "Well, by Besthra! We might as well head for this ridge to get to the key. It was Zaln's last wish that we set forth. A treasure like that'll allow us to buy an army and crush Cthan and his scum. The dragon treasure is to be discovered by Thrules, not Behundrians."

Vetra grinned at the snarl that spilled from Lehundr's lips. Evidently the half Thrule resented the prospect of splitting the treasure multiple ways.

Aus clicked his tongue with skepticism. "There hasn't been a jackleg prospector come through Dragonskull that tried to discover the treasure and succeeded."

"But this time there's a map," said Besu.

"But likely a fable too," assured Samos the priest-shaman. His bone-carved femur-staff bobbed in his hand while magical amulets draped on gut-cord around his neck jiggled with his every motion.

"If we don't try," Jhara said, "then nothing is to be gained."

The Thrules looked at her with surprise. Some peered with envy at her sleek, toned body which was glitter for the eyes; the swell of her high breasts pressed in appealing fashion through her tattered jerkin and she held herself erect like a young barbaric queen.

For some reason, her words affected the Thrules in a curious manner. There was a fierce note of passion in Jhara's voice, and her confidence was such that stirred the dispirited hearts of these Thrules who were too used to persecution and failure.

"Best we get as much distance from those vengeful Behundrians as possible," advised Vetra. His warning glance was enough at the Thrules who gazed too long on Jhara. Two had limped over to rummage among the supplies strapped to the packbeasts. Vetra and Dunon joined to take inventory. The company had dried food and grains for a few days, several bladders of water that had not been slashed by the leaping, looting Behundrians and various other necessities: pots, loops of rope, torches, wineskins, blankets and weapons.

Dunon pointed ahead to the waves shimmering in the heat. "East along the ridge then. The eagle ridge is north of here. First break in this ravine we branch off! We cannot reach it today, but maybe tomorrow."

"Then let us move," said Vetra, "lest those fiends rout us out or try to flank us."

They followed a series of wild goat paths along the ridge before the desert scrub broke off and gave way into a flatlands. The road, the Great Highway, ran straight as an arrow and the last shoulder of ridge rose up from the sands to grant views of both sides, particularly the shallow bowl north and into the land of desolation.

Vetra marveled at the vast, breathtaking solitude of the windswept terrain. Nothing but animal paths, red dirt, tumbleweed, and the odd cluster of towering cacti or gum tree. Ridges sprawled in the distances in a sinking haze of twilight.

The east-west road wound to their right like a ribbon of glinting silver. Then branched north.

On Dunon's advice, the pack followed the lesser road north. After an hour's brisk slog up the valley, the sun was a flaming ball sinking on the horizon. They had not ventured a league when signs of human activity became apparent. The pack drew back, crouching under a stand of withered eucalyptus whose shadow cast a dusky blanket over the hot sand.

Enemy soldiers wearing helms and glinting mail bore falchions and crossbows. They walked the perimeter like lords. A fence surrounded the compound with broken posts in places, but these had been stitched over time with wire.

Black smoke swirled about wreckage and bodies. Corpses, mostly Thrule, lay broken and mangled, pecked by vultures which clustered upon the sand dunes.

Dunon, Gefzad and the others crouched in restless groups in the desert scrub, grimacing in hate.

The soldiers had irreverently set up a camp around the huge, chipped and worn dragon statue that marked yet another sacred oasis of the Thrules. It was a small Thorian mine too. The water was pumped by means not dissimilar to the last pump site, the same machinery used to control the working beasts that hauled the ore. A tall, wood-framed rig towered thirty feet high on a small mound, with thick ropes looped over its summit that a dozen oxen pulled through a clever pulley system. It was an operation designed to filter the ore dug from the ground while camels lugged wheeled drays nearby to transport the Thorian ore out to Dragonskull or elsewhere.

Samos gazed sourly upon the enterprise. "The Behundrians blaspheme the old ones, by corrupting this site. You see, outlander, how they take our water? The dragon lords used this water for sacred purposes to lave their holy ornaments and purify their bodies. Much of the ritual is lost in time and beyond our knowledge. We revere these waters; they are life-giving. The spirit of the dragon-lords though deceased, gave us permission to use the lands that were once theirs. So it was said in dream quests by our shamans."

Vetra frowned at such ceremonious mystique. He had not much to say about the glorified devotion, so deigned no comment.

Gefzad, as if he sensed the mercenary's critical attitude, growled his endorsement. "They drain our oases! It's our water. We were here first. The Behundrians forbid us to use our own water, for their own greedy purposes. Can you not see our frustration? Can you not fathom our hate, our anger, and why we revolt against these pigs and take command of the pipe heads?"

Zren had shambled forth, like a moth to the flame of confrontation. His eyes burned on Vetra, who, though now unofficially an ally, he had no love for.

Vetra rubbed his cheek with a reflective scowl. The pumps and the water gushing from the open-mouthed pipe was singular, and the three-score armed guards with their spired helms and plumes who moved about with an air of lordly arrogance, no less.

Smoke billowed up over the low-lying trees to the east. Vetra frowned. Another mine? Doubtless the smoking ruin was that of a site that had been attacked and overrun by invading Thrules, if Cthan's informants were to be believed. Such signs meant that Cthan and his vigilantes would be coming to avenge the mine's capture. Whether they would venture on and track their steps and attack from the rear was another matter. Vetra recalled the wild look of fury on the sheriff's face while he battled him tooth and nail; also his boasts back at the trader's post that he would end the Thrule's little rebellion once and for all. He doubted much he was a man who would give up his vindictive duty.

"Let us storm in and attack the soldiers," suggested Lehundr. Vetra caught the sly look in his eye, as if it were a covert way to ditch the headstrong Thrules and secretly make off to the tomb.

"Best not rile them," urged Besu. "We are tired and wounded. The eagle ridge lies yonder." He gestured beyond the guarded mine.

"They've killed our people!" raged Gefzad.

Samos silenced the argument with a jerk of his stave. He gave an imperial rattle of his neck amulet.

Slinking among pulpy flowering aloe vera, they skirted the miners' camp, Vetra leading, next Lehundr and Jhara, masking the jingle of their weapons.

A wild, angry shout went up in the compound. Vetra turned. A glint off a Thrule sword had betrayed them.

Vetra gave a scathing curse. They burst out of their hiding place, crouching low to the ground. Bolts came spraying from the fence line as bowmen on their high perches took aim. There was a loud thunk then a groaning as a Thrule fell flat, throwing his hands up, a chunk of iron through his back. The skulkers fled like dogs, and the defenders of the mine sent horsemen out to ride them down.

The packbeasts ran amok and some of the retreating Thrules halted, kneeling and took aim. One bolt caught a rider in the throat and he tumbled from his mount in a gurgling mess, clutching at his neck. His body lay splayed in the red dirt. Two others came crashing down with their black steeds through the knot of scrambling Thrules, and more Thrules fell.

Vetra and Besu rushed in and struck up at the horseman. Besu hacked from one side while Vetra ran his crimson blade in a fierce uppercut and caught an exposed leg. The rider screeched and bent over, gurgling in pain, his upper thigh streaming blood.

Jhara had the foresight to snatch the reins of the terrified horse. Any extra mount would give the rebels advantage.

The last rider kneed his horse round after the quick deaths of his peers, then turned in a cowardly retreat, deciding that the small band was not worth dying for.

"Into the scrub, before they send more riders after us!" screamed Aus.

"Frightened sheep!" called Dunon, shaking a fist.

"Never mind them," Vetra growled. Though his brows lifted in surprise, thinking that from the enemy's perspective they too were little more than cowards.

No retaliation came from the guarded complex. Too few of an enemy for the Behundrians to make the effort. The Thrules gathered themselves in a tight knot, death hovering over them like a black cloud.

Vetra wiped the sweat from his face. "A bad turn of luck. We lost five back there. The Behundrians spotted us. Now they have an indication of our presence, and may come after us, if they think us a serious threat."

"Easier now they know the direction we're heading."

"And the packbeasts have fled," announced Besu sourly.

"We'll find them," assured Aus.

"Our pal Cthan will come seeking revenge for the loss of the mines," panted Dunon.

"Are you forgetting the havoc you created back at the pipe?" Vetra questioned in wonder. "They would have to split their forces to repair the pump and defend it while charging us."

Reluctantly, the Thrules left the bodies where they were and melted into the wild foliage ahead of them, a low shrubbed panorama forming a vast net to the north. The scrub thinned; the weary fighters moved from island to island of sand, along worn trails between strands of brush.

A keen-eyed scout, following a trail of broken vegetation and hoofprints, caught sight of a swish of tail, then he gave a muffled shout. Vetra caught a glimpse of two beasts wandering aimlessly. A moment later a group of Thrules came bursting out of the shrubbery to retake the packbeasts. To their relief the supplies were intact.

Twilight was almost upon them. Many leagues had they to cover before an organized pursuit caught up with them.

Besu, the old Thrule, suggested that they find a place to camp.

On Vetra's lead they crossed a low ridge, placing more distance between them and the enemy who guarded the mine.

A soft blue haze hung over the gumtrees and cypress, casting the lands in muted shadows. Samos, versed in such things, selected a cleared area to camp for the night, protected by spirits and barred on the east by tall gumtrees.

They unpacked their supplies and tended to the wounds of their company, wrapping cloth around bloody arms and cut thighs, disinfected scratches and gashes with dampened cloth sprinkled with herbs and potent grasses that Aus and Samos had gathered.

The tenting gear was unraveled and laid out on a flat sandy area near the trees. The extra horse Jhara tethered to the tall gumtrees by the packbeasts. Both beasts hung their heads in gloom and swatted tails at the last few flies that buzzed in the dusk-laden air. There was some argument over whether they should light a fire. In the end, they decided light one, Dunon believing the Dragonskull men would not venture out for a night attack, or even face the hazards of the desert at this hour. His feeling was the Behundrians had suffered enough losses, and had not the Thrules' instinct or skill of surviving the desert. A watch was posted on the hills, to look for sign of invading enemies.

Several Thrules under Samos' direction laid stones down around the campsite while the magician sprinkled drops of sacred water in the four directions, North, South, East and West—an offering for protection, as was Thrule custom. Water, precious as it was, was the life-blood of the desert gods. The Thrule magician, sinister in his jingling, bone-sewn garb and his mud-caked hair, dug an inch-wide trench and poured sparing drops in ritual fashion from his canteen. A long flexible sapling was arched over to create a crude portal under which everyone ducked to cross the trench and enter the campground.

By a small fire they dared to cook broad beans and mutton. Others still, created crude lean-to style shelters, with hides and blankets strung overtop, using the trees as braces.

Losses had been heavy. Despite the lack of gaiety among this group, they sat around the glowing embers, humming folk songs and staring into the gloom.

Dunon raised his hands for attention. He gave encouragement to their flagging spirits: "Stand tall, you doom-mongers! A score of us are left, so let us be happy for that. We've survived an onslaught and where others fell, we live and should rejoice at our fortune. Do not forget that we are Thrules and hold the map to gain us Dragon Forge!"

Vetra lips curved in a smile as he saw Lehundr squirm in his seat on the fallen log. Jhara squinted in boredom.

Murmurs of approval rose among the surviving Thrules. Only a few retained their solemn and gloomy faces, among them Zren who did not feel uplifted in any way by the lecture.

The discovery of the map had prompted a lighter mood. Many wished to forget the death of Zaln, their leader. Camaraderie and a united purpose made the Thrules come alive while the night deepened and the whine of night insects grew. Even Dunon believed they had lost pursuers and no enemy roamed within leagues of their hidden camp.

Some wineskins were passed around, and the stiff kick of the desert mead burned hot trails down their throats. They did not stint on it. Before long, tongues were loosened and feet and hands began to move.

The half moon was already a golden globe rising over the low ridges and the desert glowed with an eerie light. Akin to the gloaming on the misty downs Vetra recalled, of his native Tolizia; it was a moving sight. One Thrule brought out a small battered zither from a saddlebag and strummed a few tentative, plaintive chords. Others soon joined up in a refrain and a slow dance. Men were whirling in high-kicking dances, toe to toe. Vetra wondered what it was like when their women were with them.

The mercenary gazed around him. These nomads were people

who were always prepared for transit, in grief or celebration, with ponies laden with supplies and cured hides ready to become rude shelter or whisked back on a pony when enemies came upon them. The nomad's life was one that few dreamed of, sleeping under the stars, moving from place to place, locked in an endless movement of caravan and packbeast, seeking out food and shelter, water and safety, never having any designated place to call home.

Vetra smiled gamely. How was he any different? The last time he had stayed more than three days in any one place had been back in Trallgate and that had been brief, on recalling the altercation with Rufus the smuggler and the scandal which ensued with a certain noble's daughter. He frowned at that and brushed the memory aside. True to form, here he was in a band of vagabonds in the middle of a war...

Vetra sat like a carven idol, grim and moody in his restless thoughts while the Thrules and their blood-grimed companions drank. His eyes roved constantly in the desert, alert for shadows and movement where every clump and bush looked like some cutthroat creeping from the wilds ready to leap out and hack out his throat. He sighed. His muscled strength lay dormant under the tattered, grimy desert garb of his, but he was ready to uncoil at the slightest sound of danger. Such wariness had kept him alive for more years than he could remember...

Jhara had come to sit by him and he shifted with grudging welcome. His eyes stared in moody intensity into the fire and fled off into the moonlit knolls.

Jhara's voice intruded on the peace. "So many weak men in Dragonskull. You're strong and noble."

Vetra grunted. "If you want noble, think of Bekr the Berserker. He fought the Brusites across the Rouge banks at Brine-Halt at the cost of their own lives."

The girl chuckled and clicked her tongue. "What do I care about Bekr? You were noble enough to save my brother. Fight a war that is not yours. I think that's noble."

Vetra grumbled at that and rubbed his jaw. "Why do you care anyway?"

"Decent men are hard to come by these days."

"Come," he muttered. True to his word he fetched swords and positioned her in front of him, moon over his shoulder, the dying fire to one side. It was time to teach the girl some art of swordplay.

"Like this," he said, coming behind her and taking the hilt in his hand and placing his hands over hers. He lifted the sword, blade pointed down. "Watch your flanks, protect your vitals with a strong block." He swung with authority. "Watch for feints and quick flicks, like this!—" He twisted sideways on the balls of his feet, facing her, letting shimmering steel batter her sword. It nearly knocked it out of her grasp. "Develop a rhythm, girl, don't waver!—" He sped back behind her and crossed over nimbly. She stumbled, trying to keep up with his feet that moved like those of a panther.

By Dergath, she was going to be a force to be reckoned with, thought Vetra. But he didn't want to let her know. He knew, give her too much praise, and somewhere it would sabotage her growth, perhaps end up getting her killed.

He remembered his own trial-by-fire training by the old Grayhurst, master and soldier in his own right, whose bloody campaigns had been without number, and at whose hands he had faced trials at best grueling. His father had taken Grayhurst into his company to train his son—or knock some sense into him. The many bloody bashings and thumpings he had received at that badgering hand—to 'temper his stubborn pride'...he preferred not to tell.

She fixed him a coy glance. "Do you find me fair?"

Vetra narrowed his gaze.

Pressing herself close to Vetra's muscled girth, she smirked. Vetra, slightly taken aback, could feel the warm pulse of the girl's heart in a completely unexpected turn of events. Without warning she pushed her lips full on his.

Vetra loosed a gusty breath. Without preamble, he grabbed up the quivering girl and herded her into the bushes, much to the surprised exclamation of the Thrules. The mercenary found a cleared area not far away. He spread her on a mat of sand and leaves. Before long, the sounds of their passion rose to animal heights, raking the stillness with its primal beat.

Jhara's languorous moans and cries of laughter burst upon the glade as she followed his muscular shoulder, along his rippling arm, to his strong hand that moved from naked thighs to buttocks.

There came a skullish face peering through the folds of foliage, then the rattling of beads and murmuring curses that spoke of outlanders soiling the protection on the very soil he had blessed with magic. The shaman lurched back on a snarl from Vetra's lips. The mercenary's gleaming blade flashed violently. The shaman disappeared back in the shrubs, and Vetra went back to his pleasures, his passion undiminished. Nor the girl's, whose pale skin gleamed in the soft moonlight streaming through the twisted branches of the gumtrees. Their passion escalated to a new rhythm in tune with the distant howls of the desert animals.

The moon rose a notch higher. Two flush-faced figures finally emerged from the brush. The shaman was nowhere to be seen, nor was Zren. Facts which did not bother Vetra.

A feverish heat rose from Jhara's sweaty skin and sultry curves. Her dark, burning eyes had the potential to enslave a man.

"The Kirns say drink helps a man overcome his fears before battle," Vetra remarked distantly, swaggering forth to swig a gulp from the wooden cup on the fallen log. "More the act of love, in my opinion."

Jhara made a husky avowal.

"Keep my extra sword. You'll need it. You've earned it. I'll show you how to use it properly later."

"You mean it?" Her eyes lit up.

"Of course! You'd think I'd joke at a time like this? We're in the midst of war. Come on, let's dance." He gave a hearty grunt, a sound deep in his throat then offered his arm. "That'll get the rest of that minx-energy out of your loins. I see it has no end."

She laughed and grabbed his arm and he pulled her up to the dance area, a squared section of cool sand that felt good on their bare feet. Makeshift drums were beating with hypnotic rhythm. Many Thrules had joined in dancing. A lively melody, unknown to Vetra's ears had him reminiscing on days of youth in many a tavern on his journeys. He thought he had heard all the strange melodies and rhythms of the lesser-known tribes.

Vetra failed to see Zren's burning gaze fall on him and the girl, gyrating in the heat of merriment. The Thrule's eyes were sullen and looked with resentment that an older man, an outlander had captured the girl's interest.

Later that evening, Zren went off to a quiet, private place while the embers glowered, to lash himself with a thorn-tipped branch and in a fever of murmurings, recount his vows, taught him by Samos the shaman, to remain pure of spirit and redeem himself of sins. To pray also to Turga, the quiet, wrathful dragon god for revenge on the shame and humiliation caused by the outlander and his female harlot.

When the moon rose higher still, Vetra spoke in low tones to Jhara. "Your father did well."

Her face fell. "He passed away a year ago. Cast out of the league of protectors. He came to Dragonskull an innocent Mercian trader and died penniless. Someone murdered him. My brother Aeke and I have been on our own since."

Vetra frowned. "You're worried about him, aren't you?"

"Much so, I admit. I left him with friends of mine. I hope he's well."

"Likely he's faring better than us," grunted Vetra.

"If he keeps his hands off the vendors' apples," she muttered with a laugh. "Hold me. It has been a long time since I felt the touch of a strong man."

Though the hides spread unevenly on the ground, she came next to him and thrust her warm back against his bear-like chest. He roused with a grunt, surprised at her unfettered way of showing her need. He clasped her in gentle arms, his fingers tracing suggestive lines down her thigh, and he thought with a wry breath, "Let us enjoy this interlude. Tomorrow may not bring as gentle tidings."

IV: Tomb of the Ancients

The way to the vale of Zabenzar was cut with dry gullies and boulder-strewn ridges. A strange range of sparsely populated woodland rose up in their path—a deadlands in its own right. At one time the blackened trunks must have been healthy eucalyptus. What had killed them, Vetra did not know. Dunon suggested a blight had passed through these lands long ago. Besu, who was more knowledgeable about such matters, remarked that fires had ravaged the area, taken the trunks and hollowed out their cores. It was apparent that over the years, these trees had developed a resilience to fire. Some still showed green leaves in the tops. Smooth, ghostly limbs twined from stem, like withered bones of skeletons. The odd lizard darted underfoot with long tail, sliding behind one of the trees, or down a hole of one of the blackened trunks. Overhead the squawk of a desert bird came as an eerie intrusion; likewise the shadow of a circling buzzard, appearances which set a forlorn mood over the company in the sweltering heat of the noonday sun. They broke out of the trees and stood panting at the fringe of the wood to see a rugged canyon wall facing them.

"Call a halt!" Vetra wiped sweat from his brow. It had been two days since the attack at the mines and his eyes burned with a vengeance, squinting under the yellow glare.

"I think we're lost," called the old Thrule Besu at his side. His bowed frame slumped on a charred log.

"I think that landmark is familiar," muttered Lehundr. He lifted a finger to the canyon face. "Is that not the eagle ridge crest depicted here in this hill mesa?"

Dunon stirred; Jhara hissed an excited breath.

Eyes scanned the area; indeed, the shape of the hills and its eagle-winged formation resembled a section of the ancient fabric at Lehundr's ribs, all purple and gold, with its cryptic collection of images

"It's the only place remotely looking like any place for a tomb," Aus said. "We might as well investigate."

A trail wound up the cliff, cut crudely in the form of a ledge into the crumbling rock.

They set feet up the path, though there were many grumbles among the company. Like outcasts on a singular mission, the Thrules trudged up the desolate track, boots crunching on pebbles, the sun beating down on their backs.

Vetra looked over the edge. A sprawl of boulders and prickly foliage promised a quick doom should one fall. A queasy feeling crawled in his gut at the sight.

The trail curved around the far side of the cliff, veering away from the valley. The ravine was quiet, save for a soft sigh of wind brushing the cliff's sides. The path widened to twenty feet. Ahead in the narrow gully loomed two rounded boulders rising three times a man's height in precarious poise. Both looked menacing, balanced as they were on sinister angles. Positioned to ward off intruders? Vetra scowled. Or only a natural formation?

Regardless, the boulders nearly blocked their path, only a narrow gap between them.

Samos gushed out a jabber of warnings about the cursed nature of such boulders. "They're jinxed", he cried.

Vetra rubbed his jaw with great weariness. He had not expected such a timorous reaction from the Thrules. It seemed even the shaman was doubtful about treading here. An omen—likely men would avoid this way believing it was cursed. What better place to hide a tomb? Vetra allowed himself a grin. Possible tombs that had not been rifled in these long ages? He flourished a fist. "A small team and I will go on ahead," he muttered. "Dunon, Besu, Lehundr and Jhara."

Zren's red hot face pushed forth. "Why shouldn't the rest of us go? We've come this far."

Vetra shook his head. "Cthan and his dogs could be marching up the valley soon to liberate the Thorian mine. I need you here to watch the valley and signal if necessary. It's not hard for them to track us here."

Besu gave a grim nod. "Aye, better to take no chances."

A flicker of resentment flashed in Zren's eyes. "Why not keep back your precious girl then?" He spat at the outlander's feet. He flung a finger at Jhara and glared with envy at her.

Vetra's mouth curled in a sneer.

Zren capitulated, shrinking in the mercenary's shadow.

Despite the shaman's gibbering and amulet-waving, Dunon waved them through.

They left the packbeasts behind, and the majority of Thrules were invested with instructions to make traps, triggering piles of rock to fall down from the steep trails and defend the gap on the other side should enemies be sighted.

Jhara and the three Thrules slipped through the crack. It was all that Vetra could do to squeeze sideways between the two mammoth boulders.

He stared up the valley and turned warily to Lehundr. "I don't like the fact that we can't see the valley from past this barrier. With a Behundrian army on our tail—" he left that dangling.

"Nothing we can do," the half Thrule muttered. "As you said, we have the scouts."

Jhara struck light-footed up the trail with inexhaustible energy.

Vetra called her back with the others. "Slow down. We don't know what dangers lie ahead."

Jhara reluctantly dropped back.

Eagles made their nests in the low crags rising to either side of the canyon and screeched at the intrusion to their domain. The canyon was well-named. Vetra looked down at the rough crumble of shale and chips at his feet. He had a feeling no one had been in this corridor for hundreds of years. The whole canyon had a dead, eerie feel to it, as if it were separated from the rest of the lands and sinister eyes watched them from realms unseen.

Before long a daunting cliff rose to their left. Sculpted out of the rock jutted a fearsome, weathered face in full relief. It might once have been that of a dragon with its great gaping mouth and hollowed-out eyes rising head heights above them. At one time the entrance had been sealed but the giant snout had cracked and toppled, maybe from an earthquake, leaving only a crumble of boulders at the foot, blocking out the dark path that led into the stony maw.

The three Thrules regarded it with spell-struck wonder. Besu muttered while fingering the oil lamp he had brought along. Primitive, old beyond imagining, the gateway to the tomb was awesome and mystifying—and creepy enough, thought Vetra, unable to stop the shiver that crept over his flesh.

Lehundr crawled past the boulders and made two steps into the dark interior. The four plunged after him into the darkness. Lehundr led with bluff confidence. The entrance opened up into a small domed cavern. Vetra's eyes widened in the gloom, his blood quickening to the echo of booted feet on smooth stone and the mysterious weight of ages.

The sprinkling of daylight from the entrance revealed a massive stone sarcophagus looming at the far end of the chamber. Besu lit the lamp with trembling fingers. Any jewels or gold which had lain strewn about the chamber had long been pillaged. The crate-like sarcophagus lay flush to the far wall and was flanked by serpent pillars. Draped in shadows under the flickering light, a hulking animal statue with a dragon's head and leopard's body sat watching, eyes glued ahead like an unforgiving sphinx. Vetra felt his blood pulse; he heard others' sharp breaths as they squinted in the gloom.

The sarcophagus's head was mantled with a carven dragon skull. At the foot stretched a stone tail into a darkened passage. All looked with dread, loath to enter that passage. Lehundr, for all his mettle, feared to tread over the vile, serpentish tail, as if it would come to life. Vetra reached down a finger tip, driving back the apprehension that inspired such irrational superstition. Cold, dead to the touch, the ancient stone was smooth carved and painted yellowish green from what weak light shone from the lamp or in from the entrance. He could not help but shudder at the thought of groping and stumbling down into a crevasse or some sepulchral pit of doom.

The floor gave Vetra cause for reflection. The polished paves were crusted with bones and ancient remains which altogether seemed abnormal, for no reason availed such mangled flesh. The paves showed rough scratches, but the ceiling was bare. No chute for boulders to tumble from upon high to crush a skulking thief. Dragon carvings raked the walls, wings lifted in majesty, jaws agape, eyes burning, as if portals to some inside knowledge beyond time and space. In the same panoramas the rightmost wall was smeared with ancient blood and bits of gristle and bone, unless Vetra missed his guess.

He kicked a clump of sinew and the bones rattled like fiendish dice, sending ghoulish echoes and dust around the chamber.

Jhara's teeth chattered. "Would you stop that?"

"Aye, it's disrespectful," muttered Lehundr, "not to mention jarring on the nerves."

Vetra grunted. He thrust his head into the tunnel, calling his own name. The echoes died in a dull murmur. Tink, tink. A drip of distant water—and a wash of dusty vapors, sediment and musty layers compiled from the ages. "Goes on a long way, I think," Vetra mused.

"This must be where the dragon lord who was buried in yon sarcophagus once walked," whispered Besu.

"Aye, probably where he went to feed his faithful protectors," said Dunon. "'Tis said the oldest dragons lived in caves, dark and deep, that stretched to the center of the earth."

Vetra snorted. "Or perhaps it's just some old underground cave carved by water and time. I think you two have vivid imaginations."

Lehundr frowned. Folding arms over his chest, he gripped his cloth-sewn map like a beggar would his last morsel of food.

Jhara spoke, "I heard that the dragons were gatekeepers to the world below. They were used to judge human souls when they passed the river of death for their deeds, good or evil. Men fought and died to tame them because they thought that they would have victory over death. So my father told me."

Vetra uttered a laugh. "Or how about it's all a myth? And that men built this tomb, not dragons. They dressed it up like a dragon tomb, and inside that stone crate there's at worst some moldered human bones, of a petty lord or forgotten king?"

Lehundr scowled; his mouth was drawn tight. He refused to accept that the treasure was not real and that dragons were anything less than magical.

Dunon tested the slab. "The lid's heavier than a mountain. We may never know. None of us could lift that."

"Unless we all get our swords under it and pry it off?" suggested Besu.

Vetra shook his head. "We'd bend all our blades."

"Maybe the dragon things were not the mystical creatures with untold wisdom and the wealth of ages past we think," argued Besu.

Dunon's eyes grew solemn. "Those with dragon heads and bodies of men were ancient before the stars were young," he whispered. "The dragon lords tamed the dragons and became their masters. This is one of their tombs."

The group fell silent and edged their way along the far wall.

By the arched way they could make out the tunnel which stretched off into murk. None wanted to go down there, not even Lehundr, for all his keenness.

Maybe they didn't have to. Glyphs and symbols were carved into the wall around the door. Possibly the makings of a map, and there, at a place below, alongside carven knobs and levers, lay a foot-long, sharp and hard thing, pointed like a claw, a great dragon claw.

Besu gaped. "Can it be? A real dragon claw. They're rarer than finding the gilded elephant tusks of the Kirns!"

"Now do you believe me?" gasped Lehundr with triumph. "Here are signs. This must be the key!" The half Thrule gingerly lifted the claw out of its cradle.

While they murmured and argued, none recognized the shadowy figure creeping over to the sarcophagus.

"This dragon claw must be the key to opening the portal to the fortress," cried Lehundr. "Though I can't understand the script, it's some form of dragon runes."

"Why didn't thieves take it?" demanded Vetra.

"They were looking for gold, not claws. They wouldn't have known it was the key either, unless they had the map."

Besu pointed. "I've heard the dragon fort's never been opened since it was sealed by the curse of a dragon's death, or some old dragon magic. Many a plunderer has tried to and all have failed."

"Aye," said Dunon. "Most died. It's leagues from here out in the middle of the desert."

Vetra suddenly felt a chill crawl over his skin. He peered up and blinked. He felt an unknown presence in the chamber. A razor-sharpened sense of danger told him trouble was near. He reached for his sword. There—a shift of movement near the sarcophagus. Some thin, skulking shape. Something else caught his attention—the perfectly polished wall at his side, almost too polished, and there were those vertical seams forward and back that ran suspiciously up to the ceiling, as if they were—

He gave a harsh cry. "Watch out! Fall back!"

Sliding stone sounded from underfoot. In the moment that the skulking Zren had passed his hands over some hidden lever behind the sarcophagus, the floor suddenly sank a foot lower.

A sharp choking cry rang out. Jhara somersaulted backward, landing on her feet like a cat. The floor gave way several more feet and with the others, she clawed with desperation for something to hang on to—to no avail.

Vetra fell and was knocked on his back, gasping for air. Zren tumbled into the pit too, his fall cushioned by Dunon and Lehundr who gurgled out surprised oaths.

Twenty feet up the sheer walls of the twelve-foot square prison, Vetra peered and heard a sound more terrible than the hiss of vipers—the grinding and scraping of heavy stone on stone. Two parallel walls of massive construction writ with dragon insignias, one which slowly advanced toward them with ominous implication. With savage energy he tried to mount the walls, but they were too sheer and high.

He stared in mute astonishment. Someone had triggered the trap, likely the Thrule, or perhaps it was the girl taking hold of the jeweled lever? No, it couldn't have been her. She had been tracing fingers on the map. Jhara's fingers had not yet touched the ancient runes. It was that wretched Thrule lolling at his feet. "You idiot!" He kicked him in the ribs. Zren sprawled in pain.

"Quick!" Vetra snarled. "Up the wall. Climb on my back!" He crouched and motioned Dunon to climb on. The Thrule wasted no time and Vetra yelled a harsh command at Lehundr next. Putting backs to wall and boots to the advancing opposite wall, they formed a human ladder, Vetra on the bottom, Dunon and Lehundr next, and then Zren. Jhara scrambled last over, legs and arms pinwheeling while others palm-lifted her up to grasp the rim. She heaved herself up over the lip.

Falling dust from the ceiling caught the weak sunlight and Jhara's sweat-grimed face peered over the ledge.

Vetra tossed the dragon claw to her. She caught it and set it aside, then continued to help each man out of the pit. First pulling Zren up, his fingers groping thin air. Reaching over the edge, she just managed to grab Besu's fingers while Zren kept her from falling. Besu scrambled over the top, gasping into his beard; together they formed a backward chain.

The wall was inching slowly closer. Vetra, last in the pit, bared his teeth in a growl. With no less than three feet to spare, he jammed his blade lengthwise between the constricting walls. The steel quivered, buckling fast. He hated to see his only weapon compromised—but it purchased him a few more seconds...

He squeezed himself part way up, pushing with boots on one wall and inching spider-like with back against the other. Barely had he hooked fingers over the edge when hands hauled him up and over, and the walls clanged together like jaws.

He squatted in a pained crouch on the cold stone, staring at the pit of death below him. The sound of machinery died. His sword and the lamp lay mashed down there somewhere. He cursed sore words at the loss of his sword.

Doubtless the trap had been ingeniously constructed, operating in some mysterious pulley and lever system beyond the feet of stone.

Clever minds were at work here and somehow he doubted they had anything to do with dragons.

A trap...to foil who? Would-be treasure seekers?

Vetra craned his neck, looking back toward where the crushing wall originated. A hidden chamber behind the wall?

He stooped and peered wolfishly down into the gloom beyond the wall where a passage disappeared off beside the massive, battering ram that powered the slab.

Another dragon claw was fastened on the inside of that wall in ceremonial fashion, like pieces of a puzzle. Almost fearful to touch the cursed thing, Vetra hesitated, then gripped it and tore it off its brackets. Nothing happened.

"So, now we have two of these claws," he muttered. "Like parts of a toy. So much for your key," he scoffed.

"Any one of them could be the key," Lehundr objected. "I'm guessing it's probably this one."

Zren clambered forward to have a look; the others glared at him.

"Your curiosity nearly killed us all," Vetra said through clenched teeth.

"Yet if Zren had not tripped the mechanism," remarked Dunon, "we could not see the exposed chamber behind the wall."

Lehundr weighed the truth of the matter.

An uncomfortable silence gripped the group. Jhara went to examine the lethal dragon levers on the wall behind the sarcophagus.

"Can't see what's down there," muttered Vetra. He squatted to peer down, straining his eyes in the faint light streaming from the entrance. He saw shadows of strange statues huddled in the murk farther up and more carvings on the wall. "Dergath's ghouls, what is this place?"

"We're going to need a light."

"Maybe if you use the small brand I brought along," Zren muttered with thick irony. He rifled through the sack tied at his waist and produced torch with flint and tinder.

While Besu grunted and Dunon snatched the items and lit the torch, Vetra turned to the others: "We've come this far, so we might as well explore the likes of this treasure." He pushed his legs over the edge and jumped down with the torch. "Anyone else coming with me? I'll have a look around and when I'm done, you can help me back up again."

Besu was the only one who volunteered. But Zren, blood dripping from his lip, gave a sullen grunt and on impulse jumped down, as if to redeem himself for his impulsive act.

The pit looked like a chamber out of legend, a crude, cobble-stoned dungeon laced in thick cobwebs that spread amid dense shadows underneath the floor above. The three groped their way about the chamber, Besu and Zren creeping behind Vetra. Unease had him padding like a wolf and blinking into the murk, straining eyes to see what demon or horror would jump out at them.

Vetra's keen eyes discerned a dark opening in the floor some twenty paces to the side. It was crisscrossed with cobwebs, something resembling a stair descending to unknown depths.

The cylindrical stone ram rolled on wheels and was crudely chiseled and affixed to some large stone mechanism. The ram itself was cold and rough to the touch, a work of monumental proportions.

Vetra moved on, transfixed. Following it back under the floor above, he trained the torch up.

A dragon statue loomed out of the darkness, towering heads above them on its hind legs. Clawed feet were outstretched and hands cupped in a gesture of offering—its toothy jowl carved in an austere grin. Vetra gave the thing wide berth, circling round it with bared teeth. His toe snagged on something rough and he realized his foot passed over a long seam dividing a false floor from the real one. He figured the falling floor of stone was powered by a similar mechanism hidden underneath the tons of stone underfoot. Why the elaborate engineering to ensnare a few thieves?

A large disc above with pulleys and chains hung down to fasten on the stone ram. A chute allowed a trail of boulders to fall and power the wheel. The boulders had already spilled, powering the ram to do its bloodthirsty work. Ingeniously constructed, thought Vetra. His hairs stood on end. How floor and walls retracted was beyond his knowledge.

They inched along like mice in a snake's lair, passing one springy cobweb after another and ever-present molder and frightful shadow. The chamber narrowed to a dingy tunnel underneath the floor above. They followed it for about sixty feet.

The passage ended in a sheer wall, edged by supporting pillars, old as time.

Besu pointed. "There! Over by that column, the wall!" They stumbled on to stand gaping aside a closed-off arch. Two skeletons lay sprawled in layers of dust and filth by the wall; one still clutched a corroded pickaxe in its hand. The wall was gouged with crude strikes. Obviously, the figures had been hewing a hole, digging for something—or perhaps digging to get out? Vetra rubbed his jaw. "These wretches likely starved to death before completing their mission."

He held the torch up to the wall. A grim pantheon of dragon faces and scenes met his eye: men, dragons, beasts, weapons, expectant armies and mesmerizing symbols.

Zren peered at him, his face a wild mix of angst and wonder. Besu looked like an old hunted owl, his wings clipped. They retraced their steps underneath what would have been the chamber's wall above.

A harsh grating of massive slabs sent hackles rising on Vetra's back.

"What are Jhara and those fools up to? Do they want to kill us?" He raced back down the tunnel, torch guttering dangerously close to extinction, the others at his heels. "They must have jiggled the controls!"

They came stumbling back to the death-dealing wall. But this time the stone slab was moving back toward them at an alarming rate. Jhara was leaning over the edge up top, whimpering, her face white with tension and a wail stuck in her throat. "Get up, now!" she cried. "Grab my hands!" While Dunon held her legs and lowered her down, she snatched at Besu's wrists and together the two hauled him up.

Besu scrambled to his feet then helped Dunon lower Jhara to attempt to get Zren and Vetra up.

Vetra glared daggers from below.

"We didn't cause it," Jhara protested, answering his vitriolic stare. "The slab started moving of its own accord. Lehundr is trying to reverse it now."

"Well, tell Lehundr to get a move on," Vetra thundered.

"It's starting to close over completely. Faster now!"

The Thrule looked up with fear that he would be the last left behind.

"Get up there!" ordered Vetra. Dropping the torch, he hoisted the smaller man up on his back, pushing him up with a grunt.

No sooner had the Thrule been hauled up when Vetra felt the slab push him back. He caught a brief glimpse of Jhara's look of absolute horror as the wall slapped shut.

The resounding smack of stone echoed about the chamber. Jhara's fading, sundered wail echoed about the chamber and Vetra blinked—to silence. The beat of his heart.

"They'll flip the switches and spring it open," he assured himself.

But no such welcome scrape of stone came to his ear.

Likely the mechanism had a mind of its own. He grimaced.

He stared around his gloomy surroundings, struggling to contain his frustration. The torch would not last forever. Already it sputtered at his feet, smoking and hissing. He stooped to clutch it in a sweaty palm, eyes wide. A square chamber stretched off in the distance perhaps thirty feet.

Something told him he could not depend on his comrades' efforts. These wretched traps! He should have known where one was sprung, another would follow.

His mind sprang back to the ancient pickaxe. Could he chip his way through the wall? It was at least a foot and a half of solid rock. Not easy. Perhaps a work of many hours, if not days, if the corroded metal didn't give out. What of the poor fools who tried to chisel their way through? Could he chip at the movable slab above? Perhaps where the stone joined the ceiling it was less thick. He studied the dragon statue and imagined poising on its neck and shoulders and striking upward at solid rock. He frowned. Only to have stone chips blind him? It seemed a foolhardy plan.

He prowled his prison like a caged lion. Retracing his steps back to the two skeletons, he crouched on his haunches and pulled the tool from the molder. Why? Where? To what end? What had these fools been hewing for? Did they have knowledge of what lay beyond?

Vetra passed fingers along the wall. Rough, cold. It was both inscribed and embossed with relief.

The arched door was five feet wide and sealed to perfection. The seams were tight enough to be hardly detectable. What lay beyond? Had the diggers been trying to get to an adjoining chamber?

He weighed his options and fingered the rusty pickaxe, peeling off the layers of flaking metal at its head. The tool had a stout, four-foot wooden handle; the iron was flaked with orange on the surface, but it was black and strong underneath.

He concluded that such men, despite their evident failure, had embraced a worthwhile mission. At least they carried tools, so they likely had some purpose. Hand on chin, Vetra sat engrossed for several moments in some lip-chewing thought. Were there other options?

Nothing seemed of immediate interest in the vicinity of the

tunnel wall. No chance of scaling the chute. The opening was too high, and it looked dead and dark up there. What he wouldn't give to have access to the tunnel he had shunned earlier near the sarcophagus.

Off toward the far wall, a wide staircase in the center of the hall wound down, now cracked and sunken with age. He was almost afraid of what he might find there and crept on cautious feet over to investigate. Drunken steps trailed down into the gloom, perhaps thirty feet. But that was not what held Vetra's attention. They were flanked with low-riding dragon statues, of most familiar design.

Insanely lifelike! Almost like monster lizards, but with the bodies of leopards and the heads of dragons—not dissimilar to that strange, sphinx-like guardian lurking by the sarcophagus. He saw that more of them crouched, on the level below.

Vetra forced himself to walk down the steps, on the odd chance that something might offer an avenue of escape.

No such luck. More of the repulsive things lurked in the periphery, head to tail in what seemed random postures. Some were flatfooted, other poised in mid-step with necks bent and eyes glaring, as if frozen in time.

He stared. The chamber was like an insular menagerie, of size and configuration to the one above, circular, and admitting no exits, save but one corridor which ended abruptly. The walls and ceiling of this chamber bore no carvings or bas relief, unlike its predecessors, only simple smooth stone, as if it were a chamber to house only these repugnant things. Dergath, but they swarmed around him so life-like that he had to catch his breath. Every swell, lip, crack of bared fang and sharpened claw was depicted in startling detail. The things waited in an attitude of frozen menace for what was untold centuries.

Vetra thrust the torch into the face of one of the creatures, better to study its features. The flickering light showed the black-eyed face of a dragon and sleek torso of a jungle cat but sporting the scales of lizards and an alligator tail. The legs were stubby like those of a lizard's. Though the eyes and horns were dragonish, it sported the wide snout of elder amphibians with razor-sharp serrated teeth. The stone was glazed over with red pigments. Like sleepwalkers, the watchers poised in a frozen prowl, as if they were in an induced trance. Jaws were slightly agape as if ready to mouth a toothy roar, and Vetra frowned. Such pantomime reeked of an ancient mystery impossible to decipher after so many passing centuries. He tugged at his chin. The whole place stank of menace and decay, as if upon the dragon-lord's bidding, or perhaps his death, all had come to a standstill, frozen in time.

Vetra had heard of old tales spoken by the Kirns and the Guirites, of incredible life-like statues secreted in tombs. That they were watchers of the deceased, that they had been cast in stone, or iron, or some other form by arcane wizardry too old to name. That they could come to life at will to protect their deceased masters from unwanted intruders.

He brushed aside such thoughts with a wry grunt. These hobgoblins certainly had not come to life upon his entering this tomb. Mere fables. The stuff of myth.

Yet Vetra's finger reached out to stroke the leafed stone of the massive gargoyle in front of him. Instantly he recoiled. The thing had a peculiar rubbery texture, as if made of old moldered clay. Dead but alive—? Hard but yielding? His mind reeled. Too many incredible things lurked in this forsaken chamber to make sense of. He backed away.

What was that? A sound? He retreated to the broad stair. A wretched slithering? No, nothing. Just one of those many uncanny moments when a man lets imagination get the better of him. One of the repulsive dragon statues stared at him with its eerie, sightless gaze. A sudden swish of movement, as of a tail had him whirling. He crouched, drawing his pick. A tongue flickered out and a soft sibilance... The torch guttered and hissed. Vetra blinked. His imagination again. He relaxed, loosed a breath. The sound had played havoc on his nerves—it was a product only of his hissing brand and the elusive shadows in this dim, otherworldly place.

His torch would be burning down soon. How much time had he left? An hour? More? Why was he wasting time here?

Hurrying back to the skeleton tunnel, he propped the fragile flame on the wall. Time to pursue the digger's cause. Taking up his tool, he began hewing at the hole where the others had failed.

Flakes of rock chipped on the rude paves.

Before long a pile amassed at his feet. His long-reaching hope was that the iron head would last long enough for him to hack his way through this barrier. How long had it lain here in the dust and silence?

The minutes passed. Sweat oozed from his pores. His muscles stood out like iron bands as he strained under the flickering flame. Should that light go out... The clinks landed like blacksmith's blows and the tinny smacks rang in his ears like bells with every strike. Ghostly shadows played on the tunnel walls.

All the while he felt a strange presence weighing upon his soul. He felt the intolerant dragon statues glaring over his shoulders and their visionless eyes scrutinizing him and his movements with disdain. That he was trapped here underground with them he sensed they knew and had waited for. Who knew what sinister purpose they guarded?

The minutes passed; Vetra cleared the pile of rock away with his boot. Minutes of life remained in the hissing flame. No sound of help from his colleagues. Surely they could hear his tapping? He had the sickening feeling they had failed and were forced to move on.

The torch flickered and died. Vetra slumped, back to the wall, arms and shoulders sagging. The first vestiges of panic began to crawl over his limbs. The bones of the diggers rattled at his feet. He kicked them away. A bleak feeling of failure washed over him. What a fate to die here in this darkness with these skeletons! He lurched to his feet, a snarl on his lips, rejecting such a demise. It was getting hot in this chamber. The air was less potent, less breathable. The sods had likely died of asphyxiation; two mouths breathing the same air. His head swam, his bloodshot eyes burned, and now his throat felt clogged with dust.

He pounded on without pause, merciless stroke after stroke, every muscle feeling the battering shockwave of steel on rock up his arm. There came a different sound to his swing. A thunk versus a thwack. Had the blunt head hit air? He smashed with all his blind fury. A tremor of hope bloomed in his chest. He pulled the iron free and passed fingers through a small notch. Yes! Air! A tiny finger-sized hole.

Like a prospector striking gold, Vetra hacked with zeal, surrendering all restraint, flakes of rock flying at his feet. He knelt and heart pounding, passed a hand through the arm-sized opening. The air was cooler there. A glow, very faint, almost imperceptible, drifted from behind that hole. The presence of air meant some fresher source and possibly an escape route out of this stifling burrow. He chipped some more rock and squeezed his sweaty head through and snuffed a mouthful of welcome air.

A two foot hole was gouged out, and he crouched, peering through.

Some natural light shone from a slit in the rock from high overhead.

Solid objects loomed in the dimness. More statues? He could not be sure.

He crawled through, eyes widening pools in the murk, pick raised. The hall was huge; his scuffing boots echoed cavernously. It was like a great amphitheater here, with lofty ceiling lost in gloom. The air was pervaded with an ancient grandeur and the uncaringness of ages.

He crept forward like a man in a trance and in front of him at the hall's front stood a dragon lord statue, eight feet high. On either side crouched two guardians, miniature versions of the ones in the adjacent chambers. Draped on the statue's chest was another dragon claw similar to the others but worn as an amulet. The look on the lord's face was one of solemn wonder and sublime reflection. Yet, a sadness, which struck Vetra as odd.

The statue was not dissimilar to those he had seen in the desert. Was this the last lord of a dying dragon realm?

The lord faced the outer semicircle, as if addressing a vast crowd. A proprietary hand was placed on one of the small leopard-lizard's heads like a pet hound. Vetra turned to see benches spread and tiered on high, row after row, rising from floor to domed ceiling. He shook his head in wonder. What a hall of the ancients. His head swiveled in full circle. The acoustics were perfect here, and he could hear the scuff of his boots and his heavy breathing amplified three-fold.

Wait. There—a light gleamed in the dead dragon lord's eyes. A chill crawled down his spine. The glint vanished, whatever it was. Only a glister off his tool perhaps from the pale sunlight streaming through the shaft above.

He went to stroke the claw-amulet. Two or three of the precious gems encrusted in the ornament rattled free of the ancient collar and clattered to the paves. With swift ease he picked them up and put them in his pocket.

Almost with reverent grace and trembling hand he lifted the chain and amulet off the lord's jeweled head. Why, he did not know. Perhaps all Lehundr's talk about 'keys' and treasure had affected him. This was the third dragon claw, and intuition told him it was more important than the others.

Vetra turned to peer in suspicion. Rows of spectator-seats rose up tier by tier along the back wall, connected by aisles of stone steps at some ancient time. It was a vast auditorium, a honeycomb-shaped dome, hollowed out and built like an amphitheater into the cliffside.

The vents above were too distant to make out—but had all been long sealed with stone slabs by expert masons. All except one had crumbled. Vetra wondered if these vents admitted light when the dragon lord was alive. Perhaps this was his oratory.

His eyes flicked back to the statue.

Another glint in the thing's eye?

No sooner had this flash of light dawned, than a slither of movement disturbed the silence. He wheeled around. What was it? A distinct set of glowing eyes peered from the gap he had crawled through. Teeth gnawed at the edges of the rock. Wild fear stung his gut. It was one of the reptilian leopard statues—struggling to squeeze through. What eldritch sorcery was this? A thing come to life upon the robbery of the dragon claw? Fool! How could he have been so stupid to think he could snatch an item like the dragon claw and not be punished? Frantically, he cast eyes around him for some avenue of escape. The rock he had hewn through would hold the creatures for now. But there were more of them, sawing and biting their way at the edges of the rude opening, like hounds digging for a favorite bone. The hole widened with every gnaw and bite. A snout was almost already out, and with it a bellow and snarl.

Besthra take him for sacrificing his sword! Could he put the claw back? Hardly—the guardians were awake, and likely deadlier than vipers.

He took up the pickaxe and raced over to hew the creatures back. He smashed the iron tip into the skull of one of the slavering beasts. It died, thrashing, but the first guardians of the tomb burst through, waddling on all fours like lizards. The monsters blinked and made small hissing sounds and glared at him with repellent eyes. They spat a foul black liquid that sizzled on the stone like acid and scored holes in it.

With a gasp of horror, he hopped back, scrambling for the stairs heading up to the semicircle of spectator seats. It may be his only hope, the high ground. Some globs came shooting at his chest and he jerked aside and narrowly avoided getting splattered by it. He lurched, struggling to stay erect. He could not help but tread in a pool of acid before the first steps. The sticky goo stuck to his boot and melted part of it away before he could fling it off. With a ghastly moan he leapt back, clawing at the air, aghast at the nightmare around him.

Up the stairs he bounded.

One came at him up the crumbling steps, maw agape, tongue ready to lob another foul, sizzling dollop at him. He swung—the pickaxe smashed straight through the thing's ear. He pulled his axe free, eyes burning with satisfaction that iron tip had passed through claylike flesh and pierced the brain. The leopard-lizard jerked in a bray of bellowing agony, then slumped to the stone. It gave a final spasmodic shiver then lay sprawled on the steps, tongue splayed. Vetra turned and blundered up the steps past the first tier, leaping like a deer, though he bashed his knees on fallen rock that lay obscured in the murk. Others came shambling up, tails sliding over their dead brother and rustling the crumbled heaps of stone blocking the steps.

The curve of rough-hewn ceiling where the vents glowed must be near the cliff face to afford such light. Years of erosion and quakes had loosened the rock.

Vetra scrambled up the steps where the middle section lay in ruin, stomach reeling from the heights. At one time this auditorium had been packed with dragon folk listening to a lord's speech, or being entertained with some other performance. He had to squat and catch his breath. How he hated high places. Dergath was always putting them before him! He bit back the bile that crawled up his throat, grimacing at the cruel irony of the god.

He mounted the steps, two at a time, pushing through dust and molder. He groped this way and that past fallen rock and cracked benches. His blundering rush had started a cascading tumble of rocks and debris underfoot. A whole section of seats gave out, heaving up a maelstrom of dust.

Vetra lay there clinging to edges of benches, legs dangling in space, while chunks of seats fell underneath him. His lungs heaved to the smell of dust and decay. More creatures were scrambling up after him along alternate routes. It was lucky for him they were more lizard than leopard and that their climbing was limited. The range of their spit balls was no more than eight feet, else he'd have been peppered full of holes.

Dust motes drifted like listless fireflies. He pulled himself up and checked the racing of his heart. On he crept, pick clutched in hand while the dragon-lord from far down watched with impassive deliberation.

Two guardians had now cornered him. They had sidled up from nearby stairways and flanked him, licking jowls in anticipation. Vetra hacked and slashed, snouts and claws flying, black goop spraying everywhere and him ducking the slime. He watched, heard it lap into the other beast's face, blinding one of its eyes. The thing bellowed in agony. Some sprayed on his desert cloak and sizzling smoke clouded him, momentarily blinding him. He tried to brush it off with his sleeve and nearly gagged at the rank odor. He sprang upward to the next tier in a nail-clawing attempt to save his life. An eyeless head came lurching up, fangs seeking to rip into his arm. He smashed down on it with the pickaxe. The dragon creature fell back, its face and neck still sizzling with goo. The shelf of seats gave under the monster's weight, and the rock crashed down, crushing a half dozen of the brutes that struggled to get at him. Bestial whines filled the spacious arena, highlighting the madness of the scene.

Scrabbling with the best of his speed, he crawled through the rubble. At last he made it near the vents. Every stumbling step up those crumbled, haunted steps was like a herculean effort. Sunbeams traced dust-streaked rays in the air. He leapt up on the carved, polished backs of the highest stone benches. Bracing his feet, he began chipping with mad fervor at the cleft that admitted welcome sunshine. It was not wide enough to let him squeeze through. His muscles burned with the effort. The precipitous drop showed the ruined section of amphitheater yawning below like an abyss that made his senses swim. Clang! He struck again with mighty swings. Ever did the dragon beasts below slip on the rubble and blocks of masonry, unable for the moment to edge their way higher and closer to flank him. He could hear the sinister rustlings among those shattered, broken, clogged steps, slipping and sliding on debris and emitting ominous bellows. Should they clear a path... Vetra shuddered and smashed at the flaky sandstone. His tool sent hard flakes and chips flying. He closed his eyes to avoid stray fragments. At last he cleared an area large enough for him to squeeze through.

With a grunting gasp he pushed his way through. At the same time he dragged axe and feet, ducking the black spitballs of beasts that were at his heels.

A wash of blazing sunlight stung his eyes. He could make out a patch of white clouds somewhere greeting his beleaguered sight, and he hauled himself on through the gap, his feet wriggling in air. The hisses and red snouts and black teeth came angling up.

They could not get past the narrow gap.

He crabbed his way on hands and knees down the slope, gulping breaths into his lungs.

He hung on the side of the cliff, up higher than where he had entered the dragon tomb. Below the familiar canyon spread like an engorged snake. He blinked, squinting into the sun. Untold relief flooded his body, and yet, the feeling of height sickness still clung in his gut and would not abate.

Farther below he could see the vestiges of a steep, crumbled stone trail that connected to the path in the ravine. He wormed his way on his belly down toward it, pickaxe lodged in crooks to brace himself should he slip.

After painful effort his feet touched the gravel path. Approaching the mouth of the broken dragon that marked the tomb, he heard not a sound. Not a soul.

Quite a different space than before. A pall of death hung over the sepulchral chamber. The floor was up—and the wall was back to its regular place, exhibiting no sign of having moved at all.

New bits of gristle and bone lay clumped in ghastly heaps in the floor's center, now awash in a thick pool of blood...

Vetra grimaced. The sphinx-like guardian lurking by the sarcophagus had vanished. Bloody crimson pawprints stained the floor where it had walked...on towards the eerie, ink-stained tunnel at the back of the sarcophagus. Where had the Thrules gone? What had happened to Lehundr and Jhara? He shuddered, his mad thoughts reminiscing on who or what it had dragged to that moldering corridor.

He reached down to touch the warm substance staining the rock, and knew before he touched it, it was blood.

He heard a spine-tingling slithering of non-human feet from the eerie tunnel and he backed away, feeling a shiver up his limbs. A suicide mission should he go back there.

A hundred grotesque thoughts swarmed in Vetra's mind. Likely whatever had created that heap of flesh had dragged the victim or victims down that tunnel. He would be next if he lingered too long. Ill would he fare against such a grisly guardian. Could ancient iron continue to prevail against demons that came back to life to haunt the living?

He dragged himself away from that gruesome chamber. His fingers clutched the dragon-claw in a death grip.

Not a hundred paces down the trail he knelt and swayed dizzily. He let fingers pass over what looked like crimson drops on the dusty soil. Another fresh blood trail—maybe two hours old. A hope flared in his chest that there were survivors.

V: Dragon Forge

Vetra squinted south with longing. The sun's flaming orb had swung significantly westward since he had taken up his peers' trail. From his wobbly crouch on the hillside his weary eyes struggled to discern movement. An endless plain of red dirt and sand lay before him, lost in a shimmer of haze. A blur of something else: dust clouds on the horizon, caravans and camels wheeling in a long line. Supply caravans of war? Whether Behundrian or Thrule Vetra could not tell. All practicality screamed at him to leg it back to the great eastern road and hire passage back to Lvendar. He should give Dragonskull wide berth. With what money was a concern, considering his emeralds were still back on the pony. But the thought of Jhara stayed his hand. She could be wandering or enslaved by cruel lords, likewise, Lehundr.

Yet without food and water he would not last long. He looked down at the dragon claw. The fort was far to the north of this desolate valley. That's where they would be heading, if they were still alive and if they held the other dragon claw keys. Should the Behundrians catch them, that would be another matter: the scum would either kill everyone on sight or take them prisoner, or force them on to the Dragon Fort to unlock the treasure. Rafa knew about the map and Vetra was under no illusion that they would torture them for the truth. Vetra took a calculated risk and pushed on, past the cacti and windscarred shrubbery, ever north.

The road that he had come up on with the Thrules was nothing more than a narrow, dusty track, winding up the broad, shallow valley dotted with small boulders and husks of ancient eucalyptus. He staggered on, feeling the fire of thirst, keeping a path well off, but parallel to the road.

A disquieting stillness lay over the land. Only the low moan of wind that crept around crumbled rock forms. He gazed into the distance. At his feet trailed a vague set of prints, lightly dusted over.

Before long his lips were parched and split from the heat and his legs burned, but he stumbled on despite his half-mangled boot.

Black smoke—perhaps phantom mist for all his delusion—rose over the low hills to the east. More fires? Vetra guessed the Thrules had been busy burning the Behundrian mines to the ground. He swept a hand over his sweat and blood streaked face where a claw had raked his brow and torn his left arm above the wrist. He shook the fatigue from his mind, shook out the throbbing in his arm. His belly ached with a fierce hunger and his tongue scraped around his dry mouth.

The grunt of a condor intruded on his thoughts—merging then back into the background thrum. He stumbled on a loose stone, collapsed, got up again, stumbled again. A scorpion scudded across his path, a foot from his head. He cursed, staggered up to his knees, slashing at it with his rusty pickaxe. His head spun in a dizzy spell of heat.

His vision blurred. What was this? Puppet figures in the distance shimmering of heat? At least fifty of them—ragged nomads, no more than five feet tall.

Thrules! No mirage.

Vetra stood to his full height and seemed a giant. He squinted in amusement. The desert Thrules either lacked ponies or preferred walking on foot.

"Where go you?" one demanded brusquely.

Another strode forward and passed hands over Vetra's empty scabbard. Vetra saw that they kept scimitars belted at their hips. A group of them fanned out, covering him with bows.

"Kill him if he tries anything."

Vetra weighed the advantages of trying to conceal the truth of his mission and realized there were none. Bluster would not hurt. "Fools!" he snarled at the leader. "Would you slay the bearer of the Dragon Claw?" He took a step, wielding the claw. The Thrules shrank back. "What would your gods think of you then? Slayers of the holder of the key to the Dragon fort—Dragon Forge!"

The Thrule's eyes widened. "Where have you learned that name?" With fascination they stared at the claw and suspicion swarmed over the Thrule's features. A murmur of astonishment rose from the gathering.

"He lies!" sneered an angry voice.

"'Tis a mummer's trick," others cried, lifting bows and weapons.

The archaic pickaxe with wooden handle seemed to disturb and fascinate the Thrules at the same time. He lifted it with its dried black blood. They rotated around him in a circle, murmuring in awe and indecision.

"Where have you come from? Why do you trespass on our lands?"

"Water," croaked Vetra. "Some Thrules and I, from Dragonskull, we entered a tomb back in the valley. Give me water." A familiar light-headedness threatened to have him swaying and sinking to his knees.

"We have water, but you may not get any, outlander," snapped the leader. "At least until we discover more about this sacred relic you hold. You came from the Valley of the Dragons you say. Maybe you stole this dragon claw from some wealthy collector and are fleeing the law, feeding us a lie, only to slit our throats in the night and steal our gold."

"Aye, Nhfer," affirmed another, "but so odd is the tale that it may be true. Look! Here are tracks of the band that he talks about. The prints head toward Dragon Forge."

The one called Nhfer gave a grudging assent.

Vetra snorted. "If you believe anything of slitting throats and stealing gold, you're as simple-minded as those damn Behundrians. Help me find my friends."

The leader scowled.

"What was in this tomb?"

"Guardians, blood, secrets of ages past. It's guarded by ancient creatures—dragon leopards. Their skin was black and they came to life from some foul magic."

The Thrules looked at him in wonder. "You survived the Guardians?"

Vetra grunted.

The Thrule leader fidgeted. "I knew there was some truth to the old tales. You are lucky to have seen them, outlander. Only the aged mystics who induced visions by chewing the sacred mushroom have claimed to have been graced by their presence. They crawl into caves for months on end."

Vetra shrugged, a lackadaisical droop to his lips. He was hardly thinking straight, after being hunted by dragon-leopards, yet he was used to the blind reverence with which these people clung to the long dead race of their dragon people.

"And the others?" grunted Nhfer.

"I don't know what happened to them. I was trapped in a lower wing of the tomb. One of them was surely killed as I saw bones and fresh blood. You haven't seen sign of a band of twenty, travelling light with a girl?"

"No."

"She may be wounded," mumbled Vetra. "I must find them." He turned to leave.

The Thrule blocked his path and trained his bow. "You smell like lizard piss."

Vetra recalled the thick black acid that had almost engulfed him.

"There are hot springs not a league from here. You can soak your dirty hide." He gazed at the dragon claw with kindled interest. "If there is a chance, we will take it. There could be great riches to aid us in this wretched war. We must go to Dragon Forge."

Grumbles and mutters ensued and several raised their bows and shook their heads with animosity.

"Listen, you fools!" said Nhfer. "The long lost key is legendary. Many have died, starving and perishing of thirst in the desert looking for it. I will call for the brothers in the north. We have stirred up a hornet's nest here in these parts. We will need reinforcements."

Vetra saw that Nhfer sent no scout but reached for some beat-up instrument in his pack. "With what?" Vetra called. "Talk into the wind?"

"No, with this." Nhfer produced a lackluster horn from his back. "Zaln from Sunswatch gave it to me, should I need it."

Vetra stared at the horn—it was small, sleek, archaic, coiled with antique tubing, like a bugle from a far off time.

The Thrule climbed to the top of a boulder and pushed the unimpressive thing to his lips. Vetra frowned, for it made no sound, but a hollow whooshing of air, yet it was strangely lit in glorious gold when he blew into it.

"'Tis done. The Thrule bands will come before sundown tomorrow."

"Are you sure?" Vetra shook his head in doubt. "How will they find you?"

"An old Thrule secret, which you would not understand."

Vetra shrugged, indifferent to the truth of it. "I came from Sunswatch, the pump site. 'Tis lost, and Zaln is dead. I saw him tortured before my eyes."

The Thrule bit his lips. "Dead? Sunswatch fallen? So are the mines. We came from Maniswaning, and it was taken. Though we made a ruin of their precious Thorian rigs. It will take them weeks to rebuild it."

Vetra shook his head. "Not the wisest move. Unless you plan to defeat them utterly, you have made your deathbed when they come after you. These petty skirmishes and acts of vandalism accomplish little."

Nhfer rounded on the stranger in anger. "What do you know? Do you suggest we sit back and let those Behundrian pigs dominate us like serfs and take our land and our women?"

"I suggest nothing of the sort."

"Then hold your tongue, outlander. Give him water." He flourished a hand. "Cut him a piece of leather to tie around his cursed boot." A Thrule snapped to attention and brought a canteen from his pack. Vetra snatched the canteen out of his hand and chugged warm gulps of water—nectar of the gods!

"Then we head north—to the fortress. 'Tis but eight leagues away. To Dragon Forge!"

An hour's march later, with the dull ball of the sun arching a sweltering arc over their sweating skulls, they stopped at a low thicketed wall of foliage.

Vetra frowned, wondering what this place was.

Nhfer led them through the thicket, cutting bramble with his short blade, revealing hot springs camouflaged in a net of green *alphanel* fronds. A bubbling pool gave off an acrid sulfurous scent. Following with grinning anticipation, Vetra shambled on to strip down and clean his grimy skin and cleanse his wounds. Others bathed and took fresh water. It had a sulfury taste to it, but Vetra felt better.

They made camp shortly after. Though they had no packbeasts, the Thrules were efficient, but taciturn.

This company was not so merry as his own, and for this, Vetra felt a pang. No song, or merriment carried over the light wind, only grumbles, stares and solemn predictions by this crew of nomads. After a time, milling around a low, glowering fire, Vetra lay down to sleep. But Nhfer's slightly slurred speech and fumes of mead from his breath caused Vetra to stir. "All this blood and fire, and woe. When will it end?" Other members mumbled their commiserations.

Vetra spoke, "Do you not feel satisfied with your accomplishments, Thrule?"

The leader mused for a long time. "When I was young I thought there might have been some purpose to it all." He heaved a heavy sigh. "Some cause to our fighting. But seeing the cruelty I have, the sorrow that man inflicts on his fellows, I started to lose hope. Now, I just scurry about like a rat in a cage trying to survive, to fight the cretinous swine who push over noses deeper in the sand and every day creep closer to my backdoor. Running, hiding, fighting... It seems an endless loop."

"You think too deeply into purpose, Thrule," grunted Vetra. "You expect too much from your neighbors. The bad ones are swine, and there are all too many of them. Things seem not what they are. They will not change with your restless expectations."

The Thrule exhaled a breath. "You may be right, outlander." He stroked his beard under the loose hood, and his thoughts were faraway, as were his eyes.

"Sleep easy, fellow. Tomorrow we will reach Dragon Forge, and then we will test this claw of yours. Maybe something *will* change. For all our sakes, I hope so."

* * *

Dusk was well advanced and the stars twinkled like a web of sparkling jewels. The cicadas were out and chirping in the dry desert weed.

Vetra lay dreaming, and in his dreams came Jhara. She stood in a frost-glittering field, a maiden fair as the dawn, wielding sword, with a forest not far off, dusted with ice. He grinned, threw down his own crusted blade and caught her up and bore her down and they writhed in love in the welcoming onset of winter, and there was no feeling of coldness, only warmth, their combined heat melting the ice crystals around them.

He tossed and turned. A vague recollection gripped him of sleeping on hides under the stars with the Thrules, hearing the call of the jackals, and the answering howl of a rival pack. He woke in a sweat, the moon glaring overtop like a sinister runestone. His thoughts were heavy with the lingering question if any of his party had survived. He thought of Jhara again and a guilt pricked his heart. It left him with a sadness that had no relief—that he had failed to protect her and the others of the Thrule company.

* * *

The company of Thrules trudged ever north up the valley. Vetra followed in their wake. Shimmering waves of heat hovered always out of reach, merging with the low shrubbery in the flat distance. The Thrules gritted their teeth to the growing heat, trodding on with single-minded purpose as the sun rose in the morning haze. There were few places to hide in this open, sweltering bowl of desert scrubland if enemies sprang upon them from behind.

A faint wind came from across a nearby salt marsh, carrying with it a dry, tangy odor. The pale green desert plants faded in the distance. It was not until noon that the ruin of a mighty fort loomed like broken teeth on the horizon. At first only jagged stumps or spears of rock showed themselves, then a domed mesa, gray and blue, thrust itself out of the haze like the molar of a prehistoric beast.

"Unexpected, isn't it?" remarked Nhfer.

Vetra offered no comment.

A group of white-hooded Thrules moved about the plain, clearing rocks and arranging wooden totem forms. Vetra guessed they were preparing for a ceremony. As they neared, he saw that some were women playing with groups of children. Several of the clanspeople moved in a solemn line up the hills toward the caves to the left, dragging bundles tied with string or carrying baskets.

Twin hills ranged to the north, blocking access to the valley. On both hills reared Dragon Stones, huge megaliths, shaped like twin forks, which rose like enchanted spires in the yellow afternoon light. They glinted like ancient, cyclopean earth talismans. Casting long shadows down on the plain below, they intersected mysteriously to play mischief with the eye, as if defying natural laws, and held some astrological or zodiacal significance. At one time an ancient river had flowed between the hills, but now was dry. Stray boulders and seashells populated the pebbly earth.

Nhfer pointed to the hills surrounding the left flank of the valley. "There is water in those caves yonder. That's why the temple Thrules go there—to fetch sacred water. It was a precinct revered by the dragon-lords."

Dressed in flowing ceremonial garments, with colorful braided designs and brilliant white hoods, the temple Thrules were a stark contrast to the dark rags of the hill Thrules. Vetra noticed complex beadwork showing emblems of dragons on their breasts and backs.

He also saw the low sandy plain looked blasted as if by huge rocks hurled down from the hilltops. The whole area at their feet was a jumble of masonry and sprawling sand-filled ruins. Dragon-headed temples lay carved into the cliffs. At one time it had been a majestic city, that much Vetra could see. Metal doors and architraves had been forged by fiery breaths; he imagined such from their exotic tints. By such unusual means, metals had been melted and reformed into fabulous shapes: of dragons and giants and lords. Fluted columns and dragon-headed turrets rose like broken masts out of the ruins, teetering in drunken unison, and the lines of ancient walls and stone pathways were but the skeletal remains of what was once a great, flourishing center under the rule of titans.

As for the actual fort, Vetra's eyes strayed to a long white-washed limestone portico rising up the mesa's front with a line of columns and four great dragon lord statues. *Dragon Forge.* There was an elemental beauty and stark vibrancy to this place which seemed incongruent with its age. So remarkably well-preserved it was for something so old.

Nhfer pointed. "It was cited that the desert giants built this fortress to protect their realm, though they died off as a race. They fought here and were turned into stone, by the mighty dragon-serpent Ermgen's fire. It was said a star fell from the sky and became the avatar that was Ermgen. Dragons and their lords fought giants and took over the old kingdoms. Thus the giants languished. That is why everything is so monumental here. See there—those gleaming columns—" he gestured to the sprawl of massive pillars in the ancient city beside the fort "—they are intact—as is the great dragon hall."

The Thrule approached the other curious clan members who blinked and stood gazing. Many dropped whatever they were doing. Nhfer lifted Vetra's hand that held the claw. "All hail the finder of the Dragon claw!—the Claw Bearer!"

"What do you mean, Claw Bearer?" one Thrule cried out.

"Can it be?—the talisman to open the gates?" another hissed.

Vetra tensed in recognition of several faces, startled. A ginger-haired beauty with sun-bronzed limbs stood out like a beacon in a sea of shadows. Jhara! She was entertaining a group of Thrule children and had them enraptured, singing in her melodious voice of the legends of the lands that her father had told her.

Vetra exhaled an explosive breath, feeling the weight of days slip from his shoulders. She and others must have caught up with these temple Thrules.

Lehundr was conversing in excited tones with Thrules under the colonnade of the Dragon fort beside the great dragon door.

A circle of domed-shaped yurts stretched to the side, past the ruins and shattered columns and time-eaten stumps of masonry. This was once the dragon-lord kingdom. Houses? Dwellings? Communal halls? Vetra was undecided. Others came running from the small caves up the hills; several were hurrying down a well worn trail, tents and yurt tarps draped over their shoulders. Samos, the shaman, roved among them, directing, whispering blessings.

Knots of Thrules moved in and about in animated conversation and Lehundr had taken pains to gesticulate his theories about the dragon claws to the people who sat on the steps, their downcast heads in their hands.

When Jhara caught sight of the dustworn mercenary, she jumped up and raced over to wrap clinging arms around his neck. She hung on him with her knees bent and small feet angled to the sky. "We thought you were dead!"

"Good to see you," he said with a smile. The familiar smell of her brought back pleasant memories. "I thought you were lost out there, or worse."

Lehundr came sauntering up and gave him a brisk handshake. His cracked smile split his sun-browned features. "Old dog. How did you survive?"

"I found a hidden exit." Vetra quickly told his tale. Others approached, Aus, Gefzad, Dunon, eyes blazing with surprise.

"Incredible! We've been looking for sign of you—and gave up, I fear. We failed in releasing you from the tomb as we had our own trials with the Guardian. But you have survived—"

"Everyone says that this must be the key to unlock the door." Vetra displayed the claw trophy.

Lehundr gasped in astonishment. "So you found it. Small wonder the others failed," he mumbled.

A low, soft female voice spoke from behind, "I am Sebju, leader of the Dragon Forge People. We are the Dragon-Thrule, keepers of the Dragon Lords. You claim to hold a relic. Let me see it—"

Lehundr grabbed the claw before the woman in the white robes could examine it, and caressed it avidly in his fingers. He passed it on to the middle-aged woman who frowned, her long graying hair curling out around her shoulders. A grunt of child-like disbelief passed from her lips. Tracing its contours with trembling fingers, she uttered a startled gasp and swept back her hood. "It seems genuine. Old beyond belief."

"Then let us try the doors!" Nhfer cried with impatience.

Lehundr held up a hand. "Hold! You need this. The map speaks of three dragon claws. We have two." He held up the other scored and ancient dragon relics.

"You brought them?" asked Vetra in a hushed whisper.

"Who is this?" barked Nhfer.

"The one who had the map that led me to this—" Vetra lifted the woman's hand that held the claw.

Nhfer passed eyes over Lehundr with a frown. "What would a half Behundrian want with dragon claws, and why have half a care of our heritage? Except to steal our treasures?"

Lehundr objected to the accusation but Jhara clutched his arm. "He has everything to do with it, Thrule, and we would not be here, if it were not for him." Her features clouded as if struck with a sad thought. "Besu didn't make it," she told Vetra quietly, hanging her . "He was snatched by something hideous and dragged off and mauled. It was horrible! The leopard-sphinx, or Guardian of the tomb, came to life. It got to him before we could—"

"I know," Vetra consoled. "I saw the crimson remnants of the struggle." He looked around at the hollow-eyed group. "Where is that rat, Zren?"

"Gone," snapped Dunon. "Disappeared after our escape from the tomb."

"You mean after all the trouble we went through trying to save his hide, he up and leaves?"

Dunon nodded. "He was ashamed of what he had done, particularly to you, and couldn't stand our cold glares. I would have done the same thing, if I were in his shoes. We shan't see him again."

Vetra shrugged with indifference.

"The Behundrians will be coming up the valley before long," warned one of Nhfer's aides.

"Right, I heard that hound Cthan boasting that he would take an army up and strip every flab of flesh from our hides," murmured Aus.

"Let him try. We laid waste to plenty of their mines," rasped Nhfer. "Though many of us died in the doing. All of what you see is what's left of us, barely fifty, when we were three hundred!"

One of the Thrule women consoled a crying child in her arms. "Why do you bring this evil upon us?" she wailed. "We don't want your wars! This is sacred land to us, and the old ones—they ruled the dragons."

A chorus of sympathetic protests went up among the clan women.

"War is war, woman!" Nhfer shouted back at them. "We cannot control or predict what and where it will strike. Pack your belongings. Delhas! Nesthu!" he snarled at his assistants. "See that the children are prepared for travel. At dawn's light they will go north with you, to seek a place of safety. The Behundrians must pay for their insolence!"

Shocked murmurs rang among the women. "This has been a peaceful haven for years! We are the caretakers of the dragon lords."

Another hissed, "If you force us, so be it. But why not flee to the hills with us?"

Nhfer snorted. "And tuck our tails between our legs like whipped dogs?"

"At least you'll be alive," returned one of the more influential women. She was taller and more composed.

"Do you have that little faith in us?" Nhfer asked with sad incomprehension.

"No, it's because I have too much faith in you, captain. You will give your life to support our independence. Knowing that, I'm sad that you will spill your life blood on sacred soil, if that is what is asked of you."

Nhfer growled, but he curbed his tongue. It was clear in his gaze that he saw the possibility of it and was moved by the genuine concern in the woman's eyes. His lip firmed into a sullen scowl. "No matter. If death is to be my fate, then that I must accept."

Vetra saw the hopeful faces vanish and the feverish whites of their eyes glint underneath their monkish hoods.

"Take the girl with the others." Nhfer jerked a hand toward Jhara.

Jhara stepped back, steel flashing in her palm. "The first one that touches me, dies," she hissed.

Nhfer blinked, raised brows in surprise, as did others of his company. Low, nervous chuckles spread through their ranks.

"The girl stays with me," grunted Vetra.

"As you like, outlander," muttered Nhfer. "But her blood will be on your hands."

"Let us focus on the effective things we can do," said Vetra. "If the Behundrians fall on us, then those high pillars over there are an ideal place to put your best marksmen. We can dig pits to ensnare careless invaders. This narrow tract of sandy plain is a perfect ambush ground." He snarled. "The Behundrian host must pass through this vulnerable neck to get to the dragon hall. We will trap them here! Pick them off like ripe fruit. We will hide up in the crags with our spears and bows and rain holy terror down on them. We used tactics like this when I was stationed in Sarnhill, on the Sahir border."

A flicker of resentment passed across Nhfer's face, as if he disliked being counseled on strategies of war, but he held his tongue. Perhaps the Thrule was afraid of looking inexperienced in his men's eyes. With a wave of his fist, the Thrule leader ordered his men to comply with Vetra's wishes and assist him in any way they could.

Despite the unhappy faces of the retreating group of women, and the crying children, and the wails of the angry wives, Vetra closed his ears to their tears and sobs. Many would not see the men of their family again. He had witnessed this all before.

"I need a sword," he muttered.

Nhfer motioned to Euth who pulled an extra blade off his packbeast.

Vetra examined the weapon. It felt light in his grip. The blade had a wide end—too wide for his tastes—but it was a wicked instrument, nonetheless. The broadsword was always his weapon of choice. But the curved falchions of the Thrules would do just as well if it came down to a fight.

Down wide avenues of fine sand, Lehundr and the temple Thrule leader, led Vetra through the ruined city over to the Dragon fort, accompanied by various other Thrules. Dunes sculpted by winds curled over the gleaming white vertebrae of dragon tails. Vetra and others pushed deeper into the ancient sprawl of tumbled blocks and walls. More often than not, his keen eyes saw more: scattered bones, a monstrous skull tilted in barbarous fashion, half submerged in sand, or shattered by a broken column, or an elongated snout protruding out from a grave of sand. It was a place that snakes and lizards made their playground, scuttling among the scattered stones and dried earth.

They mounted the steps of Dragon Forge and began a long march down a marble terrace, a few hundred feet. White limestone, buffed smooth as glass, glistened in the intense sunlight. Tall, proud statues of dragon lords stood in a long line at intervals down the court with austere dragon faces and arms cupped in offering in front of them.

Vetra stared at the entrance to the temple, and could not help but be engulfed in a sense of wonder for the construction that spanned ages beyond his imagining.

A thousand years had passed of lashing wind and sun, and still the structure bore a look of gleaming vitality, unbroken and true, something which could not be explained by natural upkeeping. Surely it must have been forged under the protection of advanced sorcery! Its shadow cast a somber hue over the plain, as if steeped in a memory of ancient antiquity.

Sebju spoke in a whisper, "Long ago dragons warred with men over land and the precious water supply of the oases. As you see, bones lie strewn over the plain that was the last Dragon Lord outpost. We temple Thrules call it the *Temple of the North*. Bleached and sun-dried by centuries of sun and wind, it now lies mostly covered by dust storm after dust storm, and their secret was forgotten, by all but a few."

She continued in a proud voice, "The Dragon Lords sealed up their secrets and treasures in their dragon mesa. It was once a great covered fortress, of iron and stone. But it had been battered by invading armies, forgotten but for the low, squared-off vault that shows now. Still the portal stands, invested with carved, copper double-valves, initially fired and cast by powerful dragons' breath."

It was lined and coated, as Vetra now saw, with their own gleaming white bones, the most resilient things in the world, withstanding the test of time over rock, and the legendary Thorian. Vetra gazed at the key in his hand, supposedly a talisman existing to unlock this portal, one that had been lost for ages.

Vetra followed Lehundr toward the middle of the colonnade, his bootfall echoing off the polished stone. The dragon door, unlike the gleaming walls, was reddened as if bathed in the ancient blood of dragons. Massive ringed handles faced inwards like great ox-yokes, for equally massive hands, as if the doors were handled by giants.

Vetra rubbed his scalp. A score of paces away, an ancient dragon lord statue stood fixed in timeless majesty. Palm held open, the giant stood enthralled, riveted in a gaze of sublime contemplation. A tall man with a dragon's head carved in stone, it sported a bronze girdle about his waist, a sculpted boomerang tucked within.

No keyhole was apparent in that solid door and Vetra paused, puzzled. There were no visible seams or signs that indicated whether it opened inward or outward. The temple Thrule leader solemnly passed the dragon claw over the smooth face of the door. The door neither budged or wavered. Lehundr grabbed the talisman from the elder's hands and moved it in different directions, jamming it in faint grooves that showed on its massive face.

"No human hammer will break that gate, half Thrule," the wise woman said, chuckling, throwing back her weathered white hood. "None knows where such stone was quarried from, or how such metal was forged. Some say the eldest, most powerful dragons, breathed fire and brimstone on them and blasted them with their fiery breaths, making them indestructible."

It seemed probable, looking at them now. Vetra stood back, impressed.

An hour later, feverish, fruitless efforts had failed, resulting only in disappointment and no budging of the door.

"Maybe we should think of trying something else," grumbled Nhfer.

"Or adopt some other profession than grave robbery," murmured Vetra.

They had gained no more access by late afternoon and they sat slumped, chin in hands, scowling in dissatisfaction. A shout came up from the plain.

Those whom Nhfer had summoned came marching over the gap where the two hills to the north met.

Vetra blinked in surprise. He saw their numbers approximating the order of a hundred, a welcome addition to their war band. He felt a twinge of relief, for they were a hundred more than he expected. A weary bunch too, for they had traveled much distance, non-stop and in haste, he guessed.

Nhfer greeted them with warm words and exchanged embraces with Vasuth, the leader, and nods of head and broad smiles with certain of his peers. He introduced his companions to Vetra, Sebju. They nodded and clasped arms, the Thrules clutching boomerangs, with only a few spears and bows among them.

Vetra gazed with curiosity at the newcomers. When he saw their meager, limited arsenal, he winced and massaged his temples.

"Not enough bloody bolts," he muttered.

"Boomerangs will serve us," asserted a proud member of the new company.

"Boomerangs will do you no good against those savages of Behundrians and their camels in close-quarter fighting," argued Vetra. "Make spears from the deadwood at least. They lack the metal heads, but are better than no weapons at all. I'd advise sharpening and hardening their tips well. Twirl them in open fires." He motioned to a zealous, gleaming-eyed Thrule, who gripped a prime example of a spear in hand.

"Aye, Claw Bearer," said the Hill Thrule.

Vetra did not care for the title, but let it pass. A faint strain of condescension edged the tone: an unnecessary attitude, considering he was helping these vandal Thrules who had gotten themselves in a mess through no fault of his own. A part of him wanted to walk away from this dusty plain and never look back, and let them fight their own misguided battles. But he always fought for the underdog, and that was definitely these nomads. And there was always the spoils. But the thrill of the chase was his real inspiration, as was it the heart's drive of any mercenary.

After instructing them on spear-making, he went on to set up archer hides atop the pillars, also lead in digging snare-pits. These turned to be shallow ovals hollowed in the sand upthrust with pointed stakes. They covered them with withered branches, goat hides and a false floor of sand. He went so far as to oversee some crude catapults operated from the caves, and collect larger stones to roll down on enemies from the craggy hills and crumbling pinnacles of rock. He sank wearily on a broken stump of column, squinting against the sun as it sank in a weltering sea of red.

Lehundr sat down aside Vetra some moments later. "We'll not see a gold speck of the treasure once these Thrules get their share. It was me who found the map. 'Twas me who had the vision!"

Vetra shrugged. "We haven't even penetrated the blasted vault yet."

"Which is why I think we should work through the night, crack it open, carry out what gold we can and steal off under the stars."

"A brilliant plan, Lehundr, but it may be these very Thrules who keep us alive, if the Behundrians are haunting the desert to the south. Unless you are thinking of crossing the wastes north into Sahir? With an armload of riches and nosy Thrules all the way? All the gold in Behundria won't buy you water out there, or food."

Lehundr clenched his fists with fury. "It was unwise of you to give up the claw. The old woman has it now."

"You already have two claws!" grunted Vetra.

"I don't think they're the right ones. Decoys maybe. Your claw is different from the others. You said you found it draped around a Dragon Lord's neck, hidden in a secluded chamber. The others were in plain sight, too easy to snatch."

Vetra gritted his teeth. "That claw didn't work." He shook his head in incomprehension. "Take whatever claws you must and do what you like with them. I'll not have part in your plots."

* * *

Before the women had left with Delhas, several of them had prepared a feast for the defenders of their lands who stayed on: dates, mashed figs, dried mutton. The threat of battle lingered heavily on Thrule shoulders. All felt that tomorrow would bring red maelstrom and slaughter to the hallowed grounds.

In the early evening Vetra further trained Jhara in swordsmanship by the ruins of the dragon-lord's hypostyle hall. "Use the same motions as you would with the knife," he instructed her. "Better not change your technique that much. Just use the shorter blade, remembering you have longer reach."

"It's all new—but I'll adapt." She clutched Lehundr's blade with zeal, nodding with a grunt of raw vigor and came at him in a rush.

"Easy girl!" he chided. "You'll exhaust yourself." He parried her short, aggressive thrusts. "Feint in like this—" he made a quick sweeping motion "—then draw back." He drew her into a defensive crouch and turned in an unexpected circle to edge around her lean hide, with the blunt edge of his sword touching her neck. "You see—your opponent wouldn't expect this."

Mouth hanging slack, crouching low, she repeated what she had seen, improving her technique.

"That's it," he encouraged. "Make your opponent waste his energy, not yours."

She gave an exasperated cry. "I always use my cat o' nine tails! If some dumb mule gets too close, whack—" She whipped out the ring-hooked weapon to clash against Vetra's outstretched blade.

Vetra glared. "Perhaps. But don't rely on that thing. It can be thwarted easily. Some 'dumb mule' can come in and snatch it out of your hands, like this." He shot forward, hooked out his sword and her whip lashed around the gleaming flash of its attack. With a lightning-fast yank, he grabbed it and pulled it, jerking her off her feet.

She snatched the whip back in anger. "That's not fair."

He stepped back with a laugh. "Fair? Are we back to that again? Watch that temper of yours. It won't serve you in a battle."

"It could also save me," she argued. "If I see red, I can fight like Mother Dalki, demoness of the hunt. So I was told by my mother."

"Well, she's right, and she's also wrong. You could miss the obvious and end up dead." He wiped sweat from his brow.

Dunon and Nhfer and other Thrules had been watching the sparring, whispering among themselves like adolescent boys, the odd lewd comment inserting itself in their conversation. Both he and Jhara ignored them.

"Come on—it seems we need some privacy from the spectator gallery. We'll wait till dusk when the little boys have gone to bed." He found a shrubbed-off area and lay down with Jhara in his arms, resting, feeling her soft warmness pressed against him, his back to the cool sand, though with one ear and one eye always open.

Twilight brought a salmon glow creeping over the naked desert. The thrum of activity merged into that pleasant bustle and cricketsong that the hill Thrules knew best. Temple Thrules mixed with hill Thrules and men's high voices, laughs and spirited arguments rose over the sounds of desert instruments, zither and palm drum, and the crackling of cook fires. The temple Thrules had rolled out casks of ale from sand-covered holes near the foot of the hills. Samos and the Sebju participated in sprinkling a protective trail of spirits around the common ground, the same spirits brewed from a cactus like plant that grew in these parts. Vetra and Jhara chose to join the company, languid and unhurried of stride.

Scouts had been posted as far as two leagues down the valley to warn of any attack. But none came. The security cushion of advance warning nonetheless lessened their worry of ambush, and allowed the men to relax.

Some of the women had refused to travel north with the others, and Sebju and story-tellers of the hill Thrules revealed tales of their heritage, mostly for the entertainment of all:

"We dragon-Thrule come from an ancient race, long before the Behundrians or the Sahirians came and wrested this land from us, and set us scurrying to the hills—We knew much about the lore of this hallowed land, and how the giants came and founded this city long ago, and died in war with dragons, leaving their treasures with them. Plates of gold and iron meld were then fused on dragons' hides which made them invincible. Stone dragons, colossal statues, piles of bones. The city of Dragon Forge was but a shattered rock when the last dragon lord lay in his tomb..."

Vetra could see the city had been a major center...with its dragon-headed temples carved into rock cliffs, its wide ways and stone-carved avenues that hosted dragons, giants and men at one time.

"It was said a great smoke came over the land when the islands of the sea erupted and spewed filthy ash into the air—and this earthy plain, then a leafy green paradise, turned to dust and cinders, and a coldness settled over the lands. Men turned to war with dragons. They came with a vast host before Dragon Forge. The Dragon Lords raised their hands to the sky, and the dragons dipped down at their command from the clouds to smote the army ranked before them. But the black blood froze in the dragons' veins when the champion of the men, Percias the mad witcher, launched a glowing ball of power into the air which beguiled the swooping beasts as a flame does moths. They flew into its dusky interior, consumed by sorcery, to fall as one, cleaving mighty domes and cloud pillars of the city of Dragon Forge, as you see before you.

"The Lords quivered, their magic fled them, then men with pikes speared them down like marlins...All except one, the most powerful lord—Macemas, who turned within to his abode of power and closed the vault forever."

Murmurs rang through the gathering; many asked how Percias had won favor with the men.

Sebju's voice tolled low and serene. "The Dragon Lords strove among each other, vying for control of the realm. They were not immune to vice. One betrayed his master: a certain protégé and coming lord bound under Macemas. He contracted Percias, the witcher from old Angoram in Mosete, to build him a weapon to usurp his superiors and make him king. The witcher granted it to the aspirant but betrayed him and withdrew his talisman, the magical orb, and he teamed with the men, who he knew could defeat the dragons and their lords, and thus deliver him the wealth of all Dragon Forge..."

There was a pause as many blinked while absorbing the tale. The Thrule magician Samos clapped his hands. He regaled everyone with a few entertaining tricks, letting a hawk land on his shoulder and then outstretched arm, and after encouraging it to clutch up several objects the magician had secretly stuffed up his sleeves, let it fly about their heads, dropping things: seeds, papers, ornaments, from its beak and talons. To the tune of amused applause, Sebju brought out her story tellers, and Nhfer his jugglers and Vasuth, the other hill Tribe leader, let his acrobats perform a comic routine. Some men, drunk on mead early on, fell into the fire and shouts and laughs went up in wild peals as beards and hoods were singed. Vetra gave short shrift to the antics; for all the time his warrior's brain worked on the problems of tomorrow.

Vetra and Jhara and Lehundr enjoyed, or more aptly suffered politely through, the entertainment and conversed some, mingling with the fiery-tempered Thrules and their reckless sports, but Vetra grew restless, as men indulged in ale and grew boisterous, perhaps preparing themselves for the trials and fighting ahead, with its uncertain outcome.

It was easy to evade notice of the two Thrule sentinels who watched the inner perimeter. He did it more to test his powers of stealth, than out of necessity, though Jhara certainly got a kick out of it. Vetra had much experience of getting past guards in his day.

He moved into the shadows, with Jhara at his heels, away from the hubbub, shouts, laughter and song.

The two weaved their way up the hill that hosted the dark stones and they fought and trained under the forked megaliths limned against the rising moon. Though the landmarks towered like devil tridents under the ghostly light, they paid them no heed. The eerie radiance lit up the sand like molten silver.

At the feet of the nearest megalith a gap opened where a crumbled stairway angled down to gloomy depths. An entrance to another tomb? The passage was half filled with sand, Vetra saw, out of which poked a dragon snout.

"What do you think their purpose was—the dragon lords?" asked Jhara. She wiped the sweat that still poured from her brow after their vigorous sparring.

Vetra shrugged. "What do you think?"

"Why did they die off? I don't believe Sebju's tale about mad dragons and witchers and orbs is true. Did they die in vain?"

"They're remembered still centuries later," Vetra observed. "Our dwarfish Thrules somewhat idolize them, so in that sense, no, they didn't die in vain." He looked up at the garland of stars pricking the heavens and reflected. "It's quite likely, some species altogether more alien than us, might look down on our bones and see our moldered towers a thousand years from now and think the same of us." He grinned at the thought.

Jhara's lips parted in a thoughtful breath.

Vetra caught a sudden glimmer of motion down in the valley. He peered, surprise dilating his pupils. On the terrace before the portal to Dragon Forge, a tiny figure toiled under flickering torchlight, tinkering with hammer and claw. Vetra shook his head, wondering if the half Thrule would ever find his pot of gold. If he did, he'd vanish like a bird in the wind.

He and Jhara slept on the hill under the stars and the warm desert air, their bodies twined in a comforting embrace. Jhara squirmed her lithe body into Vetra's chest while he clasped her tight and drew in the lush fragrance of her hair. She whispered sultry words in his ear and wormed her way closer into the crooks and strong folds of his muscles, and he burned with the feline heat of her. It was all the mercenary could do to keep himself from falling into a torrent of passion, given her pliant advances and strong lust for him. Something he had no intention of resisting. For some moments he forgot the horror of yesterday and the trials to come.

VI: Red Sands

Pale light was spilling over the barrens when Vetra and Jhara sauntered down to find sleepy-eyed Thrules ranged about last night's fires. Sporadic groans emanated from dust-caked lips.

"Up, you fools," growled Vetra. He bared his blade. "The alarm could sound and you hounds would be caught unprepared."

Grumbles and curses passed among the hooded men. They eyed the mercenary with sullen respect as he moved through the camp with ease and authority. The girl trailed flush-faced behind him.

Hardly had the two snatched a few wedges of cactus fruit and handfuls of dates when a shout arose from the shimmering plain.

Scouts came riding in on desert ponies. "They're here!"

Eyes darted to the south. The sign of distant dust clouds rose like smoke on the horizon.

"To your positions," ordered Vetra. He and Nhfer scrambled onto the open plain, drawing their swords. The Thrule leaders rallied each of their detachments and moved them into position. As the minutes fled by, the rumble of hooves grew steadier.

Vetra and Nhfer steeled themselves with their limited forces to face the approaching Behundrians. Jhara and a red-eyed Lehundr joined the main force of Thrules up the sides of the hill breasting the mesa to await and ambush the host at the appropriate moment. Some of the Thrules lay hidden up in the crumbling rocks and peg-like pinnacles overlooking the dragon fort, while others ran up the shale-flaked paths and crouched behind the fallen columns and cyclopean masonry, or barricaded themselves atop the designated pillars with crossbows and bolts. The dust cloud ranged closer; camel riders and foot soldiers took form. Through the haze and the promise of crippling heat, slaughter rode toward them.

Dozens of camels and horses broke through the mirage of dawn. The roans were driven by white-turbanned riders, some Kirns and

Guirites, the latter Behundrians from what Vetra could see. The rest, a mixture of races, marched on foot.

The enemy had brought reinforcements—some three hundred strong, forcing a collective gasp from the defenders. The fifty Thrules, for all their mettle, shifted from foot to foot at the sight of the host. Flags and banners flew from the backs of the enemy riders, the blue and red of the Southern Behundrians: a flag much different from the corrupt satrap of Behundria whose reign beyond the northern hills did not extend to these lawless southern wastes.

"Fire!" an enemy rider yelled, and the first bolts peppered the air. The crossbowmen knelt and reloaded.

Curses flew among the arrayed soldiers and those of the Thrule resistance fighters.

Nhfer crouched at Vetra's side, watching the spectacle unfold through grim eyes. He and the Thrule leader had earlier rehearsed a tactic to draw out the Behundrians while others would ambush them from the crumbling slopes. The pits were ready below and the marksmen hunched behind their barricades on the pillars, bolts ready to loose.

"Stand firm," Vetra reminded the uneasy Thrules. Nhfer motioned to his men. They glared at the gathering enemy and whirled shiny blades before them, as if to give them confidence.

Samos, the Thrule magician, readied his stones and his bones of magic.

Cthan, the sheriff of Dragonskull, came riding like a bold king on a shaggy roan at the head of the vanguard. He peered around with insolent self-assurance, like a lord grown fat and cocky with the fruits of success.

"I know there's more of you, you mangy rats!" he yelled. "I can smell your cook fires and taste your rotten meat. I can see your rat prints in the sand. We have your Thrule," he bellowed with contempt. He made a savage flourish and one of his riders yanked a cord tied to a blood-streaked man bound and lashed and sent his heel into his back. The man fell to his knees.

Zren!

"Give yourself up!" Cthan's voice boomed again over the ruin of stone. The impudent tone echoed off the face of the dragon fortress and sent a rumbling anger among the Thrules. "You cannot win. You'll be slaughtered to a man!"

Vetra's fingers clenched on the hilt of his sword.

"If you want this wretch alive, bring us gold and proof of the treasure from the dragon ruin. We know you have it. This scum of a Thrule babbled on about some dragon key, but we had to force it out of his mouth." He rode over and slapped the head that was lolling. He gave a cruel laugh, a wolfish, half-taunting guffaw.

"We have no treasure," called Vetra. "All the keys we sought turned out useless. We have nothing to give you. Go back, Cthan. Go home. There's nothing here for you."

"Liars!" boomed Cthan in a bantering, hysterical laugh. "Do you take me for a fool?" His laughter grated like the slither of a sword from a unoiled sheath. "We'll burn this place down and ferret out every one of your sand-hugging hides. You bed with the weasel, be prepared to have your pelt skinned!"

The arm came closer and a mirthless smile flitted across Vetra's face. Let them walk into the trap. Behundrian falchions glinted in the blazing light and the tramp of booted feet grew louder. Camels grunted in the toiling ranks. Vetra held his breath; he sensed victory, despite the odds.

Cthan rode on, confident in his high saddle. He hurled more insults at the approaching line of warriors, hoping to rile them into a fight.

One of Nhfer's headstrong Thrules crouching above in the rocks, stepped out of hiding, and in a moment of trigger-happy passion, fired a bolt, taking Zren's captor in the throat. Zren stumbled and fell, then he ran. A cry broke out from the Behundrians. One caught up with the runaway and jerked his rope back with a proprietary tug, as if he were some pet on a leash. It had Zren landing hard on his back.

Vetra cursed. Their position was compromised now; there was no choice but to attack. He wanted to lead them further up into the ambush but the idiot Thrule had loosed prematurely. Dergath, but he would pay! Vetra threw down a fist. The Thrules on the slopes stormed out of hiding and streamed down like a pack of wolves, blades hefted, bows trained.

The boomerangs sang out like strange birds from a far star and swift destruction fell upon the Behundrians. Those that found their mark, broke necks or smashed limbs. Others that missed their mark flew back toward the throwers to land clattering among the rocks. Hands snatched them up, or some were caught in expert flight by Thrules who wore heavy gloves.

The defenders continued to swarm down, as crossbows loosed from both sides.

The unmourned Thrules fought helmless, and for that they suffered losses. The Behundrians wore no mail or iron helms, but their chests were padded with tough leather jerkins worn beneath their loose, light-colored vests which stopped a jabbing scimitar tip or whirling knife hurled from far.

The marksmen, bedded on their high places on the columns, rained bolt after bolt into the seething fray. Some caught camels' flanks and sent riders careening sideways and elicited screeching brays from the crippled animals. As horses rode in, the dragon fort was cut off from access. Horse and camel rode over the sand-covered hides and fell in the pits impaled on sharpened stakes. Footmen also fell prey, shrieking to their doom, while others pushed behind them. The crossbowmen rose with swift assurance from behind their stone barricades atop the ruined columns and released streams of bolts, killing dozens. Riders and footmen alike fell with iron in their gullets and limbs.

The Thrule magician threw his stones and spell bones into the raging horde. With an odd whistling movement they sank into small sinkholes in the sand. Foot soldiers watched aghast as rivers of flame beetles and fire scorpions came burrowing from their holes to crawl up their legs, wherever the bones landed. The creatures came swarming in, and the attackers cried out, clawing at their backs, legs and arms. Quickly the Thrules drove in and cut them down.

Where the last of the magician bones fell, they erupted in a yellow singeing flame that lit up like candles amid the front lines.

Vetra grimaced. He ducked a spear arching through the air which plunged on to pierce Samos's neck. The wizard gave a high-pitched gurgle and sank, bloody froth wheezing from his throat.

"I want that sorcerer's head pinned to my saddle!" howled Cthan.

The hill Thrules fought alongside the plains Thrules as one. Around the Behundrian flanks they circled, to hamstring enemies and plunge steel into thighs or exposed flanks. The Behundrians surged forward. With brute force and greater numbers they plowed their camels through the Thrules like scythes through wheat, despite the traps and crossbowmen the Thrules had posted. One Thrule marksman fell with a bolt through his chest; another slumped, arms flung forward as a spear plunged through his spine. The protective stone shields raised the day before were crumbled, riddled by bolt fire from the ground.

The boomerangs flew true but were less in number, and did not wreak the same terrible damage as before.

Vetra ran into the fray, roaring like a lion. His falchion rose and fell in red waves. He took blood and lives, parrying and blocking thrusts to his vitals, penetrating through leather padding to bare flesh beneath. Blade-wielding Thrules and bowmen poured in behind him, inspired by his fearless assault.

Dunon and Nhfer fought shoulder to shoulder. In a moment of ill chance, Nhfer fell as a Behundrian's saber ripped upward through his chest and he was trampled under the boots of the charging Behundrians. His men gave fierce cries, but kept on slashing and hacking with inhuman strength. Their rage rose and showed in the hewing, steely resolve carved on their faces.

Dunon wavered, blood-stained and torn, narrowly side-stepping a curved sword aimed for his neck. He shook the blood out of his eyes and, helped to his feet by Gefzad, forged into the fray, clanking swords with the spitting, one-eyed Rafa.

Vetra stepped in to block Rafa's strike that would have disemboweled the smaller Thrule, then thrust blade forward to engage Cthan's henchman.

Vetra's corded muscles rippled and lent him strength for his every savage strike. Jhara fought behind him like a hellcat, whipping her cat o' nine tails, taking with it wads of Behundrian flesh. A burly Behundrian charged her, veins popping on his brow. He was enraged at his colleague's death, the man she had just slain.

Jhara twisted like a snake; she spun outward into a crescent kick, smashing his face with the edge of her heel. The man crumpled, and was run through by a nearby Thrule. Jhara's cry rose above the clank of steel.

Vetra saw Cthan in the forest of heads and he pushed toward him like a moving shadow, beating his way with bull-like intensity. If he could take down that pig-headed tyrant, this battle would take on an altogether different flavor.

Such happening was not to be. The surge ebbed sideways. The mercenary was swept along with the mob like flotsam on a sea, as a new wave of attackers entered the scene.

With a dogged fanaticism, Cthan led his charge, thundering orders left and right in the hot wind and thrusting a fist forward. "Forward! Kill them all! Take not a man alive."

The Behundrians roared their war cries and their thundering charge was like the crash of boulders down a ravine. Their combined momentum hurtled them forward like a runaway deluge. It took the Thrules by surprise and hurled them back with fury.

Men screamed and died like corn stalks flattened in a hailstorm. They fought in close-packed knots, the leather-helmed Dragonskull aggressors towering a head over their robed enemies.

The butchery came and went in appalling waves. Steel fell and blades chopped like cleavers; lives drained away as blade lifted and thunked in men's sides. The sands of the Dragon lords ran red that day, not with Dragon blood as men had spilled in the past, but with human blood. Could the Dragon lords witness such desecration to their hallowed land, they would have rolled in their graves, sent their mightiest dragons to hew down the barbarous men who fought here.

The Behundrians with their superior numbers were edging out the smaller force, rallying together in a final pitched wave despite their losses. Their last camels tore through the Thrule line, trampling any who stood in their path. Jhara and Vetra were brushed aside in a flurry of hooves and slashing swords and whirling dust. Vetra was pitched onto his back, scrabbling to avoid the clomping hooves that would surely break his bones. A warning tremor shivered in his head. This battle was lost. He grabbed the girl by the arm and pulled her toward the dragon fort. He twirled his sword, and gave a thundering call for retreat. The camels could not mount the steps; it was apparent that a last stand at the dragon fort was all they could hope for. Vetra and Dunon and Lehundr and others staggered in a dust-choked frenzy, avoiding pits where dead men stared up impaled on stakes. They slid their way through a lake of blood-soaked Thrules and robed Behundrians lying bent and broken.

Knots of Thrules fought still in the dust and mayhem, cut off from the main retreat.

Vetra gave another bellowing roar and he and Jhara and Lehundr and a motley band of Thrules clattered up the central steps, their backs to the portal, holding the one key that Lehundr believed unlocked the mighty gate.

Stumbling backwards down the limestone way, thirty of them, ragged, cut and dusty, beat back the howling mob. They raced for the last stairway edging out on the ruins of the old city where they might lose their pursuers among the dunes and fallen masonry.

Vetra brought up the rear. He smashed his sword on heads, stabbing and hewing limbs, taking cuts and bruises as he retreated down the ancient terrace. The way was narrow, flanked by a low balustrade and intermittent statues, but in their favor while fighting in close quarters.

A quick glance ahead showed a carpet of dead on the blood-drenched sands. Thirty Thrules were already reduced to half their numbers.

The survivors ran along to the dragon gate in a fierce rush of hope.

Lehundr jealously drew the dragon claw from his vest and began scraping it along the impenetrable portal.

To no avail.

Vetra slashed an invader. With a wolfish howl, he kneed another attacker down the steps into the sandy bloodpit below. The howling Behundrians who dared to come near the dragon hall, felt the bite of his dripping sword. A dizzy veil of crimson swam before Vetra's eyes; his lungs heaved. The sun beat down like a scourge. The raging horde had exhausted their supply of bolts it seemed, or their crossbow men would have picked them off like flies. He saw Thrule bodies sagging over the tops of the pillars like straw puppets, pin-cushioned at last by volleys of Behundrian bolts.

"Hold the stair!" shouted Vetra, panting. "If we lose it, we're doomed."

The invaders flanked them, cutting off their escape. They were pinned to the terrace. Vetra hoped to make it to the end of the terrace and lose them in the ruined city, not a stone's throw away. Only three sets of stairs gave access to the temple, one in the terrace's middle and stairs at both ends.

A bloody wretch of a figure came staggering up the step—Vetra sucked in a breath—the figure's arms were bound and a long bloody rope trailed from his neck. Zren. His hood and garments were torn and shredded. It seemed that the Thrule had killed his captor and had managed to scramble his way through the mad melee. How? Vetra could hardly guess. Surely a testament to the Thrule's ruthless craft, no doubt, luck. Vetra winced at the sight of Zren, his hooked nose mashed, one of his eyes fused and swollen shut.

Snarling, Vetra cut once at the cords that bound his arms to his torso and the Thrule gave a gasping sigh, flexed hands and lacerated arms while Vetra severed the rope dangling from his neck.

Behundrians charged in with ruthless force and defenders' blades were hard pressed to keep them at bay.

Zren gurgled out a sound of renewed vengeance. His keen eyes burned with an unquenchable fire; they had not lost their sullen passion. A flash of steel and a chopping thunk and Zren deftly snatched the blood-smeared blade from the dying man's hand that Dunon had slain.

Leaping off his camel, Cthan pushed aside his own men and came charging up the steep dragon-stone steps like a blood-mad bull. His blade met Vetra's in a clash of blind fury. The two strained and heaved, slashing and parrying, until they closed together, fierce adversaries breathing hot air into each other's faces with swords locked high over their heads.

Vetra twisted on his hips. Nearby, Dunon closed with two sword-stabbing Behundrians—"Die, you mongrel curs!" He lanced his blade through the closest man's guts.

Cthan cried out with a piglike grunt when Vetra's knee rammed viciously in his crotch and knocked him down the stairs. The sheriff toppled over into others, sending his men reeling to the sand.

"Open, blast you!" cried Aus. "I'll drag this claw across your throat." He snatched the claw relic from Lehundr's hands and raked it across the glinting stone.

"To hell with the claw," cried Gefzad. "By Dergath. I'll kick this door down. Open! Damn you, open!"

Jhara rushed about in a frenzy. Her eyes narrowed on the statue, then blazed in a freak hunch. The Thrules had been focusing so much on the door that they had neglected the statue. She grabbed the claw from Dunon, and pushed it into the outstretched palm of the dragon lord.

Nothing.

One of Cthan's rogues hacked through the rebel net and knocked the claw off the palm. Jhara howled in frustration. She laid back her whip to slash at him. The man rose, blade gleaming in an angry hand to cut her throat. The rogue fell in a crimson tide as Vetra's sword arched in a deadly sweep and sliced him from shoulder to navel. His blood ran slickly over the fallen claw.

Jhara reached a desperate hand for the claw. More men rushed in to savage the mercenary. Jhara flailed her whip in a fit of panic, snatched up the blood-drenched claw and slapped it back in the statue's hands.

Almost instantly came a rending screech and groan of stone, as if tortured metal and buckling forces from deep in the earth were alive. Then a slither, as of massive gears winding and stone grinding below. The portal slid open.

Vetra's mouth twisted in satisfaction. He drove his sword through the last of the attackers and pushed ahead. The claw needed only a blood offering to open the door. By what sorcery, he could barely guess.

With a breathless gasp and wheeze of stale, gushing air, the gray slab that hadn't moved for centuries yawned open like some mouth of a prehistoric fish. In their goggling fervor, Vetra and the others pushed through. Spears clattered on the steps behind them. New bolts whined and whistled over their heads. Swords clanked about the opening that was fast jamming with heaving, roiling bodies. Thrule blood spilled, as did Behundrian. Vetra was the last defender through. He grabbed the claw from the statue's hand as the door started to grind shut.

Not fast enough.

Cthan, wheezing in pain, managed to stagger through with a clutch of his fighters and sent steel into a Thrule's gut and kicked the dying man back and away.

The heavy door slammed shut and Thrules and Behundrians were plunged into near darkness.

VII: Trove of the Forgotten Ones

Vetra stared into the shadowy interior, slack-jawed. Blood trickled down his cheek where a blade had flicked a hair width from his left eye.

A dim watery light leaked around the edges of the portal—perhaps the mechanism in its extreme age had grown faulty. Groans and livid curses rang off the echoing stone of the inner vault. Men pounded at the door, trying to win past the portal with their fists and weapons. Others who were trapped inside slashed in blind desperation at what they believed were enemies, sending sparks along the cold stone walls.

Vetra ducked whistling blades and stumbled ahead through the cobwebs with the others, straining his eyes in the gloom. The hall was about twenty feet wide, equipped with a lofty ceiling running up into darkness. Lehundr, Jhara and Dunon slunk beside him—others he guessed included Zren, Aus and Sebju. All hunched, awaiting his order, their lungs heaving, as did four other Thrules.

Dragon bones littered the long corridor; their boots crunched on them: a twisted mess of dragons and men, helms and swords and shields. A battle had been fought here, that much was evident, a scene untouched for centuries.

Vetra glimpsed the small details of this last stand: a rusted battleaxe, the handle cleaved in twain, a fallen shield held up over a man's helmed skull to stop possibly murderous dragon's teeth. In his mind's eye, a sword poking up from a skeletal hand plunged into the white underbelly of a bellowing beast as its tail thrashed in agony. Ahead, more haunted ruins loomed; even this far in, the thin light streamed from the cracks around the massive portal to bathe the cobwebbed interiors in a ghoulish glow.

Vetra urged his comrades down the hall, his feet crunching on bones and skulls. "There! Make for that back passage."

There came the tramp of men's feet and the rustle of arms from behind.

"Listen! I can hear the Thrule rats," came a nearby voice that sounded like Cthan's. "Follow them!" The voice yelled again, with disgust: "So, you have no treasure, eh? You pack of coward spawn. No key to the dragon fort? I knew you were liars!"

Even then as the sheriff's voice broke, men came clattering after Vetra and his crew. Despite all their spells and wisdom, dragons had died defending their sanctuary against rogues such as the sheriff, Vetra thought with a snarl.

He mounted a short flight of steps and paused at the landing to look back down the stair littered with broken rock and pale bones— only to hear the shuffle and stamp of feet and the angry murmurs of bloodthirsty men.

"Get a light," Cthan yelled from the darkness. Fumbles and shouts ensued, then a slap as a heavy hand smote a henchman.

"This place is cursed," cried a voice that sounded like Vilivet's, the rogue from the Dragonskull market. "Did you see the old dragon skulls, the half man, half dragon bones?"

Cthan spat with disgust. "You halfwit. Curses? Really? Get a grip! We fight these rats to the end and we win. I want that treasure—for the damage to our pipeline, for the deaths of our comrades. I hold them ransom for all these insults." He cupped his hands to his mouth. "Vetravincus! I know you're there. Why scurry and cower like your fellow rodent? Come out and fight, like a man."

Vetra's fist whitened in anger on his hilt. He hated the truth of the bully's words—but it was foolhardy to engage Cthan now, as much as he despised him and being branded a coward. They were thrice his number and thrashing blindly in the dark would only mean death. Better to lure these fools into a trap ahead—hopefully something would materialize—if it didn't get them first. Jhara opened her mouth but Vetra silenced her with a hand over her lips. He ushered the others up the stairs and bade them halt before an arched doorway to their left. He hoped that a last-minute plan would avail itself. If not, Dergath help them...

A faint gleam showed in that passage beyond.

A strange bubbling, almost a gurgling murmur of water echoed about the ancient stone, accompanied by a warm waft of humid air.

To continue past the landing would lead to more stairs snaking down into murk, thought Vetra. Already, faint sounds were stirring down that eerie way—low rusty bellows, sinister croaks and scuttling, things not human. A tingling shot up his spine—rustlings as those were not dissimilar to the leopard-lizards he had heard back in the dragon tomb.

He ducked into the passage where the glow burned stronger. Down a low ramp they crept after him into the bowels of a huge cavern.

They beheld a fantastic scene.

The inner sanctum of the lost dragon empire! Deep in the heart of the mesa, ceilings rose crusted with riches, jewels beyond imagining—countless sapphires, endless diamonds, opals, rubies, emeralds, smatterings of shiny jet, lapis-lazuli and jade which provided garish color to the panoramic maps and designs portrayed there. Dragon gems, the plunder of ages glittered with shameless appeal on high. Treasures fetched from all corners of the world, Vetra saw, anointed in lonely splendor and protected for untold centuries.

Dergath, what a horde! He had seen treasure troves before, but never like this. If it could be quarried, that prospector would be rich beyond his dreams. But how to reach the cavern's ceiling where the wealth shone? The walls rose vertically from the floor without chink or crack where a boot could gain purchase.

Before them spread an enormous bubbling pool, some manner of giant hot springs. It radiated a peculiar brazen luminosity, thus the source of the glow earlier. In the center, accessed by a broad stone ramp, rose a stone island on which stood a crystal-like pedestal of petrified bone, shimmering green, orange and white. Its quality was unique, of an otherworldly radiance, as if activated to life with the fey opening of the portal after centuries. In spite of the countless jewels overhead, here was what the dragons valued most—water!—thousands of bubbling barrels of it.

Vetra glanced quickly behind him. No sign of Cthan.

He edged toward the shore of that strange pool. In the mysterious light cast by it, he discerned the dim, familiar faces he had come to know of late: Aus, Gefzad and Sebju, the venerable leader of the Thrules who had fought alongside the men with sword and survived. But she wore a face set in grim fatality—that she and others would not survive this crypt.

Vetra hissed through his teeth. He turned to the vast pool. A lattice of stone walkways spanned the waters, from one to three feet wide. Like a spider web, these lesser walkways branched out from the central island to intersect each other, like an intricate mosaic.

Each way gave passage across the water in its unique way. A broad stone ramp gave clear access to the island, at first angling down on a shallow grade from where they stood peering in awe, before it spread over the bubbling waters. Almost on impulse, Vetra set feet down this path and Jhara ran close by with Lehundr.

Zren hunched in a defensive crouch like a cornered animal, peering up with his one good eye, the other swollen over, lips pressed in a scowl despite the glistening wealth.

"That eye will do you no good in a fight, Thrule," muttered the mercenary.

Zren grunted. "I can see well enough, thank you."

Lehundr's face lit with greed at the wealth, but dimmed upon seeing the difficulty in chipping the priceless gems out of the ceiling.

"How could anybody build such a place?" Jhara whispered. She turned in surprise. "Where are you going?" She strode after Vetra with darting eyes.

Vetra made no answer.

Lehundr spoke in a voice of hollow wonder. "'Tis surely the heart of the dragon lords."

Great dragon king statues looked down from the far edges of the cavern where their stony feet touched the water. The ceiling was a rugged dome crafted of blasted rock, embedded with untold crystals, and as Vetra's eyes probed deeper, he could see the pattern of the star maps and the legends of the dragons woven in the crusted weave of gems: of faraway kingdoms, glorious and singular, a story of Dragon history told from the beginning. But it was so vast a panorama that Vetra's struggling senses balked, unable to absorb in any single glance the immensity of it all, and he staggered back.

He turned his eyes away. The water had risen over the stone walkways, if these even were human or dragon-lord walkways at one time. To peer down upon and contemplate the pool? Or up at the magnificent maps of ages, and stars? The water's surface seemed in constant turmoil, bubbling with a feverish energy of its own. Why? Vetra did not know.

But the perfectly carved pedestal...and a shining globe hovering a foot over it, about three feet wide, on whose circumference shimmered a veil of transparent water—or yet some type of filmy, magical glass. Impossible, but true.

Vetra shook his head to be sure he wasn't dreaming. Jhara's fingers clutched his arm. Her lips parted in a gasp. The orb defied the mind's reasoning, an apparition of mindless impossibility. It was as if all forms of laws of nature were broken. Inside floated a golden dragon's eye, suspended in some transparent medium. Liquid? Air? Vetra could not say. It was as if held immobile by some incomprehensible sorcery—and fashioned of intricate detail.

Vetra went to reach for it, but an inner voice stayed him. At the pedestal's base on the dusty cold stone sat a circle of small dragon skulls plated with gleaming silver, eyes inset and glaring with flaming garnet. Vetra saw human skulls set in similar fashion at each junction of the walkways over the water, perhaps the gory trophies of past skirmishes between humans and the dragon lords.

The invaders from Dragonskull stormed in, reeling at the sight of scintillating jewels and brilliant color. Three dozen of them at least stared gasping; at the head, Cthan's eyes were lit with rapacity, his jaw clenched in critical wonder. His fingers flexed on a dripping falchion, ready to exact his thirst for vengeance.

Vetra's eyes roved for sanctuary, some strategy to foil these boorish marauders, but before him only the waters bubbled and the steam rose over the long, yellowish pool. The mosaic of stone walkways seemed at best random, some unpredictable labyrinth architected by minds of the distant past. And yet, perhaps this was just what they needed...

A ledge with sections of steep stair switchbacked up the tail end of the cavern to the ceiling, like that of the dragon tomb. For what purpose? A frown curled Vetra's lips. A ritual stair in bygone days? Dragon lords ascending and descending from some hidden entrance or exit? Could they use them to make an escape?

Vetra gave a violent start and lurched back as he nearly stumbled over one of the skulls at his feet. He snapped out of his reverie and murmured under his breath, "No time to probe the mysteries. Let's lure them into the waterways." He motioned a swift hand. "You two, Dunon and Lehundr, draw them away hither—" he jerked his head toward a distant statue on the side wall. "Over there. Jhara, you follow me."

Stealthy as a panther, he skirted around the pedestal and took to the main path toward the cavern's far wall. Jhara struggled to keep up with him.

The ragged, blood-tattered Behundrians charged up to the shore and halted before the bubbling water, their eyes gleaming upon the gems above. They had not yet spotted the scattered band loping down the walkways. With circumspect glares, thirty of them threaded their way along the main waterway to the island where the pedestal stood and the steam rose in ghostly wisps. Several of them murmured in suspicion at the magical construction and the chilling array of skulls set at its foot.

"What's this eldritch fane?" grunted Cthan.

"Worth a fortune!" Vilivet cried. He reached for the shimmering eye in the white-lit globe, but Cthan slapped the twitching hand away.

"Keep your dirty paws off that eye. It's mine!"

Rafa hunched at his side, a hooded figure leering like a jackal with his one beady eye. A bloody patch lay draped over his missing orb, taken by Jhara's scourge back in Dragonskull. Other Behundrians crowded around the pedestal to gawk rapaciously at the impossible treasures gleaming on high. A few ran back to the shore to try and scale the wall and chip out some of the gems glistening from above.

The luminous eye had got to Vilivet's brain. He drew his blade and sneered, "Says who? I'll kill you, you dog. I have just as much right to the treasure." He jumped back, grunting. "Hey, what do you think you're doing?" His eyes blazed as Cthan drew his own saber. "'Twas I who saw the eye first."

"Be careful how you speak, 'dog', and watch your insubordinate tongue," hissed Cthan with danger in his voice.

"Why? You arrogant slug," spat Vilivet. "All the deeds I've done for you? I ought to slice you in two. The Thrules aren't half as stupid as you think. They knew there was power here. They sought out this key that Rafa harped on about, having some fool map that he claimed he almost had in his hand. The eye thing's proof of it. Rafa! Here, help me wrest this golden nugget from its socket, and we'll take the magic for our own, and—"

Cthan upended the butt of his sword into Vilivet's teeth, smashing them back in his throat in a spray of bright crimson. The rogue pitched sideways, staggering back, and slipped into the water. Blubbering, flailing like a fish, he choked out a blood-flecked cry, his sword flashing in a palm aching yet to gut Cthan, but some disturbance came arching over the water.

The Thrules watched in uneasy silence from a safe distance. Vetra couldn't decide whether the foaming roil was some type of jellyfish or octopus, but it wrapped opalescent streamers around the villain's thighs. There came a wretched screaming and terrified thrashing as Vilivet scrabbled to gain the walkway. The thing in the water, whatever it was, must have mutated over the years, Vetra guessed, judging from the elongated tentacles and the ghoulish suckers on each end. Now it pulled down the screaming ruffian to his death into the bubbling water.

The Behundrians recoiled and hopped back from the edge of the water. They sucked in air, brandishing their swords.

Cthan's face wrinkled in corded knots and his hard features locked in a strange sneer. "He was a fool, Vilivet. Serves him right for defying me and believing in the likes of ignorant superstition." He glared about him at the men who still looked on in horror. "Well, what are you waiting for? Let that be a warning to you fools!" he cried, waving his sword with fanatic displeasure. "Don't get too close to the water. Who knows, you'll end up like Vilivet." His words caught in his throat as his eyes caught a whisper of movement— Vetra and his gang, pushing toward the back of the cavern. "The rogues! Well, what are looking at? After them!"

The ragged Behundrians stared in reluctance at the walkways but hurried forth, cringing at the possibility that they too might fall in the infested waters.

Cthan's hand reached for the mystical eye.

"Beware the old ones," Rafa mumbled in his ear, pointing spellbound at the shimmering globe and what fate it had in store for them.

Cthan's hand stopped inches from the eye. "What old ones? It's a myth. Nothing but outworn statues, old skeletons and fossils dredged up to scare old women."

"You're mistaken," said Rafa in a quiet voice.

Cthan rounded on him. "You too, Rafa?" He glared at him in wonder. "I expected more from you."

Rafa opened his mouth, but Cthan cut him off. "Get them, you idiot! What am I paying you for?" With raised sword thick-smeared with blood, the sheriff stomped after his henchman and beat the backs of three other laggards with the flat of his blade.

A sinister shuffling came from behind them near the back of the chamber. Cthan wheeled about and his twisted features frozen in blank-faced dismay. A curse caught in his throat, one full of regret.

"They live still? It can't be—" His voice trailed off.

Out of the gloom shambled seven primitive-looking reptiles. Dragon-leopards—the guardians of the chamber, like those of the tomb that Vetra had prowled. They crouched on all fours with dragonish heads lifted, the torsos of leopards and clawed feet of lizards. A look of madness shone from those iridescent eyes that darted all ways at once.

With a need for distance, Cthan plunged after his men, abandoning the treasure of the golden eye.

The six dragon guardians fanned out to examine their numerous prey, who they considered invaders of their realm. Already they had cut off any escape and a silent unblinking stare passed among them. A deep-toned rumble echoed from their cavernous throats. Tongues flicked out in unison. With slow, lizardlike movements three of the largest shambled across the water, straight up the main path while the others stayed back to guard the exit passage.

Vetra and Jhara exchanged glances and hurried on; others of their band slunk deeper into the maze of walkways. The guardians reached the isle and fanned out toward Dunon and Aus, and now Cthan and Rafa circled their way like weasels, far from the oncoming brood.

Vetra crouched on his walkway before a human skull, eyeing the waters and the approaching enemies with grave concern. He wondered what sinister creature watched him from below. Jhara hunched at his side, breathless, her ginger hair matted with sweat and blood. "What do we do?" she cried in a strained voice.

"We wait. No choice."

Jhara's fingers tightened on her whip.

From under the tangled mass of his matted black hair Vetra looked to see the gleam of defiance in her fiery eyes, and his heart burned with a fierce pride.

CHRIS TURNER

VIII: Jaws of Death

Vetra turned to face the oncoming horrors. One spat a ball of viscous phlegm down an adjacent walkway to affix itself to a nearby Behundrian's vest. Ooze soaked through the man's middle; he slapped at his chest in wild desperation. "Agh—get it off!" His horror-brimmed shriek filled the air. "It burns!" His fingers smoked on contact and the sizzled flesh gave off noxious gray vapors.

Vetra cursed. He sprinted onto an interconnecting walkway just in time to avoid gobs coming his way. Waters bubbled, carrying a sulfurous stench. The chamber was unbearably humid; the air pained his lungs.

"The guardians have increased our chances!" his hoarse cry echoed over the din. "Make for the ledge where their fangs can't get us."

He stared with bloodshot eyes at a distant place across the luminous waters. Shadowy shapes circled closer, glints of wheeling light reflecting off a dozen swords. He bared his teeth.

At places along the opposite shore the steaming pool ran flush to the crusted wall; elsewhere the shore widened allowing room for fighting men to move. To this place Vetra wished to flee, for the ledge wound its way up, away from the pool and the dragon beasts. The shore sloped before the far wall where colossal dragon-lord statues stood in solemn procession, staring in reflection at the sinister waters.

He and Jhara had scrambled as far away as they could from the circling fiends without being flanked, but now steel would have to decide their fate.

"Slay them!" Cthan shrieked in hoarse fury from a walkway not a dozen paces from where they gathered. "Catch them and cut off their privates, you fools! We cannot relieve this cavern of its treasure with these salamanders spitting acid at us. Kill the outlanders! Kill all these wretched Thrules."

"What do you expect us to do?" sneered Rafa. "Pull them in with our teeth? They have feet as swift as wolves."

Cthan scrutinized Rafa with a rancorous grunt. "Fifty gold talons for the first to cut off the outlander's head. Twenty for the girl's. No—take the wench alive!"

A roar went up among the swarming Behundrians and they came charging hard down the walkways at both fugitives.

A quick glance told Vetra that only a head-on assault would make any difference. Throwing caution to the wind, he ran to meet them. Rejecting the odds, the mercenary swung his sword in whistling loops and drove in hard and furious. His blade struck bone in a splatter of crimson; sword met sword in a clanking echo around the skull-littered walkways. Raging blades bit into flesh while steel smashed through sinew, driving the foremost attacker back like a mule into the other Behundrian jackals.

The man died instantly and his guts spilled out on the stone. His colleagues seethed forward, struggling to get around the standing corpse that was wedged between opposing forces, eager to stab at the berserker and win their reward.

Vetra roared and drove his blade more fiercely into the cluster. He could see the bearded dead face lolling in front of him. He could smell the hot rank breath of the men behind. Jhara's whip snapped past Vetra's shoulders and cut into Behundrian flesh. Their fates hung in balance; men's muscles strained and grisly shrieks rent the air. Dragon guardians snapped, gnawing at the enemies' backs. Vetra felt the mass of men surge and a chill wave of horror as the line of Behundrians shivered under the first beast's mauling assault. He released his lock on his attacker's sword arm in a sudden twist and unleashed a flurry of slashes. The next man fell dead, ribboned with cuts. Another took his place, his blade arching, but was soon cleaved to the bone. The mercenary showed no mercy. The blood flew from his blade and boiled in his veins; a battle lust was upon him, and for the moment he was unstoppable.

Fortune did not favor the blood-drenched Behundrians. For all their numbers, they were hampered by this lack of space and the lizard attack from the rear. Despite their initial advantage, another of the brute dragon guardians appeared, lumbering up from a side path like a ravenous ghoul. The thing ripped into their flanks, and the ones in the back screamed and fell, hands outstretched, clawing at stone as they either slipped into the lethal waters or the monster rended them with teeth and claws and dragged them away in its jaws.

Vetra saw a creature shaking its maw like a dog and a screaming victim tossed like a windblown leaf into the pool.

Vetra gave ground, snarling as dying men pushed forward like zombies. They struggled to escape the snapping jaws, the sharp claws and trampling feet. The first two in the thing's path died horribly, crushed and mangled between sets of serrated teeth. Down they went trampled by its clawed feet.

Sandwiched between foes, Jhara fought tooth and nail at Vetra's back. Yowling like a banshee, Jhara kicked with savage force and lashed out her whip at the three rogues who tried to grab her and pull her down.

Vetra abandoned his fight. The wall of flesh was pressing in on him. He pushed Jhara aside and smashed his bloody falchion like a club into her nearest attacker's face. The other he kicked in the stomach and sent him gasping into the waters. The Behundrian reached for the ankles of his fellow man to save himself, only to end up pulling him in too. Vetra ran with the girl, barely keeping ahead of the mad rush of the surviving horde who drove from behind, while the dragon guardian made grisly work of anybody left in its path.

"Fight back to back!" he snarled at Jhara over the din of the tortured screams and eviscerated bodies. "The narrow walkways give us an edge over their numbers!"

Down the walkway they scrambled. Vetra's feet skipped past an intersecting path, his eyes roving for solution, knowing a wrong turn could be their last.

Another ball of black mucus came slapping at their feet,

perilously close. He stumbled sideways to avoid it. Not a dozen feet away, three Behundrians crouched on a narrow walkway, weapons drawn, cringing. They realized they had taken a wrong turn several steps back, now they stared into the snouted face of one of the waddling beasts that had swung past a narrow bend and was fast gaining on them.

Vetra wasted no time to observe the carnage. Behind them, yelping attackers wheeled in confusion. Boots rang on stone.

The girl turned and feinted and cut a man just as he was bearing down on her. Vetra marvelled at her fluid skill. She moved just as he had taught her. In a quick follow up lash, another chunk of flesh ripped free from the man's sword arm. He wailed, clamped a free hand to staunch the growing gush of blood. Twirling, she ducked the man's strike, and sent him howling into the steaming water with a swift kick. Immediately a swarm of spidery tentacles engulfed the writhing body. The blubbering shrieks were lost in the hiss of water.

The man's comrade shrank back, the whites of his eyes showing fear, blade hanging limp.

Vetra sucked in a breath. The slimy things must have infested the waters since the demise of the dragon lords. He couldn't for the life of him imagine what had impelled the lords to allow such vermin in their splendorous hall.

He raced on, fingers hooked on Jhara's arm. They clambered for a point along the far edge of the cavern, but a half dozen Behundrians read their intentions. Vetra found the way was soon cut off. "Is there no end to you rats?" he cried, sneering at the enemies who blocked his path.

Cthan's rogues leapt forward and snarled, striving to cut them off before they could get to the next crossway. Too late. They leaped over a narrow gap of water onto a cross path which headed back toward where the men quailed, struggling with the dragon guardian.

Vetra cursed this place. The irregular web-like layout of the walkways made it impossible to predict any enemy's movements for more than a dozen steps. A sudden turn down a crosspath or a doubling back down another could leave a man sandwiched between foes.

A long stretch of open water lay between them and the three Behundrians. The stone path had sagged over time. None wished to chance that water and the loathsome squid creatures that teemed within.

Vetra weighed his options.

The doomed trio slashed at the dragon guardian that was menacing them from behind, trying to keep it at bay. No such luck.

A glob of acid spewed from a gaping maw and hit a man square in the temple. He danced a devil's jig, howling, clawing at his face which melted away in a waxy ruin before the astonished onlookers could react. The gasp died in his throat. Black goo sizzled from his flesh and he sank, twitching, legs draped over the side, his arms the other. In an instant, crawly, green, plant-like tendrils pulled the sightless body under.

Vetra and Jhara halted in dismay. Water foamed over the stone at their feet.

To race across that long sunken stretch invited disaster. No matter—the beast decided it for them. It charged across, unafraid of what dwelled in that frothing cauldron. Vetra stood grimly poised to face the thing. Jhara held back attackers at the rear. Sucker-vine tentacles hooked onto the running beast's forelegs and claws, but these were stamped to oblivion in its angry dash toward them.

Vetra staggered back, pushing Jhara hard into him and onto an intersecting path that sank into water not three strides out. He wheeled and crouched low as the beast's head reared up to smash him from the side. Had he stood where he was, he would have been mowed down by nothing less than the driving force of a battering ram.

A noisome wind hit him as he ducked under that looming wall of flesh and ripped his sword across the thing's throat, and while dark fluid spurted forth, dripping on him and staining the decayed stone, a slippery white tentacle arched from the water to grab its twitching leg.

Wild cries sounded behind him.

The thing died with a hissing gurgle, blocking the path.

Vetra shoved Jhara back. Taking a run, they leaped over its humped back. The Behundrians came after them howling. They bounded over the beast's glistening hide with another raging dragon beast snapping at their heels.

Vetra and Jhara leaped between winding paths, the stone lapping with blood and corpses. Vetra's feet slipped in a wide pool of blood. Jhara crashed into him. Her whimper and sob sounded in his ear. "We're doomed! There's nowhere to run."

They pulled each other to their feet, and the blood drained from Vetra's features. Another monster with fanged snout bore down on them. The skin of his back crawled. They scuttled down a cross path and Vetra cringed at the meaty sounds of carnage as the beast tore into fleeing Behundrians. Whatever sorcery animated these brutish killers, it could only have been brewed from the blackest pits.

He closed his ears to more gristle-rending sounds and his hand fled to his blood-matted scalp, a growing lump gathering there where a grazing rake of sword had glanced off his skull.

"Come on," he muttered at Jhara. "We don't want to fall into ruin like those unfortunate sods."

"Cthan's rogues will catch us and corner us!" she protested.

"Move!"

They scrambled over corpses and a menacing whoosh flew past their heads. Vetra looked back to see a hill Thrule's boomerang catching the loping beast full in the eyes. It stumbled out of control and splashed into the frothing water. Grinning with satisfaction, Vetra clapped the approaching Thrule on the back. He saw the sweating man had a healthy supply of boomerangs strapped to his back. "Great throw, friend!"

Vetra's sharp eyes took in the scene in a glance: the fleeing figures, the hacking blades, the shambling beasts. His mind registered all. How to win this fight? Lehundr and Aus were knee deep in hewn corpses and cloven skulls. Aus, the Thrule marksman crouched and stabbed and launched boomerangs at advancing foes. Zren raged like a ghoul, his sword gripped and flailing, tossing ear-heavy curses and hacking with unfettered lust. Of the Temple Thrule leader there was no sign; Vetra assumed she had fallen.

His inner sense told him to take a weaving course toward the clotted path where Dunon, Gefzad and Aus battled not a stone's throw from the cavern's edge against a guardian.

Arching and twisting in its confidence, the monster got too close to the water and found its foreleg gripped by a probing tentacle. With a mournful croak, the beast bit at the curling menace, but more tendrils came lurching out of the water. Like sucker vines, they were alive with force. Festoons of the snake-like things wrapped around its other leg, then its neck, and slowly dragged the creature into the seething water. Its head came bobbing up. There it thrashed, seeking release, sending keening moans into the air. But snaking cords soon webbed over its snout, fangs and into nostrils, and it dropped from sight.

Vetra closed with two blood-drenched attackers. His sword found soft flesh beneath the leather. One attacker gave a last sighing gasp and Vetra put a foot on his chest to pull out the blade. He slipped on the spurting blood, lost his grip, was unable to pry the weapon loose from the breastbone in time to prevent the blade from falling into the steaming water. Instinct took over. He kicked the corpse away and winced as his only weapon bubbled away into oblivion.

The mercenary's eyes roamed about the chamber. He felt naked without his sword. Not long would he last amid these fiends without familiar, protective steel. His flesh quivered with the thought of being rended by these foes.

Six feet out in the water, another guardian thrashed, struggling to stay afloat. Crossbow bolts stung its neck. Now its snout and humped back rose above the steaming bubbles. Vetra's eyes caught the glint of scimitars lying not far away on the stone walkway, in the hands of dead men, mauled by the guardians. It gave him an idea.

"Skirt around that way!" he shouted to Jhara. "We'll meet at that adjacent walkway." He stabbed out a finger.

"It's insane!" she cried. "You'll be eaten alive." She saw what the mercenary was planning—and she caught him in a convulsive grip.

"Do it!" cried Vetra.

No sooner had he uttered the cry when a blade came whistling by his head. He made a last savage leap.

Over the guardian's head he launched himself onto its back, now crawling with great, green, slimy tendrils. Even as the shiny, flesh-flecked teeth snapped up to chomp him, his feet were in the air again and he was lunging for the opposite walk. Where was Jhara?

He came slamming down on the crude-cut stone, his boots in the water, and the fingers of one hand clawing on the wet stone. He half expected the creature's lips to vomit out deadly goop.

He pulled himself up and over, legs burning with pain from the scorching water, and the feel of sucker-vines latching onto his leg.

Scrambling to his feet, he jigged around, a frantic fury upon him, smashing boot heels down on the crawly things that wished to twine around his ankles. He grabbed an abandoned sword and beat it against the things creeping up his legs. He shook the horror out of his head, feeling his limbs quiver.

No time to lose.

Sword in hand, he regained his footing and lunged for Cthan and the rogues who guarded the junction. Jhara was alone and against many. He cut the first opponent down in a wave of red, cleaving flesh to the bone, then faced the others.

Cthan darted away, laughing, directing others to take the place of the dead minion. "Hold him! The fool has nowhere to go." He raced back toward the island, where the dragon eye lay.

Vetra caught a glimpse of that fathomless orb, pulsing away like a ghoulish, living thing. It vibrated as if it were of demented, elemental origin, alive and quickening, shining a weird translucent glow.

Cthan had been lucky, or smarter than his hapless men. He and Rafa bolted along a narrow ledge that lapped over with water.

Leaping over those sections, with the intent to skirt around the guardians, they closed with Lehundr and Aus, and the boomerang thrower who came rushing up to assist them.

Dunon, Gefzad and other hill Thrules saw the Behundrian enemies storming up to murder Lehundr and Aus. They came at Cthan and Rafa from the rear with howls of rage on their lips.

Cthan gave a rancorous roar. He turned to engage Dunon, who was snarling from lips caked with froth. Dunon turned at a whizzing blade that sliced close to his ear. He stumbled, tripped by a foot snaking out.

Gefzad jumped over and caught Cthan's whickering blade. It would have driven into Dunon's ear. Cthan's blade slid rasping over Gefzad's hilt and Gefzad's finger was shorn off. His blade again locked with Gefzad's. With a quick, snake-like flick, he ran the Thrule through the chest. The gape-mouthed man toppled across the pathway with a squashy thud.

Vetra watched as jelly-like forms swarmed over him, the man's face a parody of comic surprise. Cthan booted him out of the way. The rogue came driving onward. Dunon was inches behind and tried to jab past his man to get to Cthan's jugular, but the path was too narrow and he could do little without suffering damage, nor do much for fear of skewering his own man.

Ten feet in front, the boomerang thrower parried Rafa, and realized that even with a patch over his eye, the man was more than his match. He drew back in defeat.

"Retreat!" came Vetra's pained voice rising across the water. He called to Aus who was spidering his way back with Rafa's opponent to regroup. There both he and Dunon were but two dozen paces away on a parallel walkway.

Lehundr pulled back the boomerang thrower and ran with Jhara, to Vetra's place of cover.

The boomerang thrower slipped and Rafa, seizing the opportunity, ran a sword through his back, his face lit in fierce triumph. Aus gave an agonized bellow.

"Forget him!" cried Vetra. "To the ledge! The beasts can't follow us up there."

Cthan turned and glared at the mercenary. "You're a dead man!" Hearing Rafa's triumphant cry from not far away, he shambled off to the pedestal where gleamed the dragon's eye. Dunon and the two others came spitting curses after him, blades flailing. "Coward! Fight like a man!" Dunon cried with frothing anger at Cthan's back as he stumbled after.

Cthan ignored such insults. He strode with blade hoisted with an imperious grin to carve out any Thrule flesh that would thwart him.

The rest of the Behundrians, crowded by circling guardians, foiled Vetra's plan of regrouping. They cut off Dunon and Aus, with a wall of bristling blades.

"Up the ledge!" Vetra thundered in frustration. He and Jhara reached the opposite shore while Lehundr puffed behind them. Now the shadow of a towering dragon lord statue fell over all of them and they scrambled past its massive stone feet. They reached the ledge that wound up the cavern wall.

Up the crumbling slope they scrambled, a crust of fallen jewels crunching underfoot, sparkling in the luminous glow of the water. Cthan's men saw what they were doing and gave angry shouts. Cthan gesticulated in wild fervor. Half of the forces raced to cut them off at another stairway leading to the same ledge. Vetra clenched his fist grimly and hoped the others could make it in time.

There was an advantage to this route. The sinister dragon lords could not scale the wall, and the Behundrians would be hard pressed to take them on the high ground.

The plan was flawed. Foes were coursing behind them, and up ahead on the straight section of ledge, squeezing past dead bodies, encircling the defenders in a knot. A flash of figures appeared in the dimness and he and Jhara and Lehundr raced to meet them.

They were backed out on a ledge. Below the waters boiled. There was no way to escape.

On the death of Cthan's rear guard, Zren had managed to worm his way through the battle and up the ledge. Panting, with new cuts and bruises, he was like a dripping beast, and Vetra almost cut him down, crouched as he was, lips asnarl and streaming sweat and blood.

"Fight with Jhara and protect each other's backs," Vetra ordered him.

The Thrule listened, for once.

To his credit, Zren had knocked Rafa's man aside and had just saved the mercenary from a direct hit. He was willing to waste himself for the girl whom he eyed with most possessive fanaticism. Young, impulsive fool! thought Vetra. He would get them all killed with his headstrong impulses.

Bellowing a savage war cry, Vetra wheeled and smote in reckless abandon, giving Jhara space and time to crouch and round-house kick, "Die, you ass-licking dogs!" she cried, and she thrust a boot out into a bearded face. Vetra heard the crunch of bone. Rafa rounded in, grinning, lunging in to trip her.

Jhara fell with a thud, crying out in surprise, the wind knocked out of her. Her cat o' nine tails licked out, but Rafa caught the twirling thong as it curled about his sword and he yanked it out of her grasp. She squealed in frustration as Rafa pounced like a tiger, flicking her hateful weapon over the edge.

The girl crawled away but Rafa pulled her up shrieking by the hair.

Zren came stabbing in like a wild man and Rafa snarled with fury at the fierce passion of the man's attack. Rafa gave ground, stabbing wide-eyed, but his men shouldered in and booted the Thrule back.

"Away from me, you stinking cur! Back to the reeking pools where you belong."

Gashed and seething, Zren leered. He swung two-handed frenzied sweeps of blade while Rafa dragged Jhara back into the protection of his knot of rogues.

She writhed in his cruel grip, her face pushed over the ledge overlooking the pool, but he clasped her tighter and encircled her with his ape-like arms, crooning a foul proposition in her ear.

Vetra lunged forth, but too late, blades kept him in check too. Lehundr crowded behind Vetra, his hilt quivering in his bloody fist.

Cthan paused below, a saturnine croak of laughter on his lips like the hyena who has cornered the rat. The smug insolence of the man showed on his face. He stared up at the vice his men had sprung on the rebels while others of his forces contended with the dragon beasts.

Toward the center of the island he sauntered leisurely, a pleased expression on his face. Three of the guardians were down, one guarded the exit and only two remained to harry the walkways, these far away and under the control of his men.

"That's right, Rafa," Cthan called up savagely. "Hold the bitch. She's a she-cat." The sheriff's one eye lingered on the guardian that menaced Dunon and his men at the other end of the ledge. "I'll see what this precious dragon eye is all about."

Rubbing his hands in satisfaction, Cthan paused to appraise the glimmering globe and its treasure. "A fair march to this god-forsaken place", he said in hoarse enthusiasm, "and losses to go with it, but well worth it."

"Aye," gloated Rafa, yelling down from his ragged patch on the ledge. "These Thrules will pay for our losses. And this filthy outlander—" He shook Jhara vindictively as a dog does a rat and flashed her a lascivious smile. "In quarts of their own blood, and in bed favors. Starting with these mangy rebels before us, trapped in this treasure den."

Rafa relaxed his grip, overconfident in his advantage. It was an open invitation for Jhara to strike and with a snake-like jerk, too quick for the eye to see, she twisted out of Rafa's grip, ramming elbow into his teeth. The man howled and Vetra lunged forth, knocking one of Rafa's henchman off the ledge. Vetra cut through another man and ground a heel into Rafa's foot, catching the flailing arm and bending it backwards.

One of Rafa's remaining henchmen grabbed Jhara from behind and put a knife to her throat.

With a savage wrench, Vetra pulled Rafa down to the stone so he was on one knee, gasping in pain, putting blade to his throat. Lehundr vaulted over the two of them, and his curved falchion quivered inches from Jhara's captor's face.

"Drop the swords!" barked Cthan, seething at the sudden assault on the ledge. "Let my man Rafa go free, or my other man will slay the girl. That I promise!"

Jhara protested, struggling with feverish desperation. "No! I got you into this mess, following you here. Don't give into this monster! Let him die, Vetra. Let me die. Kill all these vermin."

Cthan laughed cynically. "He's not that much of a hero, doll face. Besides, that wouldn't be very heroic of him, would it, 'Vetra'?" he sneered. "Our knight in shining armor cannot live with himself, responsible for the slaying of a girl, could he?"

Vetra growled. It wouldn't be easy for him to sacrifice the girl, that was true. Was there another way?

Rafa's henchman now had the screaming rebel over a precipice. Vetra reluctantly released his hold on Rafa. The thug unruffled himself from Vetra's grip and shook out the hurts.

"Now hold her this time, you idiot. I give you a few simple tasks and what do you do, get your eye gouged out."

Rafa snarled and turned in malicious distaste on the girl. "You're a tasty piece of meat. I think I'll take out my pound of flesh on you later." He ogled her sleek body, her luscious curves pleasing to him. He fondled her breasts like a drunken soldier in a brothel. "Do you remember how you gave me this, you wretched spitfire?" He jerked a hand to his eye, lifted the blood-torn patch, displaying an ugly red socket.

Jhara turned her head away. Though she struggled, there was no overpowering that brute who now held her and thrust her arm cruelly behind her back.

A voice from the haunted past, echoing dim and terrible, suddenly smote the chamber. Or was it only in their minds? Vetra did not know.

"So, this is what mankind has evolved to after a thousand years?"

The startled Behundrians peered around in abject wonder. Strangled murmurs hissed through their teeth.

Vetra looked around in no less surprise. But he could discover no source for the mysterious voice that rolled in doomful waves in his mind. A stir began to form in the waters abreast the pedestal.

Scowling into his beard, Cthan reached out with impatient urgency toward the mystical, glowing dragon eye.

Through the ethereal film, his hands thrust with bold intent to seize the eye for his own. A keen thrill of ecstasy rippled through his body and lit up his face.

"A life's fortune," he hissed in marvel.

The iris of the eye was cut like an exquisite diamond. A ruby pupil fitted dead center glared forth. Like a cosmic egg it glowed, solid gold, silver, or both—one could not distinguish. The treasure harbored a shimmering aliveness that tantalized the beholder. Just as Cthan was about to withdraw the prize from the globe, a fierce wave of agony and horror passed over his face. A searing blast of radiance burst from the eye and lit up his face. From a distance Vetra squinted, the flare was so bright.

"I see your bloody past!" Cthan raved. "Dragon wars over eons!" It was as if he came to understand all of the dragons' secrets in that one flash and greedy grasp. A secret not meant for man. The eye lit with the brutal sum of knowledge of the eons that the dragons had lived, and died and warred. All blasted into Cthan's brain—embodied into one blinding pulse, like a hundred possessed lightning strikes.

With a choking cry the sheriff stumbled backwards, his lips mouthing shrieks of pain. The skin of his palms stuck to the white-lit egg, so supercharged it was with heat and mystical energy.

The rogue's eye sockets hung in red and dripping flaps. Smoke billowed from his hands, his eyes scalded by liquid light.

The sheriff of Dragonskull jerked about like a mad puppet, stumbling back in blind terror, as he learned how the dragon lords became rulers of the earth, how all the battles they had won and fought were in vain, and how they had been lords of the sky and the earth ever since the beginning when the oceans boiled and the first islands rose out of the sea to become the fabulous continents on which the first humans stood.

The eye fell from his grasp and hung suspended in the sulfurous air to return in magic force like a faithful sentinel to perch inside the globe.

At the same moment a liquid column of strangeness rose from the pool at the stone's edge. A water spirit? One of the feral jellyfish-like horrors? Vetra was at a loss. The thing was a giant cyclone of raging water at first, then an amorphous mass that bulged and formed the dim outline of one of the dragon lords, tall and imposing, with eyes unblinking, arms folded across chest and staff in hand.

The dragonish head tipped in grave judgment, staring down at the fly-sized humans. A shimmering yellow halo surrounded its watery form, this solemn giant of all creatures.

CHRIS TURNER

IX: The Dragon Lord

Cthan groped back blindly, as if aware of the foaming rush of some horror in close proximity. With pathetic whimpers, he pawed for his sword, his senses still intact, but his eyes beyond repair. He found his blade where it had fallen and gripping it in a clenched fist, swung wildly at an apparition he could not see. His blade passed right through the will-o-the-wisp without drawing a drop of water.

The thing ignored him as if he were no more than a gnat.

Vetra elbowed Rafa in the ribs, taking advantage of the moment. He seized the man's sword. While he was doubled over, he sent him reeling into the hot springs. Lehundr ducked a whistling blade just as Zren surged through the pack and rammed his head into Jhara's captor. Jhara gave a wild screech and in a burst of hysterical strength, pulled herself into a ball and brought her assailant rolling over her back. Vetra plunged steel into his throat and kicked the dying man down the slope.

Jhara scrambled past Zren and Vetra felt her shudder pass over his body as she brushed close. She shook with fierce outrage, her fingers digging into his back.

At the same time, words came into Vetra's mind—thoughts forged from the hidden wells of the subconscious, a deep rumbling sibilance like low waves breaking on an ocean:

"None can lift the dragon eye so waste no efforts. 'Tis the jewel of our heritage, the heart blood of our race, the greatest treasure we have known—excluding the water that gives life, for the eye links soul with body, body with earth and air. We are centuries dead, our memory is preserved, and still you have brought a blight upon us..."

Rafa floundered in the water, quivering and thrashing as his flesh burned. He clawed his way up the shore, his flesh raw, red and seared. Swarming green and white tentacles crawled over the gang leader's shins and began their evil work. He clawed at them with his quivering fingers, tearing clumps of flesh. The things wound tighter about his legs. He pounded his fists with strengthening intensity, tearing with fingers now bloody. His gruesome shrieks were awful to hear as he struggled in vain to get the ghastly things off.

Up the path Vetra, Jhara, Lehundr and Zren clambered, blocking out the sounds of Rafa's and Cthan's wails. They skidded up higher while the Behundrians stared in speechless horror like stunned deer. Vetra bowled through their startled ranks, leaving two writhing on the jewel-crumbled stone. He, Zren and the girl vaulted over them.

Dunon and Aus scrambled up a stair running parallel to Vetra's and now cut down the last resistance from the back even as Vetra barreled through.

More invaders, rousing from their shock, rushed them, grunting and hacking up from behind. Vetra herded the others up a set of steep, crumbled steps and turned, chopping the pursuers down from the narrow stairway. He was getting slowly pushed up, his back to his peers.

"We need to climb higher!" he bawled.

Dunon motioned. "To where?"

"Doesn't matter! They can't surround us on the narrower ledges."

The voice from the ages boomed again:

"*People from this far age—feast thy eyes on Naklion, our Dragon Heart. I am Macemas, last lord of Aslante. But only in memory do I impart this message. Take your wars and skirmishes elsewhere and wrest no bauble from our tomb, lest my curse befall you!*"

All gaped in wonder as the voice reverberated through their bones.

"*We, the lords of the dragons, have languished; our reign passed a millennium ago. Yet all must live together in this world. Leave in peace! Whether in life or death that you understand these words, take this memory with you— that whether dragons or their lords live or live not, you are the masters of your own destiny. Nothing comes to pass that is not a form of your own doing...*"

Dunon gasped and clambered up higher behind Vetra. "What manner of creature is this water devil?"

200

Vetra grunted. "Something to mash our brains."

"The dragon lords have left a remnant of their past, you fools!" snarled Lehundr, "—a living, conscious memory! None heeded the call for peace ages ago."

"Get higher!" Vetra yelled.

In the midst of clanking blades he gave ground inch by inch. A long, ghastly line of guardians advanced like hungry predators from the exit tunnel. The mercenary grimaced and gripped his blood-stained blade tighter. Doom crawled at every corner of this forsaken pit.

The water god seemed to watch them with detached interest. Vetra expected it to kill them all in an instant, and drown them in lakes of quicksilver. But it just rose higher, a shimmering tower of judgment.

He craned his neck upward. The crust of jewels glinting like fireflies to the senses was tantalizingly close. While he slashed down at the Behundrians still fighting for a cause without a leader, the dragon pool seemed to cool, and billows of steam flattened in peculiar fashion. An ominous scrape echoed from overhead, like a heavy stone slab lifting off an impregnable tomb.

Vetra's eyes narrowed. He saw a patch of open sky above them, pale sunlight momentarily blinding him. The water lord shimmered and compressed its liquid form into a long, rippling spiral, up around Cthan, who flailed blindly with sword raised like a madman as the dragon guards advanced on him. Up it rose, like a living cobra, swirling like a whirlwind to disappear in the opening and was gone.

Vetra's senses reeled. He shook off his dizziness, a fear of heights returning in full. Sweat streamed off his face; his stomach heaved with nausea.

The rush of booted feet came from below. He edged back and struck all the harder at a leather-helmed skull that bobbed up. He pointed to the opening, then at the sky, and his parched throat gave voice to a hoarse shout. "There! Our only chance out of this burrow. Quick! before the portal closes."

Like harried rabbits they crawled up the stairs, quivering fingers reaching for the opening. The Behundrians came roaring after them, scrabbling at their heels like bloodhounds.

"Cthan's dead!" blurted one. "Our reward is gone."

"Let's kill these rogues and be out of here!"

Water hissed in the pool below and the Behundrian's wild curses were lost in the wrathful echo of the dragon lord's exodus.

Through gritted teeth, Vetra held the throng back, his blade whistling wild arcs of death. Dunon helped Jhara up the hole, while he and Aus and the others pushed Zren and Lehundr through. All were up and out and Vetra leapt, fingers clutching the opening's rim. Feet dangling, he kicked at enemy blades that licked out at him like vipers. His friends snatched at his arms while hands from below sought to use him as a ladder. Vetra smashed these with his boot heels and a tumultuous wail rent the air as a man plummeted to his doom.

He was out, blinking in dazzling light. The open sky yawned above them and the searing heat of the desert beat down on his skin.

The stone slab was too heavy to pull over to stop the snarling Behundrians who seethed up in a mad, feverish wave. Vetra and Dunon hunched over the opening like vultures, slashing at fingers that tried to hoist themselves up. Dying shrieks echoed below; more fell to crash down the stairs and to the cavern below.

Vetra stared about, his eyes wandering to the place where the dragon lord had drifted. He shook his head, saw only a film before his vision. His eyes stung as he looked into the overwhelming, golden light.

The dragon lord glided like a solemn wraith across the skullish, scar-topped rock of the mesa.

Halting at the summit's edge, *he*, or whatever it was, traced circles in the air with its slightly clawed hands. It had shed its watery body, yet its skin glistened as brightly as before. For all intents and purposes, he was now a real flesh and blood dragon lord, stern-faced and regal, and majestically rendered out of thin air. He lifted a hand in the direction of the two megalith fangs perched high on the adjacent hills. An unearthly aura surrounded him like a wizard from another age.

The Dragon Lord stared out over the edge of the cliff rising high above the plain. On the battlefield below, the straw-like figures of Behundrians, drenched in blood and sorrow, gasped and stumbled away in terror at the sight of the apparition. Searing light came lancing from the megaliths, arching out and striking the dragon bones that littered the ruins below at the warriors' feet.

Like ants before the raging storm, the fighting men scurried on all fours, gusting curses. But no such easy escape was given them.

The somber words from faraway spoke, splitting the fabric of the air, the fabric of their minds and the monstrous intonations rose and fell like deep musical waves:

"Fools! Ignorant fools! Do you flee like vermin without a moment's understanding? Die now, and start afresh in your incarnations. Tragic repercussions are in order. Suffer for your actions in face of these Thrules who have struggled to uphold the heritage of the dragon lords. Now they lie broken like dolls on a god's playground. But they die not in vain..."

These words came as not human born, but from an incomprehensible place beyond the stars.

In his days of life, as centuries ago he had moved in magical ways from hill to hill and tomb to tomb, the dragon lord moved now, the same which had discovered secrets and forbidden pathways far under the earth—the same which had forged the labyrinthic ways under the Dragon fortress of *Aslante* whose vastness and mystery mortal minds could not fathom.

"Time to die..." came the disembodied, almost hypnotic voice. *"Our knowledge is too advanced for you. On your journey of life let you plod in an endless cycle of war, strife and grief until ultimate awakening dawns."*

Maybe he was some great lord or magician, who knew? Vetra stood spellbound. The knowledge of such things was beyond him, and lost in the gulfs of time.

"Dead brothers. Rise again!" Like a thunderclap the voice came over

the sunburnt plain. The speech was lost in sand, air and cloud and the last dragon lord's murmurs washed over the shallow valley to end in a final command:

"Rise brothers, rise!"

And the dragon skeletons came to life, bones clattering together in an animated collective, tinkling like a thousand sinister wind chimes. An army of them creaked to life, rippling to unnatural form by some unseen magic the dragon-lord wielded after many ages of rest. The dragons' fierce sun-bleached skulls tilted skyward, seeing a firmament not witnessed for a thousand years; then their necks swiveled to assess the fleeing remnants of the Behundrian army through their empty eye sockets.

A horrific murmur rose through the Behundrian's ranks. Skeletal dragons vaulted the rocky molder of their ancient death beds, springing after routed soldiers who ran in sheer terror. Ageless, undead creatures of bone and teeth rent flesh and crushed skulls, tails sweeping, snouts ramming, soldiers' armor and weapons proving impotent.

These enchanted specters then took to the air, bony wings spread like monstrous bats, flapping at air that should not keep them afloat, and soared low and high, searching for enemies to kill. As they swooped and dove like merciless raptors, they slaughtered in numbers the invaders to their sanctuary.

From his majestic perch the Dragon lord watched all this with no apparent emotion. Perhaps the briefest flicker of understanding fled across that imperturbable face, that the doom claiming these warriors sprang from the same source governing his own demise eons ago.

When the shimmering lord had seen enough, his eyes glowed once more and his pulsing vision sent out the signal to the megaliths on the hill. The animus left the dragons, and like one they fell, their bones scattering like broken twigs over the dismal, corpse-strewn plain. There came a hail of bone on the last scrambling men, crushed and hammered to pulp beneath a storm of undead remains.

Vetra and his company watched aghast.

Satisfied at the death and destruction, the dragon lord walked on solemn feet back to the open slab and Vetra and his ragged fellows drew back with awe and apprehension. Under the natural light of day, the dragon being was a complete replica of one of the old, carven lords of the elder age. The perfect folds of the flesh on his face and naked shoulders and thighs glistened in the sunlight and burned pits in Vetra's memory: the chilling dragon's mane of scales and his corselet of fur, and the clawed feet.

There was no place to run so Vetra clutched his sword, ready to fight or die. "Kill us, if you must, fiend," he murmured. Muscles taut, he shouldered Jhara out of harm's way and faced the menace. Pulsing with instinctive self preservation, Jhara uttered a soft sob. Lehundr gazed in trance-like stupor while the Thrules shrank back, expecting instant death, swallowing dry lumps in their throats, bowing their heads in reverent terror.

The apparition briefly studied the defenders, though those seconds seemed to last a hundred years. Then its kohl-shadowed eyes gave them a blinking appraisal and shimmered back into its watery, mystical form. Like a column of liquid nothingness, it coursed wraith-like back through the black gap and the sad, shrieking cries of the doomed Behundrians trapped below rang out like a gallow-man's song. To a man, their white eyes blazing in desolation, they tumbled back before the unfathomable terror that was the dragon lord of Naklion, and the heavy slab slid back and closed with crushing finality forever.

The Thrules shuddered and shrank back. Jhara gave an exhausted moan of relief. "Am I in a dream, or in one of Dergath's afterlives?"

Vetra gave a grim laugh. He sheathed his sword and faced the Thrules. "So, your dragon lord crawls back in his hole with his riches. Who would have believed it?"

"You should pray to your Dergath that you still guard your head," came Aus's retort, which Dunon and Lehundr endorsed with nods and hoarse "hear, hear's".

"Let us count our blessings then and be gone from this sorrowful place," murmured the half Thrule.

White-faced, they all threaded their way down the side of the mesa, squinting under the unforgiving sun.

Thrule reinforcements were making their way from the north, hundreds of them streaming down like ants from the hillside with rune-scribed boomerangs on their backs as they surveyed the dead. The broken bodies lay strewn from rim to rim in the valley, among the ruined columns and the toppled masonry and the bleached, lifeless bones of the old dragon lord empire. Vultures had already started to gnaw, hunched about the crumpled shapes in the sand, tearing chunks of flesh in red beaks.

Vetra stared dazedly at the dragon temple—an old, silent mausoleum, its facade of stone glimmering in strange, inexplicable mystery. Regal and austere, it stood towering over the dragon lord's last stronghold and the insignificant band of survivors with an ancient, ominous grandeur.

The dragon claw was gone. Gefzad, Nhfer, Samos and Sebju among others had perished. The great gate was closed, doubtless never to be opened again. The Behundrians were trapped within, like the last unfortunate invaders from bygone days. A chill ran through Vetra's body as he envisaged the horror they must face at the claws and spewing acid of the guardians.

He scratched his head as new questions arose. Macemas had spared them, for reasons which were not quite clear. Was it not by his hands, and his companions, that they had spilled blood on sacred soil? A foul taste fluttered at the back of his throat as he eyed those who lay in mangled heaps before the dragon door, buzzing with flies.

He stepped back with a grim shudder, shaking his head, a hollow feeling in his chest.

His limbs and torso tingled with a dozen cuts. He limped over to where Jhara slumped in an untidy sprawl with others on the steps. Her bare arms and cheeks were dust-caked and smeared with blood; her leather pants were torn, her hair tousled like a drunken doxy's yet she grinned with a lively gleam in her eyes. She had escaped mostly unharmed as had Lehundr, who had a cloth circling his brow and a splint wrapped around his arm, which was either sprained or broken.

The Thrules rounded up the surviving Behundrians to take as prisoners; they helped bury the dead and gave treatment to those Thrules who were injured.

The leader of the arriving company, Arast, approached and addressed the bedraggled group of survivors, "Hail, battleworn. By Zeldra and Dergath! A war of wars you have fought here. I was loath to drive my men faster, lest their hearts give out on them. Pity we could not lend aid. Where is Nhfer?"

"Dead," mumbled Dunon. "Sebju is slain too."

"These are ill tidings!" he cried. He hung his head and wide fingers played idly over the double falchions at his belt. He was a broad and heavy-limbed man for a Thrule and he rubbed his chin with a sweaty hand. "Nhfer summoned us on the magic horn, and we came as quickly as we could."

"Though tardily," Zren pointed out.

The leader flourished a sword. "It is as it is, boy! Men on foot can only travel so fast."

"The last dragon lord has come and gone," announced Dunon with a weary groan, "and will likely never appear again."

The Thrule's eyes glinted. "Macemas, the damned? At this forsaken place? It can't be. Tell me about it!"

Dunon told the tale, motioning to the great dragon fort behind him and tracing measurements in the air describing the size of the guardians. Several of Arast's men gathered to listen spellbound and Lehundr eagerly took up the tale. Vetra and Jhara added their parts when the leader pressed for details. Aus and Zren picked up the story at certain key moments.

After the tale had been told, the chief eyed them with amazement and returned to the battlefield with his men to oversee the cleanup, still shaking his head in awe.

Vetra sighed and turned to face Dunon: "The Behundrians will come searching this place to carve out the jewels when news of the interior reaches Dragonskull."

The Thrule uttered a hollow laugh. "They can try, but the dragons will defy them even in death. You saw what happened to Cthan and his villains."

Vetra shrugged. He could not refute the fact. "That will not stop their thirst for Thrule blood."

Dunon squinted at the dragon fort whose timeless presence had persisted throughout onslaught after onslaught. "The dragons of all beings realized that water was the most precious resource in the lands. More valuable than gold. Or all the jewels of the world. That's why they built this impregnable sanctuary rich with water and gems. They celebrated beauty and life, and presented it in monumental grandeur in the greatest hot spring in all of Behundria and Sahir. They saw the evil that rubies and emeralds and the like wreaked on the greedy hearts of men and grew wary of its lures and perils, and thus hid them away. As the spirit of Macemas pointed out, men like Cthan have still not learned the primal truth."

Zren shook his head in contempt. "The dragon lords are dead, old man, as are all the marshals of Dragonskull, as we all should be. 'Tis a flaming miracle we are standing here right now."

Vetra snorted his agreement. "It's some part of a greater design, which only Dergath knows."

Aus, bursting to get something off his chest, offered an egg-sized garnet to the blood-stained mercenary. "I nabbed it on the way out. You deserve it, I think."

Vetra shook his shaggy head. "The treasure belongs to the dragon lords, not I, at worst the Thrules. Keep it!" He caught the look of painful disapproval etched on Jhara's face.

Dunon shook his head with a laugh. "The bulk of jewels will stay with the dragon lords behind that impregnable wall."

Aus's eyes dropped. "I don't feel right to keep it, Dunon. Cthan learned the error of his ways, when he attempted to steal the mystical eye of the master dragon lord for himself. I have a feeling some doom will come of this." He cast his eyes to the sand.

"Maybe," said Dunon. "You did what you did, perhaps no more than what a nobler man would have done."

"What will you do?" Vetra asked Dunon.

"For now, the captive Behundrians will take the place of the bullocks at Sunswatch and draw water for the Thrules."

"They will rise up," Vetra muttered. "Reinforcements will ride across the desert, ferret you out."

"Let them—we will be ready."

Aus flourished a hand. "We will be ready! We will fight until the end of time. We may die and flee to the hills, but until then, we will continue our vendetta—or retreat north, living in yurts, not the sheltered sacred caves of Zabenzar. We have the map, the garment and a glimpse of the old treasures of the dragon-lords. Their secrets, we know now to be real. The fact that we are alive, tells us much, that the dragon lords are our allies."

Vetra stared and rubbed his chin in admiration for these brave nomads whom he could not help but think were a trifle mad. "Then Dergath be with you!" He laid a hand on Aus's shoulder and gave Dunon a friendly gesture which the Thrules gratefully returned.

With a crinkly eye, Aus pursed his lips. "It'll be sad to see you go, outlander. As far as men go, you're a deserving one."

Dunon murmured his agreement. Zren made no effort to control his grimace and stalked off with cursing grumbles.

"Let us clean up this mess and go," mumbled Aus. "We have many weapons to forge and plans to make. Send riders to the hills on foot to Hruen! Call the other Thrule clans from the north! They will be needing to come down and help us for the aid we have given them in the past. We have offered them sheep for slaughter and supplies when they have had need of it."

The Thrules turned their ponies to the eastern road, but Lehundr hung back from the milling group, pulling at his blood-flecked beard.

"What's wrong, half Thrule?" Vetra inquired with a wry grunt. "Will you not come back with us to Dragonskull, or do you hanker for another shower of dragon bones falling from the sky?"

Lehundr shook his head. His brow creased with warring thoughts. "I grow weary of rogues and swindlers in that dusty town. Cthan has fallen, and an inevitable new order will arise, but the trader's post will decline back into its old habits, I fear. I will head north, my friend, to Vespia, that spire-ridden capital of Sahir. From there? Who knows? A fresh start and a chance to buy some fortune." He scrutinized the mercenary whom he had come to know as a friend. "And you, Vetra? Will you seek more bloody misadventures?"

Jhara broke in sourly, "Aye, will you go with this vagabond and seek out your death?"

Vetra thought for some time, his brows lifting at Jhara's comment, then his gaze drifted to the red glow of the setting sun. "I will take you as far as Dragonskull, Jhara, but no farther, nor will I tarry there. I must return west—to Lausern, the pits and scum dives of Lvendar."

Jhara's lips parted in a desolate look. Her eyes dilated and her lips quivered in despair. "Take me with you," she pleaded.

His eyes passed over her sleek, muscular lines. Keen approval showed in his gaze, but in a brief glimmer of foresight he glimpsed a foul scene: her flesh bloodied and torn during one of his bloody, underground campaigns. "As tempting as it, girl, I fear not." At the look of her crestfallen expression, he added, "The dark places I go are no place for you, as fierce as you are. You're young, inexperienced, have many adventures before you, and many fair men to meet. Maybe you'll take a fancy to one of these hot-headed Thrules." His eyes strayed to a group of hill Thrules digging among the wreckage where Zren stood motioning in heated argument.

She looked away, her sour expression saying all. "They're too short."

Vetra laughed, but quickly stifled his amusement. "Continue your sword practices, Jhara. Find yourself a good teacher, as rare as they are in this world. Dergath's cats, woman, with your skill, you could teach the art yourself!" He paused, shifted, his sweat-draped leather under his mail shirt becoming an uncomfortable burden. "Maybe that headstrong Thrule, Zren, will make a decent swordsman himself one day. He flails like a fish and blunders like a newborn ox, but somehow I see potential in him. You could teach him. Show him how to move and feint. Your zeal and restlessness reminds me of myself in my younger years."

She beamed at the roundabout praise, and a glimpse of the old Jhara came reaching once more in her eyes. There was comfort and protection in the mercenary's gaze, along with the ever-present lure of high adventure, but also the keen promise of death.

"Go then, Vetra. I see where your heart lies. Bloody quests, fighting for the underdog, killing for hire, nothing permanent or satisfying there for me, likely the thrill of a long line of paramours to go along with life on the road. I will remember you, if that means anything. If you remember anything of me, think of a woman who wanted to be at your side, enjoy our trysts, fighting as an equal. It seems you have much to do. Go! I will not hold you back. Nor will I go back with you to Dragonskull—others will make the journey and I will go with them. Return to Dragonskull one day, if you wish. I pray that our paths meet again."

Vetra hesitated, then collected himself, his mouth carved in a crooked grin. "Until our paths meet again then." He tipped his head and walked off. Dergath, but the ways of women were inscrutable.

* * *

So Vetra turned to the dusty road south, but an afterthought struck him, and he halted and turned back to seek out the tearful young woman. The weight of something familiar jingled in his pocket. The others had left, and she was alone on the steps, sitting chin in hands, in despondent self pity. Vetra approached, put on his most amiable face. "Here are three diamonds and rubies that came to me in the dragon temple. They came from about the stony neck of one of the dragon lords." He pushed them into her hand. "Take them and buy you and your brother freedom from the streets of Dragonskull."

An expression of wonder softened her gaze. "You don't want

them?"

"I've enough good fortune to last a lifetime." He clapped a hand on his sword, calmly remembering all the death that stalked him through the years, a silent partner treading in his shadow.

She mumbled a dry response. "Nine lives of it. If I could count the times I thought you were dead back in that cavern." Her features frowned and a faraway look clouded her eyes. "Should I be worried about curses and the like cast on these gems?" She flashed them a glance. "Aus seemed serious about that and I heard you agree with him."

Vetra shrugged. "The jewels fell from the dragon lord statue's garland. I see it as an offering he gifted me with, rather than a theft. The spirit of the lord gave them of his own free will. Otherwise I wouldn't have felt compelled to snatch them, and would probably have died back in that dim chamber. It would have been my tomb as well."

Her lips slackened in a grin. "Then go with my blessing, and I thank you. Be gone, mercenary, before I tear up!...a warrior should not cry on a day of victory and good fortune, should she?"

He took her in his arms and her forced veneer peeled away. Her breathless sobs poured out against his chest; her hot breath stormed on his neck, and Vetra, for all his faults in the arena of love, drank in this woman's passion like a stag at the lake, an antidote to the grim business of his trade.

"Come on, Dragonskull's a long ways away!"

THE HUNTRESS OF CAERLIN

1: Isks of doom

A gentle breeze rustled the treetops and Risgan the Relic Hunter paused to take a breath. He called ahead to his four companions to wait up. He clutched the handle to his enchanted wagon, a kind of barrow that carried the caged witch, Afrid. Her eyes glowered in distaste, rich with an unpleasant hue behind those dark withes of thorn. A godsend that her magic had been stripped by the piece of nephrite he kept stashed away in his pouch. But was the effect permanent? Her three foot height did not diminish her menace, despite confinement in that square cage of tough thorn.

"Seems Afrid's in a rotten mood this morning," mused Kahel the archer, lumbering forth, scratching an itch on his sweaty brow.

"Bully for her," said Risgan.

"Aye," mumbled Jurna the journeyman in a dark voice. His bushy brows dipped in a scowl. It seemed his memories of old wounds inflicted back at Thornkeep were still quite fresh.

Moeze the magician looked back at the trees from where they had come. "Thornkeep, bah! Perhaps, I shall learn useful spells from this hag before she gets her just desserts."

"Better luck talking to the devil," grumbled the archer, counting his precious arrows. Too few of them for the dangers that lurked ahead. He shook out his shaggy mop of red hair.

Afrid hissed between the thorn bars and rattled her cage with an unwholesome fervor. The witch's baby face and youthful skin seemed uncanny for one so utterly wicked and cruel. Her snake-like hiss had Risgan recoiling.

213

"Relax," Moeze chided. He flicked his fingers in the gesture of a spell...a bright green spot grew on the witch's brow. "Aiee!" she squealed in anguish. She clammed up after that.

Kahel laughed.

Risgan only stared at Afrid with dislike. He recalled how the witch had turned on the philosopher Delpit and transformed him into a mindless slave. Left him some shell of a man. Effectively killing him.

Risgan sighed. *And what of his own fate?* Pursued by Pantius's bounty hunters across the lands, he was little more than an outlaw. They had chased him practically to Afrid's doorstep. He and the others were lucky to have escaped Thornkeep, abode of the dark sorceress, and then only by the skin of their teeth. Aside from the fabulous gem in his pouch, he had only the black boots, leather breeches and jerkin on his back.

He studied each of his four new companions with fresh wonder. Kahel, Jurna, Moeze and Hape. Strange how fate had brought the five together. Bonded after their narrow escape from the witch's lair, they each guarded an inner fire for survival. Jurna, a journeyman, tracker, dark-haired and shaggy; young Moeze, a questionable magician, tall and spare, whose magic had not helped them much on their journey; Kahel, a grim-faced archer with a thick red beard, who was swift and strong; then Hape the Homeless, a thin-boned drifter, something of a vagrant whose meek temperament was offset by his knowledge of the wild lands.

Risgan turned his attention back to the witch. The powers of the nephrite stone had reversed her aging process, given her the face of a baby and the body of a four-year-old. He patted the sealed pouch at his side that housed the spell-laden nephrite. He too had handled the gem briefly and felt its taint. Mercifully, he hadn't been affected as much, though he felt his skin softer than usual and an uncanny spryness in his step.

Hunger had struck early that day. The wayfarers hunted quail and hare in the broadwood and scattered glades. Larger game if they could find it. A chill mist rose from the hollows and vales, leaving the lands naked. Before long they had a fire crackling in a sheltered lee by a small wooded hill. But they had scored only two small hares to glut the hungers of five ragged men. Few words were traded among the fugitives. It was time to move on, find more game and seek shelter before evening.

A glade of wild huckle-flowers loomed ahead. A lone dead elm stood tall in the center. At the fringe of the clearing, twitch trees soared on high, green as firs, willowy as willows, soft as deadmusk, a screen for stags and elk to hide behind and creatures much more dangerous.

The air was fresh and the spring birds chattered in numbers in the high boughs, adding a pleasant ambiance to the dwindling dawn.

Risgan knew better. These woods were as perilous as any in the four lands. He hoped to escape them before long.

Better hope for the devil! Though Jurna's tracking skills had, up till now, proven infallible, they found themselves utterly lost, heading in a northerly direction at best. Their bellies growled with greater hunger. Moeze yawned. He tugged at the hem of his wide sleeves. He fidgeted in his loose robe, grown rank and soiled from confinement in Afrid's keep for days on end. Brows furrowed, he murmured anxious words, as if playing over some mispronounced spell in his mind. Hape doddered listlessly at his side, wrapped in his brown, tattered monk's robe, mumbling phrases of encouragement to himself in no less cryptic manner. The tall twitchwood trees bore witness to the company's passing, heedless as the wind, silent as ghosts.

Hape sighed. "We'd best drop lines into the creek and wait an hour for some trout."

"Quiet," muttered Kahel. He turned to Risgan. "What do you want today, falcon or hawk?" His face showed a facetious grin.

"Neither. I prefer wild boar. The meat has a succulent flavor, gamy but tasty. Roasted, of course."

Kahel chuckled. "You'd not like to be surprised by one of those violent beasts."

"Not as bad as isks—"

His words were cut off as a flutter of motion caught Risgan's eye—a shrub rustling at the edge of the glade where the twitch trees thinned. He pulled his comrades back into the brush.

A slender figure poised in a bent-kneed crouch. A hunting bow was in her hand. Drawing an arrow from her quiver, she steadied her aim upon what looked like a majestic stag grazing a bowshot away. A smaller shape, a young foal with black and white pelt, ambled out of the bushes. It lifted its head then came trotting forward to brush its parent's muzzle, as trusting as ever. Risgan's eyes widened. Not a stag, but a full grown unicorn. The huntress lowered her bow.

"Wait." Risgan held Jurna firmly back.

Awestruck, the maiden advanced, only to pause a dozen feet before the mother and her foal. The mother unicorn nudged her young one forth; it sidled closer to greet the newcomer. The huntress dropped to a knee, then began to pet its black mane. She cooed with delight as it snuggled closer.

The mare's hide shimmered a deep purple hue; her proud white horn arched high. While the huntswoman patted the youngling's mane, the mother wandered over, as if intuiting no great threat.

The woman wore brown breeches and leather jerkin that blended well into the surroundings. A cascade of brown curly hair trailed down her back.

"That lass looks as if she knows the land," whispered Jurna. "Let's go question her. We're lost, let's admit it."

"And you the master tracker," jeered Kahel.

"Be careful not to scare her," Risgan warned. "The woman looks a bit skittish." Though he noted she moved with a grace and a defiant upward tilt of chin.

"No more skittish than the unicorn," Jurna observed.

"Be careful not to spook the unicorn. I've never seen one up so close before, let alone a foal."

"Maybe she possesses magic?" suggested Hape.

Moeze huffed out a laugh. "I detect no magic."

The maiden, wild and beautiful as the forest, continued to charm the young animal. The mother moved closer but halted at Risgan's approach. The mare lifted her head, cocked it on a suspicious angle then thumped her hooves. The young woman's head turned in surprise. She snatched at her bow, gazed at the newcomers, no more than a shaggy band of forest rovers come out of nowhere. Her hand drew the bowstring taut. "Halt! Stay where you are!"

A flutter of wings echoed from above. Risgan's head rose. A dark shape loomed out of the cloudless sky. His jaw tightened.

"Isks. I hate isks," Kahel growled as he nocked an arrow.

The gigantic bird dove toward the maiden and gave a raucous croak. The air seemed to bend with the advance of the black-feathered predator, a monstrous raven-like creature, several times larger than a man, with a huge, tapered beak.

"I can manage this." Moeze said as he lifted his silver disc. A crafty glint shone in his greenish eyes, as if seeing his chance. "*Nastanderlist. Exeunt!*"

Risgan reached out a hand. "Don't—"

A gleam of magical radiance sputtered out of Moeze's crystal disc. It smote the tree next to the huntress, surprising the winged predator. A boom of distant thunder came from afar; a pale silver light seemed to touch the top of the trees near the bracken where she and the unicorns hunched undercover. The nearby twitchwood tree split and toppled, nearly crushing them all, leaving the isk unscathed.

"You idiot!" Kahel cried, cuffing Moeze on the head.

"Ow! What was that for?"

"Focus on the isk!" said Jurna.

The huntress took aim and fired; her arrow grazed the isk's belly, prompting a screech. Kahel's first arrow caught the beast sideways on the wing, but it deflected off, falling harmlessly to the ground.

She fired again; this time the arrow plunged deep in the flesh above a talon and stuck there, stirring the beast to frenzy. In a flurry of outstretched wings, it flapped down to gut her. She ducked the murderous sweep of its claws while the mother unicorn reared, striking the beast with its sharp hooves in the beak.

The bird croaked and reached out to gore the mother in the vulnerable flank. She gave a shrill whinny and arched aside, hooves flailing. A trail of blood dripped from her sleek flank.

A second grayer shape, an older isk, veered down with equal menace.

Then another. The bird landed aside the young woman who leapt sideways and drew her blade, slashing out with fierce desperation. The young unicorn bolted in panic for the thicket.

A horn blared through the dense trees. A thunder of hooves pounded at the end of the glade and Risgan snarled, tightening his fist on his club. A score of horsemen came galloping forth, garbed in a mixture of green leather to ragged furs, shouting and readying bows.

Two other dark shapes veered down from the sky. Shadows of terror to join the existing three isks. With hooked beaks and grasping talons, they dove down upon the riders. The long, moving shadows of their wings stretched far across the glade. One swooped low and raked the foremost horsemen on their helms. They had barely time to nock arrows and take aim. Another marauder smashed a man screaming from his mount while another lifted a man from his saddle and flew westward over the treetops.

The horsemen wheeled about, hurling challenges and brandishing swords. Some scattered as arrows flew. A red-fletched arrow caught the nearest beast in the wing. Risgan raced toward the woman and ducked under a strike of talon, clubbing the offending member, beating its claws back.

The huntress dodged, but not fast enough. The creature clamped talons on her shoulders. It lifted her two feet off the ground and she cried out in pain and dismay.

Risgan staggered with club clutched in hand. The girl was moments away from being lifted forever out of reach! He tossed aside his weapon and grabbed on to its talons before it lifted free.

Clinging to a gnarled claw, he purchased firm hold for his life. The woman, white-faced, struggled inches away from him. Jurna smashed his club against the hovering isk's talons before it flew off. Moeze stood a stone's throw away on the grass, rubbing his magic disc. He directed a magical push to thwart the isk. Hape chucked rocks while Kahel nocked another arrow.

Another harsher blare of a horn sounded as the thunder of hooves came closer. "Let me go, you filthy demon!" cried the huntress. She wrenched her bow free as the isk flapped upward. But she could not take proper aim. The beast circled wildly under the club blows and arrows from Jurna and Kahel, trying to lift higher and free, hampered by the reduced power of its injured wing. It strove to shuck Risgan's weight off.

But it could not.

Risgan felt himself buffeted every which way. His world was slipping sideways. Then he caught a mad glimpse of mingled gray sky and earth in his horizon while the awful reek of the bird's hide filled his nostrils. Hanging there desperately, he reached with one hand to snatch at the dagger at his waist. He stabbed again and again into the hard flesh of the exposed leg. The isk gave a hoarse shriek. It loosed its victim. Risgan and huntress fell end over end onto the soft grass.

* * *

Risgan rolled to his knees, shaking the daze out of his skull. He tried to reorient his senses, but nearly collapsed. He reached for the huntress moaning beside him. Dark figures came running. The isk was in the air but a blur in his memory. He struggled to gather his wits. The beast fought, feathers and blood flying every which way, struggling to elude the rain of arrows from the running and mounted figures all around. In a last-ditch attempt for prey, the isk dove and snatched up the young unicorn, confused and looking for its mother, and bore it aloft while the mother limped away, whinnying in distress.

Hape stumbled over to gather the young huntress up.

"Away from her, vagrant," shouted a surly voice on horseback. A wolf-furred man leaped down to kick Hape back, a gleaming, blood-caked sword in hand.

Jurna fumbled for Risgan and managed to haul him to his feet. He shoved the fallen club back into his hands.

A horseman's arrow hit home and the isk gave a screech of rage. The young foal wriggled out of the isk's grasp and fell in a splayed heap on the ground. But very much alive. The mother gave a whicker of delight and galloped over to gather up her young. Arrows whizzed off in her vicinity despite the isk attack, but fell short of the mark. The hunters vented howls of frustration. The isk was not so lucky and fell under a hail of arrows. Its massive form thudded to the grass. Both wings broken, it flailed around like a beached fish.

The horsemen circled the creature, raining arrows into its feathered hide. A handful of women were among the band. Others jumped down to hack at it with blades.

Surprised at such fury, Risgan watched the riders garbed in worn leathers and steel caps vent their rage. The lead hunter who had spoken the harsh warning to Hape wore a crude wolf fur cape draped about his massive shoulders. His black boots were heavy with mud and he wore a great scowl on a scarred face. Dusty brown hair hung down to his waist under a gleaming helm. His hand lay not far from bow and broadsword at his side. His cap looked more polished than the others and was dressed with feathers and makeshift wolf ears. A band of his other wild horsemen wheeled about, guarding more of the same feverish look in their eyes as each warily scanned the sky. But no more of the beaked marauders came. The surviving isks dwindled to specks then disappeared over the willowy treetops.

Risgan paused to assess his wounds and those of his companions. Aside from cuts and bruises, remarkably they had emerged unscathed.

A druid approached on a black stallion adorned with a blanket dyed blood-red and woven with designs of stags and unicorns on its borders. A single antler horn rose from a conical cap of copper color that contrasted to a gray staff clutched in his gnarled right fist.

Another horseman rode up behind, having the haughty mien of a tribal chief. The multi-hued emblem of a stag dueling on its hind legs with a unicorn adorned his leather jerkin. A signification of rank? Risgan could not tell. He swayed on his feet. The chief hopped off his mount and gathered the young woman up in his arms. "Arcadia, child! We thought you were lost. Are you hurt?"

"Nothing but a few bruises and sprains, Father." She wiped her brow and grimaced, pawing the grime off her leathers. Her chest heaved. Her tousled brown curls hung in disarray. Grass stains and a bloody crimson cut marred her bruised cheek, but she still looked as lovely as ever. Perhaps even more so now after witnessing her brave show and fighting spirit. The chief signaled to the horsemen to bring water and cloth to cleanse her shoulder and wrap the wound.

One of the green-vested riders reined in his black mare and jumped down to attend her. "Arcadia! What on earth has happened?" Pushing forward, he clasped her arms—a handsome youth with striking physique and long dark hair tucked under a peaked hunter's cap. His face creased in distress, his cheeks flushed and gleaming with sweat. "Why did you run off? We were worried sick." His sword hung scabbarded at his hip, along with a curious-looking golden arrow which caught Risgan's attention.

Arcadia lifted a hand to wipe her split lip. "I saw a movement at the edge of the forest. I broke away from the hunting party, thought it an unusual looking stag. For some reason I felt compelled to follow it. Then I saw it was not a stag but a unicorn! I could not believe I almost killed it. Rather than frighten it, I stayed very still...to my delight...it came to me."

The hetman, Arcadia's father, responded in a scolding tone. "That was foolish. The woods are dangerous places, child. As that isk is testament. Never do that again."

She winced in frustration. "I'm sick of your men, Father. Always dogging my heels as if I'm a child. I've already lived sixteen years. I want to hunt on my own. You follow me around like a nanny."

"Better that than have you in the belly of an isk," the hetman grumbled.

She gave a rebellious toss of her head, then looked away.

The leader of the wild horsemen jumped off his snorting mare and struck the young huntsman a reeling blow on the face. It knocked him backward. "Get away from her, you fool! She's mine. You possessed the golden arrow. Why did you not shoot?"

The huntsman, lean and wiry, shrugged off the unexpected blow and bent to steady the maiden whom he had jostled. His long, loose green-leather jerkin was in direct contrast to the stinking furs of the man who had slugged him. The horseman snatched the golden arrow from the younger man's hip before he could object.

Risgan's eyes widened at the sight of the diamond tip on the golden arrow. As any relic hunter's would. Before the huntsman could lay hands on it, the lead horseman tossed it to the druid who gazed down with stern judgment from his horse.

"My lord Mygar, I—" The young hunter stammered.

"What? Spit it out, fool!"

"I could not harm Arcadia, sir. The foreigner was clinging to the isk's talons. If I risked a shot, he might have fallen—lightening the load, allowing the isk to fly out of range—"

Mygar, the lead horseman, cast him a stony glare. "If Arcadia, the hetman's own daughter and my bride to be, were carried off by the barbaric thing, you think her fate ripped apart by the savage beast's brood would have been any better?"

"My lord—"

Mygar struck the young hunter again. "You sniveling simpleton!"

"Leave him alone," cried Arcadia, surging forward.

The druid nudged his horse past Risgan to intercede. "I will point out that Arcadia's life has been spared by the providence of the gods...Somehow in the form of this foreigner's intervention, not Lokbur's indecision."

"Bollocks! Nothing but priestly rhetoric," Mygar cried. "He's a coward and a bungling fool." The cluster of wild horsemen huffed in agreement while they rode around the group in a circle while the green-vested men of Arcadia's clan grumbled.

"Enough! Blame is useless at this late hour," called the hetman. "One warrior has been carried off to his doom and several nurse injuries. The black-feathered beast will take the victim to some foul eyrie in the hinterlands, likely from there slowly rip him apart to feed its younglings."

Risgan looked down at the dead bird. Its black-feathered fury was quenched forever, its yellow eyes glazed in death. The isks were mean killers with the black face and long gray beak of the wild rook. But many times larger, and sported the dull, yellow eyes of the predatory great gray owl. Although he'd encountered many isks in his travels, avoiding many close scrapes with them, he'd never gotten used to the baleful, yellow eyes that could mesmerize a man. Scavengers, slayers and butchers. Making falcons and eagles seem as tame as quail.

Mygar flourished an accusing hand. "Likely you rogues attracted the isks and almost got Arcadia killed."

Jurna growled in anger. "'Twas nothing like that."

"Who's this vagrant then who was reaching for her?"

"His name's Hape. I'm Risgan and this is Jurna the Journeyman. There's Kahel the Archer. We are wayfarers, nothing more. Hape only intended to assist her to her feet."

"Do not forget me, Moeze, your practicing magician," piped up Moeze.

"Magician, eh? So you say." Mygar glowered. "You seem a suspicious lot."

The hetman climbed on his horse and trotted forward to gaze upon them with undisguised puzzlement. "Who are these men, Mygar? I did not catch their titles."

"Wayfarers, they say." He snorted. "A load of bollocks, if you ask me. Look at their soiled and tattered cloaks. They smell like a pack of sewer rats. Probably down-of-luck bandits who haven't bathed in weeks."

The hetman stroked his chin. "No doubt. They do look like thieves and bandits on a mission. But their part in this debacle is still under question."

"I say we roast them," threatened another of Mygar's hunters, a ragged bully with squinting eye and spittle pooling in the black gap in his front teeth.

The young man, Lokbur, who had been struck moved to soothe the hetman's daughter, despite Mygar's venomous leer. "Are you okay? How fare you? Did these men harm you?"

Arcadia shook her head. "They're not bandits. This one here is a brave man. All of them are. If they hadn't—I would be—" she trailed off, swallowing hard "—I would have been the one carried off along with Gronjil. They have strong magic. A tree split in two. It startled the isk."

The hetman frowned. "That seems an odd, if stupid thing to do, child—you could have been crushed by the tree—making them only more guilty of this mess."

Moeze stirred, raised his disc in a curt manner. "Take care, lord, lest I weave a spell to coat your bearded chin with a golden itch. You cannot slander us so easily."

The hetman's cheeks flushed red. "An insolent mouth have you, magician."

Risgan winced, glared at the mage and signaled Kahel to elbow Moeze in the ribs.

"Agreed, lord," said Risgan. "The stripling is but green in the art of statecraft. Somewhat junior also in spell-casting."

"In what capacity do you serve?" the hetman demanded.

"I am Chief Risgan—leader of this small band, a hunting band like yourselves, on an expedition from Zanzuria, my homeland. Our travels have taken us far and wide. Suffice it to say, game has been scarce. Hunger and losing our way brought us to this glade where we spotted your daughter and hoped to ask for directions."

"Indeed, judging from your impoverished looks that might explain some mysteries. I am Thäene Vardot, 33rd hetman of the Caerlin Clan, 20th chief of the Vithibri Tribe." The words rolled off his tongue a little too pompously for Risgan's tastes. "You've crossed into our hunting territory—a trespass of serious consequence."

"We only wish to pass through your lands in peace," assured Risgan.

"Point taken." The hetman sighed. "It is too late for last wishes though."

Moeze stepped up to assert himself. "I am senior magician of the—the Crystal Circle—and demand to be heard." He stabbed a thumb to his chest in affirmation.

The druid sputtered to contain his disbelief. "That is preposterous. Only seasoned wizards can exhibit magic. Yours is nothing but fledgling magic. Seize the swine!"

Risgan fluttered his fingers. "My humble associate apologizes for his indiscretion. He is young, lord. You can't fault him for his ineptitude. He's just learning."

The hetman held up a hand. "I'm afraid it's more complicated than that, Risgan. Your crimes number in the many. Interrupting a Thäene's sacred hunt, jeopardizing the safety of a hetman's daughter, trespassing on clan property. Repercussions are in order."

Risgan creased his brow. He chewed his lip at the litany of accusations while Kahel fumed, baring his teeth at Moeze and fingering his bow. A murderous look crawled over his scarred face. Jurna stifled a yawn; pale-faced Hape visibly shuddered.

Mygar raised an impatient fist. "Enough of this charade! I say we take out our grievance on these louts—in blood and coin. How much gold do you have on you?"

Risgan scowled. "Not much, I'm afraid."

"Then blood it is! Strip them, lads—of garments and weapons."

"Stand back," threatened Kahel, raising his bow. He aimed at Mygar's breast.

"Now look what you've done," hissed Risgan. He shouldered Moeze aside.

Moeze gave a helpless shrug.

"Leave them alone!" Arcadia cried. She leapt in to defend the outnumbered band. Men from both sides hesitated and looked to Mygar and the hetman for further direction.

Risgan blinked in astonishment. Heaven help Mygar, as fierce as he was, if he were to try to tame this wild fox. Upon closer inspection, he could see Arcadia's soft leather was of the finest quality, a hunter's green for camouflage. Her vibrant brown curls were thick and luxuriant and fell every which way in not unattractive patterns down her slender back. It left her quite stunning in her trim garb. But not entirely dismissible was the stubbornness and fire that lurked under the surface of her flushed face.

One of the few young mounted women had ridden up to listen to the talk and sighed as she spoke, "Sister, you are always the defiant one." The woman's chest rose and fell and she raked over Risgan a sultry, calculating glance that seemed to contain more than a hint of approval. Risgan returned the look with an appraising nod of his own.

"Says the scorched kettle to the boiled-over pot," Arcadia muttered.

"Enough!" cried the hetman. "You two shall not square off here." He waved a weary hand. "Today is a sacred day for the hunt. We must salvage what we can. The rest of the matter will be decided back in Caerlin. You men will come with us!" He waved his heavily-jeweled hand at Risgan and his comrades.

The lead huntsman prodded them along. "Come on, all of you!"

* * *

Things were not looking up for Risgan and his band. More mounted hunters had joined the company. Some went on ahead while five remained to encircle and guard the prisoners.

Risgan looked back to see Mygar's men hacking the head off the fallen isk as a trophy and leaving its steaming entrails strewn on the grass. Grumbling men milled about, stewing about the loss of their fellow hunter. "We'll conduct ceremony for him back at the village," muttered Mygar. "'Tis an unexpected loss."

"Perhaps it will appease your bloodthirsty god," suggested the druid.

"It should have been me," murmured Arcadia.

Lokbur stared aghast. "Don't say that, Arcadia. Nobody should have died." He hung his head. "I feel responsible for this. Had I fired the magic arrow—"

"Do not blame yourself, Lokbur," Arcadia soothed. "'Twas I who snuck off from the hunt, compelled by a whim." She flashed him a disarming smile and touched his trembling hand. There passed a faint but brief look of intimacy between the two, then it was gone in the blink of an eye. Arcadia mounted her horse, the reins of which one of the other clansmen had handed her.

The woman's watery eyes and trembling lip told of the shambles of the day. "At least the unicorns escaped." The curved longhorn bow hung slack at her side. She stared at Risgan. "Despite your noble intentions, wayfarer, your deeds have stirred up more unrest in our broken clan than ever."

"And if it wasn't for Kahel's arrows and Risgan's heroics, you'd be deader than the isk," pointed out Jurna.

She looked away, but with a sniff of reflection.

Risgan turned at a flutter of movement from the brush. A white tail flashed among the twitch trees.

"The unicorn has returned!" one of Mygar's men cried. "After it!" A host of horsemen spurred forth to chase the creature down, their bows drawn and swords lifted.

Kahel shook his head. "What animal in its right mind would be dumb enough to linger here?"

"It's no unicorn," Risgan said.

A priest beside the druid reined his horse forward to stop them. "Driadis curse you all," he shouted. He waved his staff. "The old gods will rise in their graves to haunt those for molesting their sacred animals."

Mygar trotted forth to face down the priest. "What do you plan to do about it, knave?"

"Out of my way," the priest snarled. "Somebody has to defend the traditional ways." He turned to smack the insolent chief across the head with his staff but landed a stroke on the shoulder instead.

Mygar grinned and leaned in, raising his broadsword. The druid's staff came down again and Mygar blocked it with his blade. This time he leaned in to smash his gloved fist into the priest's face. The priest slid to the ground, dazed and gasping.

"Uncle, no!" cried Arcadia, hurrying forth.

Mygar spat on him. "I say that Wülv, our fanged wolf god, fine spirit he is, spits on the old gods. 'Tis the head of Wülv with his hoary wolf ears and slavering jowl that adorns your shit altars and fanes now, not that feeble teat-sucking Driadis."

One of the green-leathered men gave a fierce cry and galloped in to avenge the vicious sacrilege. The gesture caught Mygar by surprise and angered as he was at being struck, he mustered a wild swing and parried the bold thrust, then he reversed the sword and ran the rider through. He slid out of the saddle with a cry and a thud.

Arrows trained on each other from both sides. The ragged men looked to their hetman for a signal to attack.

Vardot merely looked away, lip quivering. Mygar's eyes gleamed with derisive intensity. Arcadia knelt to console her uncle, holding him in her arms.

"Remember Driadis, my child," the priest croaked. "Dark times are upon us. Pray to the goddess Driadis." He wheezed out a bloody gasp, then looked at his hands where blood flowed from his broken nose.

"Anybody else have a bone to pick?" challenged Mygar.

Arcadia lunged forward with a strident shriek, her sword sweeping out in a killing arc. Mygar parried her blade, then jumped down to face her, his grin ever wider. "Come on, my bonny lass, that's no way to treat your future husband."

The clash of steel echoed through the glade as she surged in to strike him down. The huntress chopped and slashed and Mygar defended his ground. The wicked smirk continued to crease his leathery face as the two swords cried out with each parry. He put one insolent hand on his hip and defended, stroke for stroke, with blade clutched in the other.

"Ah, a spirited wench is what I want to warm my bed! Can't you do better than that, Arcadia?" He leaped aside, then dodged her vicious swing as she turned to spit full in his face.

"Stop this nonsense!" her father bellowed.

Arcadia ignored her father's outburst. She drove in ever more furiously.

Gutsy mettle this maiden showed, Risgan thought, as he watched in admiration. She displayed skills beyond her years, a natural at the blade. But Mygar was faster, and slier, and ever more experienced and meaner. He twisted on his heels and snuck inside her guard and brought his gloved hand down on hers, ripping the sword from her grasp. With a grunt he tossed it away into the bushes. He stared at her, eyes fuming. Then he bowed. "Very nice, milady. We should do this dance more often."

"You disgusting brute," she spat.

"And so complimentary."

She sprang at him, teeth bared and nails outstretched.

He caught her by the wrists then flung her away. "Deal with her, Vardot! Do you hear me?"

The hetman hissed and signaled two of his men. They came running in to restrain Arcadia, despite her mortified cries. "Let me go, you stupid fools! Who is the enemy here?"

Several looked to Vardot for a signal to attack Mygar, but the hetman just shook his head. A sigh rippled through the gathering. The druid looked on with a face of stone.

Vardot sat atop his mount, teeth clenched. "Have you enough bullying for one day, Mygar? You've killed one of my men and maimed my under-priest. Are you satisfied?"

"Very much. There will be more violence if you don't heed my warning and show some respect and control your vixen of a daughter. Isks fly and the hunt is not yet over! Onward!" he barked at his hunters. "The hunt for game must continue!"

The horsemen returned from the thickets, admitting that they had found no sign of a unicorn. The hetman's green-clad men groaned in disgust. They gathered up the fallen horseman and the wounded priest.

At that moment another horn blared through the trees. A clot of new figures came charging into the glade—more of Mygar's company by the look of them: lean-jawed, heavy-muscled, steel-capped men dressed in furs and leathers.

"News, lord," cried the leader, a tall, sinewy man with bronze rings on his arms. He drew abreast of Mygar. "A pack of stags run loose in Falgron's glade. Jorgu, the old marksmen, got a piece of one—" His mouth dropped upon sight of the carnage. "What in the name of wild Wülv has gone on here?"

"Never mind." Mygar gave him a brisk flourish. "We'll be moving out of here soon, Svengar. Prepare your men—the wolf-hunters." Cheers of enthusiasm coursed from the fur-cloaked hunters.

"Guard this popinjay, well," hissed Mygar, pointing the tip of his sword at Risgan. "My horsemen and I will deal with him and the others when I'm back."

Svengar grumbled. "As you wish, lord."

"They will have a proper trial," warned the hetman.

Mygar shrugged and gave a harsh laugh. "They'll feel the bite of my sword, is what." He turned and raised his blade to the sky. "The hunt goes on!" Springing upon the back of his horse, a broad-chested brown bay, he rallied his wild hunters. They roared in answer and turned to speed off.

Arcadia raised a shrill cry: "Not so fast! We must look after our wounded. The animal totems speak that—"

Mygar reined in, peering at her with narrowed eyes. "What do you know about animals and their spirits, woman? I've spent twice your years herding them and killing them, and wandering about these wilds like a priest of the hunt."

"I know more than you think, Mygar."

"Hear, hear," cried the green-vested men of Arcadia's clan. The other wild horsemen, savages of Mygar's clan, jeered in opposition.

Risgan's brain spun with the wide schism in this group. Half were for appeasing Arcadia, half against. Grumbles of dissent rang like deerhide drums. The hetman's face clouded over.

As the remainder prepared to leave, another cry came. Those of the hetman's green-vests brought the cart forth carrying an agitated Afrid.

"What manner of loathsome creature is this?" the hetman demanded.

"Thäene Vardot, meet Afrid, erstwhile witch of Thornkeep," Risgan said. He made the introduction with a low, mocking bow.

Afrid hissed.

"You don't say?" The hetman gaped. "Her reputation precedes her. 'Tis' a spiteful crone I see, with a baby's face."

"Agreed."

Even the antlered druid had trotted forward to grant Afrid a more careful inspection. Though it looked as if he liked little of what he saw.

The hetman gave a weary sigh. "Tolfgard! Mesin! Bring the witch along with us. They shall all return with us to the village. Let us make haste!"

* * *

So the hunt proceeded without incident, though Risgan watched the hetman and the small band of Mygar's hunters scour the skies with wary eyes. Only three stags did they flush out from the thick brush, beasts whose carcasses were well pierced and slung over the backs of spare horses. Risgan's mouth watered for venison roasting over a crackling fire, but he knew that was a pipe dream.

The huntsmen designated as guards drove Risgan and his company hard through the wilds. The peeling gray bark and thin wispy branches became a blur in his mind. Finger-like twigs scratched his cheeks and caught at his leathers. The natural alleys and corridors through the hag birch and twitchwood grew dim in the coppery light as Arcadia rode alongside them, flashing them occasional glances, as if pitying their ignoble treatment. "It's not normal this happens," she said to Risgan. "It won't be long now. Our village is but a half hour away."

"That's good to know," Risgan said, loosing a noisy breath. The hetman trotted ahead with his clansmen in a dark mood. His uncommunicative druid rode at his side, while Mygar and his wolf-furred hunters ranged off elsewhere to hunt. Only ten of Mygar's guard stayed behind to watch the hetman and his prisoners, but that was enough. The chief's subjects also watched Risgan and his company closely. Risgan made note of Jurna's itchy fingers on his sword and Kahel's gleaming eyes as if they contemplated an escape. At this point it was folly and he jabbed an elbow into Kahel's ribs, warning him that impulsive action would lead to death, surrounded as they were by the horsemen's drawn bows.

Dark billowy clouds moved in from the north. By late afternoon all the golden light had disappeared from the sky as they neared a freshwater river. The arms of the forest opened up to look out upon brooding flats where a long low salt marsh spread. Deadheads rose among the mire. A bridge provided access over the sluggish stream that emptied into the marsh.

A wooden wall surrounded two sides of the village with trees and water on the other sides. Archers poised above the entrance gate, bows at the ready. The gate swung open; the horses trotted through.

A group of longhouses lined the river while bull reeds and pussy willows sprung up near the shore. Hale, leather-clad women and eager children came out to greet the hunters.

The day was still warm, not much wind so midges swarmed; a faint reek accompanied what breeze there was, bringing the waft of rotten vegetation and human waste.

Odd place for a settlement, Risgan thought.

The hunters dismounted and hung the spoils of the hunt from branches to drain them of their blood. Other carcasses looked to have hung there for some time and were pulled down for the communal feast, soon to be roasted over fires. It was a good thing, for Risgan's belly ached with hunger. In the meantime, the hetman ordered bowls of broth brought for the riders to tide over their hunger.

While they gulped the offerings, Risgan noticed a scout hawk circling overhead whose lone piercing cry rang shrill in the late afternoon. It scattered the other birds in the twitchwood and flew down toward the hunters. Where were the dogs to help them hunt? He asked as much to the gathered hunters and one of the Caerlineans replied,

"Dogs make short work of game. Their teeth tear into the spoils before we can get there."

Risgan blinked. "Makes sense."

"Train them then," said Kahel.

"Easier to make pigs fly. At least the dogs in these parts."

Jurna grunted. "Your king seems to enjoy the likes of hunts and horses and hawks. I'd have thought he'd make hounds part of his retinue."

"We have no king, only a hetman."

"So we've heard," growled Kahel.

To the side of the common ground facing the huts loomed a hulk of scorched, blackened stone which looked something like a temple or monastery.

"That's Driadis's Sanctuary," said one of the hunters. "Or what's left of it. Burned by invaders. We used to favor the goddess Driadis. Now our druids worship Wülv. We switched to the wolf god at the coming of the outland tribes during the great migration. Their shamans taught us the wisdom of the wolves and eagles, and the importance of the hunt."

Risgan nodded in comprehension. The variety of gods, heroes and animal totems he had seen during his travels had been too numerous to recall. They had come and gone like flies.

A boardwalk stretched out into the salt marsh; in Risgan's estimation a region which sported an eerie gray and unwholesome look. Why they built their village so close to it was a mystery.

The hetman seemed to perceive some of this and inclined his

head in a sagely way. "Once this was a swale of fruitful bounty and supported us well. The land was well drained with freshwater creeks. The muskrat competed with the sharp-toothed beaver; both multiplied and dammed the rivers, flooding the area for miles. Even today we cannot control the devils. Every time one of their dams break, two more spring up. Ever do we fear we must leave Caerlin and forge some new settlement. That day will come soon enough. Then there's the marauding isks..." He trailed off, his face pinched in displeasure, perhaps with the foul memory of Arcadia snatched up in grasping claws.

The druid picked up the conversation in a grave voice: "The isks nest across the great eerie divide in the dead firs beyond the hummocks and hills we call the Swalestrike. Perhaps attracted by the fresh meat." He motioned his hand at the squalid village and gave a bitter laugh. "Even their greedy talons and slavering beaks cannot cull the beavers. We keep sharp lookout for the isks and from time to time they carry off our children when our hunters are engaged. Even though we despise them, they are sacred birds."

Risgan frowned. "These isks seem a menace not worth the risk."

"'Twas not always like this." He sighed. "They used to be mighty protectors. Hasifer the Traitor played them a trick and incurred their lifelong enmity toward humans and thus an everlasting curse."

"Indeed," said Risgan.

"What...you question our lore?" the druid snapped.

"Nothing like that." Risgan held up a hand. "I merely assert that being a man of the world, having hunted fabled treasures far and wide, my very existence depends largely on the truth of such legends."

"Is that so?" The hetman's words echoed hollowly.

Upon explicit orders, the horse guards took Risgan and company to a spacious but gloomy hall within a large wooden longhouse. Timber beams supported a high ceiling. A hearth stood at the side, now cold with ashes. An elderly judge with white hair and a visible stoop bent clearing the ash and coughed at the sight of them.

"Thäene Vardot, Arcadia, welcome." He bowed. "I trust the hunt was a success."

"Indeed it was."

"I see you have brought back some friends."

The hetman nodded curtly. He gave a quick summary of the isk attack, the casualties, the near escape of Arcadia, and the presence of the unicorns and outlanders whom he introduced one by one.

The judge rubbed his chin. "I see. Present their cases then—" he gave a long sigh, as if dreading the thought of hearing five defenses in one day.

Risgan and company were allowed to say their part, then Arcadia gave her account with animated flourishes. After much haranguing and questioning back and forth, the hetman called order to the assembly. "Judge Kjarn. What is your verdict?" He paused. "Wait, I want to hear it in private first."

They repaired to the antechamber and both returned, the hetman wearing a brief scowl. "After listening to Judge Kjarn's esteemed opinion, I concur that action must be taken."

The hetman, his round face flushed, lifted a finger to lips and gave a sharp exhalation, "Risgan, seeing as your company inadvertently trespassed on our ancestral lands and provoked an isk attack which almost lost me my daughter, I sentence you and your men to hunt down and kill fifteen stags of excellent quality in the upcoming hunts. Three for each member of your party."

Risgan choked on his tongue. "What? This punishment seems excessive. Clearly we are innocent of any crimes."

Arcadia leaped to her feet. "I too, Father, must object. Risgan was instrumental in saving my skin. You heard my testimony."

The hetman held up his hand. "Is that ingratitude I hear? Normally, the punishment for this number of transgressions is severe: a minimum of one year in jail, often accompanied with torture. But in this case, I make an exception, even though these outlanders interrupted a sacred hunt and let a valuable unicorn escape. The adjudicator's word and mine are absolute."

Risgan nodded with a curt growl. "As you wish, Lord. We acknowledge your—leniency." He turned to leave, quelling Kahel and Jurna's disbelieving stares. He cut off their grumbles with a wink.

"One question," said Moeze, unable to resist the urge. "Can we use sorcery on these hunts to speed up our taking of the fifteen stags?"

The hetman harrumphed. "Ordinarily, no, especially considering your unproven magical skill, Moeze. "In a nutshell, I formally forbid you from exercising any form of magic."

Moeze sputtered but Risgan raised a finger and cautioned the magician to silence. "Young Moeze is most vocal, lord, and for that, I apologize. He accepts your wishes. I will see that he complies."

"A wise choice, Risgan. See that you do."

Risgan drew Moeze aside and hissed. "Fool. Do not annoy the chief any more than you have to. I've told you once and again not to practice magic that involves risk for others. For that matter don't practice magic at all until you are better versed in it and healed from Afrid's vile spells."

Moeze sagged. He hung his head, muttering a terse word. "As you wish, Risgan. In the end it will go the worse for you and the others."

"There is still the matter of this witch." The hetman gestured toward the thorn cage. "The crone exhibits a fiendish aura which disturbs my sensibilities."

Risgan sighed. "Pay no heed. Afrid's suffering penance for her past deeds."

"And what does penance have to do with her sinister aura?" he intoned. "Why the grimacing rictus? The baby face?"

"Trade places and find out," snorted Kahel.

"What's that?" The hetman scowled, noting Kahel's brazen tone, but choosing to bypass it.

Dodonis, Vardot's druid, rubbed his chin. "I might have uses for such a specimen in the days ahead."

Jurna laughed. "Valuable only as a freak show oddity."

The druid ignored the comment. "I request a transfer of the witch to my hut, Thäene."

Kahel gave a barking laugh. "Go right ahead, druid. She's all yours."

"Not so fast," said Risgan. "Afrid is under my protection and I'll not have her mauled."

Kahel sneered. "When did you become the hag's guardian?"

Vardot called for order. "The caged witch will go to Dodonis for future study! That is the end of the discussion. In the meantime, you can make use of our humble grounds. I'm not an ungenerous man. We have an obstacle course, training ground, workout area, private sparring grounds, baths and a temple to Driadis. Though that now runs with wolf heads. There by the marsh, some fishing piers and equipment are at your service so you can contribute."

"We'll consider it," said Risgan.

The hetman studied them with care. "You'd better. You would do best to offer us service and participate in the training of our hunters, particularly our younger members. Your skills may accelerate your release. Now we have to contend with Mygar's brutes who have moved in on us." He grunted with distaste.

Risgan gave a strangled cough. "Why don't you repel them?"

The chief frowned. "Easier said than done, outlander. They're canny as wolves and immune to ambush. All too well have they become versed in swordsmanship and bullying intimidation."

"And versed in crass behaviors," piped up Arcadia, "as some of our females are well aware of."

Vardot mumbled under his breath. "I know. How I would love to drive the lot of them into the swamp..." He balled his fists. "We are at their mercy. Nonetheless, they offer protection and hunting skills to our community, so a fragile harmony exists."

"Very fragile, Father—and I wish you'd just—"

"Perhaps there is something you can offer," the hetman interrupted, toying with his staff. He gazed at Risgan. "If so, the judge may reduce your sentence. We make our young undergo a rigorous practicum to ensure they are fit for the hunt, that they can defend our village from warring tribesmen like these apes who currently control us. Little good our martial skill has availed. Anything you can assist in this regard will be helpful."

"Understandable."

"What is ours is yours, as I have said. But do not try to leave the perimeter of the village. Our guards will repel you, and you'll be punished. Not to mention what Mygar's men will do if they find you have deserted."

Risgan gave a crisp nod. He accepted the situation as it stood.

"Your quarters are being prepared this moment. We have set up accommodations for you in Kevil the blacksmith's longhome. He will billet you."

"That is most kind of you, lord."

He gave a curt nod. "Come, let us prepare for the feast."

With a regal inclination of head he strode away in the direction of the common ground to deal with the many petty issues that every chief had. Squealing pigs, two lame dogs in a fight, a field hand squabbling over a few turnips his neighbor had pulled out. Risgan felt glad that he had not the weight of a chief's duties on his shoulders. Being leader in more than name of this small band was enough of a challenge. Thinking of which, what was he to do about Moeze's infatuation with dangerous and inept spells? They could be the ruin of them all.

Shouts came from the common ground. A scout scurried up, his ruddy face glistening with sweat. "My lord! Terror flies—isks, four of them—they ravage the village!"

"What? Don't just stand there, man, arrow them down!"

He fled back to the battle. On brisk feet the hetman stormed over. Arcadia, Risgan and his band followed close behind.

The common ground writhed to the tune of chaos.

Three giant birds had swooped low, bone-claw talons grasping and raking the straw-thatched huts, tearing holes along their ridges. Villagers ran screaming for their lives. The birds, fast of wing and long of beak, eluded the huntsmen's arrows in the fading light.

"The birds seek vengeance for the death of their brother in the woods!" called one of the huntsmen.

Villagers crouched, wielding blades. Some aimed bows. The arrows skidded off the birds' tough hides. Only a few caught the feathered flesh and stayed lodged, but even those barely deterred the birds' menace. The ten horsemen Mygar had left behind from his company circled on their mounts, drawing the isks out. But their arrows failed to penetrate the tough hide.

Risgan clutched his club, waving it back and forth at the hideous black creature that dove at him all too closely.

"Can you not do anything with your magic, druid?" spat the hetman.

"My lord, the isk is an ancient bird impervious to magic."

"Bollocks! Do something, you fool!"

Arcadia snatched the golden arrow from the druid, who sat atop his horse dazed in inaction. She drew back the strings and it flew in a rainbow arc. The gleaming tip pierced the lead brute in the chest. It gave a ghastly shriek, sagged. Then its massive hulk fell to the ground in a feathery, heap. With wings flapping uselessly on the ground, it crawled along the grass. Miracle upon miracle, the golden arrow emerged of its own volition from the isk's breast and in a looping arc returned through the air back to Arcadia's hand. She strung it again and took aim at a second beast. It swooped to rake her with its talons but Kahel wheeled in and sent a spinning arrow straight into its eye. Lokbur's arrow twanged next, catching it in its side as it careened off in a screeching rage. Villagers came running with angry curses and hoes and axes in their hands, chopping the fallen bird in a frenzy of pent up fury. The beak snapped out and took the legs off one overzealous villager who got too close. He bled out in an instant.

"Kill it, you fools!" the hetman cried.

Jurna stepped up to jam his sword into its beak, silencing the creature's fury forever. Kahel and Lokbur stood at the ready to pepper it with arrows. But the thing moved no more.

"Two attacks in one day. A sinister omen," cried a distraught villager.

In eerie synchrony the other birds swooped low and snatched two huntsmen off their horses and rose aloft from whence they had come.

Risgan stood dumbstruck as the two marauders disappeared into the horizon. A lull descended amid the cries of the wounded. Men's shouts dwindled to angry mutters. Others made slow movements to repair their damaged huts and longhouses.

Lokbur strode up and spoke in fevered words. "Lord Vardot, we will have to launch an offensive against these vile isks sooner rather than later."

"The journey is long and the risk high," asserted the druid.

"Risks we must take, Dodonis," mumbled Vardot. "But not now. Mygar still hunts and we must gather meat and hides for the long winter."

Risgan gazed in wonder upon the hetman's daughter and the fabulous weapon she clutched. Already its diamond tip and shaft grew redder and duskier and seemed to scintillate with an aura of mysterious power. "This arrow you hold, what magic does it possess?"

"Its magic is not fully understood," the druid said.

"And yet even its power is not enough to kill these creatures," scoffed one of Mygar's guards.

Arcadia spoke as if in trance: "It was said the arrow is the trophy of Queen Razastaf who bathed in the magic pool in the woods of the dryads in ancient times. The waters gave her powers of foresight, wisdom beyond her years...and mystical experiences. One day—"

"One day she brought the arrow to her pool and it became ensorcelled," finished Mygar's man. "We've heard the story before."

"She had it fitted with a diamond tip by the best jewel-smiths," continued Arcadia, ignoring the remark. "It sat through the ages until it was stolen from the palace by a Zerulian thief."

"A quaint yarn," scoffed Kahel.

"Yarn or not," contended Jurna. "If not for the courage of this hetman's daughter, we'd be isk bait or weeping tears of blood right now. Seems as if this arrow and a true aim from a maiden's hand saved the day from these vicious creatures."

There came murmurs of agreement.

* * *

The roaring fire blazed amid the grumbles of the villagers, males and females alike, as the huntsmen shared their accounts of the day's happenings and the coming of the unicorns. The druid murmured some prayers in a foreign tongue for the three who had perished. Cedar, sage and wild twitch sprigs hissed and crackled over the fire. The hetman ordered the release of three flaming arrows over the marsh into the deepening dusk.

Heads bowed and a silence was given.

Tables and benches were hauled out and laden with food, bowls and barrels of mead. Some small state of revelry returned to the clans but with extra bows and quivers at hand. Soon after, isk meat roasted over spits and joined the overflowing platters of succulent venison. The trophy head was carried off and tied to a stout post overlooking the glade as a deterrent to other marauders.

"Do you not think it an overly brazen challenge to more of their kind?" asked Risgan, between mouthfuls of meat.

The hetman growled an oath. "'Tis the only thing these foul isks understand. Slaughter and death! So let them feast their eyes on the head of their kin if they return. We'll be ready."

Risgan and members of his band looked upon the mounted head with doubt and wonder. Blood dripped from its severed neck and ran down the dark wood of the post, the sight almost enough to spoil his appetite.

Mygar came riding in with his mob of hunters. He waved his blade, a sneer on his lips. Not a scratch was on him from the dangers of the day. A majestic stag with a top-heavy rack of forked antlers lay stretched over the unsaddled mount tethered behind his own horse.

"Looks as if you fools have lost more men to the beaks of the isks," he called jocularly.

Angry grumbles issued from the Caerlinean hunters.

"And fat lot of good you were," one dared to cry out. "The men you left here were next to useless."

"I cannot be at five places at once," Mygar said. "Can't you weaklings fight your own battles for a change?" He laughed. "Peace! Here's more meat for roasting. Let's make merry and wash our hands of the bloody affairs of the day."

"Not so merry, today, Mygar," called out Arcadia.

He raised an eyebrow. "What's that, my fancy bride-to-be?"

She looked away, fuming, refusing to look at him.

The hetman lifted his cup of wine and made a toast to all gathered. "Four prime stags, four ribbons. That's what is awarded the best hunters of the day. The stag, the symbol of beauty and prosperity, has offered itself for our sustenance. None match its supple grace, save the unicorn." He lifted a ringed finger in the air.

"Except the unicorn," repeated Arcadia, shaking her head. "And these foul brutes would have killed them all and made doormats of them."

Risgan nodded, commiserating with Arcadia's frustration.

Mygar merely shrugged.

Ale guzzling competitions were soon in full swing, starting early this evening. Risgan motioned to one of Mygar's bearded rogues, Svengar who was laughing, downing a huge jack of ale that spilled foam down his jerkin. "Who are these dolts? Where did they come from? I don't like the look of them. Here in your village they are like sharks among minnows."

Arcadia expelled an angry breath. "They're not part of our clan as my father explained. They just think they are. They came from the east a year ago, hooligans and warmongers. Expelled from their own clan, the Svengari, following a blood feud. Mygar rallied them; he assumed leadership. He came to us all blood-smeared and yelling in his foul tongue, a fierce, uncouth barbarian. Since then, he has installed himself here with his wolves as our 'protectors'. Pah! He rules and my father is nothing more than a puppet. That bastard over there to his left is his lieutenant and nephew, Svengar, a man as mean as a rattler. His uncle obviously taught him everything he knows."

Risgan peered over at Svengar, a sinewy brute with bronze warrior rings on his arms and hair like his uncle's down the middle of his back. Though this was dirty blond with a dyed strip of black, it had no less menace and denoted a rising champion of the hunters.

Mygar and he clasped hands.

"And the druid?"

"Dodonis is halfway between the two, my father and Mygar. He's split between the old ways and the new. Ever looking for a chance to grab at some power and opportunity at the expense of anyone who gets in the way.

"A pack of thieves and vipers," Risgan muttered. "Your tale sheds more light on the situation at least."

Lokbur came by to pay his respects to Arcadia. His face had a red welt which he tried to hide in an awkward fashion. He seemed almost shame-faced about it.

"Arcadia." He tipped his head with a forced smile.

"Lokbur. I thank you for coming to my defense back there."

He nodded grimly and looked at her with obvious fondness. "Ever am I watching out for you, huntress. Seems you're a magnet for trouble." He gave a tense laugh. "Remember the time you got into the bee hives a few years back, licking your fingers of honey? Ha. Oh, what a mess that was. How many villagers got stung?"

She chuckled. "Too many. I remember well, Lokbur. All just follies of a rebellious childhood. Remember when we used to hold hands by the river? I fell in and you rescued me. You pulled me out by the hair and I smacked you good, if I recall. We'd talk for hours, catch fish in the sun, then bask in the shade, sometimes even sneak a kiss, or two."

"I remember." He grinned and blushed with clear enjoyment of the moment from the past. "We were not even twelve or thirteen." His eyes glazed over and grew bright and dreamy at their shared memories. Then they dimmed, as if such things were only ghosts of yesterday. "And yet, thirteen is an unlucky number."

His voice was drowned out by the drunken whoopings of the wolf-hunters. "We got four stags today, not a bad haul, but could be better," clamored one.

Risgan murmured under his breath, "Pity to slay such magnificent beasts."

The hunter, one of Mygar's rogues, overheard the remark and gave an angry shout. "Who are you to make a judgment on us, outlander? Would you rather eat turnips tonight?" Others laughed.

Risgan shrugged. "I was merely appreciating the majesty of the beasts."

"And the isks are majestic and we slay them too."

This raised jeers. The fur-cloaked wolf-hunters catcalled.

Dodonis the druid spoke in a commanding tone, waving his staff. "The unicorn leathers and hide are magical and essential for our charms and spells."

Svengar flashed Risgan a contemptuous glance, "I say we slay these knaves, as Mygar suggests."

Others of Mygar's band voiced their agreement.

"Silence your tongues," the hetman called. "They have undergone a proper trial and are under my protection."

"You forget," said Mygar in a quiet voice, "we don't obey you." He approached, his eyes glassy with mead, somewhat placated by the spoils of the day. He lifted a hand. "Peace, comrades. It is a time of feasting and celebration!—didn't you hear?" he roared, slurring his words, "your 'chief' has said it himself, a sacred day for the hunt. The outlanders will live—for now!" He raised his sword high and cast Risgan an evil look. Risgan bared his teeth, not liking what he saw.

"Brute," hissed Arcadia. She turned her head aside.

Traditional wrestling matches began, accompanied by music with lute and drum and other instruments that Risgan had not heard before. Some with long hollow cylinders carved of wood and a place for a musician to blow into.

Caerlin clansman built a second bonfire that soared up into the black night, dispelling the gloom and chill of the change of season. Children ran freely, wearing hats and eye-patches, playing blind man's bluff, with Arcadia playing monkey in the middle—all to the delight of the children. She even got her sister to join in, then Jurna and Hape. Others played a variation of hide and seek while rowdier youths bobbed for apples in barrels filled to the brim. Moeze went even so far as to demonstrate a magic trick or two, but Risgan came up behind him and offered a cock-eyed smile and whispered in his ear. "Moeze, I know you like to impress the children, but stick to the disappearing bead under the three-cups-trick, okay?"

The magician frowned at him, then smiled. "Yes, Risgan, simpler is better." He tapped his chin. "And yet, this is not what I expected—but certainly better than taking residence in Afrid's lair. Speaking of which, I wonder how our hag is faring?"

Risgan gave a brief mutter. "As you witnessed, she has been confined to the druid's hut. Douran only knows what he will do with her. Frankly, part of me is relieved to have her off my hands. I only hope the idiot does not let her escape."

"Aye, pray that he does not," said Jurna.

Kahel lifted a cup of mead to his lips and drained it in a single gulp. "Bah, this is mere goat piss! I've tasted stronger water than this."

Arcadia laughed. "Let's see you say that after twenty more cups, archer."

"Why, mistress? You challenging me?" he chuckled.

"Judging from your size and capacity, no."

Kahel smiled, a rare act for him.

Musicians brought out deerhide drums while others clutched lute and fife and started up a lively tune that had many tapping their feet. A chorus of singers joined in. The village folk kicked up their heels and danced around the fire. A high-spirited mood had them striking up a jig that involved deep knee bends with hands on hips and high-flinging kicks. Risgan chanced to make eye contact with the lady

Thrulia, the hetman's older daughter who watched with some interest. With a shrug, he sauntered over, knowing he had nothing to lose. So, he put on his best smile, eager to start up a conversation.

"Lady Thrulia," he said with a bow. "We have not formally met. I'm Risgan, a relic hunter of small repute."

"Pleased to meet you." She lifted her had in offer. "Shall we dance?" He accepted and they promenaded with the others around the fire.

"You have the look of an adventurer to you," she remarked. "The fit, wiry type with a dash of sandy-haired mystique thrown in. It speaks of mischievousness. I'm a good judge of men...Those vagabondish leathers of yours—they have the looks of an outlaw."

Risgan shrugged. "Others have said as much."

She nodded. Perhaps a handful of years older than Arcadia, Risgan guessed, but she exhibited the same fiery spirit, the same bright inquiring green eyes, and slender figure, though she was not as tall, but no less striking.

"You are an odd sort, Risgan. You have the gentlemanly quality of an older man, yet the look of a far younger one."

"It's an odd combination," Risgan said, bowing again. "I take pride in my upbringing at an early age."

"Oh? And from where do you come that demands such upbringing?"

"Zanzuria." He grinned. "A fiefdom several leagues distance. Perhaps you've heard of it?"

She nodded. "In name only."

"A proud kingdom ruled by a proud man. Although sometimes I wonder who rules: him or his queen." He chuckled.

"Lady Farella is quite a handful—from what I've gathered."

"Oh, she is."

"Zanzuria...one of the old kingdoms, blessed with an opulent palace and elegant gardens. One day I hope to see it and experience its charms. Our humble village of Caerlin, as you can see, is not much to speak of." She arched her back. "But—it's not often that a woman rules a kingdom, is it?"

"Farella is a spirited maid."

"More than I?" she asked in a playful voice.

Risgan spun about. He lifted his long legs in one of the scissor kicks demanded of the dance. "I do not like to compare women. Not very gentlemanly, you see."

She chuckled. "Don't shove your foot deeper into the mire, sir Risgan. Let's just enjoy our dance."

"Of course." Risgan was relieved to drop the conversation, which he found bordering on stressful, considering the carnal nature of his liaisons with the lady Farella, which Thrulia seemed so cunningly to have guessed.

Thrulia's long rose-colored hair gleamed in the crackling flames. How he would like to stroke it. The flushed faces of the dancers mooned around them. Risgan tried an innovation to the 'kick' which earned her laughter and everyone's admiration.

"You seem quite adept at those high jumps and kicks."

"And I no less envious of your dexterity, milady."

"Indeed, have you danced the *riga* before?"

"No, this is my first time."

She sputtered out a laugh. "Of course."

She drew in close and gripped his waist and spun him around.

Risgan stumbled, surprised at the bold maneuver. But he quickly recovered and echoed the move, grinning and twirling her with more force than she expected. Was she testing his mettle? When she landed on her feet and turned back to face him, she was slightly breathless. He grabbed her and tossed her high in the air. Wild cheers rose from the spectators, many of whom had stepped back to observe and give them more space.

"Well, wasn't that fun?" he asked with a broad, disarming grin. "But you, lady, you have not said much of yourself."

Thrulia shrugged. "What is there to say, sir Risgan? I am a hetman's daughter, no more, no less. Destined to become some poor huntress like my sister, though I'll never be as good as her. Likely my father will wed me to some savage boor like that thuggish, lank-toothed Svengar over there. See how he watches me with an obnoxious leer pasted on his ugly face. He makes my skin crawl."

Risgan's head turned as the dance steps slowed and indeed he saw the chief's lieutenant crouched with his bearded cronies over grogs on tree stumps for tables, eyeing the women with lascivious interest and trading rude jests.

Risgan's expression grew somber. "I'd rather see all hell freeze over than you wed to that mongrel."

She grinned. "That is sweet of you to say. Yet somewhat of an inevitability. As it is, I feel sick at heart knowing that Arcadia must become bride to that savage brute of a chief." She shivered at the thought. "Even the rebel that she is, he'll break her spirit."

"Can nothing be done?"

She frowned; a pained look surfaced on her comely face. "And what would you have us do, Risgan—declare open war on these animals? They'd tear us apart. We must appease them, as my father has stated."

He grunted, pondering this defeatist attitude. He missed another step and almost pitched himself into the fire. He regained control and faced her with a faint smile. A fight lost was better than slavery. But what could he do? Leave them to blunder along with their own battles? For the moment, he'd watch and wait and enjoy these halcyon moments with this captivating maid while he had the chance.

Mygar, inebriated, staggered about, his hair askew, deliberately dancing with every female in the two clans but his future bride. Perhaps to spite her? It suited the hetman's daughter just fine. She sat out and rebuffed all dance partners save Lokbur.

The dance came to an end; sudden loud shouts erupted from a disorderly cluster of Mygar's huntsmen as another fight broke out, apparently over who claimed title to the last stag slain in the hunt. Mygar allowed it, even encouraged it, punishing the loser with a cane-whipping. Risgan and his men were not alone in their sullen misgivings about this rowdy clan.

The hour grew late and even more boisterous tumult echoed from the Svengari huntsmen, though many had returned to their squalid camp next to the village on the shores of the swamp. Risgan, enlivened by the dance and a growing passion for Thrulia, drowned himself in grog. There seemed to be no end. The hypnotic voices of Jurna and Moeze blurred together in a background hum of boasts and threats, the clash of swords in mock battles becoming one; all the while the two bonfires continued to burn as the raucous music progressed to the rhythmic beat of drums, and whistling and wheezing of multiple wind instruments accompanied by the drunken singing of ribald verses decidedly off key, until Risgan had finally had enough.

He and his crew stumbled back to the blacksmith's longhome and flung themselves on the dusty blankets slung out in front of the hearth. The fire had long grown cold. After a time, the master of the house came stumbling bleary-eyed upon them where they snored away. Risgan sprang upright at the sound of the blacksmith's sandal scuffling on the dirt.

"Sorry sir, not my wish to wake you," the blacksmith apologized. "Just wanted to check everything was alright."

Risgan nodded and yawned. Likely not checking on their comfort for altruistic purposes. Rather, verifying that they hadn't made off with his valuables, despite the assurances of the hetman that they were not thieves or murderers. "Quite alright, master Kevil. I always sleep with one eye open."

The blacksmith wandered back to his quarters with a doubtful glance over his shoulder. Trust, it seemed, was not easily gained in this village.

2: The Magic Arrow

After a hurried breakfast of hot meal and oatcakes, Kevil hustled Risgan and his gang off to the fringes of the village. "Where are we going?" Risgan asked.

"You'll see. Hetman's orders." The dawn's pearly light filtered through the trees to pierce the mist and glaze the trampled grass a washed-out silver. On cresting a small rise, Risgan stared with some awe upon a tall palisade with stout, close-set poles—a gigantic corral, about three hundred feet long. It was shaped in the form of a long oval of sand, mud and grass clumps. Several complicated walkways, towers and observation platforms formed parts of the wall. Evidently the villagers had the craft of clever builders.

Within, several animals, horses and riders milled about. Also of note were stacked bales, targets for archery practice and what appeared to be a track and obstacle course for training purposes.

At the gate, a watchman beckoned the newcomers in. Risgan gave a cheerful smile and Kahel shoved past him with a surly grunt.

A variety of weapons hung from the inner palisade: swords, axes and shields. A dozen young hunters spurred their wild-eyed mounts forth, amid much clamor and gesticulating. In the high-spirited tumult, they whipped lassos over their head to take down young stags, in preparation for live hunts, capturing either young deer or horses for breeding and training purposes. Others drew their bows and fired arrows from their mounts at the targets. Others stood at a hundred paces and aimed at smaller or larger targets depending on their marksmanship. A group to the side wrestled with each other or sparred with mixed weaponry—sword and staff. Risgan's crew stood about, watching with curiosity and amusement, along with several others who had gathered to watch.

A mixture of male and female hunters of both bands, young and old, participated. The clansfolk, it seemed, gave no preference to gender or age.

Kahel sauntered over to examine a trio of young hunters aiming longbows at targets about fifty feet distant. With steely-eyed inspection, he sized up a blond-haired youth wearing red cap and green jerkin who consistently kept missing his target.

"Let me see that bow," Kahel grunted. The boy obliged. "Your bow's of good quality but you're holding it wrong."

"What do you mean?" The boy looked up at him blankly.

"Watch." He raised his brows. "You don't believe me? Try it." He positioned himself behind the boy and placing hands on his, guided his fingers along the smooth curve of the wood. "Grip the middle hard, boy. Yes, like a sword! Squint with your one eye, straight along the shaft as close as you can. No, aim a little higher, yes, that's it, you were shooting too low."

As a team, Kahel and the youth aimed and the bow twanged.

The arrow struck the edge of the target high to the right with the fletch quivering like a peacock's fan before it fell to the ground.

The boy blinked in surprise. "Wow, did I do that?"

"Of course. Your turn. Try it solo."

The boy bit his lip and squinted in deep concentration. His arms trembled, not used to seeing so many eyes on him.

"Wait—aim a little higher," admonished Kahel. "Hold your breath and stop your quivering. You're like a tail-wagging puppy. That's it. Now shoot!" The boy's arrow caught the edge of the butt closer than the last shot. Certainly far from a bulls-eye, but a significant improvement.

"Wow!" The boy shook his head in sheer amazement. "I've never got that close before."

Kahel winked at him. "Keep practicing."

Arcadia chanced to ride up next to Kahel and flashed him a wry smile. "Quite the bedside manner you have there, Kahel. You could become a good trainer."

Kahel shrugged. "I doubt it. Not my calling. But others have said as much."

On one of the raised platforms rising over the gated section, a group of youths huddled, staring down at the stags running in a penned-off area below. Mygar's brood, judging from their worn brown furs. A few stags were loosed from the side and then caned on the rump to get them running. With grins and mutters the young hunters took aim, fingered their bows and fired blindly with blunt wooden arrows and small, low-powered bows. They seemed to have not much more force than slingshots.

Under the scrutiny of a scowling, cold-eyed teacher, they fired one after another while the instructor barked out brutal criticisms on points of technique and style. "Too slow, Jikrak. The stag's already far out of kill range."

"No! Too fast, and stiff on the draw, Egrek, You're a lousy disgrace. Look, even the stags are laughing at you!"

The youth pouted and hung his head. The sniggers of his friends were demeaning. Wiping his snotty nose, he took aim and fired at a large buck which raised its rack of antlers at him. The animal leapt up with a snort, battering the platform and almost toppled Egrek, then bounded to the end of the corral, only to be pegged by his wooden arrow with blunted end. The beast tucked tail and snorted but was unharmed at that distance.

Kahel grumbled. "Look at them. Easy to take pot shots at a bunch of penned-up animals then laugh and joke about it after. It's as if hunting big game is like bagging birds. It's not the same."

"They have to learn somehow," sighed Risgan.

"I agree though," said Jurna. "I wouldn't do it like that."

The Caerlineans didn't approve of the panicking stags and grumbled loudly at their treatment. The stag was a revered animal, not to be abused. There was little they could do in the wake of Mygar's savage ways and his program of versing the young clan members in live target training. Competition among the young hunters was fierce; improving their skill and speed seemed the priority, all of them eager to join in the hunt and be recognized among the senior hunters of Mygar's band as worthy.

Risgan watched Arcadia trot up on her gray mare. All eyes trained on her.

Horse and rider moved as one, as if she had a secret communion with her steed. Her skill was well known among the clan and something of a point of jealousy among others, including her sister, Thrulia, whom Risgan had taken even more of a shine to. Or perhaps it was the other way around.

On horseback Arcadia could easily outmaneuver the men, having ridden since the age of five. Her long hair rippled across her shoulders with every move of her proud mare.

Risgan had heard whispers that both she and Thrulia had descended from the blood of warriors. It seemed hard to believe, given this defeated and gutless hetman who had sired them. He could only conclude such traits must have come from the mother's side of the family.

After a few swift turns about the track, the riders dismounted and brandished their blades. Arcadia joined the sparring, an excellent swordstress who could best or hold her own against any or all of the others, save Svengar and Mygar.

Competitive sword play was in progress; several youths paired against one another. Ever were the younger contenders eager to challenge Arcadia, for it was considered an honor. The clink of blade on blade echoed across the sand and eyes turned to follow the matches very closely. Arcadia whipped her blade faster than the eye could see. Her blade whirled and she snuck inside her challenger's guard to halt her swordtip before his nose. "Okay, who's next?"

"*Me!*" called out the nearest young man, tipping his woolen cap and clutching his sword with defiance. He swaggered forward, wearing a cocky grin. Arcadia bowed and the youth echoed the courtesy.

They sprang back on the balls of their feet, brandishing their blades. The young man struck first, confident in his attack. Arcadia gave some ground, letting him rush in. She sidestepped and parried his thrusts then snuck in a left and right sequence of her own and in no time she had him backpedaling, tripping over his heels until he blundered and she slipped under his guard and the blade caressed his neck. "Yield?"

"I do," he hissed. His voice, a defeated whisper, was not so soft to escape the ears of the spectators. The others murmured in wonder and cheered.

"And now how about me?" drawled a low voice. Risgan blinked in surprise to see that it was the huntsman Lokbur.

A wide grin spread over Arcadia's face. "You'd like a drubbing, my lord?"

He bowed low. "I'd be honored."

She laughed. Before they could engage, Mygar pushed in and grabbed Arcadia in a bear hug. He laid his lips on hers so hard that she could barely breathe. It ended in a sloppy kiss and she wrenched herself away finally, gasping, wiping her lips of his slobber. She slugged him hard in the chops.

The others watching laughed and cat-called. Arcadia, quivering in rage, uttered several unladylike remarks. Mygar stood there, laughing uproariously, smoothing out his reddening cheek.

"I love it when you're angry, Cadie. Such a vixen! You and me will go far. I'm in love! Love, do you hear me? Love!"

Svengar, his brawny lieutenant, howled a wolf's laugh. "I believe you are, lord. Such a pleasant sight. It must be spring."

Lokbur mustered a wild leap forth and with a crazed shout, drove in to attack Mygar, sword flailing.

Mygar parried and grunted, striking back with force. "What is it with you, puppy? You want to play? The worse it'll go for you." He lunged in with dangerous speed, slashing several overhead loops. Lokbur was hard put to defend against such furious attack. Yet he parried every stroke blade. Such was his animosity and fierce love for Arcadia that he held his own and it granted him strength and luck. "You're a pig," he taunted. "You don't respect our people." In he rushed, impassioned, angered by the foreign lord's audacity.

But pretty words could only go so far against such a foe. Mygar, not treating the assault seriously, struck again and again with negligent ease, moving in inch by inch with a lion's yawn on his lips.

Ducking Mygar's whipping blade thrusts, Lokbur smacked the giant in the chin, a firm crack across the mouth that had Mygar stepping back and licking his bloody lip with a crinkly grin. "Nice shot, Lok. Wülv's praise. You're getting better. Must be all those oat cakes you're eating in the morning." He laughed, drove in, snorting and grunting with a wild brute strength and smashed the sword out of Lokbur's hands. He kicked him hard in the chest then clouted him with his leathered fist on the side of the head. Lokbur's face grew very purple at the force of the hit. The chief's fist rose and fell, pummeling the younger man until Lokbur's mates jumped in to defend him with savage cries.

The spectators roared. It looked as if full-scale war would take the entire Caerlin clan but then horsemen broke in from both sides broke to separate the two parties.

Risgan, appalled, remained impressed that the whole line of Caerlin members jumped in to defend their clansman.

Mygar gave a rude snarl. "Louts! Idiots! I'll not waste my time fighting stupid cretins like you one by one."

The druid watched from the back of his russet roan with a shrewd cast to his slitted eyes. For a fleeting instant, Risgan saw amusement flash in his face, full of disdain and indifference.

"Seems our young hunter has his hands full," murmured Jurna.

Lokbur staggered out of the knot of figures and slumped down at a nearby table, taking a cup of mead from a barrel. He downed it in a gulp. He looked badly roughed up, his hair matted and blood trickling down his cheek. Risgan came over to check that the young man was okay.

Lokbur's voice came as a hissing rasp. "She makes eyes at me but I have no idea if she even likes me. Maybe she is just playing me for a fool? Maybe I'm clinging to nothing but a boyhood infatuation for her." He seemed to not care about his own wounds, only that he had been disgraced before Arcadia.

"By 'she', I assume you mean Arcadia?" Risgan sighed. "Don't be too hard on yourself, Lokbur."

"Easy to say. Mygar humiliates me at every step. How I'd like to wring that weasel's neck!"

"So would many."

"What do you suggest?"

Risgan sighed. "Well, easier to wade through that swamp than fathom the complexity of the female race—which is tantamount to saying easier to become a master magician—just ask Moeze." He gave a mocking chuckle.

Lokbur frowned. "Judging from Moeze's skill, I highly doubt I shall."

"Moeze's capabilities are steadily growing," observed Risgan. "Afrid was rather hard on the young buck. He's had a rough handling, so give him some encouragement."

"Did someone mention my name?" A pale face bobbed in—Moeze, a figure in a blue-silver robe.

Lokbur blinked as the magician butted in, eyes gleaming and long, slender fingers clutching a silver disc.

"Need a trick done, a magical incantation written, or curse counteracted? Moeze is your man."

"Not today, Moeze," said Risgan. "Perhaps tomorrow, or next week?"

"As you wish." He bowed with a small curl of lip and glided away.

Lokbur took Risgan aside and spoke in a hushed whisper. "Some practical advice, Risgan, on how to deal with women would be welcome." He rubbed his sore jaw.

Risgan steepled his fingers on his brow. "Lokbur—think of it like this. Women like to be sought after. It makes them feel valued. You've got to give them that feeling of being special, or else they don't feel you care for them."

"Oh, ho, you seem to know a lot about this, Risgan. Sounds

good, but can you give me specifics?"

"Use your head!" said Risgan with impatience. He slapped a palm on the wine barrel. "Get plucky, Lokbur. She's a hetman's daughter! Raise the bar high and higher for Douran's sake."

"You're right, Risgan." He hung his head and ambled off, rubbing his bruised chin.

Risgan frowned, wondering if he'd given the young man a bit of wrong advice. His own success with maidens had been sadly lacking of late.

In all of the four sections of the training grounds—archery, rodeo, horsemanship and sparring—Risgan's companions found a place, as did members of Mygar's and Vardot's clans. Risgan and Arcadia favored the sword, Kahel and Thrulia the archery butt, Hape remained much enthralled with the horse racing, a skill he'd give his eye teeth for.

Moeze was intrigued with the druid and his beguiling jeweled staff, and he approached to trade lore. Dodonis at first fixed stern eyes on Moeze, then gave a slow nod. They went off together, Dodonis's hand on the young magician's shoulder. Meanwhile, Jurna perked up at the talk of several hunters discussing tracking skills in the woods.

"Haven't you heard of setting snares while you scout?" Jurna asked. "That way you can trail-blaze but set certain hunters to pick up the spoils."

Risgan smiled, catching a snatch of the conversation. Jurna and one of the younger huntsman before long became instant friends.

A strident voice intruded on Risgan's train of thought: "Raise your sword, archer! You think you're so fast?"

Risgan turned to raise his eyebrows at Kahel. The archer was practically spitting curses in Svengar's face.

"A deal better than you," Kahel growled. He moved in fast.

"Let's you and me go a round or two then." Svengar's silver broadsword rose in a slithering rasp from his scabbard and caught Kahel's darker blade.

Risgan scrambled over, alarm showing on his face. A sick feeling coursed through his gut. He had a sinking premonition that such a duel may spell the end of them all. He jumped in without a second thought. "I will fight you, Svengar. Raise your weapon!"

Mygar bustled forward. "No," he blurted. A sinister grin spread from ear to ear. "How be you and I go a round, relic hunter? Thus far you've been a big mouthpiece in this village with little action."

Risgan scowled. A hundred eyes watched their movements. To back out now would imply cowardice.

He shrugged and bowed. "As you wish, my lord." He drew his sword.

"My lord! Don't insult me with your fake deference. You mean it as much as my grandmother's dead dog. On your guard, outlander!" He came in slashing at Risgan with a breakneck speed. At the same time Svengar roared and charged Kahel. Their blades met in a mutual, resounding clash.

Risgan barely had time to parry. Sweat poured from his feverish brow and the hair behind his ears as the fur-clad huntsman came charging in, grunting like a hog.

Risgan ducked and rolled. He narrowly avoided decapitation. Mygar was playing for real stakes. He lunged in again and again and Risgan danced about, favoring defense over offense, thinking to play the cat and mouse game where the mouse avoids the cat's paws. This tactic seemed to infuriate his enemy all the more, a game which Risgan relished playing, if not for the fact that one slip could mean his death. But during the dodging and baiting, Mygar slashed the pouch at Risgan's side and all Risgan's magical relics tumbled out on the sand: his pale blue wishbone, and some beads and the lumpy dusk-colored nephrite gleaming a sultry red glow.

Risgan hissed and hastily stooped to cover them up with the black fabric, then he cursed. He rolled aside, barely escaping Mygar's blade. But the baleful, glowering gleam of the nephrite did not escape the huntsman's notice and he paused and uttered a loud oath. "What's this evil witchstone, outlander? Some talisman you're guarding for your magician? Let's have a look at it."

Risgan quickly snatched up the black fabric and stuffed it back behind his belt.

"Nothing to concern yourself about."

"I'll be the judge of that. Let's have it." He laid into Risgan, pushing him back with a series of scythe-like strokes.

It was an unfortunate happening, this sudden exposure of the nephrite, for Risgan had been careful to keep the relics hidden. His teeth ground and with renewed vigor he parried and slashed, catching the huntmaster on the side near the hip, slitting leather.

Mygar, in a fit of rage, spun and crouched low; a boot heel flicked out and caught Risgan in the kidney. Risgan gasped, almost doubling over. Ignoring the pain, he sprang in and as Mygar let down his guard, he leveled his sword tip at the chief's neck.

"You yield now, 'lord'?"

"Yield, my ass!" He scrambled to his full height, swatting the flat of Risgan's blade away. Risgan gritted his teeth, ready to run the blackheart through. But he held his composure, knowing he'd be skewered to death by Mygar's men if he attempted such a bold move. Already the chief's fiercest hunters had gathered round, grumbling in rancor, their blades drawn. Not wishing any further escalation, Risgan held up a hand in a sign of peace. "Let us call a halt to this idiotic roughhousing."

"Fair enough." The Svengali chief grunted in accord. "Enough of these puerile games. We've work to do."

Svengar and Kahel let their blades drop, huffing like stallions, neither of them likewise winning an advantage.

"You stupid striplings!" called the chief at the gawking spectators. "Back to your exercises. We've got hunts to train for." He shook a fist at the youngsters on the platforms and the others aiming at targets. "Kaergli, Minas! Take the outlander to the druid and divest him of his occult talismans."

Someone ran to fetch the hetman.

The druid watched the goings on very closely and gave a crafty nod. Mygar's men joined in lockstep with Caerlin's men to escort Risgan off the grounds. The druid followed along with an eerie relish, rubbing his wrists, a bright gleam in his eye.

Risgan decided he did not like Caerlin's druid.

* * *

Chief Vardot's men accompanied Risgan to the druid's hut, a high, conical dwelling of straw bales and mud. A rank odour assailed Risgan's nostrils upon entering: of earthy herbs, incense, old ash, and something more peculiar. A brazier hung close to the side, a hearth too, unlit and dingy. Old bags and bins of saltpetre lay aside bowls of fat and a long tableful of many talismans and tools: antlers, pincers, stones, gems, clay bowls, herbs and unguents, liquids and pastes.

The hetman, who had joined the party, addressed the outlander with a twitch of nose: "Yes, Risgan, you have been summoned here for two reasons. Barring your useless magician who has exhibited a fledgling and dangerous magic, it is clear that you are somewhat of an occultist, a man harboring magical adjuncts. As you know, spellcraft and magic is strictly forbidden by laymen in the village without my authorization, furthermore controlled by our druids, in this case, Dodonis. Hand over the witchstone."

Risgan swore under his breath. "Impossible, lord. The item in question is quintessentially an heirloom, of great sentimental value."

"Be that as it may, I must insist on the relic." The hetman nodded and signaled to his attendants who unsheathed their swords.

"Very well, lord. If I must."

"Ordinarily I would not care about this, but Mygar is quite adamant about the seizure, and seems to bear some vendetta against you. If he is to be my future son-in-law, I must contrive to keep the peace."

"It is a misguided way of thinking, but understandable, lord." Risgan rubbed his chin. Imbroglios. Too many of them.

Upon relinquishing the piece of nephrite somewhat reluctantly, he licked his lips with discomfort and stared. He unwrapped the black cloth and the talisman fell out on the table, the size of his fist, gleaming a rare glow. His heart pounded. It was a most valuable piece, dangerous if fallen into the wrong hands. He didn't realize how attached he had become to it. Perhaps the magic had infected him more than he cared to admit? The spryness in his step and extra vigor was due to this gem, beyond doubt. He hadn't experienced such freshness of spirit for years! He must get the bauble back. He felt confident that an idea would come to him.

"And this pale bit of bone?" inquired the druid, pointing to the other relic shaped like a fishbone that had spilled out.

"A good luck charm, nothing more. Surely you do not want to confiscate that too?"

The druid waved a hand. "I'll let it go. Anything else?"

Risgan shook his head.

The druid reached for it, but thought better of it. For the moment he gave it only a cursory inspection.

Wild cheers and drunken shouts drifted from the common grounds, and Risgan imagined Kahel and Jurna indulging in too much swamp-rot grog with the other hunters.

"Oafs," murmured the druid under his breath. "A waste of a life all that ale-guzzling so early in the day. You, I trust, are not of that breed?"

Risgan shrugged. "That depends on the circumstance."

Afrid hissed from her cage of thorn. Risgan stared at her with a contemptuous resignation. She had the face of a young imp and looked ever in fouler mood than before, if such was possible. Risgan instinctively reached for the sealed pouch at his side, noting the cursed nephrite hid there, was there no more.

"A wretched creature," muttered the druid.

"She has committed great sins," agreed Risgan.

"No greater than any of ours," the druid sighed. "Each man or woman thinks his sin is less than the one beside him." Dodonis signaled to his attendant. "Bring in the prisoner." The attendant bowed and left.

"Stay with me a while, Risgan. I wish to show you something."

Dodonis shifted to the table, wise enough, Risgan noted, to use gloves instead of bare hands to handle the nephrite.

A crafty glint entered the druid's eye, as he surveyed Afrid glowering in her cage. "Yes, my little witch. Soon you may yet help me in certain tasks invested upon me by Mygar—this new talisman may help along the way also."

"What tasks are these?" barked the hetman.

"Nothing which you have not already instructed me in. Only to appease his whims."

The hetman glowered with the memory.

Risgan curled his lip in disgust. "You would do well not to enlist on the witch's help. She's treacherous. Shall I expound on her deeds?"

The druid held up a hand. "That is not necessary."

The servant returned. A giant accompanied him, hauling in a captive whose head was covered in a baggy brown hood. The man, an older slave, Risgan guessed, was thrust forth heavily roped at the wrists and wearing heavy shackles on his ankles from which depended a chain in the hands of his hulking captor. Risgan had never seen a man so large and tall. Risgan stared up at him in awe, evoking the amusement of the druid.

"This is Warscax, our jailer."

The giant gave the chain a proprietary yank. "You asked for this knave, my lord?" The jailer wrinkled his nose at the stench. "You'll want to bathe him soon enough."

"To where he's going, Warscax, he will hardly need it," Dodonis commented dryly.

The prisoner snarled with hate.

"Spit all you want, Moginax. Your fate awaits you. You slit the throat of Verix, our talisman-maker. Remove the hood."

The giant pulled back a flap of the hood to expose a crooked nose and leering mouth.

The grim captive rasped, "Verix was a cheat who frauded my sister and deserved his fate. His magic power tricked her."

"No matter. It is not your call to take another's life."

The prisoner spat a wad of green filth at the druid's feet.

"Very pretty. Recalcitrant to the end. Pity. That is why you must die."

"I care little for your dogma or the laws of this society," said Moginax. "Wülv, your false god, has done nothing for me. Only dress me in filth and with rags and pile me with ignominy. I spit on knaves like you and your hetman who break laws every day, like allowing these filthy raiders in our village."

The hetman bristled. "See to it that he is punished."

The druid had no answer and looked away with a glassy stare. Risgan felt awe and pity for the condemned, who looked one step closer to death.

Dodonis ripped back the hood more now to reveal a surly face with red welts, pocks and scars. Dodonis gripped the nephrite with a thick leather glove and shifted it toward the prisoner, raking it across his pocked cheek and bare arm.

The prisoner stiffened, opened his mouth for brief instants they gurgled several incomprehensible words. He hawked another wad of filth, jumped and jerked about spasmodically, yanking at his chains. His gray hair stood on end then became a shiny brown color and his skin looked much younger and his eyes blazed and gleamed with vitality.

The druid stepped back with wonder. "The magic of youth and age. So, the sorcery is real!" He turned to Risgan with a new look of appraisal and twisted the gem in his palm to expose its lighter side. He raked it cruelly across the prisoner's other cheek. Moginax loosed a howl of anguish and stiffened and his hair seemed to grow to a lighter shade of gray.

The druid gave a sharp inhalation. Rubbing his chin, he frowned at the glimmering relic, whose mystical dusky-red glower could inspire the imagination, especially of the ambitious. "So, I must keep this object in my possession for further study."

"Have it as you want, Dodonis," said the hetman. "I'm weary of spellcraft and have no head for this magic. See to it that Risgan meets me in my chamber after you are done with him."

The druid nodded. "Very well, lord."

The hetman turned on his heel. Dodonis had few more words to share with Risgan and ordered Warscax to thrust him into a back cubicle, little more than a closet. Risgan, waiting at the door, gnashed his teeth in fury, trapped as he was in the dark. He heard many grunts and howls and pleas. A flapping and scuffling, as of vials and pots tumbling off the table. He winced. Some time later, the door jerked open and the druid stood akimbo, lips parted, hair askew and his chest heaving. The hooded figure lay slumped in a heap and Risgan feared he had killed him with his liberal application of the nephrite's magic. "I have no further need of you," the druid said. He gave a brisk flourish and signaled to the jailer. "The magic is alive and well. Take him back to Vardot."

The Caerlin guards escorted Risgan to the hetman's longhouse near the communal hall. A break had been called from the early training session, for several of Mygar's men loitered about the communal grounds, plopping apples in their mouths from the dinner barrels or ogling the Caerlinean women. Risgan waited in impatience before the hetman's door. The sound of angry voices ensued, slipping from under the cracks.

"Mygar comes from a powerful line of warriors," said the hetman. "His family lineage is on the Herstag side of the wolf. I have promised you to him."

"It is ridiculous," came Arcadia's voice.

"I have promised you to him...to keep safe the clan and peace in our land."

"Then you're a bigger jackass than I assumed. They make a mockery of our customs, Father, camp next to us with their boors and motley clot of wild animals, and even harry us, goading us on their hunts. Do you think they'll stop at me, Father? He'll demand more and more of you—until you have nothing left."

"Perhaps, but I know of no other way at the moment. You do

need to marry."

"It's Lokbur I love," she cried.

"Lokbur?" the hetman snapped. "Forget him. He has good intentions but can do nothing against Mygar's mettle. You saw what happened to him today."

"Why don't you fight him? Are you that cowardly?"

"And be cut to ribbons? Is common sense stupidity? He has too many wild men. He watches us like hawks. We aren't what we used to be, Arcadia."

"Then let us train, Father. We'll trick him, ambush him."

The hetman's weary grunt came back as a muted hiss. "We've been through this before, Arcadia. I admire your spunk, I really do, you have the fighting quality of your ancestors in your blood, particularly your mother's. But it's not enough. We can't win this war." He sighed. "It's a shame Malcina passed so suddenly."

"Better to die fighting than to be a kept animal," she muttered. There came the sound of breaking pottery and the door jerked ajar. Arcadia stormed out, almost bowling over Risgan. She pushed past him, angry tears in her eyes. The golden arrow rattled in her quiver. "Out of my way, you outlander."

"Milady—" said Risgan.

"Go! I don't want to see anybody now, or listen to any more dogma."

After the outburst, the hetman ambled out with a weary step, running his fingers through his hair, damp with sweat. He was in no mood to see Risgan or any others and flourished a quivering hand. "Go back to the training ground. I'll see you in the evening." He closed the door.

With a shrug, Risgan hastened from the hall after Arcadia. He caught up with her, out of breath. "Milady, wait."

"You," she huffed. "I told you to go away. You can do nothing for me."

"Are you sure?"

"I'm sure."

"Milady, If I can help you in any capacity, I will."

"What can you do?" she wailed. Her face was a tear-streaked mess. Her hands thrust in her vest and fixed on a charm in the shape of small unicorn figurine which she worked in her palm. "I pray to you, mother Driadis," she said, "that you will send these wretched invaders far away. That you will guide me on my path and tell me what I should do." She closed her eyes and murmured several prayers in a tongue Risgan had never heard.

At that moment, Risgan saw a strange light in the sky at the fringe of the forest. The form of a unicorn, he guessed, the head at least, but with the body of a woman. He blinked to ensure he wasn't hallucinating. She floated up into the boughs and stood on a branch clutching a golden arrow. He blinked again and rubbed his eyes. "There!" he cried. "Look! Arcadia, a sign." And yet, when he looked again the image was gone and the huntress was striding away.

Risgan wet his lips and cast her a solemn gaze. An urge of whimsy came over him that he could not fully explain. "I have the wishbone," he blurted. "I am not without means. I will employ the magical might of this talisman to make things right between you and Lokbur." He pulled it out, pale blue shimmered, and yet, it looked an almost ordinary thing. "It is the only thing your father and his druid didn't confiscate from my person."

She stared at the talisman with curiosity. "What is it? Is it better than my unicorn charm? It seems not to work any more and I grow doubtful of Driadis's power."

A brief flare of memory surged in Risgan. He recalled the unfortunate predicament leading to his exile. The Pontific's wrath. The heat of the Lady Farella who had been at the heart of it all and who had left an impression on his heart, which he could not rid himself of.

"I acquired it at the market in Zanzuria some weeks ago. The rest I'd rather not say. They are sensitive issues."

She shrugged and turned toward the enemy camp.

"Where are you going?"

"To face down Mygar."

Risgan blinked and ran to get Jurna. The journeyman loitered by the communal well, waving his sword and trading angry words with one of Mygar's hunters.

The two caught up with Arcadia and together approached the wolf chief's hut where among others he lived with his wild band in the makeshift camp. The place was a shambles, dogs roaming around sniffing piles of garbage, some smoking heaps. Stray fires burned and crackled, over which huddled figures roasted river eel. A band of crude huts lined the river bordering on swamp; hunters milled about with their women, ragged-haired and unkempt, hints of rough song and rude talk lurking about the periphery.

A stag head was nailed to Mygar's door, the carcass given to his stray dogs to devour. Risgan curled his lip. Arcadia's mouth hung loose as the dog's muzzles tore at the meat and the naked ribs of the carcass with growls in their throats. "You butchered that stag for your own sport."

"And what of it?" said Mygar. "The dumb beasts are here for sacrifice."

"The gods will curse you," she spat.

"Not my gods," Mygar laughed. He thrust out a long arm and snatched the golden arrow hanging in her quiver. "From now on, I'll be the guardian of the magic arrow."

She gasped, reaching for it. "You can't."

He slapped her hand away. "I just did."

"It's sacrilege. The arrow is the symbol of our people."

"Not any more. I'll use it to slay these pesky isks that invade our skies. So far you've been incompetent and haven't managed to thwart the leader of the flock." He tossed the golden arrow to Svengar who came ambling up, and they both laughed.

"Take it to Dodonis," Mygar instructed. Have him ensorcell it with richer magics. By eventide of my wedding, we'll have cleared the skies of every isk from here to Bazuur!"

Arcadia turned away in disgust. She marched off, fuming while

Jurna cast the chief and his crony a chilly glare and Risgan hurried after her.

Risgan caught up with Arcadia and made efforts to speak but she jerked back in anger. "That louse has stolen the symbol of our ancient power. It will demoralize the clansmembers and weaken us even more."

Risgan gritted his teeth. "I will get it back for you."

She blinked at him with amusement. "Are you some miracle worker, relic hunter? First my love life you promise to repair then you pledge you'll return me my clan's magic talisman? Pah! What can you do?"

"You'd be surprised," Risgan said dryly.

* * *

Later that day, Risgan ducked back behind the shadows of the blacksmith's home and unwrapped the wishbone from its black cloth. He rubbed it until it was warm in his palm just as the peddler who had sold it to him had instructed him. He closed his eyes. With all his strength he wished that Arcadia might have her dreams realized. It was a longshot. Whether the magic was potent enough to fulfill such a request, Risgan did not know. He only knew that if it worked, it could save this village from disaster. He also knew it only worked if the bearer believed in the magic. He had seen it work in the hands of the Pontific's young son in the market of Zanzuria. A miracle had happened. He snickered, recalling the horrified shrieks of the courtiers as they crouched bare-assed in the market.

That evening when the blacksmith Kevil had retired, Risgan gathered close to his companions around the hearth and spoke in low whispers. "We must retrieve the golden arrow—for Arcadia and her clan."

"What, are you crazy?" Kahel griped. "Why should we risk sticking our neck out for these people? They hold us here against our will and would slay us if either of the two warring chiefs demand it. I don't know why we are not contemplating an escape right now."

Jurna looked at Risgan. "He has a point. We could probably

sneak past their scouts this very minute."

"Except we'd have to collect my relics...which are in the druid's hut now along with the arrow, and we still have Afrid to deal with."

"Sod Afrid!" sneered Kahel.

Risgan ignored Kahel's outburst. "I have ulterior motives in my thinking, Kahel. I'm thinking three moves ahead. The golden arrow is a weapon that we can use against Mygar. He's our real enemy. Steal it and we have leverage against him—then we can escape. If we try to sneak out of here, they will come after us with their horses and men and cut us down. Without it, it will be a tough road with many risks. We can kill two birds with one stone, and get my relics back."

Kahel turned away with a growl. "Count me out."

"Fair enough. Hape?"

"Me? Why me?" He looked around blankly, seeing their expectant looks.

"They will not suspect you, plus you are good at creeping around in the dark."

"What? And you aren't?" Hape was clearly not pleased with the arrangement.

"Moeze," breathed Risgan, "this time you and your wonky spells can come in handy. Pay Dodonis a little visit and draw him out. Get him off balance while Hape grabs the golden arrow." He smoothed his hands.

Kahel shook his head in disgust and walked away.

"Moeze? Are you in?"

The magician gave a silent nod.

"Good, then I will work as overseer. Jurna, you are backup. Stay here and hold the fort. Run interference if things go sour." Risgan took him aside. "Convince Kahel to help you, if you can."

Jurna grunted with a grin. "Right."

Hape sighed and made motions to creep out in the dark.

"Hape, wait—" Risgan grabbed his shoulder "—don't forget my piece of nephrite. I must have it back!"

Hape gave a crisp nod.

Jurna looked at Risgan in bewilderment. "Are you obsessed with that thing? Something unhealthy about that relic. It has a dusky look to it."

Risgan pursed his lips; his youthful hands clenched. "Let's just say, Jurna, it is more important than you think." He forbore telling him about its sinister youth-and-age magic and the hold it had on his own. There was no way to communicate such things without raising alarm.

* * *

The night was wholly dark, black as the burnt pot, and the moon, a waxing crescent, lay obscured behind ragged clouds. The communal fires had burned low and voices drifted as mere murmurs, ghosts of the night, with straggles of drunken men returning from their revelries to their lodging to recoup for another day of hunts and training.

Crouching low, Risgan crept on stealthy feet. Moeze and Hape loped after him across the common grounds past the bridge to the other side of the village where the druid's hut resided. A golden glow spilled from the open window. The druid was still up, hard at work. Risgan gave a short sigh. Perfect. He grinned. Ducking between a pile of firewood and two squared-off compost bins, he motioned the others forward. Moeze clutched his silver disc in a pale hand. He rapped on the door and Risgan ducked back deeper in the shadows.

The druid answered. "Who is it? Oh, you? What do you want?"

Moeze bowed. "Moeze the magician, at your service, Dodonis. Pleasant to see you. I hope the evening is treating you well—"

The druid held up a hand. "This is no time for a house call, Moeze. Be gone, I am busy." He moved to shut the door.

Moeze stuck a foot in the door. "Wait! My associate Hape the Homeless and I, have come to discuss business—

"What business?"

"Magic, what else?"

The druid sneered at that and cast the intruders dire looks. "I haven't time to waste on tyros. Why are you two skulking like spiders in the dark? I have an important task entrusted me by Mygar—which will have no end, and this cursed witch of yours, is not cooperating."

"You don't say? You mean, Afrid? I can help you with that."

"How?—You know her spells?"

"By heart. All of them."

The druid scowled and looked left and right. He worked his lips then beckoned. "Come in."

Risgan covered his mouth in a snicker of triumph. Hape and Moeze doddered in.

Risgan risked a peek through the window. The golden arrow sat on the table amid pots of steaming liquids and unguents, glowing a golden red. The druid had been dipping its diamond tip in some mixtures, but seemed entirely dissatisfied with the results, judging from his flushed scowl and his animated gestures. From what Risgan could grasp of the ensuing conversation between him and Moeze, it seemed that Mygar had entrusted the druid to infuse the arrow with an extended magic so that he could kill all the isks in one go and gain ultimate power over all the clans. A lofty goal. Risgan curled his lip. Dodonis was just arrogant enough to think he could pull it off.

Moeze gestured and laughed with carefree ease, showing a face of cheeky confidence. Lifting his disc, he rubbed the magical shimmering side.

The druid's face darkened in a scowl. "Put that away, Moeze. What are you crazy—"

He had no time to finish. An explosion racked the confines, blowing up in everyone's face.

The three of them went flying. Hape banged against the wall. The hut dipped, sagged and seemed to press outwards, as if the most foul wind blew through it, tousling the druid's sandy-colored hair, and rifling the straw bales and pitching him backwards. Moeze was thrown sideways.

Risgan gasped in horror as he saw the smoking hole in Afrid's cage. She staggered out, eyes agleam with fierce triumph.

Risgan gave a sharp intake of breath. Here she was, crawling across the mud-packed floor. He was about to burst in, but stopped. Let Moeze and Hape handle it. The plan would either sink or swim on its own two feet. He heard Afrid's hissing and blubbering like a baby in an attempt to mouth spells to lay waste her enemies in the hut.

"Contain that witch!" bellowed Dodonis. "Idiot!" He groped about in the smoke. The sounds of shouts and the pounding of feet of villagers grew. "What were you thinking, magician? My precious sanctuary—my herbs, staves, ruined!"

Moeze bit his lip. He coughed and lifted his blackened disc in the direction of Afrid. To no avail. The magic was spent.

Afrid stumbled out of the hut whose door now hung on its hinges. While the druid's attention was diverted, the magician's fingers grabbed at a black-wrapped object that had tumbled to the floor.

The village grounds swarmed with figures. Hands tried to snatch at Afrid. She slipped through their fingers like a greased pig. She fled off into the night. All was an indistinct blur; figures rushing hither and yon and Risgan skulking by the pile of firewood and the waste barrels of compost. He laughed when he heard the screeching oath of the druid and a similar howl of an enemy huntsman victim of Afrid's teeth.

Moeze and Hape tottered out of the hut, blundering into Risgan, soot-blackened and scratched. Risgan steered them away from the hut. Moeze and Hape were out of breath, their eyes gleaming in the dim light from the dying fire. Other torchlight brands bobbed nearer.

Risgan seized the arrow from Hape's nerveless grip. "Good work, Hape!"

"A messy night's work,' Moeze professed.

"And the other item?"

Moeze shoved the black fabric in his palms.

"Good lad!" Risgan's lips curled in exultation. "That nephrite means more than you can think." He tucked the package under his belt. "Quick! Let us bury this arrow while the hubbub is about. Back to the blacksmith's! When our druid finds the arrow gone, there will be hell to pay."

They bumped past several panicked villagers eager to discover the source of the explosion. "Hurry!" Risgan hissed.

He turned to address the villagers in an overloud voice, "There's been a fire and a terrible accident! Fetch buckets of water from the swamp. You there, young stalwarts—form a brigade!"

While the village youths filed in confusion to obey, Risgan motioned Hape and Moeze on, then trailed after with a sly grin.

Jurna was waiting in the shadows, crouched by the door. Kahel was inside snoring. "Took you long enough," said Jurna. "Well?"

"The good news or the bad news?"

Jurna rolled his eyes. "The good news, Risgan, please start with the good."

While Risgan hastily buried the arrow in the shadows back of the longhouse, Hape told Jurna in a few words what had transpired at the druid's hut.

Jurna went suddenly tense and looked left and right. "So Afrid's escaped?"

"Vanished."

Jurna sucked in a wild breath. "That's bad news."

"She—"

Risgan put a finger to his lip. "Quiet. We've not time to waste on Afrid now. Quick, inside."

* * *

A rigorous search of the fugitives yielded nothing in the morning. The obvious suspects had been ruled out—Moeze and Hape. No magic items could be found on their persons. Vardot and Mygar stood around arguing, glaring daggers at one other.

Risgan took Arcadia aside to whisper in her ear that he had buried the arrow behind the longhome and described the place exactly where she could find it.

She blinked in surprise. "Relic hunter, maybe you are a miracle worker after all..."

Risgan tipped his head. "At your service. The least I can do, milady."

Afrid was still at large and nobody knew where she was.

Kahel stood about in slack-jawed wonder, his throat thick with a derisive snort. "How far can a baby-faced midget get?"

The question sat heavily on the members of Risgan's company. They knew only too well the witch's capabilities.

After a time Mygar gathered his hunters and brandished his sword. "Move out!" he bawled. "We can't be worried about some dumb witch and a missing arrow. The hunt goes on! Be ready in a half hour."

* * *

The day dragged on. Gray skies stretched from horizon to horizon, east to west, investing the twitchwoods of Fandar forest with an eerie silence. Majestic trunks ranged to either side with thick ropy bark, trees too old to fathom, trees beyond the clutch of time. Boughs creaked to the movement of vagrant winds.

Risgan and his band were not outfitted with mounts as he had earlier hoped. Instead Mygar and a dozen of his grubby, fur-cloaked rogues forced them to scout on foot with many huntsman's bows trained at their backs as horseman kept them under constant watch. Risgan, Jurna and Kahel were prodded along as the main band rode behind them with bows trained ahead. Kahel alone had his bow to scout ahead and flush out animals while Jurna kept his hunting gear and sword for tracking, and Risgan his knife, sword and club. If Kahel tried to shoot at the horsemen, he would be quickly arrowed down. So, Risgan and Jurna made no attempt to escape.

Moeze and Hape had stayed back at the village. Moeze was still detained under suspicion of colluding to steal the arrow, Hape deemed totally incompetent at such thievery.

Kahel's dark scowl bore testament to his disgust with the whole thrall of indenture and his wish to be free of this damp, woody place. "This land and its endless salt marshes and midges has none of the charms of my eastern hill country," he complained.

"Perhaps you shouldn't have wandered so far afield then," posed Jurna.

"And what of your own falling afoul of Afrid? It doesn't count? Speaking of which, I hope that hag has wandered far and will cause no mischief?"

Risgan held up a hand. "I have no doubt she's up to more shenanigans. Dodonis will have a fine time catching her."

"You think so? I don't trust that hedgehog farther than I can throw a paper bag. Conniver's got his fingers in every pie in the oven."

"Shut up, you weasels," growled Svengar. "There's hunting to be done, not gibbering. You're scaring the animals."

"What animals?" croaked one of the huntsmen. "There's not a gopher in sight in ten miles."

Jurna knelt and felt the soft earth. Certain patches showed the outline of the hooves of stags. "Look, stags roam these lands. These prints are fresh, not an hour old."

Mygar jumped off his horse to examine the tracks. "So it is, tracker." He cast Jurna a look of new respect.

Risgan waved a fist. "Onward then. Let us catch these four legs and be done with it."

Mygar looked at him with amusement. "We'll go when I say we go, outlander. Don't give my men orders." He gave his men a curt nod. "Onward, Svengar."

Risgan shook his head with a bitter laugh. Oaf. He mumbled under his breath, then traded meaningful looks with Jurna.

The next two hours passed with fruitless return. No stags, no unicorns. Not even a measly hare. Perhaps the animals shunned Mygar's stink and and the land on which they trod? Risgan couldn't quite comprehend it. Likely it was the isk attacks of the other day that had spread a taint over the lands.

Ever were the hunters' eyes turned to the sky, dreading the swoop of another renegade isk. None came, perhaps daunted by the loss of their unlucky brethren not three days ago. Arcadia had gone off on her own again, much to the vexation of Mygar. "Where is that wench?"

Svengar shrugged.

Kahel grumbled. "This is useless. The stags are too aloof and canny today. Let's all spread out to flush them out."

"No, we go as a group," muttered Mygar. "I don't trust you rabble to beetle off in the bush—or scare the animals off."

Kahel shook his head. "At least, let us fire-flush the stags out then."

"What are you talking about?"

"What, you've never heard of fire-flushing?"

The horsemen flashed the archer blank looks.

"You know, set some bonfires at strategic places—spook the stags? Get them running out of their places of hiding, so then your hunters can take them down."

"Sounds like a worthwhile plan," one dusty horseman grunted. He rubbed his chin. "It might work."

"Of course it'll work," scoffed Kahel. "Just make sure you don't burn the woods down. Otherwise you'll have no stags to hunt."

Mygar took a breath with an effort of patience. "That goes without saying! You think we're a bunch of idiots here? We'll try out your idea, but not today."

"Why not?"

"Because I said so." He gave his head a mulish shake. "Might burn the forest down."

Kahel just shrugged. "You'd be surprised. I've seen it done before."

Mygar rolled his rangy shoulders. "I said, we'll try it out one of these days. Keep your eyes trained ahead."

Upon Kahel's continued glare and no sight of game, he sighed. "Okay." He signaled Svengar with a brisk chop of hand. "Go! Escort these outlanders. Light some fires, or whatever tricks he speaks of." He squinted at the sky. "With rain coming, I don't see how effective anything involving fire's going to be."

A grim smile broke out over Kahel's cracked lips. Risgan grinned.

* * *

The fires were set and the hunters drew back into the thickets, waiting with drawn breath as smoke drifted to their nostrils. Motion came from the nearby woods. Kahel beckoned them down.

Two stags came bolting through the underbrush. "There!" he cried. One of Mygar's men's arrows caught the fleeting shape high in the midriff. Svengar's arrow nailed the second.

The horsemen reined in on Mygar's signal and circled the fallen prey. They looked on in triumph.

"Chock that up for our count, Mygar." Risgan said with triumph.

"I might," said Mygar. "But I'm thinking that these two stags are largely a product of my men's efforts, not yours, building fires and whatnot."

Kahel lanced him a silent glare while Risgan and Jurna rumbled oaths from the depths of their throats.

Arcadia happened to gallop in on her gray mare. Her heart sank when she saw the slaughtered animals, especially as it triggered the inevitable memory of the head tacked to Mygar's door. She had lost all desire to kill animals. Her quiver was still full of arrows and her hair held a garland of twitch sprigs and a may flower.

Mygar roared in displeasure. "What have you been up to, little flower? Collecting herbs?"

That got some laughs out of his men.

"None of your business," she said.

Risgan allowed himself a grin as he cast her a thoughtful glance. Her left hand dug into her jerkin pocket. Probably fingering that unicorn amulet of hers. He didn't doubt she had been praying to Driadis more often than not. He knew the feeling, praying to gods, magical powers. His own hand strayed to his wishbone many a time and not without some success. The magic was real, though he hadn't a clue how it worked.

Ever since the attack on the unicorn, Risgan noted how Arcadia had been less keen on killing animals. Specifically, she had refused to take part in target practice in the last two days as if she had lost all appetite for blood, unlike the other enthusiastic hunters.

Only two stags had fallen to their credit. A poor showing if Risgan ever saw one. Stomping out the fires, they all made their way back to the village, practically empty-handed.

Tempers had flared upon the low yield of the day and a palpable tension settled over the group. Jurna accidentally trod on Kahel's heels and Kahel rounded on him in anger. "Careful there, journeyman." Kahel wrinkled his nose. "You reek of burnt ash."

"What, and you don't?" said Jurna.

"Quiet down back there," called Mygar. "A day's a day. Sometimes the hunt yields few fruits."

One of the hunters muttered, "We'd have got none without Kahel's innovation."

Mygar hissed and gave his head a sour shake. Risgan thought it was a sullen acknowledgment of the truth.

Tired, exhausted, scratched by brambles, the companions examined each other and their soot-grimed faces with weary scowls. Their ragged leathers clung to their skin, soaked in mud from plunging through creeks and marshland.

Risgan, dissatisfied at the turn of events of the day, frowned. At this rate it would take weeks before they could wipe clean their indenture. He planned on getting away from Caerlin before then and its breed of roughnecks. But maybe not too soon with luck like this. He fingered his wishbone and discarded the idea of using it. An overused magic was a weak one.

A fugitive form, a wispy white tail and a white and black body, eased out of the brush. He could not be sure, but he guessed it must have been the unicorn. Why was it following them? Didn't it sense the danger? He opened his mouth to alert the others but closed it once again. What was the use? These brutes would slay the creature without a moment's thought. It was bad enough to have to kill stags, let alone majestic animals such as these. At least the villagers, unlike these barbaric hunters, used the meat and hides for sustenance and clothing, whereas Mygar and his bullies would nail their antlered heads to doors and hunt them for sport.

* * *

The wedding was fast approaching and much preparation was in order: a grand feast and celebration that included dancing, drinking, various entertainment, acrobats and a new village play, whose subject matter still remained a mystery. The call for extra stags and drink was on and hunters scoured the woods searching for any game possible. Vardot could expect extended peace with the alliance of the factions so he was particularly pleased. Arcadia was not pleased and she sat with Thrulia by the fire, downcast and wringing her wrists. Risgan a put in an encouraging comment as did Jurna.

Moeze told stories around the fire of the old magicians of Romaric. A topic that aroused some small emotion, but even this did not cheer Arcadia or others like her sister. Risgan was about to ask Thrulia for a dance, but he thought better of it. Better to let her console her sister. Kahel approached with an armful of sprig and threw it on the fire, sending it crackling and hissing. A tart smoke wafted in Risgan's direction.

Arcadia waved a hand to ward off the stinging cloud herself. She leaned into Risgan, brushing his arm. "It seems your magical wishes have availed one thing at least," she murmured, forbearing to mention the arrow.

Risgan leaned over to whisper in her ear. "The item is safely hidden?"

She nodded.

Risgan loosed a breath. Thank Douran, she had recovered the arrow. He hoped it would take down many isks. "Do not give up on the other matter, milady. Miracles are known to happen."

She shrugged. "They'd better happen quickly, Risgan. The wedding is in five days. It will have to be a rather large miracle."

He turned to see the enemy chief stumbling over on heavy feet. He plopped himself down at Arcadia's side, wrapping an arm around her shoulder with an oily leer. "Arcadia," he jeered, slurring his speech. "So good to see you. Why so dour? Not becoming of a pretty maid to shed tears. Aren't you happy? Your nuptials should be a source of joy."

Arcadia shirked away as if the rank-smelling chief were the bearer of some plague. Svengar moved in to take a seat at Thrulia's side. He was wearing his usual foxish grin.

Risgan stiffened. His hand instinctively reached for the handle of his club. But he hesitated, recalling what had happened to the last horseman who had crossed Mygar.

Lokbur spoke in a frost-laden voice, "Don't you have other business to attend to, chief, like stripping hides or gutting eels?"

"Go back to your cave, Lokky boy. Your place is back there in the outhouse." Svengar laughed along with other hunters of Mygar's band who had gathered. The chief leaned in to place his lips on Arcadia's ear in an oily kiss. "Come, Arcadia, my dear. Let us repair to a more private surroundings so we can test each other's mettle before our nuptials." He laughed, an ale-ridden laugh, gross and reeking, as he placed a meaty mitt on her shoulder.

She drew back, looked him up and down in contempt. Jerking to her feet, she pulled loose of his weaselly grip. "Frankly, my lord, I'd rather bed down with the goats out in yon yard."

Mygar's face went red despite his drunken mood and his teeth rattled in his mouth. He snatched at her wrist and painfully pulled her back down beside him.

Risgan lurched to his feet and Lokbur was at his heels. Risgan reared in and smelled the grog on the huntsman's breath. "You're drunk, Mygar. Go back to your quarters rather than regret doing something foolish in the morning."

Mygar gave a raspy chuckle. "Oh, is that right? Get away from me, you puppy." He slapped Risgan back and shoved Lokbur aside.

Risgan drew his club. "I'll not stand by and see a maid's honor sullied by a conceited boor."

"You won't will you?"

A dozen figures appeared out of the shadows—all Caerlin men

bearing swords and bows.

"Very touching," said Mygar. "Get out of my way, relic hunter, or you'll regret it." He drew his knife in one hand and his sword in the other. "The wench's mine. Her father's promised me, and she'll learn respect, by Wülv!"

Svengar stepped in, his eyes darting over the grim gathering. "Come, my lord. Not the time for a squabble in our drunken states." He grabbed the chief by the arm.

"Hands off, you mangy dog."

Svengar swore. "Let it go, Mygar, none of us are in the mood for drunken rows tonight. Tomorrow we'll spill blood, and plenty of it."

"Piss on tomorrow!" Mygar spat. He imitated Svengar's whiny voice, "Blood I'll spill any time, Svengar, anywhere. You're a damned sissy." He swept off his nephew's arm and hefted his blade. "I'll go when I damn well feel it. Or do you want to play chief now?"

Svengar's shoulders drooped. Yet Risgan could see the rage etched in the scarred face and his fingers clenching on his sword with the urge to smack sense into his drunken uncle.

Moeze twitched his nose and held his silver disc close. In the blink of an eye, Mygar's face became suddenly very furry and rosy as if he had sprouted a new beard. The chief scratched his cheeks like a hound with fleas and began to bay like a dog.

Arcadia began to laugh. "My lord, I didn't know you were auditioning for the comedy hour at our wedding."

This earned chuckles among the Caerlineans as Svengar dragged the cursing, scratching Mygar away.

Risgan shook his head and patted Moeze on the back. "Good riddance, Moeze. Always a new surprise with you."

The magician smiled. "Sometimes spells can come in handy, can't they?"

"They surely can,"

Risgan's cheer was shortlived. He dreaded the wrath of the chief in the morning when he was sober.

3: The Last Hunt

The final hunt of the season was on and Risgan and his men were only seven stags away from fulfilling their indenture. All five trudged ahead through the green and silver trees, clutching bows, swords or knives while Svengar and eleven of his mounted hunters took up the rear. Moeze and Hape accompanied Risgan and the others this time, dragging their heels and grumbling. Risgan had appealed to Vardot, stressing the need to work as a team, without which they were losing out on capturing stags. It was stretch of truth, but they had a better chance in numbers at escape and Risgan had a plan.

No freshly-slain stags slumped over Svengar's or the other huntsmen's mounts. Mygar, mercifully, was absent. Only his right hand man rode with the group, the brute Svengar with the scar down his left cheek, and bared muscles with tattoos despite the chill air. The plan was to meet up with Mygar's team later that afternoon.

"Pick up your feet," Svengar growled, "we've got many miles to cover and the stags aren't going to catch themselves."

Risgan kept walking without a backward glance. His throat was parched and his belly groaned with hunger from lack of proper breakfast. All of them woke up a little too late to get full fare and somewhere lady luck had failed to give them leftovers. Somewhere there had to be some good news in all this. In the huntsmen's eyes, Risgan saw only resentment, that they couldn't ride free and full out to catch the stags.

Moeze sighed. "Even my cursory magic is failing to flush out these crafty stags." He gave a weary frown. "Why is it that every time I try to help out you people someone always grabs my shoulder and cautions me, or says, 'hey, Moeze, please relax and don't strain yourself?'"

Risgan spoke in a casual tone. "Your magic is too profound, Moeze. A master mage is not to be enlisted in such plebeian applications as this. Even that trick with the beard last evening was beneath you. You should be saving kingdoms and rescuing princesses from fierce dragons!"

Moeze straightened his back. "Yes, right, Risgan! How could I forget, and I'm glad somebody recognizes the fact."

Jurna tried hard not to cough.

Arcadia came pounding out of the brush on her gray mount after some mysterious venture.

Svengar turned and swore at her as she came reining in. "Woman, you should be back with the others! There's no solo excursions allowed. You heard Mygar, unless you wish to directly confront your future lord."

"I wish to confront no one. Unless it's only a stupid policy—I'll ride free where I wish." She fixed him a glare. "Besides, it's dull riding with you and others—my 'betrothed', for example, is a dreadful bore. All he talks about is halters and arrows and bows and swords and how much fresh meat they're going to take and how much ale he can gorge at the next campfire feast. I'd rather go off on my own. I urge you to show some respect. Being a chieftain's bride can have its perks—or can rebound on you should you displease me."

He laughed at that. "You're Mygar's whore, nothing more. Or soon will be. You'll have no status once you're under his heel."

She grimaced at the prospect. Risgan took pity on the maid. If it were him, he'd run away before marrying that lowlife, Mygar.

Ominous black dots roved high in the skies well out of range.

"Isks," groused Kahel. "There can be no doubt what's on their mind."

"Aye, scavengers," hissed Svengar. "What else is new? Why do they wait?"

"They fear our arrows, lord." One of his henchman lifted his sword. "When we are most vulnerable, they will strike."

"I know that, dolt. I just didn't give them the benefit of that much intelligence." He grunted. "Curse the thief who took the magic arrow. Now we have no surefire protection against the beasts. If they swoop all at once, we're doomed. One of us will likely die. I'd skewer the whole lot of those miserable predators with that arrow."

"Pretty boast there, Svengar," said Risgan. "Can you back it up though?"

"Quell your tongue. Let's get this hunt over. A sour feeling brews in my stomach. I like not the taste of it."

"Nor I being downwind of you," muttered Kahel. One of Mygar's hunters laughed.

The hunters spurred on their mounts, forcing Risgan and his band to lope along at a faster pace. Before long they were huffing and puffing like whipped cattle. Arcadia looked on with heartfelt sympathy. "Give them some slack!"

Svengar gave his head a stubborn shake. "Mygar told me to work them hard after last night's escapades. What is that extra quiver you carry on your back, lady?" He tipped his head in an insolent way. "Surely you don't plan on bagging a hundred stags today?" He laughed.

She examined him with cold grace. "Perhaps I will, Svengar."

One of the black-toothed men next to him hissed. "Svengar, there." He pointed—it was the same unicorn from the glade on the first day. Its slick white pelt was smeared with old blood from the isk attack. A magnificent creature, with its sleek flanks brimming with health and a golden corn proud and true on its head and wild, blazing blue eyes. The crafty beast stopped just short of bowshot as if it were goading them. Risgan gazed at it with an air of uncertainty.

All eyes turned to the slender shape poised at the edge of the woods. They were downwind of the unicorn so it hadn't detected them yet.

"That animal'll land us a pretty prize," said Svengar, "its hide and head nailed to Mygar's door."

The hunters grumbled their agreement.

Svengar gave a cruel leer and lifted bow and took aim, but Arcadia spurred her horse to intercept, a shriek on her lips. She knocked his bow arm, fouling his aim. The unicorn skipped away to the copse ahead unharmed.

"Foolish witch!" he cried as his arrow slammed harmlessly against an exposed rock.

Wheeling his horse around, he tucked bow in his saddle and snatched at his sword. "You'll pay for that insolence. How dare you?" He charged after her but she spurred her gray mare on through the woods and bolted for the open ground after the unicorn. "Ride, Spinifex, ride!" She laughed at Svengar's feeble attempts to catch her. Her mastery of a horse far outweighed his.

Svengar gnashed his teeth. "Don't just stand there, you fools! After her! I want the wench caught!"

The horsemen reined in their mounts and crashed through the underbrush. Kahel took opportunity to charge into the thickets in the opposite direction. A grunt of satisfaction rumbled on his thick lips. Risgan and Jurna took to their heels on diagonal paths with Hape and Moeze splitting between the two.

"Get them!" Svengar roared. He spurred his horse and kicked out at the huntsman's beast next to him. "Nastra, after those ragbags."

"Haha, lost your wards, have you?" crowed Arcadia back at him. "Mygar's going to skin you alive." She brandished her blade as she galloped on. "Won't be just me he beats silly," she yelled. "Which is it going to be, Svengar, the outlanders, or the unicorn?"

Risgan continued to crash through the underbrush, Jurna not far behind. The sound of whinnies and men's curses echoed on their heels. What to do? So many variables. Risgan's brain spun.

He dodged around the tree trunks, scratched by many brambles and thorn. Leaves slapped at his face. Gradually the shouts and the horse hooves faded away and he began to hope that maybe they'd win free.

Round up the others. A voice spoke to him. There was safety in numbers.

"Moeze." He hissed at a moving shape deep in the thickets. "Quiet down." He gathered the shivering magician to his side.

"An arrow missed me by an inch," Moeze quavered.

"Don't worry, you're alive. Where's Hape?"

"Back there." He pointed to the dark tangle of trees.

Risgan winced. He tugged the youth along. If only Hape didn't wander too far. There was a hunched brown-robed shape shouldering his way through the trees. They hurried toward him. He was unharmed, a fierce and pale look of triumph on his face though at his new found freedom.

Kahel and Jurna stalked out between two ancient massive twitch oaks, whose roots clung to the leaf-covered soil. They wielded their swords and bow. Jurna had no difficulty tracking Risgan and the others.

"Good, we're all here." Kahel patted Risgan on the shoulder. "For once, I'm happy to see you, relic hunter. Let's make as much of this as we can. Starting with as much distance as we can get between Svengar and his goons."

"What of Arcadia?" asked Risgan.

"What of her?"

"We should hunt for her. They'll harm her."

Jurna barked out a laugh. "They'll never catch that wild one—nor us, if we're crafty."

So they wandered through the mysterious elder woods until Arcadia's fierce mare broke out of the underbrush. Her face was flushed and a glow of triumph burned in her cheeks. She had doubled back and managed to outflank Svengar and his men.

She drew beside them. "Quick! Follow me, if you wish to be free of those rogues. They'll be coming for you and they're not far away."

Risgan broke out in a wild grin. He scrambled after Arcadia with the others on his heels. He gestured to Hape. "Come on, Hape! Move your butt."

"I'm coming, Risgan—as fast as I can."

Arcadia plowed ahead through the thickets, over brooks, fallen logs, hills, dells, brackish pools, hollows, across untouched glades, through forests older than time, ever stranger and more enchanted, always far ahead of them, and she seemed to be following something.

At last, they came to a glade deep in the forest. Risgan estimated they'd wandered for an hour or more. Only it was not a glade. Risgan peeled back a screen of vines to peer on a vast ruin of shattered pillars and a great dome-shaped building in the middle. A temple appeared somewhere out of time: a hundred feet high, four hundred feet long. Riddled with spires and crusted gems. But the stone walls were blackened with age and infested with ivy. Shrubs grew from the cracked courtyard leading up to its main entrance where a black gap spoke of a ruined portal.

The huntress drew them no farther and she sat atop her mount, staring in mystified silence. Out of breath, Risgan turned back to gaze upon her. "How did you find us?"

"The unicorn," she said in a breathless voice. "I followed it here. Why I don't know."

Risgan choked out a startled cry. "The unicorn? How?"

"None of us will know." She lifted a trembling hand. "There, that's the temple of Driadis." Her voice faded to a whisper.

"How do you know?"

"The legends speak of it. Lost. A fable." She blinked, her eyes full of wonder. A small tear glistened down her cheek. "None of our clan has ever seen it. The unicorn led us here. Our twistings and turnings so far from our hunting grounds must have led us here."

"Where is this unicorn?" said Kahel. "I've not seen hide nor hair of the animal since Svengar chased us."

The weather had begun to shift. A cold wind blew and with it, a freak rainstorm. Hail came thundering down from the gray skies, pounding on their heads, driving them to shelter under the trees.

Unusual for this time of year and the ragged company grumbled.

The sound of hooves clattered on shattered rock. "Down!" hissed Risgan.

Arcadia checked her horse and she scrambled to duck beside them. She clicked her tongue; dutifully her horse backed behind the thickets out of sight. They crawled behind a rubble of stone, some ruined outbuilding where a cover of twisted branches blocked the force of the rain and hail. The temple lurked a few hundred feet away.

The forms of three mounted riders rose from the rain mist and ice pellets.

"Of all the wretched luck," Risgan muttered. They'd tracked the unicorn or followed the huntress. Or perhaps she'd followed them here.

"I seem to have underestimated that louse Svengar's tracking skills," mumbled Arcadia, ducking lower in the dead leaves.

The horsemen drew nearer. The echo of voices sounded over the patter of rain. "Curse this falling ice," one railed. "The black wolf Wülv speaks. The gods are angry with us, Svengar. Angry."

"To Douran's tits with your fear and superstition, you fools. There's no 'wrath' of the gods. You've been duped by those pious druids. What gibberish has that priest Dodonis been feeding you?"

"They fled this way," growled the third horsemen. On Svengar's signal, they moved out of earshot.

Arcadia peered out upon the ruined courtyard and lifted a hand. "That unicorn," she hissed.

Risgan risked a glance and saw the graceful creature poised at the black gap leading to the massive domed temple. It sniffed the entrance, one hoof raised, then turned about, flashed them a queer glance before venturing into the dark gap. Why did it do that?

Arcadia's jaw dropped and she rose to gather her mount.

"Where are you going?" Risgan hissed at her.

"To draw the hunters away."

"Why? Wait here."

"No. Remember, I have a mount, and you don't."

She cut him off, hopped on her horse, and clicking her tongue, urged Spinifex out in the rain, a short canter in the ruined courtyard.

Risgan shook his head. He saw the horseman clacking closer. "Stupid girl. She'll get herself killed."

"If she wants to sacrifice herself—"

Risgan waved Kahel to silence.

The voices drew nearer.

"They came along this side path. There's somebody lurking about," grunted one of Svengar's horsemen.

"I can see that, monkey-brains. Their mud prints are plain, but there's a jumble of them that disappear in various directions. But they seem to lead to—Look! Well, I'll be a flying monkey. That vixen bitch huntress. After her!"

Risgan squinted through the screen of vine-covered trees and caught in the daze of the moment, he watched Arcadia clatter over on Spinifex and disappear into the ruined temple. Svengar and three of his horsemen whipped their horses hard and Risgan groaned in dismay. They waited tensely, expecting her to come out of the side, but saw no movement. All was dead still, everything too uncannily quiet here in the lonely wilds.

Risgan swore. "A trap. She's trapped! I know it. We can't let her fight them alone, Jurna. Svengar's in a murderous rage. He'll kill her. You saw, she lost him his prize, the unicorn."

"He's right," murmured Jurna.

The freak hail storm had changed to drizzle. They clambered after her, like weasels, through the wind and rain, across the courtyard of stones and weeds poking up through the cracks, the witch shrub with wild purple flowers. Kahel shook his head, wondering aloud at the folly of women.

Jurna ducked inside the jagged black gap, then Risgan. Hape clambered in next. Moeze gripped his silver disc and Kahel shouldered him aside, moving into the half darkness like a thief in the night.

A thin, watery light streamed down from broken casements, notched squares cut in the stone. Even in the dimness, Risgan perceived the presence of spirits here beyond the ken of human understanding. The place was overgrown with weeds and choke vine. Tendrils had broken through the floor and curled up the walls.

They wormed their way forward on their bellies, hardly daring to breathe.

Crumbled pillars ranged around them, forming something of crude circle. Elsewhere the stubs of three rows of ruined inner pillars rose. In between the tallest foremost, a cracked statue of a unicorn stood rearing on its hind legs. The effigy was awe-inspiring, if not scary. An altar, some low slab of marble propped up on carved unicorns' legs, rose out of the splintered stone like a monolithic ghost of the past.

This cavernous space was huge and littered with broken masonry of sublime and eerie design, half-broken statues of leaning pillars. At one time the place had been beautiful, a work of art, with magnificent paintings on the walls and designs carved in the domed ceiling, but these had all cracked or disintegrated, or lost the battle to vines over the ages. A pool of water lay in the centre, investing the air with a musty smell. The rustle of rats bristled in the gloomy distance.

Risgan stared on high, trying to make sense of the dim shadows. Giant statues of unicorns and half unicorns with human bodies lined the upper galleys. A stair had once given access to the tiny, vine-shadowed windows on high, but it had long disappeared, crumbled to ruin and lay toppled in stony desolation. No way of getting up to those windows to pluck the gems that to a relic hunter's eye would be worth a rare fortune.

An agonized snorting alerted him. In the near distance they discovered new horror: Arcadia's horse, Spinifex lay sprawled in an pitiful heap. Evidently the mare had slipped on the shattered tone and broken its hind leg.

Where was Arcadia? The animal, still wheezing and struggling, would have to be put down.

Shouts and the clack of steel echoed from within. *The huntsmen.*

"Come!" Risgan snarled at the others. They picked themselves up from their bellies and raced after.

There before the altar four figures loomed.

Risgan held up a hand and crept closer, urging his comrades to stealth.

Svengar brandished the golden arrow, plainly wrested from Arcadia, and his two henchmen pinned her against the wall. She looked lost and defeated, her hair tousled and a bright red welt across her cheek where she'd been struck. Her arrow was snatched again, at the mercy of these ruffians, and her horse lay mortally wounded.

"Let's have some sport with the woman before she's wed to our 'lord'." A mean-eyed lout gazed at her, licking his lips. "She looks a tender morsel. No one'll know, and I'll make sure she doesn't talk, won't I, mistress?"

"Get away from me, you pig!"

A faint smile tugged at the corners of Svengar's lips but he scowled. "It's a pleasant thought, Burkit, but I'm not in the mood for such rompings, especially in these dank precincts. Such an unpleasant environment. God, I hate these holy places, especially moldering ones. Though I'd like to see her punished and humiliated, if not cowed for losing me that unicorn. Strip her!" he ordered.

"With pleasure, lord." The mean-eyed man leered and ripped at her jerkin and bared a breast while the other held her.

Svengar sneered. "Where's your unicorn god now, lady?"

"How about here?" Risgan looked down at them cheerfully from the altar. He'd crept up behind it and crawled up the back. "I'd wisely suggest you unhand the woman, Svengar, and step back slowly, unless you wish my bully-boy archer here to lay you full of wood."

Kahel stepped out of the shadows with his bow and Jurna at his side, broadsword brandished. Hape and Moeze were next to appear, Moeze's silver disc whirling.

The hunters growled and froze. Arcadia twisted in her leather and covered herself up.

Svengar whirled about. "You? Outlander. I have bones to pick with your mangy hide." He nodded to his henchman. They did nothing to obey and he growled a gross insult to let Arcadia loose. She stumbled past Svengar and lurched, reaching for the arrow, but he pulled it back at the last second and leered at her. She spat in his face.

She came running toward Risgan, on the verge of tears. Risgan grabbed her and held her in his arms. "There, are you hurt, milady? Moeze, see to her!"

Risgan signaled to the journeyman. "Jurna. Divest these cretins of their weapons."

He gave a cheerful nod.

"Milady, you are hurt."

The huntress clutched her left arm and shoulder. "'Tis nothing, Risgan. Those brutes, I thought they were going to—to—"

Another echo clanked from down the hall. Horsemen by the clatter of their hooves. The members of Risgan's company crouched, tensed.

Svengar grinned. "Well, relic hunter. Your move. It seems matters move to a new condition. What will you do?"

Risgan thought fast, his eyes darting right and left. Even as they did, some horrendous sliding of stone came to his ears, like fingernails dragging across an endless chalkboard. A massive stone fell, creating a booming echo, blocking the entrance and much of the light with it, plunging them in deeper gloom. Dust billowed and men shrieked.

Svengar and his men bolted. Bedlam broke out in the half gloom.

Risgan hissed. There was no mistaking that hulking form, walking his black mount. *Mygar.* Two shadows and more followed him. Horsemen. Others crept behind him at his heels.

But the crashing boom? Mygar or one of his henchmen must have triggered an ancient snare. Risgan and his allies grimaced and crept for shelter. Now they were all trapped in this preternatural temple of some ancient goddess.

Risgan rallied the others with silent gestures and he ducked behind a rubble of a fallen pillar with Moeze and Jurna at his side, checking his breathing, daring not breathe. He didn't know where the others were, he just hoped they would stay quiet and keep out of sight.

He heard Svengar hissing to Mygar in the gloom. "So you found us."

"Not hard to track your blundering trail."

"You know of this place?"

"I'd think some foul crypt or temple to their pansy-faced god. How do I know?" Mygar's eye roved to the arrow Svengar clutched in his hand. "Where did you get that?"

"Arcadia had it on her."

"Arcadia?" Mygar blinked. "What do you mean?"

"She was here, and is still lurking about somewhere. I tore it from her grasp before—"

"Before what?"

Svengar licked his lips. He looked away.

"Damn you, you stupid oaf. You let her escape?" Mygar leaned over and smacked Svengar hard on the mouth.

Svengar whipped his head back, wiping the blood from his lip. "You're getting good at those pot shots, Mygar. Even for one who struts around like some lumbering animal who can't even control a few weakling clansmen."

"Careful there, Sven. You're treading on thin ground."

"And so what if I am? Those ragbags stole the arrow from right under your nose. I got it back. Now they are laughing at you."

"Where are they?" the chief snarled.

Svengar flung up a hand. "Here somewhere with the girl. The same grubby thieves who you let live. Mr. Big hunter and chief."

Mygar's eyes kindled with wrath. "Svengar, you're an ungrateful cur. I gave you everything! That title. That horse, loyal men and command, and what do you do, you mock me?"

Svengar's face twisted in confusion, perhaps regretting his words, but the ball had rolled down a slippery slope and there was no stopping it now.

Yet Mygar was distracted and his eyes rolled with greed at the sight under the vine-covered stone. Serpentine was embedded in the altar, a deep jade hue. Such was worth a fortune in the open markets of the cities.

"Burn this place!" bellowed Mygar. "Loot the altar, carve out those emeralds. I want them now!"

"But lord," spoke one of his men, "the jewels have lain here for an age. No one has taken them. Perhaps they are cursed."

"Shut up!" Mygar swatted him away. "Take them and be gone. Driadis be damned. We'll ride to Caerlin and burn that bloody pigsty to the ground. Stupid traitors."

A sinuous shape suddenly rose from behind the vine-covered altar, glowing a pale luminous blue. A slender figure rose from the gloom in a swirl of misty gray cloud, wearing the head or headdress of a unicorn, but having the body of a woman, nude to the waist.

"What sorcery is this?" cried Mygar in a brassy tone. The horses bolted, spooked by the apparition.

Svengar laughed. "So, Mygar, are you going lame on us? It's the druid's work, this ghostly spook. Or that incompetent magician's."

"Moeze?"

"None other. Last time he was skulking about the druid's hut accused of being accomplice of the thievery of the arrow—Now he's here. Though how that nitwit conjured this up is beyond me."

"His magic can still kill." Mygar stared fearfully at the hovering apparition.

"He couldn't burn himself out of a paper bag. Him or his puerile pyrotechnics."

Svengar's eyes bulged white and he clutched his throat and bent over double. His two men recoiled, grimacing. The goddess rose, or rather the unicorn who was the goddess rose, a luminous avatar that cast cold unicorn eyes upon the villains before her.

Mygar sneered. "Out of a paper bag, eh, Svengar? You silly fool! There's magic here at work. Look at it. And you've insulted the gods."

Svengar wrenched himself out of the invisible grip clutching his throat. He choked on his tongue, gasping for air. "Wizardry!" he croaked. He clawed for his sword. "Search this place. Flush out the magician." His head turned. A sudden motion came in the dark. "Ah, there he is. Lop off his head."

Risgan gave a warrior's cry and surged in, smiting Mygar's men. Moeze was on his heels, his silver disc shimmering.

"A barrel of mead to the man who gives me that magician's head," cried Svengar, "served in fresh blood!"

Risgan's club thudded against the fur-cloaked hides of his enemies. Jurna was at his other side. Kahel drew the string on his trusty bow and plugged arrows into the fray while Arcadia faced off against Mygar's closest hunter.

"Ah, my little flower," called Mygar. "You are here. I was beginning to think Svengar a trifle mad."

Arrows flew at them but Moeze's spinning disc cast a warp on the air and caught the arrows in its glowing swath. Risgan's heart stopped as one curved aside, aimed for his chest. While the men stood stunned, Hape ran up behind them and conked them on the head with rocks.

The battle raged; men died and cried out as blood splattered the crumbled altar of Driadis and ran thicker still. And still the goddess floated on high like a nimbus of wonder, as if reluctant to intercede in the petty squabbles of foolish mortals.

Svengar gained control of his senses and fired the arrow; it missed Risgan's head by a hair—the relic hunter could still feel the wind of it—as it ricocheted off the gray stone behind him and smashed some hanging stone projection. It must have struck some lever, for a strange grinding sound echoed in the hall. The floor underneath the fighting figures jerked sideways; everyone was knocked off their feet.

True to its enchanted form, the magic arrow came sweeping back along its rainbow arc and began its descent back to the bearer. Svengar lay nose first on the cold, moving stone, his face a ghastly grimace as the worst was yet to come. The arrow's light illuminated the ancient hall in multi-colored clarity. All saw the floor slide back, as if by magic.

Risgan teetered on his heels, swaying, catching at the last minute the edge of floor, as the stone opened up underneath him. Hape and Moeze jumped to safety, grabbed an arm each and hauled Risgan up. He lay there gasping beside Arcadia and the others. Mygar and his henchmen plunged down in the pit with the wails and groans of Svengar and the last survivor in his ear. Two had cracked their skulls on impact.

The survivors gasped as one of the horses fell too, breaking a leg on the floor of a great rectangular pit, fifteen feet deep of sheer sides. They untangled themselves from a knot of arms and legs and blinked; Svengar crouched, shaking his head, snatching at the magic bow that lay at his side and fitting an arrow in its strings.

"What is it?" demanded Jurna in puzzlement.

"I don't know. Some pit. Arcadia?"

"Never seen anything like it," she murmured.

Risgan cautiously peered over, only to see the glint of the magic arrow of Svengar's aimed his way. He pulled his head back. The arrow shot up and whizzed by his ear to smack somewhere else up on the ceiling. Risgan swore. It came arching back into the pit, its diamond tip unscathed.

"That thing's dangerous."

"Rotten losers," Jurna grumbled.

"Let's kill them all." Kahel gripped his bow and drew near the edge of the pit in a bent-kneed crouch to peg off Svengar.

"Wait! I'm sick of killing," cried Arcadia. "We've done enough killing." She stepped in front of Kahel, blocking his shot. "It's a miracle any of us are alive. Only the fruits of the goddess's work. I've been praying to her. Perhaps that's what this is all about. Maybe this is what she's planned for them."

"What about the arrow?" snapped Jurna. "It's down there with those scum."

Arcadia pinched her lip. As much as any, she was reluctant to let the arrow go. It seemed that a war of wills passed within her.

Jurna gestured. "I tell you what you do, huntress, let them starve down there. Come back in a month or two and get your arrow. Then they'll just be a bag of bones."

She wrinkled her nose at that. "It's a gruesome idea."

A curse came from below, as of acknowledgment of the idea.

Risgan looked down and ducked at the sight of Svengar pointing the arrow up at him. He rubbed his chin, racking his brain for a solution to the problem.

"They deserve nothing more than to suffer a cruel fate," rumbled Kahel.

Mygar shook his fist up at them. "We can pick you off all day!"

Risgan shrugged. "It's your call, mistress."

She bit her lip. "They'll stay here. I'll send for some horsemen at a later time, if I feel pity in my heart."

"If we can get out of here," Moeze pointed out.

Kahel shook his head. "I still say we should kill them." He crept over to the edge, dipping back with a growl. "We have the high ground. I can peg Svengar off from up high."

Risgan pulled him back. "No. Arcadia's decided."

"You're a fool, Risgan."

"Well, I've lived this long."

"One day too many, I think."

Mygar clashed his sword against the wall. "Shut up you imbeciles and listen. Help us out and I'll show mercy. If not my men will come and kill you all—even you, milady, for my patience is not inexhaustible."

Risgan looked down at him coldly. "Let them cool their heels in that crypt. Might teach them some lessons in cruelty."

Mygar bellowed, "You'll pay, you filthy outlander. I'm going to tear you limb from limb with my bare hands, even if I have to rip every stone from this damn dungeon." He leapt, purchasing for handholds, but only slipped back.

Jurna gave his head a sad shake. Moeze studied the three prisoners with a philosopher's curiosity, as if wondering how such an intricate predicament could have been orchestrated. Risgan pondered no less the intricacies of fate.

They made their way to the entrance, only to find it blocked, as Risgan guessed, by a massive slab of stone jammed tight to the edges with no chance of moving it or squeezing around the sides. It was in the shape of a unicorn goddess, fallen headfirst from on high. The horn had pierced into the flagstones, effectively pinning it in place.

Risgan looked left and right. "Where is the unicorn?"

The men stared at each other dully. "We've not seen it."

"But you saw it come in earlier, did you not, luring Arcadia into this dank place?"

No one had an answer. Arcadia just looked away with a puzzled frown.

They passed the wounded mare, snorting and thrashing on the cold stone and Arcadia knelt to console Spinifex until she could bear it no longer. On a heart-choked nod to Jurna, she looked away as Jurna ran it through, putting it out of its misery. The young huntress clasped hands to mouth and wept.

* * *

A solemn mood fell over the companions. Hating to see the huntress cry, Risgan inclined his head in the direction of the back of the temple. "Spread out," he whispered. "Hape, you take Moeze down that way and see if you can find an alternate exit. I'll console her." He turned back to the others. "Jurna, Arcadia, let's go this way."

He put a hand gently on her shoulder and guided her away from her dead horse. "Milady."

She wiped away a tear and snuffled, brightening as she pulled back the vines that covered the broken pillars and stared entranced at the rows of script carved there. "Look, there's more writings on these walls."

Risgan frowned.

Shattered tablets lay in a pile at the foot of a small shrine flanked with marble unicorns on their hind legs.

"This is the craft of the old gods," Arcadia murmured. "Driadis and Argonos whom we used to worship until the warrior druids came and infected our tribe and forced us to worship their gods."

Rows of animals were inscribed on the ancient walls, at one time dyed with pigments of various colors: unicorn, deer, fox, bear, wolf, raven, stags—all in communion with the goddess in the wilds.

"That old script conveys the lore of the animals—the unicorn, wise and compassionate, the bear strong and true, the wolf sly and mysterious. All are sacred to the forest and play their part in the overall scheme. To kill them, especially the unicorn, is a sacrilege."

"What of wolf furs and the leather that you wear?" jibed Kahel.

"Maybe the wolves should shear men of their hides for use as rugs for their cave dens, I think."

"It's an interesting concept," mused Risgan.

"Look...on these tablets are written the teachings of Driadis the Great."

"How do you know?" grunted Jurna.

"I studied the scripts. My mother was adept before she died. She imparted me the gift."

"What does it say?" Jurna asked.

"It says, 'Seek virtue in kind hearts. Forgive the wounds your enemies have inflicted on you, though they will never be your allies.'"

"Right," Kahel snorted, "like anyone's going to forgive that scum Mygar and his gang. Does it say we should maybe give the brutes a charity hug for all the woe they've caused you and your clan?"

"Enough, Kahel," said Risgan.

Arcadia laughed. "You have a way with words, Kahel. I'll give you that."

Risgan paced back and forth, seeing no solution to their dilemma. His pacing brought him past the endless rows of figures and script and closer to the altar and his fingers instinctively reached for the wish bone in his pouch. He closed his eyes, rubbed the pale bluish bone and wished for a miracle.

"Staring at a miserable altar isn't going to help us, relic hunter," muttered Kahel behind his back.

Risgan nodded and turned with grim resolve, forcing a tight

smile, almost tripping over the thick vine that crawled across the floor. "More of Mygar's horsemen may be lurking about the shadows and it won't take them long to find us."

"They can't get in though, can they?" Jurna pointed out.

"If they do—"

At that instant the altar trembled and a pale blue form rose again, its luminous glow lighting the ancient stone. A slender woman garbed in leathers of the hunt rose this time, but with the same headdress of a unicorn.

They stepped back with croaked murmurs in their throats.

"Goddess!" Arcadia gasped. She immediately dropped to a knee and bowed her head.

The luminous figure nodded and lifted a pale hand. "Child, do not flee, there is nowhere to run." Risgan blinked and stopped dead in his tracks.

The head turned to gaze upon Kahel and Jurna who had raised bow and sword at her shimmering form. Slowly the weapons hung slack in their nerveless hands. Moeze approached and stood pinched-lipped. Hape was at his side, his mouth hanging speechless. Risgan sniffed and licked his lips, his mind in a turmoil, a flurry of thoughts racing down shadowy corridors.

The disembodied voice spoke, "The huntress and the outlaws have finally teamed up. I'm glad of that."

"Wh-what do you want?" Arcadia asked.

"I want nothing. It is more, what do you want?"

" I—I really don't know."

"Isks haunt the skies and you don't know? The power of Driadis wanes in these dark days, and you have no desire?"

"Goddess, I—"

"No need to backpedal, Arcadia. The isk is the dark minion of Wülv, you know it, child—an instrument of terror, rapine and bloodshed, and the embodiment of cruelty. Spawned in the underworld itself, through the devotion of ignorant worshipers who don't know what they pray for. The unicorn, the splendid avatar of

Driadis, is ever pure, protector and healer that watches over the forest and its innocent denizens. Anyone who reveres the unicorn is brought luck and prosperity. So it is taught by the priestesses of the old ways. Those who go the way of the isk and worship death are rewarded with blood and pain—like those wild huntsmen who languish in the pit, the ones you fear and the ones whom you fight."

Arcadia stammered. "But—"

"You abandoned your old gods, the Driadis whom your mother showed you at age six. That is why your sacred arrow has been snatched from you and even now lies in the clutches of your enemies."

"But, I had the arrow," she protested.

"By whose grace did you have it?"

Risgan recalled the strange light in the trees back in Mygar's camp and what had prompted him to win back the talisman. He stifled the rasp in his throat that grew to an ache of sadness.

A tear raced down Arcadia's cheek. "I didn't abandon you, goddess, I swear. I say a prayer to you every morning!"

"And that is why I protect you, child. Never fear, the others who worship false gods will fall prey to isks and worse. Close your eyes and dream. All of you!" She gave a gentle command, soft but firm.

Risgan felt his head droop. After a short time and a sharp breath later, he dreamed he was in a lake, swimming with a raven-haired beauty of such enchanting presence as to make his breath catch. She dove with ease into the clear water; he followed her with strength and speed, kicking and diving deep, and they visited many fabulous underwater realms: kingdoms of coral and seaweed and stone. A million years seemed to pass in the blink of an eye. Risgan yearned to kiss the fabulous maid and learn her secrets and she turned about with brazen energy, a challenging smile, a fluid heat, and their lips met for an instant, only an instant, then he was whisked back to the present, this strange, fey hall of the goddess, and her unicorn statues, left still feeling wet and damp with seaweed on his skin and the sultry press of the maiden's warm lips on his.

He wiped his mouth and licked his lips, yearning for that moment when he could still feel the sweet damp taste of her.

The presence of the floating goddess was so peaceful that he wished he could dwell here forever. But that was impossible, and he was snatched back at the sound of a familiar voice.

"What in Douran's name?" Moeze snapped out of his trance, blinking in astonishment. "What was that all about? I recalled being in a horse-driven carriage. My father had given me a strange toy—a wondrous, fabulous unicorn! All white and gleaming of polished porcelain. A magical thing, some curio from yesteryear. It captivated me and I grew up wanting to be a magician. How crazy is that?" He shook his head, as if not knowing what was reality or fantasy. "I've heard it said that sprites can ensorcel a man's mind in the forest, but…"

The goddess smiled at Moeze's evident bafflement. "Yes, Moeze, they can. What would you like it to be—real or imaginary?"

For once, Moeze was at a loss for words. His silver disc sagged in his hand.

Hape murmured, "And I was in a bower aside a pool of water amid the trees of my childhood, surrounded by great animals of the forest—bears, wolves, tigers and lions."

He shook his head in wonder. "Parts of it didn't make sense, but then a weird feeling came over me as if I awoke from a poignant dream."

"We all experienced some wonder," admitted Jurna.

Yes, all of them had been whisked off to some place or time in their past, thought Risgan.

Kahel grumbled, "Nothing but sorcery. Tricks of the mind," he refuted. "This unicorn woman before us isn't real. Just an apparition." He turned to Arcadia. "Say it, huntress, what fiends of imagination did the magic pull up for you?" But Arcadia would not talk. She only wore a puzzled expression, as did Jurna. Both were so moved by the experience that they looked away from each other and would not share their experiences.

"Goddess, you confuse me," Arcadia began. "I hew isks, and even hew men and spill their blood yet you ask me to be a 'protector'? It makes no sense to me." She clutched at her brow. "My head reels with the discord of it all."

The goddess shimmered and showed a kindly face. The unicorn horn on her brow shimmered and her eyes were bright. "It is not an easy thing to grasp, child—the cycle of life and death in this strange, violent world is ever complex. Even the greatest philosophers have come to no reasonable conclusions. They shake their fists at the gods and curse fate. But it is not fate—it is destiny. Only this can I say: while you are hunter and warrior, you must fight the moral fight and kill when the need arises. While you are protector, you must protect the weak and just causes, as your heart guides you to."

Her form began to fade.

"Riddles and maxims," grumbled Kahel. "What are we but just playthings to the gods?"

Arcadia wailed and beat her fist on the altar. "Wait, goddess, wait, how can we escape this place?"

"In my home you are always free, child. *Follow the light and the secret way out will reveal itself to you.*" She shimmered and faded and no more.

Kahel jeered. "Don't make it too easy for us, goddess."

Risgan sighed.

"One thing for sure," intoned Arcadia, "I will protect the ones worth protecting more than ten times the amount I kill!" Her voice echoed with the thunder of defiance.

Risgan nodded his approval. "'Tis a good plan, milady."

Jurna consoled her with a rough pat on the shoulder. "If it means anything, huntress, I think that's what the goddess was trying to tell us."

"But what does she mean, the secret way will reveal itself?" muttered Moeze.

"Don't look at me," Jurna hissed. "Maybe time to put some of your fancy pyrotechnics to work here?"

"Oh ho." Moeze lifted his nose in the air. "When you're in a bind, you solicit my expertise. Forget it, Jurna. Every other time you've rebuffed my services as if they're a plague of ages."

"That's all in fun," the journeyman persisted. "No time to get uppity, Moeze. One of your firecrackers will do, just bust a hole in—"

But Moeze had already stalked away.

"Magicians!" Jurna threw his hands up in exasperation.

"Forget him," Risgan bawled. "We need to find another means." He pulled Jurna and Hape aside and whispered in their ears. "Hape, you're a rat, good at quarrying and burrowing and finding hidey holes and secret exits and tucking in for places of the night. Find us a way out of here."

"Right."

"Jurna, you help him. I'll take on Moeze and Arcadia and try to talk some sense into our magician."

"Follow the light…follow the light," came Moeze's echoing voice as he mused. "What could that possibly mean?" He tapped finger to lip.

Hape caught up with him and tapped his shoulder, "Well, the only light is coming from those windows."

"True, true, and what of it, Hape?" Moeze bit his fingernails. "How to get up there? The staircase to the upper gallery is crumbled, you can see it as well as I, and it's a good thirty feet up."

Risgan huffed. "Hey, I thought we were going to split up and try working in groups?"

They ignored him. Kahel grunted and shook his head. "Even if we could get up there, Moeze, how would we get down? We'd break our ankles jumping that distance down to the courtyard."

Arcadia gave a despondent sigh. She plumped down in the molder, her head in her hands. The others looked left and right in despair. It seemed hopeless.

Hape rubbed his chin, finger to his lip. He gazed from the wall to the rubble then to the vines that crawled everywhere, then back to the window, his eyes glinting in a sudden inspiration. "What if we could use this vine somehow. Loop it around to make a—"

Arcadia and Hape's eyes met. "A rope. Of course. Are you thinking what I'm thinking?"

"Good one, Hape!" Jurna clapped both of them on the back. "We make an excellent team. We'll fashion a rope of the strongest cords. Why didn't I think of that? Kahel, if we can tie enough of those vines together to hold our weights, then we could pull ourselves up."

"We'd have to hook it up there somehow." Kahel's eyes, narrow slits, grew to pinpoints in the dim light. "Possible. Just possible, journeyman. If we could snag it on that projecting beam up there…"

Risgan mused. "Or you could try that unicorn's horn."

"Easy," Jurna affirmed. "We could create a grapple of sorts with some of these fallen blocks."

Risgan and Kahel withdrew their knives and began hacking at the stoutest vine crawling on the walls and floor. Jurna and Arcadia twined them together.

"We need a rock as ballast, to tie the end to," asserted Jurna. "Before long they had thirty five feet of vine gathered in a coiled heap. Kahel took the end and tied it around a suitable block, knotting it tight.

Like a sailor whipping a ship's anchor, he whirled it at his waist and tossed it on high. The rock smacked into the crumbled ledge above and sent broken bits of stone raining on their heads.

"Ow, you clod," groaned Moeze. They fled, holding hands over their heads.

"Careful, already!" hissed Risgan. "This place is already a walking booby trap."

Kahel grumbled and tried again. His second attempt yielded better results.

With a grunt of satisfaction, he tossed the grapple and yanked it back at the appropriate moment to get it looping around the unicorn's horn. No easy feat. He gave it a firm tug and grinned in approval. "Not bad, if I say so myself. "Holds my weight. Any takers?

Risgan looked to Arcadia. "Milady?"

"My pleasure."

She gripped the vine and began the ascent, grunting with the effort. The vine swayed; eyes looked up and Risgan held it taut. At last she crouched on the narrow ledge, breathless and waving down at them. Jurna was next. He grunted his way up; then came Hape, Kahel, Risgan and Moeze who was afraid of heights.

The magician swayed on the ledge, wiping his brow. "Agh. Don't feel too good, Risgan. Never been a fan of heights."

"Well, don't look down."

Kahel shook his head, mooning his eyes.

Risgan risked a glance and saw the trapped huntsmen down in the pit glowering with rage at the fugitives making their escape. They shouted curses up at Risgan and his band. Risgan and the others patently ignored them.

Risgan pulled the vine rope up and fed it through the nearby window from where cool air drifted in. He couldn't help but notice the gargoyle-like realism of the nearby unicorn whose stone horn had saved their skins, half leaning over the edge of the ledge. The work of a master craftsman. This one sported wings and yearned to fly over the forsaken temple and its time-eaten grandeur like an angel. After double-checking the line was snug, one by one, they climbed down, hand over hand, to the dark puddles of the court below. Risgan paved the way, the first to stand on solid ground. He held the vine and called notes of encouragement to the others.

The sky was gray and the drizzle had abated but a chill wind still blew through the courtyard, rattling the bushes and tousling their hair.

Arcadia shivered and wrapped her arms about her waist. "As much as I adore Driadis, I'm glad to be out of her house and back in the fresh air again."

"Not so lucky our chums back there," said Risgan, jerking a thumb to the looming dome that towered above.

"My heart bleeds," said Kahel.

"Let's get as much distance as we can from here. Arcadia, we need to see you back with your father."

Arcadia's eyes lit with gratitude. They loped off at a respectable pace, their boots crunching on the shattered flagstones. They left the ancient temple far behind…though Arcadia's mood was as gray as the sky at the loss of her good steed Spinifex.

* * *

"My aching head," groaned Svengar. "Who in the seven hells built this pit?"

"How should I know?" Mygar scratched his brow and wiped away the blood that trickled down his scalp. "I should club you for triggering that trap."

"Me? It was you." Svengar rounded on him and each looked on with daggers of contempt, fists clenched, ready to bash in each other's skulls. They crept about, exploring the wall with their fingers, ignoring the third man of their party, one of Mygar's troop. No handholds worth mentioning, just some ancient cracks running far up the marble. Also a black tunnel carved in the stone wall that wandered off into illimitable gloom. The smell of rot and damp wafted to their nostrils.

Mygar poked his head in and pulled it back out, wincing with disgust. "Ew. Stinks down there. Like wet dog or something."

"Should we explore it?" suggested Svengar, studying its crudely rounded edges. "Could lead to some way outside this ruined temple."

"After you." He nudged his boot at the two dead men lying at their feet with cracked skulls. "Maybe it does and maybe it doesn't." The only other survivor swallowed the lump in his throat, the whites of his eyes little pinpricks of light, darting left and right in fear.

"How do you suppose the floor gave away?"

Mygar shrugged and gazed at the notched grooves inches from the top of the pit where the disappearing floor, the thin sheet of slate, had mysteriously slid aside. "Levers, tripwires, ropes weighted with blocks."

There came an eerie sound to their ears, like some claw or nail scraping on stone.

"What was that?" Mygar blurted. He whirled around.

Svengar just shook his head, sick with apprehension.

Another noise came. This one like a low growl. Some hellhound creeping through the dark. Mygar swallowed and shook his head, massaging his aching temple.

Mygar tensed, his fearful scowl betraying the fact he thought it was some predator. "Where does this damn, wretched tunnel lead? I've heard stories about ancient beasts, Svengar, kept hidden in these temples to punish the sinners. They'd sacrifice the blasphemers to them, then feast on their skulls during the full moon and commit rites to worship the god after the sacrifice was made."

Svengar scoffed. "That was ages ago, Mygar. You think these pansy-faced Driadis do-gooders would stoop to such atrocities? I doubt it. How long ago was it? What beast could—"

The growl came louder from the tunnel, and this time accompanied by clacking feet. Many feet.

Svengar drew the golden arrow back in the bowstrings and trained it at the black gap. He gave an audible gulp and the third man quailed at the lumbering shape of a troglodyte monster emerging from the tunnel. It was some hairy, four-legged thing with spikes protruding from a humped back like a monster porcupine. Svengar grew pale. The creature scurried forward, spider-like, with beady yellow eyes fixing on them like daggers; tusks, fangs outspread and curled back like a sickle.

Mygar thrust the rider forward. "Kill it."

"Me, lord. How shall—?"

"With your sword, you idiot. What else? Your nails, your teeth?"

"I don't think—"

Mygar kicked him forward. "Do it, man!" Svengar took aim. The arrow flew and plucked the beast in its side. It stuck out like one of its quills. Not a killing blow, the thing's hide was too thick for that, but it slowed it.

Not enough for their comrade to escape though. It hunched,

tilted its spiny back and a volley of quills shot forth. It peppered the nearest man in the chest and face. He sagged back in agony. Some passed around his body and stuck in Mygar's arm. He gave a wild shriek. Another lodged in Svengar's boot, another in his lower leg, prompting a lurid howl. As they hopped about pulling out quills, the monster pounced on the fallen man, its teeth and tusks digging deep.

While the monster devoured its victim before their eyes, Mygar took a running leap, immune to the terrible screams and the blood. He springboarded off the monster's back to grapple for handholds in the cracks higher up on the wall. His fingers clawed the ancient stone and he pulled himself up over the lip while the wrathful beast swatted at his heels. It turned its attention to Svengar. The lieutenant gasped and dodged the giant hedgehog-like creature's claws, scrabbling his way up the wall, shredding nails and flesh. He willed his fingers to find handholds within the crumbling cracks like a cat with fire under its tail.

Mygar reached down and hauled the gibbering man up before the beast could tear at his heels. The two lay panting on the vine-ridden stone. The monster leapt up at them, snarling like a rabid dog, but the walls were too high and it couldn't reach them.

True to form, the magic that bound the arrow lifted it up and out from the monster's wound to roll at Svengar's side. The hedgehog thing swatted at the stone, blood slathering its ugly jowl. Its hunger was sated. Back it crept to the tunnel, leaving the mauled carcass of the huntsman behind on the bloody stone.

One by one Svengar and Mygar wiped the spittle from their lips. They shook off the stink of death from their skin. "Let's go," mumbled Mygar. "We've lost our bows, but the outlanders have shown us a way out of here."

Svengar gusted a savage curse and began hewing at the vines with the knife strapped at his belt.

* * *

By and by, a band of Mygar's horsemen caught up with Mygar and his nephew who were leg-weary, blooded and ragged beyond recognition. They slumped by a stream of purling water in exhaustion.

"Lord, what is the meaning of this?" the lead rider called down to them.

"Fools. You could have come a little sooner."

"Lord, we tracked you—"

"Shut up, man. Give me your horse. Ride with Svengar. The others can't have gotten far on foot." His lips spread in a vengeful grimace. "There will be blood to pay and a terrible reckoning to come."

* * *

Far away in the direction of Caerlin, Risgan and the others struggled through the wilderness, over creeks, hollows and through untouched glades ringed with old growth. Ever did the denizens of the land survey the passing troupe with a feeling of strange curiosity, the great hares, owls, foxes and badger, for they felt fate hung in the balance and the woods would not be the same after the passing of these strange human folk. The isks had been ever circling the treetops, eager for blood, growing hungrier by the minute. The animals were wary of this; none could miss the baleful yellow eyes that sought the sight of fresh prey: those on foot rather than horse. Doubtless the isks had young to feed and many miles lay between them and their eyries. For the fugitives it was still a long way back to the village.

"Step it up, Hape," rasped Kahel.

"I'm moving as fast as I can, Kahel." Hape pulled up his brown robe, ragged and unkempt at the hem, trailing in the mud and the wet leaves from the recent rain.

A new sound greeted them. The thunder of hoofbeats. Risgan paled. There came with it a gleeful but vindictive promise of victory.

"There they are, lord!" shouted the lead scout with triumph. He reared in his saddle. "Just as I promised."

Jurna looked back with a growl of hate in his throat. "Now we're done for."

Arcadia raised her bow. She pegged off the first of the lead riders. At the writhing man's side, Mygar rode straight for her.

Arrows sang. Risgan and Kahel ducked and a horseman cut Jurna off and slashed a sword down at him. The blade clanged on Jurna's shiny steel. With a fierce yell he lunged in and smote the rider in the leg while another circled in to finish him off.

Moeze raised his silver disc. The talisman flared but the magic seemed to fizzle out with a raw hiss. Moeze cursed and looked at the disc with fury.

There came a rushing wind, like a funnel of disaster from the sky. In a chaos of whipping wings, the isks swooped. Like stormcrows of doom they whistled through the treetops, their talons raking away twitch leaves.

The horsemen wheeled aside, their roans and bays rearing in fright.

An anarchy of motion struck the small glade and Svengar's golden arrow went awry, catching Mygar in the leg. The chief gave a savage cry; he spilled from his mount, cursing in agony. Clutching at the shaft, he hobbled away, but was caught in the crossfire of Kahel's arrows and the fury of the isks. A giant bird, half black and half gray, landed in front of him and opened its beak wide. He lifted his sword, but the hulking creature clamped the blade in its beak, shook its massive head and flung the weapon off into the bushes.

Mygar's eyes mooned in terror. He bolted for the trees, but whatever hobbling strength he had was not enough to save him and the isk lifted wings after him and snatched at his sinewy bulk and bore him aloft. With a final wail to wake the dead he struggled, his legs kicking like a puppet dancing on a string.

"Fool!" cried Svengar, shaking a fist up at him. "See what happens when you don't kill your enemies!" Svengar was both anguished and gleeful at the sight of his uncle being carried off. His horse stumbled in a gopher hole, throwing him clear. He lay there in the wet leaves beating his fists on the ground in frustration, cursing the freak fall that had lamed his horse. He took hold of his senses and sucked in a breath. Clutching his bow and magic arrow, he grinned in maniacal triumph as a new reality surfaced in his mind.

He ran toward the knot of confusion, drawing his sword while Hape and Moeze scurried for safety. Three great isks dove to intercept, their shadows falling like lead weights over the woodland glade.

Risgan hastened in with a battle cry, smashing his club at a rider who tried to haul Arcadia away by the hair. Arcadia stuck an arrow in an isk that dove at Moeze. Crouching in disbelief, eyes blazing, she ducked a claw that swiped at her shoulders and loosed a shaft into the back of an unhorsed rider trying to despatch Jurna with a steely blade.

Svengar bellowed, "Isks take you all, fools! I control the wolf-brothers now. I'll usurp that weakling father of yours, unicorn lady. You'll become my new bride." He scrambled after Arcadia who scurried for safety after Risgan, Hape and Moeze while Kahel held the attackers back, shooting arrow after arrow into the midst of the winged horrors. Svengar laughed a wolf's laugh. "I'll break you in, you haughty—"

"Agh!" His boast was cut short as a sinister shadow loomed behind him and reaching claws grabbed his shoulders and hauled him aloft despite his fierce struggles. He shrieked once and the cry was torn from his throat. He ripped his sword from his scabbard and hacked again and again at the thing's talons, but nothing seemed to gouge that crusted bone and gristle that lurked under the hide of the elder isk.

Arcadia stared appalled at the humps of men slumping dead or twitching mortally wounded around her. Gray-black feathers floated in the air like dandelion fluff. "Wretches. Let me be free of this nightmare." In a last clutch at sanity, she stooped to seize the golden arrow that lay aside Svengar's fallen bow.

Risgan urged the others on, a great gash on his cheek under his left eye. "Leave the isks to their feast! Let us not join them." In desperation they rallied together and stumbled on through the trees, dreading to look back at that place of death.

The fate that awaited the two chiefs, dangling like wriggling worms in the claws of the mighty isks caused Risgan's heart to shudder.

Arcadia gripped the golden arrow in her hands. A sad look entered her eyes, as if the words of the goddess fled through her mind and gave her no comfort.

Ahead, the ageless trunks flanked them while an eerie maroon light filtered through the wavering boughs.

* * *

The exhausted party came to a halt before a woodland stream and drank deep of the cool water that flowed over rounded stones and down into a deep, jade-darkened pool. On they scrambled, through the sylvan depths, heedless of their wounds, fearing the return of the isks. Jurna sported a cut on his right arm where a huntsman's blade had sliced a thin, grazing stroke; Arcadia, Moeze and Hape nursed multiple bruises. Kahel had a gash over his right eye and a flap of skin hung loose on his arm where an isk's claw had gouged through his leathers.

They picked up their pace as the sun became a glimmering ball behind them and the woods a silent bastion of protection. Risgan marveled at their luck; they'd survived the isks and Mygar's attack, and the horror of being entombed in Driadis's lost temple. He also recalled the wish bone's magic and knew that it and the power of Driadis were behind them. He could not discount the enigmatic disappearance of the unicorn with the telltale blood smear on its flank at the temple's entranceway. The gloom had just swallowed it up. Where had it gone and how had it found that lost, fabled ruin?

Unless the unicorn and the goddess were one?

Moeze seemed to pick up on something of Risgan's restless thoughts.

"You can never conjure up a goddess, Risgan," he mumbled philosophically.

Kahel gave a skeptical snort. "If you're talking about that entity back at the temple, how do you know it was a goddess? I saw a shimmering apparition that could have been anything—even your magic for all we know."

"You're too much of a skeptic, Kahel," scoffed Hape. "When will you learn? You saw the unicorn as well as we did. It came back and led us to Driadis and lured Mygar there. He and his rogue lieutenant are dead, in the bellies of isks."

"All random happenings in my mind," grumbled Kahel. "Anything could have caused that."

"Oh?" Risgan laughed. "It could have been, Kahel, just plausible. Maybe."

"But somehow none of us think so," said Jurna.

Kahel just shrugged.

Arcadia nursed a doubtful frown.

On the way back to the village, as the fleeting light slanted between the swaying boughs, the company heard a soft whickering drift from the brush.

Jurna pointed between two massive twitch oaks. "Look, Kahel—your friend."

He gaped. "That miserable foal—" his eyes grew wide and shining. "I—"

The young unicorn reared on its hind legs, pawing at the air. Its deep blue eyes stared right at the archer. Perhaps a token of thanks for earlier deeds? The mother with the wounded side came out of the brush to stand beside it. It lifted its nose to sniff at the air.

Kahel shook his head.

"No need to speak, Kahel. Save it for your bedtime stories."

A slow grin crept over his hard-chiseled features. His red-bearded cheeks suddenly crinkled in mirth and he burst out in laughter: the second time in two weeks, a record for him.

"Come on, let's go," laughed Arcadia, while there's daylight about. I want to see you off on your journey."

* * *

The party approached Caerlin as the last light was fading, a much dog-eared troupe, dragging their feet and nursing aching bruises. What was left of Mygar's riders had not returned, still out looking for their master. It was just as well.

Arcadia cautioned them to silence and led the way forward. Past ghostly trunks and fallen logs. A voice called out of the shadows.

"Who goes there?"

Lokbur reined in, his sword flashing in his palm. His jaw sagged when he saw Arcadia and he leapt off his roan to embrace her. "Arcadia, you have returned!"

Risgan saw his eyes blurred with what could have been tears. Relief and incomprehension were writ there, and something else. "I thought you were dead!" he cried.

"No, Lokbur, it'll take more than a few thugs like Mygar to kill me."

"Mygar—what's this talk? Everyone's looking for him."

"They won't find him."

"You mean he's—"

"Remember I am favored of the goddess. I have Driadis behind me."

Risgan bowed his head. "Only too true. Lady, we have completed our oath to you. We've seen you safely back to your village. Now, we'll take our leave, at least before your father gets second ideas about detaining us longer. As much as we like Caerlin, we do not want to spend the winter there."

"Of course. It goes without saying." She nodded and gestured to Lokbur to let them pass.

"Hold!" cried Lokbur. He held up a palm. "A parting gift—to you all."

"But—" Arcadia shook her head and caught up with him to whisper something in his ear and he nodded and whispered something back.

Risgan and his men gazed in puzzlement as he rode off back to the village.

While they huddled in the shrubs and as violet gloom crept about them, the huntsman returned bearing something with him.

He approached, out of breath, drawing a barrow-like cart behind him, supporting a square, thorned cage. "A little surprise for you," he said with a glint in his eye. The bars had been repaired and a small surly figure darted within, hissing and spitting.

"Afrid!" Jurna smacked a fist in palm. "Now there's a sight for sore eyes."

"I found the little witch skulking around Dodonis's hut earlier today, no doubt up to no good."

"Plotting some foul revenge on our good druid, I think," said Moeze.

"Good work, Lokbur. A relief." Risgan shook his head in amazement. "Now we're spared her midnight hexing."

"She's that bad?" Lokbur lifted brows.

"Worse."

"I think you'll want to say good-by to Thrulia too, Risgan?" Arcadia motioned to the bushes behind him.

He turned and gaped.

Another figure stepped out of the shadows, biding her time while the business of Afrid was squared up.

Risgan blinked and blushed. "How did you know?"

"You think we women are just dunces?" chided Arcadia. "I saw how she looked at you. No less how you looked at her."

Thrulia's doe eyes flashed. She held up food for them, venison and a pot of ale. Her face was flushed pink. "Risgan, good to see you."

"And you too, Lady. You are looking ravish—I mean, stunning, gorgeous as ever."

She curtsied and smiled. "And you as dashing as ever, relic hunter, despite the grime and cuts on your face and arms." She sighed. "In another life I would have taken you as my husband for your noble deeds—and not only that..." She scanned him from head to toe, and let her tongue flick over her lips. She halted her scrutiny and her eyes darted to her feet. "I'm not expecting you'll be staying?"

Risgan sighed, a low sibilant murmur. He held her in his arms. Gently he kissed her on the cheek. "No, milady, this is not the time. Certain deeds need attending to, involving a gem and a price on my head. In fact, the Pontific of Zanzuria is most displeased with the way I left town. There'll never be enough miles between me and his bounty hunters."

She nodded. "I understand." Although she likely didn't. "We thank you for all you have done. You've returned my sister, ever the mischief-maker she is."

"And you, Arcadia, what are you plans?" Risgan asked.

"Now that Mygar and his henchmen are no more, Lokbur and I will marry. I'll be damned if I let my father pawn Thrulia or me off in an arranged marriage ever again."

Lokbur and she looked in each other's eyes. They clasped each other again in a warm embrace.

Risgan peered through the trees and saw the village bonfire rising higher with fresh wood and torchlights gleaming and the scurrying of swift feet as if some great tension was in the air. "What will you do about the rest of Mygar's band?"

"We'll manage," said Arcadia. "Without a leader they'll be crippled and ineffective."

"I admire your spirit, Arcadia," Risgan murmured. "Why do I get the feeling you'll be the next queen of the Caerlin people before long?"

She grinned.

Lokbur lanced Arcadia a glowing look. They kissed in another heated embrace and all of Risgan's band clapped and laughed, even Kahel, the gruff Kahel.

Lokbur lifted a stern hand; his lips worked with emotion, as if he regretted their going. Arcadia was no less moved, her throat choked up, and a tear even came to Thrulia's eye. "Go, you outlaws, you have our blessings."

The mournful wail of the hunting horn echoed through the trees. "Quick! The rest of the Svengari hunters are coming! Back to the village. Take your witch and be gone. She's an omen around here."

Lokbur nodded. "Best to sneak out now while you can at dark."

"In those foul woods?" asked Moeze.

"I admit it is not ideal, but the consequences could be worse." Lokbur gave a brisk flourish. "Take the hidden path by the river, past the rapids. Then ford it over the stones at the place we call 'Milestone's Tomb'. That will get you far beyond any trackers our hetman may set after you."

Risgan nodded. "A good plan, Lokbur. Afrid may be getting a little wet, but so be it. Farewell." Wasting no time they made a beeline for the river, with Hape huffing, and Moeze mumbling and Risgan carting Afrid in tow.

The horn sounded again, and Risgan paused and turned to gaze back at Arcadia one more time. "Mistress," he called. "You're not a huntress any more, I can see it in your eyes. What will you do?"

She hesitated, rubbing her chin, licking her lower lip. She stepped over to address him personally. "I'll become a priestess, relic hunter, not like the pious ones that serve Dodonis. But one who devotes her energies to the stars and studying the animal mysteries. I'll help protect the sacred beasts. My allegiance lies with the unicorns. I'll bring them back. One day they will wander the forests without persecution from any hunters."

"My best wishes to you," said Risgan. Now it was his turn to pause. "But do priestesses marry? I thought they were supposed to be virgins?"

"I'll marry, Risgan, never fear!" she laughed. "I'm the priestess who makes her own rules. Even against my father's wishes. I will take over his rule one day. For now we must suffer through his blundering. But his power wanes every day and he will not last long as hetman. Then I will change the ways of the clan forever."

"You already have."

Long after Risgan and the others had taken to the trees, darkness spread over the land like a gloved hand. Risgan gave a long sigh.

"That's one noble and courageous lady."

"Yes," Jurna murmured, "too bad there weren't more of her kind."

Kahel lanced them a steely look. "Are you lugs going to yammer on, or shake a leg? The moon is up and I don't want to be picked off by any straggling isks."

ENCHANTRESS OF RURNE

I

In the evening's gloaming, Taar glanced furtively over his shoulder. The tall, fern-like trees were like witches' broomsticks pointed to the night sky; the terrain, over which the stars were just starting to show their frosty glare, was unfamiliar. Dark forests and musky lowlands, so unlike his native Jinjan sprawled everywhere. Jinjan—so pleasantly graced with rolling hills, golden countryside and glistening peaks on an aquamarine horizon, seemed very far away.

The thin dirt trail that dogged his feet gave him no solace. Mischief and mishap laced its very ambiance. His well-worn boots were fire-blackened; his mulish tangle of hair fell in singed clumps, which a skirmish in a burning fane had not helped. Doggedly, he kicked at the wet dirt, full of odors, taking vengeful breaths from a dry mouth.

Lights glowed ahead: a small hamlet? A good sign. Not much farther could he tread without food and rest. For three days he had been on the trail of a crew of rogues who had murdered Perias—his master, Alassian forest monk and self-studied magician who had initiated him into the Sizocerene arts of sorcery. Over the crumbling Fallen Wall Taar had ridden and on past the deserted village of Boarspirit, finding it burned to the ground and picked clean by God knows what hands, human or not. After picking up his assassins' horses' prints, he had followed up through leagues of wooded hills and windy crow-haunted valleys. Beyond its limits of endurance he had pushed his bay where it had foundered on a hill, leaving the warrior stranded, forced to travel the rest of the way by foot.

The wineskin at his belt was empty. Darkness was upon him; the prospect of shelter seemed questionable.

The sky was a remorseless shroud showing only a plum-hazel band of cloud on the western horizon. In the fading glimmer, Taar noticed a grim raven perched on a goblin-ash. The creature contemplated him with eerie introspection. An omen of evil? Perias would have chuckled. *"Ah, Taar, you are a clever man; full of gloomy predilections and strange twists of fate. You came to me seeking wisdom, knowing that in this dark world, man cannot live by sword alone. Mage?—Sorcerer?—Monk? Ha! What are these but foolish words spoken by naive souls scrabbling after fame and fortune. Think you to grasp the Alassian philosophies? Are you worthy to master the arts, and conquer the senses?"*

Even while nursing his own pangs of doubt, Taar had assured Perias he *was* worthy—Perias who had listened with a bark of amusement. He had set a grueling initiation for his acolyte. Once the silver-haired monk became aware of Taar's keen ambition and his drive for liberation, he eventually acceded to his request for teachings.

Three years had passed. Now thanks to Perias's tutelage, Taar harbored a decent command of a few useful spells—good enough to ward off the fatal leap of a creature, though there remained a humbling awareness of how scant his command of magic was.

Knots of sorrow twisted Taar's guts. No more was his dearest teacher alive left to guide him. Now only an apprentice's devotion sent a bitter friend upon a grim mission.

He tightened his fist about his pommel. How his master's slayers would pay for their heinous act! From end to end of these cursed lands he would traipse to exact revenge!

The lights ahead grew to fangs of flame. Smoldering over the rim of a crumbling wall were thrust-up torches. As Taar approached the courtyard, he saw an empty place, unmarked by any living creature, enclosed by a huddle of ramshackle wooden huts. The smell of roasting venison wafted from under the door of the local inn, evidently the village's largest structure. The portal was twice the height of a man, made of burnt stone and green timber. He could neither see through the grimy ground-level casements nor past. They emitted only a dullest yellow glow. The misshapen troll's head nailed to the door caused Taar no great surprise: such was common in these backward frontier-lands.

The door gave way with a creak. Taar footed his way down a flight of steps and past a witch-oak beam, under which he saw more crudely-carved heads. His eyes took in a stuffy room with the logs crackling away. Around a rude hearth eight or nine figures huddled, engrossed in private amusements. Roguish-looking, thick-bearded men. A silent person sat apart, dressed in dark leather, possibly a woman, though Taar could not be sure. The figure's back was turned to him and plunged into shadow. The smell of musk-ale was thick enough to be carved with a knife. A row of boars' heads mantled the cracked elm wall behind the innkeeper, whose belly protruded over a grimy slab of oak. To his right, a bevy of iron-bound wine barrels was stacked high.

On Taar's intrusion all laughter immediately faded and a heavy silence reigned. Nine sets of weasel-eyes peered over at him, but Taar did not mind. He sauntered over to the bar, cast an exaggerated swing to the length of silver blade sheathed in its jeweled scabbard— a blatant assertion that an accomplished swordsman was present. One who would bat not an eyelid at some fresh practice.

The landlord seemed amused, leaned over, intrigued by the newcomer's heavy tread. His unfriendly gaze lingered. The dark, saturnine face of Taar did not reassure him; it told of grievous tales, as did the scars that marked the right forearm and the gash on the left cheek. Thick knuckles gripped the custom-gilded pommel of his blade. Tousled hair the color of sand ran down his neck of tanned ocher; the lips were proud and curled back under a hawk-like nose. The ashen-gray eyes gleamed with a tragic sense of adventure—with unwritten respect for the wonders of the world.

The innkeeper mumbled, "What shall it be, traveler? Goat mead or boar's blood? We don't see many strangers wandering into *Hunter's Rest.*"

Taar did not reply; the man's dialect was strange. He made a curt motion to the keg of ale. "Ale—no blood."

The innkeeper twitched his fingers. "A mug'll be two penzers."

Taar threw a bronze coin on the carven bar slab. It rolled to a halt, glittering in the flickering light of the oil lamp stuck between the boars' heads.

"Ah, a man of coin!—my preferred kind. One mug of Hunter's ale on its way."

Taar's voice twanged in the local tongue like strung wire: "I'm looking for two rogues, possibly three. Thieves. Men in a great hurry. Probably wouldn't have stayed any longer than to glut their bellies with a few scraps of meat."

"Perhaps I saw them and perhaps I didn't. What does it mean to you?"

"They have something of mine, which I want returned."

The innkeeper gave a grave laugh. "Well, that's fine and nice." He leaned over the table and put a meaty hand out to his mouth. "Hey, Roraol, Corben. Listen, this slanty-eyed Jinjan here says—"

The landlord choked on his last words as Taar's mallet-like fist shot out, grabbed the innkeeper's wattled neck and lifted him to put his head level with the up-strung boar heads. "Quietly now, old fool. Let us speak if we have something to say, otherwise let us hold our slippery tongues."

Amid the gathering, five stools scraped back. Five men sprang upon Taar; crooked scimitars and knives flashed into their greasy palms.

Taar whirled. "Easy lads. I'll take any of you, one or all if I must." He unsheathed his sword and bared its naked steel, glittering in the fire's greedy flame.

The local ruffians halted, not liking the feral look in the stranger's eye, nor the way in which he wielded the grim, silver, rune-lined sword while effortlessly holding the burly landlord aloft.

The landlord muttered a strangled croak. "You'll hear no words from me. Unhand me!"

Taar gave a gracious tilt of head. He hooked the innkeeper's leather neck-flap on the boar's tusk and let him hang there while the innkeeper's rancid boots dangled in mid-air.

The tall figure whom Taar had noticed before sauntered forward and caused the swordsman small surprise. At first glance, she was a scintillating creature in any light that Taar had ever seen. Wavy hair parted in the middle, red with tawny streaks flowing to the right, oyster white to the left. Twin dirks lay tucked in her silver-green snakeskin belt. Rising from ankle to neck rippled a costume of black leather, smooth as satin and as tight as rope, emphasizing brazen hips and taut, shapely breasts.

"I know of your thieves," the stranger announced tersely. "They are not all men. One's an old witch, and the other two are hired ghoul-men. I saw them yesterday around sundown. They were taking to the western road—to Zantius then on into Shnuor's forest when I arrived in this stinking hole of Trollnook."

Taar strode forward, incensed. "What is this, woman? Speak!"

"Patience," she said. "You'll not catch them at night. Let us sit down and converse."

Taar grunted; they took stools at a table farthest from the muttering, seething locals. Taar was puzzled, for he rarely took anyone's command so readily. He sniffed at the air. There was the strange scent of myrrh in the air about this female. Balsam also? Hickory? He thrust his speculations aside. "What of these people? How did you see them, and what makes you think they are the ones I seek?"

The woman answered glibly, aware of the burning fervor in the foreigner's eyes. "I can tell you their names. Wislox and Daig— villains from Cutter's Pond. The old crone is a changeling—calls herself Welfstang. What feud would you have with these lowlifes?"

Taar's lips curled in a sneer. Undisguised hate brimmed in his scarred face. "I am Taar, swordsman and mystic from the east. They killed my master for the Tu-Steev, a magical knife cutting through steel. I knew little of my master's slayers, only that there were three of them, by the sign of the footprints they left outside his forest hut."

The woman nodded silently. "If I wasn't already engaged in business of my own, I would go after them with you, for I owe dear Welfstang a debt."

Taar waved away the kindness. "No thanks, I must go." He rose to leave but she put a hand on his arm. Her grip was hot and strong and Taar felt many peculiar sensations creeping up his arm. He felt languorous pleasures, heated baths, scented oils, fleshy, luxurious sex . . . The dazzling clear-cut gem clasped on her index finger caught his rolling eye and gleamed with the intensity of an enflamed city. "You must stay with me the night," she asserted.

Taar's teeth flashed in surprise. "What does the honor? Surely not the beautiful scar running cross my cheek?"

"A man's outer scars mean nothing," she sneered. "'Tis the inner man which is of importance to me."

"Profound words, lass," he grunted, looking her over with growing interest, and not without some attraction. "What's your name, and why are you here alone amid these rogues? The minute I leave these premises they'll be up to mischief with you in no time."

The woman laughed, her sultry mouth a display of mockery. Her laughter exemplified as much concern for a man as would a lioness staking a herd of goats. "Let's just say that these bullies have grown wise not to lay a hand on me."

"As you say," Taar replied, blinking.

At the bar, the innkeeper's cronies were managing to unhook him from the tusks. The landlord landed with a thud on his butt bringing the stuffed head toppling down on his head. Pitching the trophy aside, he glared at Taar with malice. "Found a new friend, have you, slanty-eyes?" He heaved himself erect. "Be careful with little Sowela here; she might prove a little more coltish than you expect."

Taar guffawed. "I think I can cope with one lone girl, innkeeper. You on the other hand—" He downed the last of his ale and expelled a breath "—are hopeless. Let's go—Sowela, if that's your name. I shall gladly take up your offer, but I need some rest and recuperation before tomorrow's hunt."

From the corner of his eye, he caught a strange shimmering light, causing his eyes to drop to the glistening emerald upon the woman's finger. It tickled at the edge of his imagination, sending roaring passion up through his loins. He started uncomfortably. Who was this alluring minx?

A nameless stir still flared in his breast. The innkeeper's vindictive smirk caused him to frown as he left.

CHRIS TURNER

II

Out in the chill, Sowela led Taar west along the main road toward glowering purple trees framed on the horizon. He was surprised that she had no horse, but he made no comment. He saw the *Hunter's Rest* sign shivering in the vagrant breeze, also the stanchion from where he had snatched a blazing torch.

Sowela stopped before a footpath cutting into the wood. She pointed a jeweled finger: "It is three or more leagues west to the frontier of Danzinia and to the city of hundred-spired Zastius."

Taar whistled. "The Danzinian border lies so close?" He did not realize he had made so many leagues since the Sekkian uplands.

The swordsman rubbed his chin; his eyes narrowed to slits. "It is said that if a man keeps traveling west, he reaches the Purple Sea—a place where ships sail to the islands peopled with strange tribes amid mountains of jet."

"Of that I would not know," she commented. "Shall we go? Rurne lies this way." She lifted a white hand to the trail.

"Rurne? Into that gloomy tangle?" He gave an incredulous grunt.

"Of course? Where else?" She tugged his arm, leading him under the beckoning eaves. They left the smoking torchlights of Trollnook behind with the swordsman feeling a small pang of misgivings.

His suspicions were not without substance; more puzzled than ever was he to learn that the alluring Sowela would live in such a remote place as Rurne. Where? Why? It made no sense to his logical mind.

The trail was thin and little used. Over willowy boughs and ages of fallen leaves they trudged with the harvest moon waxing like a bloated pig. Warm mist, blue in comparison to the sallow glow cast by the moon, hung in between the old trunks, gnarled and weathered. Dank chill and moss sprouted everywhere. Spidery leaves swayed in the unholy rhythm of breezes and cool vapors coursed through the narrow, tree-crowded aisles.

Taar did not know how long he trudged with Sowela along this mysterious route, only that he ever disliked the eerie presence of the twisted bushes and the strange birds hovering over his shoulder. Like two wraiths he and his guide moved as one through the ever-thickening gloom. He gripped his sword, glanced about uneasily. Pale waist-high mushrooms tottered on thick stems and grew in disquieting numbers. Ringed fungus gripped the trees like lampreys. The tangy smell of musk drifted in the air; something more sinister too which Taar could not identify. Rotting things lying deep in hidden troll-haunted swamps that had not seen the daylight for centuries. Overhead the canopy stretched, and always did his enigmatic companion lead him with an effortlessness born of self-assurance farther and farther toward the glowing moon, which was like a gleaming eye lurking in a witch-breed of stars. While his belly grumbled with hunger, every wayfaring instinct told him that this forest was a place of lurking evil.

More primal than ever did Sowela appear in the exotic moonlight. Her hypnotic eyes seemed to wander over his muscled torso and burn like an expectant she-wolf's. Her movements were lithe and surreptitious; her arms hung by her sides, her carriage seemed slightly bent and insolent; the trees, more her secret companions than nameless items of flora, seemed to bend to her passage.

Taar's sudden desire for her flesh flashed again and the woman's seductive aura became a promise of rapture, to which he was drawn like a magnet, feeling a lover's ache for the warm, inviting woman-ness lurking beneath that soft leather. Always at the edge of his awareness was her churlish laugh, a sound enticing his imagination, while her scintillating ring glittered in the torchlight and mesmerized his waning will. Her smile was a mischievous leer, promising fey fortunes; her scent worked sensual magic on his will and enveloped him in a cloak of passion.

No longer could he withstand her fierce attraction. He made a clumsy grope for her waist but she slipped away like an eel.

"There shall be time for that later, Taar of Tumestoi—there will be time—at Rurne." Her chuckle was instinctively chilling.

Not for years had Taar felt such heated passion. The woman was probably leading him into some deadly trap, as did everything his twenty-five years of martial training tell him, but a man like him caught in a spell, was a dangerous combination. His legs dragged him forward with a force of their own—beyond logic and reason, to a place called 'Rurne'. He gritted his teeth, cursed his random fortune, and wondered what had brought him on this unearthly pilgrimage.

Long had Sowela abandoned the hunter's trail; now they marched as one through virgin forest thick with elf shrub of pale, water-beaded bark and of girth he had not seen before in his native Jinjan. He swung his torch, risked a look behind, watched beguiled as the trampled ferns seemed to rise again like living automatons, masking any signs of their passage. The trees were black as stalks in a pikeman's row and seemed to stride forward, close rank, to form a protective shield around their selected guests.

Taar shook his head. Just an illusion. He was fatigued beyond measure and depressed at his master's death. Surely he was given over to languor by the dark, unfriendly place and Sowela's bewitching presence.

The brooding arms of the forest gave way. A rounded hill stood wrapped in krall-bush and twisted conifer. A narrow path wound alongside the hill and up to an ink-stained hedge. A tower or spire, all shadow and dusk, seemed to rise skyward like an ogre's bastion over the crest of the hill.

Down the path Sowela led him, then along the edge of what appeared a dark pool, as unmoving as glass.

Taar's jaw dropped; round the hill he saw a strange sight: a jungled castle of antediluvian grandeur cut into the mossy tree-slope—whether crafted of mud or stone he could not tell, for the lofty battlements marveled the eye and ranged upon high. On the crenelations spread gigantic trees whose tops reared like dumb bells and whose monstrous roots prowled down the weathered stone like hard, ropy vine. A tower squirmed among those trees, tilting upward toward the sky, completely covered in vine, much higher than the hill itself. From its summit a single window glared with a yellow glow and wafted smoke that caught the amber bloodshine of the moon.

Who had crafted such an eldritch place? Surely not this enchantress who tugged him along so gaily, with such purpose?

Under the hill's shadow, Taar was led across an esplanade of shattered tile then under a great iron-toothed gate. Each gatepost was capped with bears' skulls and other spine-shivering skulls. Ghoulish lanterns, lit by unknown means, ranged upon an iron trellis that straddled the walkway. Taar discerned cold gray-iron stone growing out of the old gloom.

While four-winged condors fled against the mourning moon, out of the coppery shadows suddenly emerged a great moving shape bearing trident and ball and chain. The thing was blacker than black and had no distinguishable form. Taar only guessed that it was powered by some evil force. He stepped back, drawing his sword but Sowela waved a hand. The guardian, fell to submission, and let them pass.

Under an archway the two moved, past the guardian, cool as death, then out into the dark spaces beyond. Bare basalt spread underfoot into an unlit chamber crowded with dark walls and python-like roots. A flight of weathered steps appeared behind an archway, spiraling up into darkness. There were no lights in this keep and Sowela led Taar by the hand, a duty and privilege which he could not refuse.

Up and up the winding stair they climbed, with Taar's torch guttering in the small drafts, into the clouds it seemed, and the memory of the yellow glow atop the tower burned in his astounded brain.

"Since you will be staying the evening, I demand of you a task."

Taar growled in protest, "Who says I'll be staying the night. I'll not do errands for a witch!"

A scathing sound hissed past Sowela's pursed lips. "Oh no? You who hunger for my flesh? Carefully now, or you may end up like the others."

"What others?"

Sowela grabbed his wrist and pulled him along up four more steps into a circular chamber lit by three torches hanging on brass sconces. Taar felt weak, he could not resist her pull. The floor was mud-brushed stone and full of dust and emptiness save for a domed hump that covered some fiendish, shadow-haunted entranceway cut downward into the floor at a forty-five degree angle. Sowela gestured toward the passage—a command more than an invitation. Taar crept forward, more cautious than afraid.

He thrust his torch under the overhang and craned his neck to see past another rusty iron grate. There in that black pit lolled many men, though now nothing more than gibbering creatures. Sinister moans slobbered from their lips; eyes were like vacant pits, spy-glasses, grim vistas into dead brains. Gnarled, thumbless hands grasped the bars and shook. Snakes and other creatures dwelled in that rank pit, creatures which had had their ways with the men, for even now, one man was missing an arm and was tugged back by a malevolent force as a brown, wedge-headed thing slithered up his leg.

"Black demons of hell!" hissed Taar. "What manner of inhuman filth lies in here? He hauled himself back, his eyes blazing with wrath. "Have you no mercy, vixen? Why do you torture these men so?"

Sowela flicked a contemptuous finger toward the bars. "Regard all the weak fools who have failed in their attempts at my 'mission'. I keep them locked up so that their tongues won't wag at the *Hunter's Rest* as to what a delightful creature I am."

Taar made a hateful lunge. Sowela stepped aside, slapped his rugged face: a blow as hard as any man's.

Taar snarled, stabbed out a fist as such would knock a man flying to his knees, but found his arm pulled back by invisible strings. Another smarting blow struck his cheek. He staggered back, cursing. The enchantress had cast some foul spell over him. He reached for his pouch—looking for Perias's magic pebbles. His hands would not obey. His few paltry spells seemed uselessly ineffective in her midst. This she-devil was stronger than he would have imagined. Her weight and size were pure illusion. The seductive attraction pulsing in the pit of his stomach was not an illusion. Suddenly the magic cast a cold shiver up his spine. How could he harm this fair flower rooted so impudently before him?

A moan drifted from the dungeon, jarring him out of his reverie.

"Would you like to join them?" she inquired. "I myself would consider myself fortunate to be the one next on trial."

Taar shook his head with resentment. "Why not pen me like the others then?"

"I need a man of strength. A warrior, like you. You are perfect for my needs."

Taar laughed, a harsh, metallic sound. "There are many 'warriors' in these naked lands."

"Perhaps. But not like you. There is a cold passion running in your blood. One coloring your soul a black-orange, and even a green, and that is rare. I see in your aura a man who travels past dooms and pits till death calls, as it does your master's murderers. 'Tis that tenacity which I like. When I saw you in that reeking dive I knew you were the *one*, the one spoken of in the *Book*."

Taar scoffed. "What book?—and I curse your conniving means, woman."

She ignored the remark. "Others would be fickle; they would abandon my cause at a whore's call and I would be forced to chain them with my magic and keep them alert to their cause. Should I waste time fettering cowards with spells? No!" She laughed like a wolf, the snarl of ancient savagery. "It spoils a man's initiative. We shall do the deed by blood bond."

A dirk flashed in her hand. She slashed a piece out of Taar's fine roan-leather jerkin along the upper arm, exposing the brown skin in the torchlight. Running the blade along her own thumb, she drew blood, then jabbed the tip of the jeweled knife under his unyielding skin. Taar felt a prickling in his arm which shot up into his throat as the blood of hers met the blood of his. Pounding hell-fire racked his body. A strangling blood bond formed, wrapped stronger than any chains to this mysterious woman. Like nothing was her mesmeric ring compared to this sinful sap that flowed now through his body— ichor that was joined in everlasting union. He felt an insatiable allegiance to this creature, as if he would travel the ends of the world for her. Woe! How could he have been so unlucky?—so naive? What foul fate had he incurred?

"While blood flows in my veins," she croaked, "you shall truckle to my bidding. So it was spoken that one day I would twice join with a resolute man of the sword who would come to liberate me from the demon's curse."

"Demon?" rasped Taar. "What's this about a demon?"

She looked at him, her large, amethyst eyes filled without pity. "Poor fool. You have no clue. Long ago a spell was laden on me— one so strong that I could not break it, though I had many great gifts and marvels at my disposal. I was but a child of seven that one day I wandered too far in the woods and became lost. A place not unlike this, though it feels worlds away. I fell to the turf sobbing in my sleep, in a vine-knitted copse where I awoke from the most horrible dream, if dream it was, for I had witnessed something too terrible for words, that no child should ever see." She paused in bitter reflection. "From then on, the seeds of a dark path were instilled in my spirit . . . and they tempted me. Aye, I was to be the most formidable sorceress in all Tandarland. But alas, the demon saw to that. I can barely venture a league from Rurne without his energy glutting mine. I must walk free of this curse!"

"I refuse to be your glove-puppet."

"Try, but you will fail."

Taar was silent for a time. He summoned his spells but they had deserted him. Whatever influence this devilress had over him, it included his command of magic. "I will do this deed of yours, witch, though I know not what it is."

Toward the growing light they climbed, Taar struggling with feet of lead; the enchantress dogged his heels, brimming with a sense of exultation.

III

The two emerged into the tower's crows' nest, a circular chamber of high-peaked roof and mud-like walls, bare save for two emblazoned tapestries chased in gold. Taar saw vines creeping in past the windowsill. Thorned branches played twining fingers down the stone floor. A black cast-iron pot boiled over a glowering fire while silver-green smoke fumed out from the open window. A soft divan reposed nearby, alongside an oaken desk littered with folios and iron-bound books whose pages were lit by twin candelabra. An alabaster altar stood aside the desk, glowing with candles and torches and populated with pantheons of strange semi-human figurines: nymphs, dryads, beasts, snakes, reptiles, all manner of beasts adorned with countless gems glittering frost-like in the candles' guttering glare.

The floor, Taar saw, was covered with a heavy mat on which was inscribed various glyphs and strange symbols: of crescent moons, stars, candles, sickles painted in red, black, yellow and orange, underscored by ancient writings beyond Taar's ken. Some of the more cryptic runes he recognized as markings of the black tongue of Koppor, spoken by those demon succubi people who crafted the ancient Ziggurats of the southern wastelands.

The enchantress led Taar past the altar and over to the desk where she buried her eyes in pages of runes of spell books.

Taar gazed disconsolately out the window. He saw wispy branches trembling in a chill draft far below. A pool was as still and ominous as black ice. No twinkling lights of villages bade welcome in those long leagues of lonely forest. It seemed he stood miles above an endless wood, trapped in a dream, in an isolated, vine-covered tower.

On the sill Taar picked up what looked to be a sinister clock powered by a beaker of sand. Its face showed time by hands carved of human finger-bones. He toyed idly with the curio, tipping it sideways and watched dully as the sands shifted and the claw moved back half an inch.

Sowela leapt over and snatched the ornament from his grasp. "Leave this alone. 'Tis my life-register! Now listen to the spell that describes the mission with which I charge you:

"Let he who is brave enough to face the underworld blight with steel alone, be the bait! Hear, o necromancer! Scream the summoning with eyes wide! Unleash the mystery of Reclamation. Into the shrine of jade and onyx shall the demon's force be bottled. Thus speaks Ancast the witch!"

Taar shuddered, listening with disgust and confusion. "What need you of me?"

"Fool! If the demon notices me, he'll know it is a trap. Which is why I need somebody else." She pointed to the frothing cauldron. "Those smokes are my efforts to concoct the potions of the *Reclamation* to thwart his terror. As I hinted, I was cursed by words that should have never crossed my lips. I was only an adolescent then, a natural in the Black Arts, but delving foolishly into the realms best left untouched, I fell prey to *Horkinhar's* wrath. I harbored not the knowledge to combat the unheard-of territories with his sinister force."

"Whose wrath?" sneered Taar.

"A demon of the night worlds, beyond Tethys!—a demon whose name I am loath to whisper! Do not repeat his name, for you shall know the terrors of the gulfs beyond, swordsman." Her violet eyes lost some of their menace and glazed over like ceramic. "How he lusted for me! I was the most sexual creature he had ever encountered. He could not take his mind off me . . .

"He sentenced me here in jest, to Rurne, his wretched hill-keep, so that I might be his plaything on the night of each full moon. This is his castle; these are his rooms; so I have taken residence for an age. The demon-king lets me tinker with my potions, but oh, how he laughs at my feeble attempt to foil his everlasting curse!"

Taar smiled without remorse. "Such are life's vicissitudes."

"Shut your mouth! You must face the creature. Together we will defeat the menace or perish. Only because I am strong can he enter the mortal realm. Each moon he takes my feminine force, adds it to his own power in order to combat the material barriers at the threshold of the mortal and spirit plane. This is your task! Bait the ghoul, draw him into my trap so that I might walk free from his curse, and fall prey to no more of his insidious lusts."

"Alas," declared Taar sourly, "this is a thing beyond my ability."

"You will do as I say or suffer like the rest!" She strode briskly over to the altar and selected an eight-inch bottle crafted of jade and banded with onyx and gold that seemed to glow with an inner light of its own. "This is Ancast's vessel." She placed it at Taar's feet. Into the cauldron she plunged a ladle and splashed frothing liquid in a circle about five feet in diameter around Taar and the bottle. The liquid hissed. Some of it ate through the mat and up came a turquoise smoke that stung Taar's eyes. The odor was of the same pungent hickory that he had perceived upon their introduction.

Sowela cried: "Here stand you with the bottle to face the demon. The shadow shall not be an easy foe! While he is distracted I utter the spell and his force shall be snatched into the bottle."

Taar scrambled quickly out of the circle.

"Swear it!" she cried.

Taar swore it. Nothing else could he do.

Sowela glanced at the clock and gave a satisfied nod. "The demon shall not come till midnight. In the case that you are to fall to him, which sadly is a high probability, I shall at least taste the warmth of your flesh."

Letting her soft leather slip to the floor, she leered. As naked as Eve she stood, fully revealed as a lithesome ivory nymph. Her silken breasts were ornaments of pure living blossoms, her lips sultry slashes of pink-rose, her multi-colored locks swung down to exquisitely-shaped, honey-sweet hips. Though Taar despised the treachery of this witch, he was not of quality to resist her.

Perias would have agreed. Down onto her velvet divan she drew him, where, against her enchantment, Taar was powerless. Her embrace was like a torrent of fire. Through Taar ran an electric current, of mingled hate and lust and other irreconcilable emotions raging in a moon-tower of abandon.

Time seemed to pass like eons in a land of exotic splendor. In their erotic embraces neither Taar nor Sowela were aware of the chilly cloud that came shuddering through the window, and came creeping across the floor like a snake. Nor were they aware of the grim, loathsome thing that spawned in that slow-swirling mystery. It inched its way slowly upon the two lovers on six silent hooves.

In her passion, Sowela felt a faint movement tickling her naked breast. She glanced aside to see a huge goat-like head rear over Taar's lean shoulder. Three curling ox horns grew from a blasphemous crown; unblinking orbs seared forth blazing blue light. The sight rendered the sorceress senseless. Her limbs seemed petrified like wood. Never before had her master arrived before the hour of twelve! Then she remembered, how her new lover had been toying with the time-teller by the window, and spasmodically she rocked beneath him and let loose a frightful screech. Taar whirled and beheld a depraved sight: a red-furred monstrosity the size of a horse with a llama's neck, a goat's head and a bull's body. Blue-gray mist swirled about its high, spiked hooves.

Snatching for his sword, he let the Alassian blade arc a gleaming path upward, shearing a furry leg to the bone. The lifeless limb flew tumbling across the floor. But the demon only raised a yellow-bearded jowl and laughed—a bloodcurdling guffaw that froze blood to ice. Forward Horkinhar limped on its five remaining legs, and then, all at once, a stream of serpentine tentacles erupted from its back and rippled out toward the divan.

Taar made hacking play at the rush of tentacles and checked the first rippling appendages, but was not in time to prevent the blade from being snatched away. A new battalion of gummy loops flew through the air like coiling arrows and rippled around his muscle-taut form. Before he could counter, a score of writhing appendages slithered about his thewed shoulders, then as quickly, slipped under Sowela's slender, naked waist and whipped her up into the air. The foul links constricted the two together in a repulsive, mocking embrace. There they floated two feet over the divan, stuck together like two luckless pieces of serpent meat. The coils wrapped tighter and Taar's incredible strength was squeezed out of him.

The first ghastly touch of those gummy loops brought a blinding, snapping madness to his brain, plunging him into an erotic world of shadows. Perias had warned him of the world of the *Shadow*—where the air was a medium of weightless water and pulsed with an otherworldly, sub-aqueous light. The demon thing loomed like a puppet born of nightmare, and Taar could perceive Sowela locked in insuperable loops, but she was only vaguely formed and half human herself. Her soul had been ripped away for so long by this blasphemy of the nether depths, that she was long on her way to losing her female form and taking on the characteristics of his abysmal, perverted world.

Fighting back his horror, Taar heard his master's voice echoing in his brain:

"Remember, Taar, never speak your name aloud in a demon's presence. Show fear only at your peril. Mortal weapons are useless against them, as you will discover. Embrace the magic as I have taught you. Mayhap Taar, you will succeed in confronting your worst nightmare, hidden terrors as you can never imagine!"

He could have cried out, for when he squinted through that watery light, there was poor Perias joined in the ranks of the dead, sad and withered. His head was dangling at the stem, his limbs racked with awful wounds.

Then his form shimmered and the scene changed to one of the past. The surroundings were murky but the characters clear. Taar could see himself and his master, riposting in mock battle around a magic fire in a glade before his hut. Perias was throwing pulsing orbs of green light at him while he parried with his ensorcelled blade wiped thrice in the magic of Rlon.

The image faded; he was gone; now the old man was caught in a web of treachery, breathing his last gusts of breath while two bloody-handed brigands slashed down on his quivering limbs with rusty mattocks, and in the background a cackling old hag made off with his enchanted scimitar.

Whether it was a side effect of the *Shadow* or not, Taar saw other people gathered about like zombies: friends, old acquaintances, relatives, all emaciated and grisly memories in all aspects of death and undeath to the point of revulsion.

Taar was thrust back into reality. He knew no greater horror than the glaring, goat-like face that bent so close to kiss him, and the squeezing, strangling coils that tightened ever around his bulging thews. Gagging in the demon's reek, he spat the words 'Ank Urgh Akula!—' the words Perias had given him. Then he sagged, wincing with the pain of the effort of speech.

The demon's slavering mouth stopped an inch from his throat. A hideous guttural voice rang forth from blasphemous gulfs: "Who are you, insignificant flea, to parrot the Chant of Dismissal?"

Taar gurgled incomprehensible words—the last he knew of the old incantation as ancient and evil as ever that Perias had taught him.

The demon shook with anger and dismay. Taar felt an inch of coil give slack, and welcome air return to his lungs.

Horkinhar howled: "Ank is only the first word of the Chant! Know you not the rest?"

"Zost!" Taar gasped. The incantation was so close to completion, but so far. Death was calling.

Squirming in the serpentish coils, Sowela howled her fiercest invocations. Her prince laughed with macabre ecstasy. All her magic seemed to have abandoned her in the presence of this bane. Taar could feel her heart beating against his breast, feel her animal-like warmth flooding him with a power that he had never experienced, but her soft skin was stained an unctuous green from the demon's slime, and he grimaced with loathing at the thought of the countless grisly couplings this woman and her demon had shared.

Horkinhar pranced forward, its horned shadow looming over the two like a nightmare's climax. "Tell me your name, plaything, and let darkness enfold your myopic being! Can you not hear it? Listen! The gongs of doom toll for your soul!"

Sowela wheezed. "Kill the infidel, Horkinhar. The swine tried to take your mistress by force!"

Taar's breath raged between his teeth.

Through wide, glaring eyes, the demon saw the jade and onyx bottle lying on the enchantress's mat and an evil intelligence began to dawn in his consciousness.

"Take you by force, did he?" The gigantic goat's head swiveled mirthlessly in Sowela's direction. "You seemed to be enjoying it, so I recall. Why not cuddle a little closer?"

Reptilian muscles jerked and coils constricted with hideous elasticity that made both of them writhe in pure agony. Sowela's body was contorted into a hunched ribbon. She gasped, her eyes wide with limitless fear. Taar squeezed his eyes shut and felt his bones on the verge of snapping.

The demon gave a cruel laugh. "If such were possible, you, boy, would rather die than tell me your name. But what need I of your corpse when I have an earthly trophy beyond imagining?" The bloated, yellow-bearded face drew close. Out flicked a rasping tongue that licked Sowela's pale, sweat-beaded cheek. "My little sylph! How you have much to make up for your indiscretions!"

Four coils unwound and Taar rolled onto the divan and bounced to the floor in a shrunken heap. But the very same coils wound quick as spider's thread about the girl, who loosed an unearthly shriek that sent shivers down Taar's back.

That was not all that pricked the small hairs on the back of Taar's neck. Unexpectedly a black, swirling void seemed to open up from nowhere on the mosaicked mat. Taar swore. He caught a glimpse of a blasphemy of goat and bull hopping away on five legs toward the gap. The demon made a last monumental leap into the whirlpool, taking with it a naked, writhing form struggling on its back, looped in slime-sheened hoops of wrath and doom.

Taar watched spellbound as the demon took its prize into black nothingness, then down into whatever depths such things go. The void shimmered in violet haze and speckles of gold, then vanished.

Taar squinted about in an unreal daze. The chamber stood still as a mummy's tomb. The fire was cold ash. The candles guttered in a soft, chanting wind that wafted from the window. The blood pounded in Taar's ears. He tried to reclaim his sanity, but could only shake his head in apathy. Surely he must be witness to some foul dream? The overturned bottle lay on the floor. This was no idle dream. He picked it up and was about to put it back on the altar when sudden anger took hold and he hurled it through the window. He seized the clock, and threw it too, and they both fell smashing on the rocks, crushing Sowela's last hope for emancipation from Horkinhar's eternal lusts—but of that he could not know.

The chamber was becoming frightfully cold. Soon the candle would extinguish, leaving him in darkness. Shivering with exhaustion, Taar gathered his garments and his blade.

IV

Moans of distress echoed faintly from the stairwell and reminded Taar of the huddle of men imprisoned half way down the tower. He snatched up a faltering candle and scuttled down the murky flight on rubber legs.

He was directly above the tower's armory. Under the domed chamber he found the prisoners as before: gibbering and moaning, imploring him to pry open the grate. He paused, held his breath. A force of dread waxed thick in the air and was advancing with speed.

Rurne's guardian was returning.

On noiseless feet, Taar crept over to the stairwell. He could feel an ancient presence—the same crawling menace when he and Sowela had entered the gate-guarded keep—a black shadow darker than dark bounding up those time-eaten steps. No doubt the guardian was aware for the first time of the terrible turn in its mistress's fate.

A helpless rage washed over Taar. Where was he to run? He thought to hold his ground, bare his sword, but in wise practicality, he quickly hid in the shadows, knowing that against this creature he was no match.

He pressed himself against the prison grate, crouching so low that only the top of his head could be seen above the level of the floor. Twelve paces away, the malevolence lurked, brooding, scanning, sizing.

The thing poised, waiting like a hungry predator. Taar moved, his eyes flicked upward a fraction.

Its bulky mass filled the entire C-shaped stairway. He also discerned a yellow pinprick of eyes and the thrust of a horn pitched in a dense mass of a million silently-buzzing black flies. So this was the guardian's form! But he could not be sure, so eclipsed was he in cumulative horror of what he saw before him.

The dark monstrosity hesitated, sensing an unfamiliar presence.

Taar sagged. How could he fight a foe he hadn't a clue what it was?

He felt the warm touch of his magical beads in his pouch. If he were to roll them in his open palm, perhaps he could cast some kind of primitive telekinetic ripple. Rubbing the three scorpion-stones together, he whispered an old spell. The fires on the torches flared but their shafts did not budge. He scowled with disgust. So weak was his magic, so short had been his training!

He considered his options. Engage the beast? Hunker in the dark, hoping to stay undetected? Doubtless the ghoul, which was fast sniffing him out, would be more than disgruntled to discover him here and not Sowela, if indeed this were her abhorrent guardian and not some ghastly plaything bestowed upon her by the demon king. If the latter were true, he was done for. A prickling sensation tingled his skin, and a memory in a dimly-lit ale-room, where he had heard a frightful tale whispered by a well-traveled wayfarer who had witnessed the rites of Kopporian shamans on high hills chanting cantraps to summon minions worse than their masters—minions endowed with powers that made freezing a troll on the spot and blasting it into oblivion seem a childish exercise.

It did not occur to Taar that this creature was neither Sowela's pet nor the demon creature's, but something more elementally ancient, something that had inhabited this hill before men had walked the steppes and roamed the hills.

For the moment, the creature's intent was bent on the high tower. Its impending presence vanished out of the chamber.

Frantically Taar began hacking at the prison's locks. Ever and again he struck with his blade, pried at the rusty prongs and iron bars embedded in the overhanging stone. The layers of rust were still enduring and would not give. Within the pit, five living men howled in dreadful anticipation, their white faces lit with pasty expectancy, their parched lips working in turbulent distress.

But now, the creeping shadow fled back toward the tower's middle, alerted by desperate sounds ringing below. Taar grimaced, feeling cold anguish well in the pit of his stomach. Back from the grate he edged and the men's frustrated cries were heartrending. Curse the witch Sowela!

Horkinhar's call sliced the silence. The demon was returning. An echoing boom rocked the chamber and Taar fell to his knees. The tower groaned like the creaking of a hundred ships bending in a storm. All about him the walls heaved and buckled. A great slab of grayish stone toppled, missing his head by inches. He jerked back two steps, down the stairs, hoping that by chance the menace would not dog his heels. He hated himself for his cowardice, but there was no choice. Impossible to free the men and escape at the same time. Down those cursed stairs he leapt, taking four at a time while the cut in his upper arm throbbed.

Aching within him was Sowela's infectious bond. Her lustful presence was as of some fleeting past. Poor doomed Sowela!

Grimly, he pushed down the mounting panic growing in his breast. Out from under the overgrown arch he fled, staggering like a madman past the iron-trellised hedgeway, ducking tumbling stone and dodging fallen limb. Twice he was almost sprawled senseless by massive trunks plummeting from high. On another occasion, he was almost buried by a storm of basalt.

On he stumbled.

Standing a hundred feet back from the hill, he halted, gasping for precious air. He looked over his shoulder. The slope was a shifting mass of chaos and destruction. Huge trees uprooted and sheared. The castle swayed, gave one last abysmal heave then came crashing down into shards and clouds of gray dust along with the men who were imprisoned there.

Taar shook his head in black defeat. Had the wretches deserved this useless doom? The demon Horkinhar had seen to the destruction of Rurne's outpost—a final vengeance on man now that Sowela's task was done.

What had become of the black shambling thing, Taar could not say, but he doubted that it had died in that crumble. Soon it would be lumbering after him on noiseless feet.

He limped off into the forest like a broken crow; only the sallow moon floating in a sky of pitch remained to recall Sowela's deeds and what had gone before. A distasteful ordeal all in all . . . now another awaited.

V

In the days that followed Taar caught up with Perias's murderers. The rogues were sheltering in a wood near Traghem, hunched around a small fire, munching fried pheasant wings, licking their lips.

As promised, Taar took his initiative grimly, approaching the campfire without stealth.

The two lackeys, Daig and Wislox, jumped to their feet. Rushing him with daggers bared, they hurled insults, but he fascinated them with Perias's Singing Stones—talismans that were his master's legacy, greedily guarded like a last breath. When the eerie sound found the knaves' ears, they both fell, garnet-eyed, before they could unleash any assault.

Welfstang was another matter: the changeling was downright evil, and already he could feel his arms sagging, weighted like stones before he could prepare his vengeful incantation. Green patches of light webbed Taar's mind like a spider's lacework. Through the daze engulfing his brain he could discern Welfstang's body transform into some huge form of winged malignancy—half amphibian, half kraken, with slavering blue tongue and horned ears. A semblance of the Tu-Steev blade was clamped in her beak.

The warrior fell to his knees. He clutched his own weapon for frontal protection. His sight went dim. Welfstang's soporific power had thrust out feelers like a hundred sprites. As Perias had taught him, Taar traced perfect figure-eights with his sword—so lightning-quick that nothing could be witnessed of their humming arcs, but a blur of steel. They formed a pattern of a near impenetrable screen. For long hours he had drilled on this very pattern of defending against dark attack when blind-sighted by changeling magic. Changelings and their fey magic were old when the world was young, and this fiend was no exception . . .

The monster's Tu-Steev broke through his enchanted net and

sheared off the tip of his blade. The blade bit in further to saw off his left pinky.

Howling in pain, Taar could feel warm blood pouring down his ear too. An earlobe dangled shorn. The fury of his attack, however, had unnerved the attacker.

Taar experienced screeching triumph—his broken blade cleaved through gristle and bone. The flurry of fetid wings ceased. He hung in limbo, while his beleaguered sight returned.

Squinting in the smoky darkness, Taar saw the changeling at his feet quivering, a wretched crone of misshapen dimension. Her sightless gaze stared past his own, dwindling to nothing. A glaring green gash showed in her side.

In the hag's overconfidence, she had invaded his net. What an arrogant, foolhardy thing to do!

He pulled the Tu-Steev from the crone's mouth. The knife was warm, curved, an object of scimitarish origin, gleaming with a magnificent effulgence. The sad, dwindling moonbeams held no match for its brilliance. Fingering the hilt, Taar shore off the changeling's head, burnt it in the fire and buried the embers in a deep pit, as it should be, so it could not reorganize itself into some frightful rebirth.

He found the garments of Welfstang's hirelings useful for wiping down his dripping blade. The corpses would be eaten by crows.

After bandaging his knuckly stub with strips from his vest and available musk-spruce sap from the trees, he covered the Tu-Steev with snakeskin and placed it in his own pouch, knowing that its merest brush would slice off another finger.

Cautiously, he began weaving his way through the forest. Weary steps were all that sounded in the tangled wood, guiding him on a path back to Jinjan, yet strides tempered with satisfaction, and in sync with a faint pulsation in his veins.

AHRION'S MINIONS

I : Night Shamblings

The war-chief came to with a start, nursing his throbbing temples. His instincts were good: to roll free and defend his vitals, but he was on his left side, bruised and aching, with the scent of a dying fire in his nostrils. Slowly, before his eyes, vague shapes began to form. Things that he would rather not have seen. Where in Balael was he? He had no memory of anything. No bawdy taverns filled with ribald song or naked wenches and brawls. Only a headache of agony pulsed in his throbbing skull.

But wait! What of his Huughite horsemen riding at his command toward the pass? What of the enemy falling into pools of their own blood? Now his memory was like some distant dream. He had fallen . . . yes, blacked out. That was all he remembered. Now several ghoulish shapes shambled toward him. What could the pasty mutants lumbering on bare feet want of him, Dereas, leader of the Huughite clan? The swamp-haired thing had craters of pustulated sludge for skin and webby stubs for fingers and black and yellowed lumps for teeth. The dull opal eyes stared at him with an unnatural vacancy. Its three-toed feet were swollen, the webbed hands flexing. What the devil did the thing want of him?

The war chief leaped to his feet, struggling to avoid the clammy touch of its fingers. He groped for the dagger normally tucked in the baldric at his back between his shoulder blades. But surprise . . . the dirk was not there. Nor were his poison sac or stun-powder. His left wrist was shackled. Only a few mere yards of slack chain separated him from another bedraggled man to his left, drenched in shadows. All he could do was claw himself to a sitting position, then peer into the gray face that was almost on top of him.

The creature, now accompanied by others, grabbed for his wrist.

Dereas recoiled. Though feather-light, the touch was clammy like a corpse's and cast shivers up his spine.

"Back, zombie! Back!" he cried through a mask of hatred and froth on his lips. "Back to the cursed swamp you crawled from!" But there was no going 'back' as he tried to shove the thing away.

The creature blinked dumbly; its slack, wet mouth offered no response to his insult. Being the ghoul it was, it could neither speak nor understand human tongues. The brute only stared past Dereas, sightlessly, as if such a thing were beyond it. It could care less for humans. The only reason it had come to paw at him was to check that its captive was alive and had not succumbed to the death stupor of Phygus. There was a long journey ahead.

Such dim reasoning was all the thing was capable of, for it was a slave—to dark sorcery. The thing, in essence, had barely once been human, although this particular fiend was perhaps more fortunate than others of its kind that remained behind in the dark distant keep to do its wizardly master's bidding.

Dereas heard groans coming from a place near him. He turned and peered in the shadows, grimacing. One of his comrades was awakening: a rough-hewn warrior with tangled beard and a thick camel-hair tunic and leather sandals—a Kechian, if he did not miss his guess, and an archer from the look of his over-muscled right arm. "What the—where?"

"Brother, better that you had stayed unconscious," Dereas muttered.

The dazed captive struggled to his feet, baring his teeth in a grimace of anger. "By the dogs of Zecrates! Who are you, warrior, and why I am chained to this cursed leash?"

"Dereas is my name—" the warlord said, "Dereas of Asgolin. Who are you?"

"Derken—of Keshalt."

"Well, save your breath, Kechian. Unless you wish to argue the matter with them." He lifted a finger at the shambling ghouls, of which there was now an obscene foursome.

"Demons from hell!" cried the archer. He kicked his immediate neighbor awake. "Get up, fool, unless you wish to be mauled in your sleep by an undead horde. Get up!"

The captive next to him jerked himself up, groggy from his drugged sleep. The figure was scarcely amused at his plight. He had scarlet hair and wore an iron-studded leather jerkin, a Tluthe—another finely built warrior, though not so burly as Dereas.

"Who are you?" demanded Dereas.

"Svanctus, from Jasaroth."

Dereas grunted. That made three of them. This one was certainly better dressed than the Kechian. Now another captive, long-legged and dark, curly-haired, lay slumped on the other side of the fire. He looked to be some kind of barbarian Pirean, but Dereas could not be sure in the shadowy light.

One of the shambling ghouls lit a torch and began stamping out the fire. Shadow-thicket on either side of the glade wavered in vagrant breezes. The ghoul's bare feet crunched on the embers and sizzled as its toes burned, but the creature paid no heed and there remained only an awful reek of charred flesh as the fire was slowly smothered. The ghoul cared little for singed flesh. The repulsive reek was enough to make the men-prisoners gag.

The leader of the ghouls tugged on the heavy chain that linked the four slaves. It pulled with a force strong enough to half drag the half-sleeping man along the dirt. The Pirean staggered to his feet. With a grumbling oath, he filed along the chain, brushing his bleeding ribs that were lacerated by sharp stones.

Dereas was next in line. He did not wish to move as the chain sprung taut. Four solidly-built men surely could overpower the strength of a few ghouls?

But three of the four jailers pulled out leather whips with cruel iron-tipped stars at the end. They snapped them on the captives when they disobeyed. Dereas, like the others, was forced to stumble along like a goat, suffering his fair share of lashes before surrendering to their will.

"Ha!" grunted Derken. "You have grand aspirations, war hound, to be so rebellious." He plodded on just behind his companion. "What do you think you are going to do—chew your way through your bonds?" He gave a throaty chuckle. "I've heard you horse riders are dumb enough to try things like that." That brought a croak of laughter from the Tluthe. But it was not an easy laughter. Idle banter was few and far between among this motley group; there was nothing here to cheer them up.

Dereas's face tightened into a grim mask. Corded muscles rippled along his back. The mocking banter he ignored, but what were these undead horrors that could chew through flesh but yet chose not to? They trudged on like mechanical monsters through the nameless barrens. How did he get here? Perhaps it was the memory of his youth as a slave-raider and being caught long ago that cast such awful memory over his soul. The memory of the chilling touch of the ghoul did not help. To have gone from chieftain, to zombie's slave galled him more than any shame could. He shook off his anger, and sweat dripped off his mane of copper ringlets.

The company plodded along the hard-packed sand. Even the fiercest nomad feared to wander this god-forsaken soil at night. Past crumbled rock formations, and boulders that reared up like menhirs in their path—it was nothing more than a barrens of peril; tales told of an old world which had survived through the evils of time.

Stars peeked out from behind moving clouds. Stark mountain peaks glared down on them from the north, which they followed upon a dim, sandy trail that barely gave the captives enough girth to travel by. It was no secret what type of a path this was. It was an old death-slave trail: once used to transport the hordes of captured unfortunates indentured to the southern kingdoms.

The prisoners fell often and gouged their shins and held up arms to fend off blows and whip lashes as the ghouls drove them ever on. The ghouls' tireless pace left their legs burning with exhaustion. But when the torches began to burn low, the leader halted the train and fetched another torch before forcing them to resume their march through the foothills without water or rest.

It was true that none of the prisoners knew exactly where they were. The Pirean barbarian thought they plodded through distant mountains above the frontiers of ancient Shaele. But none guessed where it was they were actually going. Only Derken dared whisper his suspicion to his peers.

"We plod to the realm of Phygus," he murmured.

"Phygus does not exist," mumbled the Pirean, whose name was Jhidik.

"Well, then speak, man, if you would know more. Share your wisdom, if you are a prophet," cried Dereas. "What plans have they for us?"

"No plans. It is the will of Phygus—the cursed Phygus." Derken scowled and shook his head like a beaten heretic.

Svanctus the Tluthe loosed an anguished moan. Without warning he bolted out of line and fell, pulling the Kechian out of lock step with him.

The maneuver was construed as a flagrant ploy to halt the caravan. The ghouls rounded on him with whips and sting-charms—small enchanted weapons of bone, hide and stone that the prisoners came to know well.

"Don't touch me, ghoul!" the frantic Tluthe gibbered. "I'll go on, I'll go on!" His words meant nothing to the slavers. They gathered round him and forced their clammy hands on his body: his back, his shoulders, his wrists. They poked him and prodded and stunned him until he was a cringing, stammering mess. After they left him humbled in the dirt, the only words that would ever spill from his lips were, "I'll do anything, anything, but just don't touch me!"

"Of course you will, you silly Tluthe," laughed Derken. "What other choice do you have?"

The incident was a forgotten, but it was one that left a dark stain on Dereas's memory. He remained brooding, glancing back with an inexpressible horror upon the shuffling wretches. His eyes caught the gaze of Derken and a strange empathy passed between them. Here were two very different men from different cultures caught in an eerie web of fate. Each discerned the threat of the other; each was aware of his own battle-mettle, and vulnerability. Dereas treated the Kechian as a sarcastic churl who would need keeping an eye upon, and he retreated into his own shell.

The Kechian seemed amused by the Dereas's moody reaction. "Why waste your anger on these mindless fiends?"

Unlike the others, Dereas soon forgot the Tluthe's grief and forced his attention on the lands around him. Ever did his mind stray to the quality of revenge he would extol on the slavers and their depraved master. The sorcerous arts that bound these ghouls were potent. They were not to be underestimated. Cold cunning had taught the war chief to survive, but what retribution the Kechian had for his foes was anybody's guess. The archer's mordant gaze showed disrespect and ridicule at every step, prompting Dereas to swallow in distaste.

There was to be no solace tonight. Stone crunched under men's sandals. The stars wheeled and as the night breeze rustled, blowing dry air around the crumbled rock pillars, the single torch held by the lead ghoul continued to gutter, with only a small night wind moaning as it whipped about the sand formations and carving shadow-breath among the weird, twisted rock shapes. They were the only players in this game of destiny.

Dereas at last spoke, for he could not stand the oppressive silence any longer. "Can any of you men guess when we will drink our next mouthful of water? What plans do these fiends have for us?"

The Pirean answered, "I'll wager that it's nothing good."

"Very good, Pirean," Derken grumbled. "We have all night for quips."

"Maybe. But would you bet on it?"

"I don't know. Seems as if no supper of boiled cactus for us tonight. Heehee. We'll march until sunup, or until we drop. All the time in the world to gab."

"They'll silence us before long," muttered Jhidik. The Pirean frowned and lowered his voice. "I was in less of a daze than you when I was kidnapped by this team of undead scum. A heavy sack was thrown over my head. I was clubbed and carried off in a cart. 'Twas on a black night on the Basgion docks as I came from Brave Beard's Inn. I was thrown into the hold of a square-sailed galleass and there we made way to what hellish port I cannot name. Carried overland, for leagues, blindfolded and sold to the highest bidder—in the slave camps of Numenon. I knew I was in Numenon for I recognized the sound of their gravelly voices. *"Here, here, matey, how much will you pay for these fine catches?"* Jhidik trailed off his mimicry.

Dereas listened with clamped jaw. He urged the Pirean to continue.

Jhidik grunted. "How I made my way into the clutches of these fiends is another story, for I was drugged and beaten. But I remember making contact with your company not long after. A vile trade was made...I came into the hands of these ghouls. When I came across your squalid huddle, I knew that like me, you were dead men. Drugged like sacrificial lambs, bewitched by some breed of the foul poppy oil, I knew, as I feared, that some terrible evil had befallen us all."

"But how?" cried Dereas in dismay.

"We lay out in the chill of the desert, tethered hand to hand to spikes driven deep in the ground. While some rude curs made banter and coarse jokes inside their yurts, I decided to play along and maintained an air of defeat, hoping for new information and a chance to make a break for it. For the most part you were lucky, swimming in your dream sleep of the red poppy. You could not hear the unimaginable suggestions the slavers made and their nightmarish jests. You were largely unaware of the torture and the hopelessness that lay before us. I was not so lucky . . . If Svanctus could tell his tale, he would . . . but he is gone. His mind tumbled over the brink a long time ago."

The chronicle only gave the Kechian cause to sneer.

Dereas could hardly contain a shiver. He wondered what misery was to come at the hands of these human slavers. Surely it was they who had cast him into the hands of these ghoulish overseers? If so, they would pay dearly when he caught up with them!

"Aye, Pirean," mumbled Dereas, "it seems as if you weren't the only one to be waylaid. I remember riding with my Huughite warriors but days ago. We were risking a night raid on the enemy who held a command tower in the Besmeran Pass. All of a sudden a menace was upon us. Winged demons came dropping from the sky! Come to think of it, I smelt treachery from the get-go, before we came to that shadow pass, but I heeded not my instincts. I was thrown clear of my mount, along with three of my men. Where they went I knew not. I remember clutching for my life onto a shrub. My feet were dangling over a precipice. I watched two of them, tumbling to their doom, the poor souls, then lying smashed on the boulders below. I grasped. I hung on—"

"Don't you wish you had joined them?" chortled the Kechian.

"Shut up!" Dereas lunged for him only to add three more lashes to his hide by the ghouls who had come shambling. He cursed them; he cursed Derken. The warrior stared sullenly at the whip-yielder who stalked ahead of him. Then he was yanked back into line by the inexorable pull of the rattling chain. He was forced to reminisce on the great gap in his memory—when he had slid off his mount into that interminable abyss.

The grinning Kechian did not add to the pool of tales that evening . . .

* * *

By and by the path grew less distinct and Dereas knew that they were leaving the main mountain trail. He could only believe that their doom was fast approaching, that already the men were beginning to flag. Panting and weakened after the effects of the crushed poppy and from hunger and fatigue, Dereas feared they would not last the night. It would only be hours before they dropped in exhaustion and did not get up. The war chief vowed that he'd make these wretches pay, that it would not be he to be the first.

A set of hostile howls drifted from the distant hills.

The men's eyes and ears trained into the night-stained darkness.

The jailers did not stop. They drove their charges ever on in the spirit of haste. The howls grew louder, sending the short hairs rising on Dereas's neck. He stumbled on with the rattle of chain, over roots and rocks and felt the sting of his captors' whips on his backs like a thousand angry bees.

There came no warning. Only a pad of stealthy paws. Soon wolves were gnashing out at them everywhere.

Toothy, snarling beasts with frothing jowls. Gray shapes with yellowed fangs dripping mad white-froth. Be-deviled eyes glared out from the gloom. If these man-eaters could stand on their hind legs . . . Dereas did not finish the thought . . . No, these were not ordinary wolves. They were steppenwolves: creatures of the haunted peaks of Shaele. Killer-bred from crypts of southern Phygus where witches such as Hexir, the old one, had called them on a whim from her underworld lair on some blood-stained night.

"Had I only my freedom and a sword!" Dereas rasped, "by Balael, hound and ghoul would die in lakes of blood!" He lifted the chain to catch a lunging beasts' jaw as the wolf rounded on him. From his lips bellowed his war cry.

"A lot of 'ifs', barbarian!" cried the toothy Kechian. He twirled a loop of chain to lay low a yelping marauder.

Dereas bared his teeth. He whipped iron links into a wolf's skull, hearing bone crack. He almost split the metal right them, so great was his rage. The primal force of his strength pulsed off him like a madman. "If you don't keep your mouth shut, Kechian, I'll feed you to these vermin myself."

"Temper, temper," the archer grunted. "We mustn't—"

With a savage twist he wrapped a coil of chain around a leaping wolf's neck and pulled. It was a move only a disciplined fighter like him could manage.

The neck snapped like rotted wood and the black-maned crown of the beast hung on grisly shreds. The torso heaved and convulsed before it lay dead.

Jhidik ducked, swinging chain with brutal efficiency at Dereas's side. He cried out as a wolf grazed teeth across his left forearm. The Tluthe, already in weakened condition, was taken down by a pack of wolves. A ghoul clambered to save the human's life, but he was pulled down in the fray. The wolves were quick to work their death magic on Svanctus and he was in no position to hinder them from the pleasure.

"For god sake's, help him, Kechian! You're the closest!" Dereas's shouts died in his throat above the din.

"And have my throat cut and blood drained by these vampire curs? No way! I'd say the Tluthe should satisfy their blood lust for a while."

"Heartless coward!" Dereas roared. He leapt out to aid his fallen peer but there was no time to avenge him. The man was doomed and already another beast had lurched out of the darkness and clamped jaws on Dereas's forearm. The warrior's leather saved him from serious punctures and he managed to duck as the beast continued on its flight and smashed against a nearby boulder.

The Kechian laughed. "Not a coward, just practical."

It would have been a very short end to the companion's nightmare had something not extraordinary happened. Indeed the captives and ghouls would have been slaughtered if their fiendish leader had not been pulled under a mass of writhing, rending teeth and claws and now wrestled with one of the fiercest werewolves.

The fanged horror suddenly whimpered and lay limp. With the ghoul's algae-like touch, the werewolf's spirit was snatched away in a sorcerous whorl and the undead leader replaced it with something of its own essence. The wolf was now a thing more ghoul than canine and its matted fur gleamed in the moonlight, a baleful gray-green like its killer.

The hideous tongue lolled from its jowl. Now it reared on its hind legs a length and a half over the tallest of the men, perhaps in mimicry of its undead slayer. The walking carcass reeked of putrefaction, half loping and shambling on all fours, a half demon, half animal and worse than either. It struck out with teeth and claws at its brethren with a ferocity that could only be born of supernatural forces. Those victims whom it savaged never rose again. It carved a devastating swath of death, as wolf upon wolf fell before its terrible fangs. Some it chewed whole, their necks falling off, others it bit deep into sinewy hide and spat out grizzle, while others were lucky enough to be knocked senseless, with necks broken as it grabbed them in its teeth and flung them as the hound does the rat, to die beaten and smashed to pulp on the rocks below. At last it crawled hunching from a pile of blood-dripping hides.

The Kechian almost died beneath a murderous claw swipe as a surviving wolf leapt through the air and caught him unawares.

The rest of the werewolves began snorting and baying. The remaining pack fled, tails tucked between legs. The steppenwolves, having witnessed the carnage of their leader and its hideous transformation, were of mind not to return to that place too soon.

Whatever was left of Svanctus was not worth burying. Dereas and Jhidik kicked sand over his remains and dropped their heads in sorrow. The ghouls gazed on at the carcass like sleepwalkers, as if death were an everyday sight to them. Being undead, they knew only the place between life and death, an endless eternal void wandered by ghosts and elementals, and so the body was left where it lay in a dripping wretched pool. The ghouls were content to have won the battle—one minion in exchange for a human life.

The party regrouped. The torch-bearing leader shambled on. He tugged ever at the chain while the wolf that was turned were-ghoul loped at its new master's call.

Behind, trudged Dereas, pondering his fate while the others trod at his heels. A whip-yielding ghoul took up the rear. Two zombies kept watch at either side of the prisoners, swift to brandish whips whenever any flagged.

The ghouls tramped on through the highlands of Shaele, mile after mile. The humans cared little from where they had come nor where they went. Their sandaled feet scratched at the sands; bloody shins were caked with dust and racked from frequent falls. Where the shackles held, the wrists remained puffy of chaffed. Indeed to those devils, they were no more than a hapless drove of cattle . . .

II : Guardian of the Keep

The final ascent to the blackstone keep was long and tasking. Like a waiting wraith the tower loomed ahead of them, hewn from the very mountain itself, flanked between twin spires of rock. From the heights of a solitary window gleamed a sinister glow.

The trail continued onward down to mist-haunted Phygus. How strange that in this direction they could spy no more desert lands, only pyramids and minarets rising above a cloud of choking forests. The ancient edifices glowed with an evil cast, accentuated by lanterns hung by zealots. Back from where they had come, the prisoners staggered on a dangerous maze of twisting pathways that weaved their way before an ominous ring of steep cliffs. How the slave paths connected to this forgotten stretch on the Shaele border was beyond Dereas's knowledge.

The ghouls began to grow excited as their destination loomed nearer the mysterious castle. They almost danced with glee, uttering grunts and snorts from salivating mouths in a gush of guttural mishmash. The fiends coerced their captives toward the keep at a reckless pace.

'Hold up!" crowed the Kechian. "I can only move my feet so fast."

"Look at them, Dereas," cried Jhidik, appalled. "What could be exciting them so to keep them prancing about so?"

"Who knows, Pirean?" Dereas muttered. "Nor do we want to."

"Like it or not, we shall learn soon," Derken sneered. "Now listen, there'll be a welcoming party to surprise us with a ball and chain—"

"Shut your mouth, Kechian, or I'll split it in—"

"Look!" muttered Jhidik. "Pteradons! I loath to utter the name, yet I know them by sight. The same winged monsters that snatched my grandfather, before they lay low our clan."

Dereas gazed spellbound at the circling pack of prehistoric birds and his heart jumped. They had long pterodactyl beaks and hovered not far enough away. He was a western-warrior. Never before had he beheld such dinosaur-like fowl. Their wing span was three times his height. Their razor-sharp beaks were sharp enough to puncture a man. Hooked talons dangled, making clacking noises as the nails rubbed together; these were perfect engines of destruction.

The creatures held no interest in dining at this late hour. Little did they know they were the eyes and ears of the keep-master, and kept faithful watch over his domain to his lonely purpose. Unbidden forces had not beckoned them to glide brashly through the gates. The primitive fowl all flew back to their unwholesome tower-eyries where bells had once clanged and watchmen had once kept guard with bows trained. Now an age had passed. Castle Basilurk had fallen to disrepair and terror and housed nothing human for an eternity, since the coming of the necromancer Ahrion. Ah, sweet black-tongued Ahrion! The magicker who could ensorcell the most cunning king, subdue the brawniest warrior, beguile the most chaste maid. Long ago he had abandoned the lesser magics, given up his puerile obsession with fire and ruin. He had striven to conquer the darkest arts. It had not taken him long to stumble across the forbidden witchcraft of Phygus. There he had viewed the unknowable, the hordes of rune-spells carved in ancient, phosphorescent blood upon dust-ridden tomes of papyrus. There he had read them, and learned them by rote. As could be expected, he commanded foul spells of dark oblivion and committed atrocious deeds under a host of blood red moons. He had even slain his revered teacher, fixed it up that her tongue should not wag, for if she should ever thrice name him...his doom was sealed.

As a youth the magician had come from land-locked Omirus, yet none knew where his earliest travels had taken him. Was it to the haunted island of Thrakon? Or by ship to far eastern Thiran, or beyond across the mysterious Pzison Sea to fabled Mnglai and the unknown eastlands? Was it by the power of more malignant winds that he took sail over the western seas to the isle of Cinnamon Death and back again before crossing the land of tomb-ridden Shaele and on into dreaded Phygus? The answers were not known. Gaining necromantic power and hypnotic prowess, Ahrion merely took what he wanted with less than a conscience. Working his way up among the ranks of the Phygusian priests, he had murdered many of them and had stolen their secrets . . . until but a short time ago, when he had disappeared from the ranks of men to be never seen or heard from again.

Until now . . .

Guided by their new ghoulish hound, the ghouls forced the haggard prisoners through an iron-wrought gate and ever onward over an old wooden trestle. The bridge was spotted with arcane runes, writ in what appeared gaudy ochers of some long lost tongue. The trestle granted passage over a murky stream which coursed in the blackness below. Though it was inhumanly dark in the wee hours, the captives swore that the shivering waters below harbored animation; indeed existence coursed there, though not the existence that any civilized person would call 'life'. Glittering eyes blazed there, and Dereas swore he caught the rustle of shark fins, parasitic tendrils and stinging tentacles festering in the liquid abyss down in the murk, things that paralyzed a grown man by filling his imagination with pure terror.

They were met at the castle's main gate by the doorkeeper, a fierce gargoyle that Dereas thought was more bat than bird. Five hoary horns crowned its plated skull. On four scaly legs it shambled like a lost animal from a parallel universe. There was no exchange of pleasantries from this beast, save for some throaty growls. Nor was there any sign of camaraderie or idle small talk among ghouls or gargoyle.

The condition was to be expected. In this eldritch district the creatures were slaves to a higher power and etiquette was not part of their function.

Prisoners and ghouls made their way through a dim-lit main hall, excepting the gargoyle whose task it was to guard the door. The captives were not to lack company; another gargoyle slunk out of the darkness and it accompanied them as they made their way up a wide-winding staircase. Doubtless the steps spiraled their way up to the black tower...

Torches lit the way. The air was thick with must, enough that kept dust motes moving under the glowering torchlight. The prisoners could see remnants of the human age, of steel armor hanging in the cobwebbed corners, of long-forgotten kings and powerful monarchs frescoed on the walls. Yet blasphemy clung to these crannies. Circles of heathen symbols writ in profane inks were crudely scratched out from a once immaculate marble floor, as if they had been 'mistakes' of an earlier spell-hatching or necromancy gone bad. With each new terrible step the prisoners rose higher into the tower and the armored statues ranked about them grinned back through their visors, with the heathen runes like stick drawings drawn by childish fingers on their steel breasts.

The stairs ended. Soon they stood blinking before the tower eyrie. It was surely a room with a view. From the great window the stark outline of thinly glowing peaks and ancient pyramids stood limned against a pale yellow sky. Mazes of test-tubes brimming with evil-frothing liquids hung on cluttered benches. A cauldron of smoky elixirs bubbled away in some corner of the room. Candles dripped gobs of wax on a flagstone floor. All about them came rustlings, as if dark things scuttled about in the murk. Their host, a blue-robed wizard, rose from behind a low table.

Dereas then saw for the first time the infamous Ahrion. He was young, almost boyish in appearance, wearing a flaxen crop of waxed hair, long and streaming in a single neatly-combed tail to the middle of his back. Yet there was nothing juvenile about the presence of the figure. He was like all the precocious wellspring of his kind—a necromancer who reveled in the dark arts. Like a dank cloak, evil followed his shadow's every step. He wore a silver cowl and a pair of scarlet slippers. The workbench he hunched over was an altar of sorts, housing twin candleholders crafted from the skulls of beasts and imbued with a scope of terrible instruments: tongs, wands, amulets, pincers, elixirs. Incense coiled round the wizard in pale golden rings.

A long while passed before the figure spoke. "Ah, Grendil, my ghoul! How pleasant it is to see you. There have been days lacking your creeping presence. I was wondering when you would return. But what is this? You have fulfilled my mission and brought me a trio of humans! But only a trio? Faugh! Did I not tell you I wished four specimens!?"

The Kechian took the opportunity to speak. "There were four, Your Excellency. But the fourth, Svanctus suffered a bad turn—a nasty encounter with some wolves, which laid him out, did it not, Dereas?"

Dereas fought back a resentful growl. It was all he could do not to strangle the Kechian.

The wizard demanded an instant explanation. "Grendil, what is this nonsense? What do you mean 'a nasty spill'?" His attention shifted from his lead ghoul to round on the Kechian. "Speak up, lest I tear that tongue out from your mouth!"

Sensing peril, Dereas took a brave step forward. "What our friend means to say, is that your ghouls failed to protect us. One of our numbers, a Tluthe, fell to the fangs of a steppenwolf lunging out of nowhere for our fresh blood."

The wizard cast an impatient gaze upon the lead ghoul. "Is this true, Grendil?"

Grendil attempted a mumbling appeasement, wagged his head and gibbered from time to time. But what good was this to a creature without a tongue? In a fit of rage, the sorcerer grabbed the ghoul's head and pressed cheeks with both palms while shaking it horribly. Tears dribbled from its eyes—tears of terrible knowingness of what fate awaited it. The three humans watched in amazement as greenish stuff oozed from the creature's eye sockets.

"You simpleton!" chided the wizard. "Oaf! I can read it in your egg-headed, pig-hollow brain! I told you to avoid Hexir's mischief, didn't I?"

The ghoul seemed not to respond. It was a horrible sight to behold a wizard in a tantrum. Slowly, he proceeded to squeeze the liquid from the poor ghoul's head into a foamy pulp. The more the necromancer squeezed, the more disfigured the zombie's head became. Until finally it spurt a horrible mess of liquids out of its nostrils and mouth, which before long, became a thin flat slit, hung with eyeballs slewing on the cold stone floor. All the time, a terrible orange fire grew in Ahrion's hands, burning and singeing whatever remained of Grendil's skull.

The wizard let the corpse fall to the ground. It struck with a dull thud and he washed his hands of the filth on the tablecloth.

Magic items spilled every which way. Meanwhile the corpse continued to sizzle its remains into a reeking pool. Rats skittered out from the cobwebs and the captives were appalled to see them lap up the ghoul-liquid in delight. The prisoners all had to turn their heads—except Dereas, who was immune to these horrors; he had seen much death and cruelty in his day.

"Let that be a lesson to you sniveling infidels!" Ahrion shrilled. He wagged a jeweled finger at the two blinky-eyed ghouls that cringed in the shadows, hopping from foot to foot. "Next time, heed my warning."

Peering at the grim-eyed lot before him, the necromancer kicked one of the lick-lapping rats out of his way and stormed over to inspect the prisoners. "That these vermin sup in my workroom is despicable!"

Derken calmly showed a mouth full of blackened teeth. "Too bad you killed the wretch so soon, magician. You missed the true story about how the ghoul tamed the werewolf."

"Silence, ape!" roared Ahrion. "I'll feed you to the werewolf myself. Much work is to be done here and proper explanations are in order. We will let gargoyle and ghoul fight over your remains later. Now, tell me your names—and origins, all of you! You first!" He pointed at Jhidik.

The Pirean gave a surly grunt. "I am Jhidik, scout from faraway Pirea."

"And you?"

"I am Dereas, war-chief from northern Asgolin."

The wizard's eyes strayed keenly on the Kechian.

"Derken, humble archer from blue-forested Kech. At your service."

Ahrion studied the bedraggled crew with a thoughtful air then he turned his attention upon the Kechian. "So! You would claim a sense of humor among this motley lot? Perhaps you would care to assist me in a small problem."

"The concept is certainly not outside my grasp," the Kechian announced magnanimously.

"So it would seem," exclaimed Ahrion. He rubbed his chin. "So here is my dilemma. One of you three should start my experiments— but which one? Should it be the Pirean? The Asgolin warrior?—or perhaps *you*?" He flung out a finger at the archer's feet which shot forth a blue ray.

Derken paled. He did not like the accent on the last word, nor the bolt of fiery magic. The necromancer uttered a comic exhalation. "Come now, let us refrain from timidity. Nothing to add? No quip or timely repartee? Tsk, tsk, Kechian! I'm highly disappointed in you. I thought you had more mettle than that, cringing like a little schoolboy before the yardmaster."

Beads of sweat trickled down Derken's brow. His face had paled to a shade of ivory. Dereas and Jhidik were no less apprehensive and cast each other glances in tense inquiry.

"Surely not I, my Lord," beseeched Derken, caught in his own game.

"And why not? Would you offer your comrades as sacrifices then?"

"Now that you mention it . . ."

The wizard snorted. "I like a man with humor. Though I should have guessed."

"Wizard, I'll have you know that—"

"You'll have me know nothing," Ahrion thundered. "And don't call me 'wizard'. I find the title pretentious. Now on your knees, you mangy cur. Start begging me for mercy, or be a snakeskin ornament before long wrapped round my baby finger."

The Kechian gulped and was sinking to his knees, cowed under the brilliant aureole that glowed about the magician. Fire slashed forth from Ahrion's hands, burnt to hissing shards the chain binding the prisoner's wrists. "Now away, you jackals. I wish a word with this man. He is my chosen one..."

The ghouls dragged Dereas and Jhidik away, who objected with all ferocity. Dereas stole a look back; he saw the wizard donning a nightmarish helm with twisted horns as he gazed into his victim's eyes from red gleaming orbs of his own. For the first time Dereas felt compassion for the archer. The Kechian was trembling on his knees wrapped in a hellish circle of runes while the wizard, mumbling and throwing powders and vials of liquid, snatched up a staff, and sought to lay an evil hand on the archer's sweating brow. He chuckled comically. Even Derken in his insolence did not deserve this fate at the hands of a certain madman.

The ghouls prodded their persons down the stair to the chamber below where another gargoyle relieved the ghouls of their vigil. Hand in hand, the warriors were shuttled away to some unnameable part of the castle. The ghouls shuffled off in cobwebbed shadows while the gargoyle prodded Dereas and Jhidik down to the dungeons. The guardian tossed them in a foul-smelling cell, where a single torch guttered above the bars. The monstrous bat-bird of a gargoyle lumbered in to chain their ankles to massive iron balls. The grill shut tight; the creature retreated to stand watch outside.

As best as possible, Dereas examined their dank cell. His only discovery was that the chamber was impregnable. He slumped down in miserable defeat, burying his chin in his hands.

"Well, at least we're alive."

"But for how long, Jhidik? Are we doomed or are we just doomed?"

"I'd say we're snake-bait unless we can convince our ogre outside to open the grill and give us a free pass."

Dereas gave a harsh laugh. "Fat chance of that." He slid over to the iron mesh and gazed bleakly out at the silent gargoyle. The monster turned a notched eye to him and glared back, letting out a low rumble.

"A highly inadvisable plan, Jhidik," Dereas muttered. "Look at the size of him. We're as good as lost if we don't figure a way out of this. Listen, we have to come up with a way to defeat it! Who knows what scheme the wizard has in mind for us, after he deals with our archer. You and I are the last hope."

Jhidik chewed his lip. "Alive we are valuable commodities to this madman Ahrion. You saw yourself, the grisly fate that the ghoul faced for letting Svanctus die?"

"I did," said Dereas. "Listen. We shall pretend to do battle with each other. You come at me like a fiend. We force the creature to come lunging in, opening the gate, to break up the scuffle. If I predict properly, his neck will be on the line if the bat-goblin thinks it will fail."

"A good beginning, but what then?" Jhidik stirred restlessly.

"We shall improvise. Think, Jhidik. I'll first feint an attack on you. You pretend to fall and be hurt badly. Hopefully the ruse will be convincing. If in the moment he hesitates, I can attack him with this ball and chain. When I cry out, you leap and attack from the flank. You get it? I'm going to need all the support I can get."

"You'll get it, warlord. You will." Jhidik rubbed his chin grimly.

"Yes, it is risky, but what do we have to lose?"

Jhidik gave a resigned shrug.

"One more thing."

"What?"

"Make it look good, or we're rat fodder."

They continued their conversation in low tones, making no

chancy assumption that the fiend outside the door was not savvy of their language. As they prepared their assault, Dereas shot covert glances from time to time at the bat creature. He had the innovation to indulge in a game of chance with Jhidik using flakes of mortar as betting chips. Satisfied that he caught the creature's attention, he launched into a tirade. "You stupid hillman!" he yelled at Jhidik, shoving him back. "You lost the first round, now you're trying to cheat me? Give me back my chips."

"What are talking about, Dergath scum? You lost, not me."

At first Dereas pretended to snatch back the tokens then gradually he let his banter grow to wild shouts and escalate to blows.

"Miserable monkey!" cried Dereas, clipping Jhidik on the side of the head.

Jhidik swatted at Dereas; Dereas fell gasping.

The guardian peered in, warning them in growls and snaps of teeth to pipe down.

Dereas and Jhidik ignored the pleas. They laid into their quarrel with both fists. By the time the real fighting began, the monster had thrown back its horned head and gave a hissing bellow. It thrust clawed paws through the iron-barred window, threatening to topple the stone wall down on all their heads.

Dereas smiled. The prisoners continued to throw punches and trip each other and loose insults. Fumbling with the lock, the beast lumbered into the cell, fixing its burning eyes on Dereas. The warlord knew too well that their fates hung in limbo, if that beast decided to end his game.

But just as the bat-gargoyle was realizing its life was forfeit should the foolish humans be harmed in any way, it jumped to haul Dereas away from Jhidik.

But Dereas rolled away. He forced the beast to scramble deeper into the cell.

Unsure of what to do, the beast sidled from foot to foot, uttering frantic mewling sounds. The possibility of crushing them with its clumsy hands was enough to cause it indecision. At Dereas's signal, he made a hostile lunge toward Jhidik. Crouching, he swung a slack loop of chain in a half circle around his head and lashed out higher to avoid braining his friend. Jhidik took the cue; he executed a magnificent fall. Dereas spat a mouthful of blood on the Pirean's neck—an embellishment which he had rehearsed mentally, by biting hard on his inside cheek.

The monster perked hairy ears in alarm. It blundered over to throw Dereas aside and aid the Pirean.

Dereas seized the giant ball and raised it high over the gargoyle's hunched shoulders, crunching it down on the ridged skull.

Jhidik rolled out in time, barely avoiding getting crushed by the bat-ogre's weight as it fell. The creature writhed, mortally wounded, but it was not ready to die just yet. It sought to drag Dereas down to oblivion with it. It heaved on the chain, gasping its last breaths, dragging Dereas closer to its snapping jaws. Despite Jhidik's repeated blows on its head with the chain, the beast did not relinquish its hold. Then it expired as Dereas crashed ball on its skull one final time, and the warrior-chief sucked in a grateful breath. Morosely he gazed: only a mere six inches from doom...

The gargoyle lay still; the door to the dungeons lay open, but the heavy ball severely limited their movements. He and Jhidik were still anchored together by chain. The realization was a crushing one, but at least they were free! They crawled out to the main corridor and guards' station and with mad haste began scouring among the molder and the thick webs and ancient bones and rusted chains, looking for some instrument to help them.

Before long, Dereas's hands fixed on a sizable double-headed battleaxe lying off in the shadows. His muscles strained. He lifted the rusted weapon and brought it down hard in a shower of sparks on the chain links. The old iron split. The colossal stroke severed them from confinement. They laughed in exultation.

Dereas cautioned them to silence. Like stealthy rats, they crept back through the moldering passage, back to the upper hall where the wizard made his abode.

No ghouls or gargoyles were in sight. They loped through the murk, with freedom at their feet!

III : Birth of a Minion

The fugitives curved their way through the dungeon corridors, stepping gingerly past bones, skulls, and wracks of torture instruments. They scrambled by rooms of tarnished weapons and treasures undreamed of, guarded by strange idols and stranger gods. From one such room, Dereas snatched a broadsword, and Jhidik seized a falchion and flat-bladed short sword. Time did not permit them to examine any other precious oddities in those rooms that would bring them riches in the markets of Numenon. Ahrion doubtless would be alert to their absence. With no surprise, they heard an inhuman shout. Dereas paused, cocking his head. The fabric of the air was torn with agony. Each knew that it was the Kechian's cry. They bowed their heads.

The howl died, something akin to a dying beast. They reasoned that their comrade had died with it.

Dereas kicked open the door to the main dungeon hall. Together they hotfooted it out into the halls beyond. The stifling oppressiveness of the lower halls lessened, but hardly were they graced with any more comfort here. Ahrion stood atop the spiraling staircase, peering down on them with a baleful purpose. At his side hunched a new minion—a black and grisly thing, winged and pointy-eared, gesturing at them with an outstretched claw, uttering an inhuman screech.

"Welcome, friends. You are just in time," greeted the wizard with familiar exuberance.

"Hurry Pirean, if you value your life!" hissed Dereas.

They coursed a hasty retreat, bounding down the stone steps, each hoping that the other knew where they were were going. The keep was enormous and they took many wrong turns down one gloomy corridor after another. At last they gathered a semblance of their bearings.

But not without Ahrion's minion hot on their trail.

Too many indecisive branchings had brought the beat of unholy wings on their backs. In panic they fled. The scratchy thud of nail and claw against rough-hewn stone sent shivers up their spines.

The hall veered left. They stumbled down a dust-caked Doubtless hallway flanked with armor and spears. The winged behemoth was on them, soaring inches over their heads, a nightmare from a phantasmagorical world. Now they could smell its primitive fetor as it swooped low and sent Jhidik sprawling with its talons. The creature landed with a resounding thud in front of them. Wings and fetid body barred exit out of the nightmare shadows. It was huge beyond belief, towering two heads over their own, with wings spread, bat-like ears twitching. They faced their worst fear. The thing's teeth were like yellow fang-incisors of the wolf ghouls which had attacked them amid the peaks of Shaele. The grubby skin was matted with animal-like fur, ears pointed up like a devil's. Two roving hawk-like eyes were Tyrian purple and glowed with a vampire's lust, yet with a mindlessness that sent chills up Dereas's spine.

A new wave of horror drew about his soul. The face was one they once knew: the Kechian's, the sardonic grimace unmissable, with a goatee still carved in the inhuman physiognomy, despite the bestial transformation that had taken place.

Without calls or laments, it launched itself upon the two with the bestial savagery of ten. It was Jhidik, crawling on his hands and knees, who it attacked first. For scant seconds Dereas was unable to stop the mighty momentum of its charge. The creature's wattled legs were like corded trunks, its wings flapping with enough power to break limbs. The malevolent fangs drooped and slavered, enough to snap bones.

Ahrion should have been given credit for his mongrel of death. Yet his *minion* was not invulnerable to attack. It met Jhidik's upthrust sword with a brutal cuff of a crusted wing. A fierce cry broke from its mouth as it swatted and the blade sang out of the Pirean's hand.

Jhidik cursed dumbly as his sword clattered away on the cold stone and the creature fell upon its quarry without a moment's thought. Eager to rend flesh with its flexing talons, it hopped closer, thrusting beak in to lay bare the life of a pale victim. But Dereas moved like a coiled jaguar. He heard the anguished cry of his friend and uttered the war cry of his people. Then he flew at the winged fiend with every bit of his strength.

Quickly he made it know pain.

The broadsword sang deep into the hoary spine. Out spilled a river of blood. Wounded beyond repair, the creature half hopped and flapped, between its teeth shrieking dreadful syllables as it flew back like a viper, springing upon its enemy. Jhidik wormed his way along the flagstones, struggling for breath. With seconds to avail himself, he steeled himself for the final onslaught. Dereas was not unprepared. He stumbled backward, almost losing his balance. He would have perished then and there had he not had the instinct to roll clear, shield himself by the wall, thus avoiding the crushing weight of the hulk. He did have the sense to flail out his broadsword and hack at the thing until the monster's wings were shredded pulp and its blue blood spilled darkly on the floor. A long time it had been since blood had flown so thickly in Basilurk's halls . . .

"Kill me, warlord," gasped the creature, wheezing in uncontrollable spasms. "You know who I am."

"I know you as Derken."

The thing gave a hoarse wheeze: "Those who are still alive in the world of men know not what it is like to have lived in a husk of a demon..."

In the throes of its dying, the thing's eyes betold a woebegone tale of shadow and pain and Dereas was moved to pity. "I will kill you gladly, Kechian. I have wished it from the very outset. But not for reasons of earlier spite. You are an insolent oaf—but you were at least human, which is something you are not now. You are something of wraith-spawn. In the fey name of Balael, I liberate you!"

With a Herculean thrust, he ran him through to the spine and Derken gasped his last breath. There was a smile on the Kechian's face as his spirit dissipated into the ether, voiding the horrible devil's pact that Ahrion had forced upon him. So did Derken die and know peace—as a man, not a demon puppet of Ahrion. The warrior's spirit flowed as a thin ethereal mist from the wracked corpse with sorrowful stars for a garland. The lighted aureole rose, escaping through a nearby window to make way to the plane beyond. There came a lull—then a terrible silence.

"Shades of Balael," hissed Dereas.

"Hurry," called Jhidik. He staggered up from his crouch, nursing a swollen knee. "It won't be long before that devil Ahrion senses the demise of his minion and comes after us!"

"True, but can you make it? Your wounds are serious."

"Never mind me! Just pray that we can outrun that wretched wizard. Hark! I can hear his banshees already."

True enough, an unearthly screeching grated on their ears. The din slowly began to build. Now an ear-shrieking whine filled the stone hall.

All turned heads to behold an electric image—a glowing necromancer bending over his fallen minion. A cry formed on his lips. With it, a smoldering grimace of hate crawled over his young face. "Who are you to bring death to my minion? To Hexir's hell with all of you!" The wizard thrust a flare of blue magic perilously close to their feet. They hopped back with curses on their lips. Ahrion's amazement was rich, but his anger was degrees beyond. With a voice laced of canniness, he began whispering spells.

Dereas of Asgolin called back: "Know that I am warlord of the Huughites, sire to the ancient Tukosothians!—neither I nor my companion will die in the rot of your accursed halls, Ahrion, so farewell! Save your magic for lesser fools."

"You are deceived, Dereas of Asgolin, for you have not yet undergone your 'trial'."

Dereas did not like the sound of that warning. He grabbed his friend by the arm; they rounded a corner. They fled to new sounds of terror. The wizard's laughter echoed in their ears. "Try, try, little mice. Try to flee, but you can't!" Dereas caught glimpses of a pantheon of twisted creatures come after them out of all the crypts the wizard had ever kept hidden in the bowels of Basilurk—monsters of all sizes, shapes, and forms, fiends come to life before their very eyes, things that should never have been, roused from the dead or some dismal, unholy slumber.

The fugitives skidded to a halt. Gaping at the main portcullis, they saw the rusted iron had slapped shut after their passing not hours ago. The iron-paled threshold gleamed in the starlight, impregnable with the bars drawn so decisively down. The bat-like guardian was present, hunched miserably aside the grate. It looked like some monstrous troll out of a huntsman's nightmare. With curses and swings of blade, Dereas baited the gatekeeper, drawing it away from the portcullis, eluding its clumsy swats while Jhidik, yelling to distract the beast, aimed an expert throw at the lever that controlled the gate. The Pirean gave a chirrup of triumph as he saw the flat end of his short sword strike home.

They dove head first, rolling under the rusty pales as they groaned upwards. The guardian's claws were but inches from their necks. Across the bridge they scrambled for their lives, heedless of the giant pteradons that circled overhead. Their relieved lungs sucked in the cool mountain air. But the winged sentinels did not hinder them, nor did Ahrion's brood of darker things accost them as they raced across the rune-crusted trestle. Ahrion's creatures lingered at the threshold but they did not dare cross the dire waters. Dereas frowned with puzzlement. The necromancer stood at the gate, coaxing his creatures to continue, but they cringed in the light of dawn and he leered at them with distaste. "You are not fit to be messengers of mine," he began, and his mouth worked terrible spells to punish them.

"By Balael, I fear we are lost!" cried Dereas. "Look, the devil is not a stone's throw away and he seethes, ready to unleash his diseased minions in the hundreds upon us."

"Nay," replied Jhidik. "They are creatures of shadow. Look. The light does not let them advance. They are afraid to pass."

Dereas shook his head. "But why? How? We are sitting ducks. Why do they not follow us and devour us? Where are his ghouls?"

The Pirean sucked in a breath. "Why are you so quick to name the things? Look out!" Behind came the tramp of Ahrion's ghouls—a half score of them, shambling and gibbering in blasphemous unison. Dereas turned, shot a mad quick glance, his jaw quivering. So...others did guard the bridge's hither side. With hysterical strength, he cut the marauders to ribbons as they flooded in a tidal wave upon them. Jhidik's sword flashed crimson, hewing heads and limbs with frenzy. The brood lay twisted in groaning heaps, clumped in bright bloody swaths. Lungs heaving, Dereas calmed his naked terror. Was there no place to flee in this world from Ahrion's creatures? There came an ugly silence, punctuated only by the grim moaning of wind, and the cold gurgle of water far below.

The fugitives held their breaths. Across the bridge the winged minions ranked in the hundreds aside their master Ahrion. But his minions did not advance, though they flapped and hissed and stamped, and threatened to charge the infidels in one seething storm.

Dereas turned bloodshot eyes skyward. A glint of warm sunlight was shafting ever stronger over the eastern mountains.

Jhidik's breath came in labored gasps. "I have heard that magicians of his sort have no power outside their own domain. Their own netherworld is limited. Ahrion's threshold lies on hither side of this river of darkness—that bubbling brook lying so far below us is not a natural thing. Past that circle, I feel he can do us no harm."

"The victory is ours then. To the gods—to Balael!"

"To Kizoi!" muttered Jhidik. But his mood became somber. "Perhaps, this time we have escaped, Dereas. But I fear none of us will ever recover from our battle scars."

Dereas looked in dismay at the swollen welts his comrade had taken on. He could only loose an angry curse. "By Dergath's wrath! It all starts to make sense now, Jhidik. Four strong men, each from a different race—to be Ahrion's prized minions!" He spat in distaste, the echo of his words were all the more hateful to his own ears. "We were to be his minions—his messengers—underlings. We were to await his beck and call night and day."

"Yes, his pet ghouls," Jhidik wheezed. "They who were once men, the slavers which brought us here. We were lucky we didn't become brainless jackals like them."

The two limped down the hillside, each offering his support for the other. Dereas could not help but feel a sense of pride for Jhidik and satisfaction at being alive . . . yet a hollowness crept into his soul. He stole a glance back at the black keep and felt the wrath brimming again ever deeper in his core. Ahrion's gaze burned deep into his own. One day he would return and raze this slag heap to the ground. He would destroy this blackhearted Ahrion. Yet why did he feel so little solace in having cheated death this time?

Danger and anger boiled in synchrony in his brain, rendering him confusion. Proper revenge had not been exacted. For a long time he resisted the urge to charge back across that bridge and demand justice.

The impulse of fools...

Not today. Not tomorrow. He would attempt no such crossing. With pain lancing in his right limb, he stared at the shackles clamped on his wrist. They would be shattered soon enough. He had only to discover a proper instrument to crack them without breaking his own wrist.

"Yes, Jhidik," the war chief rumbled. "We shall walk free for this instant. But we shall not forget those who perished today, nor the mercy of Balael that it was not us who died..."

BEASTSLAYER:
Rise of the Rgnadon

Prologue

"Our seers translated the ancient tablets from forgotten tongues—and they spoke in hushed whispers of a time before man, when a great flood rose flashing through the valleys, a cataclysm, some hundred thousand years ago. The rain sloughed from the heavens. The great glaciers cracked and shivered before bolts of lightning. Tempestuous gales blew around a globe on fire.

"Hear me, O valiant people of Xatu, that when I say the ice splintered, slid, melted in massive shards, the waters rose!

"The animals, stripped of their habitat, swarmed to Vharad, the only standing island in a sea of azure stretching as far as the eye could see. Some beasts burrowed into the ancient mountain and founded the tunnels below. Others fought for resources, scarce on a windy, water-cursed world—but only the reptiles survived—to evolve into creatures of nightmare, a horrendous brood, relying on strength and size to survive..."

—*Legend of the Flood, the mountain king*

CHRIS TURNER

1: Night Raiders

The beast within...the beast without,
Slay one and one slays the other!

—Old Huughite saying

Long before the sun sank Dereas knew something had been following them. Every instinct screamed that stalkers roved the skull-domed hills. Clear to him as the call of the jackal howling at the moon. His gut spoke loudly that two forces of independent origin worked against him and his band of riders, one human and one not. His instinct was never wrong. Facts spoke from a turned stone, a strange clawed print, a broken bush or weed, or the fretful way a scavenging bird would suddenly screech and arc to the blasted hills to the north.

Such marauders could be stalking, lurking behind the next hummock, or crawling flat on their bellies unseen beneath the gillhorse weed, or stealthily crouching at a high vantage, ready to pounce on their naked flanks or pepper them with arrows. And possibly then, something even more sinister.

Masking his rising concern, Dereas muttered to his lieutenant, "We must mount an assault on that wizard Alrion before long."

Jhidik's face remained expressionless. He rode abreast him as befitted a trusted second-in-command.

Dereas coaxed his mount a little faster. "'Tis time. The eve of the new moon of *Alperon* is upon us. It has been almost a year since you and I escaped that cursed realm of Phygus! Saeth's teeth, but I vowed I would put a sword through that sorcerer's guts."

"That you did. I owe you my life, for what you did back at that keep, Dereas, strangling that gargoyle fiend who was our jailer." The Pirean warrior gripped his reins and crouched in his stirrups, scanning the coppery dimness. His sun-bronzed face frowned at the rising wall of stone on either side of them and the ever-deepening shadows. "These hills are a phantom's haunt."

Dereas could see that his lieutenant hated the low moan of the wind, which was nothing more than a wraith's whisper in this world of haunted canyons and crumbling outcrops.

"It's a world away from those pleasant vistas of your Pirean homeland for sure."

"Evil things are about," grumbled Jhidik. "Ever since we found your village burned to the ground and we scoured the plains hunting for allies and gathered such warriors as we number now, I have felt eyes probing me. I value your cause, Dereas, as much as any man, but how I wish to be back among the green trees and the clean rivers flowing with salmon and trout!"

Dereas managed a restless smile. "We persevere, Jhidik." He winced, reaching out a hand to slap his comrade on the back, but then he peered up at the darkening sky. "'Tis odd, what war can do to a man. It fuels his courage; it burns off his petty sense of identity, his mediocrity. But it also brings out the darkest side of him, the beast, the wandering, primal animal."

Jhidik's eyes narrowed. He looked none too easy under his chief's gaze. "All these evil calamities smack of wizardry at work. Recall, we did not part on amicable terms with Ahrion."

Dereas shifted in his saddle. The name spawned a spur of hate in his heart. Ahrion! His lips peeled back to spit out a gob of phlegm; it brought a sour sting to recall the men lost in the days past to the jowls of demon hyenas and undead raiders. To unnatural blistering fevers or inexplicable storms, or cursed to fall off their mounts at full gallop. The war chief suspected it was the result of the wizard's magic. "We must smite where we can, face our enemies wherever we must!" And yet, a part of him considered deviating from the course of this hateful, rugged trench.

The high, shaggy-shouldered mounts they called the *belamyl* snorted as they fought the reins. Heavy clouds thickened the sky and a scathing wind bit at the war band's leathered skin. Crimson sunset stained the ancient hills a dark ocher, a color that Dereas liked little, for it was the color of the banner-emblem of the dead wizard's circle.

Up ahead the gully split into two. A narrow file wound up to the left; ahead the ravine coursed in a stony jumble to disappear into a pool of darkening shadow.

Jhidik's keen eyes caught sight of tracks on the trail and he swung an arm out to his chief.

Dereas frowned; it was an ill sign. He stopped his men. Dismounting, he fell on a knee and examined the sinister three-toed tracks in the dry soil. A shiver of loathing crawled up his spine. Could more of the undead fiends from the gorge have tracked them this far? His face creased in a scowl. It seemed unlikely, unless sorcery was about. He did not doubt Ahrion's necromantic power to warp events from a distance, especially after witnessing the sickening transformation of a Kechian archer into a ghoul before his very eyes. When he and Jhidik had been imprisoned in the wizard's keep, it had been nip and tuck that they'd escaped.

He sent Lavg, a gaunt-faced scout, cantering on straight ahead.

Black Balael! None of their riders could follow the higher ground, nor trot comfortably on the heights of the ridgeline—it was too roughhewn, not to mention impossible to get the heavy-hoofed belamyl up the steep inclines. Worse, Sil had not returned from his reconnaissance a half hour ago. What had become of that first silent scout? Had he fallen to the claws of one of those three-toed beasts of yesterday, or some other horror that haunted these ravines? Only yesterday, a scrabbling detour after a freak windstorm had led them into a skirmish with a band of half human raiders, with grizzled goat skulls crowning their heads. The fiends had slaughtered a third of their band and blood had flown in plenty before they had turned, fought the devils and cut them to pieces.

If the warrior still lived, he would have to catch up to them, following their prints in the thin soil and sand. As it stood, Sil's hoofprints had petered out some way back on a stretch of rocky gulch at the feet of a stone statue of an ancient king.

Craning his neck, Dereas had a sudden feeling that evil dwelled in that dusky gap straight ahead and wished he hadn't sent Lavg on up so hastily. He made up his mind. He could not halt the company a moment longer. To wait here was death. He was risking the lives of his men. Shadows were teeming, ripe for wicked purpose and the powers of necromancy. He could feel it in his bones. Yet he hated to spare another man on another doomed mission.

He regained his saddle and urged his mount into the narrow ravine to the left, avoiding the trail of fallen boulders strewn to the side. Many a somber face of his company fell in behind him.

He regretted the course of events that had forced him to push his riders farther than ever before to escape the teeth of dangerous foes, to the remote territory known as the Vhale, a broken country of hills, scavenging jackals, roving nomads and feral hyenas. This desert was a land forgotten by kings, a fringe of the larger Thiran wastes which stretched thirty leagues east, to end at the shores of the mysterious Pzison Sea, the end of the world, or so it seemed.

Jhidik murmured in a confiding whisper: "Perfect haunt for these living dead!" He loosed a gravelly curse. "When you almost fell to the claws of those shamblers back at the gorge, I was thinking this was the end of us. The moment Dereas Beastslayer falls, 'tis the day I burn my sword and a sad howl goes up in the world of Darfala! Are we so cursed that we must ride under such a black cloud?" He shook his head in bemusement.

Dereas's frown grew. He chewed his lip and motioned his men on, hefting his three-foot broadsword. His eyes stared unblinking in the gathering gloom.

Geylor, his other lieutenant rode in from behind. "What are a few undead to our sharp blades? You are the Beastslayer of old! We called you that when you slew the rabid hyena as a young hunter-warrior, fourteen summers old, the wild, reckless panther you were!"

"Aye," piped up Ger, "You slew Hreta the Black's wild dogs which our enemy of a rival-chief loosed on our yurts to his amusement."

Dereas's expression became harder to read. He reached around his saddle and tore the *gareyr* axe from its halter, whirling a practiced loop. He signaled to his ragged band to change course down a wider, winding ravine. He peered at the long line of riders, cantering in double file behind. This was his 'new' Huughite clan. Resurrected after his village in Asgolin's fall, these spirited mercenaries were a prideful bunch—lean-muscled, bearded and armored men. Helms framed the confident features of their faces; their spears glinted in dying light, their swords easy to access from worn scabbards; they were a brood dressed in hides and cloaks, leather underpadding and light-ringed mail—men determined to ride into slaughter, give all to the ghost should their chief decide it.

Dereas looked at them with approval. Down a defile and up a rocky incline the riders pushed their tiring mounts. Dereas shook the sweat out of the tangle of copper curls that amassed under his bronze bull-horned helm. Another dry gulch cut their path, spread with rugged outcrops carved with the faces of kings of past ages. On impulse he led his men into the shadowed alley. Like those of old, a hunter or tribal chief's sense of survival was the only thing that kept a man alive in these days, long enough to remember the old tales of sorrow and the calls of the dead, in these dark times of the *Saeth*.

Dereas lurched in his saddle.

What was that? A rustling scrape? Something else yet—a muffled cry that rose over the ceaseless plod of his company's hooves.

An unfamiliar beast? The creak of a bow? How much time had passed in his musing?

In an age when sorcerers or half men walked the daylight, it did not pay to daydream too carelessly on the coming of twilight. He scowled, rubbing his eyes, then wiped the cold sweat from the back of his neck. Though the gully offered a firm defense, the path was far from wide and they were too hemmed in to maneuver properly. He remembered how he had lost his bow in the last fight with the undead, a weapon he wished he had now! He gave breath to a thunderish curse. Had he made a grave error? A cold chill tickled up his spine. His company trotted two abreast, prey to disaster, should the unknown strike.

Dereas's dark glittering eyes stared in brooding discontent. Though they cantered with speed, it seemed there were ten more hollows to replace the rises and falls where hideous goats' skulls peeked from the tops of battered slopes, roped to a stone cairn. The ghoulish fanes of the desert people were painted with inscrutable symbols.

The lead mounts whickered. Had he failed his men, left them as prey for ambush? He gripped the copper hilt of his battered sword, plagued with indecision.

He motioned in circular fashion to Geylor, alerted by some primitive instinct. Attack was imminent. He gave signal to Jhidik and they crouched in their saddles, spurring ahead in a burst of speed.

A thunderous roar of pounding hooves rose above the wind, masking the clanking armor and battle cries of enemies up ahead. He and his lieutenants looked straight into a raw assault in motion: hooves skidding on rock, the muzzles of screaming horses, lurid shouts, the scrape of unsheathing swords. Dozens of riders were on them from all sides. Before Dereas could mouth a war cry, twelve of their own were cut to a man. Footmen dropped from the sheer flanks, appearing from nowhere: black, wolf-helmed figures, charging over the low ridge of domed rock like panthers to land before them. A team of axemen shimmied over a section of rock a half stone's throw away, pouncing from on high to assault their exposed flanks.

Dereas felt a wave of blood wrath. His warriors writhed to action, hands fleeting to weapons, horses rearing. He could feel the indescribable thrill in their blood, the lust of battle and adrenaline rush, death and excitement rippling through them like wildfire.

The marauders wore black shin greaves, black breastplates and wielded wicked upturned axes, as well as maces and swords. Most had triangular-shaped bucklers strapped to their forearms with corkscrew-shaped spikes fanning from their edges. The enemy helms were shaped in the form of wolves' heads; they rode a mixture of horses and desert belamyl—sturdy animals, like their own, with the shaggy slope-backed shoulders of the steppe-beast and the resilience that set them apart in climes of dust and drought.

How had these stalkers mobilized themselves so quickly? Dereas's mad thoughts whirled. With a savage cry, he drove his mount straight into the teeth of the dragon.

His first glance told him his band was heavily outnumbered, curse Balael! By exactly how many he knew not in this sudden turmoil of death. The aggressors had the semblance of mercenaries not unlike his own, with brawny arms and weathered faces: lawless men with no common cause but the wild inspiration of their leader, a dangerous mix.

The attackers' axes and maces rose in meaty synchrony and ripped into Dereas's men and mounts alike. Dereas reined in to the side to avoid the sickening crunch of a spiked ball to his left thigh. He plunged cold steel through his attacker's throat, then gaped in dismay, for at the head of the throng, he recognized a murky shape crowding his way forward: a big, stalking warrior with coal black eyes and a vindictive smile. He stood out from the rest of the mob like a lion in a pack of cubs. Grimly he sat astride his lightly armored belamyl, wearing brown-leather armor. A wolf-eared, tri-horned helm was fitted to a flap of leather and fur under his chin and around his cheeks, accouterments making him look more like a wolf than a man. A mane of russet-colored hair, not unlike his own, fled low down below his broad shoulders like a dark cape.

In the warrior's left arm he wielded a mighty broadsword, while in his right, a small buckler strapped to his forearm, studded and dented, obviously had seen much use in its killing days.

Dereas turned his snorting mount and discovered to his horror that a quarter of his warriors had been thrown or disabled—that his enemy, come out of nowhere was cunningly slaughtering them. It was his half brother, Rusfaer!—grinning like a bloodhound bearing down on him like something out of a nightmare.

Dereas gave the Huughite chant of victory and thrust his mount into the chaos, the fire catching his blood. His black-maned belamyl screamed and reared, biting hard into the hide and sinew of enemy mounts as it had been trained to do from a colt. His broadsword crashed and sang bloody hymns among man and beast, felling anything in its path. Two snarling riders rolled in to replace their blood-gored fellows and the beastslayer parried their furious stabs. He let blade, dripping with blood, run arcs of carnal triumph, in and out of faces and torsos, wreaking frothy ruin, finally to sink deep through gullets or straight into teeth—while Rusfaer, desiring the heart of his brother, caved the skulls of a half dozen protectors who bravely squeezed up from the back ranks to aid their leader. With each stroke, the enemy lord's glistening weapon felled two more howling defenders who blocked his path.

Dereas snatched a dirk from his belt and stabbed it into the ribs of the nearest mounted dead man, using it as a lever to unhorse the slumping rider. Kicking the man's horse out of the way, he saw from the corner of his eye, his man Jhidik hacking at an overzealous foe who threatened to cut legs from under him. The enemy had foolishly underestimated Jhidik as an easy mark, though nothing could be further from the truth. The Pirean was a wild hillman of the northwest, as wild as the savage race his people bred. He caught a momentary glimpse of Jhidik springing through the melee, earlier unhorsed, whooping and howling and slipping on blood and entrails—only to plunge his sword through the rider's ribs. He parried the stroke of another who thought to sneak in and smash him from above. The enemy was hacking and stabbing at air. Jhidik ducked and hopped up on a dead man's horse and with sword whirling, kept the front line intact.

Rusfaer grunted and kneed his mount through the frenzied press, trying to get to Dereas with undisguised intent. His and Dereas's swords met in clashing sparks, the bright clang of which, sent glinting blades sliding off each other with strident rasps.

Dereas's belamyl reared on its hind legs, windmilling hooves to gouge out one of Rusfaer's mount's eyes. Curses and agonized screams of dying men rose above the clanking of armor; the thunk of metal into flesh and bone was appalling. Swords flailed in gobs of bright crimson and horses snorted among their own like raging boars. Surging bodies and shattered hopes filled the hollow. Dereas, awash in the lust born of battle, gave himself over to a drunken frenzy. With all his massive strength and its intrinsic brutality, he struck and struck. Sword slid off an adversary's sword in a desperate dance, but found no hole to penetrate the oiled leather beyond the chain-linked ringed iron. He needed higher ground! His curses rang loud but hollowly. He sought for a break—for himself and for any of his men remaining—from any of this bleak scrabbling that put them in hand-to-hand fighting so fatally outnumbered. Then, in a dizzy moment of lull, he leapt from his mount and gained a higher point—four feet above where he had leapt from his saddle, ten feet from the base of the hill. Up the slope he clawed like a wild cat.

Even his brother, taken by surprise, grinned at the daring of the last act, though he was not happy with its outcome. His mount was blinded. He roared curses at his men and tilted his wolf-helmed head back, flinging orders left and right.

Dereas laughed. His quick maneuver had deprived his idiot sibling from an easy kill. Yet Rusfaer reined in his thrashing mount and thought to try a similar maneuver. It was an act as desperate as it looked, but was what saved them from immediate death, for no sooner had both warriors gained access to the slope when a spate of raucous screeches came pouring from the sky. The men struggling in the frenzy below looked up in speechless wonder—upon huge winged horrors diving from the sky—hideous bat-weaselly shapes, beaks curved as bows, trained to skewer man and belamyl alike.

The warriors stopped their hewing and raised shields to protect themselves.

It was a useless exercise. The dozen or so winged obscenities dropped on them like predatory dactyls. More fiends were swooping down by the second. These creatures were black, flying hybrids with bat-like faces and ears, bodies of weasels and beaks and wings of condors. Each was thrice the length of a man, and as massive as a titan. They gave shrill, bloodthirsty calls while their yellow-snapping beaks homed in to shred man or beast. Anything that moved were prey to attack, horses, belamyl and men, and many fell in pools of their own blood. The gully floor was stained a rich crimson.

Dereas had heard of these beasts, *Eakors*, grisly terrors from the south, but he never imagined to see them here. Such were evil spawn, carrion creatures of old, birthed from the unholy joining of an earlier race. The sinister product of past ages forgotten in the mists of time, with the appetites of raptors.

Whatever foul scent had lured these monsters to their trail, Dereas did not know. Indeed these must be famished brutes, to fly so far north from their haunts. An ill omen, or likely, Ahrion's scourge...

An ugly red-tailed beast swooped to rake Dereas's torso and he ducked the repulsive beak and the punishing claws in a pantherish crouch, growling, letting broadsword run a dangerous arc through and beyond. Notched steel caught the ribbed flesh; sinew parted in its underbelly and a left talon sheared off, squirting a spray of avian flesh.

The outstretched talon flew from the bird in random flight to smack into one of Dereas's enemy's faces. Off his mount the warrior slid, clubbed like a felled ox. A roving avian picked up the man's limp form from the gully floor and carried him away to some nameless place in the sky. Dereas grimaced in horror. The weaselly thing that had lost its talon set up a painful outcry, landing crookedly, hopping about in demoniac agony, unlike the others which squatted to feed on the corpses that bled out in the gully. In its mad spree, the Eakor spitted a horse with its curved beak and the rider was thrown clear before one of Rusfaer's black-bearded warriors jammed a pike up into the Eakor's throat. Another of Rusfaer's unhorsed men ran, sword flailing, bawling curses before he too was scooped up in unbreakable grip into the darkening skies.

For all that these winged devils were, they shared something in common, a greedy purpose, a merciless slant of eyes, a slavering vulture beak come to feast on the corpses of the dead in battle. An insatiable appetite for flesh, dead or alive.

The last feeling he had of the abomination before it was skewered in the gully was one of indescribable horror. At that close range when it had stared him in the face, Dereas could not fail to see that the creature guarded a sinister intelligence, something mirrored in its greenish, upturned eyes, suggesting a primitive, merciless intent. The older beasts, like that creature, had a set of tusk-like horns on their graying crowns, which made them look like mutant owls.

Others of his band, Ger and Munes, made play with axes about their helms, hacking the legs of those that swooped down...only to have other sky marauders snatch them up in grasping talons. The beastslayer watched three men wrenched from their saddles and lifted airborne. Whether they were Rusfaer's men or his own he could not tell, such was the confused sequence of events.

Dereas crouched on his uncertain perch. An inarticulate sound welled in his throat as he readied his dripping sword, exposing himself to the diving monstrosities. Rusfaer was torn off the ledge closest to him, and found himself in a desperate, cat and mouse fight, dangling upside down from a gripping talon, yet he still clutching his blood-soaked weapon. With superhuman strength, the warrior stuck the naked blade up into the bird's belly, followed by a spike from his shield. The winged creature danced and writhed in its death throes to crash headlong into the boulders of the hill. Rusfaer fell in mid air with it to land catlike on his feet, his fall broken by a maimed horse. The bird beast that had snapped its neck was pounced on by another vulturish brute which began to feast upon it.

The sickening stench of death and rent flesh was all around. Yet Dereas could not help but stand goggle-eyed in horrified fascination. Out of the corner of his eye, he saw Jhidik lifted from his mount, pulled from his fight with one of Rusfaer's wolf clansmen. The Pirean flailed puppet-like in that grip, unable to fend off his attacker. Another bird joined the fight for the Pirean. Jhidik's body was caught in a ravenous tug-of-war between birds.

Dereas could not tear his eyes away.

Graced with a quick, instinctive intelligence, the Pirean lashed out with his dagger into the blinking eye of his immediate tormentor and it fell with a hoarse shriek, tracing dizzy circles to its doom. The Pirean fended off the second Eakor by lashing out with his boot and hewing at its wing as he twirled in midair before it flew off screeching in frustration. To his good fortune he was close to the ground. His fall was minor, but as he stumbled about blindly on the corpse-strewn ground, more Eakors were upon him.

Dereas shouted at the top of his lungs. His furious waves were an attempt to attract birds in midflight so they would turn their evil eyes away from his bloodied comrade. A coven of them swarmed upon him with shrill outcries, loathing the upstart who straddled atop the shoulder of rock and singlehandedly stood to defy them. Beasts swooped and snapped in one collective effort; the beastslayer, teeth bared, bloody sword gripped two-handedly, was hard put to fend off their gnashing strikes and lunges. He ducked and stabbed upward, slashing at their grim beaks. Then he fell flat to the stony ground to avoid being snatched aloft. What he saw below became a seething bloodbath; one minute were dim, blood-hazed glimpses of men falling off mounts and fending off talons and beaks, the next, a blinding swoop of a hurtling shape come out of nowhere to hook a hapless rider—like the brown-bearded Rao who was caught in a vicious pulling match between two predators, similar to Jhidik. One bird had the man's upper body trapped in its beak, the other had talons gripped round his leg. The beasts pulled in fervour—Rao gave a soul-shattering cry; the man was ripped straight down the middle, drawn and quartered like a prisoner condemned to the torturer's block.

Raucous squawks fanned the air as the two birds flew off with their respective pieces. Dereas bit back the dry heaves that struggled to spew from his lips. The ragged scavengers that had not secured their own meat, swooped to gobble up bloody scraps.

Dereas's lungs heaved. He staggered to his feet, blood dripping from a dozen cuts. He hardly knew whether he was alive or dead, only that his last savage strokes had somehow repelled the invaders...

Now that the war bands were severely diminished, birds below fought over oozing body parts. No human-like figure or human-friendly form littered the defile. Dereas wished for no such ghastly end, but the truth of what lay before him could not be denied.

But what he had underestimated was the cunning of his brother. Rusfaer was born of a wolfish resourcefulness that knew no equal, a ruthless skill which few men could call their own. The beastslayer had failed to notice his half brother slinking away from the carnage while his men died and birds gnashed. He was crouching on his haunches, keeping to the wild gorse-bushes and the twisted weeds to the side, threading his way upward like a puma. He snuck up on the ledge before shattered boulders, where unaware, Dereas hunched with horror, staring bug-eyed at the scene before him.

The wolfskin warrior landed on the ledge beside Dereas. Only a boot crunch announced his presence. The beastslayer whirled and the two faced each other, crouching in fierce warrior's stance, grimed and wild-eyed, swords raised, hot breath heaving raggedly from their chests.

Dereas studied his brother with an animal's appraisal. The ghost of a thousand memories burned in his feverish brain.

"Back, you swine!" came his dry hiss. "There's nothing to stop me from slaying you, even if you are my flesh and blood."

Rusfaer flung back his wolfskin-clad head and hurled a caustic laugh. "Slay away, little brother. We are all of mortal blood here, just mere flesh and foolishness—both doomed."

With a fiendish laugh, he rushed his brother, heedless of any roving Eakors, and Dereas scrambled to meet him. The bigger man twisted sideways; at the last instant, he sent his brother skidding off to the lower end of the ledge, a space already ridiculously narrow. Dereas, the lighter of the two, started to slip on the loose pebbles, trying to stay aloft and not roll down the incline to the pit below in a blood bath with the Eakors. With a vicious grin, Rusfaer wheeled. He cut him off, spun a blinding kick and another upthrust killing stroke, but ominous screeches spilled from the air and tempered his barbaric rush.

Powerful wings knocked the two flat. Slipping on pebbles and weeds, they cursed and thrashed, each trying to throw the other off the slope, but both rolled, grappling each other like beasts. Before the ultimate could come, Dereas felt a flutter of wings. Fetid breath brushed his face as a monstrous shape swooped in and tore Rusfaer out of his grasp. His brother was hauled aloft by heaving flesh, but managed to hold on to his weapon and hack at the bird's pink underbelly. As he fell out of the snapping beak's range, grasping talons twitched and another bird swooped and tore the weapon out of Rusfaer's hands, scooping him up before he smashed to the rocks. Dereas watched his brother's weapon crash on the rocks below. While he himself continued to slide, Dereas felt the rake of a bird's claws about his own waist, and with an anguished cry, he found himself encircled in those three-foot talons.

Dereas's breath squeezed out of his pinched lungs. He was drawn airborne like a leaf in a gale, the beast's talons curling round his midriff like a ruthless python.

His leather underpadding saved him. He twisted his head around and saw a long train of Eakors dangling men and mounts in talons, alive or dead, flapping noiselessly south in a gathering of darkness. The warrior's silver-chased dirk was at his side, but he could only reach the Eakor's claws by stabbing wide. Sawing with frenzied haste, he managed to hack one of the bird's toes off, but it only clutched him all the tighter, till the warrior cried out in pain, and the weapon nearly fell from his nerveless grip. Where were the fiends taking them?

Dereas peered up through bleary eyes—he saw only the feathered underbelly of the weasel-bat horror that carried him. The reek of the mite-ridden hide made him retch. The slobbering beak opened and closed, gnashing in synchrony with the beat of unholy wings. He bobbed to a backdrop of countless stars as the beast shrilled out its cry in an abominable tongue, the tireless thrust of its powerful wings pushing a foul air to his nostrils.

The host passed over a thin divide far below and a dried up stream in a valley. Canyons showed as dun smudges across the dull, featureless lands. To the west, distant fires of villages winked; a larger settlement thrust farther out, about fifteen leagues, he guessed, on the plain.

From toe to crown Dereas's body ached. Some of the smaller beasts were not much more than fledglings—rapacious copies of their kin, well equipped to carry a full horse or belamyl in their clawed feet. But their young clutched only torn fragments of the victims, a section of a severed body, a threaded leg, or a neckless crown. The fact that these beasts carried dead carrion as easily as live caused him to wince with the monstrous possibilities, and the images that awaited them...

Sour phlegm crawled up his throat.

The myriad stars wheeled before the beastslayer's eyes and faded to pinpoints as a bloated moon poked up on the eastern horizon. It rose over the distant sea, a misshapen grinning pumpkin shrouded in a wreath of pale wispy cloud. The killers must be passing the uplands of Erath now, Dereas thought, and he spat blood. Onward into Yemestan and the plains bordering lost Karache and Kuewanishe the birds would fly. The piles of corpses such predators had consumed on the battle fields below... Dereas shuddered. The wars between iron-fisted Yemestan and her less than tolerant neighbors had been many...

For an instant the war chief's eyes fluttered and he saw the flapping beasts' lumbersome shapes on his horizon. In his dream-like daze he noted they seemed to be making slow progress in this twilit hour. They flapped continuously to keep their vast bulk aloft, unlike their cousins, the primitive condors, which could glide for miles without moving a wing.

The birds carried them far—far across a great river, an ox-bowed ribbon in the inky dusk that ran with muddy water while the desert plains fell below like a silent blanket of powdered chalk.

The Eakors, weasel bats that they were, squawked as they neared their destination; in no way were they ready to release their holds on their prey. Ever south they flew, with steadfast precision, wings beating steady cadence through the tortured night. Dereas felt a wave of despair shiver through his frame, knowing that even if his men could break free of those grips at this height, they would be smashed on the sand below. Their only chance would be to fight in a mad, unseasoned rush, carving their way to freedom upon release.

But when? How? It was all so random; and it would not be pleasant. In those few moments when the birds decided to do with them what they would, Dereas vowed to be prepared for that moment to fight for his life.

2: Vharad

Ancient mountain hidden under the moon,
What skeletons molder in your crypts?
What beastly horrors skulk in your shadowy halls?

—Vharad's Secrets, unknown minstrel

For how long the warriors flew in the clutches of the giant bird beasts, Dereas could not say. He guarded a cold memory of some wind and damp cloud fleeting by and the hoarse grunts of doomed men. He kicked and thrashed and snarled but the bird only loosed savage cries and tightened bone-hard claws around his torso. He hung limp and disheveled, bathed in cold sweat and dried blood, his gaze wandering, swollen tongue pressed between lips. He could sense that Jhidik, his warrior-in-arms, floated somewhere in the void ahead of him in that flock of Eakor nightmare, the blue moonlit edge of his baldric glinting under the tireless flap of the dominant bird's wings. But that too was like something out of a bad dream.

His tortured thoughts swam in a sea of chaos. Only one man could have tracked him so ruthlessly and doggedly! not to mention engineered the bloodbath that had befallen him and his men.

The war chief choked on his own phlegm. How well his towering brute of a brother knew him!

A swift rage tore at his insides. He had lost his tribe. Insidious forces had worked against him. True, he had raised some few dozen supporters, hardened men, loyal men, willing to battle at his side, but it seemed that he faced only resistance, from his clansmen, from the detestable wizard Ahrion.

And not leastly from Rusfaer, who had gained support of the outlying tribes by treacherous means, if the whispers among the black-gummed nomads who swilled sour goat-curd wine were to be believed.

Even Balael seemed to have turned his back on him. For that he choked back sorrow, for he could not for the life of him understand how he had fallen afoul of his god. There were many who cursed the name of Dereas Barath-o'-Bear, or 'Beastslayer' as they called him in the northern climes, for deserting his tribe.

The grim beat of his heart at this moment bore testament to how ill he felt about that unjust accusation.

He shivered at these somber thoughts as he flew through the air clutched in the talons of the beast. For in this world, like the land of Darfala herself, all was veiled in shadow, as his grandfather had told him many a time—and that all was not as it seemed...

The Eakor's talons tightened and the war chief saw through slitted eyes a misshapen peak rise out of the rose-tinted murk.

It was a sight that made him quail. For Mt. Vharad, crouching in its ominous splendor, was shaped like twin buffalo horns and its snow-peaked crown gleamed sullen orange in the breaking dawn.

Could it be morning already? The war chief shook his head. Every sense of time and place seemed skewed.

Even in these moments of aching stupor, he saw a leaden sea wallow to the east, with no barges or ships or thriving ports to grace its solemn shore. Rust-colored ridges and hard-baked soil melded into desert, marching leagues southward. Northward ran desolate plains, the grassy steppes of his homeland left far behind.

The flock was heading straight for the horned mountain whose horns were like the old bull-god Broasus's; ever did Dereas feel a soul-wrenching destination approaching. The dawn's light snuck slowly over the rim of the world to strike the summit; everything seemed different, both dreamlike and distant, for the mountain had a malevolent cast to it—also an evil reputation. In his woeful hour, Dereas was wondering how these predatorial beasts had come upon them. It was not natural...The Eakors had found them under improbable circumstances, far from their hunting grounds, if this far mountain was their home.

The birds wheeled closer, raising their tusked beaks to the setting moon. They gathered in a crescendo of screeches of recognition. Such tumult could be akin to some code or password to the guardians who protected the cliffs and they flocked to greet them. The birds veered around the lit face of the mountain closest to the glimmering sea. Dereas saw a brilliant flash of tumbling water—a great waterfall pouring down from snow peaks, nestled below the two horns that crowned the giant mountaintop. Giant statues of kings or animals flanked either side of the waterfall—only the work of myriad sinister craftsmen! Over centuries perhaps.

Cold fingers of doom touched Dereas as he felt himself falling, falling and cool wind hissing in his ears. The birds arched their way down in a series of slow undulating circles to form silhouettes against the sheer cliffs. He was still far above and could see black dots set against a dun, chalky scarp marking the mountain and his hapless peers. Further below, clumps of plumed, long-leaved trees rose up from boulder-strewn ravines thrusting down the mountain side, or jutting out from the sheer cliffs.

The birds soared and swooped, and Dereas saw they had dropped to the quarter mark from where the mountain rose above the desert.

When he caught sight of the bristly nests he knew horror. They teetered in a long clustering line, clinging to the cliffside, massive branched ovals of them. Their 'twigs' were actually branches as thick as a man's leg and knitted tightly together, like wickerwork. Some protruded like quills from nest and cliff. Dereas's heart went numb, for it could be no accident that these baby chicks housed in the vile mangers, screeching, fluttering, bald as a gibbon's behind, were crying for fresh meat, and that *they* were the fresh meat.

The blood hammered in Dereas's head. His mouth worked.

A warrior whom he recognized as Angmir set up a doleful wail a stone's throw away as he was swept closer. His parched lips bent back in grimacing rage as the Eakor gripping him descended upon those chicks in their dark nests, reaching, squawking, teeming.

Angmir struggled in the bird's foul grip. With no success. There gleamed a hundred or more nests like that one, each with four or more squirming young, and the beast lowered its glistening talons so its slobbering brood could stab up their beaks and snatch at the defenseless man.

Dereas wrestled in the bird's claws, trying to hook sinew with his knife. But even his thews could find no play in that avian grip. That he might be next in the slavering maws with their gnashing, horn-hard beaks...

The monster that clutched him had caught up to the rest of the flock; he also saw the bird that gripped Rusfaer dip in flight. Jhidik's and others' carriers were circling close to the roosting colony. The air was a frenzy of men dangling from talons and shrieking in contorted postures. The mad rush of beating wings and ruffled feathers mingled with the discord of squawks and screeches. The din was deafening, and all around him Dereas could see the expressions of fierce anticipation on bird faces with parted beaks. Jhidik was alive; thank Balael for that! But his heart sank when he saw his friend's face wince with agony as he was pushed toward a dark nest, and the awful, frightful suffering of what was to come.

The first victims, including Angmir, fell screaming into the yawning beaks of blind, beak-snapping chicks. Some of the horses, dead or alive, fell into the yawning pit of black jaws and bills—the owners of some of them, half as big as a horse itself. They ripped into the dangled offerings with twisted pleasure; Dereas's eyes grew wide at the carnage that progressed in those nearby nests. He watched men he knew torn apart and swallowed before his eyes. In a gruesome instant he knew sorrow and prayed to Balael that he be smitten down before such fate befell him.

But no such liberation came. Only the chilling thought that come his turn, there would be no recourse, only a sudden jerk of beak, a reaching of blood-stained gums, the sharp rending of teeth tearing his flesh, as a slimy, mucous-filled palate and gullet worked.

A group of squawking outriders drove in with killing shrieks to ram claws and tusked beaks at their fellows. They tried to dislodge the others' squirming cargoes, some with success, others not. The victors snatched new prizes out of the air; riotous beak wars raged, peppering the air with feral squawks as the losers were drenched in blood and feathers and went skidding back with bloodied jowls, broken wings and snapped talons.

Dereas gaped in revulsion. The sudden wing of a passing bird raked his side and almost hurled him into oblivion.

His world swam upside down. He felt thankfulness for a few brief moments more of life, but none too lasting. From the flailing of limbs and shrieks coming from Rusfaer; it was clear he discovered equal horror in being sidejammed by one of the airborne attacking birds.

Yet providence intervened...perhaps Dereas's prayer had been answered. A big ugly creature with a gray pelt and large badgerish crown swooped giddily to tear the neck out of a younger Eakor. It snatched up one of Rusfaer's howling men. The dying bird crashed into Dereas's carrier, which upset Jhidik's before it crashed into the treetops below, ripping into fronds and woody stems. It hurtled down through the treetops smashing headlong into the rocks.

The beast kept rolling down—down the rough hillside until it was a shredded mass, while the victor snatched Rusfaer's man out of the air and dropped him into a large nest of four chicks. The warrior was ripped to shreds and devoured in seconds.

Jhidik's captor careened out of control, falling and smashing straight into a hellish pit of screaming young. Jhidik was thrown clear. He rolled to the far edge of the nest.

Dereas's bird followed, crushing half the chicks in it, nearly pancaking Jhidik and his near death-twitching bird.

Dereas released himself from the jumbled sprawl of broken flesh. The injured mother Eakor's talons had gone limp and he found himself faced with a ring of blood-hungry, clucking chicks. They were twice the size of his own hard-muscled body. Jhidik was beside him, scrabbling for his life. Dereas brandished his knife, slashed left and right. Eyes, nose, throats, fetid wings, all became targets in this flesh-shredding fight for survival. The mutants were all over him! He scrambled, numbed feet trying to gain a position of defence. But there was none—trapped here like a rabbit in a pack of wolves.

The chicks squawked with hunger, thrusting beaks forward; gruesome noises poured from the backs of their throats, a sound which seemed like the cackle of a demon's laughter. The membranous pink necks showed pulsing veins and youthful flesh glowed underneath; the skin under the wings was wet and thin like goose flesh. Dander from ruffled feathers spilled in the air like chaff. Wings spread wide, the fiends hopped about in mad anticipation of a feast, some trampling on their fellow chicks in a food-finding frenzy.

Branches snapped; the nest's foundations ripped away from the cliff. With the force of the shifting weights, Dereas and his lieutenant were pulled into space. The shifting clawed feet and the slamming impact of the dead mothers had broken the balance...now the world slipped sideways in hellish doom for the gasping men as they fell through the air.

Dereas dropped slowly at first, then saw the desert loom below him, as an unreal blanket of sand. The horns of the mountain, much higher still, lay hidden behind the frowning cliffs. But the dislocated nests floated above and to the sides like twisted clouds in a vast open sky.

Dereas groped empty air, feeling his heart leap into his throat. Both he and Jhidik fell from brambly tier to tier, down the cliff while angry birds dove and tore at them, trying to snap up their flesh. But the beastslayer could only laugh—a laugh of maniacal anguish—knowing that such effort was in vain, for he was already doomed to suffer a gruesome death.

Yet he did not.

Dereas's fingers grasped a tangible thing, a limp brown form and he and Jhidik fell with it, nests and all.

The sudden confusion and violence of the nail-clawing skirmish had given Rusfaer opportunity to hack his way free from his captor.

The birds had reached such a pitch of frenzy that their senseless aggression triggered a sudden trail of casualties. Dereas caught glimpses of Rusfaer and other warriors of their bands tumbling in free fall.

The beastslayer felt fronds ripping into his flesh. A sudden stabbing pain...then a clinging vertigo as the slapping branches slowed his descent. He caught a mad glimpse of Rusfaer and the others smashing through the screen of treetops above him in a horror-plumed whorl of destruction. Then the breath whooshed out of his tortured lungs as he fell flat on the padded hide of an Eakor.

Dereas sucked a mouthful of air back into his lungs. He realized he had managed to grapple a dead bird in midflight. Whether it was the one which had carried him so far all this distance, he knew not, only that it had cushioned his fall, and had spared him the fate of a spine snapped in two.

He groped to his knees to examine his wounds. Superficial, at most. He was alive, no broken bones. The ripping cushion of tree fronds and springy nests had deadened the others' falls too, likewise the fleshy bellies of the mangled Eakors.

A handful of dizzy human forms lifted themselves groaning from the tangle of bodies. The tottering figures fought to get air back into their lungs.

"Kizoi's devils!" rasped Rusfaer. "I curse these fiends to the end of time!" He mopped blood and feathers from his eyes and hauled a gray-faced warrior to his feet who had a bloody gash whittled across his bare skull.

Dereas saw through his stinging eyes Rusfaer's men staggering in their boots, taking groggy steps about the wreckage like broken scarecrows from a distorted dream.

He shook the fog from his own head. The treetops soaring above them had shaded the dim slant of the morning light. They had landed on a broad strip of loose shingle that hugged the cliffside. A trickle of water now purled nearby where shadows played through the boulders and foliage. A pale light illuminated the winding goat paths around them. The cliff soared a hundred feet above in a phantom loom of mist.

Crumbling boulders and giant sandstone slabs had fallen from the cliff over time and Dereas's eyes now raked over weed-choked cavities and lichen-crusted boulders. The tall cactus-like flowers growing from the base of the cliff with their yellow blossoms offered hiding places.

By a solitary palm a large gaping hole loomed not far distant. It seemed blasted by magic. The hole was surrounded by a ring of weathered boulders.

Dereas's eyes had pegged it immediately. One of the big Eakors was still twitching in its struggle against death and tried to lift itself. But it could not. Its talons were pinned and broken in many places. The beast could only rise inches from its stony cradle with a barrage of angry slobberings, using its twisted wings to try to crawl closer to where the men were stirring.

Dereas moved away from that lethal beak, his lips locked in a contorted grimace. Several surviving chicks were still rustling nearby and he staggered sideways to escape them as they raised ravaged wings.

Already the survivors could hear horrid screeches echoing from above and each knew that many sinister dark shapes would be falling on them soon.

Three of the five who fell were dead—Geylor, Misten, Alapas. Crushed by direct impact or pinned under chicks these men had no chance. The others stirred with a hopeful hint of survival.

The adult Eakors were either maimed or killed. Dereas grabbed a blood-caked poniard from one of the dead men and fended off a battered chick that had risen from the rubble to snap at his leather-padded leg. He drove the tip through the chick's throat and caught a last glimpse of the corpse beneath. Beyond, Rusfaer's group struggled in the near carnage. His brother, having unhooked himself from the crush-winged Eakor that had broken his fall. He searched for some weapon to kill it with, while the maimed bird croaked strident curses.

Rusfaer, helmless and riddled with scrapes and scratches across brows and cheeks, groped around blindly, searching for a club. He snatched a bent blade from the bloody belt waist of one of his crushed henchman and ran the slick sword through the beast's heaving breast before it could wrap its talons round him.

The hulking warrior rose and panted. His puzzled expression spoke of shock that his brother was alive. In those hazy moments, it seemed from Dereas's perspective, he could only regard Dereas with the coldest hatred.

Dereas tripped forward in a frantic scrabble to tend to Jhidik who was pinned under a creature that struggled to rise before it tore off his arm.

He hauled his friend to his feet and sent his blade through the thing's eye. Wiping blood and grime from his own face, he snatched up another dagger from a dead-man's fingers and placed it into Jhidik's shaky palm; he put his back to Rusfaer and the other five of his band who tottered around grumbling curses and looking to the giant warrior for leadership.

"Quickly!" Dereas called to Jhidik and another warrior, Amexi. "Let's be away from this feeding ground. More fiends are on their way!" He saw that Amexi's face was hardened and bleak, his blond hair matted with dried blood. The multicolored tattoos of the animals and weapons on his bare neck and cheeks lay coated with a sheen of sweat, grime and cuts. Experience had told him that such a man was a survivor, aye, a fearless ally to have on his side. He had, after all, walked away minimally scathed from the fall. Training his anxious eyes skyward, Dereas scanned the lightening sky. It was pale and brooding, and one in which he gave the sacred protector sign of his god Balael.

Grunting, he hobbled amid the gathering. The three picked their way through the knotted wreckage of bodies, and dodged any lump or shape that came at them. Back along the base of the cliff they tottered, toward the cave opening, nothing more than an ominous gap in the cliff face that seemed to peel back and stare at them with joyless mirth.

The dark hole in the cliff yawned before them with portentous challenge, into the pits of hell itself. Dereas frowned at the threatening way it rejected the morning light like a wizard's curse.

"Zecrates' jinxes—" he breathed. He had heard tales of these tunnels before—into Vharad and the lost mountain, and the haunted tunnels of *Shaerm*. Likely this was a gateway into one of those dark crypts. Skalds told of catacombs too, haunted places under the mountain that peopled forsaken creatures and lost kingdoms of elder races, unimaginable to even the most graphic story-tellers.

"What an eerie, filthy place to have to die," muttered Jhidik, squinting into the light-swallowing darkness.

Dereas glared in indecision. Was it an act of chance that had brought them to this evil-looking tunnel?—must they pass through uncharted territory and on to the other side of mountain? He did not know—only that they must do something in their wretched condition to escape the gathering fiends ready to rend them to pieces.

He herded his men closer to the cave. Jhidik forced a sullen grunt. "In there? You've got to be joking?" The Pirean winced. "Curse this game leg of mine. I've heard Beren's ghouls or worse live under this mountain."

"What choice do we have, Jhidik! Into the tunnel!"

The others hesitated; even in the wake of the killing shrieks echoing nearby, the warriors shied away from that sinister hole.

"By Balael, I'll kick your hides in if I have to!" bellowed Dereas. He shuddered and gave pause. Grave tales had been told of what lived in these labyrinths under the mountain. With visible effort, he waved a bloody hand to thwart Beren and his ghouls. Better to contend with a possible ghoul or two, than fight those fiendish raptors again.

"I think it's a bad idea," came Amexi's cracking voice barely above the squawking birds. He limped back with a bleak stare.

Dereas saw the man's watery gaze fall in a half-dream, echoing shock and terror. Amexi looked to be a man alive courtesy of Balael.

410

He shrank back from the cave's cold shadow, and like Jhidik, he peered with dull wonder. Dereas thought him half-minded to turn tail from that place and its clutch of dank vapors.

Snapping boughs and a whoosh of air caused them to look up. Dereas saw an obscene flock of black shapes tearing a path for them through the leafy treetops. Other birds wheeled a bowshot away, furious upon seeing the carnage of their kin.

The blood drained from Jhidik's face. "We're done for." His wide pale eyes scoured for an alternate refuge. "Make for cover! There along the weed-grown cliff."

"No, into the cave!" thundered Dereas. He shoved them past the lip, the straggle of boulders likened to a witch's hex ground. The three dove through—a sanctuary of blackness that swallowed them whole.

Their first sensation was a dampness, then the feel of loose stone beneath their desperate feet as their eyes adjusted to the gloom. Dereas braced himself for the worst and shouldered his comrades onward, nerves tensed from the harrowing fall through the trees. The sounds of flapping wings and vulturish squawks were fast on their heels but muffled. They clawed their way slowly past boulders and tinkling streams deeper into the eerie confines of the cave. It was a tunnel as wide as a bailey's gate, and as it opened up, Dereas saw as wide as it was tall. Their ears rebelled at the tumult of the shrieks of pain and vicious tearing sounds that gathered behind them.

Looking back, Dereas caught a glimpse of one of Rusfaer's axemen hooked by a nightmarish tusk and hauled aloft.

Dereas clenched his weapon with numb dismay; he stifled an urge to scramble back. The howls and rending flesh and cries of terror of Rusfaer's remaining riders flung wide about the entrance to the cavern, sent chills up his spine. Those men were tossed into maws and fed to the chicks which scrambled about in hopeful numbers. It was enough to bring a lesser man to his knees. Dereas also caught a glimpse of Rusfaer himself and two of his last mercenaries brought to senseless unreason racing into the black confines of the cave.

The beastslayer turned his head. He bit back a gushing nausea, loathing to think what the bird creatures would do to his brother.

He pulled Jhidik along. Amexi stumbled but a few feet behind. The bird-beasts devoured whoever remained in their path and clawed and smashed at the rock of the cave entrance and stalked on up the tunnel, heaving their loathsome bodies against the stone. There was sharp clacking of sharp talons, then croaks and shrieks as the fiends hopped and flapped their way deeper into the blackness, hoping to snag some remnant of the fugitives.

The warriors scrambled on in gasping frenzy, clawing their way in what little light penetrated the cavern. But there was nowhere to run—only a high pile of rocks barring their path, black and chiseled. At the summit of the pile Dereas spied a small crawlspace, fit for maybe a man at a time, and with it some hope. The pile spilled down to a loose mass of crumbling debris and old decayed egg shells, and bore an evil cast about it.

In the darkness, Dereas saw dim ruby red eyes bobbing behind in feral intensity. He felt shivers of doom tickle at his back. The coldness of the Eakor's gaze could not help but bring a sheen of sweat down his neck, but neither could it gain the beasts passage past what looked a Y junction. The small boulders they had passed seemed to have been caved in from above, or perhaps they were man-hewn blocks.

"Follow me!" Dereas growled, not knowing whether anyone would. He clawed his way up through the musty closeness. A frantic scrabbling of men's boots and nails clawing on stone clamored at his heels. Through the crawlspace he pushed himself, down into the unknown gloom.

He slid down a slippery slope of pebbles, bones, shells and varied rubble. At least one form came skidding after. Where were they? Dereas shook the daze out of his eyes. He had slid into a shallow pit. Amexi wallowed at his side while Jhidik groaned in the nearby litter.

A greenish glow bathed the area in uncertain light. At one time this pit appeared to join the tunnel on the other side of the cavern but now it was nearly sealed. Why? Above their line of sight reared a dusky opening: a side way? Above and to the left showed another passage, almost too small to pass, but from which issued the curious green gleam, of source unknown. Muffled gurgles ran from deep within that burrow from where the water trickled. Yet Dereas felt a strange comfort in the faint glow, which in itself encompassed the seeping water. At the head of the cave mouth, five feet above their heads, a cryptic symbol carved by rude tools pointed in a direction roughly east, toward the sea. The actual ceiling remained a blur of darkness in the vaulting heights.

The chamber brought a puzzled frown to Dereas's haggard face. The musty, ancient odor brushing at the air carried with it a feeling that nothing had crawled here in an age. Dereas trailed his fingers along the wall, feeling the grooves of many stacked blocks. So, not a rockslide after all, but cut stone blocks piled up in the direction of the junction to block the tunnel. Yes—deliberately done, as if intelligent hands had been at work here. Why? To block the entrance to prevent creatures from invading the cavern? Another question surfaced. Which creatures were being blocked, and from which side? The large broken egg shells that crunched underfoot indicated that some menace had for a time lurked deeper in the darkness.

Dereas shivered. In face of such evidence he felt sweat drip from his brow over the implications. A quiver of exhaustion ran through his aching muscles. No creature larger than a man could pass through the cramped hole. This much he mused, along with the recurring suspicion that this side of the cave had been unoccupied for years...

A clatter of pebbles broke the eerie stillness. A sudden shape burst through the crawlspace. The intruder slid down the pile of debris, panting and gasping. A man! Dereas tensed. A fresh wound glaring out from his forehead indicated a close scrape with an Eakor. Another figure came tumbling next, a small knife clutched in hand, coughing blood and cursing. Both were men of Rusfaer's band.

The last to crawl through was Rusfaer himself. Dereas sucked in a hostile breath. He gave a choked cry and leapt with sword swinging.

Rusfaer, sliding down the ramp of pebbles, landed with his boots on the backs of his men to brake his descent. He sprang to his feet like a cat, a four foot blade gripped in his twitching palm, cutting loops in the thick half gloom.

The warrior was bareheaded and his rusty hair trailed down a massive set of shoulders. A scarred face gleamed, burnt with years of sun. His eyes glittered like balefire and in the weak light, looked slitted like a pike's. His right arm was bloodied from elbow to wrist, and the leather padding beneath his mail was torn and soaked with blood.

The warrior grunted and faced his enemies, blinking in the gloom to which his eyes were readily adjusting. He saw Dereas and clenched a fist on his hilt, ready to parry his blade, his mouth set in grim anticipation. The two warriors circled each other. Jhidik and Amexi crouched in the shadows, breathing in gusts, Amexi clawing for some rusty weapon. Dereas saw his rival's face crinkled with a neatly laid grin of false mirth. His eyes took in the situation in a ruthless second, assessing the domed chambers and its blackened ceiling that glistened with quartz crystals and geodes of amethyst.

"Well," he said, "what pack of rogues do we have here?" His voice boomed like hammers in a smithy. "Shall we draw straws to see who cuts whose throat first?" He let his sword trace jocular circles in the air. His ragged men followed suit, huddled at his side, brandishing knives.

"Let's start with yours," Dereas rasped. His fingers flexed and his blade swept out.

Rusfaer rushed to meet him, sword raised and dripping to the hilt in Eakor blood.

Dereas sprang to cut him down. Their swords met in a ringing clang that sent echoes rocking about the chamber. Rusfaer's blade, rippling from low to high, raking mail rings, cut a quick stroke for Dereas's throat, but the beastslayer dodged the swing. He rolled under that strike and parried with a sense of ease. He stepped away unscathed from a dismembering sweep, quite used to his brother's flamboyant, brutal attacks.

Rusfaer's cheeks were red with anger, and he turned and came reeling in for a definitive strike. Dereas's dodged. His light mail caught the rake of steel. His counterstrike hit home and his brother blinked in surprise. Normally such a blow would miss him by a half inch; now it grazed eight ringlets, nearly shearing them.

Dereas spun in a wide circle, ending in a catlike crouch. The twang of Rusfaer's blade still resonated off his mail rings as he planned his next move. He could smell the sweat on his brother's wolf skins draped over his mailshirt, amid the blood and bestial heat of hate brimming from the awesome form, but the lighter man pushed back, elbowing his enemy in the ribs, disarming him with a cunning jab and tight wrist lock. Rusfaer grunted, long blade slipping from his fingers—to clank on the litter of shattered skulls and thigh bones underfoot.

Dereas saw his traitor-chief brother assessing him with new respect. But with a blank-faced smirk that was born of a false look of surrender, the bigger man spun backwards and roundhouse kicked the loose blade out of Dereas's startled fingers. The two circled each other. Dereas stared into the bearded face, his chest heaving. He heard his brother laugh, a gravelly sound that sent the hairs up on the back of his neck. He returned the same blank stare on his brother's wolfish countenance. The two were weaponless, Rusfaer panting and masking his violent impatience. He charged, hands clawed like an eagle's. Then he grappled Dereas, muscles strained like bowstrings. They fought in near darkness, rolling in the detritus and filth, the bones and skulls and victims' tattered garments kicking up generations of dust and molder into each other's eyes. All the while Rusfaer's entourage feinted in and out, cheering and calling rude taunts, waiting their turn to chop Dereas at an opportune moment.

Blades whistled aloft and Jhidik and Amexi held the two rogues back.

"Stay your blades, you dungmites!" bawled Jhidik. "Let it be a fair fight."

"I'll kill you, you bloody bastard," Rusfaer yelled in Dereas's face in hate, trying to chew off his brother's ear. "You don't deserve to live!"

"You couldn't kill a newborn lamb," sneered Dereas. He gripped his brother's head in an arm lock. He too was rolling, wallowing in bones, helms, weapons, anything of the rubble underfoot—yet starting to feel the giddy rush from the weight and tireless strength of his brother's pythonish grasp.

"You would have been plugged full of arrows already," Rusfaer mocked, hissing through bared teeth, his thrashing starting to loosen Dereas's grip, "but we spent a dozen quivers, fighting off those cursed marauders from Kembashwe clan already."

"Your boasts are shallow, brother," wheezed Dereas, trying to reaffirm his grip. "We would have gutted you long ago, had not some foul wizardry played its part on your side."

"Foul wizardry? You are mad! Just simple tracking skill." The rival warrior's thick lips were frozen in a mirthless snarl.

The beastslayer felt an explosive anger, but his eyes widened in recognition of the truth of his brother's claim. He felt his grip slacken; his mind warred in a sea of conflicting thoughts. A bestial snarling and pounding of wings reverberated across the stone without, prompting a curse from Jhidik. Then Amexi wielded his blade and they rushed to pull the two apart. "Hold up, you stupid fools!" called Jhidik.

The fighters staggered to their feet, their chests rising and falling like blacksmiths' bellows. Six sets of eyes rounded on the cavern's dome, from where the sounds came. Each glared in confusion. Nose to nose, sweat dripping from their bruised limbs, they were two kings in a small tomb—easier to have two lions pacing the same den.

Angry tumult grew to a sliding of pebbles and broken shells. An awkward shape burst from the crawlspace—one of the smaller chicks which squirmed free, and now bore down on them. Its webbed wings were spreadeagled and it raked at the rubble as it scudded down toward the exhausted men.

The thing sprang at one of Rusfaer's warriors, its beak parted and pecking at the man's blood-grimed face, nearly taking out his eyes.

"Talemeon's ghosts!" the man bawled. He turned his head, slashing out blindly. The tall grim-faced warrior was one of Rusfaer's senior clansmen. "Is there no end to these vile creatures?"

Rusfaer snatched at the dripping blade at his feet and speared the squawking killer. The others set to taking up femurs and using them as clubs to pulverize it to red ruin.

The sounds of fury rocked the chamber—a hundred wings smashing on the ancient stone. A blood-flecked beak snapped through the crawlspace, then a single glaring eye, red and furious at not being able to squeeze through. The chick's dying only infuriated the brood on the other side of the wall. The death of one chick would be the death of them all. Dust fell in sheets from the very ceiling with every crunch of the fiends' beaks and tusks on stone. The beat of their wings crashed against the tunnel walls. The blocks seemed ready to cave in and crush them to death and each man ducked, mumbling prayers to their favorite gods.

"We can't stay here," muttered Amexi, his weapon quaking in his grip.

"You think?" Rusfaer growled.

The brothers glared at each other. Not one trusted the other any more than a famished beggar could toss a moldy crust of bread to a gull. They were fierce figures in this stifling murk with the blood of chieftains running in their veins—skilled warriors and leaders in their own right.

"You may want to kill each other," Jhidik chided, "but I suggest we pool our resources in favor of staying alive."

"What do you suggest then, Pirean?"

"Balael has spared us. Agreed? So, let's see what we're in for then?"

For a tense moment, Dereas and Rusfaer stared one another

down, shafting daggers and grumbling oaths. Rusfaer slammed his weapon in his scabbard, muttering a foul grunt of agreement.

Gripes grew to cursing, but even the most foolhardy could see the logic of the Pirean's argument. Glares of enmity gave way to hopes of survival and what more they might do to save their necks.

Dereas saw Rusfaer's rabble wore leather pants—torn and ripped and grimed with blood and offal. Their eyes blinked in the murk. Rough, unsmiling faces returned Dereas's glare. Despite their ordeal, the beastslayer remarked that these stalwarts of Rusfaer's band seemed afflicted with only superficial wounds—cuts, scratches, bruises, scrapes and abrasions. Yet the newcomers, Hafta included— for Hafta was the surly warrior who had been near clawed by the chick—seemed on edge and ready to plunge a dagger into anyone's ribs. The other man was short and red-haired with a small tail of unkempt hair. This was a rogue called Draba. He wore short ankle boots and leather chest armor in the fashion of a Tluthian plainsman. He seemed by nature to be more important than he was, with a quirky smile that was a sour slash on a thin face, an indicator of one who fought dirty, and with conniving intent. His sardonic stance and pocked face denoted a slippery foe who tended to bluster, trickery and roguery. Indeed, the beastslayer wondered where Rusfaer had dredged up these rogues, for this short rascal had more the look of a Yemestan thief than a windblown, free-spirited man of the steppes. His mate, shifting on limber legs, the one they called Hafta, was blue-eyed and dark-haired and had fair skin with a nose ring and cropped ear lobes after the fashion of the rebel hunters of the eastern climes, possibly a Scidonian of the old spear-hunting tribe on the Pzison coast and its neighboring isles. This was a man in sharp contrast to Jhidik who was dark-skinned, hawk-nosed and wore only a loose jerkin of oiled leather under his mailshirt as most of his Pirean brothers favored. Amexi kept his distance, a man born and bred of Asgolin, his quick fingers flexing on his hilt with nervous anticipation at the croaking sounds without. His mailed chest moved to the rhythms of the code of roguish honor that lurked within these adventurers.

In a haste of panic the survivors fell to examining their surroundings. Blinking like owls, they searched this way and that for a way out. In the process they stumbled across all manner of helms, rusty swords, old bits of clothing, gold-trimmed tabards, frayed ropes, harnesses, broken cuirasses, musty accouterments, chin guards, and a myriad other things that may or may not have been of use—all amid the litter of egg shells. One great domed shell was half intact, suggesting an egg as big as a watermelon.

"Eakor's eggs!" snorted Rusfaer with disgust. "Whatever was in here, obviously cracked these eggs and feasted on them."

"On men too," Jhidik growled. "Judging from these skulls and gouged helms and ancient weapons and bones, warriors fought and died here." He gave rise to a scowl. "This looks like a grown man's femur here. Look at this batch of skulls! Bones smashed as if the meat was sucked out of them. How long has this ghoulish feasting been going on?"

Rusfaer shook his head in disgust. "Who knows, Pirean? We can assure ourselves it has been for a long time, perhaps decades. There's no fresh meat here that I can see, or smell. Just an indicator that—"

Dereas barked, "What's that?" At the sounds of talons clawing on stone they gripped their weapons with sweaty hands. It seemed more of the bloodhungry birds were attempting to surmount the pile of rubble and squeeze their way through the opening. Another beak gnawed halfway past the crawlspace, flaking rock at the edges. Dereas saw a trickle of speckled dust fall. Then flakes of stones. The rock overhead shivered in a disconcerting way like the tremor of an earthquake.

The men stumbled about, boots crunching on the ancient egg shells in frantic unison; all tried to gather as many items as possible before quitting this chilling pit while the sounds raged above. The tunnel that housed the green glow seemed the most hopeful but this was dubious, for it carried a reek of the ages, and an evil rising among other disturbing airs. As to the crawlspace, it looked as if the stone blocks, cut by human hands, was off limits.

Dereas frowned. If the portent of the bones and stray armor were any indication of past events, it did not bode very well for their survival. Dereas stalked about warily; he and his brother avoided each other like badgers. Each kept as much distance as possible and combed the area with distrust but calculated level-headedness, arming themselves with knives, swords, shields, anything that could be of use. They mumbled curses at the dimness and the lack of proper torches here in this musky sinkhole. All eyes scanned the darkest crannies for any activity. Any extra rusty weapon was better than none. Dereas peered into the shadows. Nor did he like the pernicious look on Draba's face when the rogue unearthed a curved scimitar from the rubble—a murderous weapon with a broad, double-edged blade as long as his forearm. The rogue rejoiced in the find, and Dereas frowned, for Draba was a man he would not trust farther than his eyelid.

Lost in a reverie, the wanderers sifted madly through the layers of rubble, an accretion of years of forgotten hopes and dreams.

Amexi and Hafta discovered a pair of double-headed axes which at first glance seemed like prizes, but they soon discarded. Lighter weapons were better matches for their cause.

Rusfaer advised them all to take a mix of weaponry: tulwars, maces, cudgels—in case they needed them to use as tools.

Dereas could find no fault with the argument and gave a curt nod.

Rusfaer fitted himself with a tarnished, dented steel cap. He tamped it on his wild locks to replace his lost wolf helm and also a pair of silver greaves to replace his torn leather shin guards. Dereas commandeered a wicked, two-pronged spear that felt light and easy in his grip.

The two turned their back on the crawlspace, mentally saying farewell to their life of sun and wind.

"Without food and fresh water, we won't last," remarked Hafta idly. "Maybe two days at most." The warrior glared around the chamber, tugging at his nose ring. Dereas saw he was the most heavyset of Rusfaer's crew and had a sardonic twist to his mouth with the many scars there.

"Never mind, it can't be far to the end," Rusfaer grumbled, "if an end is where these cursed tunnels will take us."

Jhidik mustered a cryptic murmur. "If we don't run into more jackals like those bird-fiends hungering for our blood."

The sounds of grisly croaking receded as the brood realized it was next to futile to break through the solid rock without shredding their wings and dulling their beaks.

"Wretched beasts," rumbled Rusfaer. He looked sharply over his shoulder. "Though I have heard of this filth, worse than Haghordian harpies, I have never heard of them roving so far north."

"Nor I," muttered Dereas.

"Or I," said Jhidik.

"So why come for us then?" Amexi scratched at his brow.

Dereas waved a hand. "Stranger things have happened. Let us be thankful to have our lives."

Hafta and Draba were absorbed in their rummaging, oblivious to the conversation. The two almost knocked heads stooping to seize the same jewel staring up glittering from the debris, an almost perfect oval. Their eyes had set right away on the prize of the topaz which glinted in the rubble. Their argument over it grew to blows. The fight did not abate and if things had been left to chance, they would have knifed each other for possession.

Rusfaer sprang forward to bang their heads together. "You dull sots. No sooner are you out of the beasts' jowls than you are fighting over a miserable bauble. Ah, Kizoi—these are the knaves I recruit by necessity!"

Dereas shook his head.

Rusfaer wiped his sword on a moldering garment and exclaimed in a blustering voice. "Out of the fire and into the cauldron's broth, eh, brother? Are we then to grope about this cursed darkness forever while ill beasts gnaw on our heels? Saeth's teeth!"

The remark earned Rusfaer no reply. Hafta muttered; Draba voiced rude murmurs; he rubbed his aching head.

"Let's see then where this other tunnel goes," advised Jhidik, "and what this glow is."

Out of the pit the water's gurgling grew, and they strained to squeeze their bulk through the opening that housed the greenish glow. They all peered into the eerie tunnel beyond, with doubtful stares.

The passage ran far off up into the shadows, a dim and uninviting corridor to nowhere. The deep gouges in the rough walls could have been the mark of primitive tools as easily as elder beasts' claws. Before it twisted out of sight round a sharp bend, they caught a glimpse of the thin rivulet of pale greenish water trickling down its middle, to disappear into a narrow cleft at their feet. The strange thing about this water was its magical phosphorescence, the same that bathed the entire corridor in its weird greenish glow.

Dereas felt the hairs stir on the back of his neck. Magic? Elder sorcery? A waft of danger sent the hairs rising further on edge. An evil drifted in the dust and silence of the past. Casting uneasy glances about the dank rock, he regretted that the black passage ahead seemed the only choice for them at this moment.

"All in favor to follow the stream?" Jhidik asked.

No one readily answered.

Dereas stooped in front to take the lead and Rusfaer jostled his shoulder and sent him sprawling into a small pool, massed at the foot of the stream.

"Watch where you're walking, you clumsy oaf!" yelled Dereas. Springing to his feet, he lunged at his brother, his face infused with anger. His tattered cloak dripped water and he bared his dirk.

Jhidik planted himself in between the two. "Easy now! Let's have no more roughhousing. There's no cause for bloodshed."

Dereas's breath heaved in and out. His tigerish anger hovered on the verge of exploding into violence. Rusfaer maintained a sly smirk, entertained at the sight of his brother so riled by what he considered a small offense.

The thick silence grew between the two. In between the spasms of rage bursting at the edges, Dereas forced calm upon his nerves, if only to ensure their mutual survival by upholding an unspoken truce.

There was a subtle vetting going on here in this group. Two chiefs vying for power. Dereas was not ready to relinquish leadership to his pig-headed brother.

The warriors were affected by the silent power play; Jhidik leaned in, assessing the two chieftains with sober reflection, tugging on his chin. The others gathered in a huddle and traded low murmurs, unsure how to handle this situation. Dereas was of mind that it proved better to show allegiance to one's respective master. Yet leadership and loyalty were fragmented in this small group, and the more support for a strong leader, the better. It was evident that Rusfaer's crew worshiped him in a savage way and that Rusfaer's own wild ferocity was to the cause, known across the outlying tribes as a force of impulsive action. And yet, fragmentation was never a good thing in a group where danger reared its ugly face.

The sun-weathered leather baldric on Dereas's shoulders wafted a sulfuric odor on contact with the water. In his nagging thirst, every cell screamed at him to kneel and scoop up handfuls of the cool water lapping away. Yet he resisted the urge, knowing that poisons or contaminants might lay him low. A man poisoned was no good to anybody. He thrust the desire off, tending to Jhidik, who was far worse than he looked.

Further examination revealed a festering wound on his lieutenant's left thigh, causing him to wince with every movement.

"That leg needs attention," Dereas told him seriously.

Jhidik grunted offhandedly. "We need to find a way out of here, Dereas, not fuss about with minor flesh wounds."

"I admire your selflessness, Jhidik, but it won't serve here. Squat down. There's a fellow!" He set himself to fashioning a splint from the flat edges of two short swords appropriated from the rubble pile earlier. He smeared the wound with a rude poultice of mud from the stream's edge and secured the blades about his friend's thigh for which the Pirean gave a relieved sigh. The warrior's crinkly grin was one of genuine gratitude.

Rusfaer and his ruffians stared on with disfavor, muttering at the display of warmth, before they trundled up the tunnel. They left the others in the heavy shadow.

"To Zecrates' two-toed sloths with Rusfaer," grumbled Dereas. "The lout obviously can't spare a moment for the wounded." After binding the splint, he snatched up the spear and with a motion to Jhidik and Amexi, stumbled on to catch up with the others.

Bitter silence grew—to breaking levels, until Dereas at last rounded on Rusfaer, "Well, 'brother'! Why have you not tracked down these depraved kidnappers of yours and put them to the sword? Instead you waste time hunting me?" The beastslayer's snarl was like a lash on the thick air.

Rusfaer halted to face him, his face a maelstrom of uncontrollable fury. "If it was so easy, I would have done that by now, don't you think, *brother*?"

Dereas scowled, looked away.

"The cowards who fled and left me for dead with nearly a split skull were long gone. The only thing that saved me was an extra layer of steel I put in my helm, which my father, *our father*, always told us to have. I wrapped a cloth around my aching head and stumbled on. But the trail was two weeks old."

"Did you not send word out to the clans?"

"I could barely get onto a mount without pain bringing me to my knees. I remember the faceless riders, nine of them—beneath their black cowls, I could read the sneers on their ugly faces, the lust in their bodies and what they planned to do with Pameel. Most of all, how they had planned this crusade from the very outset!"

Dereas grimaced. He felt his brother's angst; he would wish no such pain on anyone. He remembered Pameel of old, a queen and beauty among women, her dark hair, burnished and flowing like a river down her shoulders, a mass of springy foam, and her eyes a spellcaster's flame, as sultry as a cat's, shining with bright intelligence. Her delicate features were enough to win over any man, her lithe movements rich and her scarlet lips and curvaceous body only perfect parts of a seamless whole. The image burned in his brain with surprising clarity, and Dereas felt strangely inclined to regret his harsh words, knowing that his actions had indirectly played a part in her tragedy. For once, he did not have words to answer his fiery brother.

Rusfaer had not always been like this. A year lost wandering tribeless and with family broken and heart split had buried his carefree wildness, bred in him an resentment beyond conception. It shrouded any sparkle that might have burned bright in him. Perhaps his brother's loathing of himself and his failure to protect his tribe, and his family, had pushed him to a level of rancor beyond bitterness. Dereas shuddered at the idea, for he did not share this awful weight of loss on his brother's shoulders—even his vague conjectures of what his brother had endured were nothing compared to the reality.

Dereas tore himself away from Rusfaer's glaring scrutiny and moved up the tunnel. The scowl on Rusfaer's face deepened.

Every footstep in this inhospitable passage raised the hackles on Dereas's back. His eyes narrowed and roved the shadows, searching for pits and traps and any signs of dangerous movement that might bring predators champing at their necks. The seemingly bare and desolate corridor with its droppings of egg shells every fifty feet or so, on the surface did not portend any direct threat, and yet, it did not inspire much confidence. Things long dead and a threat long vanished seemed to haunt the very air and stir the ancient molder and rubble that dusted the tunnel.

He shook off the crawly feeling. He went over the details in his mind of what he knew of Pameel's kidnapping and the events leading up to her capture. He had done it a thousand times since he had returned to Asgolin.

It was strange that the clanswoman's disappearance had ultimately hinged on the demise of his and Rusfaer's father over a year ago.

Rusfaer quivered in rage not two steps away with his eyes blazing, a sworn enemy, and even as he turned to lock eyes with his brother in the tunnels under Vharad, he remembered the night Rusfaer had lost the confidence of the clan members during the great gathering of the peoples. Denied chiefdom, Rusfaer had left with his wife and mother on a cloudy evening on impulse. His small band had been waylaid by the members of a rival clan, who, hearing of the upset in leadership of the Crow Clan's reign, had planned an ambush. Their motive, to gain control over the antelope-rich lands by undermining the clan's bloodline, was dastardly. How they had accomplished this, Dereas did not know. Such tactics had proven common amid the nomads...

As if reading his brother's ruminations, Rusfaer crept close to him and whispered in his ear, "Listen, Dereas Barath-o'-Bear. After they snatched Pameel, they failed to put an end to me. The last vision that swam before my eyes, I saw two black-cowled riders leading the others. One with tapered, coiled beard, another with a star-shaped scar on his left cheek. They were leaders, overlords, cowards and filth, with the emblem of the Snarling Cougar and the Horns of Victory on their breasts. I vowed I would take vengeance on those cravenly scum. They left me for dead, my life force bleeding out—I also vowed to deal with you, brother, for forcing me and my mother and my wife out of the clan."

Dereas pushed himself away. "Lies! We never forced you out. You opted to go of your own accord."

"What other choice did we have? You do not know what it is like to be second in the clan. What it is like to wear the mantle of shame, when you, the eldest son, are denied your own chiefdom. No, not you, pretty cherub, the golden apple of my father's eye. You were the one who could do no wrong." A harsh shadow fell over Rusfaer's face and his mocking tone working itself into his deep-throated voice only grew. "I have always been the dark horse of the family. Let's face it, so I have always been, so I will always be."

Rusfaer had a way with words and Dereas felt his impassioned testimonial pushing the others to sympathy. Now the giant seemed to master his grief, and went on in a menacing voice:

"Take heed, brother. For I have not yet finished with you. Did you ever care to ask how I survived that nightmare? They had no interest in my mother. The marauders left her for dead, sobbing in the dust. If it weren't for her bravery, neither of us would have made it to safe ground."

"Then she lives still?" Dereas asked with wonder.

"She lives, but we were sorely tasked to make it to Knotran. My mother was never the same after that."

"Ill tidings, indeed. Closayne is a good woman." Dereas frowned, afraid to ask of his own mother. "Where is Klaistrous Barath-o'-Bear then?"

Rusfaer's face moved with a flicker of tension. "You have no need to worry for her. She is safe, with the others, at Azim."

Dereas could not help but experience relief, also a panged memory of Closayne and Klaistrous battling it out at the council of elders over which son would be chief. It was testament of the power and status women had in the clans. He wished it had been Rusfaer's mother who had won.

"Most of the women and children got horsed out before Asgolin was burned," admitted Rusfaer. "So I heard. It was the Spotted Lynxes who attacked Asgolin, maybe others, curse their hides!—they killed many of our warriors and fled with our belamyl and supplies and burnt our idols. They meant to make an example of us—because of our father who defied them. Whether it was they who waylaid me, I do not know. I have no definite proof."

Dereas's jaw hardened. A thousand thoughts fled through his mind.

Amexi's deepening scowl indicated Rusfaer's words affirmed his own suspicions. "Before my brother Brar fell to a Lynx arrow on the day of the raid, he told a tale of betrayal within our ranks—of Lynx sympathizers living among us, bribed by gold dust. We were alerted by riders mobilizing in the hills. Jequen, your father's advisor, ordered the women and children spirited away in your absence. We thought it best that it should be so, and his hunch was correct. I wandered weeks in the steppes after the battle, hunted and wounded before you found me. I haven't been able to verify that our womenfolk survived, nor was I able to track them down."

Dereas's pulse hammered in his head. Despite Amexi's testimonials from days before, the combination of facts was overwhelming. "Then we have a common enemy," he said.

Rusfaer only grunted with an offhand wave of hand.

A wave of sorrow hit Dereas. Asgolin and a thousand childhood memories stirred in his heart. Asgolin was his village of a hundred yurts spread along the Nascombe river, the sacred fire grounds burning strong with the antlered fanes to Balael and bronze cauldrons smoking herbs and animal fat...How could it be leveled? Asgolin, whose great fires ever stayed lit, roaring, celebrating life and the fruitful tenure under Balael!—now only a cold windswept ruin. He had seen it so many weeks ago when he and Jhidik rode in, and he couldn't believe his eyes—a blackened charnel ground, his people dead or enslaved by enemy tribes or wandering the plains lost and forgotten.

"Your father always was a hothead," muttered Amexi, "also a fool, pitting you two against each other. 'Twas his private joke—at the camp feasts in fits of drunken revelry he boasted of it, naming first you then Rusfaer to rule when he was gone. Then, when he was sober, he bantered that you two should hack it out between yourselves. Always a gust of laughter quick on his lips."

The flame in Dereas's eyes kindled and Rusfaer shouldered forward, his face lit in a cryptic grimace. "He was a fool, Xanithe, and a womanizer, but an iron one, and a man great among men." He stood in the dim light, chest heaving, as if defying anyone to refute it, and his face flushed, heavy with the urge to charge on with his heady tirade. "So I recovered, with my mother's aid, with a wicked scar across my scalp." He rumbled on about how a shaman had wandered leagues to find him and had coaxed him back to life with magical herbs and sickening pastes ground from mushrooms. "Aye, this man also gave me much more to hope for—teachings, wisdom on the path of life and death—teachings that you will never learn, brother, teachings that I will use as hammers, when this world is consumed, to crush any enemy in my path! This I vow on my grave—or when the *Saeth* takes us all!"

So Rusfaer's speech split the heavy silence and seemed to amuse only Draba, but Dereas pulled himself away, unsettled by the fervor of his brother's outburst and the bestial look on his face.

Rusfaer glared at him and Dereas forced himself to glower back, though his heart could not stand behind it. The two of them drawn from the same blood could hardly bear being in the same cave together, not to mention the same tribe. Only their dilemma made it imperative to work together, and to leave vengeance for another day.

The beastslayer plowed on in the greenish gloom ahead, frustrated with the direction the argument had taken. The tunnel weaved and showed slick dark walls, oozing with trickles of the same dark-green water glowing with magical impetus. He thought to see animals or strange reptiles carved in the walls, but sidling closer, tracing fingers on their damp contours, he saw they were so crude as to be unrecognizable. Rusfaer had caught up and nearly trod on his heels.

Dereas whirled on him with a savage cry. "It still does not explain why you waste time hunting me down rather than finding Pameel's captors? I see you moan and groan and blame me for all your troubles while you do little to get her back."

Rusfaer's breath hissed sharply between his bared teeth. He leaned in close and his wolfish eyes blazed with a fire worse than Asgolin's death pyre. "Careful with your accusations, brother. We scoured every hill, every ravine looking for her. All traces of Pameel were gone, disappeared from the very sand itself. Our enemies denied any knowledge of my beloved or the episode. My few horseman could not find her among the rival clans. But there was a rumor that a black shadow had come, a shadow back from the dead. You. For moons your hide had been away, given up for dead. Though I never gave up my search for my raven-haired beauty, it was you I wished most to cross paths with. One of my scouts spotted you and a band of your riders. It was a stroke of luck!—too good to be true. And we followed. Now some sort of a reckoning is upon us."

"And what good has it gained you?" mocked Dereas. "A sealed tomb in a haunted mountain under a blood moon."

"Poetic now are we, brother?" sneered Rusfaer with a jaunty flourish. He pushed himself forward, hands gripped on his knife. "Perhaps it was ever an opportunity to see your sniveling face for one last time before I gutted you."

Dereas looked at his brother and glared. "Why are you so blackened with hate, Rusfaer? Can you not see that I am not your enemy?"

"Who are you to claim anything?" he snarled. "You're a deserting mongrel who is not fit to be chief."

"Listen, you idiot! After I was crowned chief, I left on a hunting expedition for antelope and fresh meat. 'Twas a joint venture—to scout out our perimeters, scope what had been lost during our father's neglect. Five days I was gone—five days to be there and back, during which time I was waylaid by some dog-vomit of a magician—Ahrion, and I was brought to some faraway place in the west—Phygus. I wish to forget every moment of that horror. I was sold into slavery, by ghouls. As were you waylaid by jealous opportunists, it seems we both had our enemies at work, but different ones—"

Rusfaer shook his head in disbelief. "You lie! Whatever the case, words are moot. In your absence, I could have ruled the clans. Instead I was passed off. I *should* have ruled. I could have protected the clan! For a time I wandered lost in the wastelands, delirious, consumed by sorrow and out of my mind. Now, I fight back, though without a ruler, our people are scattered or struck at the heels by enemies, beggared in our own territories. We live as thieves and outlaws. The Bear, Lynx and Cougar clans harry us like vultures.

'Twas not supposed to end like this!" Grief cracked his voice and his eyes pinched shut in sorrow. He raked his sword across the black tunnel walls and the shrill scrapes echoed about the ghostly shadows. "This is not the way of the warrior!"

"But it is, brother. We cannot deny what has passed. The hardest trial is to face the scars of past pain. I cannot back up the wheel of time, or shift things that have already happened. Even Balael can't juggle fates."

"Don't try to understand the gods or counsel me!" roared Rusfaer. "Your words do not console me or return me Pameel. Nor does it change anything, or return me in any way my birthright to rule the clan!"

Dereas shrugged. "Have it as you will." He jerked a thumb at his two grime-faced men. "You have your two wolves at least, I mine." He made a grand sweep to include Jhidik and Amexi who had been listening and now beamed with pride.

A shadow of understanding flickered in Dereas's heart, a memory of a long-lost association. The two brothers each stared at the other for a few seconds; then the sneers resurfaced, but for an instant they were snatched back to an earlier time, a magical place where the wild wind blew in their hair, and the free sweep of the steppe was before them, and their eyes and young hearts flamed with the thrill of the chase. They stalked a herd of antelope that ran amok before the beating of the hooves of their snorting steeds. It was a moment of peace—a hint from the past, when times were happier and histories simpler—and then it was gone like a breath of wind.

"I vow if we escape," hissed Rusfaer, "that we will have it out, you and me. On the battlefield. One on one, in single combat."

Dereas crooked his mouth in a sneer. "So we shall, brother." Though he did not wish it. There was no joy in any aftermath fighting his bear of a brother. A terrible sadness smote Dereas, as of a hammer arching out of the sky and sundering roots that had once run deep.

The bad blood between the two still festered; this half-hearted truce would have to do for now.

And so, the estranged group trudged up the cavern in a glowering silence that lasted for all too many heartbeats.

3: The Mountain King

A spell was laid,
To save a people,
In a sunless hall,
Where a king slept,
And a terror dwelt!...

—The witcher of Yarim-Id

No untoward blur of movement or fang of demon or ghoulish claw disturbed the greenish gloom painting the way ahead. Each of the company took stock of his surroundings and nursed his own private thoughts. The trickling water at their feet continued to emanate a luminous glow, and ever was it a source of wonder for the haggard men. Past another twist they stumbled and onward: up a rough hewn lone shaft, spidered with murky shadows. Twice their height, the tunnel narrowed to half that in places where no branches or junctions appeared. It was carved by what looked at first sight, primitive hands. The rudely-etched bestial carvings sighted earlier had slipped away. No bas-reliefs or art adorned these aged walls that crowded them on both sides, and Dereas loosed a soft breath, suspecting with an uneasy thrill that the hewing belonged to an earlier age.

He frowned. A shaft worn by underground rivers? By beasts or man? All possible, yet he thought to detect the signs of activity more contemporary—crude claw marks scraped on the wall, sinister jagged scratches, a half inch deep. The tunnel appeared scored at places both left and right. The warrior entertained some furtive speculations, and no small amount of theorizing. Maybe there was some hint of truth to the legends, about a shadowy menace that roamed the bowels of the myth-shrouded mountain—of headless goblins with pincers stalking the dark, devouring any soul that passed. Such tales brought shivers to his spine, those campfire stories and ale room tales of old that haunted mysterious Mt. Vharad.

He could only steel himself against such unimaginable horror and turned his eyes to the arching shadows. Spear clenched in a tight fist, he saw, under the greenish glare, petrified shell creatures embedded in the walls around him, from whose fat, fibril-fringed bodies the companions shied. Rocks and chips had flaked from the walls and ceiling over the years, creating a detritus of molder and rubble.

It made for slow going, but they plowed on. Amid the water-smoothed rubble and ancient snails, more crustaceans were embedded in the rounded stones—spiraled volutes, shellfish, and other weird sea life.

At a curve in the tunnel, the path widened and they gladly forged ahead. No stir or movement touched the desolate passage, and yet, there lay somewhere in there, a crawling sense of lurking peril. Each man was lost in his own reverie; none uttered more than a low grunt now and then in face of the eerie silence and the echoes careening back at them. Jhidik's grimaces indicated that he was having no pleasant time coping with his injured leg. They sat after a time with their backs against the wall to rest, listening with one ear trained on the inscrutable purl of the mysterious stream trolling at their feet. The faint odor of ancient must rose from the damp stone. A small sound clinked ahead. Dereas's hand fell swiftly on the hilt of his sword. Heavy slabs had fallen to either side, shelter for any manner of creature, around which the cool waters tinkled with quiet ease and lit the chamber a sullen green.

Nothing more came to their ears, yet they strained them in the darkness for a long time. "What do you suppose that was?" muttered Amexi.

Dereas did not answer. The dimness brought an unsettling chill to his heart.

"We have to eat sometime," grumbled Rusfaer. "Let's see what we have. Come on, cough up your wares!"

With much grumbles, they took stock of their rations, and

revealed what they had, appalled to see how little it was. Dereas carried an emergency stash of dried sour goat curd on his person in a small pouch, likewise Rusfaer's man, Hafta, who produced some dry cornmeal bread, and Jhidik, the same. They held no water. Only did they hope to find a clean source, or things would go badly for them. The others had lost their emergency rations, or neglected to carry supplies. Draba was surly of this fact, and tried to take more than his share when lots were divvied. But Rusfaer rapped his knuckles with the back of his sword. "Wait your turn, greedy guts," the giant growled. "You get to eat exactly what the others do."

The bandit-man scowled. Even his weaselly eyes burned to a bitter pulse at his chief's reprimand. But he contained himself. His thin lips muttered some rude words, choosing not to defy his lord at this tense time, especially in front of the others.

The company split the last rations and Dereas hoped the slim pickings would get them to the end of Vharad. The hope was perhaps extravagant. Starving men were no good as fighters, Dereas knew. If it came to that.

The trickle that seeped down the center of the tunnel seemed to grow in passing and caused the wanderers new wonder, glowing with its uncanny inner light. The tunnel steadily slanted upward on a small grade. Jhidik knelt and examined the water. "The stream carries a wash of phosphorescent particles. Evidently the source of our greenish glow. It doesn't smell toxic. It may even be potable."

Dereas squatted next to his friend. Curiously, only when the water was in motion did it seem to radiate this fey luminosity. Squinting down at an isolated puddle that pooled at his feet, he saw that the water was black as night, but when he swished it with his toe, the small pool shimmered to the tune of an otherworldly green. A marvel!

What fortune, the magical water.

Their eyes had adjusted to the gloom now and they could distinguish vague shapes in the spaces ahead: pillars of rock that buttressed the tunnel's flanks—stray carven boulders fallen from the craggy ceiling or hewn from the sides, or points along the tunnel which opened onto mini caverns.

Dereas thought the feature odd and he stared with curiosity, edging around the peculiar columns carved now with the likenesses of strange gods, snakes and toads, salamanders and newts. Some had one eye, others two, others stood with legs numbering up to four. These depictions were feral looking, avatars perhaps, Dereas guessed, or carvings which at one time served as deities for some race, and yet evoked such a repellent horror in the pit of Dereas's stomach that he felt compelled to look away. But then most gods did, did they not?

He recalled the savage, ghastly caricatures he had seen many a time inscribed in temples and caves about the lands.

The knot in his throat grew and he swallowed it. A crawling malaise wormed in his veins, thinking of all the nooks and crannies of this shadowy world that carried hidden evil and votive ghastliness. All the mysterious effigies and worship grounds, the secret lairs, the blood-stained altars and twisted temples that teemed in nameless caves, or forests and jungles, high mountains or ice caves in the far north bared to wind and soul. Here, in the world of Darfala strange gods lurked and cavorted and howled in mocking laughter at the hapless lives of prideful humans. And yet these same occult entities were brought into incarnate form by willful monks and wizards through arcane worship, either mumbled as hymns or through the monotonous power of cultish incantations. Whether such acts were blessed or cursed, these rituals were the food offered in exchange for power and wealth, lust and glorification, prizes or banes. Whether through prayer or black magic, or devil worship and many unimaginable alternatives, mattered little, Dereas concluded...

Balael..The word slipped soundlessly from his lips. The name was pure on its own, even as it came ringing in his inner ear, but when he mouthed it, it rang off the cold stone, echoing in the close chamber like a breath of winter ice.

Most of the other races knew Balael as some obscure pagan

figure of terror and myth, but Dereas knew he was real—the true warrior god, whose wolfish bark contained untold power to fill the waning light and top up the strength of a warrior with courage and fortitude in times of darkness and terror. Now, in the time of the *Saeth*, it seemed as good a time to call upon him...

Saeth. A word barely kept lingering on the tongue of even the bravest warrior, the name of an age darkest to humankind.

Dark wizards, dark magic...

'Twas the mantra of the *Saeth*...

A chill ran through Dereas's body. He fretted with his spear as his mind drifted to Ahrion and the sorcerous black keep in ziggurat-haunted Phygus where he had been imprisoned, seat of countless evils and lineages of black sorcerers before, of heathen priests, heretics, and lost and deranged souls. Ahrion! The name sent a waft of tickling fear in his breast. It held evil power. The many nefarious sorceries the wizard had committed! Ahrion, the primordial necromancer, had brewed untold horrors in his dread chambers. For the hundredth time Dereas pored over the fact that were it not for this fiend and his far-flung magic, he would not have had this strife with his brother. Perhaps he could have averted this tribal disaster in the first place? Was it not during his time of imprisonment at the zombie-patrolled slave camps of Ahrion and later Basilurk keep, that Rusfaer and Pameel were waylaid by unknown kidnappers?—It was a time when he could have, as resident chief, ordered an escort to accompany his brother safely to their new home. Instead, his forced absence had kindled Rusfaer's wrath and he had stolen off in the night with his bride away from Asgolin, without saying as much as a fare-thee-well.

Nay! 'Twas useless to try to impress these facts on his brother's mind. Rusfaer was a lost cause; already, even as he watched him trudging sullenly up the tunnel, it was clear Rusfaer was hopelessly addled with pain over the loss of his beloved. And yet, Dereas's mind raced with the possibilities of fate, shaking off the what-ifs and should-haves that could have come to pass.

His eyes instantly lost their glazed look. His reveries were shattered by the clink of Rusfaer's sword on something hard on the loose shale.

His neck jerked around, eyes lingering on the irritating Draba who took pleasure in cracking some of the larger eggshell fragments with his ugly blade. The pastime was something he had adopted evidently from his mentor, Rusfaer.

Jhidik waved the two to silence, hissing a harsh word over the clash of breaking shells. "Quiet, you sods! Must you alert every predator within ten bowshots of our presence? What devils dwell down here we haven't a clue, any of which likely have long ears."

Rusfaer glanced whimsically at the Pirean, as if he were some specimen to be studied. "Something addles you, lame man?" He jerked a thick thumb toward one of the larger shells and snatched it up in his bear-fisted hand. "Well, something dragged these miserable eggs in here and it obviously had to be something hungry."

"These must be those wretched birds' eggs of the Eakors from back at the roosts," grumbled Hafta.

"Another splendid deduction," huffed Rusfaer. "There seems to be a pattern to where these eggs are dropped though," he mused, his eyes kindling in interest. "Doesn't look like the trappings of a mindless beast's hunger to me, or any random foraging. It's as if the eggs were placed here deliberately."

Draba's mouth twitched. "'Tis unlike what those vultures would do."

Rusfaer ignored the complaisant smirk on his henchman's face, the shadow of which seemed to pop up at his elbow or shoulder much too often.

Dereas was not altogether trusting of Rusfaer's capricious rascal either, and trusted him even less in this cramped space. His swagger annoying, no less his condescending grin and cocky quips. Likewise, Hafta's grimace of distrust and constant sheathing and unsheathing of his weapon. Rusfaer's stride was much too aggressive, that too, the mean lurch to his shoulders. It brought up pangs of old memories that the war chief wished to forget. His brother had a pent up rage of dark brooding inside him that spoke of a violence ready to uncoil in a blinding sweep of fury, sweat and death.

The company drew to a halt. A three way junction loomed before them; one branch led to a pit into half murk, another straight ahead narrowing to follow the source of the mysterious stream. And yet another yawned into eternal blackness. The vapors exuding from the last opening were cold and damp. A sound, barely perceptible, emanated from it, the chitter of a soul-despairing cry—one longing for release, strangely human, and yet somewhat reptilian.

Dereas clutched his spear tighter. The hairs prickled on his scalp. The backdrop of vague splintering sounds followed this cry, as of shells being smashed with great hammers. The less than inviting discords had him halting in his tracks, plagued with a grimace of uncertainty.

"I think best we avoid that way, comrades. Let's be away from this horrid place."

There was little objection. Something unusual clung in Dereas's memory after the feeling of the last junction. It went beyond even the suggestion of unimaginable woe, though it was indefinable to his warrior's instinct.

Up the main passage they trod, their boots sloshing in the phosphorescent water. The tunnel wound inexorably on, following anything but a straight path. The passage curved, looping back on itself through solid rock, narrowing its way and twisting, widening at times to sections as large as a cavern and a place where they would gape at the numberless, natural, gem-crusted formations clustered on the ceiling and feel the welcome drip of cool water lapping down on their sweat-doused heads as it seeped from high places. The water, as it turned out, was pure, and they drank it lustily.

No concept of night or day graced this cheerless place. All felt helplessly disoriented. Stomachs roiled and muscles ached. Their last meager meal had been devoured back at the T junction perhaps an hour ago or half a day. Time had become meaningless.

A new junction appeared out of the gloom. Now they caught a glimpse of a stony mass jutting out of the claw-hewn wall. The anomaly was a shapeless lump, low and smooth at first. Squatting before it, Dereas traced the outline of a primitive snake's head with a single eye, the whole effigy gaping like a slug. The carving was cold and serpentine to the touch, almost like sculpted ice. With the look of some sacred deity out a wizard's dream or other, it was fashioned in the shape of a water fountain or some spout. From the snake's mouth dribbled more of the magically-lit water which trickled out to join the main confluence.

Dereas cupped his hands. He let the cool water play through his brown-knuckles. He splashed it on his sweaty brow. Two small human skulls were directly fixed to the rock beneath the proto-snake. The whole exhibit had the look of a devotional altar to Dereas's eye, before which beings would kneel. It was much too overt and disquieting for his tastes. More stoneworks massed directly opposite the construction on the other side of the tunnel, flanking a gaping black hole which descended downward on a sharp angle. From this opening wafted unsettling cool, fetid air, before which Jhidik quivered on the weight of his game leg, wincing.

"A pretty little statue," he muttered. "What inspired such grotesquerie, I wonder?"

A macabre moment overcame Draba, or perhaps in the whim of a vile prank, he contrived to tighten a bootlace and casually bump the Pirean with his hip, sending him stumbling almost into the hole. For a second Jhidik swayed and cried out in a hoarse voice before he was pulled back by Dereas.

"You careless, miserable sod!"

Draba's lips curled in surprise. "Careful there, one leg," he cautioned, reaching out with a comradely hand. "The mountain holds dooms around every corner. You, my friend, are living on borrowed time."

Jhidik pulled himself away from the villain's clutch and struck out with a fist. "You idiot!" He rounded on the smirking rogue who was a head shorter and who leaned on his sword a casual distance away like a cocky weasel. Draba's wicked blade flashed in his palm.

Dereas intervened with speed. The tip of his spear quivered in front of Draba's nose, already penetrating the man's guard. "What's with you, lout? Next time you try a stunt like that, you lose a hand—or an eye. Are we clear?"

The simpering smirk on Draba's face showed he was not, and Dereas could barely stop himself from lashing off the fool's head, especially after just being recently tested by Rusfaer. The blinding urge to push steel through that prankster's heart became overwhelming. He managed, teeth gritted, to relax his twitching fingers.

Rusfaer and Hafta snorted at the amusing display and turned away, unimpressed with their peer's impetuous behavior.

Draba resented the slight and sought to recover his dignity. "What's wrong, captain?" he jeered at Dereas. "Your lame boy here can't fight his own battles?"

Dereas's expression grew snarling and dangerous. "No," he said with a menacing laugh. "I'm sparing 'my lame boy' from spilling your guts on the cold stone. In fact, I'm sure he'd do it before you could spit sideways."

Jhidik grinned. "That, or heave your carcass down this wonderful hole," he said with a sinister grimace.

"Oh, is that it?" snorted Draba. "Well, it's easy to—"

A blade flashed in the Pirean's hand and pressed up against Draba's pulsing jugular—with the blinding speed of a snake.

The lout licked his lips, as if pondering the seriousness of the warrior's boast. That he could be caught off guard by not one, but two men, one of them lamed, inflamed his blood. Yet he turned a notch cooler as he saw the raw-edged look on the Pirean's murderous face.

The scowl grew on Draba's round chin, and he crimped up his lip, like a small boy whose bullying had gone sour.

"Seems as if I'm the only honest one here," he complained.

"Truth is, your gimping man's a liability to us. He'll only slow us down—or get us killed if something goes awry in the tunnel—say some beast does try to maul us. I was only doing us a favor, culling the herd, so to speak."

Dereas recoiled at the level of Draba's audacity.

Jhidik took three jerky steps forward. "The only favor you'll be doing us, you dunghill cock, is slitting your own throat." The words poured forth in a gush of choking anger.

Dereas had stopped listening. Out of the corner of his eye, he had noticed Rusfaer's careless grin during this whole episode. He stared, puzzled. The smile had faded to a surly frown. Was it genuine reproach on his brother's part, or a quick cover-up for his complicity in the affair?

In a quick upward motion, the beastslayer threw down his spear and hooked arms under Draba's armpits—slamming the bully hard down on the rock, back first.

Draba wheezed out a gasp, eyes starting from his head.

The full weight of the war chief pressed on top of Draba and Dereas hissed air through his teeth straight into Draba's bloody ear. "Don't ever try to goad my men again. If you do, rat, I'll cut you to pieces and shove you down that hole myself."

The flustered bully, still gasping for air, uttered no retort. He groped painfully to his feet, staring defiantly at Dereas whose eyes were dark as death. Withal, Draba's eyes seemed slitted and promised terrible repercussions to come. The weaselly face was contorted in a disturbing grimace, yet at the same time, not understanding why Rusfaer's expression remained so impassive.

The shattered company took up their journey again. Draba moped his way along mechanically, nursing a bruised back and battered ego.

The matter seemed settled, but Dereas's spirits remained cloudy. Draba's spiteful aura and muttered oaths were indicative that he sheltered a grudge that would fester and threaten to undermine their mission.

None felt sorry to leave behind the oppressive fetish. With the wary steps of hunted men the wanderers followed a path of silent gloom, always on a slight upward slant. The surrounding rock became drier and smoother here, the air fresher, perhaps indicating a break or opening somewhere in the rock to reveal open sky. There was a sense that the walls had been chiselled in more glorious days, and with some precision, thought Dereas. Obviously the artisans who had chiselled these effigies had been meticulous, he reflected, judging from the craftsmanship and the sturdy stone trestles now fitted above their heads which likely kept the rock from caving in. Smaller side passages appeared from time to time, but these they avoided. An indefinable feeling of emptiness permeated their bones. There was a fear of getting lost too, and Dereas's senses swam with the thought of wandering these frightful tunnels in aimless circles.

The tension between the war chiefs had not lost its grip. Amexi's and Draba's muttered curses grew to sneers as knife play broke out over a petty argument over who had tread on whose heels. Draba had wrested the blade out of Amexi's hand and had almost plunged it into his ribs before Dereas came sprinting to lock arms with him and knock the dagger clear, bending the shorter man's wrist back. He sent the troublemaker sprawling to his knees, panting for breath. "When will you learn your lesson, you squabbling oaf?"

Rusfaer found the whole incident entertaining and his smirk indicated no less. All the time Draba's wrath had been brewing to seething levels. Dereas did not treat Draba's behavior lightly. Men were known to go mad when entombed underground, or so he recalled from grim tales and folklore of his people, so he grudgingly overlooked the incident. This time. He knew his man Amexi would not instigate so fevered a reprisal over something so trivial. The hothead Draba was much to blame for the incident, everyone knew it, and the beastslayer kept one eye trained on him.

The company filed along in grim procession. Dereas stalked in front and Rusfaer and his surly cohorts in rear. All men hoped for an end to this abominable march and the close confines, far away from the bloodthirsty lust of the Eakors. Dereas was confident to take the lead in the fractured band, sometimes interchanging with Jhidik or Rusfaer when the urge came upon him.

In one section of the tunnel, the path was ripped in half, likely caused by an earthquake. They looked down into a yawning chasm, a plunge into empty blackness with no visible end.

Dereas peered over the rim with trepidation; Jhidik lurked at his side. They heard no sound, no tinkle of water in those unknown depths. The small stream that ran from the other side dribbled down the sheer face in meek, noiseless patter. The others crept closer to the edge. Too far to leap, Dereas thought. A rash move to take a running leap and try to hook fingernails on a wet surface across the black pit, a vault which would likely lead to a grisly end. They must crawl one by one precariously around the side across the ledge where the trickle ran, using whatever handholds they could find.

Dereas tossed his spear across first, which clattered noisily onto the rocks across the gap. The walls were clammy, foreboding. Dereas made the first tentative steps, wincing in chagrin. He halted and gripped the wall with his free hand, but recoiled at the dank feel. He crafted careful, lithe steps and set hands methodically, scabbard scraping on the rock behind him.

Twelve feet only. It was child's play, at least in broad daylight, but on a ledge with parts crumbling and drowned in greenish gloom and only a few inches wide at places, it was only with nerves of steel could one cross.

Dereas arrived safely. Hafta and Jhidik made skittish steps next, almost slipping to their dooms as Dereas, snatching up his weapon, thrust out his spear so his white-faced comrade, who was thankfully within range, could grasp it. He reached and grabbed Jhidik by the belt. The muscles on the beastslayer's shoulders knotted as he encircled him underneath the armpits. Rusfaer, following on Jhidik's heels, refused Dereas's hand, as did Draba, hating the sight of his enemy, let alone any helping hand from him. Draba went so far as to impress everybody with an idiotic acrobatic leap for the last few feet, only to pin-wheel back into the void at the last second and had not Rusfaer shot out a hand and grabbed his mail shirt, he would have perished. "Smarten up, you idiot! Save your antics for another time."

Stung by the remark, Draba gazed up at his chief with a smug, almost beseeching look. His air of false pandering was not lost on the big warrior. A strange dependency existed between the two. This Dereas could see, one which he could not quite understand. He flashed both Rusfaer and Draba a stare of mild perplexity, passing eyes beyond to the murk in which they must grope.

The last was Amexi inching himself halfway across snail-like. On the narrowest part of the ledge, a small chunk of rock crumbled loose from his left heel. He almost slipped and fell face first into the abyss. Like a spider, the warrior hung there, tottering for several seconds, finally pulling himself up, trembling and blinking in the gloom with sweat pouring into his eyes.

Dereas helped him the last few feet and he and Rusfaer peered down into the black, bottomless pit once more. They expected to hear a tinkling or splashing or some pebble crashing against the primordial rock or stone or deep water...but none came.

A frowning silence overcame the company; heated grumbles melded into scowls. All perked their ears to hear what was not to be heard.

Though none could be certain, the keenest among them might have heard the tiniest ghost of an echo plink far, far below in that illimitable darkness.

A thud? No, thought Dereas. A distant slither of ancient scales?

There was a stir of movement, definitely something solid. The rattle of ancient breath perhaps?

It was not definitely and instinctively clear what it was and Dereas jerked a hand to his scabbard. He felt his pulse quicken. His flesh crawled at the thought of what possibly had been alerted.

With the utmost noiselessness, the troupe slipped away from the eerie gap, plagued with misgiving.

Jhidik's leg was not improving. It had stiffened considerably during the last arduous miles of stumbling through the dark and Dereas and Amexi took turns helping him plod his way through the endless twisting passages. It seemed that they were going in circles, and that the tunnel was a foul trick of the mind. The splint that Dereas had fabricated for the Pirean had held up, but was not altogether perfect and he had to stop many times to tighten it. But it was slipping and blood had seeped around the edge, staining the old fabric. A rank, septic odor wafted from the wound and caused him to conclude that the gash was festering, possibly already malignant. "It needs to be cleaned, Jhidik," he said seriously. "I'll risk dousing it with this weird green water, but it could make it worse. The liquid could be contaminated."

Jhidik waved a hand. "Let's do it then. We have to keep moving."

Dereas complied; his efforts, he hoped, would make a difference.

The tunnel weaved relentlessly upward and Dereas thrust his hunger from his mind. He clambered up a crude staircase of natural ledges, some which had been carved out skillfully in the naked rock. He wondered, who crafted them? The others followed with grudging unease, Jhidik trying to hide his limp. The war chief swung a confident arm to motion them onward. With sullen grunts, Rusfaer and his band stalked behind, grumbling curses. Their heavy tramp was like the plod of feet made of lead.

The six scrambled up a shorter flight of stone steps where the peculiar green light seemed to glow with even more intensity.

Weapons drawn, the group crowded into a long narrow hall where they beheld a gigantic carven facade of smoothly-polished stone. The wall rose hugely out of the dimness, rearing many times a person's height, up from a jumble of toppled columns and blocks sweeping along the base of the opposite wall. The troupe wandered spellbound across the paves, hands on their hilts, bearing the strange weariness of travelers from a faraway land; all the while large drops issued from the high ceiling and the strange waters glistening down the facade trickled into the middle of the hall. It was a strange sight—the wall bore an air of ancient antiquity as if it had been revered over long centuries.

An austere altar rose out of the gloom ringed with pedestals holding stone bowls, some long-toppled. These stood eerily, looking much like bird baths. An earthy smell permeated the chamber; odd underground plants with black- and dark-green broad leaves grew from various cracks in the facade. Dereas noticed several squat, bush-like plants also poked up from the cracked pavestones. The curious flora was nourished by the falling water, a weird find to be growing in the dimness? After prodding them with the flat of his blade, he saw that they were not figments of his imagination. A mosaic underfoot showed the faintest reminiscence of a coiled snake, the flagstones tainted with the passing of ages and spread with lime and budding stalagmites, well worn and damp from the dripping water. Closer inspection revealed that the high facade was carved with what looked like a pictographic history of a forgotten race—gatherings of people, ceremonial fires, a primordial sun rising over a nation and a horned mountain that was obviously Vharad. Strange archaic script was inscribed beneath the pictographs, elaborating every scene of the past employing symbols of moons, stars, sickles, hammers and animals of all breeds. Dereas saw carved on the final block to the right, almost flush to the floor, a gigantic stone serpent rearing with its strangling coils bound around a group of a hundred stricken faces.

He stiffened. His blood tingled at the ghastliness of the image. Some deep primal cord of recognition stirred within him, given more fuel by the pall of primitive superstition of the distant past oozing from the very pores of the stone around him.

Rusfaer clomped about in grumbling impatience; he finally stumbled upon a gloomy alcove inset into the great facade. It was about eight feet square and he motioned for all to gather. Something had stirred him. The chamber was replete with webs, dust, and a dim feeling of tragedy. Inside, Dereas saw a stone pot bolted with iron ring and accompanied with frayed ropes, large enough for a miniature person or perhaps a child to squat inside. What was this strange vessel? It looked strangely akin to a sacrificial ground, what with its flanking, slightly angled stone slabs ideal for directing runnels of blood of intended victims—somewhat of the same that Dereas had witnessed in obscure temples and blood cults as far to the west as Lunra, bordering Phygus, and scattered across ancient Darfala. The room itself contained dilapidated stone torch holders and candelabra stationed equidistantly at knee height around the chambers as if they were ritual ornaments. Amexi, suddenly disinterested, chose to explore elsewhere.

"A curious parlor," remarked Rusfaer grimly.

"Aye, what do you suppose it is for?" asked Dereas, a part of him already suspecting the answer.

Jhidik shrugged. "Some barbarous votary stage at best."

Rusfaer forced an ominous laugh. "Seems odd for that. No carved runes, no bas-reliefs. Almost like a cell, I think."

Dereas felt his nerves jump at the mention of 'cell', recalling his experience with Ahrion. A revulsion hurtled up his spine, made the hackles on his neck rise. He kicked a layer of the gray dust away from the base of the pot, fighting a sudden urge to back out of the chamber. "Look here, at this old blood," he growled, "on the flags— and drops of it as if it was spattered from the lip of the open crock."

Rusfaer grimaced and involuntarily swiped at the vessel. "'Tis an offering receptacle—for their gods, I imagine, or whatever fiends they worshiped, like this ugly snake here—" he slapped a fist on the ghastly effigy coiled in the shadows.

Amexi's cry came leaping to them from the main hall.

Dereas, wired-edged with apprehension, was first out of the chamber. He halted to see the blond warrior recoiling from a bulky shape tucked in the shadows farther down the hall. He raced to investigate.

At the base of the facade loomed a sculpture of a seated dwarf carved on a great throne. He was sitting eternally as if he had sat there for a thousand years. On his crown he wore an oversized wreath, woven of broad leaf shapes similar to those growing from the cracks in the wall, while over and around him writhed in lifelike coils, a sandstone serpent, in a poise like an obscene garland, not dissimilar to the hideous serpent carved in stone they had seen earlier. The snake's mouth was wide open, fangs exposed like bristling scythes. Its curled tongue slithered out to nearly tickle his ear, as if he were some martyr or defenseless gargoyle. His placid eyes were closed in a slumber of ages, as if in trance or offering to the snake.

Dereas stared, bewildered. The first sight of the artist's depiction evoked a pang of repellent horror in him, for reasons quite evident. Although the symbiosis of dwarf and snake was not altogether apparent, it was too real to be casually dismissed. He scraped the edge of his sword across the glistening stone as if to test that the effigy was actually stone and not flesh.

The blade clinked and slid harmlessly off the carving's hardness.

Dereas hissed. "I swear that the figure and snake could jump right out at me."

Rusfaer, swaggering at his side, chuckled. "You're getting maudlin and jittery today, little brother."

"One tends to be in unfamiliar places," growled the beastslayer.

Jhidik, lost in his own thoughts, gave a musing grunt: "Not just this, but any of these carvings could be dead ringers for real men and animals. Look, they almost shimmer as if alive. It must have taken ages to carve them."

"The work of years," marveled Hafta.

Dereas stooped to look the stone man more carefully in the eye—a portly figure of middle years with an artless grin. "And who then is our sleeping beauty? He looks to be the 'dwarf who could do no wrong'."

Amexi laughed. But as Dereas turned to sheath his sword, the eyes of the statue fluttered open. The beastslayer almost choked on his breath. "Here, what's this!"

Amexi gasped.

"Sorcery? Saeth's teeth!" grunted Dereas. "What black wizardry thrusts itself upon us in this burrow?"

Rusfaer hissed. He brought back his broadsword to lop the thing's head off.

"Wait!" Dereas cried. He caught the edge of the arcing blade on the steel of his guard.

The dwarf slowly shook his head as if waking from a deep and foul dream. The whisper of bared steel and the sudden glimpse of the armed men about him left him with an expression of astonished wonder. He recoiled from the carved snake as if suddenly seeing it for the first time. He disengaged from the strangling loops, his waking consciousness now somewhat registering the terror at discovering where stone ended and flesh began.

Likewise, the dwarf's face registered the shock of one stung by a dream-memory too gruesome to recall. Something which he tried to hide, thought Dereas. His skin seemed grown pale, almost withered from living in a sunless world.

Dereas held up a cautionary hand. "Hold up! The gnome's as baffled as us. Look! He loathes the snake." Kneeling in a crouch, he stooped to glare into the vacuous gaze. "Who are you?"

The dwarf stared back at him blankly. "I—I am Fezoul. A king I was once, if memory serves. King of Yarim-Id. It was once Xatu. But I am not sure. And who are you?"

"I am Dereas—" answered the beastslayer. "Nevermind who I am. How did you come to life, and what are you doing here?—Are you a stone, living man? Or a sorcerer of some kind?"

"I—I don't—remember."

"You must!" yelled Rusfaer. "Liar! Only a simpleton or trickster would plead ignorance of something so basic!" He hitched himself forward, his blade flickering at the monarch's throat. "Is this a temple or a wizard's lair?" His brawny frame quivered with impatience.

The little man shrank back from that daunting presence, his face carved in a grimace, as if pondering an unsolvable problem.

"Answer me!" cried Rusfaer.

"Neither one!" cried the dwarf. "I believe I have slept overlong."

"I don't care if you've slept through ten Zecrates' hells. Tell us what we want to know!"

Dereas and Rusfaer shook their heads in exasperated wonder. Each reached to shake the dwarf—Rusfaer went so far as to slap his face and try to knock some sense into his brain. But the bewildered figure just moaned and whimpered. His speech was disjointed as if he were befuddled or under some mysterious spell.

Dereas and Rusfaer, both dumbstruck, fell silent for some time before they tried another approach.

"Where are all your people?"

The king blinked in confusion, as if struggling to recall a terrible memory. "Guards! Come hither, and seize these—"

"There are no guards," snarled Rusfaer. "Answer us, little man."

In defeat the king threw down his hands. "They fled, long ago—or gave Pygra her sustenance through the years. Where is Pygra?" he cried with a visible shudder.

"Who's Pygra?"

The king's eyes grew wide with reverent terror. "You don't know Pygra? She's the first snake under the mountain. Everybody knows Pygra! They must have been eaten by her, or maybe—"

"Or maybe what?" demanded Rusfaer harshly.

Fezoul could not bring himself to say 'what'.

Rusfaer slammed his fist on the serpent's head. "And why are you the only one left here in this abominable chamber?"

The dwarf's mouth opened but no words came out.

Rusfaer grunted and snarled an oath. "Come on, let's go! I've had enough. This cowardly midget knows nothing."

The adventurers turned to leave, foraging for a last few clues left in the shadowy rubble, but the little man, peering disconsolately from stone snake to armed men and back to wall, forced words from his quivering lips: "We used to appease the serpent!—a sacrifice on the first day of the lunar month—thrice every season." He seemed to pale, pondering the lost grandeur of his kingdom. "Certain holes we cut in the cliffs of the east face, to admit light which would tell us of the angles of the sun so that we could accurately gauge the time of the equinoxes. The first equinox when the ice melt was at its peak, we would triple our offerings."

Rusfaer's eyes burned like red hot coals. "You sick sod. In that chamber, yonder?" He stabbed a fist out toward the sacrificial niche.

The king nodded guiltily. His gaze shrank under that formidable glare.

Dereas grunted. The quivering monarch did not seem like much of a king.

Burying his face in his hands, the dwarf cried out, "Please understand me. Pygra left us alone; she did not molest us for a time but we became more sycophantic to her demands. She wanted more sacrifices! More sacrifices..." His voice trailed off in a sick, braying murmur. "Certain dissidents among us were unhappy with the arrangement—they broke off from main group."

"And why shouldn't they?" roared Rusfaer, anger flaming his cheeks.

Fezoul nodded in meek accord. "They were never seen again—though there was evidence that our colleagues burrowed deep into the mountain, down the south branches of the tunnel. They became—something—something grotesque...and horrible."

"What else?" snapped Rusfaer, the snarl on his lips, a blacksmith's rasp.

The king swallowed. He seemed to have collected his wits. Indeed, Dereas noted that whereas before the dwarf could hardly speak, he now had found his tongue, an elegant one at that. His golden curls seemed to hold back the sweat of ages on a wrinkled brow. He wore a gown of white and purple silk, cinctured with a wide purple belt at his waist, quite sizable for an individual so small. An unusual jeweled amulet stemmed from his neck on a beaded cord featuring a fabulously cut diamond or quart crystal that hung in its center.

"Being King of Yarim-Id," came his slow, solemn words, "our resident witcher, the Groon of Xatu, concocted a spell for me, that I might be protected, to live on—to continue our race into the future when this nightmare was over. Pygra would one day vacate the tunnels or die from hunger, for lack of humans to devour. The Groon cast the spell on me, that I might dream for a hundred years, as a stone man in the guise of a living monolith. She would enscorcell herself and become my future queen. I was to be obeisant to the snake, to outlive the curse of her reign, and survive the nightmare. 'Twas her last act before she died—eaten alive by Pygra. I think she was eaten."

Revulsion shook Dereas. "How did you tolerate such a blasphemy in your lifetime?"

"The arrangement was—" but the squeamish voice of the king could not finish the thought, nor could he stop shaking in his hobnailed sandals, bright tears budding in his brown, oval eyes.

"Answer, man!" cried Rusfaer. He whipped out his sword wrathfully close to the dwarf's ear.

"'Twas foretold!" he yowled. "'Twas not always like this. We worshiped snakes, yes, but only harmless ones. We worshiped the ancient reptiles, the turtles, the crocs, the geckos, the mansors, the great leptoids, the iguanas. All the serpents of the earth we paid homage to, by far our favorites. Then the lizards, for we saw that the scaled ones guarded the wisdom of the hidden ways. The snake that slithers through the cracks in the stone and hibernates for an age, 'twas the most crafty, and lived still to stalk and snatch at the young chick in the egg. We feared them, but we also worshiped them."

Jhidik shook his head in sad wonder.

The mountain king shrugged and hung his head. "Pygra was only a small viper then, an eight foot terror, prodigy of mischief and stealth when we first found her slithering in a deep, dark pool far below. We fed her rats and moles and other scavengers from the deeps, things that we could catch easiest in the tunnels. We penned her in our Lizesium, that small chamber yonder, where your rogues were poking about before—then the Reptilium, the gilded mini temple above this hall, rife with pillars of gold and forbidding statues of reptiles and other half men and serpents as she grew bigger. But she broke free, or some careless guardian of the temple had left the cell lock half-cocked on its grate and she wriggled free to become queen of the night! Many thought she squirmed into some hinterland hole and consumed a foul liquid or some potion in a deep dark place. That it had made her grow to vast proportions. She grew and grew, and demanded more sacrifices from us and became drunk with evil ambition. Our most venerated village elder, old Banalbe, told us that we must appease our new, terrible guardian, lest she rear up in malice to bite us, strangle us, or curse us—we must worship her unfailingly, and satisfy her lusts, so he said, whatever the cost, even if it meant death to our own citizens, snatched away in the night never to be seen again. Oh, woe!" He hid his face in his hands and whimpered. "I did not condone such grisliness. Nor am I a murderer, none of our courtiers were. Our sacrifices were for the greater good. They did not work, as I discovered."

The king jerked himself queasily back to reality, stiffening under the intense glare that Rusfaer cast him and the smooth-carved snake only feet away. He said in a gloomy voice, "She roams still, our Pygra, feeding on whatever creature she finds in these murksome tunnels. For she did not die. I can feel it in my bones, her presence—even now, in my dreams. Always a slithering shadow, at the edge of nightmare, a snouted apparition, with one eye shut, one eye glistening with a bestial hunger, a seething phantasm, a succubus from the cauldron!"

"Very charming," snorted Jhidik.

"Where is this abomination of yours now?" demanded Dereas.

"I know not," the king answered in a monotone. "Where our bane lurks is a mystery many have tried to solve. None have penetrated the fastness of the mountain or learned her secrets. If I knew, I would rest easier, for I have been in my dream-daze for decades, as you witnessed."

"Think, man, think!" cried Rusfaer. In one terrible jerky motion he reached over to shake the bemused monarch like a doll. "The monster must be around these filthy halls somewhere. Or are there more of them? We heard strange rustling sounds earlier in a pit that went endlessly down."

An expression of cold anxiety bubbled up on the mountain king's face. "Woe on woe! Only ghosts of terrible things dwell in Minro's chasm. Doubtless you have awakened them—and me in a late hour of my spell! I must go, with my mind growing dim and fading, barely able to keep up, or recall a distant face or one safe tunnel from the next... I must endure with the threat of Pygra on my shoulders—whether she prowls, or sleeps!"

"Sleep if you must, old man," rasped Jhidik, "but if we come face to face with this snake of yours—"

Rusfaer pushed past the Pirean to get at the dwarf. "Enough chatter! So you admit you are no use to us alive or dead then, you foolish ape? That you might not even know the way out of this mountain?"

The mountain king pawed off Rusfaer's hands arching about his throat. "No, I didn't say that!"

"You did, and don't lie about it!" the hulking warrior cursed. He rounded on the dwarf, lifting him three feet off the ground.

Fezoul's body shrank in the iron grip. Legs pinwheeling in the air, his face contorted in a beet red blush. Coughing and sputtering, he pawed out a feeble hand. "I didn't say that! I can give you life. I can guide you out of these halls to the hither side of the mountain, if you wish."

"Tell us, then!" cried the New Wolves' chief. He threw the king hard to the paves where he moaned and tried to suck air back into his ravaged lungs.

"Tell us!" Rusfaer roared.

"Yarim-Id has many cross-tunnels," he gasped, "—side ways that will lead you to your destination—or to your peril. You must tread like humble field mice with pads on your feet. Stealthily, swiftly! No, you mustn't make a sound! Who knows what lurks or where the great Pygra may pounce!" At that, the king cast a terrified glance over his shoulder where the shadows were deepest. A mannerism that was his wont, as if Pygra or whatever was the demon of his nightmares, would slither forth, ready to snatch his quivering frame.

"Guide us well then, old man!" Rusfaer rasped with a vengeance. "'Tis your neck that rolls first—" and he prodded the king none too gently with the tip of his blade. The others grumbled and hissed, herded the king toward the exit, none too yieldingly, trusting the monarch no further than they could throw their own boot, or anything in this dark, disquieting hall.

The king saw that what they said they meant, and Dereas frowned anew. He saw the odd figure rose no higher than his midriff, guarding the placid golden eyes of a philosopher enraptured by a theory.

Dereas motioned the company up the double stair that looped back over the hall. "This way."

Before they took to the stair, the beastslayer halted the king: "What is this light that exudes from these seeps of water?"

The king seemed puzzled by the remark. "You can make light by putting the water in these bowls that are ranged about the altar. Stir it with your finger. You'll see. I'll show you the way! It will glow."

Dereas snatched up a bowl from one of the pedestals and filled it with the running water—water which he found warm to the touch, neither sulfurous nor acrid, but slightly organic in smell. The liquid tingled his fingers when he stirred it, as the curious dwarf had described. A dim greenish light, slightly yellowish in tinge, shone true.

"Magic..." He sucked in a deep breath thick with wonder.

The others were no less amazed, and took bowls of their own.

"Can we drink it?" inquired Amexi, licking his lips.

"Of course!" Fezoul stared at him with surprise, answering in what Dereas guessed to be the confident tone of his people. "Why not? 'Tis the wellspring of our heritage." He uttered proudly, "Has been for centuries." His eyes fixed critically on the strangers' faces, blinking in some distaste. Their wounds and dark scratches seemed to stir a memory in him; no less their blood-smeared limbs and overall gaunt look. "You look to have had a run in with our stone birds, the weasel vultures. Forsooth! Those flying fiends are evil personified, martinets for intruders. You have the appearance of famished wolves about you."

"Wolves? Who said aught of 'wolves'?" snarled Rusfaer.

"I would wish it that you were not so loud," said Jhidik.

"I'll say it less nicely," threatened Rusfaer, lancing Jhidik a dark look and tipping his sword in the dwarf's direction. "That he should shut his—"

"Eat too if you are hungry," interrupted Fezoul, disarming the big warrior. "Take aplenty of the Razenbush! 'Tis a weed known as 'Arizoi'. It grows in these halls. The oil is gone from the bronze lamps, I see, else I would cook you up some over these braziers." He signaled to the iron tripods beside the pedestals where they had taken the water.

Lulled by the king's artlessness, Amexi and others gazed longingly at the prospect of food.

Rusfaer motioned the dwarf grimly with his sword, suspecting trickery. "You eat first, 'king'."

"Gladly," obliged Fezoul, who had not eaten for decades.

The king skipped over to a crack in the facade and pulled a handful of the tough, black weed from the stone and stuffed it in his mouth like an antelope chewing its cud.

The others blinked in wonder. The king ate noisily, greedily, with a hint of green stuff sticking between his teeth.

"Wash it down with this water," suggested Rusfaer laconically.

"A fine idea," acceded Fezoul. He took Rusfaer's bowl and added a dash of the bitter leaf, remarking on the health qualities of the Arizoi plant. "It has been an age since I have eaten anything— ironically, longer than you, bully—despite your obvious gaunter appearance."

"Spare us the commentary," growled Rusfaer.

Draba complained, "Why waste time on this garrulous dwarf? I say put a shaft through his gullet and be done with it."

"Like you would have me?" sneered Jhidik. His curved blade arched suddenly toward the rascal.

Draba ignored the jibe and the proximity of Jhidik's blade. He sank into a petulant silence.

With grudging obeisance, Amexi and Hafta followed the king's lead, ripping off bunches of the coarse weed to bite off tiny nips and gulps.

"Well, it isn't so bad," announced Amexi after a time. "A roast hare would be better. Though I don't suppose we have any of that, do we Jhidik, old man? No cause to complain after surviving those bloodsucking Eakors."

Jhidik gave an absent nod. He seemed self-absorbed, probably fighting the pain in his throbbing thigh.

"What I wouldn't give for a hank of beef right now," mused Hafta. He fanned out his hands behind his head and slumped down against the high wall. The sacrilege to the sacred glyphs and carvings meant nothing to him as he took momentary respite.

Draba refused to engage in any group activities. He had grown fractious and quiet, still nursing his grudge against Dereas. With a pushed out jaw and a wounded pride, he sat apart from the others, a sentiment for which the beastslayer held no sympathy.

Rusfaer and the others ate plenty of the black, spongy leaves and Dereas molded a poultice of it to slap on Jhidik's wound. "Let's gather clumps of it for later reserve."

"'Tis not a bad idea," Rusfaer admitted grudgingly.

The mountain king suggested that they climb to the upper levels of the kingdom to explore the gallery after their meal. "I can give you a guided tour of our most hallowed halls and snatches of our culture! Though it may be but a meager glimpse of our former glory."

Rusfaer shook his head. "Time's precious, mountain man. We wish to quit this dark slagheap." He peered around distrustfully. "Curse this greenish glow anyway! In truth, my head still spins with its eerie taint. My stomach roils."

Fezoul clicked his tongue in reprove. "The path you speak of is this way, warrior. Let us go! There is no harm in visiting a few gilded halls and porticos on the way."

Rusfaer motioned with his sword, chewing loudly. "Lead us on, king, but no tricks," he warned.

With reluctance, the group gathered their light-bearing bowls and made their way to the end of the hall; Dereas hung back, stealing many a backward glance at the sacrificial chamber and the carven snake that had so intimately wound about Fezoul not too long ago.

They climbed the ancient, drunkenly-leaning steps, one by one, gazing in mutual wonder at the rich collection of carven idols, snakes and reptiles of all designs chiseled to either side, only to break out at the top of the landing under the dome of another great cavern hewn by timeless hands. They traversed broken halls and galleries with cracked pillars, and saw indeed that such spaces guarded an air of ancient molder and decay.

The galleries gave way to low, squat temples whose columns hung with tongue-flickering serpents or whose architraves were twined sinisterly with more of the same, looped about a carven figure or a hideous bird or some other monstrous thing. Adjoining courtyards and what looked work areas dedicated to stone chipping and sculpture loomed rich with shadows and lonely grandeur. Here in these estranged open spaces, chipped fountains bubbled more of the magical water while toppled urns spilled forth crudely-hammered coins and ornaments. Statues of carven sandstone and alabaster loomed with faces of birds and bodies of snakes and other combinations: these were only a few of the splendors of those halls of Fezoul's people. Here, an arcade of paved blocks with jeweled chests and arched columns, there carven stairs leading to stone landings above, rich with gold-twined candelabra and paintings of exotic fish, sea scenes, and memories of distant lands, presumably the one these people had all come from. There, side-by-side, lay repositories brimming with treasures, shell coins and heirlooms spilling onto the polished, limed stone, whose paves were now webbed with cracks and rank with the strange leafy outgrowth as below.

Draba and Hafta greedily scooped up the coins they saw, but Rusfaer barked at them. "Leave them alone. They are worthless gewgaws. Made of only cheap stone and shell. Can't you see? Not even metal. They will only weigh us down."

Grudgingly, the ruffians let the coins clatter to the paves.

A glow suffused the upper air where the water trickled, pale yellow and amber, augmented by the steady light from their bowls. A magical luminescence caught the water; it infected their mood, and spurred Fezoul's mood to quixotry. He whistled and skipped down the cracked paves like a child, unfazed by the attempted thievery of his coins. Those arching tunnels that they followed in a haze of aimless wonder were perhaps the same that graced Fezoul's people in days of yore when times were halcyon.

Nostalgia and remorse coursed interchangeably in the mountain king. He cried out gaily: "The Vitrin stream has not lost its allure, or charm! Watch and experience marvel." He sighed in an effort to absorb the jewels of his memory with an air of pride and regret.

"How close are we to the other side of the mountain?" demanded Dereas.

"Not far."

He studied the dwarf with care. Even his easy garrulity and jovial expansiveness could not hide the ripe tension writ on his face, nor the snatching of many furtive glances into the shadowy corners of the halls and alcoves. Dereas wondered how the dwarf had suddenly chanced to waken at that precise moment after so many years. It seemed odd. Searching his memory, he could only guess that it must have had something to do with his scraping the blade across the statue's smooth features, that somehow the action had unbound the spell. He watched the dwarf scratch his pudgy cheek and chin and it prompted Dereas to wonder what other secrets the monarch had not told them.

Onward they trudged through the ruined city, feeling its forsaken ambiance seep into their bones, despite the comfort of sustenance and liquid in their bellies. How much time passed they did not know, only that the king led them on, and his gait was a skipping half caper ahead of them.

The cavernous halls held the look of deserted terraces to Dereas, lonely with only the eerie purl of the water, dribbling down the sculpted walls. Such seeps issued from the highest extents, the snow peaks, the mountain king had told them. Dust motes clung in the air, stirred by the wake of their passing, and now a cold draft, a breath of the underworld, seemed to seep from the very cracks dipping deep in the earth. There was a cold dreariness about this abandoned place which clutched at their marrow, a cold of antiquity that caressed Dereas's skin with a carrion claw. It made him shiver and finger the scars of old cuts on his limbs and brow and he thought of the memory of dark things that still crept within the earth. What Dereas did not know was the scope of this menace Pygra, which had fascinated and terrorized the capricious king. He just wanted out of this wretched place. As did everybody.

He gestured with his spear. "When we reach the other side, will you come with us, mountain king?"

The dwarf's eyes misted and his dreamy expression grew uncannily distant. "I am bound to Yarim-Id," he confessed at last. "I cannot leave the mountain. So the witcher decreed. Her hundred-year-old spell bound me to that. As long as Pygra lives, I must abide here—I, a stone man, wrapped in the thrall of Pygra's stony coils, a servant of the beast."

Rusfaer glared; he gusted air from his nose. "Your snake is dead. Never fear, dwarf," he promised with a guffaw. "We will get you out and prove it to you."

Dereas persisted, "But you can guide us out?"

The mountain king stared for a long time, then gave a brief inclination of head; though his vacant, puzzled expression troubled the beastslayer. "I am thankful to be alive," he murmured at last, as he made a silent prayer to the unseen gods that lurked in these subterranean halls.

CHRIS TURNER

4: Haunter of the Deeps

There are places of the earth that people were not meant to tread...

—Huughite proverb

The wanderers left the crumbling galleries and once-ornate arched colonnades behind. At last the mountain king took them to a wide staircase crooking down to a tunnel similar to one they had quit not long ago. The passage loomed blackly before them, draped in damp streaks, bringing little cheer. Fezoul guided them warily, for his face was drawn and the dim passage surely evoked old, disquieting memories in him. He cupped his light-giving bowl of Vitrin tighter in his trembling hand. A small seep of luminous water trickled underfoot, though thankfully they guarded their bowls.

The narrow tunnel curved, ever danker and more depressing than the forsaken kingdom they had left behind. Snakes, beasts and other disturbing carvings jutted out in stark relief from the walls. Such images prompted the wanderers to gaze anxiously at the many side ways that seemed to branch out in all directions at once.

"I don't like the look of these passages," remarked Jhidik.

Fezoul tossed the Pirean a conciliatory glance, though Jhidik seemed little mollified by that and the king's nervous accompanying laugh.

A particularly wide passageway which Dereas could not be sure was a continuation or offshoot of the main tunnel, had him licking his lips in suspicion, for he thought he heard a strange rattle of pebbles echoing from far down the passage—also a hiss of disturbing intensity that gave way to an unwholesome slithering. When he stopped in his tracks, the sound disappeared. Fezoul jerked at the noise, as if a ghost from the past had caught up with him. Only the faraway plink of drops disturbed the thick silence. Fezoul gulped heavily at the air and pulling at Dereas's mailshirt, looked back

463

longingly the way they had come.

Dereas resented the dwarf's timidity and Rusfaer vented his own disgust at the king's cowering conduct. Hafta continued to glare distrustfully into the gloom of a side tunnel. After a time, with only the tinkle of the stream, Rusfaer gave a surly grunt. "Just a bunch of rats, I gather." He gripped his sword, waved it at the king. "How did your people come to live in these wretched tunnels anyway?"

Fezoul sighed. "'Tis a long tale. Do you have the time?"

"What else do we have?" Rusfaer stared sullenly at Hafta. It seemed the mysterious visitor had departed, yet the grimy-haired warrior continued to jerk his head sideways at every cross tunnel they passed.

The mountain king blinked nervously in the dimness. Gazing at Rusfaer, he seemed to take his cynical leer as a sign of invitation. "Our ancestors from the southern marches fled to Vharad to escape the persecutions of king Yutomay."

"Yutomay? Never heard of him."

"He was king of the desert realms of Yismin fifty leagues south as the condor flies—a simple-minded soul who had set his deranged magicians and spellcasters on us—ever since our statesmen tricked him into signing over the fertile lands bordering our territories."

Rusfaer gave a sneer of contempt. "Now you're a dead race, persecuted by a disgruntled king many years in the grave. What's that say about you, having fled from your enemies to these rat holes?"

Fezoul's twitching fingers reached to clasp his amulet. "And what are you doing here, but fleeing?"

"I 'flee' from no human enemy or mortal man. Freaks and bloodthirsty devil birds, maybe."

Dereas interrupted. "What of your homeland then?"

Fezoul gave a wistful sigh. "Ours was a land rich with olive groves—vineyards, date palm trees too and comely women. A veritable oasis in the midst of the hot baking desert. It was a land where pyramids reared, built to honor the living—not the dead like those of Phygus—or distant Lunra, with her timeless spires adorning the palaces like the jeweled citadels of lost Cyamar. Yet a land much a mother lode in *phosphoron*, the rare magic light-giving metal that crumbles to a powder which we took to seed Vharad's streams. This is what gives the waters their glow. Yutomay's magicians could not penetrate the rock of Vharad, nor its eternal solitude, or its eerie mystery. The dripping dampness and its dark secrets thwarted them."

"What of the Eakors?" asked Jhidik cynically. "How did you win past them?"

"Even then, the Eakors were a menace, haunting the cliffs of the mountain. Did you see them? Yes! They came from a diseased breed of condors that searched for prey in the dark ways under the mountain. They in-bred with the beasts that lived in the purple gloom, creatures under the mountain that became the hybrids they are now—" His voice sank into a solemn whisper.

Dereas recalled the bat-faced slavering countenances of the weaselly-avians and shivered. "So what happened to your people?"

"Most of them were taken to the bowels of the earth by snakes or other terrible beasts. Our first witcher," Fezoul recalled, his voice a dreamy and distant murmur, "had a vision while under the influence of Ayoma, a narcotic stalk that grows in the damp cracks of the deepest tunnels. She translated a tablet that detailed the history of Vharad. It told of a realm populated by giant reptiles! They dwelt here of old—Mazoma, the ruler—half serpent and half crab, having the agility of a salamander and the cunning of a scorpion. The creature reputedly roamed the dark and was said to have ancient powers. It dug the main, oldest tunnel with claws, pincers and teeth. We hollowed out the passageways naturally over the years with our primitive tools, our axes and hammers and wedges, to construct the bestial temples. Temples in the form of Mazoma and the elder reptiles, which included Pygra, Mazoma's successor. Our race became a shorter breed, akin to the dwarfs as you saw earlier carved in the entablature of the temples and facade, and what you see of me."

"Mazoma?" Rusfaer uttered mockingly, "another of these mythologies of yours? Like Pygra?"

Fezoul's lips pursed into a thin frown. "Be careful of what you speak," he warned. "Pygra is real, and the gods don't appreciate your blasphemy."

"Blasphemy?" Rusfaer barked. "Against a beast that reputedly swallows humans? And what do you call your human sacrifice? Soul healing? Don't try to sell me with your hypocritical dogma, you rotten pygmy. We haven't seen any of your snakes yet either—only heard strange sounds, possibly bats or the odd pokey little rodent. The only bones and skulls we've seen are lifetimes dead, if not centuries old... In truth, I think your Pygra is a myth."

The mountain king grew crimson in the face. He threw his arms down in vexation.

Dereas ordered a halt to the pointless debate. Fezoul almost whimpered, "Pygra is not dead! She sleeps only, as I have mentioned before." Dereas frowned. As of a force of habit, the once king, Fezoul, looked over his shoulder, making the sign of the Seven Crosses, a protection hex—two fingers crossed with eyes closed. He twitched his left ear and faced east. Then he shivered as if a cold waft had drifted up from a cranny to brush the quivering folds of his pallid face.

Rusfaer, impatient with displays of superstition, prodded the king forward with the point of his sword, his mouth wry and weary.

The musical echo of running water never ceased. It increased noticeably past a sharp twist in the tunnel. To the keen ear came also a rhythmic scraping of stone on stone, as of some cart wheel trundling on bare rock.

Dereas's muscles knotted. The mechanical creaking sounded unfamiliar in this out-of-the-way place. He pulled his blade free of the scabbard and quickened his pace, long legs carrying him far and fast. In the wider dimness of the tunnel, he stumbled upon a large stone wheel mounted to the wall, tall as a man. The bottom lip was raised three inches off the ground. A complicated series of stone flumes guided the water down to turn the wheel. It was crafted of light, porous stone and was set in slow, creaky motion by a flow of luminous water cascading from the flumes above. Slowly the water caught the cupped grooves on the wheel's outer edge and set it turning. The curious nature of the device caused Dereas to scowl and rub at his chin. Another mechanism was powered behind it, something which he could see inset into the stone wall.

His frown deepened. What was it for? Who could have built such a mechanical innovation?

The king's eyes lit up when he caught sight of the wheel, his lips curling in a sign of keen recognition.

"*Sunsvaere!*" he cried joyously. "How long has it been?—an age since I have seen our hallowed timewheel. How it guides our theosophy! It drives the core of our astrology."

"How does it do that?" grunted Jhidik skeptically.

Fezoul shed light. "It not only tells us the seasons and the time of day but gives us an indication of the fates and workings of the world." He tapped his nose in a knowledgeable manner. "When one is underground for moons on end, 'tis easy to lose track of time. The sun and moon's setting, the comings and goings of the stars, all keep us in touch with reality."

Dereas turned his eyes back to the queer device. He could see many pulleys, wire cords and gears intermingled above, in and around, working in complicated fashion. For what? To power other accessory metal disks adjacent to the stone wheel? A dial, or some kind of stone claw, was pointed at a marker placed on the nearest section of wall. This was engraved with symbols and numbers which the mountain king explained. "They are control markers and adjustment tuners," he said with the studied look of a scholar. Now his expression turned to gloomy awe. "Aie! Less time has passed than I had originally guessed. My long slumber has become suddenly shorter..."

His jaw dropped in crestfallen silence. "Can it be?" He staggered back, squinting at what the dials and markers were telling him. "The time of *Tiramon* is upon us!" he cried, rubbing his eyes. "The

Laughing Monkey besieges us! See how the claw points to the region of Zaporerian in the constellations of the Archer? Eighty years to the day have passed since I first lay in my liege hall as a stone man!—the ultimate offering to Pygra!"

"Incredible," remarked Hafta cynically. "That must make you what—about a hundred and fifty?" He wiped sweat from his brow and swept the unruly yellow locks from his eyes.

"All very interesting but what is it to us?" demanded Draba with a cold disregard for the mountain king and his plight. No word had he spoken since traversing the dwarf's great hall.

Fezoul ignored the remark. "'Tis as I feared. Eighty years! Alas," he moaned in woe. "The spell of the witcher was laid on me for a hundred—which means you have awakened me twenty years too early. Now I must age with the threat of Pygra haunting my shadow."

Draba gave a churlish laugh. "You are forgetting my blade. Fall on it, if you wish to end your misery." The rogue clanked the tip in the ground and leaned on his sword, distrustfully eyeing the indecipherable symbols that were carved on the water wheel and those on the wall opposite where a brilliant, natural light fell.

Rusfaer jeered, adding little sympathy, "Poor you, little mountain monarch. And what of Pygra with no one to eat? Here, Pygra, come, Pygra, fresh meat!" he chanted derisively.

Draba laughed again.

Fezoul bit his lip, pushed down his despair. "You cretins understand nothing of tradition and philosophy. Notice here," he went on furiously, choking back the hurt of their cynicism, "our scholars built a light gauge to accompany the time mechanism. A light funnel too."

He pointed out an ornate slit carved in the smooth rock face. "See the broad vent cut angle-wise above the Time Wheel? Sunlight pours from there and shines on the wall face opposite." He hooked a plump hand forth to illustrate. "'Tis but a few hours after noon—so the Claw of the Luminon says."

"How do you know that?" demanded Amexi in disbelief.

"Look at where the light falls on the wall," scoffed Fezoul. "Its band dips below the median marker, engraved on the stone here, thus and so. We are close to the northern face of the mountain at the moment and the sun is beginning its descent."

"How can you—"

Fezoul resolved the warrior's perplexity. "The vent above the wheel stretches back several dozen feet on a series of twists and turns. Our glass blowers constructed special reflective panes inserted ingeniously in the shafts to direct the light from one pane to another down the shaft, and facilitate our readings. Once these vents were eagle havens and shelters for other creatures, I reckon, before being weathered by centuries of rain and wind, thus steering the light down the shaft, which lands on this patch of wall." He held up his hands once again in proud exhibition.

"'Tis said our architects designed ways of inserting mirrors in the vents and adjusting them over a period of time via pulleys and wires synced to the rhythms of the wheel. To permit more accurate readings—though how they accomplished this is beyond my understanding."

Dereas's brows arched in admiration. He stooped to peer over Fezoul's shoulder who was studying the markings and projected bas reliefs in greater detail while making adjustments with a small lever that jutted out sharply from the stone.

Rusfaer pushed himself forward, fingering his gleaming sword. "We don't have time to philosophize over your arcane inventions, old man! Which way? Time passes. With or without your magical wheel, we must win free of these foul tunnels! We are no closer to the end of this maze than when we quit your dead kingdom!"

Fezoul seemed disinterested in the warrior's tirade. Draba seemed carried away by his chief's words and clenched his hilt with ever more fervor.

Dereas, for a fact, had been squinting to where the mountain king gesticulated and recognized a patch of sunlight streaming down from the rectangular slit to land on the tunnel face opposite the wheel. His lips parted in amazement. Even the small amount of light was bright enough to hurt his eyes after being immersed in darkness for so long. "Balael!..." he whispered. "Ever since I stepped into this stifling burrow, I thought I would never see the light of the sun again."

Rusfaer flourished a negligent hand. "Well, you got your wish, Beastslayer. We may not see any more of such light, so, I suggest you soak it up. We should leg it out of here before we run out of juice. We can't live on black bitter cabbage forever."

Dereas's lip twitched. True, his brother had a point, but it didn't undermine Fezoul's machine in any way or the knowledge which might help them in times to come. The beastslayer gazed anew on the stone wheel and recalled certain calendar systems that graced temple ruins he had seen on his travels. He thought this one in comparison quite unique and advanced in its complexity. His mind drifted back to a network of carven crystals he had seen dangling on wire in the temple of Telagorim in the shattered hills of Pastorech. Tinkling in the wind, the crystals had cast dizzying beams of colored light on a smoothly-polished wall marking out symbols at a certain hour. They were purported to tell a story of the fate of the ancient people who worshiped stone and the majesty of natural outcrops, according, at least, to the glazed-eyed oracle who dwelt there.

Moments passed. Despite the eeriness of the tunnel, Dereas found himself transported to a magical place, his reverie placing him gently before a quiet glade with a fair blue mist rising over a river. A figure approached on invite to the tryst. The sheen of hazel eyes, the flash of a bright smile, the expectant laugh of a lithesome maid like a tinkling brook...it was all a dream, and yet, the tangle of her shimmery hair as she alighted from her mount, was a balm to his spirit.

Fezoul's brow clouded. "Wait, if I remember...No, let us advance. There is no other way, but forward."

"What do you mean 'but forward'?" called Rusfaer. "I thought we were already going 'forward'," he cried out with dismay.

Something in the aspect and configuration of the cryptic symbols and the inverted serpent lit up on the wall caused Fezoul to stare enigmatically. "The Time of the Snake has passed..." he murmured the words over and over, basking in a cryptic frown. Surprise and fear crept suddenly over his face like a black cloud.

His pale lips curled in horror and he looked about him in dismay, as if he would topple in a swoon, for it seemed he had never known a time without Pygra.

The mountain king shrugged off the vision with a sudden jerk of his shoulders. He stuttered something half intelligible, something about 'foolish outlanders' and 'eerie reptiles' and 'forbidden magic in the tunnels of Yarim-Id', before he became lost in a moody silence.

The tunnel yawned ahead and Fezoul gestured them on, an endless pathway with an unknown destination.

Back and forth, down twists and turns they trod while Dereas dimly recalled legends of Vharad and the labyrinth that weaved under her black mantle. A half-forgotten memory surfaced of the secret lore of the old world that the Witch Hadrneas had imparted to him, much unknown to his father.

The slow creaking of the wheel faded to a murmur, the sound replaced by the dull clopping of boots and the mesmeric purl of the stream flowing inexorably down the tunnel's middle. The water level had lessened, Dereas noted, and seemed of slightly lighter hue after being siphoned off by the Time Wheel and funneled to various cross tunnels as they passed. A sort of monastic quiet pervaded the ghostly surroundings.

"Black Balael!" cursed Rusfaer. "Damn to Kizoi's hell all this darkness! Why is this wretched water so green? Makes me sick. I want to retch."

Hafta groaned. "I also feel like heaving."

"'Tis the life-giving water of Xatu," Fezoul said sternly. "It comes from the source of the mountaintop. A mantle of ice covers the dome of the skull mountain. The daytime sun melts the ice and causes the water to seep down through the cracks and follow the secret ways. 'Tis said," he confided not without a shiver, "that if anyone laid sword to Pygra and the blood of her victims mixed with her own, she would open her mouth and inject a fierce spray from her teeth to cast the color of the stream a pure green."

"A lurid lore," mumbled Jhidik.

"Always Pygra," Rusfaer snarled. "Why not Mazoma or Yutomay? Are you obsessed with this snake?"

Fezoul exclaimed vehemently, "Maybe that's what makes you sick, bully. If the water were another color, it would imply that the serpent was ill, or had consumed the blood of a creature other than what she was used to."

Rusfaer snorted his disbelief at the concept. "Or maybe the ice is just naturally green?"

"A wives' tale, I think," scoffed Hafta.

"Do you believe all this mumbo jumbo about Pygra?" growled Rusfaer, nudging his brother none too gently.

The beastslayer's face betrayed no hint of opinion.

"'Tis true! What need is there of belief?" asserted Fezoul, his features congested in agitation once again.

"Listen! What's that?" cried Hafta.

A slithering and an ominous rustling echoed as of the stir of pebbles in a distant corridor. The loose rubble seemed to rattle under the press of an enormous weight.

Dereas swore. He saw a side tunnel yawning two yards to the right. Inside was a litter of yellow bones and large, broken eggshells, around which the dribbling water forked from the main tunnel to disappear in a black haze. Dereas scratched at his stubbled chin, frowning. Perhaps Pygra had been here? It was the first sign of eggs so deep into Vharad since they had entered the mountain king's realm.

Rusfaer seemed not to notice. "I heard nothing—except maybe the scurry of certain rats. How about you, Draba? You are keen of ear and a good judge of spooks. Go on up the tunnel. See if you can spear us some rodents. Borrow Dereas's spear if you must. This way we can have us some sustenance." His quip earned him some laughs from the others. "Or maybe scoot down this bone and egg-littered corridor that has Dereas's teeth chattering."

Draba started to retort, then stiffened, jarred by the sudden sight of a large, sinister shape rattling down the side way he was closest too.

Dereas froze too. He was staring down the cross tunnel, eyes ablaze—at the place where Draba had seen the furtive movement.

"That was big." Draba's round mouth curved in an expression of shock.

"How big?" Rusfaer scoffed, not even bothering to look toward the tunnel.

"What do you mean, 'big'?" demanded Amexi.

Fezoul's voice shrilled out in hysterical terror. "He saw something!"

"Shut up, you lily-livered coward!" shouted Rusfaer.

Fezoul blinked. He looked about to keel over, his eyes white with fear. A small whine escaped his puckered lips. Almost as if the dwarf had become an oracle, another strange sound echoed in the cross tunnel, this time closer.

"I beg of you," he whimpered, his voice choked with a sob, "let's go back. Forget this hare-brained scheme of yours. It is insane! Take the road back to where you came in from the north. The Eakors are much less merciless than Pygra. I swear to you! It's the better way. Yes, the better way!" He caught Dercas's sleeve with a surprising strength and raked his fingers claw like over his mail shirt.

"We go on!" Dereas bellowed, shaking off the cringing king's fingers in disgusted impatience. "Snake or not."

Fezoul cast a longing glance back toward the Time Wheel, now long receded in the folds of darkness. He gulped down his fear and bowed his head, ashen-faced.

In the inky shadows, Dereas perceived Rusfaer's smugness as he twirled his blade.

There was no sign or sound of the terror. The tunnel proceeded on a slight downward cant through a series of twists and turns that had even the big man's sense of direction beguiled.

By and by they came to a massive cavern, rich with hanging stalactites, tips pointed as icicles. The water's flow ended in a glimmering oval pool. It was no ordinary pool, Dereas observed, black as midnight and long as evening shadows. At the far edges where the water was still, its mystical surface reflected the cavern's richness with an unsettling likeness. The place was imbued with an ancient solemnity, he thought, eerie as a golem's abode.

Despite his earlier fear, Fezoul's interest peaked at the sight of the water. He hunched himself forward like a gnome with a new vigor, mumbling to himself.

The Vitrin stream split and trickled down to fan paths left and right across the near mirror-smooth face of the pool.

Dereas, much exhausted from recent events, stopped to splash cool water on his haggard face. The others followed, to wet their tongues. All seemed gripped with an odd apprehension and a silence too thick for understanding.

Ringed around the pool's edges were small, ankle-high cairns of stones and gems—masses or collections of them. In the middle of the pool rose a forbidding fane, hulking like a grim misshapen totem out of a ghost king's palace. It was built of bleached white bones—human skulls evidently and various other bones interlaced. Bone fragments poked out of the rude mass to form a hideous face—eyes, button nose, beastly ears, with femurs denoting tusks that jutted out from the forehead of the hoary skull. A ghastly horn rode below a ludicrous chin, likely some sort of blasphemous goatee.

Dereas instinctively recoiled and reached for his sword. He peered in the water to see tokens of random offerings there: bracelets, amulets, gemstones, shields, knives, tools, even a score of baleful skulls, dwarf-size, but these could have as easily toppled from the macabre fane. This was ruder construction than any he had ever seen, not in any way as refined as the desolate ruins of Fezoul's people or those he had seen in faraway Lunra. This shrine heavily veered toward sorcerous in style whereas the others of hard stone and polished edges, were more commonplace.

A tunnel, gaping ominously behind the fane, twice as high as a man, loomed blackly on the other side of the pool. No water coursed in or out of this passage. To get to it, would mean wading through the eerie Vitrin pool, something he cared not to attempt.

Dereas felt his throat constrict. "Balael…"

The mountain king muttered his final reflections. "The pool then still exists."

"What is this pool?" hissed Dereas.

"A mirror to the other side," Fezoul murmured. "Many of our ancients said it was a confluence to the afterworld, a place of power, a soul-portal. They urged our citizens to provide offerings to the spirits on the other side for those who had died in Pygra's coils."

"Gibberish," rasped Rusfaer.

"Others went mad," went on Fezoul, "made it their own grisly shrine as you see." He thrust a trembling finger out at the disturbing tower of bones. Shoulders drooping, he was beset by some nervous anxiety that was eating away at him. His throat worked as if swallowing phlegm. He squatted on his haunches, massaging his temples.

Dereas stirred restlessly, realizing the king's behavior was becoming infectious. His eyes traveled to the white-boned tower. Even in the ghostly glow emanating from the running water at their feet that met the pool, the water seemed to take on a duskier hue out there and he marveled at how deep the fissure underneath the fane must run. His eyes caught a sudden ripple of movement—a ghost of motion farther out. He started, for it was a blur just at the edge of sight. Behind and to the right of the chilling fane, came another.

"Look! There!" he cried.

All eyes turned to the place where he gestured, but nothing materialized and Rusfaer gave a sardonic cry. "Probably some hungry minnows, brother. Why fret? We have all the time in the world to hallucinate. I see you are getting almost as good as our sniveling king here in spotting hobgoblins."

Fezoul grimaced and shook his head in fitful anger. "It's no goblin, warrior. Much has changed since the Time of the Snake—since I have slept."

"Time of the Snake? And what in Kizoi's three hells is that?"

Jhidik moved restlessly from leg to leg. "Let's be gone from this cursed place." He limped off back to the tunnel, giving the water wide berth.

Amexi voiced a grumbling curse. "I like this place no more than Jhidik. I suggest we move on."

Draba, meanwhile, fascinated with the jeweled mounds gracing the water's edge, had paused to idly single out a particularly tall and intricate pile. He seemed less interested in the movements in the water, or the ominous fane, or any creepy echoes that may have issued from the tunnel behind it.

Dereas looked back to see the rogue's avaricious grin fill half his face. A sudden, strange blue fin surfaced on the water. Dereas jerked in surprise. A dark dome of shell emerged and two eyes on a wavering stalk peeked up quickly above the water and darted back down.

"There!" he gasped. The strangled yell froze in his throat. It was overshadowed by an unwholesome image of Draba, oblivious to the growing shape, picking up a shiny gem by the pool—then pocketing it.

"Did you see that?" Dereas hissed. He scrambled close to grab Jhidik by the shoulder. The Pirean's jerky limp had ground to a frozen halt.

"What?" cried Jhidik. "The ripple, or that stupid thieving sod filching jewels that were obviously meant for the dead?"

The two friends looked at each other, but the thing was gone. Only a more disturbing ripple emerged on the pool's surface.

Fezoul's distinctive murmur broke over the lap of waves. "'Tis the guardian of the pool!"

"Would you cease your prattle?" berated Rusfaer. "Or must I haul your chicken-hearted hides away from this minnow pool, even wade out in the water myself to spear this imaginary marlin?" In a sudden fit of fury, he stomped over to the shore, probing the black water with his sword, swishing angrily. "Look. See? Nothing!"

"Brother, I wish you wouldn't—"

But the Beastslayer didn't finish that thought.

A hideous creature burst out the water, fat as a grouper, sending forth a spray of sludgy water.

Crayfish? Clam? Neither was apt.

The blood froze in Dereas's throat, no less Rusfaer's—a terror which knotted the pit of both men's stomachs and sucked the life blood out of even the bravest man.

On spindly legs, a wild, crab-like creature scuttled shoreward, leaving Rusfaer, who stood gape-mouthed nearby, transfixed. Water poured from the beast's domed carapace. Algae and gray moss threaded down its hard outer shell to cling to its six forelegs like a grizzled garland. The water gleamed green in the monster's advance. Whether scorpion or crab, the beast was a horrid caricature of neither, the embodiment of beastliness itself.

An algae-coated pincer shot out to snatch at the warrior's thigh.

Rusfaer jerked away, avoiding the rake of those sharp nailed vises across his bare flesh. The creature scuttled forward, eager to snag any appendage, arm or boot and drag his body into the water.

Rusfaer struggled, hacked at the appendage and gasped out curses, aghast at the orange-toothed maw that was moving in on him. Hideous chirping sounds issued from its mouth as the beast's crab legs clacked and splashed around him in a frenzy.

Rusfaer's sword hammered full on the creature's leg, splintering crusty shell and joint. Then the glittering edge of the sword fell on empty water as a tentacle pulled him forward and the sputtering warrior was turned over and over in the seethe of blackish water.

And yet, all this infernal commotion had alerted some new terror in the deeps.

A rumble of horrible, subterranean ghastliness came boiling up from the middle of the mysterious depths.

Rusfaer was nearly crushed as a wall of water exploded in his face. Out of the blackness burst a gigantic, wedge-shaped head, straight up from the sinister pool, with spotted snout.

The behemoth was all scales and slimy skin, a nightmarish serpent from the pits of hell. Dereas gaped at the size of its mottled worm-like head and scale-plated snake's body. It opened its maw wide, clutched the blue crablike creature in its triple fangs and crunched. The thing struggled uselessly, eye stalks crushed, wavering under the press of muscles too powerful for even its impressive girth. The prey was doomed and could hardly be recognized as the same finned thing that he had spotted earlier poking its eldritch antennae above the water.

The pincer gripping Rusfaer's boot heel was jerked back and snapped in two as the warrior fell back in a backwash of cold water. The worm, serpent, or whatever it was, had a trunk wide as two men. It reared out of the water and sucked the monster crab down head first with primitive zeal. The captured creature's hind legs thrashed and pushed against the gummy flesh holding it, but the serpent opened its fanged mouth a tinge wider and hiccuped, or some obscene mimicry of it, and with each grotesque spasm, the bristles on its inner tract tilted and pulled backwards and sucked the doomed creature deeper into its disgusting, wattled throat.

Rusfaer slapped at the water, trying to get away from that slimy horror. But the thing's head rose up to break off an end of a gray-glistening stalactite. Then the monster turned, for an instant, to shine its one glaring eye on him.

Dereas could see in a brief flash, that the breadth of each evil loop of its coils wrapped underneath, were larger than himself. From where had it come? The snake must have slithered up from some underwater hole.

Now the mutant crab was completely engulfed by the serpent-thing's mouth. The throat worked. It snapped shut its fanged maw and dove underwater, quick as it had come, sending a tidal wave showering them all.

All reeled under that assault. Rusfaer struggled to stay afloat, grunting entreaties to his gods. He kicked and thrashed like a half-drowned dog toward the shore. His mail shirt threatened to drown him but his feet hit shallow bottom and he pushed off, head breaking the surface once more, gasping for air.

Dereas plunged into the water to help him but his brother jerked himself away, eyes mad as a boar. It was as if he had seen a horde of demons. The big warrior cursed, frothed, rocked his head back and forth in thick, slobbering shock. He dragged himself from the water and staggered up the shore.

Dereas stared in mute horror while Jhidik and the others backtracked madly up the tunnel. Now a low rumble filled the dim cavern. Stones erupted from the water, showering all in slime. The thud of mighty blows sounded shortly after.

Dereas cried out a hurried prayer to Balael. He turned to Fezoul and rasped, "Run for it, you fool!" He sucked air into his lungs. "So this is the Pygra of which you spoke?" Frantically he pulled the white-faced mountain king along.

Fezoul moaned and blubbered, "Dark things dwell in the caverns of Yarim-Id!"

Up the mountain path they fled. They stumbled, reeled, clawed their way through narrow twists in the tunnel, too narrow to admit the snake that slithered out of the water after them.

Relief blossomed in Dereas's heart —for something that big could not squeeze through a junction that slim. Could it? But there came a wallowing behind them that froze the marrow in his bones—a wash of terror, a slithering tumult, immeasurably long, sliding, lurching, banging its snout against the tunnel as if the rock were made of soft curd.

The stone shook under the monster's every heave. The booms were enough to deafen the undead, resounding with a hundred bashes of hammer on drums.

Pygra was not done yet...There came a horrendous scratching and slithering of the most unnerving variety. It came from the tunnels adjacent, echoing fiendishly behind the pool. The serpentine nightmare was not far away, a fact which could only suggest that it was capable of moving with mind-numbing speed.

Dereas felt his flesh crawl. He recalled a tunnel gaping blackly behind the pool and his mind raced. Did the passage connect to the side tunnel they had passed earlier?

He did not finish the thought. He dragged the mountain king along like a sack of flour. "Quick! Before the snake cuts us off."

"But how can it?" croaked Jhidik.

Dereas waved him off, a terrible cry growing in his throat. The eternal walls caging them in for so long and the madness of this sunless world were shredding his grip on sanity. Yet neither could compare to the unthinkable horrors of being crushed and ripped apart by that horrid serpent. Doubtless the brute knew these tunnels. How it had found some other dark, unknown crevice to slither through was beyond Dereas's ken.

Sinister movements and rustling pebbles came from beyond roughhewn cross tunnels to their right. Along the way came an eerie whistling and slithering, and Dereas imagined some monstrous thing with flickering tongue scouring every murky escape route. Booms erupted, as if a muffled, colossal body slammed itself against sheer rock. The fugitives scurried on. Blood racing, Dereas thought about what those coils would do if they twined around his torso.

Like crazed men, they stumbled back the way they had come, clawing mindlessly down the tunnel, jostling against each other, scraping shins on rock, boots splashing in cold water. Somewhere behind, Dereas heard Rusfaer's and Hafta's heaving grunts and curses.

The Time Wheel was a blot to their left. They swept by it like frenzied fiends without a moment's glance. Draba, normally sullen and indolent, had taken great pains to rush past with fleet-footed strides, his black-tarnished blade clutched whitely in hand. He was twenty feet ahead in the dull shadows when a sight brought him halting in his tracks, eyes wide with terror. An abysmal wedge of a head reared before him, a bleak mottled beak, elevated on a long glistening trunk, which was part of a longer mass of menacing, iridescent coils undulating on and on into the greenish gloom without end.

His face, a quivering mask of lunacy, betrayed a myriad emotions, each more terrible than the last. Pygra had slithered up a side way through impossible means and now thrust her obscene bulk up at them from the lower ground. A horrible nightmare she was to behold in the lurid, devilish light. The serpent's single working eye glared like a beacon; the other was fused shut, the gray-golden brown folds of flesh long melded over from some old wound or deformity. Whether the monster was half blind or victim of some plague of birth, was not known. It diminished her threat in no way.

The snake reared. Her fetid mouth opened in an 'O', gushing a rattle of ghastly anticipation. Draba gaped down a crimson-black putrid pit of slime. She snapped shut her mouth, her forked tongue darting in and out between a mesh of triple fangs.

Overwhelmed by surging fear, Draba outdid himself in the way of cowardice. When the mountain king had slammed into him from behind, he grabbed Fezoul's arms and pushed him toward the monstrous face, using him as a decoy. In the wake of that bestial gaze, Draba turned and bolted, leaving the unlucky, gibbering king standing before the white, glaring eye. For a fractured instant, the dwarf stood paralyzed in wild-eyed fear, then the serpent, though partially blind, uncoiled with venomous fangs and slimy tongue.

In three quick strides, Dereas lunged forward and shouldered Fezoul out of the way. Twisting sharply, he slashed at the end of the snake's slithering tongue arching toward the king's neck.

The reptile gave a hissing shriek, missing its mark by mere inches.

Dereas's white-knuckled fingers gripped his spear for another stabbing strike. The two-pronged shaft thrust deep into her dead eye and she gave another loathsome hiss and wormed her scaly mass forward, dislodging the spear and nearly dashing Dereas and the dwarf against the rocks. Head over heels they tumbled, her foul wind a tempest on their skin.

"Flee, if you value your hide!" Dereas wheezed, his cry drowned out by the wash of the serpent's reeking breath. In thrashing confusion, having no time to recover from the stench, they clawed their way back up the tunnel toward the Time Wheel.

Scrambling in a half crouch, the beastslayer pulled Fezoul along. Lurching, barely escaping the snake's mouth and dripping fangs, he shambled sideways down the tunnel. The snake's usual lightning strikes may have been slowed—as she had just ingested the water creature.

The snake's questing tongue probed the dim confines for their flesh. She had fiendishly crept up on them all too fast and would devour them if she could get a clear view. He ripped his sword free from the sheath and the arching, dizzying shaft of blade caught the beast's face a glancing blow off the crusty scales between eye and snout.

The snake uttered an otherworldly gurgle.

Dereas crouched, laid a sinking cut into scaly flesh, deflected a slimed fang.

Pygra sprang to swallow Dereas whole, but caught the upthrust deadliness of his blade instead. In bitter rage, she bit down on the blade, and a strange brownish fluid sprayed forth, soaking the warrior's mailshirt in gore, as she wrenched the gleaming haft out of Dereas's hands to dash it clanging against the wall.

Dereas looked up at her dazedly through a screen of filth and haze, thinking that these were to be his last memories. But the snake was clearly in agony, her bleeding mouth pouring forth foul-smelling liquid, and ooze gushing from her maimed eye.

The serpent smashed her mallet-shaped head once, twice against the ceiling. Why? To ease the pain perhaps? To everyone's dismay, the upper rock began to crack.

Shrieks and rumbles rocked the chamber. The others dashed for their lives. All save Dereas. They fled deeper back up the tunnel. An avalanche of boulders came crashing down, almost crushing the beastslayer.

He rolled just in time. The snake was on the other side of the landslip of boulders. In clouds of dust they could see her evil glaring eye, staring out at them in a sinister defiance, through a slit in the pile of fallen rock, not small enough for the beastslayer's tastes. Her sight was not lost yet.

"We are lost!" cried the mountain king. His moan was a woeful quaver. He choked on his tongue, eyes blinded by the dust that swarmed in the air. "Pygra has sealed the main tunnel! There is no way out. She guards the escape route. "We are doomed!"

Dereas picked himself up from the rubble and hobbled toward the dwarf. "Shut your mouth, you numbskull king! You are our only hope. Get us out of here. You know these ways better than anyone."

The dwarf king wagged his head in hopeless futility. "It's been an age since I've trod these glooms and my memory is clogged with evil dreams over the years. The killer fiend is a foe too great for us." He glared at the cowering figure of Draba in the darkness who itched to stumble blindly up the tunnel, but was unwilling to be a forerunner. "That dastard flung me deliberately at Pygra. You saw it!" he shrieked. He pointed a quivering finger at the cringing Draba. "Why should I help a group of ingrates like you? You are nothing but a gang of thugs—and killers."

Dereas pinched his mouth tight in anger. "You will help us, you wretch, and you will do whatever it takes to keep us alive."

Draba sneered back at them. "You were in my way, king. If anyone's to die, it should be you. Was it not you who bred, nursed and worshiped that black-deviled thing from a babe?"

The king flung back a defensive curse. "So it was ordained." His words trailed feebly, falling moot in light of the facts.

Hafta glowered at him, crouched warily at a bulge farther up the tunnel. Amexi sank heavily in the dust-clouded shadows.

Rusfaer, who had stumbled out of the darkness, ordered them all to silence, blinking in the confusion, so he could think.

"What's there to think, brother?" croaked Dereas sardonically.

He felt a gloating satisfaction at his brother's being on the horror side of things. He coughed up blood-speckled phlegm in his palm. "We are all doomed, as the king says. So what is your imperial wish now?"

Rusfaer stared at him in wonder. "You too?" The big man shook his head and glared. "Come on! I've heard enough. I'm not going to give myself over to fatalistic mumblings." He waved the others on after him.

"Better be quick to run to our deaths, eh brother?" croaked Dereas.

Jhidik cast Dereas a meaningful glance. Hafta surged after his chieftain. Up the tunnel the rest scrambled back again toward the stone wheel of time, all save Dereas. There was no comfort in this route, for the snake was thrusting part of her beaked jowl through the hole in the boulder-strewn wall caused by the avalanche. If she followed, they were lost.

Closest to the snake and her coils of death, Dereas could see clearly what she was planning. He struggled vainly to retrieve his weapon. He knew with helpless fury that it was probably buried under tons of rock.

Farther up the tunnel, Rusfaer, too, saw the threat and that they were not going to win this fight by any ordinary means. The snake was too big, too fast, and knew these tunnels like the scales on her back. Rusfaer saw the look of defeat etched on Dereas's haggard face. But the sudden slope and the old wheel hanging on the wall gave Rusfaer the hint of a plan.

Motioning to the others, he scrambled over to lay hands on the timepiece's rough stone. "Here, help me with this thing, you laggards!" Amexi, Hafta and the coward Draba who crouched panting and beady-eyed in the murk, stumbled forth to lay hands on the wheel. They put all their strength into trying to jerk it off its axle.

But to no avail. Thick ropes of muscles corded on Rusfaer's back. Veins popped out on his brow. While all of them groaned, heaving in synchrony, the thing barely budged; not until Jhidik joined in and they nudged it a few inches, but no more.

Fezoul glared at the sacrilege to his heritage. "You cannot deface our sacred stone!"

"Shut up, you weasel!" Rusfaer's shadow loomed over the king like a pall of death. "Either you help us or back off. Put yourself in the mouth of your snake, if you want."

The mountain king pursed his lips. Seeing the truth of Rusfaer's words, he pushed a space between Hafta and Amexi and bent a shoulder to the wheel. It jumped, scraped off the stone axle, giving way an inch with a sudden, grating creak.

Rusfaer let out a joyous roar. The wheel fell three more inches to the stony floor. It started to roll on its own accord, given the slope of the passage, and Rusfaer, wheezing in a dizzy frenzy, lunged to steady it so that the clunky thing would not topple and crush them all.

Amexi and Hafta struggled to guide the wheel with straining thews as it plunged down the tunnel toward the blood-mad snake—and toward Dereas.

The beastslayer was racing up the tunnel as the wheel gathered momentum, with the snake's mallet-head and muscular coils smashing dangerously on the rocks behind him.

The wheel rolled faster—a massive missile threatening to crush any idiot daft enough to stand in its path. Dereas dodged its breakneck rush, edging sideways at the last minute. His back and shoulders flattened against the stone with little space to spare as the heavy mass rolled onward toward the snake.

The wheel crashed against the base of the fallen rock and it vaulted upward just as Pygra was about to squeeze her beak-like nose through the crevice. Any chance given her massive scale-glistening body to squeeze through that aperture would have been the end of them. As it was, the wheel rolled up the crumbling slope and knocked the snake back through the opening that she was fighting to wriggle through. Pitched back in clouds of dust and confusion, she uttered a dry rattle of pain and frustration.

The wheel effectively blocked the hole and it lay askew. For now the snake slid back, thwarted...

Silence reigned in the corridor. Only the thuds of her tail and the dim trickle of water purling innocently down the path impinged on the stillness.

The breath wheezed in and out of Dereas's lungs. Up the tunnel he hobbled, bloody and dust-caked. He joined the others, nursing several wounds. Foul serpent blood had stained his ravaged mail where the monster had dripped foul ichor; his whole frame reeked of snake scent. The mountain king looked at him with an expression of awe and respect. "Thank you, warrior. You of all others saved me from a gruesome fate. Pygra is behind us now," he asserted, wiping his soiled robe. "We are safe—for now."

Dereas's smoldering eyes blazed. His dark face went a shade wilder, feral as a wolf's after the bloodletting of the snake. Chest heaving, he fingered his mailshirt which was filthy and scored, and only grunted a dissatisfied oath.

"'For now' is a very tenuous time frame," Rusfaer muttered.

"How are we to find our way out to the other side of mountain then?" demanded Amexi. "The snake has obviously blocked our path."

"A good question." rasped Dereas. "Fezoul?"

"There are other ways," the dwarf admitted. "Detours and side passages, but my memory is dim."

"Well, you'd better un-dim it, hadn't you?" roared Rusfaer.

He prodded the dwarf with his sword, ushering him with no gentle persuasion down the gloomy path.

"The first side tunnel that looks promising, we take," Rusfaer called in a hoarse, gruff voice.

Fezoul deigned no response. His private thoughts were dark and foreboding. Lips pinched back like a rat's, he cast a spate of rueful glances down at the ruined Time Wheel. They left the Luminon behind. Dereas squinted under the glare of tantalizing natural light that streamed through the lonely slit. What he wouldn't do to fly like a bird through that vent, free from this wretched mountain and its untold dooms!

Through the masked terror that he hid so well, Dereas could see that Rusfaer's fingers, normally steady, strong as eagle's claws, now gripped the hilt of his sword with a hesitant slackness. Truthfully, he had never seen his brother thus shaken. The encounter doubtless had left him less than confident. Surely a formidable human foe, Rusfaer was not a beastslayer.

Dereas's mind strayed back to that blood-stained encounter with the snake. Beyond normal means the serpent had doubled around and cut them off from the front. How? Obviously the thing had supernormal powers, to track and corner so swiftly—and violently, which meant...what chance did they have, as mere gropers in the dark, to save themselves from certain annihilation?

Dereas forced himself back to the present. He reached for his sword, found it missing from the scabbard. Stupid! He had lost it in the mad scramble back in the tunnel. His spear also. He stalked over to Draba and wrenched the wicked, curved scimitar out of the rogue's hand before he could object—reward for his bad behavior leaving Fezoul prey to the snake. It left him with only his flat-edged short sword and small notched dagger as weapons. Gape-mouthed, Draba spouted a spate of curses but Dereas rounded on him, and it was obvious Draba was not ready to fight him over it. He glowered at the beastslayer, grumbling and murmuring insults, looking to Rusfaer for sympathy, but his fear was palpable of one who had taken on the snake. Ill feelings bristled like pikes in the gloom and a grayer cloud of animosity rose over their company from the ashes of old tensions. The companions cast roving eyes at a side tunnel which Fezoul had recommended with a shaking hand.

The wanderers filled what few vessels they still had among them with Vitrin and used the greenish glare to guide their way along the side tunnel. Dereas frowned, his gaze wandering cheerlessly to the bleak, flaked, carven rock all around. He murmured as if in a dream, "In what realm do you abide, mountain king, to house these horrors?"

Fezoul grunted between his bared teeth. Through his trance-like reverie, he remained still the humbled, violated king of an ancient people. "Our seers spoke of a great flood once," he murmured in a strange, disembodied voice," —a cataclysm, o'er ten million years ago that rocked the world." His voice droned on like one possessed. "The rains came and the ice melted. The seawaters rose to unheard of levels. The animals, stripped of their habitat, came to Vharad, the godless mountain within which we stand. 'Twas the only standing island in a deluge of water, stretching leagues as far as the eye could see. Some creatures burrowed into the ancient rock and founded the grim tunnels below. They are the same we tread now. Among themselves they fought for resources, scarce on a windy, water-cursed world. Only the reptiles survived. They evolved to become a horrendous brood, all needing size and strength to survive. When we arrived, most of the elder beasts had disappeared, but there were some that slept—deep down in places, forgotten from the minds of men..."

"A joyous bit of history," grunted Hafta.

Dereas bit back a shiver, feeling the ache of familiar legends haunt his soul. Memories of the frights and atrocities in the crypts of Ahrion's dungeons were still fresh in his mind, but he flung such recollections aside. He crept on with shaky feet, in silence, guided by an instinctive wariness which the others shared, knowing that they would fight to survive—though they be but shadow puppets in a sunless, windless world.

The menace of Pygra had not lost its grip. With frantic strides and hushed whispers that echoed the grimness of their surroundings, they stumbled along the silent ways, a company ragged, cut, bruised and battered. There was a harried quality to their shambling; Hafta's face was a mask of discord and turmoil. Amexi flexed his quivering fingers and gripped the pommel of his sword as if it were the only thing that kept him sane. Draba set his round, resentful, mole-like face in a sardonic grimace, always darting looks over his shoulder to see if anything was trailing them.

Rusfaer had partially developed a healthy respect for Fezoul's mythical snake and had curbed his remarks and drolleries about it. The mountain king had sunk into an infectious gloom that could not be lifted. Dereas's stomach began to roil. It felt like days since he had last eaten. What he wouldn't do to be out on the open steppes riding in the wind! Or snug in his yurt wrapped under the furs with a good woman.

Wishful thinking, he grunted. He snapped himself back to reality, forced himself to stay alert to the long-reaching shadows and the endless, twisting corridor. Thankfully, the snake's tumult had died down some time ago.

Though they had discovered an alternate passage, it didn't sport any stream of light-giving Vitrin. But the ceiling was high enough for them to walk upright at least without banging their skulls. No signs of ancient bones or eggshells did they encounter, only darkness, ropy cobwebs and shadows. Menacing shadows played tricks across the path they walked. Even if the shadows were only deformed caricatures of their own passing, they were enough to push them all to the edge of dread. The king took them on narrower routes, longer and more circuitous, but with the comfort that the gargantuan serpent could not pass.

After a period that could have marked hours or days, they came upon a rough-hewn tunnel whose rightmost branch gaped into open blackness. Rusfaer shone his bowl down the passage where golden fragments of dust seemed to cling to its sides like fairy stardust. Blinking in curious wonder, he swept up some of the particles in his knob-knuckled hand and examined them carefully under the dim light. Their sparkling radiance implied abundant riches to be had.

Hafta and Draba squinted over his shoulders, eyes saucers as they peered, conjectures running rampant in their devious minds.

"Well, I'll be a lizard's uncle," swore Rusfaer, "I think this is gold dust!"

His comrades bent to crowd around him, eyes glowing with excitement and calculation.

"Look here, more of the stuff!" called Hafta, with greedy purpose. "And a naked vein, even a nugget. Not fool's gold." He pitched himself forward to grab at a chunk of what resembled pure gold, but Rusfaer slapped the ham fist away.

"'Tis a nugget!" insisted Draba.

Rusfaer ignored the rat-faced warrior. He grabbed the chunk and tossed it to Hafta, who eyed it with satisfaction and tested it with his teeth. "Pure gold, I'd say."

The mountain king hopped about with frantic unease, waving both of the men to caution. "We mustn't go down there! No! Lizards abound in the gloom, the haunt of the half-men."

"Half what?" croaked Rusfaer. "Another one of your wives' tales? That's the first we've heard of 'lizards'," he grunted.

The mountain king's eyes bulged like a frog's. "No, 'tis true. I don't speak of them. Because it's bad luck, after all." His voice betrayed a hint of guilt that puzzled Rusfaer and Dereas.

"Well, I don't hear the snake now," announced Rusfaer bluffly, "and I'm of mind to overlook a few lizards. Carve them up with my sword, I will. Might as well make our time worthwhile if we're going to starve and get bitten by giant clams. Well," he blew air out between his teeth, "anything to say, mountain king?" He seemed completely forgetful of the encounter with the snake. Or completely in denial.

The mountain king shook his head sheepishly, his sweaty face exuding a dull cast. "Before I was declared king, a group of dissidents rebelled from our order and our devotion to snakes. Led by the renegade Xabren, a sinister visionary, they left Xatu behind, our little kingdom in the mountain. They were bent on exploring elsewhere. They tunneled too deeply, and never returned, so it was rumored. Some say they had been affected by the dream gas whose soporific vapor blows from certain vents in the rocks. This was the last place they were heard from. Look!—" he pointed to several cryptic markings etched over the gap, stone carvings withal at the tunnel's foot. He licked his lips. "It was feared that the renegades discovered some untoward evil."

"Hold up," objected Rusfaer. "There is no one down there, old man, so let's not get our robes in a knot. There are no footprints, no slime pools, lizard prints, or lizard scales that I see, and no sounds. Listen? I think our snake is gone."

True enough, there was only the roaring in their ears of unnatural silence and an ill feeling of dread. Even Dereas, despite the romantic idea of delving for riches, did not want to explore these tunnels, especially with the snake roaming free.

Fezoul loosed a hissing whimper. "You are mistaken, chief. There are other things that prowl these deeps that you do not yet know of." And Dereas could see the fear lurking in the mountain king's eyes.

Draba, meanwhile, burning with excitement, had pushed past the group, to stand glaring down into the tunnel. He, of all, seemed obsessed with the prospect of treasure and moved his head back and forth like a weasel, scanning for gold dust.

The mountain king pointed a quivering finger at the fractured rocks over the carved lintel to the side tunnel. "Fool! Did you not hear me? Those are warning stones. A group of us erected them ages ago."

Though Dereas craned his neck, he could barely make out a petroglyph of a lank lizard with a foot over the neck of a gigantic snake which in turn, gobbled a man.

Fezoul announced, "We of Xatu, erected the cairns to warn innocents—unsuspecting folk who would tread to their doom...But look, the blocks have been jarred, defiled!"

"Maybe shifted over time," suggested Dereas.

"No!" called the haggard king. "Something is afoot. I feel it. And still, after all these years..."

"Let us look then," suggested Rusfaer. "No harm. And in the meantime, let us be on the alert for snakes, lizards and crabs—and for a major lode at least." He laughed, blissfully ignorant of the import of the wives' tale talk and the recent frights. He seemed fixed on a mission of precious minerals and a dogged stubbornness burnt in his wolfish eyes.

"This must be an old mine," Amexi remarked offhandedly.

Rusfaer jerked a thumb at the sparkles of gold dust speckling the rock. "Maybe it was a blessing, rather than a curse that old Pygra diverted our attention to this gold-sprinkled niche," he mused. "We could have ourselves a fortune here, brother!" He turned to Dereas in the interest of appealing to his silent qualms. "Nothing to guard the treasure except this timid owl—" he thrust an elbow at Fezoul who still gnashed and flitted from foot to foot. "That and a few legends of some half-baked lizards."

Dereas demurred. "I don't doubt that's true, brother, in the face of such wealth, but I side with Fezoul."

"What? You crazy fool! You could buy an army of warriors to carve out a kingdom!" He snatched the bowl lamp from Hafta's fingers and shone it down the tunnel. A bend in the passage obscured view of anything further than twenty feet, but more gold glinted and what looked like a set of steep, crooked stone stairs. Part of Rusfaer's anger seemed to dissipate in the light of so many riches. "I want to know how much is down there and how much we can carry with us." His eyes burnt with dizzying depths and springing shadows, as if the horror of the crab and snake were distant memories and the old fires burned once more in his blood.

Dereas, however, was of better memory and not so quixotic.

Rusfaer ripped out his sword and scraped it on the wall with contempt. "Go then with your coward king!" he jeered. "Be swallowed by Pygra." He shook off Dereas's restraining arm. "I will stay and investigate this corridor and lay claim to the riches below! Who else is with me?"

Hafta, Draba and Amexi exchanged murmurs which grew to grunts of accord.

Dereas gave an exhalation of defeat. To split the group was an unwanted outcome, but he knew his brother's stubbornness. Rusfaer would commit to a cause to the end, like the hound that clamps jaws onto its favorite bone. The beastslayer grit his teeth. They could ill afford side ventures, especially with the snake on the loose and the mountain king's grave warning looming darkly. Though he did not want to be left out of what could be a treasure hunt beyond his wildest dreams, he could not at the same time completely mask his trepidation.

And yet, to show fear or admit to cowardice in front of his brother would be nothing less than reprehensible. "A simple look-see and then we follow Fezoul's lead," he said harshly. With a grimace, he squelched his misgiving and pushed after the others.

Rusfaer seemed not to hear. He wound his way down into the shadow-haunted darkness, eyes scanning hungrily up the corridor. The steps turned out to be ancient roots of a deep underground tree, oddly, that had been hewn down for some unknown purpose ages ago. The ungodly wood had been chiseled into the shape of steps, how was anybody's guess, and then smoothed down by skilled hands. These they took warily. Rusfaer leading, then his cronies, Hafta and Draba, and finally Jhidik and Amexi. Dereas slunk at the rear with distrust, looking for any sign of danger or pursuit that might hound their heels. He gripped his rusty scimitar, notched, but at least serviceable, flicking out of his eyes the sweat that trickled down his grimy face. His hair fell in matted loops, eyes bloodshot webs deep to the whites. Why was it he had a harrowing feeling about this venture?

Grimacing sourly, he forced his feet to move onward.

CHRIS TURNER

5: Realm of the Rgnadon

"And there will come a time when giant beasts shall reign,
Walking the lands on two legs or four..."

—*Book of Lost Prophecies, Amar-Amon-Reth,* overlord of the age of
Saeth

The spiral stairs curved like the coils of a great python, flanked on either side by primeval carvings—eels, salamanders, lizards. Then the path leveled out into a tunnel veined with pure gold.

Rusfaer's men stalked forward as if they were lords of an enchanted palace. They held forth their light-giving bowls, gaping at the ribbons of glittering golden on the floor. Their faces were lit ghoulishly in the pale light while festoons of gold, a wild weave of them, marked the walls. Crystals galore too sparkled in great clumps amid the eerie, reptilian faces that leered out at them, carved in the naked walls.

Rusfaer gave a chirrup of triumph. Excavation on such a side venture would be arduous, chipping with swords, but the return would be no less than a king's ransom.

A blur of movement crossed their line of sight. Rusfaer held up a finger, at which his men dropped to the stone like sacks of grain. Dereas's men quickly followed.

Heart pounding, Dereas flung himself on his belly pulling Fezoul with him—so close to the dank stone that he could smell the decaying clay and the molder of ages.

He glanced over the supine sprawl of his ragged comrades. He strained his eyes in the darkness ahead, but the shadows revealed nothing. Then several lithe, unfriendly shapes darted into the foreground. What in Balael—? The creatures had an eerie, springing gait.

He motioned Amexi and Jhidik into a side tunnel. The rest of

Rusfaer's band slithered behind on their bellies, eager to be away from the menacing movement. They crept down the narrow, gold-corded way, shielding their light-giving bowls to minimize detection. In the damp confines they crouched like toads, hearing the stealthy pad of footfall grow and fade. Then, as they squinted in the dark, several sinewy shapes skulked rhythmically past a dozen paces away, as no human would. But then they shrank into the shadows, as did the men who hunched ever closer to the stone floor.

Dereas felt a chill crawl up his spine. He studied them for several seconds. The creatures had the air of lizards from a forgotten time, walking upright, hunched forward on gangling hind legs. They stooped like apes, rising less than shoulder height. Their foreclaws held bone clubs, spears or curved blades. Their fleeting, steely glint mirrored the murderous efficiency of the sabre-sharp, knucklebow tulwars of the old Singlaurian tribes of the northern plains.

The sinking feeling grew. What were these weird freaks? A roving band? Some sort of patrol? Either way, it was an ominous sign, and he recalled his earlier intuition of dread. Already he could hear more shuffling at the junction and an instinctual chill fled up his spine as of the wolf that feels trapped by the hunter in the dead end canyon.

Peculiar hammering and an invasive clink of heavy tools on stone echoed from far down the tunnel. Dereas bit his lip, for the sound came from somewhere below: amid the low, unceasing yammer of weird, guttural voices...and yet, he swore he heard the crackle of strange fires, and possibly the weirdest of all, mysterious bellows of a monstrous beast.

Cursing under his breath, he pushed forward on his elbows, an offensive reptilian musk in his nostrils. His peers and Fezoul wore panicked grimaces as they crept noiselessly down the side tunnel, away from the rhythmic, padding feet.

The light grew in this narrowed alley. A torchlit glow from the space ahead flickered across the rough stone walls. The wanderers came out onto a landing, overhanging a rock cliff. In grim concert, they peered out over the rim. A sheer drop of dark rock yawned before them, and below a strangely disturbing and massive work area and sprawling courtyard nestled in an enormous, bowl-shaped cavern.

Dereas stared, entranced at the hustle and bustle and smells. Great, smoky, bell-bottomed cauldrons brewed a mixture of stews, meats and unknown substances. Elixirs? He could not say. The odors were overwhelming, and he smacked his lips, conscious of his hunger. Yet that sweet, sour pungency of alchemic brews and aromatic abhorrence, reminiscent of the wizards and shamans of the day, dulled any appetite. Instinctively he recoiled at the fuming vapors and the thick clouds that drifted up to assail their nostrils even at this height. The others eased back from the edge in distrust and misgiving.

The area swarmed with lizards, engaged in activities of hard labor, looking tiny from this distance: a phantasmagoria of nightmare and grotesquerie.

Some of the lizard figures walked on two feet, others on four, more often the latter. Certain gangs of them wore light mail and steel-tipped helms, cone-like in shape. Clusters of giant yellow eggs lay strewn about the cavern in heaps of dried weeds, mud or sand.

Dereas frowned. To keep them insulated and protected? The eggs could be the same they saw littering the tunnels between here and Xatu.

Stricken with awe, they caught sight of a massive fort set far back against the opposite cavern wall in the inky shadows. Some kind of a barbaric underground castle carved from the glistening black rock itself. A goliath of an outer rampart protected the inner citadel, all stone and black iron, looming aberrantly, like some stone dragon of yore. Realm of the lizards! thought Dereas. It was the last sight he and his crew expected in these dim confines.

The fort was oval, surrounded by thick parapets, from which rose seven corkscrew-shaped towers, silent as death. The grim ramparts ringed three sides, the back flank protected by the opposing cliff. More giant eggs festooned the parapets, also on the tops of the towers. Some were painted yellow, others green, and the strange folk, half-lizard, half-human, bobbed along the rude pathways with peculiar relish, dragging rocks of various sizes and carrying stone buckets. Crews of the lizards formed loosely-uniformed squads and seemed to be patrolling the outer confines of the cavern—even the passes in and out, whether they be scouts or guards. A central figure, perhaps a leader, gestured fervently to a knot of the creatures huddled before the fort. The lizard-man was taller than the rest, crouched on his hind legs, a good head above the others. His short front 'hands', more properly 'fore-feet', additionally served as legs when he descended on all fours from time to time. Even from this distance Dereas could see the figure wore a magnificent gold crown with glittering jewels at a jaunty angle on his slick bald head. His robe was patterned in blue-gray and white and his bare feet gripped the stone. In one reptilian hand he clutched a scepter topped with a golden orb and encrusted in sparkling rubies and other gems.

Fezoul looked on in somber fascination. He touched his brow in a gesture of supplication. His lips seemed pinched in the briefest tinge of awe, or was it fear?

Amethyst crystals and quartz hung from the domed ceiling, and still far overhead, the space glistened with unknown minerals. Below, the lizard kingdom spread in all its ominous, alien majesty.

Along the top quarter of the cavern, a ledge-like path ran with many dizzying ups and downs and inscriptions carved in the accompanying wall. The half-human creatures entered and left along this access path, to and from side chambers—patrol-lizards, workers, perhaps scouts, hauling stones on their backs or pushing large barrows or lugging stone pails and buckets of water.

Dereas's eyes glistened. From the main cavern branched mysterious side tunnels that gaped like the mouths of ghouls—some of these going down to dark depths, beside which burned one or more guttering torches. Fire brands hung from cords on the battlements and in sconces on the fort walls and from long poles staked in the ground before the grilled gate.

The lizards had created an ingenious system of drawing water down from high places, he saw—a system of aqueducts which ran snaking from the upper walkways to the grounds below. All the aqueducts stood high on massive stone arches which reared like bowed legs of mantises. Such waterways ran from three-quarters of the way up the cavern down to the fort itself—to continue on into the common area. A particular main spillway weaved its way from the far flank of the cavern, disappearing into a squared-off hole in the fort's far end. Another length of mortared stone dipped several feet down to let drop a stream of running water before the common ground. On this spillway Dereas saw Rusfaer's eyes narrow, possibly in the hope of escaping this prison, or he thought sardonically, with the ambition of scouting out more treasure.

To bring the green-flowing liquid down to the common area was a major feat, Dereas reflected, and he saw where it was curiously distributed to various outlets in the work yard; in some, blending into a yellow goo to feed certain noxious pools.

Rusfaer turned to the dwarf and smiled cynically. "So, this is what you were afraid of, eh, mountain king?"

Fezoul stammered, "You do wrong to underestimate them." His face had grown very pale in the dim light, and his hiss faded to a quavering murmur.

Dereas uttered a throaty growl, "What's that?" He nudged the mountain king. Somewhere off in the distance, two crude pens housed what looked like giant, prehistoric reptiles.

A crawling sensation inched across Dereas's skin. A pair, if he did not miss his guess—reptiles from an earlier age, caged in separate pens. Their backs were spiny, their legs armored and their black and green hides showed dun spots on their flanks. They ranged in squalid holding pens, beasts low to the ground, with greenish necks, luminous eyes, and long slithering tongues of crimson and gold, flickering in and out in evident discontent.

Fezoul shook his head with a shudder. "I know not what these beasts are."

"Liar!" snorted Rusfaer. He turned to grip the unsettled king. "I can see the deceit writ in your chicken-hearted face."

Fezoul flushed a deep crimson.

For how long that group lay spellbound, frog-crouched in the murk, Dereas could not say. Fezoul was lost in his dull trance. In the somber shadows, the beastslayer guessed Fezoul's thoughts strayed far, to places decades back, hideous recollections of beasts and savage rites and rituals.

Draba was less mesmerized by this terror and had snuck off to examine the corridor a score of paces away—likely bored with the reptilian rustlings and the eerie activities below. He was more interested in chipping off glittering nuggets that adorned the corridor, prizes much more valuable than his peers' bug-eyed reconnaissance. In the dim passage loomed a vast repository of virgin gold, bunched like fungus or knots of the rare masom root. While the greedy schemer busied himself examining a choice vein, the others watched the goings on below in oblivious fascination. On silent feet, the lizards in the cross tunnel glimpsed earlier, crept back to their post. Several paused to sniff at an unfamiliar scent and pay heed to a human figure running fingers along the gold-crusted wall.

Dereas suddenly became aware of Draba's absence. His hand instinctively flew to his weapon.

"Where is that skulking Draba?" he hissed. A tinkling sound warned him of danger. The noise came from behind, like a tiny chisel on rock. What was the devil up to? The beastslayer wrenched his frame about. He crouched on his haunches, and quick anger leapt in his throat. "Look at your buffoon!" he hissed at Rusfaer.

The grim-lipped warrior reacted instantly, his eyes catching a glint of steel and an aggressive motion of weapon. He could not miss seeing the rat-faced lout hunched in the shadows, shining the light of his bowl at the wall, tapping at the rock, his eyes glittering.

Unaware of the lank-limbed menace nearby, the fool Draba picked relentlessly at a coruscation on the wall with his notched dagger, to pry forth the priceless gold nugget clinging to the stubborn rock. With a grunt of disgust, Rusfaer clenched a fist as Draba rocked back on his heels, showing a toothy grin. The rogue fingered the big chunk of raw gold he had just chipped from the exposed vein and gave the peering men a thumbs up.

Dereas hissed through his teeth. "Get back here, you stupid moron!"

Draba gave him a cool, cock-eyed glance.

Rusfaer stifled a curse. Dereas sidled over to brain him with the hilt of his sword, but he stopped in midstep. The shadows had writhed with an unexpected flash of movement, and his jaw dropped in dismay.

Spears and poleaxes thickened in the gloom. Dozens of slapping, padding lizard-fiends burst into the chamber, their little coned helms and light mesh chest mail glinting in the light of their torches. Leather flaps were pasted to slimy cheeks and pulled back far, revealing reptilian maws and flared nostrils.

Draba staggered back, eyes bulging in terror. With a gurgling cry, he almost knocked Dereas to the ground in his stumbling haste to get away from the teeming lizards.

Dereas shoved him away with a disgusted roar. "Get off me, you idiot!"

The blade came to life in the beastslayer's hand, an animated shaft with purpose and menace. The animal nature in him ignited and like an instinctive tiger, he lunged, muscles coiled in barbaric ferocity. He cut down a gnashing, green snouted attacker and his comrade in one blinding motion. The lizard-men's lives drained away in a crimson torrent of blood and brains onto the cold stone.

The creatures behind regrouped. They tramped over their dead comrades and lunged, snarling like hyenas.

Dereas slashed wildly, his mind lost in a fever of grim battle lust. With two hands he brought back his curved blade in a wide sweep. Arching death reached out and felled the foremost lizard who sought to sink teeth in his throat. Three more fell away howling and sprawled in crimson pools as he wheeled about to let them slide by while hacking at their vitals. A lizard tulwar scraped across his chest mail. He growled and smashed the butt of his sword into the attacker's face, splintering jowl and teeth in one gruesome motion.

The clumsy Draba took a reckless bound into a few square feet clear of lizards. Slashing with his keen-edged sword, he grunted in satisfaction as a dumbstruck lizard's throat was slit from ear to ear. Another skulking brute, crouching low, jammed a spear at Draba's ribs to stick him like a pig, but he sidestepped this thrust and chopped at the lizard's neck and it fell thrashing to the dank stone, thick blood draining like syrup.

Jhidik, Amexi and Hafta came rushing from their hidden place on the ledge, and Amexi's mouth opened in a snarl. A tooth-snapping enemy had climbed on Dereas's back and the blond warrior spearheaded it in one thrust.

Jhidik scrambled sideways to parry a gleaming tulwar from piercing his chief's ribs. With a wicked, backhanded sweep, he sliced the grinning, gibbering lizard-man in mid stride.

Rusfaer and Hafta lent their swords to the fray, roaring and bellowing. Flashing blades seared through light mail rings and bloody gashes opened in two lizards' scaled chests, vitals pouring forth like abattoir slop. They planted boots on chests and sent the grimacing, frothing lizards hurtling back on their haunches into the mob.

The pack rushed forward, torches gripped in hands and bright red teeth clacking and champing like mad jackals. Their yellow eyes glittered in the snouted ugliness of their faces, little forked tongues darting in and out of bestial maws. It was a mad, gnashing, frenzied throng, and one which brought the fugitives revulsion. Dereas lost ground. He slipped on blood and warm entrails, head-butted a lizard whose mouth came too close to his, so close he could smell its putrid breath. Another fiend hip-checked him off balance. But the beastslayer recovered and retaliated with a hard hooked punch that sent his foe reeling into the outthrust spears of two-score lizards pressing behind. A four foot shaft stuck out of the creature's chest, like a gory totem pole.

A squadron of fiends burst through the wheezing, foremost ranks, trampling the unfortunate ones in front. They wielded tulwars and clubs, big, thick, rooted things of wood that should never have grown underground.

The fool, Draba, had recovered some of his wits and gripped his dripping weapon with vengeance. He stabbed, letting his whistling blade fly into a lizard's gullet, carving flesh and slicing up through brain and eye. A razor-edged tulwar was his reward—flailing out of nowhere and leaving a widening gash on his sword arm, sending the shrieking rascal reeling back in a cloud of shock and agony. The creatures, despite their four foot height, were tenacious fighters. They ran nimbly forward on their hind legs, slashing and hacking with gleaming tulwars, guttural noises shrilling from the back of their reptilian throats. More were pouring in from the head of the tunnel. Their lightning fast attack and their growing numbers threatened to engulf the entire company in one noxious rush. Dereas and his companions were hard pressed to stay standing under that teeming mass of lizards.

"Back, I say!" Dereas roared into the confusion. "Close ranks! Fight them! Don't let them flank us!" But there was nowhere to go...

With sick frustration, he saw too many of them had swarmed the company. Now the hot, blood-reeking air, thick with the stench of death, was dense with black, glistening devils with skin as dark as bullfrogs. Nonetheless, they moved with an agility that belied their ungainliness.

Either cut a swath through this army of Stygian filth or be pinned against the rim of the walkway and forced over the ledge into the abyss below. Captured like wild pigs was an alternative too grisly to ponder and a wave of grisly terror pricked his spine. Yet somehow, a quick plummet to a splattering end seemed the least ignominious of choices. His primal instincts pulsed to new life...either fight off these fiends now or suffer a hellish death.

Rusfaer was sweating and snorting like a bull. He was covered in blood, but in miraculous display of his war-hardened valour, he surged forward, sending snarling lizards to their deaths. But he was steadily being beaten back, overwhelmed by circling enemies. Growling in sheer blood-rage, he snatched a poleaxe from a gibbering lizard and windmilled it about his head. The gleaming construction of it was lighter than a human's, almost like a hatchet, and he swung it effortlessly in his grip, his face lit with a fiendish wrath.

The lizards reeled back, grimacing and snarling. He whirled the weapon with savage strength. In a frozen moment, Dereas saw the bloodlust etched on Rusfaer's face, the unfettered vitality of his wolf-like strength. Pride burned in Dereas's eyes. Though lean lizards with eyes like savage beasts crowded forward, they fell back in ripe ruin at the rending death of Rusfaer's scythe-like blows.

The muscles in Dereas's arms corded. He chopped again and again, gritting his teeth at the glancing sweep of lizard clubs ringing against his chest mail. Dodging left and right, he whooped and slashed, inspired by his brother's courage—Balael, what a warrior!—and Rusfaer struck over and over, tenfold like a cornered animal. Veins pulsed on his naked brow; his shoulders gleamed where rents in his hide cloak showed sunburnt skin beneath. Scars stained red. Tulwars licked at his mail coat, but turned on the fine-steel rings. Rusfaer's eyes blazed with an inhuman rage, a hate for these obscene creatures. They were filth dredged from the cavernous depths below Vharad, something of human and lizard bloods mixed. The maimed reptiles whined and cringed, more from Rusfaer's reaper-like shadow and his hulking fury than the threat of his naked blade singing carnage and death.

The wild, insane fury of his attack gave way, however. The lizards re-banded. He gripped two lizard poleaxes—a second snatched from the twitching claws of a prostrate lizard, now one in either hand. He whipped them in synchrony, severing heads, lopping off limbs, goring fleshy underbellies of foes and ruining complete sections of their faces.

The bloodbath raged on, throngs of them taken out at a time.

Rusfaer cut a savage whirlwind of slaughter—bodies piled up underfoot, here, above the kingdom of the lizards.

Yet during the heat of the scramble, Fezoul had cornered himself between two slabs of rock. The meek monarch he was, he cringed and whimpered. His final act of appeal was to push both hands palms up, as in offering, as if it would stop the fiends' breakneck rush. What an imbecile! A gleeful cry rose from a lizard in recognition of a sudden opportunity. It raced to hew down the dwarf—and pounced with a howl.

Dereas caught a glimpse of the king's plight, and at the last instant, caught the lizard's upraised tulwar on his own blade, a stroke which would have impaled the dwarf to the adjoining wall. He struck the scaly aggressor like a battering ram. His role as protector blazed to life. He cut down the lizard in a jet of crimson—and Fezoul's guts were spared from draping the tunnel's floor.

Such an act was likely his undoing.

He lost his footing, cursed and slipped on fresh blood.

A leader of the throng with burnished coned helm suddenly pushed through the pack and snarled orders left and right. A flood of underlings rushed Dereas, sending him careening backwards. He caught a glimpse of crude nets and lariats being thrown over Jhidik and Fezoul. Why nets? Did they mean to capture them for some gruesome sport?

A glancing blow struck his helm. Stars flickered before Dereas's eyes. He grunted and flailed with naked blade.

He struggled to his knees, tried to rise, but staggered back as he saw the lizard captain go down in a flying spray of gore under Rusfaer's blood-flailing poleaxe.

He swayed, groped blindly. More lizards came at him, gnashing and frothing at the mouths. Before he could retaliate, a smothering press of lizardish bodies piled on top of him, threatening to snap his ribcage. He felt drowned in a sea of scaled flesh. Soles of flat padding feet crushed the breath out of him. Hot fetid fumes steamed from flared nostrils, blowing foulness on his shins, shoulders, back.

Grimaces of agony rippled on his face and anguished grunts wheezed from between his lips. He regretted letting Rusfaer convince him to probe these gold-cursed tunnels. Through the screen of arms and legs he caught a glimpse of his brother's fierce gaze—a grim interlocking of eyes. Rusfaer's expression was one of dismay, rather than disgust, as he watched his brother fall. Rusfaer struggled to free himself from the throng of lizards leaping all around him. "Balael! Cursed Zecrates! Why do you let the day dawn so dark, you black-hearted knave?" The uncouth blasphemies blasted from his rasping throat. It was all he could do to stagger farther along the tunnel.

Draba, for all his nugget-chipping motives, rained blow after blow upon the gnashing horde. But to their seemingly never-ending supply of strokes, he was smothered under a press of their slimy numbers.

Gripped by lizard claws, Fezoul shrank into a protective ball, his face sick with terror. Unable to stop the horde from twisting his thin hands and binding them with stout cord, he screeched, flailed and gibbered.

Hafta and Amexi parried the furious clubs and tulwars, but too many snarling enemy lashed out at them. Amexi sagged on his knees. Hafta fell soon after in a haze of sweat and blood.

Blackened and bruised and scored with cuts, the company was gripped and bound. Rusfaer had barely managed to carve a swath through the crush of lizards. The last Dereas had seen of him was a flailing figure in a fierce swarm of confusion, raining stroke upon stroke on the skulls of lizards, cleaving through mail, sinew, and bone. Whether the New Wolves' chief won free of that press, Dereas did not know, pushed as he was on his stomach, face down on the stone.

The creatures did not want to kill them. The beastslayer felt raspy cord lashed about his arms and wrists. His muscles strained and writhed against it, but their seething numbers gave him no room to maneuver. Too easy for the lizards to kill them outright, Dereas thought morosely. No, they just wanted to capture them. For what purpose, he could barely guess, though he assumed it would be for some horrific enterprise.

The five companions were hauled up, clammy lizard hands gripping and tugging at their limbs. The enemy chittered in their abominable language, a tongue or dialect of some unknown origin, snorting, grunting. They babbled among themselves, licking jowls, flicking out tongues, chirping in half-snapping fury. But strangely human were the words that came drifting to Dereas's ears. Uttered words that became somewhat intelligible.

"To the sacred eggs!...Ode to the sacred King...back to the King's stronghold. Long live our Lizard King!"

Dereas winced, bound like a trussed deer as he tried to filter the human from the reptile, struggling in the grips of these chest-high, repulsive, salamander-like things.

His dragnetted peers quailed. They kicked and clawed as rancid nets twined over them like spider webs and enveloped their blood-grimed faces. By sheer weight of numbers the lizard people dragged them down the winding tunnel, through a section too narrow to admit the snake. The tunnel was cramped and rank with humid breath, staired with more of the strange wood. The procession weaved down to the open cavern through a startled gathering of lizards; Dereas caught glimpses of blackened cauldrons, smoking pots, rude carts being pushed by gawking lizards. He heard the rolling of wheels, the heaving of heaps of stones and sizzling liquids. War machines hung in the periphery like giant sleeping crickets, some looking like bailey rams or compact catapults in stages of construction, for whatever purpose Dereas could hardly fathom. Innumerable eyes fixed on the captives; some had stopped to gape and grumble in peculiar, guttural speech. Many reptilian stares later, the captors dropped the outsiders in an open area at the foot of the fort. The terrace was obscured in shadow cast by the flickering torches bracketed to the long black wall. The rude pens housing the two giant primeval saurians lurked not a stone's throw away.

A group of two dozen castle guards hoisted the five of them up and marched them down through the throng. Dereas's skin crawled and his heart burned with sick frustration. He saw the light was even redder here in the common ground, casting the fort in a lurid glow. The fort, he saw, actually doubled as a black, twisted citadel decorated with reptilian gargoyles. Several lank lizards had gone inside to emerge with a retinue of lizards-at-arms and their leader.

Droves of them swarmed the common ground and Dereas and his company were caught up in a chaotic rush, pulled along closer to the outer rampart. Too many foes crowded the spaces and even if he could break free of his immediate captors, he realized he could no more thrust through that surging throng than a minnow could fin its way up a waterfall.

The sentries attempted to halt with their charges in a wide area laid with smooth stone, but were jolted back. Dereas could see they had come to a holding ground or rude terrace, worn over the years by countless clawed feet. Not more than a dozen yards stretched to the fort's wall, a bowshot to the farthest cavern wall. The reptile pen was a squalid square, reeking of dung. Behind the fort, a long stone ramp spanned a deep chasm. Squinting his eyes, Dereas could dimly make out a walkway running on a slight arch that disappeared in a high tunnel carved into the rock on the far wall.

The leader approached while club-wielding attendants beat a way for him. His jowl was firmed in a terrible glower, and with knees bent he sported a slight, primitive air. His coronet of pure gold was tilted on a rakish angle, his lizard-hide gown disheveled. His eyes were a golden hue and radiated a feverish intensity upon the expectant gathering. In no time, the commanding figure was surrounded by a retinue of fawning followers and green- and yellow-liveried bodyguards, threatening overzealous subjects back with curved blades.

"Who are you? Speak!" the lizard shrilled.

Dereas and Jhidik exchanged startled glances, bewildered at being addressed in their own language; they expected a purely primitive creature. They wrestled with their captors, each trying to wrench an arm or knee free to brain one of them or gouge out an eye, stubbornly pursuing any avenue of escape.

No luck. The lizards were not to be thwarted. They kicked and buffeted the prisoners back in their place. Cursing them, Dereas murmured grave appeals to Balael, while reprimanding himself for the foolish decisions that had brought them to capture. He hated this dim uncouth place. The mad thump of his heart strengthened his resolve to suffer whatever fate was in store for them. He put on a brave face.

A pike-lizard addressed his leader in a solemn voice with bastardized speech. He was undoubtedly a lieutenant of the guards, judging from his attire, a surcoat with a lizard insignia under mail now stained in blood. Dereas's eyes narrowed in dislike. "Sire, we, citizens of Yarim-Id, bring you intruders and lay them at your feet— offerings also, Great One, to the hallowed Rgnadon!"

The king looked from face to face sternly. No acknowledgment of the lieutenant's announcement came from his lips.

The pike-lizard gulped back his unease and he paled, undoubtedly lower in rank than most which addressed its monarch. To conceal his awkwardness and perhaps to better please, he ordered the prisoners prodded forward with pikes and clubs and personally paraded Dereas before their monarch with the shoves, bites and club taps of his henchmen.

"Hold off!" roared Dereas, piqued at being goaded forward like a common mule. He pulled at his bonds with mounting fervor, avoiding the slaps and ceremonious prods of the flat ends of the lizard blades.

The guard-lieutenant snapped, "We arrest you in the name of His Majesty for trespassing, thievery and blood-letting! Look at this, Great One—" he hissed, and made a presumptuous motion of supplication "—We found this big, light-haired cretin in the observatory—while the short one, with the grinning face, we found with sacred stones hid in his pockets."

"What?" bawled the king, his voice blaring like a horn. "That is treason!—" His eyes blinked several times. "Crowcock! Bear dung! Thief of infamy! You dare sully the secret possessions of Yarim-Id? They are not to be snatched as common pocket items by outsiders!"

Draba began to snort and utter profane words, the blood dripping from the cut on his forearm. Dereas jerked forward, straining his weight to headbutt the insolent warrior whose insults could get them killed.

Draba fixed him with a look of menace, uttering a surly growl.

"You are as guilty as a snake," intoned the king. "The sun does not shine on you here, man-things. You walk the land of Yarim-Id— realm of shadow, and yet you skulk about like common thieves without permission. Look yonder, what do you see?"

Dereas looked up to the looming towers and scowled. "A fortress of carved black stone, with overlarge eggs crowding the parapets."

"Those are the sacred eggs of Yarim-Id!" the king roared.

Dereas bared his teeth. "No doubt, lizard, but what's that to us? We are ignorant of your customs; furthermore, I demand—"

"You demand nothing! We hatch those eggs after ripe ages to become the royal citizens of our race. Each is a royal monarch in his or her own right. Ten years per egg. The highest born of us season for even lengthier periods to become sires of the morrow."

Dereas grimaced, the cords about his forearms and shoulders stretching with the strain of his muscled arms. The lizards swayed and grunted, and looked on Dereas with awe. "Vastly interesting, but what does this have to do with us?"

"Silence!" the lizard king ordered. He clanked his staff threateningly on the bare rock. He flourished curtly at his servants. "No outsider walks Yarim-Id without our notice. How you survived the tunnels is a mystery beyond me, but I smell the hand of the Eaklyds in this."

Dereas spat savagely, wondering what they could be if not the filthy, dreaded Eakors. This inquisition was not heading down a path in his favor.

"In fact, my lizard nose detects that you have the blood of the

Eaklyds on your hands!" He pushed out his chest in righteous indignation. "Do not try to deny it! I see everything!"

The lieutenant frowned nervously. "It is odd, your Grace, that the humans managed to penetrate the mountain so far. The west face is lost, has been for an age, and old Balbikor would have made short work of them."

The king shook his lizardly head. "The stone birds are guardians to our kingdom at the north gate. Recall, the weaker ones send us sacrifices, humans or beasts, dead or live as per our agreement, but they could not have gotten past them—unless—" and here he narrowed his eyes evilly on his lieutenant.

Fearing the wrath of his sire, the lieutenant gave a hasty reply, "We have offered the stone birds ample gifts. Our scouts regularly appease their lusts—"

"Obviously you have neglected your duty, and the Eaklyds have allowed intruders to win past our borders, which means—" he trailed off suggestively.

Jhidik deigned to add, "If by Eaklyds you mean those obnoxious vultures, yes," he grunted in his most sarcastic voice. "We put the lot of them to the sword. Filthy things they were—which died in the horror they deserve."

The lizard king's eyes bulged with outrage. Staring fixedly at the Pirean, he rounded on him with a wrath that they thought might have his staff ringing off the warrior's skull. "The Eaklyds share a strained alliance with us!" he bellowed. "If you have harmed them in any way, then so we must harm you. If it is destined to die by their beaks, then you must submit. To be torn by their talons is an honor. Do not seek to vex our guardians or skulk about thieving and killing here in Yarim-Id!"

Dereas cried out in an exasperated voice, "We are not skulking about! Only a simple act of necessity brought us—"

"Cease your lies! Didn't this earthworm bring you?" He pointed a clawed hand at Fezoul. "Did you not tell him, mountain goat man, that we have many secrets and wish no visitors?"

Fezoul looked away guiltily.

The lizard king grew pink in the face. "I stand by my words! By Jeron!" He rose on the tip of his toes to flourish a clenched fist. "Our living and fallen lizards demand restitution!"

The guard-lieutenant licked his mouth. He addressed the king in delicate tones. "Sire, some other distressing news comes to my attention. I can relay it now or—"

"Speak!"

"One of the outsiders—" he cleared his throat "—a big ox of a brute with a bush of rusty hair, escaped our net. He wielded one of our poles as if it were a fire stick and by Jeron, he fought like a demon! He's not a normal human. He killed off two of our lieutenants and went on a rampage to maul or slaughter a dozen of our ensigns. We figure a score of other lizards-at-arms fell to his blows before he escaped back into the tunnel. They have not returned. How, we know not, your Grace, 'tis a mystery. We tried to flush the brute out, but he slipped through our webs like an eel and must have lain hidden in the Borsom tunnels. By some uncanny luck or craft the fiend evaded even Ribik's and Gron's keen hunting snouts. I was lucky to escape his bloody handling myself, only having my chest-guard punctured and my rib fractured and this telling gash on my left side." He lifted a painful arm to show the gaping wound to the king.

The lizard king danced a jig of anger. "I don't care if Mazoma himself gouged out your heart, you weakling pip," he screeched. "Find the cretin! I've heard enough about your petty bruises—" and his jaw moved in hostile motions, champing, making feral, grinding action like a surly boar. His snout showed blackened gums and rank rows of red teeth. "Take all the scouts you need, Lolik," he bawled, "or it's on your head, by Jeron and the Rgnadon, that your skull will adorn the fort's gate this week, replacing your grandsire's sacred egg!"

The guard bowed obsequiously. He loped off, sweating visibly, scrambling on all fours to carry out his duty.

The lizard king turned his feral attention on Fezoul. "I remember you of old," he hissed, scrutinizing the dwarf with intense disfavor. "I remember you when you were a chubby-cheeked cherub of a young man. You were steward to the Consul-Crown of Yarim-Id, weren't you? The Keeper of the Seven Keys."

Fezoul's eyes lit with surprise. An inarticulate sound slipped past his pink mouth and he tried to make himself smaller in his captors' grips.

"What are you talking about? I know not of this role of *steward*," he stammered.

"Don't play the idiot with me! You are surprised?" The lizard king smirked in an effort to goad the dwarf to terror. "Through lizard potency and my priestess's sorcery I have lived well beyond my years. I became leader of this forbidding realm and the savant I am today. For an age, I have watched my kingdom grow and the number of highborn eggs atop Minulzon's keep's parapets swell. Growing, brewing, gestating," the king mused darkly . "I see by the royal purple of your belt that you have attained high status. Very good. Also the Vizon amulet around your pale neck—indeed, a stately token...and you have risen high, master Fezoul," he said with false respect. "For Fezoul, is it not? Do you not remember me?" The reptilian eyes of the king narrowed in shrewd and mocking amusement.

Fezoul shook his head like a dog, his whole body racked with spasms. "I was keeper of the keys—once—and then holder of the crown," he admitted weakly. "But I am no steward. I am the present king of Yarim-Id..."

"You? King? Never!" roared the lizard leader. "I am king! You are but the *memory* of some leader of the past, of a lost people, a broken race, transformed and merged with the blood of ours. Yours is but the bud of the pupa to us." He let the enigmatic image roll off his tongue—to the horrified understanding now of Fezoul. "You forget Yarim-Id of old includes the lizard realm, and the House of Rgnadon. The true king shall rise again. Now on the back of a great beast which shall rule this mountain and the lands without!" The lizard king's eyes bulged with fervor and he stood on the balls of his feet while his orbs had grown luminous and fanatically glassy. He stood up to his full height, arms spread and his followers' voices rang softly aloft in a thin murmur.

Fezoul, flummoxed to the point of swoon, tried to stall for time. "For a fact, you seem familiar to one I knew long ago, a certain Xabren, a clever but wayward rebel. But that could not be, for it was decades ago, and he was never seen again."

"Crokcow! Snake slime!" the lizard king laughed.

Fezoul recoiled as the lizard king collected his self composure. "I see you are not without wits. Very good, Fezoul. Very good....even if you did achieve your exalted position only by the grace of your father you are still somewhat of a king." The lizard scowled and continued in an indulgent voice: "The Vizon is a token I have not seen for an age. I have mind to snatch it from your pudgy neck right now and keep as a memento for my collection. But from this I shall refrain. No, you guard it, my weakling king. You will need it where you're going—on a voyage home, to lizardom!"

Neither Dereas nor the dwarf liked the sound of that ominous prediction. Fezoul blinked rapidly several times. Dereas could hardly understand half of what was said, but he noticed Fezoul looked like a man aged much beyond his years.

The lizard king made an abrupt motion of arm. "Swiftly! Take these two heathens—" he motioned to Rusfaer's quivering men "—to the beast chamber—you, with the bestial ox rings in your nose and this one who has stolen our property...No wait—better this one here—" and he stabbed a claw at Jhidik who bore the lank mat of dark hair and nursed the dark scowl. "He has an evil look to him and he has put brash words before me. I will question the others at my leisure. These two—" he made a curt inclination of head to Draba and Jhidik "—will be the first to become 'one with our blood'."

The guard-lieutenant nodded an acknowledgment. "Gladly, your Grace."

Dereas snatched a horrified glance at where the king was gesturing—toward a litter of giant, cracked eggs not far from the beast stall and staked-off pen where a brood of lizard imps ran about, champing wildly and snapping at each other like monkeys. What could he mean? Dereas thought wildly.

In the closest pen, the beastslayer saw that the large beast snuffed and glared with evil, red eyes and pawed at the filth. It would be thrice the height of a man should it rise and stand on its hind legs. The pens were not made of stone either, Dereas noticed—they were crafted of wooden posts only, with twined slats fastened with oiled cord between them.

Jhidik made an objection, "Here, now! We wish no part in your abominable rites."

"Silence, knave! 'Tis too late for that." the lizard shrilled. He hoisted his scepter high and stamped his wide, clawed feet on the rock. "Swiftly! The rites must be enacted posthaste! Jogen, see to it, immediately, if not sooner, for there is not a moment to be wasted."

"To tarry is folly, your Grace!" cried Jogen with placating earnest.

"See to it!" thundered the monarch. "I am irate and perturbed! The queen lizard is in estrus, as you can plainly see in her pen, and she struts in a most foul heat. The time is ripe!"

The attendants made haste, given these kingly words. Casting uneasy glances at the snorting creature in the great cage, they grabbed the two aforementioned prisoners and dragged them to a lower pit to strip them of their armor. They were forced on their knees, stone weights applied to their shins, and hosed down with buckets of rank water. If either Jhidik or Draba resisted, they were buffeted with the flat ends of pikes, made of hard white bone.

Jhidik's two captors herded him toward a small stall near the huge female lizard—a holding ground, Dereas guessed—yet Draba was taken to a place a dozen yards distant, on a cleared terrace. A giant egg, large enough to hold a man, was rolled toward the pinch-faced prisoner. At first the insolent troublemaker glared in distaste, still in shock at his 'choosing'. Then, with a rude gasp which could only have been construed as fright, he squirmed away from the egg, for something in his gaze caught a glimpse of its being cracked in three carefully-mapped-out places.

Underlings reached into the upper crack and pulled forth the milky-yellow egg-meat to drape over the prisoner from head to toe. Draba objected to the treatment and lashed out with pinch-lipped rage. But his frenzied thrashing was met with more buffets on crown and torso. His mouth was forced open, cups of the raw egg were sloshed down his throat and dripped down his breast. The rascal nearly gagged on the warm, silky mash.

Draba squirmed and roared as they continued to hold his mouth open and worked his throat with their clammy hands. The two caged giant lizards nearby in the pens a stone's throw away went berserk and gnashed at the wooden pales. They thrust webbed paws through the cracks, reaching for the outlander, as if they were galled that their progeny, the would-be meat in the eggs, would be wasted on unworthy human flesh.

"Not wasted, dear ones," crooned the lizard king amusedly as if he could read the beasts' minds. "Patience. You will see! Look up."

Dereas murmured to Hafta in confusion. "Thanks to your master who recruited this varlet, we are about to become playthings of these lizards."

Hafta hissed, "I have no control over Rusfaer. You know well."

Dereas's scowl spoke accordingly.

Draba, coughing, gagging, was beyond distraught; he shook like a man with a fever. Now the lizard king screeched another order.

In instant response a ceremonial postern gate crashed open in the fort's nearest wall and a somber procession of lizardly priests led by a stately lizard-priestess filed out and made its way toward the lizard king's assembly. She was dressed in woven-scaled headgear, orange robe and slippers and carried herself with an aristocratic bearing. She seemed to walk more upright than the other lizards, including the king. Her face was austere, but shining with a beauty that once signified a vibrant woman. In her thin, robed arms, she carried an intricate chest inlaid with pure gold and jewels. She set it down before Draba and removed a small live newt from the interior. Draba looked at it in bewilderment. She sprinkled it with a pinch of some magic powder which she carried in her robe in a glass vial and without warning, shoved the newt down his throat before he could so much as gurgle.

The scoundrel's face purpled; she uttered some profane and mystical words while the servants stepped forth and forced Draba's throat to swallow the small reptile.

Dereas stared aghast. The immediate watchers of the rite murmured in approval. The attendants finished working Draba's throat, now satisfied that the creature was indeed alive and kicking in his belly, evident from the visible lumps and swells on his stomach. They looked to the elegant priestess for further instructions.

Dereas felt his heart thump with loathing. He could almost forgive Draba his failings, knowing a similar horror awaited all of them.

While Draba's eyes bulged, his kicks and thrashes were ignored and silenced, if necessary, with blows.

"I know her!" whispered Fezoul hysterically to Dereas. "The priestess is Jamuo!—my witcher, the one who placed the spell on me of dream sleep. I recognize her of old. But how she has changed! I thought she was dead!" He swiveled his body toward the lizard king who grinned with simpering delight.

"What have you done to her, you monster?" Fezoul cried aloud, drunk with horrified sorrow.

The lizard king explained in a casual manner. "Jamuo was found wandering through the forbidden tunnels, a lost soul, ages ago. She was delirious and emaciated. It was said, she was searching for her 'deity', her savior, stumbling in the thick gloom. All her people had fled or perished, she told us. We gave her, her deity. We recognized her as a healer and a druidic sorceress. After she underwent a 'rebirthing', her powers increased and she channeled knowledge of the arts from ages past, long forgotten by men or lizards or the hybrids of this world. She sat in an egg for twenty four years, the first to perform the rite on herself. Now she is one of us—the priest-queen of Rgnadon!"

"Rgnadon? What in Balael is that?" cried Dereas.

The lizard king chirped out a cryptic laugh, "What it is, was, or shall be—'tis no concern of yours."

Fezoul shuddered, spittle sputtering down his chin. "It cannot be!"

"Oh, but it is, dear 'king'," mocked the monarch.

For an instant, full comprehension dawned on Fezoul and the mountain king narrowed his eyes in glassy wonder. "Then you are Xabren?"

"None other."

Fezoul reeled, as if the information and the events of the day had exceeded his threshold of sanity. The lizard king was the rebel who had left Yarim-Id long years ago.

"I am as old as the moon," the lizard king said quietly, "and as the crocodile which sleeps in the weeds with one eye open, I am lord of my domain." His eyes glazed over, as if going back to a place distant in time. "I dove too deep. I was separated from my group of rebels. Lost and starving, I followed tunnels of Vitrin far below the mountain and stumbled face to face with one of the old ones. A man-sized gila monster waddling on all fours. We fought to the death. I only prevailed because of my quick wits and the rocks I had clutched in my hands which I used to dash out its brains before it could devour me. The fiend had bitten me in the side, sending poison through my veins. Burning up with fire and delirious, I sated my hunger by feasting on its raw flesh, as it would have done to me. But a strange transformation came over me. I started turning into a lizard, limbs first, then torso, then face. But a smarter, faster, more human-like lizard than any of my subjects, and with reptilian stock in my blood running cold as icy Vitrin, I began to dream of creating a civilization of lizards..."

Fezoul shrieked: "You are mad! Cruel, no less, to your own lizard kind as you were to your own citizens in Xatu."

The lizard king ignored the dwarf. "Certain of us endure the bite of the Gila and feast on an old ones' lizard flesh, if we do not die from it, to become 'greater-lizards'. 'Tis an honor and only done under my command. Actually, one great Gila is kept caged in the castle in a place only I know about, for this purpose."

"Then what of these brutish horrors you cage in the pens?" growled Jhidik.

"A practical necessity. The 'middle-lizards' who gestate in Greta's eggs for shorter or longer periods, can interbreed, but their offspring, the 'lesser-lizards', cannot and therefore are expendable. They know it and accept it. Fathered by my ingenuity, they are in thrall to me, as you have encountered in the tunnels, their unfailing loyalty.

"The greater lizards, like myself, who have the blood of the Gila running in our veins, are revered. You will make superior lizardmen captains—the lot of you!—and possibly will be chosen to advance— if I decide it! Unlike some of my lesser lizards which hatched too soon."

With calm and didactic pride, the king went on: "All this talk about births and eggs...I can see, has confused and distressed you. The human is, according to our lore, dressed in fresh egg meat and forced to ingest half of the egg melt. The soft and warm nutrients of Greta's stock, who as I explained, is deep in estrus, Greta being—"

"The big female over there, we know," cut in Dereas curtly. He hoped to disarm the lizard king, keep him busy while he worked at his bonds.

"Exactly, that is Greta," the lizard king echoed indulgently. "You have a good eye, outlander, for an uncouth stranger. Perhaps you and I will have some stimulating talks before your 'rebirth'. I use the term loosely. Beside her is her mate, Kruger, or Layhoo as we call him, a scaly, horned brute, from which her eggs were produced. She has great fertility, as you can see from the abundance of eggs scattered about our domain."

Dereas grunted with veiled disgust. More of the egg slime was forced down Draba's throat and Dereas grit his teeth. If Draba gagged, the slop was mopped up in ewers and forced down his throat again.

"The ingested meat will help him gestate, of course," the lizard king proclaimed, "then to assume the form of his new being."

Dereas and Hafta and the others watched in ghoulish fascination as the demeaned warrior was shuttled on his back, knees bent and tied to his chest, then hoisted into the half egg. With ceremonious precision, the three egg pieces were fitted over him. Three attendants busied themselves with some natural glue to patch up the cracks of the shell, sheltering the captive while the sounds of his terrified shouts and maniacal shrieks reverberated hysterically from within the egg.

Dereas's jaw sagged in horror.

The lizard king explained in a droll voice, "It is expedient to say that we enclose the victim in the original egg shell for some time. It is said that his 'old' body will then become the seed from which the new being will emerge. 'Tis quite remarkable!" The king's grinning jowl turned away and he called out in a boyish tone, "Isn't that right, Zonx? Cement the shell too, Memak. That's right! No premature birthings do we tolerate."

"How will he breathe?" demanded Dereas, hardly able to speak.

"No need for breath. He will fall into a stupor and the meat ingested will do its work. But first, we must insert the egg back in—ah, but you will see!"

And while Draba's egg rocked back and forth under his desperate thrashings, the attendants drew back the wooden pales to expose the female lizard that squatted beyond. The egg was pushed, or rather 'rolled' through the crude portal and the attendants quickly retracted themselves—for Greta was not an amiable creature when she was in such heat.

Suspiciously she sniffed the egg. She licked it dry, then as if in a sudden premonition, or a primitive rush of instinct, she rolled it about, as if it were a playtoy. Moving it into a familiar spot, she reared high and squatted on the egg, pushing down gently on it with her genitals. There came a liquid squishy sound as of a large object being squeezed inside her. With a languid grin she looked about, yellow eyes betraying the pride of a work well done.

Dereas felt woozy, as if he were about to collapse. The yellow eyes that looked back from king to prisoners were wide and sullen. Hafta and Jhidik seemed to brood long over the last act, staring into vacant space while Amexi made a sick gurgle in his throat. Fezoul paled, gulping down his repugnance and his lower lip began to quiver.

The lizard king sidled happily toward the pen. "Back in the mother genetrix!" he called, his gleaming scepter raised in proud exuberance. "A miracle. A boon. Greta can take one egg at a time, sometimes two, but that's a bit of a stretch." He paused, looking idly from prisoner to prisoner. "No, we will do it the traditional way! A day's wait and a vat of Vitrin, or snail brine for her to sip, and then we'll see what hatches." He laughed and then cavorted, piping a strange, cacophonous chortle. The sound was appalling to the ear as he slapped his clawed hands together with childish glee.

Other lizard folk from the community had taken up their arms in applause as the lizard king did another mad caper. "Joy upon joy! A celebration! This calls for a jubilee. A seeding of highest order!"

Dereas grimaced with speechless revulsion. The whole thing was too much for him to absorb. The maternal lizard took offense at the clamor and circled around her cage, snarling and showing a mouth full of red teeth. She rattled the posts of the cage, her long, pug snout snuffling and the father lizard in the cage adjacent stared mutely and uttered a low moan of rancor? Despair? Anger? Melancholy? Dereas was at a loss. How was anyone to decipher the primitive emotions of these prehistoric creatures?

One of the lizard-guards near Greta's cage became overly festive and pranced too close to the posts, whirling like a dervish. The lizard's tongue shot out and wrapped about its neck and chest with a snakelike power. The captive chittered and screeched in a horrible way and efforted to pull away. To no avail. Greta pulled the hapless reveler in again and again smashing it against the wooden bars. The guard was knocked senseless, until it was a mass of pulp. With one final pull of tongue, she dragged the victim into the enclosure where she upended the corpse into her fat mouth in one gulp and raised her neck to the sky and gave a celebratory roar.

The mob screeched in exultation, a pitch that reverberated up to the ceiling. The lizard king screamed in a demented voice, "A sacrifice!" He cavorted with glee around his fellows in a spry, blithesome circle, kicking knees high like an ecstatic dancer. "Jornek! Come out and play! 'Tis a happening of its own making. Isn't it grand?"

Dereas shook his head in incurable disbelief at this chaos of madness. "Are these creatures all completely demented?" He looked to Hafta who had no answer. Jhidik's eyes grew wide in glassy, fatalistic defeat.

"Her body heat will keep the egg warm," the lizard king announced in a cheerful tone. "At the appropriate time, Greta will eject it. Thieves like your Draba may peck their way out in as little as a day, while the highborn among us culture for an age. Experimentation and trial-and-error forays have sped up our gestation period. A miraculous happening, don't you agree?"

"Is it really necessary?" croaked Dereas.

The king's snout twitched. "Doubtless it is overkill, but—as are so many rites of ours, we follow them religiously." He hooked a pointed claw toward the snorting reptile. "The new lizard creature, half man, half lizard, will tooth its way out of the egg before long. You will see! Meanwhile we shall revel before the miracle!"

The festivity went on and the companions, sick to their stomachs, tried to block out the wet-rag image of Draba inside the egg, inside the mother lizard while she fretted and stalked to the tuneless capering of the lizard horde's ritual. But no image could compare to the reality.

Dereas's eyes blinked and glazed over. He let them trace lazy circles toward the stone-and-iron mass of the castle. Lone lizards filed along the parapets with white pikes in hand. They were curved like the long, rib-like blades wielded by the sentries who had captured them. Some marched two-abreast in lock step in small squads, led by an officious marshal who peeked down to survey the grounds below. Its steel-peaked cap stuck jauntily on its skull and it held a whip in hand to punish any who marched out of step.

Beyond the rib-boned portcullis in the castle's central court glinted an enormous monster egg nestled on a golden stand. It was easy to see from this vantage, much polished and buffed, and held some macabre significance, the beastslayer guessed.

The lizard king whirled nearby and harrumphed, "Ah, you wonder of our royal treasure?" He clapped his hands in finality. "When the Great Egg hatches, it will grow into a leviathan to rule Yarim-Id! Lord of the shadows! It will eat men and beasts alive! We will be free! Free from our bane of serpents for good, to wander these tunnels and passages at will. No more snakes! No more Pygra. Only lizards!—and then, only free-roving lizards. 'Tis Pygra who keeps us penned down here in these dark burrows, corralled like monkeys in the meanest way. She likes it such. She does not know of the other secret ways out of these caverns, which we have barred, and there we will bring our machines when the time is right. She cannot penetrate our small tunnel here. She only waits, brooding, prowling, trying to catch us unawares while we are daydreaming, scouting, foraging for food. Whenever our spotters poke noses forth, she pounces!"

"Tragic," muttered Dereas under his breath.

"Behold the next Rgnadon," the lizard king cried again. "Ruler of the Mountain! The great Gnador! Ruler Above and Below!" In a thundering voice he called for all to hear.

Dereas gave a strangled murmur. "Not even your 'Greta' could have birthed a blasphemy of that size."

The lizard king flourished his scepter and his eyes flashed about wildly. "Ah, an ancient egg, a special one we discovered many years before, many levels down, in a quarter of the mountain shut off from the world. We hauled it here with ropes and pulleys via great efforts and many deaths along the way. We discovered that there was a nest of magnificent lizard bones nearby. Aye, the remains of Tyrannus Iguanus, a great reptile! We hauled the bones forth by cart through the endless night and fortified our watchtowers and battlements with the calcified crust. Look! Behold the ribs of the Seven Towers of Rgnadon. They shine with full glory! They are indestructible, fortified with the bones of Tyrannus guarding their flanks. Watch! Even our veteran guards wield bones of similar nature. Forsooth, their bills and maces and clubs. Heed well! Do not fall prey to the smack of their Tyrannus bones."

Dereas broke out in a sweat at the sight of the giant egg gleaming redly in the court's torchlight. His eyes darted wildly, half listening to the lizard king's mad dogma, half trying to contend with his rioting war of conflicting thoughts. Past the portcullis of Tyrannus bone, he could see the gigantic egg mounted on its gilded pedestal, huge beyond reckoning. It was exalted by the passing lizard folk, as if it were a statue of an avatar, or a king or god itself.

Could the lunatic king actually rely on such a creature being sympathetic to their cause? His breath caught in phlegmy rush; for such idolatry was too repugnant for his mind to entertain and his reeling brain balked in hopeless despair.

He gazed around up to the vicinity of the portcullis for signs of activity. Double guards were posted at the castle gate, but nowhere else. The forbidding rampart seemed relatively empty of troops, and no returning patrols roved. Instinctively, Dereas began to grow worried about Rusfaer. His eyes strayed to the various outposts stationed along the upper rim high in the cavern, where shadowy walkways and the aqueducts shimmered under the odd torchlit censer.

Indeed, it was curious that the lizards had not discovered Rusfaer yet. Somewhat hope-instilling at least—maybe his darkhorse brother could do something to help them—but just as easily, he might have fallen to Pygra's fangs, or been butchered long ago by the gleaming-edged tulwars of lizard patrols, that blade-happy rabble, who were perhaps only afraid to bring to their domineering king the remains of a mutilated corpse.

The queen-priestess had emerged, all decked out in flowing gown and green Arizoi leaves festooned in her hair. The lizard king was prideful of her presence and he stood zealously explaining to several citizens the story of the magic of the lizards' heritage. Dereas could see the priestess clutching her jeweled box of live newts with an unhealthy fervor. She held it to her breast in a way that was both fascinating and macabre to watch. Dereas saw, too, by the vacant gaze in her eyes, that she had lost touch with reality and perhaps a sense of identity. Was such the cost of being transformed into a lizard?

Dereas shivered. Her once human features seemed shriveled, betrayed a distinct look of something coldly inhuman, a detached mask of hybrid alienness.

The king's voice trailed on: "'Twas explained to us by the ecstatic, delirious witch of Katra Cavern, long ago in the mists of time that our alchemy of lizard gestation was a simple thing, belonging to the realm of elemental magic. So it was further enlarged upon by old Hela, our blind seer, and finally perfected by Jamuo here, our resident priestess-queen. We call it 'Neo-lizard Birth'. And all of you—" he swept an arm to encompass his subjects "—were once humans, like these brazen heretics who crouch here like filth."

The king stabbed out a clawed hand at Dereas and the others and a ripple of uneasy murmurs echoed from the gathered crowd.

Dereas stirred in his bonds with teeth gritted. "Your twisted views do not coincide with mine." He licked his parched lips with a tongue swollen and dry.

"Silence!" The lizard king's cheeks puffed and he purpled under the ears. "If you have nothing beneficial to say, refrain from giving tongue. Gizard, Frekt! Gag these brutes. I grow weary of their outbursts. Cretins as these shall be transformed into higher life forms before long. See that they are prepared. The heretics must watch!...Each will have his turn in the egg before long!"

Struggling, Hafta, Dereas and Amexi thrashed out, their muscles bulging, fierce cries on their lips while they strained to headbutt the guards.

To no avail. Lean, sinewy arms circled them round the necks and clawed hands worked to gag the intruders. Fezoul was bundled up like a leaf and strung up by his toes to the delight of the lizard spectators. They threw him in a heap beside the others and he hung his head in resigned fate, offering no struggle whatsoever. The four were tied together like hogs and roped before the newborn lizard cage in postures of total degradation. The young lizards pawed at them through the posts and licked the back of their necks, causing Dereas no end of miserable anguish. The foul rag of cloth that was squared in his mouth, was sodden with animal oil or some noxious substance. Exactly what type of oil, Dereas shuddered to think. But likely it had some association with the cardinal humors from the hideous Greta who raged not far away. Being gagged meant no communication with his peers, a serious blow.

Three other budding spry lizards that looked definitely younger than the other lizards of their kind, rustled in the nearby cage. They gnashed and clawed, chased each other around, roughhousing like fledglings.

Two cages down, Greta paced the confines, strutting around in a foul heat and she plunged her snout in a trough of brownish yellow slop, food likely—nourishment doubtless for her final 'gestation'...

Dereas shuddered to think of how Draba was faring inside the monster's womb, if he dared use such a word.

In the tomb-like tunnels above, Rusfaer limped along grimly, panting, head down and caked with blood. A poleaxe had snapped on the skull of a lizard-captain, useless in Rusfaer's blood-drenched palm. He had hurled it away with a snarl and ran, having no time to drag his heavy, rusted sword from the scabbard. But the attacking lizards had fallen back in a jumble of confusion, their wide-eyed lieutenant disemboweled shortly thereafter by a headstrong sweep of the tulwar he had snatched up from the nerveless claws of a trampled lizard as he had staggered on. True, he had broken through their slimy ranks with pure brawn—nay a pure reckless fury—which had saved his life. Now, outdistancing them, he faced a long and perilous journey through the tunnels, a warren of unfamiliar crypts, groping in the near darkness and cursing his ill luck. It was a trek he would rather not do solo, plagued by the ache of perpetual hunger.

Examining his surroundings, Rusfaer discovered he was in a place of rough, damp walls crowding him two feet to either side. A thin stream of Vitrin trickled under his blood-caked boots that at least provided some weak light. The tunnel rose often shy of his six foot height, forcing him to duck many times, squinting helplessly in the murk, or risk bashing his skull on the jagged rock overhead. Such rugged passage had him cursing and wheezing for breath. It was a course ideal for lizards, thought the New Wolves' chief.

He fingered his sleek weapon, the tulwar, admiring its material, some sort of hard, polished bone of whitish-gray. If it hadn't been gummed with the crusted, reeking, pale-cinnamon blood of a dozen dead, it would be a flawless, cutting instrument of death.

A sound?

He hunkered down, baring his teeth like a wolf.

Hakar's ghosts! Had the wretches sniffed him out again? He heard the distant pad of a dozen slick feet on stone in a passage not far distant.

Balael, but these devils had the noses of hounds! They were devils in green-black skin.

He steeled his nerves. Gripping his weapon, he could feel the sweat beading on his palms, and he slunk along as noiselessly as a panther. Nimble steps had him scampering out of range.

Through smaller and cruder tunnels he passed. Rusfaer scowled. Though shorter and lighter than a man, they were tenacious fighters, these lizards, or whatever they were. They would fight to the death with teeth clamped on a throat and were as quick as any lizard, as evidenced by the numerous bites and claw marks that scarred his forearms and shins. He endured their burning itch with sober contempt while he kept to his stiff, half-loping run, recalling the dozens of feints and lunges parried to dodge such toothy attacks, ultimately ending in sprays of their own blood and hewed skulls.

He gave a silent chortle at that last thought.

The echoes of feet persisted and seemed to be coming from a place up ahead and in greater numbers. Rusfaer's face creased in a sneer. With increased wariness, he backtracked on swift feet to a place where he had passed them at the last junction. He was not three dozen paces away when he tore a patch of his blood-stained wolf-hide cloak off his clammy skin and wrapped it around the lizard weapon he carried, hoping it would act as sufficient lure. They would find his bloody garment and the naked tulwar and think the snake had eaten him. Binding it close to the haft and another at the razor tip, he then hurled it gingerly up the path as far as he could.

He fell back in a crouch, hearing the weapon clunk audibly on the damp stone. The broadsword he wore still bore its notched edges in its blood-stained scabbard, which he regarded with grinning approval.

There came a halt of sudden steps. The big warrior smiled in grim expectancy.

Sidling quickly down the adjacent corridor, he ducked off at a sharp angle.

The creatures had detected the sound, that was for sure, for he could hear their miserable feet pounding and the gnashing of their loathsome teeth and lizardish grunts. How he hated that babble. He hurried on, in an attempt to get as far as possible from the dogged pursuit by that horde and from the weapon he had left as decoy.

Threading his way through the tunnels came with a vigilance born of the warrior's instinct and he felt a sense of dismay creep over him at the extent of the catacombs.

He halted, listening for pursuit, but none came, and the harsh wheeze of his breath sounded strange in his ear as he dared to breathe once again.

Another ghost of a sound?

The slither of wet scales on stone drifted down the tunnel carried by the dank tunnel air. His blood froze in his veins. Muted echoes of scuffling and clinking weapons faded back into the folds of darkness. It must be his imagination, he thought wildly. The light was dimmer here. The stream had dried, or taken another path of eerie meandering. There was neither dampness nor welcome purl of mountain water.

Then screams. And a hopeless pitiful whining, as tortured sobs and insane caterwaulings careened about the chamber.

Rusfaer leapt back. He closed his ears to the horrid thrashing and the breaking of stone.

The horror that was Pygra was on the prowl and his marrow turned to water.

Though he could not see what transpired in the corridor ahead, the symphony of ghastly tumult told all; he could put images and visuals to every scream, howl, and breaking bone, or fang crunching into lizard flesh, eye, skull or joint. The whimpers, the endless moans, the thick thunk of tulwars and snapping pikes, continued on and on in the dimness.

The snake was devouring lizards in droves, swallowing them whole, as if they were but bitesize nibbles before a grand feast! The memory of his last encounter with the snake was enough to make his stomach heave and his knees shake—for he knew that death by that hell was far worse than being put to the sword by any ruthless warrior. Even the seasoned fighter that he was, he remembered with grisly horror the heaving, writhing bulk of those iridescent loops, the thinnest of which was gifted with the strength of ten Azamalaen pythons.

He dared poke his head around the crumbling corner and caught a glimpse of a sight that melted the marrow in his bones—a prehistoric thing reveling in gluttonous slaughter. It circled a half dozen lizards, wrapping them in strangling loops and was crushing the life out of them, popping eyeballs, splitting skulls, wrapping grouper-like jaws about their torsos, before licking up the remains with its fetid tongue two at a time.

How could the creature be so close? thought Rusfaer with bleak terror. He scrambled back wildly. What kind of creature could possess such hunter-killer sense to scout out prey so easily, and with incredible diabolic stealth? It must be some demon! Some fiendish thing born out of the pits of the underworld. It was like the blubbering mountain king had said: when, as a young snake, it had burrowed deep in forbidden crevasses to suck on the nectars of poison and filth from the earth, not meant to be sipped. What knowledge of the map of the world did the thing have to know these tunnels so well? It had to be possessed of uncanny powers...

These and other ghastly realizations burned in Rusfaer's mind. He swallowed his darkest fears; indeed, he began to rue the day that he had mocked the squeamish king and his florid account of a monstrous snake, almost as if now he had put a curse on himself in the presence of every god Darfala had ever known.

Grimly he directed his gaze upward and mouthed every prayer to Balael that lurked in his memory. This and more—for shelter, protection, asylum, pricked with the ugly suspicion that even those enfeebled, rushed invocations were not enough to help him in the greatest hour of his darkness...

Two passages, one up, one down. Rusfaer looked longingly at the one that wound up, for it had a hopeful gleam to it, but then, as his brother and others had inevitably echoed, things were never as they seemed.

Riddled with doubt and dread, the New Wolves' warrior had mind to take the upper passage, flee these tunnels and never see the cursed lizard realm again. But he hated to see his brother mauled by the lizards, hardly knowing why. Nor could he leave his own men behind in the clutches of those scaly devils! Like it or not, he must remain or go back. He needed the mountain king and his inexpert guidance to forge a way out of this infernal warren. Going by gut instinct alone, up or down a random corridor, was not going to get him to safety, least of all not with that blood-guzzling serpent swinging her foul bulk around, ready to devour anything that moved.

His mind tumbled fitfully over the gearworks of fate that had brought him to this abysmal predicament. His shameless father who had baited him and his idiot brother, and refused to appoint a successor, had started a chain of events that had led to the exodus of their family and the loss of Pameel. Of them all, Dereas bore the brunt.

How he despised the name of Dereas, even more than 'Beastslayer' which at least was an honorary title earned by the person he had known from long ago. He hated his brother more than anyone for what had befallen Pameel, and no less, the demise of the Crow Clan. Despite his brother's honey-coated protests to the contrary, the facts remained. These maunderings about a silly wizard chafed him to no end and were obviously fabricated to gain the beastslayer sympathy. That his brother could have battled slavering zombies and winged fiends by the dozens and still survived was a yarn even Skalka, the Clan's bard, would have had trouble spinning.

Rusfaer felt a shiver of heat. He was not like his brother. He was not a straight-laced benefactor, always eager to save the world, an eternal straight shooter, always playing the hero and protector. Balael's teats! How he hated this thinly-veiled sanctimonious myth in which Dereas shrouded himself.

It was a wonder the two had lasted this long in these close quarters, he thought, without his tearing out the other's throat. He recalled a particularly galling time during the *Spring of the Goat*, the competitions in the Asgolin 'coming of age' rites years ago. They had been young then, but it was an important, honored event and seriously treated by members of the tribe. Feasting and dancing to stringed instruments and the beat of deerskin drums, all the young females were decked out with flowers in their hair and looked their most sensual, casting moon eyes on the young warriors, ogling for suitors. Dereas was the better archer and thrower, Rusfaer knew, but his brother had idiotically, unpredictably forfeited his prize, a trophy of the jeweled antlers of the morningstar bison. Why? cried Rusfaer, still cringing at the memory. To save face, owning up to a disqualifying foot fault on the archery ground? It was imbecilic and had left him, Rusfaer, the victor, even though he had been runner up—a fool's winner.

If that wasn't galling enough, there was the axe throwing contest right after. Many elders were present, accomplished hunters of the seasons, some who had led the clan in days of the 'Great Hunts'. His arm was bruised from a tumble from a horse the previous week and he had placed badly, missing the red mark on the tree—by an embarrassing four-finger widths. How bad he had looked then! even though he had unwittingly won the contest prior and carried home the bison to his family. Their peers and clansmen had cheered Dereas on, clapping him on the back for his noble forfeiture, while he, Rusfaer, received nothing but embarrassed salutes and apologetic murmurs, lukewarm nods and tilts of the head. A little thing perhaps, but it had always irked Rusfaer, as had many other things irked him in their past.

Regardless of these sour memories he could not leave Dereas alone, or his own men down there to rot and face whatever gruesome fate awaited at the hands of those obnoxious, contemptible lizards. If the beastslayer was to die, it would be by his own hands, and in a fair fight. This he vowed, and would be the last honor he would bestow.

The glowering warrior crept along the corridor like a hunted lynx from the elder woods. He grit his teeth through the ghastly tumult, hoping beyond hope that the terror not two stones' throw away, did not sniff him out and come looping after to ensnare him.

Not a hundred paces down the corridor and he bumped nose first into an iron mesh.

What's this? he murmured. A grate—a section below too—and a trickle of water seeping down a wide upright shaft.

A garbage pit left by the lizard folk?

Why the barriers? Odd...The rusted bars seemed older than what he reckoned the lizards would have wrought; perhaps it was another race's doing.

The New Wolves' chief peered suspiciously through the grate, for he thought to detect movement below.

A shadowy figure.

A guard with an unsettling lizardish snout prowled the corridor, nay a dim-lit pit, one of the lizard veterans, he gathered, taking noiseless steps, leaning forward as all good hunting animals do while on the prowl. Obviously the creature had smelled his man sweat and broken from the pack, hoping to catch the intruder single-handedly and make a name for itself.

Rusfaer scowled, though he could understand the ambition, having been there himself.

The lizard paused just under the grate and looked up the tunnel. Something in its gaze betrayed its indecision. Perceiving no threat, the lizard knelt on all fours and sipped water from the stream, like a wary dog.

The New Wolves' chief's face creased in a sardonic grimace. Easy pickings for any novice, if not for the grate. His bladder was bursting from all this dodging about with no chance for release and a sudden idea gripped him. He quietly emptied his bladder into the rivulet, the sound masked by the stream's own trickle.

Seconds later, the lizard jerked away from the warm water, sensing an acrid tinge to the greenish fluid and Rusfaer's lips curled in a wolfish leer. The lizard made choking sounds; its jaws parted in a grimace and scanned up the stream suspiciously, then scrutinized the folds of darkness, as if sensing an intruder hunching in the stillness, but then it settled back into its four-legged crouch and drank its fill. Rusfaer shook his head in wonder. How stupid could a beast be? He lay flat on his belly against the grate for several instants, before he loosed a breath. Should the creature cry out and alert its fellows— that could spell disaster, if there were any lizards left—for the snake was not far away. The lizard, despite its apparent inattentiveness— was still a threat should others swarm on him from above or below.

Rusfaer let his weight sink gently against the iron bars. It was cold to the skin where his mail and shirt were rent.

A bead of sweat fell from his brow down into the stream, washed away in the rush of water. He stiffened, not trusting his shaking limbs to not give himself away. But then, he was alerted by an imperceptible movement, a brief flash of skin, almost on the edge of his vision.

There, a black shadow! He withdrew into the dimness and stared, and then a chill crept up his spine.

Pygra! Still as a statue, a fiend of multicolored stone, a snake poised as if dead for a thousand years. The thing appeared fused to the stone wall like an iridescent megalith out of an elder time. Before him, not two dozen paces away, stalked a hunter, a killer!

The serpent had caught sight of the unsuspecting guard. Rusfaer could barely make out her beady eye staring like a smoldering sentinel in the murk-haunted cavern. She was scouting out her prey. But the guard was not yet aware of the danger that faced it...a danger that would strike the first moment it could.

Rusfaer thought quickly: If he could ease back off the grate and keep his distance, staying completely hidden, he might have a chance...when, as bad luck would have it, the snake lunged and looked up to see him staring pop-eyed before her.

He gripped his sword and pinched his eyes shut. He willed himself to concentrate on the task at hand. He let his muscles relax...but a bead of traitorous sweat trickled down his cheek and fell down through the grate, plinking off the sentry-hunter's steel cap.

The patrol-lizard jerked up in surprise. It tore off its cap and whirled its thin lizard body around, looked up, tail lashing in wrath. It snorted, raised a hand, uttered a squawking cry. At the same time the snake struck, an appalling mass of death. Slimy coils swiveled in view, wrapped round the lizard's squirming body, crushing the life out of the figure in seconds. Its face purpled, tongue protruded; the veteran lizard had but time to suck in one hopeless breath before its spine was snapped and the serpent swallowed it in one gluttonous gulp.

Rusfaer stared aghast at the swift violence of the act. His knees buckled. In the brief time it took him to stagger to his feet, the snake smashed up through the grate, a maddened python of a fiend, a blood-mad brute, hot on the trail for human flesh.

Rusfaer's gut sloshed in sick horror. He staggered back in a blundering frenzy. In one blinding motion, he swung his weapon, landing a felling stroke on the serpent's crown. By luck, it struck just above the snout—a shade lower than the one good eye, but effective nonetheless. The blade arced in another chopping sweep, turning in his hand, but singing true, leaving a gash three feet long, sheared edgewise along the wedge-shaped head from snout to eye.

The snake shrieked out a grisly howl. Her fetid mouth yawned in a purple, fang-filled oval. The serpent kept coming and Rusfaer felt himself sprawled backwards. He kicked his boots out to avoid those snapping fangs and barbed gums. The thing was almost on him. Balael! It was unkillable! How he regretted discarding the keen-edged tulwar! He flipped on his belly and staggered to his feet, cursing the most infamous of the dark gods, Zecrates himself. He scrabbled his way up the tunnel for his life. The snake's head shot forth, driven by muscled coils beyond imagining. Behind him he glimpsed her glistening loops pumping furiously as he skidded down a darkened side passage. He scuttled around a hair pin curve. The snake was but feet behind him. He raced down another. Her slippery coils ached to wrap around those ripe thighs of his, leaving a trail of slime on the wet, dank stone. If not for the snake's impaired sight and her sluggishness digesting her grisly fare, Rusfaer would have been consumed by now. The last desperate distance that Rusfaer took in that moldering tunnel was with a thundering rush. He clawed his way up a rough, rubbled path, fingernails snapping on the scabrous rock, banging his head on projections, slipping on loose bits of shale, falling, cursing, till he was a bruised, battered mess. Mercifully the passage narrowed—in truth, only a crawlspace. Barely the barest of a glow bit through the murk, even as he felt life and movement in the darkness.

His bowels threatened to empty in a loose gush. The snake was close behind him. Somewhere in that dimness lurked a fiend. What if the passage should narrow to nothingness? He did not want to think about that. The snake's tumult dwindled and her hisses and moans merged to a faraway echo. The tunnel was too narrow. The thing could not wedge her massive skull through and his long, desperate scramble had earned him several dozen feet, if not life.

After a claw-scratching scramble, Rusfaer halted and crouched on all fours panting. He sucked in life breath all around him like a floundering fish. He lay on his back on the rock, raising prayers to Balael and mighty Kizoi and Zecrates and all the gods he knew, thankful that he was still alive.

A chill thought flitted into his mind. Why did the snake suddenly turn and exit with such definiteness of purpose? Of course! Her dim brain was thinking two steps ahead of him, the cretin he was. The cunning monster! Her devious mind knew alternate ways of circumventing the barriers that riddled Yarim-Id. He looked up and peered intently and he could make out the rude outline of a yawning opening above, large enough for a creature of Pygra's girth to squeeze through and lap him up with a single sweep of her putrid tongue.

Gasping and swearing under his breath, he scrambled back toward the place where the snake had vacated the tunnel. He stifled his curses, forced stealth into his trembling feet, and hoped his intuition was right, and the snake was not there waiting for him.

6: Rites of Passage

"A thousand eggs shall hatch, and myriad imps shall squirm free of the egg ere the rise of the Rgnadon!"

—Jamuo, high priestess of Yarim-Id

Under the smoldering torches, Dereas passed several hours in the lizard compound, straining at his gag and bonds, battling blankness and despair. Such moments brought him back to the horror with the Eakors.

A sane man would reject the circumstances and retreat into a cloud of anguish. Dereas was not of such ilk. He floated in and out of lucidity, his body a battleground of pain. His spirits sagged, his mind lulled by strange narcotic fumes that drifted from the cauldrons worked by the lizard women, steeping potions and elixirs. The ghastly purple-gray and bluish-gray clouds reminded him all too nauseously of those brews.

He shook off his apathy. Though he struggled feverishly, the woody cords did not slacken and only cut deeper into his flesh, rubbed his wrists raw and turned his fingers blue. He could neither rise nor budge more than six inches from the pen posts. All the while he cringed at the ultimate punishment awaiting him: *sealed in the egg!* Balael, how he would fight to the bitter end to avoid that heinous doom! He would take down as many of that lizard crew as he could, strangling with his bare hands the last creature dragging him to that gruesome fate...

Lizards lifted long poles up the castle wall and dimmed the censers there, as if in expectation of a dark rite or another abominable event.

But none came.

Only drums and the somnolent marching beats of lizards, dark as Zecrates' night. It was as if they rehearsed for some long-awaited ceremony or crusade. Squads of the creatures drilled; others brandished their weapons in the dark shadows along the far wall of the cavern while a long-snouted captain barked orders at sparring lizards-at-arms.

The giant saurians, Greta and Kruger, paced their cages in restless aggression. Dereas saw the pens were completely enclosed and a crude doorway ran in between the cages, which lizard-keepers, if they climbed on the mesh, could slide up and down—likely to admit the large male, Kruger, for mating purposes. Behind him, a smaller pen loomed, containing three young lizards, which frolicked and chittered—the same he would be joining if he couldn't cut his bonds. Back farther still, fell a dark chasm, over which a shadowed stone walkway arched to a tunnel hewn in the far cavern wall.

Distant weapons continued to clank as Tyrannus blades slid off one another. Mail and bone blade glinted, and the sum of the sparring lizards' dancing forms writhed under the flickering torchlight, like a dance of wine-guzzling Kizoi himself...

Dereas tore his stinging eyes away. His gaze strayed to the castle.

The ramparts were carved with scenes of menace: a myriad of monstrous lizards stamping on the heads of serpents, crushing the shells of giant snails, or prying open the lids of enormous clams. Some clawed off the rippling coils of underworld serpents which had wrapped themselves around their protruding bellies. Others had come forth to feast on their sacred eggs. Dereas saw a chronology of reptilian legends from known time to the present—a recounting lost in the mists of the past. Whether the lizard folk had acquired such knowledge from their predecessors, he could not say, nor was he privy to such prehistory from his smattering of mythology. Iron spikes pierced the bas-reliefs and poked out of the bare stone, adorning the artwork, or perhaps supplementing its grotesque pictography. It was an odd mix, Dereas mused grimly, yet perfect for climbing, if one could ever get there...

The eggs on top of the parapets seemed secure in their gold wire-frame cradles—and well-guarded, unlike the ones strewn around the outer court.

Dereas gazed spellbound at a particularly dire, carved scene. Here, a brood of giant lizards fended off nightmarish serpents and protected their eggs from fanged maws. Reflecting on Pygra's grim appetite, Dereas had an idea now of what all the broken shells meant lying around the outer tunnels, strewn like gnawed bones about the dim corridors that weaved and branched in mysterious ways.

Moments passed, and the beastslayer noted the lizard activity had come to a rest and the hordes disappeared into the castle or shambled back into dark caves hewn in the cavern walls. The king who had been barking orders at various workers, had also retired to the castle with his priestess and his servile retinue. Dereas breathed a sigh of relief.

Several paces distant Jhidik sprawled, ragged and unkempt, enveloped in a thick pall of despair. Back roped to a post, he looked a poor specimen of the warrior he was, hunched in filth, grimacing in discomfort, radiating the same dread as his chief: a journey to the womb of Greta.

Hafta was strapped closest to Dereas and seemed resigned to his fate. The scene around him left him sunken-cheeked and withdrawn. His head was bowed, arms hanging slack, miserable grunts and half-muttered curses slipping from his blackened lips while Amexi lolled at his side in no different state.

From the fort drifted peculiar sounds, revelry perhaps, but of the most preternatural kind: disturbing laughter, muted booms, thuds of pain, cries of torture, hideous rapture and ecstasy—sounds he had briefly heard back in the tunnels, faraway echoes of madness from dark crevices.

Dereas shuddered. Part of him wanted to know what went on behind those closed gates. But if what transpired in the outer court was any indication of that which progressed in that black fang of rock, he would rather remain ignorant.

The caged saurians were snorting and pacing their confines like hungry beasts, smelling the blood and spoor of the bedraggled captives with ill tolerance. They knocked their armor-plated knees and shins against the wooden posts and sent shivers up Dereas's spine. The shock of their spear-tipped tails and bearded snouts clubbing the weakest supports did not instill confidence. The posts themselves were made of old mountain wood double-lashed with rope, a poor substitute for stone walls. Should any of the posts splinter...he did not like to think of that outcome. Savage beasts given free reign roaming the compound was a sinister thought. He doubted these beasts much liked their captivity.

The mother lizard wheeled in restless circles a few dozen feet from them, as if the egg within gestated weirdly. Aided by the potency of forbidden magic? Conjured by the priestess-queen Jamuo?

He could not help but think of the doomed Draba and he bit back a clot of sour phlegm crawling up his throat. His mind churned over the twisted magic these lizards conjured to dare such blasphemous unions between lizard and human. It was a sacrificial birthing of a wholly depraved nature. How many of these generations of birthings had taken place?

Dereas felt no closer to an answer. He jerked himself alert, gripped by another horrifying speculation. What if lizardom was not the only stage of their development? Perhaps there were other intermediaries? The insane king had not mentioned the possibility of macabre transitions in his raving monologue...

To his right the mountain king slumped in a squat heap, moving his sweating head back and forth. He spoke in riddles, incoherent phrases, in and out of delirium, inevitably jolting Dereas out of his reverie. Sweat oozed from the dwarf's pores, trickling down his high brow and his bare forearms in rivulets. Dereas could finally stand the smell of Fezoul's sweat and fear no longer and barked at him through his gag, kicking at him with his numb feet.

Alerted to the commotion, a lizard sentry came scurrying with his partner to test the captives' bonds.

Dereas scowled unpleasantly. Often these louts came in pairs to check up on them, that much was evident.

It was meal time and the guards stripped off their gags one by one to feed them. Only a thin gruel did they serve the haggard men, in clay pots or stone tureens. Looking down at the unwholesome mash, Dereas saw the clumps of what he suspected were the rank leafy bushes they had seen growing in cracks in the stone back in the mountain king's hall, or along the tunnel walls leading to this domain.

After spoon-feeding the victuals down the prisoners' throats, the guards re-tied their woven gags and gazed down at them with queer expressions, almost envy. The goons! Did they yearn for the grace of re-experiencing birth from inside the mother lizard? An infectious rapture shone on their slick-dark reptilian faces—upturned eyes, tongue peeking from grinning jowl, flared nostrils—and Dereas felt a shiver crawl over his flesh. The image was too hideous to even contemplate—this being inside Greta gestating—and he ground his teeth. He glared at the long-snouted guards with the sharp pikes. Hafta glared at them too with a rancor that knew no equal. Such vehemence and hate was tangible enough to prompt one of the patrol-lizards to kick him in the mouth and conk his ears with the flat of his bone tulwar. Hafta slumped sullenly, bearing the pain.

A guttural cry pierced the murk and a steel-helmed lieutenant came running and nattering on about sacrilege to Rgnadon. Such physical abuse would have continued in the ill squalor had not the lieutenant berated his lean-shanked junior for an offense against a potential subject of Yarim-Id.

Rgnadon! What could that be? Dereas's mind screamed for answers. Could it really be the monstrosity that purported to sit in the mammoth egg inside the courtyard? Was it a deity waiting to be born? Surely it must be some ghastly, horrific reptile that slept in that hideous shell behind the castle walls?

Dereas shook his head in exhaustion. He was too spent and aching to formulate any opinions. Nor did the nightmare ease out of his skull. There would be no sleep tonight, if that meant anything while on the brink of having one's humanity stripped of him.

Dereas stirred, senses alerted by the sound of cart wheels and guttural cries a stone's throw away. The ruckus issued from the castle—past the carven ramparts, a hundred yards to his left where a chasm thrust itself down to unknown depths. If he craned his neck, he could catch a glimpse of teams of lizards, marching three abreast, passing with lurid torches across a long, wide stone bridge of ancient blocks across the chasm. The throng pushed wagons, carts and barrows heaped with jewels and strange powders and liquids.

Dereas shook his foggy brain of cobwebs. What were these fiends up to? How had they disappeared into the mountain itself, as if swallowed up in some black tunnel? The lizards clattered on, fading into shadows, and Dereas was left with an insidious chill crawling in his gut, no closer to a solution to the mystery.

The hours passed. At times he felt choked by the earthy reptilian reek drifting this way. The pad of sentry-lizard feet came and went like sparrows on the wind, amid unsettling noises, or bestial cackles or clinks of machinery. And the soft purl of water streaming from the aqueducts, or the occasional crackling of fires. The echoes came to Dereas as from a distant dream. He started, muscles clenched, for Greta was bleating and mewling in a very peculiar way. The ponderous cadence of her cries reflected a macabre change in her. She made curious motions with her tail, heaved her bloated midsection, licked her hindquarters with unease. Not long after she squatted in discomfort and pumped her ribs in an attitude of animated expectation. Then just as suddenly, a glistening orb spilled messily from her hindquarters. The gleaming shell rolled on the soft leaves in a steaming mucous-clad mass.

The lizard kicked away the rank *arizoi* leaves and bellowed forlornly.

Dereas stared, entranced. A babble of excited grunts rose from the lizard sentries and workers that remained in the cavern. They rushed in disjointed packs to gawk at the great lizard nuzzling the egg with her scaly jowl. Though they had undoubtedly witnessed the phenomenon before, it seemed each new time was a sensation...

It was evident Greta guarded her egg jealously as she bared her teeth when certain 'midwives' of the lizard pack came pressing their long snouts against the posts. She roared a menacing warning and raked her claws in a dangerous paw-sweeping arc that had them scampering back from the pen, avoiding the sharp rake of her teeth which could angle between the pales and gore a face as easily as a salamander could lap up a grasshopper. She licked her gleaming egg dry and rolled it around the pen, proud as any mother, prodding it to ensure it was intact and not broken. She seemed unsure where to position the egg, mewling eagerly as if to coax the occupant to life. The shell before long began to shake and shiver.

Dereas cringed in awe—afraid of what he might witness.

Greta grew expectant. She raised her neck to the roof, uttering another celebratory roar.

Peck, peck, peck. A tiny beaked snout jabbed its way through the top of the shell—a three-fingered hand clawed out of a triangular crack, followed by a slimy forearm. The shell cracked straight down the middle and a thin milky liquid poured out on the stones. The occupant washed out with it, a swollen gelatinous mass, black and green, covered in a whitish-yellow fluid. Dereas's stomach heaved at the sight of a vague human-like shape with shifty eyes, rat brow and cheeks similar to Draba.

A miracle! A creature smaller than Draba, but larger than the lizard folk. The thing sprawled there, tail and claws among bits of shell, staring with alien wonder at the world around him.

Dereas stared in perplexed dismay. The mother stomped over to lick the lizard-man clean of his yellow slime and nudged him forward to crawl and learn, as would any reptilian mother encourage her young fresh from the womb. This he did with surprising speed.

A gang of lank-limbed reptile-keepers came loping onto the scene, thrusting long speared poles through the gaps in the pen. Greta was forced to leap to the side, thus separated from her newborn. A crew of ten independent lizard-keepers held her in this posture and prodded her back with serpentish hooks should she try to hop the spears. Inevitably she did, hoping to crush the interlopers who scrambled within. It was dangerous work and scratches and bruises escalated among the keepers, but in a matter of minutes, they pulled the confused Draba away from his mother with expert claws. Only one careless lizard had the idiot lack of foresight to get too close to Greta and had its front limb ripped off, which she shredded in a spray of blood and mash as would a frenzied wolf, much to the toothy chagrin of the gathered lizards.

The lizards put Draba, or what was once Draba, in the other pen with the 'juveniles', which gamboled about near Dereas and his dazed crew. The lizards stared at the newcomer with excitement, this new runt of the litter, though he was a hand height their superior already.

At this proximity, Dereas experienced a feeling of heavy dismay, particularly when the lizard that was Draba hopped over to the posts to stare down at him with a disturbing intensity, with a hint of familiarity that was unsettling. The big, piercing, black-slanted eyes blinked in the same way as the old Draba and shifted from man to lizard and back to the men again. The ugly gash on his right arm had completely disappeared; the lizard birth had healed his wounds. With tiny teeth and toothy grin concealed in those fleshy, slick reptilian features, Dereas could not help but get a glimpse of the old Draba whom he wished to forget.

The scrutiny was soul-stressing and Dereas's innards tingled. He could only reflect with the utmost revulsion that the lizard-lords had corrupted an entire race and were a scourge upon the natural universe. They achieved a new level of depravity in this cycle of ages. The obscene birthing had taken its course. Not only did a strange doomed sense of fatality fall over Dereas, but a sadness for this degenerate race.

The lizard Draba lost interest in the roped men outside the cage and began to cavort with his peers who fixed their avid stares on their new playmate.

Jhidik's face, meanwhile, underwent a series of dramatic emotions as he struggled to come to terms with his rapidly-approaching fate. He bucked and swayed with wild strength, lashing at the lizards and his constricting bonds; only to be buffeted back by one of the keepers. Lizardish snorts and admonitory grunts indicated that he was to wait his turn.

The ceremony did not commence—at least, not right away.

The compound remained at rest, or in hiatus. Despite the birthing, normal life went on and Dereas guessed the lizard king slept still in his lavish hall or was preoccupied with other matters.

Many fruitless hours had been spent trying to saw through his bonds, and in his most despairing moments, Dereas realized that such bonds were not to be broken. Even with Draba having gnawed through some cord at his back in a fit of whimsy, giving his arms, pinned at his sides, some more slack.

With a bowed head, he loosed a sulfurous curse, muffled by his gag, eyes pressed shut, formulating a silent wish. "Balael, if you can hear me now, you deaf laggard, then grant us release from this abominable hell! If you are any god at all, or have any influence over this age of *Saeth*, then let me carry my companions from this nightmare! If you are not just some blue wolf-headed idol of mortal's imagination, grant me vengeance on my enemies—this demented lizard king and his ghouls. If you don't, then sit in the egg for all I care. To Zecrates' Hell with you!"

The fevered warrior opened his eyes and tore his gaze about, looking with sad resignation about his dreary surroundings that spoke of death and lizardom.

Without warning, a hot flash arced up his spine...his hair stood on end. In his mind's eye he saw himself back on the blood-red battlefield, a sullen glower smoldering in his eyes. Mayhem was brewing and his warriors were gathered in tight ranks, and the enemy, a brood of huge helmed foemen, stood in long lines before their ranks, glistening pikes at the ready. Dereas Barath-o'-Bear was about to ride into battle and engage those armies of doom! He could see the standards bristling, the bloody banners waving glory and victory. His heart flamed and the blood boiled in his veins like the champions of old. Lurid memories filled his spirit like the roar of a gale and the war cry of his people sounded on his lips like a baleful horn-call.

Dereas exulted, for any invocation to Balael empowered his warrior spirit and enabled him to fulfill his destiny and command victory over his enemies. He had learned that from his countless trials in the field of war, the charnel grounds of combat, those bloody pastures of triumph and sorrow. He licked his lips with savage relish, for no sooner had he uttered the prayer than a simple, daring plan came to mind—which started with getting free. He saw the elegant potential of it, as the guard-patrol approached, unsuspecting...

Wheezing an awful curse, Dereas sat still, a great smirk spreading on his bronzed features. His faith in his one god had rekindled his heart, and the old fire had stolen back in his veins, the blood of cunning and the stealth and guile of his stormy ancestors.

Like a dead man he slumped, letting his head roll and his parched lips reveal a tip of a sallow tongue lolling.

Tureen in hand, the guard bent over the slumped man curiously, examining the dazed Amexi first, then prodding Dereas with a tulwar. The sentry received no response and it turned its dog-like snout to peer at a wheezing, nearly comatose Hafta. It was then that Dereas scissor-locked it. Clamped it in a merciless grip around the neck. The squirming body was dragged onto the stone, its scaly back bent into Dereas's lap. The lizard rapped the tureen hard against Dereas's ribs, but it slipped from its grasping hand and its choking cry rang out in the sinister dark. A grim struggle of fiendish strength ensued, with a lizardish flapping of arms and a bone-crushing grip of thews...Dereas heard a neck snap. He flipped the inert body over on its side, close to his face and bent his own neck low, rubbing his blackened lips up and down against the lizard's rough belt to peel off his gag. He dipped his unencumbered head down—to grab at the dead lizard's belt-knife with his teeth, hoping to work some of his bonds loose.

The three young lizards in the adjoining pen stared mesmerized at the sudden violence. They started to grunt and chitter in their native language, running amok in circles and roughhousing each other.

Derea hissed, knife clenched in molars. "Quiet, cretins!" He glowered with distaste and peered about anxiously. Bending his arms at the elbows, he went to work on the cord securing his wrists. The last thing he needed were these rambunctious lizards alerting the castle guards at the front gate.

Dereas worked fast, his heart beating like a hammer. If another sentry came to discover the contorted body of its colleague, the opportunity would be lost.

Hafta and Amexi stirred from their lethargy, inspired by the violence that had turned in their favor. Dereas pressed his lips in a grimace, motioning them to be silent. He pulled free his arms, gripped the knife and kneed the slack body out of the way. Once he cut the cords wrapped round his chest, he could slide himself up and then...All the while Draba watched abstractedly through the lizard pen with the google-eyed curiosity of a child. Dereas felt the press of his vacant, drooling gaze and bent to his task uneasily.

Suddenly he felt the weight of a grim, silent shadow hovering over him. He looked up. A large stealthy figure grabbed the knife out of his nerveless jaw and stared down at him with impassive scrutiny.

Dereas squinted in surprise. The skulking brute's face showed a glower that radiated a grim grin of pleasure.

"You live?" mumbled Dereas, his voice strange to his own ear.

The New Wolves' chief uttered no sound; he just stared broodingly at his brother, ignoring the excited rustle of Hafta and the startled croak of Amexi at his side.

Dereas's features bent in a twisted smile. Rusfaer! He must have slid slowly down the base of the wall closest to them, masked in black shadow. The crafty bastard! How did he get all the way here?

Rusfaer, the wolfish warrior, whose shadow-haunted face was now an emotionless mask, freed his man Hafta, then he gazed meditatively at his brother and the mountain king. Hafta raised himself to a kneeling crouch, massaging the blood back into his wrists. Rusfaer saw the half-spilled tureen and sniffed it with suspicion, upending it in one heave into his bearded maw. "I've a mind to leave you here with the lizards," he snarled after a time while he chewed the leafy gruel in wincing gulps. His voice was a bleak crow's caw. The figure in front of him was a harsh echo of the Rusfaer Dereas knew. He saw his arms and face were a mass of swollen bruises and cuts. "Kizoi, I haven't eaten in two days!" the big warrior growled. "Even this slop tastes good. And yet, not even my worst enemy would I leave to the likes of these scavengers..."

Dereas worked his blackened lips into a crooked smile. "I thank you for your high opinion of me."

Hafta glared expectantly at his chief, but the warrior who had come back from the dead did not immediately respond. On a signal from his chief, Hafta snatched up the dead sentry's bone-carved knife and freed Dereas's bonds. Dereas stumbled awkwardly into a rude crouch, nursing blood back into his limbs and coaxing life back to his prickling legs. "Ahhh," he groaned.

Rusfaer hitched himself closer to cut the mountain king's bonds. Scowling, he went to work on Amexi's with a truculent word passed between the two. The blond warrior fixed him with a questioning glare, but cracked his knuckles, smoothing out the raw red rings around his wrists where the lizards' cords had stung deep.

Hafta observed, "You look like you've been through Zecrates' six hells to elude that lizard net." His hand gripped his chief's shoulder in gratitude.

Rusfaer grunted in a low whisper, "I watched from that high perch on the other side of the cavern." He lifted a blood-caked finger. "The rituals were interesting, you being tied to the posts and that eldritch business with Draba."

"How did you get down?" murmured Dereas.

"The damnable darkness was my worst foe," the big man rasped. "After escaping those frog-hopping devils, I snatched up a chipped vessel lying in the tunnel a ways up. I scooped up some light-giving Vitrin. The fools—the watch near where we got nabbed, were not expecting me to return this way. They left most of the corridor unmanned. They all rushed to find me. Overconfident numbskulls! I slipped through their checkpoint, took another winding path, found the main aqueduct junction, a source down which I snuck. This was much later when the lizards seemed to have retired within their 'fort'." He frowned at the memory. "The horrors I saw there! The unborn things struggling, wriggling, floundering...I never want to see that sight again!"

"You were in the fort?" muttered Dereas, awestruck.

The New Wolf chief clamped his lips in a somber scowl. The sweat dripped down his lacerated brow.

Dereas turned away. He stripped the lizard corpse at his feet of its mail, hoping that something could be salvaged for Jhidik. He snatched up its tulwar and beckoned them forth. They snuck on their hands and knees toward the raised place where the Pirean sat slumped, bound too close for comfort near Greta's cage. All avoided the cone of dim light that slanted down from the castle wall.

They untied the Pirean and crouched there sullenly, alert for any signs of detection. There were none. Jhidik lifted a shaky hand to his head. He massaged his aching thigh. "I thought you'd never get here." He looked the two chiefs up and down. "You two vagabonds are looking the worse for wear. A sight for sorry eyes."

Dereas felt a smile break out on his face. He helped his friend to his feet and watched Jhidik hobble in a hangman's circle, careful to stay out of the stain of the nearby lamp. Dereas was not oblivious to the throbbing pain he saw his friend hiding. He could only guess the agony he had endured, even now suffering to put on a cheerful face, yet still ready to help them in any way he could. Dereas admired his friend's fortitude and he clasped him on the shoulder. "Here, Jhidik. You need some protection."

Jhidik wrinkled his nose in disgust. "It's too small." He shuffled to a place not far away, crouching in a painful totter to retrieve his mail shirt heaped in the dust, which his keen eyes had spotted from afar. He swung it hastily over his head and Dereas turned to his brother. "What of the castle? Obviously it hides some horrible secrets. We must get past the guards!"

"The castle..." Rusfaer's grumble faltered and his eyes went glassy. His cheeks slackened in a pale rictus of recollection. In a low voice he painted an obscene picture of the clutch of hybrid creatures hidden in the castle's undercroft, crouched behind wooden pales and stone grates: a haunted horde of jabbering misfits, part squid, crab and lizard, crayfish-men he described them as, and of the diseased crossbreeding the lizards had dared with other abominable species. Their demented king had put such abysmal schemes into effect, with the atrocious assistance of his priest-queen's black sorcery. There were other unmentionable things the lizard king kept confidential in the bowels of the keep, but of these, Rusfaer would not speak.

The others listened, dumbstruck, forgetting momentarily where they were.

Rusfaer went on in a hoarse voice. His giant frame shuddered. "I took the aqueduct down past the court and under, where the water flows to the cellars. 'Tis below the court level where that infernal egg sits propped like an ugly boil. Lizards and other creatures—salamanders, rodents, you name it, hunch behind bars, but the bulk are kept in cruel conditions, wallowing in filth and rot, wailing and gibbering like demented fiends. It's a damnable menagerie there, a whole dungeon of abominations. My reeling brain could not take any more of it, nor make sense of the miserable, ill-fated wretches at first, only conclude that the mad priestess who put the lizard inside Draba, uses these 'misfits' or dysfunctional 'rejects' of the lizard birthings to experiment on their own kind."

"But why? How..?" Hafta trailed off feebly.

"For their unholy alchemy in birthing their race. What else? And with her accursed dusts and potions. It's all so repulsive, and yet a long leap in evolution. Truth be told, that's what I saw, so I swear on the grave of Kizoi!"

"Never mind," Dereas growled in revulsion. "We have other things to worry about."

"Like what?"

"Getting out of here?" responded Jhidik.

Dereas acknowledged Jhidik's quip and waved the others away from the castle wall. He was impressed that Rusfaer had come back, even if it was for self-interested motives. It was not a stretch to say he was moved, considering that not twenty four hours ago, they would have cut each other's throats. With grudging camaraderie, he put his hand on his brother's sturdy shoulder, glad that some trust had been built. The briefest of grim smiles passed between them and they scanned the common ground, searching for a plan of action, but the New Wolves' chief pulled Dereas back.

"Hakar's devils! The patrol has returned." He ran his fingers through his matted locks. His nostrils flared and his fists clenched in frustration. He motioned the others aside. Dereas squinted up the cavern to see a glint of metal and a dark rectangular cave where a distant aqueduct met mid-level up the dome of the cavern wall.

"See there?" Rusfaer intoned. There was a flash of steel glinting off tulwars of the patrol adjacent, marching in lock step. "That's where we need to go."

"No chance now," grunted Dereas. "They must have awakened or gotten suspicious. We need to find another route."

"Wait here," advised Rusfaer. Before any could object, the warrior rushed off toward the ominous rampart which was draped in velvety shadows.

Several tense moments passed and the dark figure returned, panting. "Too many treading on the upper walks," he growled. Dereas saw his left leg trailed blood. "I doubt if we have enough stamina to try the trick I was thinking about. Already a stir is coming from the fort. The lizard king no doubt. I heard him screeching some baneful words earlier below. He will be making his presence known before long. My plan needs to be revised."

"There is a stone bridge behind the castle," suggested Amexi.

"Aye, but it has an evil look to it. 'Tis guarded too."

"I know this bridge." Dereas squinted at the stir of movement beside the stronghold—a long line of toiling lizards, carting jewels, or glints of what looked like light reflected from the distant black tunnel, across the bridge and to the postern gate of the castle a stone's throw away from their hiding place. The raw, grim faces of the barrow pushers looked anything but content, faced with their arduous task.

"What in Balael are they doing with all those crates of raw crystals?" muttered Hafta.

Rusfaer waved a fist. "We can't worry about that now. Probably for some hatching of their wretched sorcery. Judging from the masses of crystal and the rude mirrors, the use of elder sorcery numbers among their plans to perpetuate the monstrous legacy of their birthing."

Dereas gazed reflectively to the parapets where the wretched eggs glinted in ghoulish procession. "Where do they get the humans from to birth their foul race?"

Fezoul, who had said nothing thus far, struggled in his near catatonic state to supply an answer.

"From stray wanderers like yourself, no doubt," he wheezed. "Most who have had the bad luck of venturing into the mountain's maw," he added darkly. "I believe the Eaklyds bring offerings in the form of eggs or humans to the north portal where scouts, fastest and leanest, can fetch them before Pygra learns of the morsels."

"What an evil environment you cultivate here," grumbled Rusfaer.

"I can only abide in the fact that I have slept through most of this nightmare," sighed Fezoul. "I wish you had never wakened me!" His words ended in a moan.

"And miss all this fun?" quipped Dereas. "Where next from here?"

"Listen, I have a plan," cried Rusfaer. He pulled his brother aside. "Curse that lamp!" He waved a fist at the lurid censer strung on the pole near the high wall. "See those pike-bearing sentries guarding the nearest parapet in the tower?"

"Aye, what of it?"

"They will make dogmeat of us if we try to creep by the nearest corner. This scuppers any plan for escape. If we knock out the light, they will become suspicious."

"Too high to knock out the tower watch," admitted Amexi.

"Which is why we need a diversion," mumbled Rusfaer. He smacked a fist in his palm. "We need their attention on something else, maybe two things in case one backfires, then we can make our escape."

"But how?" barked Hafta.

Rusfaer motioned toward the pass, the eerie aqueduct sluicing down its Vitrin-green wash, and the zigzagging stairway that led up higher than the level to the way out, black as ravens. A gleam of burnished steel glinted from a lizard sentry's helm. "We will not easily evade those devils," he predicted. "There are over a dozen of them, and I remember how many of them, armed to the teeth, with tulwars and knives and clubs waylaid us before. They had nets and grapple hooks when they forced you down to this depraved colony."

"I will concentrate on the lizards here," announced Dereas magnanimously. "I'll light a fire under Greta's hide if I have to. The bitch is restless and ruts again for an egg. She is out for blood since all her eggs are despoiled. I'll take Jhidik, Amexi, and Fezoul and whoever will act as watch. You take your man, Hafta, if you need to. Climb the parapet, you're good at it—" He said this without guile, sensing his brother's intense scrutiny on the wall. "You were always good at climbing trees—remember the forts we used to build in Elk's woods near the buzzard cliffs?"

"Aye, and so—?"

"Listen! Scale the front face where it's in shadow. The stone blocks are crude there and hewn haphazardly, ideal for climbing. There are lots of cracks, handholds and iron rods to make your ascent. I'm sure you like those royal eggs no more than I."

Rusfaer grinned unpleasantly. "No need for Hafta. I can do this on my own."

"Take him anyway. It'll do no harm. He can hurl rocks at the eggs."

Rusfaer mulishly looked off into empty space. A curt grunt indicated he would stick to doing it on his own.

Jhidik jerked a thumb back at the fledgling lizard cage where Draba wandered mindlessly. "Looks like our friend, Draba, has got himself in a predicament. Wonder how he fared inside the lizard's gizzard? It's amazing he survived—though I think I would have rather given up the ghost, than be where he's been."

Rusfaer gusted a heated snarl. "Don't joke about him." A brief spasm fled across the warrior's face as he caught a glimpse of those once human features of his henchman staring through the bars.

Hafta shifted on his heel. "What of our little Draba then?"

"What of him?" growled Rusfaer harshly. "He's a freak. Can't you see? We can do nothing for him."

"We could kill him," suggested the nose-ringed warrior. "Put him out of his misery. What do you say?"

Rusfaer wiped his mouth with the back of his hand. After a time he pressed the heels of both palms hard into his bloodshot eyes. "The fool has got us captured by these vermin and has otherwise been an eerie and troublesome nuisance. He was one of us at one time, remember? I think there is sad irony in this situation—only a fool would be blind enough to not see it. Draba would approve if he had sense and could see the humor in it."

Dereas watched him study the primitive face that peered through the mesh at him, through the shadows and spaces between the posts. During that time he saw his brother shiver uncharacteristically.

"Leave him!" Rusfaer grunted.

Dereas made a silent affirmation. "Even as a lizard, Draba deserves life..."

"So be it," muttered Hafta darkly, though it was obvious that the nose-ringed warrior did not approve of the decision.

"Make it good, brother," Dereas mumbled under his breath.

The big man turned away, his eyes strangely lit. They were distant and glimmering like stars on a moonless night. He squared himself off to face the lofty ramparts not far distant.

A sudden sound...a clink of metal. The huddled men crouched in a tense silence. Their questing eyes squinted in the gloom. Lizards crawled and shuffled to and fro near the portcullis, ranging in and out of the castle.

Rusfaer pushed Dereas away, hissing harshly in his ear. "Go, quick, Ratslayer! You do your part and I'll do mine!"

"What do you mean?"

But the heavyset warrior was off on his feet in a loping, half-bent run. Into the shadows he drifted like a ghost, not bothering to share his solo mission. His wolfish figure was a blur in a greater swatch of darkness, his husky frame brimming strangely with a hallowed light, as if Balael favored him alone of all. Hafta crept after the lithe warrior, far enough back to avoid his chief's notice, and with no more noise than an owl on the hunt.

While Rusfaer scrambled off on his dark deed, Dereas, Jhidik and Amexi took the mountain king around back of Greta's cage. They slunk like weasels, for a menacing rattle now gurgled from the saurian's wattled throat. Amexi, careful not to rile the beast, was successful at stealing a pot of animal fat and a torch from a nearby bracket on the wall back of Draba's pen. The beast's muscles rippled beneath its enormous hide. Dereas took pleasure in grabbing a filthy rag from a sconce pole nearby. A fidgety Fezoul kept lookout.

Hunching in the shadows, the conspirators divvied their spoils. Dereas grinned like a wolf. He used the bulk of the oil and doused about a half of the mother lizard's posts, while Jhidik winced in stiffness behind and touched the flame tip of the wooden torch to each.

Greta glowered fixedly at the intruders, making nervous mewling sounds in her throat as they slunk by on their dark business. When the flames crackled at the dry wood, she strutted around her pen in foul humor. Suddenly the posts erupted in towers of flame. She reared back on her hind legs, hot red tongues licking up the posts like writhing serpents. The reptile went berserk. She burst through the flaming cage on all fours, scattering burning chunks every which way.

Dereas and the others shrank back, grimacing as the flames seared her spiny, bony back.

A roar, a shriek...a trumpeting cry. The lingering lizards in the common ground were up in arms. The raging creature bellowed forth a terrific roar. She took to rioting in the outer court, smashing lizard stragglers that got in her way, taking them down in her teeth or shaking them like a dog would and flinging them wide.

On all fours, the companions crawled and set fire to the smaller cages near the mother's pen, also the outbuildings, using oil and grease from the lamps.

Jhidik looked toward the pen farther away that housed the large male lizard. "Poppa's too?"

The giant male lizard glowered steely red eyes upon them.

Dereas gave an impish nod. "Why not?"

Jhidik laughed despite himself. Waving his brand, he scrambled with Dereas, Amexi and Fezoul in a bent-kneed hobble toward the cage. Under no circumstances must they get trampled underfoot by Greta or her agitated mate.

Lizards had finally pinpointed the source of the commotion. They gnashed, stomped their feet and brandished weapons. Toward the leaping flames they came shambling, a group of heavily-armed sentries which pointed lizardish claws at the escaped rebels who slunk back into the shadows.

"Quick! Let's get this business over," hissed Dereas. "By the scores they will swarm us! Hopefully poppa, once free, will keep our hosts at bay."

Straggling lizards put bare feet to stone to join the horde and Dereas bared his teeth. "Draw back!" he shouted in a hoarse voice. "They've already spotted us." Other lizards were drawing weapons and tramping toward them, not the escaping saurians. The beastslayer, stumbling forth in dismay, whispered a prayer to Balael.

In the time it had taken Rusfaer to slink over to the bailey wall, pandemonium had broken out in the outer court. Forced to crouch in the gloom, he had cursed and fumed in the agonizing wait for the guard to look the other way—but then he took to scaling the wall. Up the bestial bas-reliefs he toed his way, row on row of them, using the iron rods that protruded out of the stone for footholds. With panther-like strength, he pulled himself a quarter way up the wall. A final toehold had him pushing his boots into a stony serpent's mouth, then heaving to clench fingers around a protruding lizard claw.

Hidden by shadows crawling up the stone walls, he clambered up the nearest corner farthest from the spiked oval gate. Rusfaer paused to look down at the confusion below. Mayhem reigned. Dereas and the others had made good progress, he thought with a snarl; they had fired the male lizard's pen and now the startled beast swung its heavy neck back and forth like a bear, splintering the flaming posts to gain an avenue of escape. With snout singed, it hopped in agony on a rampage, racing for its mate, eager to join her carnage.

Rusfaer blinked dispassionately; his emotion gave way to gradual approval. He could not help but feel a certain fierce pride for his stalwart brother. Albeit a flawed personality, Dereas was industrious, even clever. With a mirthless laugh he reached for the stony snout of another carven lizard and swung himself up over the lip of the parapet. He crouched there waiting, the blood in his temples throbbing. Nose to nose with the bestial faces, he experienced a wash of memories he wished to forget. Likewise, he could not help but ponder what diseased imagination had inspired their carving.

He grimaced, feeling his strained muscles tremble under the trials of wall-scaling. He hesitated, careful not to slip and impale himself on the sharp rods that protruded below. The treasured eggs loomed in bare view on the parapet: strung out in a line, ripe targets. The goal of his mission lay before him, and glittered in the glare of torches. The fools who walked and guarded these parapets were distracted. They were not looking for an outlander creeping up the castle wall, or as he was now, crawling before their precious eggs, and he chuckled with a rancor that echoed his primitive vindictiveness.

The outer court sprawled in squalor and chaos. Rusfaer noted the male lizard took care of any resistance to his human companions straggling below. The attackers fled in terror from the path of that behemoth. Kruger swatted the stragglers out of the way with its front forelimbs or bashed them with its hind legs or chased them past smoking cauldrons and burning pits. Those who fought, stabbing at its nose or elephantine legs with their toy-like tulwars, were crushed or grabbed up in its greenish teeth and devoured.

Greta lurked at the cavern's end directly opposite the winding footpath—the same from where they had entered. It was evident she hoped to find some route up the cliff face, but could find no such escape. The stairway was too cramped and narrow for her bulk. A gory sport she indulged in, mangling the lizards that fought on the switchbacks up the cavern walls and that waved ineffectual weapons or bone sticks. Rearing up at the foot of the stairs, she snatched them in her teeth and flung them to their doom on the stones below. Rusfaer shrank back, his muscled shoulders tensing at the might of the saurians and the magnitude of that butchery.

While he blocked out the carnage, he dragged himself away from the precarious drop and hunched on the parapet, chest-heaving.

The tramp of enemies came from a short distance away.

He jerked round and wormed his way behind an egg. Many of the vile things were illumined in ghostly light from torches hung on iron brackets. He drew his long weapon from its scabbard. An armed guard had heard the scrape and gave a snuffling grunt. Its yellow eyes blazed upon the human hand and blur of movement before the skulking warrior could react and fling himself on the defender. Ducking the whirling blade was not enough—there came a dodge, a stabbing of lunging flesh, a grunting hack and a flash of steel. The New Wolves' leader chopped the legs out from under the hapless lizard and it toppled headlong onto the stone floor in the outer court. Brains and entrails sprawled in a grisly heap.

Rusfaer ignored the gore and din below. He peered without, saw the inner court bustling with fevered lizards which dragged heavily-laden carts and barrows of riches and chests, overflowing cauldrons, baskets and urns of gems and smaller eggs from the repositories scattered around the court's perimeter. The first hint of trouble had spooked them, Rusfaer concluded, and with a fiendish grin he loped down the parapet. The giant egg in the center court loomed like a cyclopean sentinel: a great hallowed eye directly in sight below. Cursing, Rusfaer could not help but experience a cold shudder as he scrambled forward, imagining what perverse colossus dwelled in that terrible egg. Torchlit bone towers spired up from the parapets at intervals of fifty feet, and teemed with sentries posted in the upper tiers.

Rusfaer ducked, but he knew there was little that he could do. He must work fast, make his exit before one of their deadly tulwars found his breast! These primitives had luckily not perfected the art of arrows, otherwise he would have been peppered long ago, a sitting duck in an open field.

The blood-letting continued below and Rusfaer busied himself with dislodging the nearest egg from its golden harness. Straining in the dim light, he found the egg heavy as iron, what with its eerie contents and all the garlands of jewels draped around it. But it took his superior strength to move it, being almost his own height and girth. He got the egg rolling and heaved it off the edge with a thrust of his shoulder.

It fell, spinning in midair for a second or more. Splat! It splintered in myriad pieces only paces from the mangled sentry. Rusfaer savored grimly this small victory. For the rude assaults and disgusts he had suffered at the hands of this filthy lot ran in high numbers. One, two, three, and more of the devil-spawned eggs he knocked down with an animal satisfaction. Plenty to go, he guffawed! A hundred to choose from. His smirk became a twisted leer, but he hadn't much time. Soon the slippery fiends would be out swarming in numbers and he did not wish to be caught center of attention on this narrow ledge.

Even as he entertained the thought, a host of the angry reptiles coursed down from the nearest tower to intercept him...

Dereas watched from below, crouching transfixed as his brother was forced to lay blade to the multiple foes that assailed him. The first went down in a sticky spray of blood. Rusfaer, thick with gusty snarls, easily took care of others, hip-checking them off the parapet into the inner court, or tossing them into the common ground on the other side. The cries of the dying were loud and furious and alerted more guards from the towers. Within the fortress came a rustle of movement.

Another egg dropped, releasing its contents, smashing on the stone. Dereas watched restlessly from behind an overturned cauldron, yet he thought twice whether he could help his brother or not, for the things that had crawled out of those broken eggs were not pleasant to behold. The carnage had created some furor among the reptilian spectators who stared appalled.

From one cracked shell, out rolled a gelatinous, mummy-like creature, once-human, thought Dereas. It was a ludicrous, pupa-like corpse gestating into what looked like some moth-butterfly transmutation. The thing was so disgusting that Dereas had to turn his head. Some, he witnessed, were in more advanced stages of gestation. Only one seemed semi alive and voiced a demonic outcry before it rose on its pulpy legs and began snapping at necks and ripping out the throats of snarling lizards. Had the priestess's magic gone awry? Seeded humans with caterpillars or moths instead of newts? In those eerie seconds he recalled Draba had hatched in less than a day...Whether her eldritch magic employed alchemy to produce such obscene larval intermediates during longer-spanning gestation periods, he had no time to speculate. The lizard king had been vague regarding the lizard magic.

By the time the lizard king emerged from the castle, his outer court was in a smoking ruin. Dereas's fist clenched the hilt of his lizard blade with murderous force. The king's shrill expostulations amounted to little more than obnoxious noise as he scampered about, his white and crimson robe flashing and beady eyes bulging at the destruction of his treasured eggs and the chaos in the courtyard. He denounced the deeds of the outlanders with the utmost vehemence. "Crokcaws! Badgebakes! Our sacred eggs smashed! Kill the intruders!" he panted. Screeching, dancing around in a mad circle, he provoked his subjects to wrath. "Our royal brethren would have gone on to become magnificent lizard captains! Look at what these defilers have done! Kill them all! Bring me their heads—and especially that Egg Slayer!" He shafted a jeweled finger at the blood-soaked Rusfaer who now fought alone on the parapets against a dozen or more fiends.

All eyes rose to where the mailed giant crouched to meet his new attackers. He was a fire-swinging fury of passion. Swift bellows rang on the warrior's lips. He cleaved and hewed to the bone lizard foes and spread red ruin in the frantic ranks of the defenders. The black-green lizard horde was getting slaughtered. But he had taken many hits, mere surface 'wounds' as he would have called them, but enough to draw blood and make him look haggard and battle-torn in the wake of the opposition.

"He needs help," Dereas muttered hopelessly.

"Go, then," Jhidik mumbled. He had crept up on silent feet to lay a hand on his chief's shoulder. "I am useless with my lame leg. I cannot climb these walls."

Dereas forced a grunting acknowledgment. He stood silently, looking past his friend. They clasped forearms in the long tradition of the Huughite warrior caste and free tribes of the north.

Like a banshee, Dereas wheeled up out of the shadows and advanced toward the fortress walls.

As he raced to the section of wall Rusfaer had earlier climbed, he stopped dead in his tracks. Coiling in the dusky shadows crept a willowy, mutant figure of dripping blasphemy that reared up from the eggish slime. Dereas dodged and slashed the thing, avoiding its slimy reach of egg-born weirdness..while to his ears drifted saurian roars of Greta and Kruger who caught howling lizards in their teeth or trampled them at the far end of the cavern.

The beastslayer was just in time to glimpse Hafta in a belated, free-for-all crawl up the rampart. "Wait!" he cried madly. The grim, scar-faced warrior had waited in the shadows, seeing for some time no change of guard or moment of inattention whereby he could launch himself up the wall. "Cover me," Dereas growled up at him. "Stop them from hurling their spears."

In a flash he was climbing up the rough stone, pushing hard his heels on rods and gripping stone fangs and claws for support. True to form, Hafta jumped down into the shadows of the common ground, and crouched, ready to deal with any attacker who would scale the wall, craving the beastslayer's skin. Dereas reached the end of his perilous ascent and gripped the battlements, where a crafty lieutenant awaited him, wielding a bone-white curved tulwar. The weapon slammed down where his fingers had just been.

Dereas croaked out a curse. The lieutenant's mouth opened in a brazen cry. The enemy slashed out again.

A miscalculated move. The lizard was unfamiliar with the speed or size of the grim-lipped warrior who faced him. In the blink of an eye a fist smashed into its groin as the beastslayer lifted himself up over the embrasure with his other hand. Dereas did a backward roll, which had him crashing up against a nearby egg carrier.

The egg teetered but did not fall. Dereas somersaulted next to his assailant which lay gasping for breath. The tulwar slipped effortlessly out of Dereas's scabbard to lock swords with another evil-looking captain of the parapet-watch. The lizard's eyes gleamed in anticipation. A miserable snarl escaped the jowly snout complete with green and red tongue flicking out, before it died.

Dereas had beat the horror back easily for he had the advantage of height. The next guard he pinned against an egg and ran it clear through his body.

Bright red lizard blood gushed out on the stones. The blade went on to pierce deep through the shell and the hybrid within.

A tiny gasping squeal issued forth...Dereas shivered. The egg split in two. He could hardly repress his distaste. He shouldered the egg over the parapet and the dying lizard with it, taking the miserable imp confined within. He did not bother to look down—or see what was left of the mess. Down the parapet he hurried.

A short flight of stairs later, he plunged fleet-footed down the walkway, which curved in a half spiral. The eggs that lined this rough corridor were like jewels on a crown. He was satisfied he had come this far and fled on down the way wide enough for five men to clamber abreast. Some of the eggs were larger here than others. Some glinted dully of different colors, others were garishly painted, and ornamented with gold leaf and jewels.

He did not pause to admire these trophies. He could see a straight stretch above the castle gate and halted, glaring sourly. A clot of attackers leaped about his brother who still held his own, but was waning fast. A thick sweat glistened on Rusfaer's brow. His mail was rent with new gashes and smeared with blood.

Dereas snorted in disgust. He jigged up behind two attackers who had Rusfaer pinned from behind. He sliced their knees clear through the sinew. They fell in sickening thuds, legs dangling from strings of scaly flesh. Dereas kicked them, or what was left of them, over the side. He let his blade sink into more slick flesh, cutting lizards down left and center while Rusfaer craned his neck and caught a glimpse of the stormy figure who was his brother wreaking ruin at every step. He loosed a cry of triumph. His eyes were wide with glee when he saw Dereas cutting whole swaths of lizards down that had jammed the parapet, preventing any escape. Rusfaer gave the war cry of his people. "To Balael with these devils!" His sword lanced into furious action and bit like gator teeth into glistening lizard hide, rising and falling in arcs of gleaming crimson. Dereas looked up to see a streaking sword-edge rise under the glare of torchlight, showering blood and gristle as Rusfaer's great blade split reptile-snouted heads and clove shambling bodies.

How the beastslayer cheered Rusfaer's fiery resilience! He shook his head in fierce pride—envious at the same time of the skill that his brother showed and his ruthless strength. No less did he admire that bone cleaver of his, snatched from the hands of a dead lizard! It was of a superior cutting quality than the traditional steel of his people and it fit in his hand with a lightness he did not know possible.

The two brothers circled back to back, defending a space that allowed their tulwars full play. They were like spokes of a radiating wheel turning on a hub, guarding their territory with jealous wrath. They slashed wantonly, jumping and dodging the strikes of the lizards, a dancing circle of death, taking foes out, mailed or unmailed by the dozens. If ever a foe penetrated their ground, the other warrior would leap in to strike off a limb or knee an attacker to doom or lop off a head. Some fell screaming to the flaming fires erupting below. Others tumbled on the giant egg looming close, and slipped over the parapets to the paves below. These sent hairline cracks spidering up the shell while others bounced off the surface to land in a crumbled mess of broken bones.

The two managed to batter back the horde, slipping on runnels of blood, launching a storm of cuts and strikes wherever possible. All the while they preserved their back-to-back formation with swords notched and ringing, blunted in the gloom cut by flickering torches. The tough lizard blades took the brunt of the force. The wolfish hardness of Rusfaer's attack was the stuff of legend. He was indeed a staggering, awe-inspiring sight, though now beginning to falter as Dereas saw. The beastslayer danced and feinted, his lighter frame a moving target that eluded the ever-swift lizards. But a dull ache began to arch up his sword arm. His lips were parched with fierce thirst and twisted in a battle-bitter smile. His flesh shivered in the mists of battle lust. As he rended and hewed, noble images came to his mind—the hours of sweat and exercise he and his brother had toiled and shared together, the endless weapons' training, the hand-to-hand combat, the hauling of weights up great hills, the climbing of trees, scaling boulders, stalking prey in the woods, scouting the misty forests along the foothills for game.

A lizard fell cleaved from ear to ear. Bloody foam formed on its jowl. Rusfaer went down with it...

Dereas flinched, for his brother had stumbled, missing a stroke that had slipped past his guard. Now the New Wolves' chief lay fallen under a seething stench of lizard flesh.

For a heartbeat, Dereas quailed; his concentration slipped, his arm went numb under a ringing parry. His hope faltered that his brother would get up.

A twitching hand grasping a bloody sword tore up through the writhing masses. But that was all Dereas could see. In a second, he too was swept away by a tide of lizard flesh. He caught crazy glimpses of twisting bodies falling on the giant egg in the courtyard, the egg battered beyond repair. The shell had started to buckle; wide cracks opened. A guttural cry pierced the air. More and more screams came rippling up from the throngs below. The egg started to tremble; it rocked dangerously as if something untoward moved within, awakening from a violently-interrupted incubation.

Lizards below pointed up at the two rebels. In their guttural tongues, they called for death. In desperation more guards tramped up the steps to gain the parapets from the inner court, clad in rough jerkins and steel caps.

The numbers were staggering and Dereas's heart skipped a beat. He was surrounded by lizard foes and looked back to the place from where he had come. He saw the entire area teeming with snarling, gnashing enemies. Their only escape route lay covered with maggot-like forms. Up the parapet steps lizards swarmed. Down the dusky wall they could not climb, or the parapet steps on the inner wall, without getting hewn down by lizards egging to gut them and cut off their heads. They were doomed!

Dereas's flesh crawled. Black Balael, how the day had turned evil! He caught a confused string of glimpses of Hafta and Jhidik in the court below flinging rocks at the eggs on the parapets, shattering the treasures. Oozing meat and bits of shells dripped down the walls. A fierce wave of pride coursed through Dereas's heart in those frenzied moments. It was a diversion of daring scope, he thought, but it was taking its toll. Some of the attention had been taken off his and Rusfaer's assault and for this, he managed a ghastly smile, though he feared for his friends' lives as much as his own. They faced a sea of enemies—and two gargantuan reptiles below, and there were scores more lizards swarming at their heels as if that were not enough to plague their daring rock-hurling.

Dereas howled. Smoke billowed up from the flames devouring the cages and anything combustible. He thundered a war curse. In-between hacks and parries, he kicked and tore away three struggling lizards to pull his battered brother to his feet. Dereas's white-eyed grimace alerted Rusfaer to the peril they were in.

"We all have to die sometime, brother," gasped the New Wolves' chief in a deep-throated rasp.

"Die yes—but not become one of them!" Dereas flailed his sword. A swift arc swept clean through the snout of a frothing lizard.

An ugly scowl formed across Rusfaer's face as he staggered to stay erect. He feinted left, let his dripping blade move with a primal strength. He struck with a zeal that belied the weakening hand behind it. An instinctual sweep severed off another lizard's head. Perhaps there lay a moment of lull when tiring muscles and gasping lungs had time to recoup. Not always...

A lizard guard pulled Rusfaer forward and two others jumped on his sword arm. Dereas saw his brother grimace in agony as they tried to wrest the blade from his grasp, and take him alive.

He should have been carved to pieces, but on the shrill order of some lizard captain, word was out to make a lizard of him yet—or so it seemed.

A throng of reptilian guards, sensing their chance of victory, stormed the Egg Slayer. Rusfaer thrashed. He snorted and faced them undaunted, blood trickling down his cheeks. A score of wounds showed on his arms and legs. The horde had just gained the parapets and were now eager for victory. An unusually large lizard-guard grabbed Rusfaer around the waist. Despite the warrior's savage slashes and teeth clamped into the aggressor's scaly neck, the lizard's tackle sent Rusfaer reeling and sprawling heavily upon his knees.

Rusfaer was knocked down hard on his back; his breath wheezed out in a ragged gasp. He grabbed onto a forelimb, throwing the lizard-foe off balance and started to careen off the edge. Dereas made a desperate lunge for his brother. He missed, grabbed with straining fervour onto the ankles of the lizard-at-arms to try to prevent the two from tumbling off the parapet.

To no avail. Instead the beastslayer felt himself being dragged forward by their combined weights and his clawed fingers scraping across the parapet's blood-stained stone.

The three fell from the parapet, plummeting through the swirling smoke...Dereas smashed into the giant egg, knocking every ounce of breath out of his lungs.

The egg swayed and trembled. It rocked back and forth like a foundering ship in a storm. There was something large, something fierce and unwholesomely sinister breaking free.

The pedestal crumpled and fell; the riven egg tumbled free of its flimsy housing to smash on the flagstones. It almost crushed Rusfaer and Dereas. They groped drunkenly to their knees, heads swimming in a blind daze, gulping great breaths into their lungs.

About the inner courtyard the two stumbled, casting vague eyes on a blurred scene of Jhidik and Amexi struggling far off with lizards-at-arms under the portcullis. The brothers tottered away, toward their comrades, shaken and bruised with swimming heads and stinging limbs...The piles of heads and soft torsos of other lizards that had crashed before them had prevented them from a certain death.

7: Rise of the Rgnadon

Man and beast fell into slavish degeneracy,
Twined in sorcery ancient beyond memory,
'Twas a Saeth-bred god's perfect playground,
When men and beast worship one other,
In blind fever of dominion!

—*From 'Chronicles of the Beastly Ages', Amor-Amon-Reth, the Telamon king*

A blast of rank heat raged at Rusfaer's and Dereas's backs, almost sending them sprawling to their knees. Twisting in terror, they looked up—into a horrendous red and purple face which had cleared free of the viscous yolk. The mouth yawned cavernously, its serrated, triangular teeth dripping slime.

The creature's roar filled the cavern and smote the rebel's bodies like a blast of thunder. The beast shook off the sludge and the fragments of thick shell as would a dog fling wetness from soiled fur. It stood tall on all fours, eyes blinking redly under the torchlit glare, surveying its surroundings with a dull, critical stare. Dereas thought the newly-birthed reptile looked like a thing out of Kizoi's hell, so little was it enthused at its first glimpses of lizard and human life in this squalid courtyard. It pawed the ground, fiendish eyes blazing on the staring men, while a repulsive wattled fan of skin flared outward around its neck with sharp spikes attached.

Dereas crabbed sideways, baring his broken weapon. Though it gleamed knife-like in his palms, it was useless to him, shorn in half from his fall. He gaped in incomprehension at the monstrous thing that towered over him. Without proper blade to fight it, he stood no chance. Perhaps the evil thing's early hatching had spawned some hybrid intermediary. He did not know. He only knew that looming before him crouched some giant salamander-like proto-saurian which held no classification in the known world.

His brother had managed to paw his rusty weapon out of the filth and looked ready to try keeping the thing at bay; but now, he and Dereas crouched stock still, paralyzed in the shadow of the awesome creature.

Then they ran.

In the courtyard, pandemonium reigned. Lizards fled in all directions, trampling each other in herds, grunting in their terror.

The brothers cursed in unison. They flew under the raised portcullis, bowling over heel-rooted defenders who gaped up at the birth of their coming god.

The elephantine legs were thick as logs, plated with scaly hide and it lumbered on feet that were webbed, duck-like things, not at all long, and clawed like a lizard's. The spiny wedge-shaped ridges lining its back looked strangely reminiscent of shark fins—possibly some weird, ancient defence against enemies—and if one looked carefully, it was possible to see the slit gills on either side of its misshapen face pocked with raw knots and wens.

The lizard king came marching from the court, preceded by his bodyguard paving a resolute path. They shoved aside any who hindered their advance.

Dereas engaged two of the scaly assailants scrambling to meet them. He and Rusfaer cut them down before hacking their way through an aggressive knot of lizard foes that blocked their way. Reptilian faces shone with feverish intensity. Dereas could almost taste the fetid reek that wafted from their gasping snouts. The two kept away from the wooshing tulwars, their legs pumping toward the section of wall near the pens. Their aim was to get Jhidik, Hafta and the others.

In a springing leap, Dereas cleared an overturned grindstone. He cleared a pile of Tyrannus bones, not yet made into blades—then leapt over a corpse in two strides, relieving the dead bodyguard of his curved blade. The new lizard tulwar felt good in his hand, tapered at the end, razor sharp, feather light, and it cast a dreadful pall on the lizards he met—cleaving flesh as he gutted attackers that stormed him from all sides while he bulled his way through.

The monster roared and cracked archways with its slimy teeth and tail, but now it burst out of the castle gate, mangling the top half of the portcullis with powerful jaws. The bellows of doom were in answer to the distant roar of its fellow saurians. The calls had stirred within it a primitive instinct and it pushed forward, searching every cranny for its kin. Catching sight of Greta and Kruger at the far end of the cavern, it loped to greet them in a swaying, two-beat gait, with head and grotesque body swiveling opposite the leading leg.

But 'greet' was a euphemism. Its repulsive features became a more mottled, scabrous mask of unpredictable passion as it struck out like a komodo in their direction. Greta and Kruger had overturned cauldrons and scattered lizard folk every which way, and were now caught in a rage of violence. The frightened lizards that did not get out of the Rgnadon's way were trampled or gored on the thing's bristling neck spikes.

Dereas glanced at the misshapen head and shuddered. The horror of it running loose in these close confines was blood-chilling.

Released too from his burning pen, Draba had come to life. The lizard-man was like a disoriented child and a lime-black shadow of his former self. But he seemed weirdly affected by the cursed witch-magic of the priestess. The caricature that was Draba came reeling after them, puppet-like. His lizardly frame shook with great chitters of excitement. He pulsed with what seemed intense memories from a former life, edged with a shiver of nightmare. It was the same weasel-faced Draba he had always known, but now with a lizard's oval skull and a spotted hide and hideous snout.

Dereas was appalled at the sight of Draba, now one of the detestable lizards. Rusfaer was in too much awe of the flames and confusion to give much notice to the freak that was Draba.

The lizard-man ran alongside them with a surprising speed. He darted in and out, like a dog herding sheep, nipping at their heels.

"Curse this zombie hound!" bellowed Rusfaer. He grit his teeth, slashed left and right, stumbled, grunted, and lunged again. But the obnoxious shape dodged and greeted him with a snuffling grunt and snuck in to play bite him on the shins.

The New Wolves' chief loosed a barrage of curses, arched his sword in flailing cuts and sweeps.

Dereas turned. He tried to sideswipe the creature, but it darted out of range with a sinister clucking and threw a handful of pebbles at his eyes. Dereas shook off the dust and charged on. Draba's cacophonous chittering was like the laugh of a hyena; into the press of the throng it faded as he veered away.

The lizard king, twenty strides away, seemed not to notice any of this horseplay, in anticipation of the capture of the two bloodthirsty brothers and their hack-happy rabble. Other members of Dereas's band mauled and pierced lizards near the shadow of the castle wall. Yet the lizard king's eyes glowed in fervor at the size, strength and speed of the Rgnadon, his champion. He seemed to overlook the trampling of his citizens—in favor of the creature's potential for butchery.

The monster charged up before the male Kruger and stopped full in its tracks, exuding challenge. The two reared up on their hind legs, windmilling front paws, sending deafening roars to the roof.

The two brothers crouched mesmerized, oblivious to their peril. They caught their breath and dove behind two overturned cauldrons. Here they watched the dynamics of these titans as others of the lizard kind stopped and stared in no less wordless astonishment, their weapons hanging slack, jowls drooping.

A strange dynamic passed among the three: Greta, Kruger and Rgnadon. Baying, snorting and head-butting, the males chased each other around in a ring, as if seeking dominance, as would a twain of alpha dogs do in a surly pack.

The Rgnadon was testing, even eclipsing Kruger's dominance and size. And yet still, the creature was but a babe compared to what it would become. Dereas had seen such behavior before exhibited among the wild wolf packs of the steppes. He noted that the

Rgnadon was extremely protective of Greta—he left her alone. They were obviously somewhat different species, but an unspoken bond of kinship passed between them. The elder creature was immediately wary of the new lizard on its turf. But to its credit, it opted to yield to a superior force, especially after a vicious attack left a gory tooth mark across its left shoulder. Kruger bowed its head in submission.

Dereas could not help but feel humbled in the presence of the primitive ritual.

The great beasts moved in tandem back to the center of the compound, as if in instinctual unison, to confront the lizard king and his ring of attendants.

Before the forbidding fort they halted where the lizard king stood with steadfast conviction, hands folded on his chest. The other lizards quivered and quaked, shrinking back like so many mice into their hidey-holes or behind cauldrons and barrows. The lizard king walked boldly out to greet the three giant saurians.

Was he invincible? Insane? thought Dereas.

Then he witnessed a miracle. Jaw agape, he saw that the lizard king, with a royal authority, sidled forth to mount the great Rgnadon from the tail section, with no fear at all. He clambered expertly up its bony back as if it were only a toy ladder. The Rgnadon did not seem to mind, only stamped a foot and bared its teeth, like any wild horse might do if a cocky rider attempted to dominate it.

The lizard king had an affinity with beasts. He harbored a voice of command and a presence among men and lizards, otherwise he would not be leader of this depraved race. He took a position between the dorsal turrets on the great lizard's back close to the repulsive fan flowering hideously on its neck. His brow sheened with rich triumph with this new transcendental position of power; none dared dispute it.

"The Time of the Snake is over!" he called loudly over the din of the assembled chaos. He waved his scepter like an exalted demagogue. "Pygra shall die in pools of her own blood. Die, I say! Let us see to it. The Time of the Lizard is upon us! Behold your god!" Thus the lizard king spoke, in his shrillest, loudest voice that none could fail to hear, as one who takes up the call of the mad hunt to lead men and beasts into howling slaughter.

"The New Order begins, now!"

The mob took up a fateful chant in frightful voices: "Hail the Gnador! Rise the Rgnadon!" Their demonic crescendo rose over the roaring of the lizard beasts in awe and mindless fervor.

Dereas covered his ears, struggling to block out that horrible din. The thrumming insanity of it brought a quiver of nausea to his throat. But he shook this off and muttered in a tone of bitter anger, "Let us be away from this madness, this haunted place!"

Rusfaer sneered, "I couldn't agree with you more, brother" and he grabbed Dereas by the arm and they fled, stumbling through the foul smoke, aided by a broken smoldering torch here or a glimmering mass of embers there.

They caught up soon to Jhidik who crouched in the confusion with Amexi, Hafta and Fezoul: a circle of sooty faces and blackened limbs. They coughed, assaulted by clouds of smoke billowing from oil and rags that had caught on fire.

The bunch looked haggard, disoriented: Jhidik, leg trembling, breath rasping, grimaced. A wax-faced Amexi was white as a ghost, and showed eyes darting fearfully in their sockets around in all directions. Hafta, head bowed, hunched in battered mail and torn hides, a bloody tulwar dripping in his hand. The mountain king sucked in a wheezy breath, his fingers clutching a lizard knife. All had secured weapons at least. They were desperate, bedraggled men.

"Well, rogues," breathed Rusfaer in a rasping undertone. "There are worst places to be—but we are alive. With few options. None good."

Dereas cursed. "The castle is out of reach and the exits blocked by lizards and saurian horrors."

Rusfaer grunted his agreement. "There is only one of these stray aqueducts that run up the cavern's face. We can make it up, I think. I know at least one of the spillways connects with some of the tunnels."

"Let us make the ascent!"

Amexi's quizzical frown challenged them. "Can we hope to find refuge in any of these places? The tunnels are haunted by Pygra, remember?"

"Forget Pygra!" rasped Rusfaer. "Better than remain here. Three murderous saurians rage two stones' throws away, and a thousand of these little lizards with their pesky picks and gnashing teeth are ready to rip our guts out."

"More of the pack coming at us all the time," agreed Jhidik.

Dereas bit back a snarl. "Then to your order, let's go."

The reptiles were indistinct masses in the smoke wreaths stirred by new fires. All was a disorded confusion. The reptiles could not see them, nor could the company see them, a situation which in hindsight was a good thing. Raging bellows rang in the chaos of the saurians' stand off.

The fugitives scrambled through the common ground, cleaving their way through stray lizards wielding tulwars and the smoke-wreathed gloom. They slipped and stumbled on filth and offal amid the sea of overturned cauldrons, smoking debris, and dead lizards' body parts. They paved a helter-skelter path through carved boulders and riven cobbled ways, but came to a close halt, breathing ragged gasps, at the sight of a winding ramp that swarmed with too many enemies.

They leapt back. Rusfaer's cry rang in their ears as they plowed a path toward a smaller aqueduct that lurked in the shadows. They scrambled past the roughhewn arch, dodging the spears and pikes hurled like javelins at them.

"Quick, the bridge!" cried Dereas. "It's our only chance! Make for the bridge behind the fort."

"There?" growled Jhidik. "It's an evil place. Why there?"

"Better than here!...Pray it's a place where the bane does not roam!"

"What of the serpentish horror then?" called Hafta. "It will rend—"

Rusfaer bellowed, "Run, you sods, run!"

The common ground was a flurry of activity. Grunting lizards reeled about in untold numbers. Burning pitch and cauldrons of oil blazed. A new pit doused with oil ignited in a whoosh of flames— flames which licked at the feet of an armory and the half-assembled siege weapons nestled there. The three huge saurians roared and fumed, with the lizard king mounted on the largest, screaming and bawling at the top of his lungs.

The companions raced for the bridge, on whose dark rock faces torches guttered. Lungs burning, they coursed along the littered ground, weaving between scattered knots of blood-soaked lizards, at the edge of exhaustion. Rusfaer's gleaming blade cut swathes among the advancing ranks of lizards. Dereas's blade took two at a time, steel-capped heads cleaved in a single stroke. Dereas, a wild figure of terror and wrath on the causeway, sword upraised in cleaving flight, carved gory ruin. Jhidik's blade moved in and out in no less savage rhythm, whistling like a scythe making mockery of the frenzied mob, stabbing, parrying, sundering, taking out eyes, ears, and limbs.

Up and over the causeway the companions surged, leaping over abandoned barrows, drays, carts. The stray victims they encountered fell, kicking in their death throes to the black abyss that yawned below. From the depths, hideous man-sized bats flew up, obscene things with hooded crests, peaked ears and flat featureless faces. They caught the doomed lizards as they fell, and their bodies were like none that men had seen, only gray-furred things with membranous carapaces showing the pulsing lungs beneath. The creatures were attracted by the flowing blood, relishing the carrion that fell freely from the lizard walks.

One blasphemous fiend flew close, lifting its prey in a clammy clutch. Gray skin and sinewy wing-flesh flapped. On closer scrutiny, Dereas saw these mutants had no eyes or nose, only a shark-like roundish mouth filled with vampirish teeth.

A shiver raced up his back. Teams of the creatures hooked claws, now onto a single lizard, and carried it aloft. To their rank eyries in the chasm flanks they flew. To do with those what they liked—and what Dereas dared not imagine.

At a far point on the span, Dereas saw a gang of bent-backed lizards hauling stone carts filled with crystals and rocks. The rolling crew grunted in confusion and the misshapen wheels ground to a halt. Several of them groped for bone tulwars and clubs, thinking they were being ambushed. The fools obviously had no idea the prisoners were on the loose. They were cut down to a lizard in a sea of red. Draba, the pesky ghoul he was, had sprinted up behind them and struck Dereas a glancing blow. Dereas overstepped his mark, attempting to dodge a lunging lizard. His effort was in vain as the lizard, eyes glazed in mortal agony, clutching the tulwar in his side, managed a lucky slash across Dereas's forearm. With a growl of frustration and pain, Dereas smashed the lizard in the face knocking it off his blade.

Surprise and agony pulsed up his arm; he felt a bright line of blood blossom on his skin. Rusfaer cut the attacking lizard down from shoulder to sternum. It slumped in a ragdoll heap. While its life blood poured out on the slippery stone, Dereas scrambled to catch up with the others, cursing his inattention. He tore a section off his cloak and bound the wound as tightly as he could as he ran. Though he was languishing from exhaustion, he felt buoyed by the nervous energy coursing through his limbs. Draba was nowhere to be seen.

They cleared the bridge, staggered into the black gaping tunnel beyond that loomed like an open sore. The passageway was huge, arched, probably formed by an upheaval in the crust. The tunnel was spacious enough to admit two breadths of the Rgnadon—and it was lit only by a handful of torches hung on high brackets in the rough stone.

Other stray lizards barred their path, but these they bowled over, and for the most part, the passage remained empty. The tunnel ran in a boundless straight line through near pitch blackness. The echoes of activity rang behind them, but were fading: a garble of groans, howls, lizardish yelps, shrieks, and a mournful blaring of horn. There came the smashing of many mallets on drums as the lizards gathered their forces and sallied out seeking vengeance for their losses—all in a wash of mania that defied his comprehension.

A light shone ahead. Dereas squinted his tired eyes. How long they raced he could not know. He thought he detected a small leering face thrusting itself out of the murk—Draba! What was the galling pest up to now? The lizard seemed to appear and fade away like a phantom—a gibbering prankster, one taking profane delight in setting teeth on them or foisting some mischief or sabotage.

The momentary lull in pursuit did not last long. The light became a broader beacon and the noise of pursuit louder: elephantine tramps, monstrous bays, reptilian growls and grunts of fury. The clash of weapons on mail rode on their heels and now the blowing of a forlorn horn sounded again. The pad of frenzied feet on stone echoed in the murk and followed the doomed company, then came the hooting and cheering and chanting of nonsensical phrases from the throats of mindless lizards led by a mad monarch.

From the dim tunnel the fugitives burst, with Fezoul flagging on tired feet. Their nerves were frayed, their energy depleted, but they stopped in a blaze of red light almost too bright to the eyes. It was, as Dereas witnessed: the ambient sum of countless firebrands and distant fires kindled in the upper confines of the cavern. Down below, they reflected the burnt ocher of the vast space they had entered. The cavern was dim by daylight standards; they had just been underground too long, like the beetle that crawls in the dark crevices and is blinded by the contrast of the faintest light that shines on it.

Dereas's grimed jaw sagged at what he saw. A lizard warren that went on forever—a vast underground valley and network of bridges over chasms, aqueducts snaking every which way—a transportation hub of water to every massive tower and fort in sight. An illimitable hive, a veritable metropolis under the mountain!—and all hidden from the world.

As far as the eye could see, only lizards loomed in their leather and their steel, marching on paths of rough, flinted stone to and fro like ants. They came and went from the dozens of towers in the valley up the cavern's flanks. Here, the lizards toiled tenfold compared to the inhabitants of the last cavern.

The company had skirted only the edge of the lizard's depraved world, Dereas realized. He staggered back dumbstruck.

Industrious as insects, the lizard folk had manufactured siege engine after siege engine and weapons of war. They had transported alchemic oils, bones, pastes, powders and liquids vitalized by the magical Vitrin water from all quarters of the cavern. Castles and forts they had built and war machines of Tyrannus bone and iron, while seeding their realm with imp after imp from the lizard's womb. For what evil purpose?

By the dozens Dereas saw pens and cages clustered in cavities and pits below, hundreds of glinting scaly hides and evil glittering eyes. Scores of the enormous lizards were caged there like the seed-bearing monsters they were, perpetuating the lizard race, vast and intimidating.

The lizard king was right! Dereas realized with sad wonder. They were setting the stage for an empire! Equipping an army. How had this menagerie evaded notice so long? Dereas's brain reeled.

More of the castles rose tier on tier up the sides of the cavern. Their gleaming-white towers and carven images of grim deities evoked flashes of past bestial nightmares.

Strange lights and fires flared from the tops of the towers. Parapets gleamed awash in blazing fires. Dereas felt a primal stir in his gut—that a great awakening had begun, as it had been prophesized in the old testaments of Amor-Amon-Reth, overlord of the age of *Saeth*, the Telamon king.

News of the birthing had passed quickly to the other communities evidently. A thousand great fires blazed in unison in celebration of the Rgnadon's birth. Behind the banners and drums and the lizard regalia, a procession emerged from the tunnel the fugitives had just quit. Horns and bugles blared; lizards beat bone femurs on kettle drums of lizard-skin, bashing a dreary, celebratory dirge—an echo of an apocalypse. Lizards garbed in vests and mail padded from all quarters, running, hopping, or crawling on all fours, come to rejoice and join the ghastly marching beat.

The speechless crew looked at each other in hopeless lassitude.

Fezoul's lower lip quivered. "I never imagined the lizard realm was so vast...We thought it was only a rebel's hideout, a few dozen ragged renegades. Now there are thousands! 'Tis Xabren's doing!"

"For what purpose?" murmured Dereas dismally.

"You don't know him," said Fezoul, shivering. "He's obsessed. A spirit possessed of dark impulses. A cursed maniac, and yet—a genius."

"He has really become this 'Lizard King'?" grunted Rusfaer, as if he still couldn't believe such a yarn. "You recognize him of old?"

"As you see," Fezoul affirmed, "whatever there is left to recognize... 'Tis his work, the plotting of decades. Possibly a hundred years," he added with a miserable scowl.

Dereas was so stupefied by the vista that he stood rooted with the others. They were straw men on a doomed mission. Grimly Jhidik prodded Dereas, a signal that the host from the tunnel had emerged and would be bearing down on them before long. They stumbled down a crumbling path that dropped into a steep, veering ravine, where no lizard enemy seemed immediately placed.

"We can't face such a multitude," muttered Hafta. "There are thousands of them down there."

The metallic glints of helm and weapon broke the surface of gloom in the sprawling valley. A jumble of stones and eerie clear pools met the eye.

The band shrank back into the shadows, taking cover behind some stray boulders.

"More to challenge our wits," muttered Dereas with ill-concealed frustration.

Hafta half sagged. "You yourself, dwarf, said that these citizens of yours only numbered in the few hundreds. So where have all these others come from then? Your race couldn't have seeded a whole nation."

Fezoul blinked his eyes in cheerless lethargy. "I have been asleep for nigh a hundred years. How am I to know what has gone on under the mountain in that time? For almost a century that madman has been preparing to amass an empire—and likely about to succeed."

"It looks as if he wants to rule the mountain," said Dereas with a scowl, "and the lands surrounding."

Fezoul murmured, "Xabren always raved about getting revenge on Yutomay and his followers who exiled us to this mountain of doom so many years ago."

Rusfaer pulled at his beard in reflection. "I've heard tales come up from the south of an old slave route operated by a gangster Utred the Bad. He operated out of Xarahom. Certain caravan drivers hauled their slaves, teams of them from the capital, around this wretched mountain to the cities and markets of the west—Tusegard, Marimeath. But it closed down." He fingered his blade. "Many caravans have gone missing over the years. Now it makes sense. 'Tis likely that Utred's caravans and others were waylaid by these roving fiends, that, or ran afoul of the Eakors."

The thought brought a nauseating feeling to Dereas's gut.

Amexi mused, "That, or the half lizards must interbreed with each other like Xabren stated."

Jhidik gave a curt laugh. "What does it matter? They exist nonetheless."

An unsettling horn blared not far away. They pushed on. The path took a precarious descent. All scrambled for sanctuary up a parallel incline, closer to the cavern wall. One of the steep and curving aqueducts was within reach and Dereas hopped over to scale it. The others followed. Dereas helped Jhidik. Amexi lifted Fezoul. The archway, they discovered, was low where the trail joined it—at head height, wrought of crudely-hewn blocks, quarried from the surrounding slope.

Dereas chewed his lip. He saw the aqueduct's source sprang from a series of caves high up like the last cavern, if he craned his neck, perhaps an avenue of escape.

"There are openings yonder," announced Hafta. "Perhaps a way out of this accursed dungeon."

Dereas squinted below. A mire of desolation festered in the stony troughs and dips: salamanders, pools of them, wallowing in mud slime. Who knew what other things bred in those artificial swamps?

Amexi gave a panged groan. A brown stain spread out from a patch four inches below his armpit. The mail was shredded, obviously a lucky jab from a stray poleaxe. He limped along at an even slower pace, much to Dereas's dismay. Grimaces and scowls lingered on his face and he leaned on his sword at every dozen paces or so, signs of a failing constitution.

Rusfaer shook his head in sullen resentment. "Now two of your crew are lamed and likely to hinder our passage."

Dereas stiffened at the comment. He forbore mentioning the grief that Draba had caused.

The Rgnadon suddenly swaggered out of the tunnel, a mammoth brute, sweat glistening on its mottled hide. Its fan of wattled flesh and red spikes bristled about its neck. The lizard king rode behind the hideous collar like some trained champion. The two somewhat smaller lizards, Greta and Kruger, lumbered behind on all fours in obeisance. The long scaly saurians swung necks in rhythm with the stamping fray. A steady stream of followers coursed behind, gnashing, crashing shields, wielding bone tulwars, poleaxes, knives, rocks, any weapon they could get their claws on.

Dereas gaped dumbly. Could the flight of a few humans have merited such an uprising?

No, something else was in the works—something more momentous.

He thought back sourly: the lizard king's words *"Time of the Lizard"*, had stirred the citizens to a frenzy.

Several of the bat-creatures from the chasm had winged their way out of the tunnel and now circled like a swarm of locusts above the lizard pack. Droves of them flew in on suicide angles, swooping to snatch up straggling lizards or those who failed to brandish pikes to protect their heads and flanks. Those inattentive ones were scooped up in fetid arm-wings and whisked back to the creatures' dark holes.

Dereas stared in revulsion. Several of their kind dove too close to the Rgnadon. A long neck shot out and teeth snatched winged killers out of the air, crunching them like flies in green-gummed jaws.

The lizard king pulled back, arching his head in laughing ease. He jumped up and down on a saddle hastily constructed by the looks of it.

Dereas clenched his fists. He loathed the jesting king and that ludicrous scene. A plan was in order, but what? A frustration washed over him that he had never before known. Doom was their mistress if they didn't mastermind a way out of this and escape the madness!

Gripping his brother's shoulder, he appealed to his tuned instincts. Anxiously he motioned to the levels of bridgeworks snaking their way up to the top of the cavern. "There are more of those archways running up to the higher places. Look! They bring the water down to the towers. Perhaps we can latch on to one and hope for less of a reception than when we first ran afoul of these fiends—and hopefully, not cross paths with Pygra?" Even the brief mention of the serpent roused a leer in Rusfaer.

"A risk, brother, but I see your plan." Crouched in the dim shadow of the aqueduct, the chieftain glanced at the dwarf and cast him a repugnant look. "What say you, 'king'? Does Pygra haunt those tunnels?"

Fezoul shook his head, blinking nervously under the cold glare. "I know nothing of the geography and can offer no advice."

Rusfaer shook him like a rag doll. "We expect you to guide us out of here, rat! Look sharp! Hafta, you'd better scout up ahead and warn us of any traps or nasty surprises. Our king is useless."

Fezoul bridled at the treatment. His face was moist with sweat.

The nose-ringed man nodded. "Will do." With a silent gesture, he crawled his way down the waterway and tracked off into the reddish shadows, merging into the broken terrain that masked his ascent. He shambled up a straggling path that branched up the left side of the cavern away from the spillway's dusky arches. Dereas watched while the warrior picked his way higher. The path he trod passed under the shadow of the monstrous, top-heavy fort steeped with seven towers and a central keep. It was of heat-blasted, black-polished stone that was plated with glistening bone—a thousand refulgent ribs of Tyrannus beasts, sporting dozens of spires, as it arched up to the cavern's roof, tier on tier. A menacing sight, Dereas admitted, and none that he would want to breach. It appeared that lizards like those of Xabren's brood inhabited the keep and managed it, though by the looks of the sparsely-manned parapets, most of them were toiling down in the valley.

Dereas's eyes wandered toward the gemmed ceiling. Closer to these treasures than ever before they now were, mid way up the cliff, some hundreds of feet above the tunnel mouth. Huge diamond and hexagonal crystals hung in glistening clusters. When the torches on the towers glinted, they shone weirdly, with a ghostly radiance that created mesmerizing patterns to the eye.

Dereas helped Jhidik and Amexi up the waterway while Rusfaer stormed ahead up the rough-cobbled stone. They looked for signs of Hafta below. Another treacherous patch they climbed before they caught sight of Hafta creeping out of the dimness, his face a grim mask. The boom of drums and the thrum of jabbering voices in lizard tongues echoed far up from the valley.

Hafta was scrabbling back along the rugged flints in a crouching lope with his lungs heaving when he called up from below. "There are a score of them in the tunnel that disappears into the cliff!" His voice trailed off in a strangled hiss. "Armed and dangerous. There's no way we can get past there without a fight."

"Not good," Rusfaer hissed.

Dereas sucked in a breath. "Let's double back and take the next waterway. We can climb the aqueduct the moment it shows a promising angle. It makes for a good place of fording there—" He directed a finger out to a place that ran away from the inimical fort.

Rusfaer ran his thumb along the edge of his blade. "We have few options, brother. I don't like the look of that waterway. It's overly steep and exposed to attack from all sides." He flourished his sword. "Look!" In the distance, tramping feet crunched on flint-flaked pathways and the glints of many torches careened off steel caps and lizards-at-arms bearing iron-tipped clubs.

Dereas frowned. There was no other way around, and he began to regret the path they had taken through the rough, flint-splintered pathways.

He paused and forced himself to think. What to do? Nothing but the chill trickle of water streaming down the aqueduct, room enough for four men to walk abreast—that and the echoing tramp of footfall and drums below and the groans of many beasts. The towers and stone forts yawned below in a haze of smoke and sea of fires. Flint-strewn pathways and rude steps ran through to link the forts. So far they had not been spotted, but their luck could give out at any time. Dereas felt a stab of dread in his bones. They *must* make an escape! Dead men they were if they did not act now.

With grimaces and a sense of purpose, they backtracked, while Hafta, stumbling his way alongside the archway, kept eyes trained on the activity below. Dereas, crouching so as not to be seen, loped in a half-shamble down the old stone waterway. Sometimes he slipped on the slick paves and bashed a knee or scraped his ankle. The others followed, in more or less a similar manner. Fezoul almost fell over the edge, so exhausted was he. If it had not been for Rusfaer's swift hand, catching the edge of his collar, he would have fallen to his doom.

"Careful where you tread, little leprechaun."

Fezoul dusted himself off and masked a petulant scowl.

They had just climbed down a section of spillway when a barbaric cry and stir of commotion rose from below.

Dereas stopped dead. Hafta waited crouching on his haunches.

He scowled fitfully at the raucous scene below. Both their hawk-eyes discerned that the eagle senses of lizard scouts had finally spotted them at last.

Black Balael! He heard the lizard king bark menacing orders at his minions. Armed outriders and warriors advanced in solemn knots. Risking a glance, a cloying fear gripped him—he saw the procession winding up toward the place where they stood, via a twisting path.

Dereas gazed on with sick realization. The meandering route they had taken was not the best choice, nor were the aqueducts that curled deeper into the heart of the largest forts.

"Quick!" he yelled in a harsh voice. He beckoned those who trailed behind him. "Leg it up, or die!"

With awful speed, the fugitives scrambled along the flinty slope toward the crumbling arches of the next aqueduct which would take them higher. About a hundred yards distant it loomed. Directly below lurked a mire of connecting pools, each exuding an unsettling feeling of decay and fetor. They were black as basalt, mirror-smooth, and Dereas saw, like the fateful pool that housed the crab, slick and glistening in a fey light. A ripple broke on a pool and Dereas shivered, for he could swear a proboscis or some strange, blue stalk had broken the surface.

But it caused Dereas a strange conjecture that this is where the priestess Jamuo may have bred and caught her newts which seeded the lizard race.

He struggled ahead, staving off the crawling feeling of impending doom.

He reached the base of the next aqueduct, then began clawing up the rude handholds carved along the edge of the stone archways.

Rusfaer and Hafta were first to pull themselves up the crumbling ramp and gave the two wounded men a hand up. Dereas's fingers gripped a rough cavity and he wormed his way over the lip to lie flat against the stone. A cool runnel of mountain water ran at his side. He pulled the mountain king up at last and they caught their breath and crouched there several seconds, listening to the cool trill of water.

Then they set out on their climb, straddling the chute and wishing for no sudden slips or bone-breaking falls.

Rusfaer's observation rang true. The waterway was steep and vertigo assaulted their senses before long. Weapons lay sheathed in scabbards. They struggled on. What Dereas or any of his companions had not counted on, was the blinding speed of the Rgnadon. It had gained the foot of the aqueduct, and raced alongside it, leaving the others behind, including Greta and Kruger.

Dereas stared in anguish. No sooner had they reached a third of the way up, when the beast's ferocious head loomed ghoulishly in the gloom, blotting out his view, and roaring through a mouthful of snapping teeth. A mottled, clawed limb swatted out—one which Hafta ducked with only inches to spare. He narrowly escaped a split skull. The monster reared again, loosening masonry and sending flakes of rock and dust flying. Its claws raked the crumbling stone to shreds.

"Swiftly!" shouted Dereas. "Get up higher—above its reach!"

The caves were but a desperate dash away. Clawing, grasping, leaving nails split, they scrambled on all fours to get higher, closer to the sanctuaries. The beastslayer's words gave them hope, but words could not make the ascent any less steep or fly them on winged feet. The snorting, raging Rgnadon would not stop its terrible rush on the besieged humans.

Amexi, smitten by a stab of pain, suddenly doubled over and began sliding down the waterway, face first.

Dereas raced to grab him, but his hand closed on empty air. He cursed as the giant lizard swung in, senses fixed in hatred on the beastslayer. Its eyes burned like shady orbs from a midnight sky, murky pools into the depths of nowhere. The blood-riled thing bore down on him, ramming its huge head with mighty, vengeful booms against the aqueduct. The lizard king hung on its back, laughing maniacally.

Dereas sagged. The waterbridge splintered in a thousand places, sending shards spraying down the incline. Before his feet could react, blocks of jagged masonry scattered in all directions, tumbling down the steep rise. Amexi was carried with it.

Dereas cried out a warning. He backtracked with vertigo, struggling to avoid being sucked down by the rumbling wash. He watched, agonized, as Amexi fell groaning, stirring faintly amid a pile of rubble below. The Rgnadon pushed its ugly snout forward to study the Huughite warrior.

The lizard king sat dispassionately on the beast's back, witnessing the commotion with a serenity that was at best icy. He raised his hand in a gesture of authority. "Peace, Lord Rgnadon, Peace!" he croaked in a lizard tongue. The monster paused, before it snapped Amexi in two. The beast herded the quaking warrior closer to the gathering of lizards that streamed in numbers now, to a place where he could not escape.

A gurgling cry of despair slipped from Dereas's lips. Amexi was faced with overwhelming odds and Rusfaer and the others were too far up to help. More of the lizard folk flocked to secure him. Again the Rgnadon focused its angry attention on Dereas who crouched some feet above. He scrambled to his knees, sword swinging loose as he struggled to plow closer to those remaining. The monster's head swiveled in view once again, crowding his horizon.

Dereas gaped. Teeth snapped out at him, a ravening maw ready to swallow him up. Dereas ducked. The sword leaped in his hand. The flashing blade rose and fell in red spray to carve chunks out of the monster's jowl. But still the thing came on—screaming in fury, grinding its slimy, fetid teeth.

Knowing well the after-effect of such an assault on the monster, Dereas ran with a burst of adrenaline up the aqueduct alongside the flowing water. The spillway loomed steeply and appeared almost sheer to his aching muscles. He was only feet from the cave from where the water poured out in a white, frothy stream down the aqueduct, when the saurian swung back beyond the lizard king's control and crashed its head and forelimbs into the arched bridgeworks, making a crumbling ruin of the rude joinings. In a matter of seconds the battered remains of the bridge gave way. The companions, staggering under the shock, made a last ditch effort to jump into the cave. Dereas was last to tumble in a shallow pool, feeling the icy shock of water numbing his limbs.

He staggered out, shaking off the water. He and his companions stood shivering in a large, domed cave with countless geodes which threw multivaried color from walls and ceiling. Rusfaer and Hafta roved about, stumbling, teeth-chattering, intent on investigating the surroundings for traps and foes. The dwarf stared, as if numbed. Dereas hobbled over to the edge of the ruined aqueduct, peering down to see what had become of the blond warrior. But he could make no determination in the ruby-stained shadows below—only a confusion of swarming bodies, thrashing tails and dark hides.

He stumbled back into the cave, withdrawn and resigned. Of them all, Rusfaer seemed the least affected by the loss of Amexi. Water poured from five sources on loftier tiers at the back of this cave. It filled the long pool in which they had fallen, which in turn fed the broken aqueduct. Dereas saw two tunnels running from either side of the cavern. One was lit with Vitrin, the other illuminated by crude torches, smoldering in niches recessed in the wall. The presence of the torches disquieted him because this could only mean lizards. He thought to perceive another smaller, ruder tunnel running back into the mountain, but of this he could not be sure; it was wholly dark and the cavern's eerie creepiness was unnerving him to no end.

It seemed that no foe was about, but that could be illusory. Dereas winced. No sooner had they breathed sighs of relief when the sound of bare, non-human feet on rock came pounding out of the dimness. Two directions showed blurs of movement. Dereas and the others froze. They were sandwiched between enemies.

From either end of the cave, teams of saurians burst out of the shadows—flashing curved tulwars and screaming in their guttural language. Likely they had been patrolling the maze of passageways to the aqueducts and had heard clinking weapons and cracking masonry.

The companions formed a half circle bounded by the edge of the dark pool. Back-to-back they drew their weapons, teeth bared.

Dereas examined his attackers with a hard appraisal. His dark scowl took in the horde of yellow-eyed fiends in a glace. They bobbed and gnashed before them like a colony of angry monkeys. The snarling, swaying rabble might be itching for a fight, but was not ready to commit to an attack. Twenty rank-toothed rovers circled and chittered at them with evident glee. Obviously the lizard king had spread word to the watchers in these caverns, that enemies were on the loose and to keep the passes into the crevasse monitored. A strategic move, Dereas mused in hindsight, however bad it was for them...

A metallic flash glittered in the gloom. A snouted face thrust itself out of the dimness, and the three foot curved blade in Dereas's hand bit into scaly flesh, chopping down to slice a lizard hand off at the wrist. A howl of agony pierced the air and set the mob yelping and charging. The lank lizard hopped around the knots of its enemies, knocking back its fellows as its useless blade crashed to the stone.

Hafta and Rusfaer surged forward and Dereas goaded a storm of attackers into committing with drawn blades. Fezoul clutched his short stiletto in trembling fingers, stabbing right and left in blind jabs. A howl of pain rang out. The dwarf seemed pleased with his first kill. Rusfaer wasted no time in deciding whether he should plunge forth or drop back, concluding that aggression was his best bet while being outnumbered by an inferior enemy. It had saved him once, and would again.

Novices and veterans raged forward to be cut down in a stream of flashing crimson. The intimidating size of Rusfaer had the lizards reeling back in confusion and had won him more fights than he could count. His beard was frothed in blood and his black eyes blazed.

Dereas locked swords with an ugly, green-snouted lizard. He ducked to avoid the slavering jaws and whirled the fiend into two more that tried to flank him. Its flailing tulwar ripped into the closest, slashing out its throat. Dereas kicked the first one out of the cave and the lizard slammed down the crumbling slope of the aqueduct. His blade found the soft center of the third and it died with a wheezing gurgle.

Hafta and Rusfaer worked in grim concert, clearing the first dozen of the rabble that attacked. Dereas's new six assailants pushed him back, those heaving, frothing, green and black-backed terrors, pushing him further toward the pool. He was knee deep in water and Fezoul, the fighter he was not, cowered behind the beastslayer's legs, moaning and striking out feebly with his knife.

Rusfaer gusted a snort of disgust and kneed the mountain king out of the way. He saved the dwarf from a lethal stroke that would have carved him ear to ear. One mighty sweep of his blade and he took out another that would have backstabbed Dereas, his blade jutting from between the shoulders of the dumbstruck lizard. Rusfaer lifted the dying creature off its feet and threw it out into the swirling fray of its enemies. Hafta and Dereas struck side by side, slashing the horde to pieces. It was pure butchery, this hatchwork, a seething riot of barbaric frenzy, but then so was every skirmish, Dereas thought, smashing and staving skulls with instinctive rhythm; the only warrior who was left standing was the one who had not halted his breakneck assault. So had Dereas's father told him from a young age—in the tallow-fumed yurts on quiet nights in winter, or as he had taught him on scores of battlefields on the fringes of the dusky Huughite plains.

Riddled with cuts and bruises, Dereas hobbled about to glare at the corpses floating in the pool. Some twitched, but now all lay dead but a few. Hafta winced from a long surface gash running down his right thigh, but his leather underpadding had saved him from a more serious injury. He was not lamed or lacerated like Jhidik. Rusfaer stood in somber silence, knee-deep in water, a dozen more welts glistening on his blood-dripping legs to add to the dozens already there. Little did this do to diminish his overall wolfish vitality.

Dereas's forearm ached unmercifully. The upthrust blade back in the tunnel had caused him woe, but this was the only major wound he had suffered and something he could manage, though his head still hammered and buzzed from the Rgnadon's pounding on the bridgeworks.

The companions tottered out of the pool back over to where dim light flooded from the cave opening. They caught a glimpse of the lizard king and a host of stragglers below.

To Dereas's distress he saw a group of guards hanging Amexi up on a pole and fitting him behind the king's saddle. It was a morbid standard, a warning not to defy the lizards. While the lizard king had his fill of gloating, the others remained silent as their monarch pointed here and there, motioning his troops to mount assaults from two fronts: one up the broken archway, another around the flanks to a nearby cave mouth looming a hundred feet away. Dereas could see knots of the lizards spreading out like locusts to climb the flinty slope and swarm them from the sides. He wheezed an oath. The Rgnadon had failed to reach the gap only because of the sheerness of the grade and the loose rock underneath its feet that would not permit access.

Seeing his clansman Amexi so misused caused his anger to rise. How he despised the lizard king, lording over his brood and the mindless subjects that ran this evil place of Yarim-Id.

He strode out on what little promontory was left of the waterway and peered grimly at the host, brandishing his sword.

The lizard king caught the movement and he screeched up from his beastly perch. "Come down, man-thing! We will ferret you out of your hole eventually. Nowhere can you go! Pygra will find you eventually. She haunts the water tunnels and will swallow your carcasses at will."

Dereas's shoulders rippled with contempt. "Release our man, lizard, and let us go our way." His fingers curled murderously around the hilt of his cold weapon. "We have no quarrel with you—though we should slit you ear to ear for your abuses on us. Let us call a spade a spade. Let us be at peace—your hurts for ours."

The lizardly voice squealed up in malice. "Never! We will track you forever. We will starve you out, if we must! I will send a hundred of my best warriors up to slaughter you in cold blood. Hundreds more to flush out your rabble. Better to become a lizard now and see the beauty of being a beast, than a lifeless corpse sprawled on the cold stone of Yarim-Id..."

The lizard king jeered and Dereas bellowed, "No chance!" The ghost of a sardonic smile crossed his lips. "We would rather brave Pygra's jaws than be part of your obscene cult!"

The lizard king's twitching shoulders became the beginnings of a wild shrug. "So be it, you stupid fools! As you wish—Mazen! Oraat! Take guard." He slammed his glittering scepter on the lizard's hide. "At my command, lizards-at-arms!" His roar echoed in the smoky valley. "Sound the death alarm! Sound the campaign horns! Send Bazard's squad up to slaughter these stubborn unbelievers!" The king's gaze fixed fiercely on Dereas. His eyes were distended, his face a bestial sneer.

Dereas bit back his revulsion. Every fiber of his being pressed him to spring down and rip out the lizard king's heart. In one springing leap he could do it. He clenched his tulwar, ready to enact a foolish deed...

But Rusfaer held him back. "Careful, brother. I know what you are thinking. 'Tis a foolish intention to rile the lizard unnecessarily. Let him die at the hands of his own monsters. We do not wish to stir the pot any more today, nor for baby lizard either. The creature is crazy for blood and the tide of events is beyond our control. We've survived thus far and will have another chance in the outer tunnels."

Dereas gave a miserable groan. "Tell that to Amexi!" His throat choked with grief.

"Amexi is lost," muttered Rusfaer, "as all of us will be if we do not get out of here fast. 'Tis an open sarcophagus, this cave. More of the creatures will be making their way through these rat holes before long. I can hear them, sniffing and snuffling like the filthy maggots they are. One of these times we will not be so lucky."

Dereas stifled an insult. He knew Rusfaer from long back, knew he was right, and he mouthed a silent curse.

The New Wolves' chief could see the inner battle that Dereas fought, and growled in a harsher tone, "Get hold of yourself! Men are like wheat to the scythe. Let it go. Chaff to the wind, do you not see? When a warrior gets attached to his men, he has already lost the battle. Why waste yourself on one lost sheep when Balael has thrown them into the jowls of beasts?"

Dereas grimaced at his brother's lecture. He felt his self control evaporating. All those nameless warriors, faces, friends, allies, all cut down in senseless heaps. How many more must he bear witness to? Too many lives had gone to feed the dark jaws of the *Saeth*, whisked away on demon wings, a nameless, merciless fate. How often had he seen his men slaughtered and cut down in battle? Even in the bowels of Ahrion's keep, during those many dangerous moments, he had been ready to fling himself into idiotic sacrifice. Jhidik only had saved him from himself.

A tight-lipped snarl sprang from his lips. "Maybe we should be more loyal and attached to our men, Rusfaer. That is the warrior's way. You seem quick to preach such words. If one of your comrades is 'lost', do you turn your back on him for Balael's hounds to chew?"

Rusfaer barked out a short laugh. "Hundreds of men are forsaken every day, little brother. You can rationalize it any way you want. Before you challenge me, don't forget who came back to save your miserable hide when the lizards were gnawing at your heels!"

Dereas snapped back, "I was already free by my own effort. I hardly needed you to nursemaid me. I didn't need you at all."

"Yes, you did!" snarled Rusfaer. "You think you would have made it out of that adders' nest alive?"

Dereas's world went still. His silent restraint and equanimity suddenly dissolved into a blaze of choking anger. "I should kill you for that cavalier arrogance."

It was an ill thing to say and his bile rose again. He clenched his fists and shook his hilt until his knuckles paled in the greenish light. Both warriors faced each other, nerves stretched to the limit. Soon the savage beast would be unleashed in the musty air, a cackling demon.

"Puppy!" Rusfaer cried, snorting and grabbing his brother's arm in a vicious clutch. With a wicked twist of force, he twirled his body, using his shoulders as a brace, and threw Dereas over his shoulder into the pool. The splash echoed through the chamber. Dereas flailed in the water. "Go soak your head in ice before you trade your life so foolishly for someone who's half your worth—and who's already dead."

Dereas leapt out of the water, shaking with anger. A blade was gleaming in his palm, dripping Vitrin, and it soared out, sweeping an arc, clanging against Rusfaer's who strode forth to meet him with a bull-like relish. The blades struck in a thunderous echo. Like dark, possessed demons, the brothers swept back and forth across the murky cave, hacking and stabbing, blades and bodies becoming one in an indistinguishable blur, such as mighty heroes of old. Such was their skill.

The passion for bloodsport burned strong in this chamber of the lizards...and Jhidik and Hafta strove to put an end to their ox-mad skirmish and prevent the two from shredding each other to pieces...But they were repelled.

The pent up rage and horror of the last few days erupted in one blinding rush. It could not keep the two apart. In a torrent of blood they exploded—maelstroms of whirling fire that would not extinguish, but sought to consume everything in its path.

"Peace, you fools," yelled Hafta in his ugliest voice. "You are not the enemy!"

Rusfaer surged sideways. Twisting in an agile crouch, he lashed out in a blistering round house kick at Dereas's head. But Dereas ducked with a howling grunt.

"We are all enemies in this twisted world!" Rusfaer returned with a roar. "'Tis the time of the *Saeth*, remember?"

"Hardly," snorted Dereas, "'Tis the Time of the Lizard, haven't you heard?" The beastslayer slashed a looping cut and his shouts became a sudden brainless peal of laughter, echoing soul-shiveringly in the gloom, raising the hackles on all present.

Jhidik crossed himself with the sign of the free peoples of the north. Hafta stepped back. Fezoul paled, quivering in the grip of fright.

Beast or *Saeth*...It was the dark time of the soul when the primal beast rose once again from the ashes of the damned...back in a dark time of man's past when human hearts and minds became possessed by evil voices that murmured from dead men's mouths. Voices lurking in the soulless beyond, that place which coaxed men to kill each other over a stolen apple or an inappropriate slur, even if such men were bosom kin.

The violent passion was both dreadful and fascinating to witness. An insane moment passed and the air gave way to a weird happening. Or perhaps the gods, even Balael, decided to put an end to the slaughter of two of his favored devotees...

A skulking shape crept up from round the shadowed side of the pool, bone knife in hand. The shape was unnoticed by the fighting men, or even the silent spiders that spun their webs in their shadowy corners. Too transfixed were the warriors by the drama being acted out to see the sinister shape that skittered underfoot. It snuck up and jabbed Rusfaer in the calf. The big warrior leaped back, howling, unnerved as the figure darted out of sight. Rusfaer tripped and lost his balance, giving Dereas time to gain the upper hand, holding the blade menacingly at his throat.

"What the—?" Surprise and rage fouled Rusfaer's sword play. He roared. "The lizard-hearted rogue's out to gut me!"

"Draba!" Dereas hissed.

The beastslayer too was equally taken off guard and saw, out of the corner of his eye, a springing Draba padding on swift feet off to the tunnel's gem-encrusted wall. Draba had again announced his presence. Dereas could not help but stare dumbstruck at the lizard-like face grinning and swaying in the spectral light.

Rusfaer gained his feet, cursing. His weapon was clutched in a seething fist. "How did you make it up here, you sneak?"

But Draba's gaze turned only a shade more whimsical. He seemed to understand, but it was as if human speech were deprived him. Or like an infant, he had not yet developed the knack. His beady eyes darted from man to man and Dereas scowled in indecision. The very fact of his presence implied the mischief maker was much cleverer than he appeared.

Jhidik rounded on the skulker and chased him off up the tunnel. The scaly legs of the fleet-footed Draba were more than a match for the wounded Pirean, who could barely keep up with his steps, swiftly-scurrying over the strewn bodies like a rodent.

Rusfaer massaged his leg where the blade had punctured the skin and drawn blood. "Miserable little beggar. I'll gut him if I get my hands on him. Good riddance! The lizards will either find him up there and put a blade through his heart for being a rebel, or old Pygra will make snake-bait of him."

Jhidik's voice rang from far up the tunnel. "The rotter got away. Come back here, you little squib. I'll carve your hide ear from ear!"

"Let him go, Jhidik," murmured Dereas.

The unsteady tramp of the pursuer's boots grew louder as the flustered Pirean limped back to the tense huddle aside the pool. He scratched his neck. "Can't you see? He was too early out of the egg and needs a father figure. He finds it in you two." He jerked a thumb toward the brothers.

Rusfaer made a dry sound in his throat. Hafta looked away cynically.

Fezoul's croaking murmur rose over the coursing water. "'Tis more complicated than that, I think. The other lizards are not like Draba here who has become some freakish quasi-lizard. Jamuo's black magic has seen to that. It has failed. Draba is still more human than lizard. I suspect this is true because he was released so prematurely from the egg, like the Pirean says. He is confused and doesn't know whether he is a lizard or a human, or both. With the sight of you—" he shrugged uncertainly at Rusfaer and Hafta "—it stirs a memory in him of old times, old hints of his former self."

"A very pretty explanation," grumbled Jhidik.

Hafta complained sourly, "All very intricate and fine, but what does it do for us? He's dead to us."

Dereas was not so sure. 'Dead' hung in the air with such finality...he wondered if the little prankster, wherever he was, had heard all that was said and understood much better than they thought.

The chill voice of reason began to rise in Dereas's head and his heated heart cooled a notch. He muttered entreaties to his wolfish god—"Balael, give me strength or strike me down, if I lose my senses over a little freak..." He turned resolutely to the others. "Let us make use of these wretched corpses—we leave them as an offering of gratitude for our lives. Help me drag them up this tunnel. The lizards will think we fought there and fled up the corpse-strewn passage. Meanwhile we take the other branch."

"A bit of good thinking, little brother," grumbled Rusfaer. His teeth flashed in an air of false camaraderie. "Which tunnel, then, Hafta? The left or right?"

"Either's as good as the other," muttered the warrior. "I think we'd better do it quickly or suffer the worse for it. Also a double bluff. We can take the tunnel with the torches, not the one with the stream. It's the one Draba took and we can hope they deal with the little pest in the meantime. They'll expect us to take the lighted Vitrin-rich route, not the artificially-lit bare tunnel. Hopefully the patrol that came running from there was the last of its kind."

Rusfaer grunted an acknowledgment. Dereas turned impassively to the mountain king. "Fezoul? What do you think?"

The dwarf's lips parted in hesitant reflection. He shrugged and shook the sweat out of his hair. "I think any way is fraught with danger. Pygra will eat us alive, no matter what we do."

Rusfaer gave a sour laugh. "Always a fount of encouragement, aren't you, mountain king?"

"Save it," groaned Dereas. Slapping Jhidik on the back, he motioned. "Time passes. To waste another moment on idle conjecture is useless."

Jhidik grumbled his agreement.

A few quick strides later the beastslayer was dragging a body in each arm up the stream and dumping them up the right-most passage. Rusfaer, Jhidik and Hafta followed his example. Dereas ran up the stream kicking water on the dry parts then backtracked with the intent to turn the scent off them. The ruse, hopefully,would keep the lizards at bay, and keep them safe from enemy clutches for a while. The other, torchlit path they would take, would not be a passage that was known to Pygra. Yet this was perhaps wishful thinking.

The lighted way was littered with hexagonal crystals. Dereas scooped up a couple which had fallen from above. His boots crunched on crystals, pebbles and stray bones. Depressed at the sight, he paused in reflection.

No, it wouldn't hurt...he made a quick note to himself. He stooped and stuffed another handful of stones, particularly spiky amethysts in his pocket. They could come in handy, these weapons. The heavy feel of the rocks in his palm gave him a glimmer of determination and his lips curled in grim resolve.

Nonetheless, a terrible guilt wracked his core as he took the first stumbling steps up the torchlit tunnel.

A sadness seized him, with the thought that he had abandoned his clansman Amexi to a fate worse than death. The violent exchange between him and Rusfaer had left him unnerved and he felt as if he needed to shed some dark energy. What better way than to risk his life for someone else? An infectious obsession with the thought troubled him, this feeling of overextending himself, and he shook off the sentiment in light of Rusfaer's words.

In a sudden impulse, he doubled back the way he had come. "Wait for me up ahead," he grunted, "if I'm not back in ten minutes, leave without me."

Rusfaer blinked in astonishment. "You can't rescue your blond boy from a pack of hyenas. Especially single-handedly. You saw, there's a whole army down there."

"Who said anything about 'rescuing' him?" scoffed Dereas. He twirled his blade, the corners of his mouth twitching.

Rusfaer said nothing, eyes working as if grimly contemplating his brother's words. He grunted in dissatisfaction. Frowning, he gave a great rub to his bearded jaw.

While Dereas slunk back down the treacherous path, his heart lay heavy with the task at hand. But he knew he could not live with himself if he did not at least try to do something for Amexi, even if it meant killing him. Stealthy steps and furtive glances left and right...they had him following the shadowy contours of the rugged, downward slope. Inside the rim of the cliff and down the secret ways toward the valley, he discovered a path winding tortuously down a cavernous defile. After a dozen switchbacks, he came to a stair where a tiny light glowed ahead. Crawling through a small space wide enough to admit a man, he came out on a cramped ledge, overlooking the grim lizard valley below.

On the crumbled stone spread the lizard king's horde, sprawled at a different point than before. He saw the bone-towered fort loomed up perhaps two hundred feet. The great gates were closed; new torches glowed dimly.

The beastslayer peered down with ominous thoughts plaguing him. The lizard king, a hunched mass of grinning lizard flesh, perched on the back of his reptilian destrier. He rallied his supporters with more verve than normal. Cheers greeted his passionate cries in the thousands. The lights suddenly flared on the highest of the fort's towers; then without warning the portcullis began to lift.

Amexi, he saw, was still trussed up on a pole, but was now lowered and staked to the ground. Dereas perceived his companion was still alive but very pale and grimly resigned to his appalling fate. The priestess of the lizard king's inner circle was present, standing fervently beside the bedraggled captive, draped in her pale gold-laced gown, sprinkling potions and fanning a foul blue-purple smoke that rose from the fires of her alchemies.

Dereas ground his teeth; how he hated the sight of that witch! The memory of her tainted rituals and obscene mummery sickened his soul, not to mention the vile newt thrust down Draba's throat. The shamanic fumes contaminated the area. It was a scent which Dereas had always loathed and made him gag even from this height.

He shifted in his restless crouch to an easier position and saw that the lizards had readied a man-sized egg for Amexi to crawl inside. Beside the doomed warrior, the priestess chanted and the mother lizard's eyes grew bright and hard with eager anticipation of receiving a newborn.

Dereas watched two under-priests stroll ceremoniously from a knot of gatherers to carry a chest and vials of more incense and powders. The chest no doubt contained the horrid, live newts.

Dereas stared wild-eyed. Could they be bold enough to perform the rites of inception at this moment? It was insidiously evil!

A murderous scowl contorted his features. He warred with the urge to hurl his sword into the gathering. A useless act. He fingered the amethysts in his pocket, wondering if his aim would be true...

One stone felt unusually smooth in his palm. He brought it back behind his head and took aim. He hurled it, dropping into a crouch. The projectile whirled end over end and missed his comrade's brow by a hair, smashing into one of the under-priest's skulls, bursting it like a melon.

A sea of lizards trained fervid eyes up to stare at the offender. A ripple of anger surged from below.

Dereas felt a stab of dismay. Stupid that he had missed! Now the horde was alerted to his presence and he would not get another chance...

He jumped back, almost slamming into a rigid figure whose muscled contours identified itself as Rusfaer. Whirling, he gripped his blade. The dark figure grinned at him and held out a hand in the dim light. The palm that touched Dereas's shoulder was consoling; in the other lay three more rocks ripe for choosing. Dereas snatched one and knelt to hurl again while the lizards were still hopping about in madness.

The stone ripped through the crowd to strike the leader of the supply caravan, knocking him clear off his feet.

Dereas loosed another which grazed one of the large lizards, the mother, he saw, which started to paw at the earth in fury and toss bellows in the air. The Rgnadon began to stamp restlessly and claw its way up the slope after him.

The lizard king loosed a barrage of maledictions. He struggled to keep the monster in check. A futile effort. Nothing could arrest the thing's breakneck charge up the steep slope. Bucked and heaving, the king waved his scepter up at the speechless rebels in wrath.

There came an answering hail of rocks from below.

Rusfaer ducked, grinning in fiendish mirth. He took close aim with one of his own rocks. The Rgnadon went berserk and broke the neck of an overzealous lizard scrabbling up trying to stop it. At the same instant Rusfaer's stone broke the neck of one of the lizard king's bodyguard. Another struck the priestess, dislocating her shoulder. Her shrieks of pain echoed in the cavern.

The lizard king, flustered by the hitch in his plans, shouted down in distress at his followers. "Kill them!" He barely was hanging onto his ill-tempered mount. "They have wrought violence against the priestess!"

Poor javelin throwers they were...nonetheless, Dereas felt a poignant pride in his work, as did Amexi, whose eyes blazed in wrath and who mouthed cheers from his frothing lips as his fellows risked their lives to spare him the horror of an impending lizard transformation. The clansman's muscles knotted; he blinked back his grief in a tragedy of frustration while the torches flared and fuming clouds billowed. He struggled in his scarecrow perch, thrashing head from side to side. On that pike he still dangled, toes inches from the ground, but still alive. The look on his face indicated he knew that meant certain gestation. Writhing in his bonds, he made every effort to kill himself, grab a knife, spear, any weapon he could, to slit his own throat, but he could not extricate himself from the pole...

The sudden violence had precipitated the lizards to fast-track their rite. While Rusfaer and Dereas ducked back in the caves, pelted from rocks hurled from below, Dereas caught a last, dismal image of his friend being hauled down from the pole, about to have a squirming newt jammed in his mouth and stuffed in that half open egg while the other half was fitted over him.

Dereas's heart quailed. He uttered an unfathomable cry of fury. The bitter tang of failure clotted his throat and tore at his soul. Such horror dulled a man's courage, and with a sickening realization he threw himself up the narrow tunnel. He was hardly able to bear his own guilt trudging those final steps up that torchless tunnel. Rusfaer did not share his brother's chagrin. He tagged behind, his face a taciturn mask. The two brothers shambled on in grim-faced file, up the murky twists in the passage. They staggered into the cave with the gleaming pool, where Dereas's despondent expression and bowed head told his fellows all.

Fezoul, Hafta and Jhidik held steel caps from the dead, filled with Vitrin, that exuded soft glows. A peek past the shattered aqueduct revealed streams of the mountain lizards clambering up the hillside, scouring any cave or opening where they might capture the escaped humans. The lizard king had been thrown from his mount and continued to screech orders at those below. Frantically he gesticulated like a mad zealot. The three beasts were nowhere in sight.

They were coming this way, thought Dereas with dismay. His hammering heart quickened with dread.

Madness! Utter madness! How could they escape this cursed mountain? Now the sounds of something evil smashing its way through the narrowed tunnel down the shadowy way to the left alerted him to a new terror. It was a hellion that hurled lizard-guards every which way. Dereas saw a flash of claws and a black snout poking its way through the shadowed gap in the corridor. The thing was dismantling the exit as if it were made of soft wax.

On all fours the men scrambled to round a bend up the opposite tunnel while the guttering torches on the walls flared to either side behind them. They had no knowledge of what was happening back in those thick walls of crumbling rock, but it sounded as if the whole reptile clan were hard on their heels. Greta, Kruger and the new young master likely revelled in their new found freedom rather than playing obeisance to a mad king.

The fugitives sped on fast and furious, leaving the sounds of the scraping claws and rending teeth behind. They would be safe in the smaller tunnel. Whether the saurians would lay teeth, snout and thews to the current tunnel, or find larger ones to support their size was not certain. Those awful guardians would be breaking down the nearby mantle of rock soon.

8: Tutraken

In the vaulting caverns of Saeth's mountain,
Dark things dream,
And die,
Passing into the mist of ages,
In abysses of doom...

—*Song of the Witcher*

It was not long before the fugitives realized that they were hopelessly lost. The tunnel had ended in a wall of crude, stone blocks, hung with glittering torches. They had stood staring, lungs heaving. In the center, at foot level, gaped a narrow square gap, cut through eight feet of stone, wide enough for a man to slip by. The opening was flanked with squat lizard statues with teeth bared. Half-chewed rodent bones lay littered about the chamber and dice carved of bone and iron chips lay strewn about, looking as if a game had recently been interrupted.

Hafta had torn one of the longest torches down from the wall and they had crawled through the gap. Obviously it was a checkpoint guarded by the troupe that had died at their swords not long ago. The stone blocks were similar to those they squeezed past upon entering Vharad, and Dereas could only assume the wall had been constructed by the lizards to keep the snake out.

Now the last guttering torchlights had faded from sight behind them and they were panting with exhaustion. They still guarded ample light, what with their Vitrin-filled helms. But no creek flowed through this new tunnel and they had claim to no water supply or ambient luminosity. Fezoul denied having any recollection of this murky passage or any part of this network of caves. To dampen their spirits further, they often heard dim echoes of a great bulk being dragged across slippery stone, or the great hissing weight of some leviathan glaring pensively from the mouth of an eerie junction or crumbling cross tunnel.

Shudders went up among the haggard men and sullen grunts grew to hostile jostles and insults.

Where the main path would split or show multiple pathways, the company would hear rattling rocks or blocks being scraped across stone, the fervor of a scale-crusted reptile surging through a dim passage.

The men retreated into their own private places of terror. The perverseness of the disturbances pointed to only one source—Pygra, and served to raise all of Fezoul's fears. "We are the forsaken children of dead Xatu!" he cried. He trembled like a leaf in the wind, stumbled on pained feet, in the forefront with Hafta, tugging at Dereas's hem like a frightened maid. Perhaps he was recalling the grim fate he would have met at Draba's cravenly hand. As it was, he was keen on keeping the distance between himself and the snake at maximum distance, with warriors behind and in front. All the while, the companions noticed they kept on a slight grade, going up.

The wanderers took to the less spacious tunnels, hoping this would deter the slithering menace that most surely stalked them. But this was not always possible, and the semi-wide to wide tunnel that yawned before them was not reassuring.

"How long to get free of this wretched mountain?" growled Rusfaer.

"I don't know," the mewling king stammered. "These tunnels are unfamiliar to me. Doom awaits us. We are all doomed!" he moaned.

"Oh, doomed is it, again?" Rusfaer snarled, raising his palm to backhand the king. He threw his hand down in disgust. "You're a hopeless case." Bitterness edged his voice.

"Doomed, I say!" maundered on Fezoul. "The snake knows I am loose—the last citizen of Yarim-Id." His words trailed off to a murmur. "The fabled Xatu, our lost city, cries out for salvation. Can you not hear the voices of our people's ghosts? The slithering of the fiend's passage? I can feel it in my bones. We are all doomed!"

"Shut up, you spineless hound," warned Jhidik. "Your whickering grates on my nerves."

"And 'tis a devil of a bore," affirmed Hafta.

The king paid no heed and Rusfaer grabbed him around the head and muzzled him tight against his chest that he might not alert the snake, or any other frightful creature that had ears for his yammering. Dereas cringed at the snuffles of Fezoul's hate through Rusfaer's foul, tattered wolf's-hide during those moments and his whimpering and sobs knew no end. Rusfaer ignored this dull tumult and wiped the dwarf's protests from his mind, forging ahead with fierce steps, his other free hand gripping his weapon.

As always, at a split in the tunnel, they halted, distrustful of the yawning gap rich with dank vapors and the spoor of serpent. "Which way now?" Rusfaer grumbled. He released the king none too kindly.

The dwarf shrank back, gasping, gibbering, saying he did not particularly know or care.

Rusfaer's black mood erupted in a snarl. "Think, dwarf, think!" he cried venomously, shaking him like a dog would a lemming.

"I can't think when you are shaking me like a rabid wolf!"

"Never mind! Our lives depend on this," muttered Dereas grimly.

Fezoul wore his misery badly. He wet his lips and quivered, a wash of fear plainly clouding his reason. "We can't go back. Lizards patrol, they lurk everywhere, and snakes...snakes and lizards. Oh, the nests are too close."

"What nests?" growled Rusfaer.

"The Eakors! They will pick us up like flies."

"Oh, are we back to Eakors?"

The New Wolves' chief scowled and exchanged meaningful glances with Dereas.

The dwarf's lips were peeled back, showing blackened gums. His eyes glowed with an unwholesome fervor.

Dereas thought dehydration might be the cause of Fezoul's malaise. The dwarf had become somewhat delirious.

"Your Eakors are old news, dwarf," exclaimed Rusfaer harshly. "Have you any new news to share?"

Fezoul lisped in a toneless voice, albeit one a tad eerie, "Lizards everywhere, lizards and snakes, snakes and lizards." He repeated the words in a mumbling monotone.

"He's mad!" declared Rusfaer.

The mountain king looked around him, his eyes darting with crazed mirth. He looked up and down the dim tunnel for any hint of shadows that looked like ghosts or serpents. "The only way out of here is up," he cried. "Up, up, you lizard beaters! Up and up! The mountain only goes up!"

Dereas and Rusfaer looked at each other in frowning confusion and muttered curses under their breath. Fezoul did a little jig, with elbows flared. Spinning on his sandaled heel, he laughed gleefully while Dereas threw his hands up in defeat.

The mountain king had stripped himself of his amulet and with a wild look in his eye, spun it round on its cord like a playtoy. Dereas thought: he was hopeless, a detriment to their mission.

The tunnel narrowed and the walls closed in on them like the mouth of a serpent itself. The passage flanks bore overtones suggestive of bestial snouts, ears, jaws and claws—demonic slab-sided torsos jutted out at them in odd juxtaposition; they all imagined such teeth and snouts craning out of the shadows to maul them. It made for slow progress and Hafta's torch had all but burned down to a stub, leaving them in near darkness. Jhidik had dropped his steel cap long ago, locked in a futile fight with Hafta. Stumbling on in his limping condition, the Pirean was ill-equipped to carry Fezoul's helm-lamp, which left Dereas's and the mountain king's lights to guide the group. That in itself made for a feeble illumination.

A sudden thrumming had Dereas starting in his tracks.

Tiny feet? A patter of padding feet?

The sound came from a fox-sized hole directly ahead of them where the wall joined the floor.

The others ground to an anxious halt. A sudden squeaking clamor had them jerking in panic. Burly shapes, a whole horde of them, burst suddenly out at them like a nest of weasels.

Hafta crabbed back in fright.

Rats! A fervid lot of them, whitish in color, each as large as a possum—spooked by the company's footfall.

The vermin teemed in one whirling frantic mass, scampering and racing underfoot like frenzied gremlins in a mad heat.

Rusfaer, nerves taut, stabbed out at them. He speared a swagbelly. Jhidik, mortally afraid of large rodents, swatted with the broad side of his blade. He sprang back in revulsion as he slashed ferociously, crushing two more underfoot with his hobnailed boots.

The rats skittered down the tunnel, stampeding in a swarming throng. Their clicking claws diminished and the shrill din with it.

The company listened, breath heaving in their chests. No sounds of pursuit, from lizards or serpent, only the distant pad of squeaking rats.

The companions gathered their senses. They were so weak from hunger that they were wobbling on their feet. True, they had picked and eaten tufts of the leafy, dark green *arizoi* plant that grew from cracks in the tunnel walls, but this was meager fare and certainly not enough to feed grown men. Dereas feared that being famished to the bone and suffering the privation they had, would bring them to the point of collapse.

In a fit of frustration, Hafta beat the torch on the ground to burn the hide of a limp, mangled rodent. As it sizzled, the smell of roasting flesh had the men's mouths watering. He grabbed the creature impulsively by the tail and started to toast it over his torch. The others gazed dreamy-eyed at the roasting rodent, licking their lips with longing. And yet, in no time they were taking turns braising meat on their own swords. There were three rats to a man: unpalatable fare, but in their ravenous condition these hunks of coarse gristle went down their gullets in well-needed, grimacing gulps.

They set their backs to the wall, legs outstretched, chewing their rubbery fare, skewered on swords with a certain, subdued satisfaction.

Rusfaer, in between gulps, jocularly suggested they go back and fry some of the lizard hides gutted back at the geode cavern.

The joke did not go far. Dereas in his musings, pondered over the possibility that this very instant, the lizard corpses were part of Pygra's own diet. He shuddered, thrusting the thought aside as he glared at his half-finished rat, which he tossed aside now, his appetite suddenly dulled.

Lulled by meat and the warm glow of a hunger momentarily sated, they lay down in mutual exhaustion, unable to keep the weariness out of their bones any longer, with Rusfaer muttering grudgingly he'd keep first watch.

An unknown time later, Dereas jerked awake, startled by an unfamiliar sound. A sudden, shadowy shape ripped through their company, snapping at their shins and poking at them with a shiny blade. The figure was like a shiver of wind—curses and reptilian chitters filled the air. Dereas scrabbled to his knees, jerked off his feet. Snatching for his sword, he groped for balance. But the blade came not quick enough and the shape bolted under his knees, upending his and Fezoul's cap of Vitrin, plunging them all in near darkness.

There was a tangle of legs and a waving of arms. The half-eaten rat that Rusfaer had been gnawing prior to dozing off was ripped out of his ham fingers. The big warrior lurched to his feet, stumbling and cursing a sulfurous oath. The hellion sped on down the tunnel, leaving a dusty cloud and torch smoke in their faces, as if it had never been.

Dereas sat for long seconds in a wretched silence. A chill ran down his spine as a childish reptilian laugh echoed back through the murky tunnel.

The hand of Draba was in all this harum-scarum roguery.

"That little spook," hissed Jhidik through his yawns, waving a fist. "I'll lay the rotter full of good iron when he comes nipping at our heels again!"

"You will, will you?" Rusfaer gusted, venting a derisive snort. "You have to catch the weasel first. He's a lot faster than you think."

"Faster than a speeding lizard," Dereas jested.

The Pirean snorted, "My patience is long wearing thin."

Rusfaer shrugged and croaked out a laugh. "You'll need more than 'patience' with that pesky sneak."

Needless to say, it was less than humorous to be left in the pitch dark with a horror that was Pygra lurking about. Dereas groped his way through the sudden blackness, tapping with his sword. The others stumbled about on their hands and knees, grunting like hogs in a lightless pen.

Now without light and confined to a steep, stone-littered tunnel with nothing but rats and a mischievous trickster haunting their every step, they were like old men tapping blades like canes.

With appalling suddenness, a familiar serpentish slithering echoed from a distant tunnel. Dereas held his breath. It was a hair-raising sliding of slimy coils on rock—from far back down the way they had come. He felt a slimy tingle to his skin and the air freeze in his chest. Ironically, it came from the place that Draba had disappeared into.

The sounds of the snake ramming its massive beak on stone should have been familiar to them by now, but not the childish reptilian chittering and eldritch laughter that rose above the tumult. It was like something out of a dark dream and Dereas's face creased in an ugly grimace. He swore it was as if the lizard boy had lodged himself in a crevice and was actually *goading* the snake.

He crouched in the murk, his teeth bared in disbelief. How could the imp have managed to survive such an encounter? Or even conceive of such a ploy, if such it were, to bait the serpent? It was madness!

As if reading his brother's mind, Rusfaer muttered an uneasy curse. "How I hate the murk and the march into sheer gloom. Quietly now. Let the imp get himself mauled by the snake. 'Tis not our time to die."

Dereas stared into the inky spaces idly, his jaw loosening. "Not our time to die," he echoed mechanically. Lips peeled back, he pulled the mountain king out of his frightful crouch and bunted him forward, a frail figure whose tongue seemed to have frozen to his palate.

"Your little bogeyman is a menace," hissed Fezoul.

Dereas waved a weary hand. "'Twas your rebel's priestess's sorcery that made him so."

"Aye, turned him into a ghoul," growled Hafta without warmth.

The mountain king shrank back in his grimy robe, having no reply to offer that sullen group.

They felt their way along the rough tunnel walls, crawling on all fours like blind moles. Slowly and silently they arched a path away from the wretched tumult. So far no surprises or screeching rats had caught them unawares.

The moments passed in a progression of painful gropings and stumblings and their parched lips and aching muscles grew.

For how long had they crawled? Dereas squinted straight ahead into empty blackness. He shook his head in utter weariness. He rubbed his eyes in surrender. Not many times in his life could he count a hundred, dread thoughts swarming in at once. He felt a man on the rack, his fingers scored on rough stone and shale, his palms raw from supporting his sagging weight. The others too were haggard and disheartened, knees bruised, faces blackened with grime and filth, creeping on through the pitch black tunnel in wretched single file with the echoing fright of a serpentine thing haunting them jowl to toe. Lizardish drums had begun to thump, distant and booming, adding to their crawling fear. Such thuds heralded the fresh beat of the 'Time of the Lizard', thought Dereas. Even the acres of surrounding rock could not contain it. Like the throb of doom, it rose and fell, each cadence terrorizing their souls and chilling their blood.

Their only grace was that the tunnel was too narrow for the bloodthirsty serpent to slip through, but it was no joy to crawl on all fours through its endless drift without light, and with only a dreadful watchfulness that seeped from the crannies, following them on closely guarded heels like a salivating phantom.

Whether little Draba still lived to walk away from the trap the snake sprung for him was debatable. Perhaps his horseplay had finally caught up with him. Who was to know in that weird, soulless place? What foul god had manufactured this sinister warren? thought Dereas. Mazoma? That Draba had made it his playground, despite the horror of the snake, boggled his imagination. It was clear his new lizard-honed eyes were uncannily sharp and could flesh out the patter of a scarab beetle in the murk and make a wolf's gaze into the moonlight look like the blind starings of a bull ox.

The men of Dereas's company still wished to live, unlike Draba, not die tangled in the coils of an abysmal snake...

Aching and stiff, the wanderers took weary turns leading their way through the stifling murk, feeling damp stone ahead, hoping that nothing untoward would leap out at them and tear them to bits. But the wish was somewhat naive, considering the violence of the past, and even then, the swish of something sinister surprised Jhidik who jerked back in grunting confusion as a rock spider scuttled across his trembling hand.

The Pirean cringed and vowed that if he ever got out of this burrow, he would squash lizards like bugs. But such were the sputters of fools, thought Dereas and he shivered at the thought of facing those repulsive halfbreeds ever again, nor did he ever want to see the open maw of the thing they called 'the Rgnadon'.

Dereas felt increasingly cramped and stifled in this rats' den. At times he felt his head fogged like a harbor ghost-misted at dawn. He cursed the closeness of the air which was too rank for his liking and he cringed at the thought of crawling days on end through this sunless labyrinth, driven mad by starvation and terror.

Even so, he sensed Pygra's breath ever at his heels.

It was something he felt rather than knew, for his instincts were sharp, as a Bosselian lynx, its blood pulsing in a timeless hunt for prey. His broad shoulders twitched under the threat of butchery that could erupt at any moment. He could almost hear the sounds of rending flesh and snapping bones, nay the gong of fate of slaughter, booming at his feet, groping for his throat and tearing out flesh and sinew. He could hear his brother grunting ahead of him, like a fretting sow. He smelt the sour-sweet reek of the mountain king's sweat pouring from his skin. Deliriously, the dwarf scrambled on, struggling to stay abreast of the others—a large part of him wished not to stray an inch from a human body in this den of horrors.

At last, a faint glow finally winked out of the murk that stretched like an unending blanket into the distance. The glimmer of light radiated from a high place overhead—a square patch, like the casemented bars of a high prison wall.

In a spurt of hope, Dereas and the others crawled up through the last stretch of tunnel, nursing scraped knees and bashed shins. Their scrabble was like that of men lost in the desert wastes who see a mirage in the hazed distance of a well and crab toward it in hope of slaking their thirst.

The musical tinkling of water came to their ears—a sound rich and cool and refreshing in this world of forbidding stone and drafts. Dereas poked his head through and saw they could crawl into a dim chamber. It was lit bluish-green and rich with a modest waterfall that fell foaming from a height of thirty feet to empty into a small dark oval pool, black as pitch, in the bowl-like hollow below.

Down the slick rock they scaled their way—with shaking feet, searching for footholds and plunging trembling fingers into wet niches to crouch on a bare spot on the ground where they lay in heavy silence for a long while.

Their musings were like the reverie of gods, who breathe dreamlike thoughts.

They seemed to have found some oasis in a hostile world, a reprieve gifted by the hand of a merciful god.

After a time, the company stooped at the water's edge and

quenched their thirst, washing away the grime from their faces and bloody limbs. Dereas blinked—after rising from the pool and walking on numb feet over to the waterfall, he scowled at two grotesque statues carved of solid stone straddling either side of the plume of water. They were carved in the likeness of 'bird men'—disturbing, squat, anthropomorphic figures, no larger than a man himself, gripping serpent-twined staves of omen, wearing grim, primitive faces. Their goblin-like wings were tucked in at the back, like seraphims from a violent time of the past.

Rusfaer, hunching at his brother's shoulder, grunted in the ghost light and was the first to speak, "Here's a lovely pair of shrews, if I've ever seen any. More grotesque things to haunt our dreams?" He winced through his teeth.

Fezoul smoothed the flaxen locks on his sweaty scalp and gestured in bemused fascination. "They were carved an age ago, these effigies, I suspect. Guardians. Etched from the oldest stone of Yarim-Id itself."

"The trail ends here," muttered Jhidik indifferently.

"We've never come to a dead end before," announced Hafta, "especially one this intricate. 'Tis odd."

"What isn't odd in this hellish place?"

Hafta clucked in a rasping tone:"Let's search this grim burrow. There's no time to dawdle. The lizards are coming. Can't you hear their wretched, booming drums behind us?"

"Yes, Hafta, we all hear it," growled Rusfaer. "If it's our time to die, then let us die. I will stand and fight, make no mistake." He hefted his heavy sword, letting it glint with green fire aside the frog-colored glare of the rushing water.

Dereas snorted at his brother's contradictory and brainless chivalry. "Foolhardy to die when we can use our wits to live, brother."

The uncanny glow of the water continued to bathe the chamber in its unearthly radiance. It was a source of fascination for the men, whose falling sheets illuminated the slabs of slanted rock around them in a ghostly grandeur.

They all examined each other and their surroundings with nervous fatigue, and not without a flicker of brief distrust and a certain distaste, avoiding the pool, not knowing what creature or creatures lived there.

It was a wise move. For the horrors of Yarim-Id pounced with singular and furious purpose. The high place from where the water fell was difficult to access, Dereas saw, because of its steepness, thus not a practical target. Above the cave mouth from where they had entered, loomed sheer rock carved in a myriad, evil faces not dissimilar to the ones that gazed forth from the grim guardians. The place from where the water issued was barely large enough to admit a man.

"No joy there," Dereas grumbled pensively.

"There must be a way," murmured Hafta. "We can't sit here idly!"

"Don't get your breeches in a knot!" chided Rusfaer. "We have enough troubles as it is, without you and our mountain king lifting your skirts at the slightest sound of a wood mouse or beetle."

Hafta bridled at the comment and mumbled a half-strangled oath.

Fezoul stared at the carven statues and his memory seemed suddenly jogged by a tremor of the past. He stroked his round face and fiddled with his sleeve. "I remember, once—there was a legend told by our mystics, of a 'hidden way'—a mist-veiled universe in itself—a portal to the damned, some passage behind the 'Falling Curtain'."

"What brings this high myth to your fanciful mind?" sneered Rusfaer.

"'Twas told by our earliest explorers," explained Fezoul. "'Twas passed on by philosophers and bards of generations of repute. This 'falling curtain' most certainly means this waterfall."

"How so?" grunted Rusfaer. "Seems an awful stretch to me."

"You have not heard all," exclaimed Fezoul. "The legend spoke of half birds and men, statues that would one day mark the portal to nevermore."

"All very nice," remarked Dereas, "but your portal to 'nevermore' seems a very vague fable and smacks of a mummer's whispers... How does that help us now? I see no 'portal' or hidden universe, only a gleaming roil of frothing water."

"'Tisn't babble, Beastslayer, but the words of the old ones, their counsel," retorted the mountain king. "The legends were always honored by the skalds, whose visionary depth disguised profound truth in their poems and riddles."

Rusfaer grunted in skepticism. Sheathing his sword, he blustered, "Well then, mountain king, let us see—" A few nimble strides had him straddling the nearest bird-man's stony lap. With shoulder braced in the crook of its thick, bull neck, he jammed his sword backhandedly through the water.

There was no answering clank of metal on stone.

Rusfaer grunted. The gathered men blinked in puzzlement.

Hafta blundered up to perch ox-like alongside his glowering chief. He tested the waters with his own weapon and the blade passed through the rushing water, with again no answering clink of rock. The two exchanged quizzical glances and eyed the strange rush of water through narrowed lids. Hafta, with a cheerful salute, took a daring leap through the icy water, his body swallowed in a wash of greenish foam.

Dereas stood jaw agape. He counted the seconds pass.

Reflecting. Perhaps Hafta alone had dared plunge clean through the other side, because of over-impatience, to be away from the brooding crypts and endless tunnels and the grim echo of lizard drums. He did not emerge for a time and Dereas began to worry for his life. He hopped across the narrowest neck of the pool to mount the sinister bird-man's twin on the other side of the falls, which crouched repugnantly. He stared back at Rusfaer. The brothers brooded with conflicting emotions. Both felt insignificantly impotent and bewildered and Dereas felt naked under the somber gaze of those bloodless statues.

Dereas twitched, readjusted his grip on the muscular-ribbed shoulders of the gargoyle. Just as he was about to plunge in after Hafta, the New Wolves' henchman staggered out, a sodden heap of dripping muscle. He crouched at the feet of Rusfaer's guardian, his long tulwar clenched in a white fist, wearing a massive grin on his hardy face.

"There is a tunnel. You wouldn't believe it!" he gasped. "Blackness, and cavernous echoes, but straight and dry. Hurry! You must see for yourselves." The warrior's matted locks bounced and coiled on his shoulders and his dripping mail and overcloak made him look like a bear-man, thought Dereas.

Hafta plunged his frame back in, and after a brief pause, they all took their turns, including Fezoul, deciding to brave the tumbling froth. And so, they left the somber bird-men behind.

The beastslayer's first sensation was a pricking chill as he dropped down several feet into a shallow depression. The initial shock of the icy water raining on his skull almost stopped his heart, but he shook out the water and stumbled on, banging into Rusfaer who hunched nearby and erupted into a spate of curses.

The tunnel was narrow and the fugitives were forced to crouch, familiarizing themselves with the perimeter of the passage. A dank, earthy smell permeated the cramped confines. Yet an eerie greenish glow illuminated the bare walls and the uncluttered confines, compliments of the Vitrin stream that ran lightly up the middle. Far ahead another rude opening emitted a wan light, perhaps a hundred yards distant. They clambered to reach it, their dripping weapons brandished and their boots sloshing on the puddles in the wet stone.

Fezoul stumbled on shaky feet, teeth-chattering and moaning in a familiar malaise, but they ignored it. The melodic rush of the falls behind them faded to a dull murmur as they stumbled toward the faint watery glow.

Hafta was first to burst through the opening. The others crowded at his heels and pressing at his back out the end of the tunnel, they halted, spellbound. Below, lay an awesome, unexpected sight—a sepulchral place, huge beyond imagining, haunting and desolate...

Rusfaer in his foul eagerness, almost fell off the precipice that yawned at his feet. Rocks, pebbles and flakes of shale crumbled under his weight and tumbled down into a never-ending abyss. He caught himself in time, and extended his flailing arms only to be pulled back by his startled but alert companions. They all stood dumbfounded at the edge of an empty, lost world.

Far down in the depths below, dropped a blue-black chasm. Gulfs of shadow spread endlessly from right to left. About a hundred yards across the fissure they stared at another rock cliff that wound up into the inky darkness, like some towering tomb. A pale light fell from above, from a source unknown. At their backs reared another parallel cliff, rising into gloom untold.

They sensed ancient death in this world, a forgotten primordial place, dreary and somber, imbued with an ancient silence as thick as the dust of ages. A mountain within a mountain, marveled Dereas, and he stared frozen-mouthed for long seconds, from ledge to far wall in a haze of incomprehension—in the inner sanctum of Vharad they stood, at the edge of a mystical, inner peak.

Blue-black shadows dominated the vast, open, airy space that ruled this kingdom. The purl of greenish water lulled their senses. For behind them, on the ancient rock face, the opening from which they had emerged, was flanked by huge, carven bird-men of similar configuration as those in the last chamber. These figures were ten-fold their mass though and allowed the mountain waters far above to pass between their legs in hallowed blessing, none other than the purling source of the glow they had glimpsed in the tunnel. At the statues' stone-clawed feet wound a narrow, chalky ledge, three-men-wide, tracing a slow, rising arc around the rim of the inner mountain which split at several junctions to disappear into the yawning stone cliff at various intervals. Each junction possessed a gaping cave eerier than any they had seen thus far.

Rusfaer was the first to murmur, "At least the lizards won't be able to stalk us in here..." His words trailed off in a cavernous echo, lost in the open gulfs. He looked awestricken, yet half-relieved, and trying without success to stifle the vertigo he felt, looking down into that bottomless drop.

"Nor can that pesky cur, Draba, track us here," remarked Hafta.

Dereas wiped the river of sweat from his brow, his face crinkling in a mirthless knot. He was weary and uneasy and his mouth was set in a somber twist. "I wish I could believe it. Seems wishful thinking to me."

Rusfaer grunted. Jhidik's eyes glazed and remained trained on the way ahead. "Methinks there's nowhere to go but up."

"Where else?" grunted Rusfaer. "We have lizards and serpents at our backs and rogues and rats weave in between."

Fezoul started at the mention of serpents, gazing fitfully at the descending path that curled around the cliff. Rusfaer caught the expression of anxiety on the dwarf's face and barked out a wolfish laugh, "What gives, mountain lord? Would you rather take the low road?" He waved his sword in mocking display to the slick, wet path where Fezoul's eyes had been goggling so long, the place that wound down forebodingly in the other direction, a grim passage of darkness.

Fezoul opened his mouth, but closed it again. He seemed stirred by a vague thought that brewed there. It was as if he knew something was wrong and he tried to cover it up—with awkward apprehension and wringing of wrists and darting of shifty eyes.

"Well," barked Rusfaer, "out with it, you leprechaun! Like it or not, we are well used to your secrets by now."

Fezoul, plainly offended, remained clam-lipped. Rusfaer grunted resentfully and they threaded their way up the dusty path, casting disquieted glances at the gloomy caves that yawned unnervingly to the side.

The strained silence grew to anxious sighs and grunts among the company—and clearly, Rusfaer's glowering resentment fell fully on Fezoul and his batch of endless secrets and reticences—until finally Fezoul burst out in a gurgling rush: "If you must know, our first explorers stumbled across this realm generations ago! We knew it was obvious other proto-humans inhabited the mountain before us. We found their bones in nearby tunnels and their artifacts."

"When was this?" inquired Dereas.

"Within the first year of our landing here. I have not personally verified it, or visited this place before, but I know of it—'tis *Tutraken*. So it was called of old. 'Twas ages before that an older people lived here—after the great flood, when the world was young. They died out, perished for reasons we do not know. 'Twas they who built the strange statues, the bird-men, so to say—in their own image."

Rusfaer's brows bristled in derision. "What brings you to this conclusion? How do you know?"

"We know because it's a simple matter of logic and tradition since our witcher—"

"Hey, how'd you like that, Hafta?" Rusfaer interrupted with a harsh laugh. He tapped his henchman on the shoulder with the flat of his blade. Down the trail he sauntered and postured rudely before the glowering megaliths with sword a-swing. "How'd you like being one of these monkeys with wings?"

Fezoul grew hot under the collar. "Do not mock the gods of Yarim-Id," he warned.

"Oh, are they gods of Yarim-Id now?" Rusfaer guffawed harshly. "And a moralist among our crew? You are a repetitious mule, sir mountain lord. You picked the wrong company for that—" and he heaved a gust of sour distaste. With visible contempt, he stalked up the path, twanging his sword on the cliff wall, as if to wake the 'gods' that Fezoul so secretly revered.

Dereas pulled at the wet haft of fabric that tugged umercifully at his neck. The echoes of Rusfaer's tumult could be heard for bowshots and alert whatever horror might be listening in the immeasurable spaces. He and Jhidik and Hafta made fretful steps to catch up to the New Wolves' chief to stop him. Fezoul fell in behind.

A strained scowl crossed Dereas's brooding face. What was this strange, solemn world of the past? It was awful, mysterious, likewise, guarding secrets untold. In the dusky blue shadows tumbling down in the immeasurable distance lurked a hollow silence that was unnerving, like the moldering emptiness of a lost, forsaken, tomb.

This dim world of the past was not to his liking, and it brought an ache of melancholy to Dereas's heart.

Balael but he wanted out of here! Into the world of the sun!...

With images of sunlit vistas crawling before his mind, Dereas truly thought he could see slits of sunlight shafting from far, far up the cliff, similar to the vents that powered the Luminon, but he could not be sure. A hallucination of the mind likely, or some trick of the imagination from being confined so long in these lightless tunnels.

While these speculations went on, the familiar *thrum, boom, thrum, thrum, boom* came throbbing in distant menace.

The sound was repeated, in triplets. The companions listened aghast. Far down under the rock they had just traversed came the haunting, echoing rhythm of doom—Dereas breathed and shrank into his cocoon, scrunching deeper within his torn cloak and ringed mail.

Jerking his head about, he put a knuckled, heavy hand on an ear. Was it the snake he heard pounding through feet of rock, or was it the advance of the lizards?

Dereas tried to squeeze the impossible from his mind. But could not. That the serpent Pygra could squash her impossible girth through a crevice half her size, was unthinkable. And yet, he had heard that reptiles could suck in their breath and compress their whole body down to the size of a wormlike thread, to capture the smallest rodent, and squeeze through the smallest burrows.

Wives' tales! Dereas complained to himself...Or was it the wretched drums of the lizards that flaunted their progress of dominion, and their vengeful intent to convert them all to lizards?

He gave an involuntary shiver. Perhaps neither—for also lingered the mental image of some other unimaginable horror that perhaps watched them in this sepulchral world of ancient recollection.

9: Death in Accursed Tutraken

On silent feet, death stalks,
Like a chill draft,
Seeping through dusky passages...
O' daughter of the night, listen you!
For none escape the claws of Saeth's children!

— 'Rhyme of Saeth's Children', poet of old Tuyokton...

The ancient ledge was carved by a lost race out of time—hewn by the same people who had crafted the ageless, winged ones that brooded below in their stony hours of dreams. All wondered of their making, even Rusfaer, who was not much of a historian.

Up the narrow trail they trudged on a slight grade that had them breathing sharply and wiping cold sweat from their brows. The path wound inexorably around the timeworn cliff, like some coil of a primordial serpent. Deep in their hearts, they knew that they were high above the lizard kingdom of mad Xabren, the somber realm of his diseased sorcery.

And still, their feet trudged with heavy purpose. Each knew he faced a senseless, futile race against death, one likely he would lose. The barest of drives kept them stumbling on, pure survival the goal, and yet, there came little other purpose beside that to this desperate crawl.

They paused to catch their breath, ears sharpening at the splintering sounds of rocks and the distant rumbling and crashing of massive stones in the nethers below. Such tumult did not inspire much hope that their wretched flight would succeed, so they quickened their pace, tightening their strides against a foe that was unbeatable, despite their exhaustion. Nameless chills ran up their spines and loosed claws of fear in every step.

Something was coming up the ledge. Fezoul knew it and he

clutched the primitive amulet around his neck with dark prayers on his lips. Rusfaer, somber, bent-kneed in the thick shadows, grunted and waved the group on, a brute of a man with his teeth clamped in resolve.

At the sound of more muffled booms, the companions ducked into one of the gloomy caves that seemed ever-present on this lonely, precarious ledge. The interior was just as dry and dusty as the other gloomy pits they had seen, shaped like a seashell, but showing no adjoining tunnel into which to flee. It was a niche carved by hands or claws that had never seen the light of day...

Back up the ledge they scrabbled, searching ever for sanctuary. Another cave they discovered, one flanked by more winged guardians, albeit of lesser mass and girth than their grim-eyed cousins hunched in the shadows below.

A quick blur of movement caught Dereas's eye. Down the ledge came a rustle of flints and the tinkling of tiny stones falling into empty space.

Dereas froze in his tracks.

Into the cave they ducked. The ambient light dimmed quickly as they made these first staggering steps into a chamber of unusual girth, for there was no water here or light-giving Vitrin, only the pale light of the portal from which they had entered.

They passed with stealthy tread hundreds of yards before any paused to see if anything had followed.

Down the passage they crept, and a cold fear pierced Dereas's heart, for an immeasurable form had blotted out the faint light of Tutraken, for an instant.

The feeble light returned.

Had the thing passed?

Dereas started for he could not for the life of him fathom how such a serpent, if it were the serpent, had followed them all the way here, to this dusky, shadow-cursed place.

Silently into another cross tunnel they pushed their way. The glow dimmed swiftly as they made their way into the shadows. The realm of Tutraken was behind them with its yawning precipice and its haunting airs of desolation and grandeur.

Hearts pounding, they risked a look back round the last bend of crumbling stone, and Dereas glimpsed a slither of movement—a frightful scaly shiver in the dimness, of some iridescent material lighter and limned against a darker patch of wall—and then the flash of an enormous tail.

He jerked back, eyes starting out of his head. He gestured the others back into the cave with a trembling hand and suspicions confirmed.

"He saw something!" howled Fezoul.

"Shut up!" warned Rusfaer, raising a club-like fist.

"It's Pygra, isn't it?" Hafta grunted.

"Yes, 'tis Pygra. What else would it be?" Rusfaer growled, suffused with rage.

Dereas's rugged face looked stripped of hope. Even after all the efforts they had made—the snake had not given up.

"Perhaps you are right, mountain king," he groaned at last. "We are without salvation..." His voice trailed off in a dim murmur. He hunched down on the cold stone, glaring helplessly at a mark on the opposite wall.

"Well, have you gone completely yellow now, brother?" mocked Rusfaer. "Like our defeatist king?" His voice rattled in Dereas's ears. Insult upon injury leapt about the cold stone. "Or are you just settling in to have a little nap while we sup on centipedes and wash it down with our own pee?"

Dereas leapt to his feet, confronting his brother with cold contempt. They glared nose to nose, waves of animosity brimming like whitecaps on a raging sea.

Rusfaer grinned in his wide, bold way. Scowling shamefacedly, Dereas stepped back into the murk, dispirited and feeling empty. He gripped his blood-crusted blade and crouched grimly before the bend in the tunnel. It was all he could do to ignore the irking jests of his idiot brother.

Rusfaer smiled plainly, amused at the fact that he had riled him. "I like a man with spirit, beaststabber. If there's anything you have, is spunk."

Dereas glowered at the remark. He pushed past Hafta, intent once again on seeing the company through this nightmare. He struck up the tunnel, and By Balael, he was not going to be baited by his taunting brother!

All the while Jhidik and Hafta remained stone-faced. They trailed behind in a cloud of brooding silence.

The tunnel widened; Dereas pointed harshly and struck up a side tunnel. Hafta crept on his heels like a sullen, glowering wraith. Each shafted nervous glances over his shoulders. Every dozen steps Hafta would pause to jerk about warily, as if expecting some slithering horror to jump out at them like a fiendish wraith. The whites of his eyes glowed with a frowning intensity, like eagle orbs glaring in the sepulchral light. At times he looked as if his mind were thick with cobwebs, then his head would bob like a bird's, nervous tics crawling over his shoulders, almost as if he felt his own death imminent around every corner.

Dereas scowled. He pulled nervously at his weapon. He had seen such looks in men before they died—cold, vacant, fish-eyed gazes into nowhere. Whether on the battlefield, in single combat or duel, it was all the same. He saw his own desolation reflected in the older man's harsh-cut features.

Nor did he like the look of the ominous tunnel yawning up ahead.

Not more than a few hundred yards had they crept up the wide, lightless passage when terror and death greeted them with open arms.

Hafta loosed a bloodcurdling cry. A battered, skin-riven, skullish crown rose over him, ghoul-like, huge beyond imagining, suspended from a mass of coiled loops. He leapt back, a manikin of fright. The coils were as thick as giantwood trunks, undulating with a fiendish allure and sickly, deadly stealth.

Stumbling over his own heels, Hafta was instantly enveloped in strangling loops of springy serpent flesh before he could even lift his blade.

Dereas swung a defensive arc of bone-carved blade at the writhing shape but the other's choking cries shivered his soul, echoing about the stony crypt in horrible symphony.

Hafta was hauled back into an abysmal wash of murk, coils rippling over his man-flesh. His screams were horrible to hear: piercing, agonizing peals of them, as bones cracked and sloppy, guttural feasting began.

His wheezing gasps and the final gurgling sobs were a blur in Dereas's ears. They left a ghoulish imprint on all their minds, as they raced up the tunnel, not knowing where they could flee.

The beastslayer felt as if he were about to upend his stomach. He clawed his way up the corridor, and Rusfaer, white-eyed, surged no less swiftly at his side. He would not look at Dereas, only abandoned all hope of salvation, shaking his sweat-matted head like a dog.

How had the fiend gotten so close to them, Dereas asked. All the twists and turns they had taken back in the inner mountain...had they all been in vain?

It was a question with no answer. The blacksome tunnel was filled with the gluttonous rasping of bristling coils and unwholesome scales slithering.

The snake was still not done.

With heart-rending panic, Dereas gripped a claw-like hand on the last amethyst in his mailshirt. He waited for a right moment to prepare himself while Jhidik and Fezoul stumbled ahead in sheer terror.

The serpent undulated coils after them, a pall of pure killing death, a reek preceding all.

Dereas was slammed backward, swept up by a noisome loop of tail. Pitched back against a projecting spar of rock, he felt a sharp pang in his back.

Raging hisses filled the chamber. The monster reared over him in a grisly, ghoulish anticipation. Dereas crabbed back, shaking the pain from his throbbing spine. He swept the haze of dizziness from his eyes as he hurled the crystal. It smashed a hole straight through the serpent's twitching eye directly into the yellow-jellied flesh. The snake thrashed and hissed—deprived of sight forever. It bunted and scraped its anguished head on the ground, trying to remove the prickly missile, dull the pain of its world and ward off the endless sleep of utter darkness. Where its universe had been at least sheathed in gray, wounded by Dereas's earlier spear-strike, now it was utterly black...

Dereas felt a tinge of savage triumph at the deed, though he knew it was probably his last.

The great reptile surged forward, feral as a titan. Her formidable sense of smell was awesome. How it would guide her now on her lusty pursuit for living flesh!

The snake arrested its coiling advance. She flicked her questing tongue, hissing in and out in momentary confusion.

Dereas could feel her weighty thoughts: Where had her prey gone? Where would her dim primitive instinct lead her next?

After a dramatic pause the serpent slid her grisly hide forward in a lightning-fast sidewinding motion, her horrific snout tilted in a direction that she thought was theirs.

Dereas breathed in a gust of horror, shaking the gloom out of his skull, for he saw, or rather felt, the cumulative evil that exuded from that beast's vast bulk.

Rusfaer's mouth moved in a strangled oval close to his brother's ear. "I think we should be beating a hasty retreat!"

With alacrity the two of them fled up that grisly tunnel. Dereas coiled fingers round the mountain king's wrist. They sped for their lives, bypassing an evil-looking side way rearing out of the shadows, discovering the way ahead even more lightless and rank with the reek of serpent spoor than before.

Pygra slid on blundering coils about a twist in the tunnel, her unimaginable weight bashing against the tunnel walls, flaking chunks of debris off like wood chips from a tree under the axe. Despite her inconceivable mass, she drove on; her endless, scaly bulk sliding with tireless energy, rippling thrusts of tail and sinew.

Jhidik, shambling behind in a half-loping painful crouch, was next to feel the snake's tongue rake the back of his calves. He sagged, gave a convulsive heave, gasping out in sheer terror.

Dereas reached out fingers and hauled him half sprawling to his side. At the same time he kneed the mountain king toward Rusfaer. If the snake's middle had not been caught in a sharp bend just seconds ago, the Pirean would have been snake bait. As it was, Jhidik darted into the black mouth of a nearby side tunnel—but this was by no means an escape route. Not two dozen strides in, they were all repelled—by a firm wall. Blocked!

The desperate crew scrambled swiftly to the side. They pressed backs against the chill stone, waiting for the inevitable—smothering coils to whip around them. Blood rushed to Dereas's brain, a horrible panic rose in his throat. Hardly daring to breathe, he hoped the horror had not spotted them enter the lone cavity. But the sounds of the snake's breath was a death rattle not far away. Its slithering rush had slowed and the rattle of its ghastly scales grew in volume.

The brute stopped short, as if something else had alerted its attention. A small black-green shape suddenly darted from a cross tunnel. It kicked the monster's tail, as if it were a plaything. The figure raked the glistening coils with a bone-white weapon clamped in a pinched, reptilian hand, then it pelted it with some rocks before backing away—rocks that appeared to have been stockpiled in its rude belt.

The snake turned, hissing with rage, her queer, flaring nostrils bristling in bewilderment and sniffing at what she perceived was an overweening, scrawny shape, spinning around in circles on its heels, chittering and dancing, like some elf, in an ungluttable glee at catching the attention of the snake.

Pygra, driven to ire, unfurled her vast coils and heaved her brutish bulk backward.

But this was easier said than done. Easier to thrash and bare fangs than turn her squat trunk and massive loops about the narrow confines of the tunnel. A kick and three knife slashes in the dimness and the figure was gone and the snake managed to squeeze her head past her own loathsome coils and snap her slavering jowl forward. The little scamp had perhaps underestimated Pygra's speed and wrath, for there came a squealing shout as if the serpent had caught up with her badgerer. All was a blur in Dereas's mind. He tried to decipher those mad events and the sounds that preceded it, but the echoes that fled in and about the ghoulish tunnel were indecipherable.

The snake shivered her tail. She slashed out with her fetid snout, then lapped hissing tongue against the narrowing walls, finding it increasingly difficult to turn and redirect her mass rather than storm a victim straight on. Draba darted away back down a side tunnel like some fleet-footed gazelle, far enough away from the snake's probing tongue to avoid mutilation. Quick as firelight, his lizard feet pumped, his forelimbs danced, spinning wide circles, as Draba thought it was a game, cackling in his pubescent, chittering tongue and darting away in merry spirits.

Dereas edged around the side of the cave. He glared in appalled wonder. How had the fool managed so dextrously to evade the snake? Did he not know what he was playing with?

Rusfaer's jaw was clamped in disbelief; he clenched and unclenched his fingers on his blade with brooding reflection.

Upon hearing that lizardish chatter, Dereas felt a peculiar chill tingle up his back. Somehow in the course of Draba's transformation, he had reverted to a child, like a rodentish chipmunk playing in the trees, a place of the past. How old was he? Seven, maybe younger?

Because of his size and speed, Draba seemed able to outwit the snake, and crawl forth in his smaller frame from a niche or rude tunnel unscathed, like some sprite. Eager to taunt it, while it would mash its invincible skull and viperish beak against the rock, trying to ferret out the fresh meat. When the snake was losing interest, the pest would melt into the darkness like some gremlin up the tunnel and be gone to lure Pygra again. Dereas shook his head. Draba's eyes were like a cat's; he needed no Vitrin water to light his way, or light bowl to guide him.

In his lizard hand, the wayward imp had clutched a small bone dagger, probably nicked off a corpse somewhere along the nighted way.

Fezoul, creeping at Dereas's heels past the lip of the cave, moistened his lips. "Thank Jeron for your mischievous comrade. Without him, we would all be dead."

None questioned this. They wondered what next the little sneak would try.

Rusfaer, with a gesture of finality, prodded them up the crumbling path. "No time to lose," he hissed. "Let's be gone, while our fiend stays busy."

Out of their cramped hidey-hole they darted into the black mouth of a side tunnel crisscrossed with shadows and dust motes. This was by no means a sanctuary. They ran headlong into another sheer wall, and Dereas frowned to himself and forced himself not to cry out in frustration.

They doubled back panic-stricken to a junction, only to find this too was blocked. Dereas saw there was an intersection farther back down the dusky passage up which they had scrambled, but maddeningly that was within the snake's lurking radius. It appeared they were trapped, with only Draba's snake-baiting to give them any reprieve.

Dereas halted, flattened his back against the wall. The tunnel was dim, only the fleeting glimmer from one of the cross tunnels bathed the dusty stone ahead in a somewhat navigable glow. It was fifty feet away from Pygra's current stalking grounds. If they could get there to the cross tunnel—twenty seconds' stride at a loping run—they could all escape, otherwise, it was sure death. They would be serpent fodder as soon as the monster finished off Draba and came after them.

The snake was distracted however, and the beastslayer sank into his lynx-like crouch and edged his way sideways along the wall. He motioned his surviving, wide-eyed peers along in the shadow. At any moment the serpent might lunge...But maybe not. Beads of cold sweat budded on his forearms; his blood-grimed forehead dripped sweat.

Rusfaer Wolfrunner stalked forward slowly, like a half-crazed animal, his blade tilted low and thrust forward in merciless, killing readiness.

But no such fanged strike came.

They slipped into the side tunnel with no more noise than cats, grateful to be left standing. Their chests heaved in relief, while the hair-raising baiting and patter of lizard feet faded from earshot.

Now they were down to four, minus Draba. It was a crippling realization and left them all depressed. A sinking sensation pricked Dereas's heart, for the loss of Hafta was a blow. He had been an excellent fighting figure in their group, a solid and dependable anchor of reason and veteran fighting ability. He was one of the few among them who was not too injured to fight at full capacity; but now no more—as he sadly realized. It was water under the bridge. Not to be dwelled upon. Dereas's heavy heart strove madly to keep faith, and yet...he shivered guiltily at the thought that the mutant lizard-boy, who was likely already dead, had saved their skins...

It was a long later time, after many hopeless hairpin turns and dead ends, that Dereas started to think they had taken another wrong turn. The mountain king's directions had proven inadequate. Though they never saw trace of Draba, his cackling, bordering on chittering, had drifted again out from the darkness. At least the quasi lizard-man was still alive. The company stood frozen like statues at an impasse, muscles clenched, shoring up their strength.

Fezoul flung himself to the cold floor, gibbering to his bestial gods. All were still unnerved by the death of Hafta and the reminder of how he had died and the atmosphere generated by Draba's tumult was less than consoling. It sent chills up their spines.

Rusfaer was growing unhinged. Especially in light of the sheer wall of rock facing them. He had been growing prone to muttering to himself at random times, as Dereas noticed, and breaking out in chill sweats. Draba's frightful chirping had crept under his skin. The echoes that drifted out of the darkness of a cross tunnel would have Rusfaer grinding his teeth with a fury that everyone within earshot could hear—and then, the snake's slithering echo would rise and fall in rhythm with the banging of her skull against solid rock...It was ever a nightmare and all could feel the rage and promise of strangling coils of the snake slithering after them. Of them all, the strange cold sweat would bead the most profusely on Rusfaer's brow. White-eyed glances he cast over his shoulders...his meaty fingers would hook on his hilt as if stricken with a malaise, prompting his unpredictable moods to turn volcanic and he would lash out at Fezoul, or Jhidik, if any break from routine or passing comment were not to his liking. Draba's mischief had reached an apex when the eerie runt had shot out of nowhere, thrown dirt in his eyes and rammed Rusfaer sprawling in a rank pool. At that point Rusfaer had completely lost control.

He had run up the tunnel, cursing, roaring and smashing his blade against the rock, drawing sparks. "By Balael and the blood of accursed Kizoi, and hedonistic Zecrates, come out of your rat-hole, you little hobgoblin!" he had bellowed.

But the grinning prankster had shown no sign, nor was there any answering chitter or patter of feet. All had grown deadly silent then, accustomed to Draba's eccentric appearances and disappearances, but less so Rusfaer's random rages. Now Dereas winced.

For Draba had emerged again after they had backtracked to the next cross tunnel, crooning some child-like song in a lizardish tongue somewhere up that bleak, nighted passage.

"He is out to curse me!" grumbled the warrior. "I have seen it in his beady eyes!" A ghastly grimace twisted the New Wolves' chief's face. He flung oaths left and right, cursing and shrieking into the maddening darkness.

Dereas ran up and shook his brother like a rat. "Shut up! Get hold of your senses, you idiot." His hissing warning echoed down the murksome tunnel. "These rants will get us killed. Remember Pygra roams, blind or not, and she will gobble us whole. Your little Draba was a New Wolf warrior, transmuted by evil magic, no more, no less. He's no spook, or ghoul, or some figment of your imagination. From what hellish place the witch's sorcery came, we know not—" the beastslayer's words rustled darkly in the gloom, drifting in the air like restless bats.

Rusfaer held his chin in his hands, gripping his matted beard with a restless frenzy. He pulled fingers through his sweaty locks. "No, brother! He's a changeling, some mischievous, cursed sprite. It's a sign yet—a sign! He's an instrument of the lower forces, the demons. Do you not see? Balael has forsaken me—he has relinquished us to the beasts."

Dereas opened his mouth, but closed it again. He remembered his raw wounds in the wild ride through the gully of the Vhale on horseback which seemed so many eons ago. How he cursed and cried out at Balael's unresponsiveness. The withdrawal of his god was one of the worst feelings of his life—and the aftermath, the thrice-damned Eakors which had forced him on this insane adventure.

The beastslayer sank back on his haunches and Rusfaer turned his back on him, mumbling angry prayers to Balael and maledictions to Kizoi. The man's wild eyes stared into the gloom with a desolation that approached mindlessness.

Perhaps he and his brother were cursed, thought Dereas. Either the mountain would be the death of them, or life on the run as cursed renegades would bring them to ruination...

It could have been hours, as easily as days that they wandered up that tunnel, delirious and mumbling imprecations, moribund and parch-throated. Their flight for survival and Pygra's relentless pursuit entailed few variations. Up, up, and always up—as Fezoul had madly murmured. They felt their ears pop with the pressure of the height they had ascended, and their aching feet plodded on and their breath ran short. Dereas could swear his ears felt dulled to sounds by the increase in altitude and the dizziness that rode the wings of hunger, fatigue and privation.

All the while, the group never knew what surprises waited around Vharad's next crumbling corner—Pygra had taught them that, as had the saturnine Draba. One never knew what the fiendish rascal had in wait for them, leaping out at them like some snouted gnome, cavorting like a lunatic dervish. That, or Pygra rearing out with her leering gaping jaws. The snake would spring upon them again, that was for sure, Dereas thought sourly, striking like a cobra, worming her way like a coiled mist through tunnels she should not be able to navigate. Those suffocating loops of hers would get them at some time.

The tactic of losing themselves up narrow passageways was fast losing its effectiveness. The snake was starting to anticipate those crude maneuvers. More and more she despised Draba's feints and dodges, judging from her hisses and thrusts, as much as she did their harum-scarum evasions. Sooner or later their luck would run out and safe corridors would make themselves scarce.

The snake Pygra herself was becoming short of patience with Draba scurrying up or down tunnels into those little niches of his, places she could not follow. The serpent went to greater lengths to catch his miserable hide. His lizard-born, razor-sharp eyesight was an advantage she lacked, and this galled her...stone blind as she was now. Her old yellow eye was almost fused shut, certainly blind, but she could smell—fiercely at that, and her tongue, though shortened from a spear's slash, provided a sense of spatial perception that none of her skulking prey possessed. Had Draba been a bit more cognizant of her strengths, perhaps he would not have made such an egregious error leaping out so overzealously one time in his blithe, jaunty horseplay. She, the primordial snake, was a creature of the darkness that could hunt indefinitely. No tunnel was her master, or too distant for her to pick up the spoor of fresh game. No living creature was too cunning to elude her grisly traps...

At some moment in time close up the tunnel, Rusfaer had leapt out, sword bared, prepared to face down yet another familiar patter of feet.

He gripped his sword and planted feet firmly.

Then Draba came springing out, wild-eyed.

But Pygra was on the hunt, a slithering shadow a stone's throw away.

The serpent whipped out her loathsome head and trunk, materializing from behind a crumbling mass of sandstone adjoining the foot of a cross tunnel.

Rusfaer let out a yell. He felt the color drain from his face. Scrabbling back in mortal fright, he fell back into his brother, who in turn jostled Jhidik. Draba was caught in open peril under the weight of that awful shadow, flat-footed with nowhere to run. Rusfaer instinctively slashed out with his sword, whirling blade, unwittingly cleaving thin air, barring the lizard's access with his gleaming sword, and the sickening crunch of coils caught little Draba broadside as he tried to leap to safety.

Dereas would never forget that incredulous look of shock on Draba's thin lizard face. It was a last glimpse of expressionless horror, an innocent air of blind astonishment. The snake caught him in its fetid teeth and dragged the diminutive form away. Draba was gone in a heartbeat. The snake poised imperturbably, swallowing—a morsel so small as if Draba had been a bread bite to a man. Her wedge-shaped head swayed on a glistening trunk. Her dead eye loomed with chilling, blood-curdling scrutiny in the dark.

The beastslayer swallowed, closed his eyes with a sadness and fright and took a sharp breath.

"Still think you're cursed?" he breathed hollowly, glowering at Rusfaer who licked his lips and stared blankly at the swaying menace in front of them, as they pulled each other away from that place of reeking death.

They shambled on all fours up the shadow-cursed tunnel, darting into a cross-tunnel. Fezoul gibbered madly; Jhidik clawed and limped his way at their heels. Pygra came after them, a horrible slithering mass in the murk. They could hear her rustling somewhere in those frightful folds of darkness, lashing her coils against stone walls in feverish delight, sounds which drove them to sheer madness. They would have died long minutes ago had it not been for Draba's last prank—or for the inordinate number of near unnavigable sharp turns that kept her sizable bulk at bay.

The snake pinched her tubular bulk with ripping strength through narrow ways, hissing impatiently around harrowing bends. She was not able to slither along fast enough to follow her scrabbling prey, to their fortune, as relentless as she was in her pursuit. They slipped and squeezed past a hole that could barely fit a man; they fled into a wider tunnel. Behind they could hear the pounding, quaking echoes of the snake against unyielding rock.

Through loops and dips in the tunnel the stragglers came out, panting and wheezing on a dim promontory that joined the bleak ledge, a familiar perch, with expressions somber. They stood blinking on the upper reaches overlooking the great chasm that they called *Tutraken* that they had quit long ago, but at a higher point than where they had last left it. They had arced a huge distance around its brim, the rim of the inner mountain. All for the sake of a few more morsels in Pygra's maw, Dereas thought miserably. Now they emerged, hollow and ghost-eyed. They followed the ledge with somber resignation on its upward climb, fevered ravings spilling off Fezoul's lips. The sheer drop down those unscalable cliffs was heart-numbing, enough to drive any one mad. Not a man among them could ward off the thought that when it was his turn to face Pygra's gullet, clad in ghastly loathing of fear and nightmare, he would die horribly.

"Little Draba's time came to an end too soon," Jhidik rumbled, shaking his head. In his slack palm his dulled weapon dangled.

Dereas turned his gaze from the lightless chasm to face his strangely solemn brother. He frowned. "Draba saved your skin back there—all of our miserable hides truthfully. Though 'twas you who killed him by surprising him with your bared blade."

"I don't play nursemaid to my men," Rusfaer muttered savagely. "'Twas his own fault, baiting the serpent unnecessarily. It could have been any one of us that fell back there—" But the warrior's words hung hollowly in the air and bleak echoes fell in their wake down the vast chasm of Tutraken.

In disgust and some guilt, he stalked up the path, grumbling. Dereas gazed moodily after him, sensing the weight of the world shackled on his brother's shoulders. He knew the thought of Pameel disturbed his soul in those restless moments. Only the strange light gleaming in his eyes reflected the inner fire which kept Rusfaer from ultimately succumbing to crippling madness and grief. They had lost three of their number now—and likewise more soon. The snake was behind them, a deathly shadow...but for how long that luxury would last, none knew.

Nor did they pause to gloat over the advantage. Up the ledge they shambled, like lost souls from *Saeth's* hells.

With increased regularity small square caves made their appearances, cut sharply into the cliff face. But these they saw with apathetic eyes. Within lay triangular stone slabs, crude altars of sorts, blackened by age-old fires and peppered with decayed stray animal bones—presumably reptiles. Listlessly Rusfaer prodded these bones and his sword lay limp in his hands as they crumbled to dust right before his eyes. With a wordless grunt, he grumbled, and up he marched on with the others who followed his lead in somber monotony. Countless images they saw carved in those walls, once painted with bright pigments, but now pale and dulled by eons of moisture and decay.

The cliff face fell into shadows and they thought to see strange faces carved in its knotty hollows—of gods and celestial beings, winged lords, bestial and half man, interwoven in a frightful pantheon of scenes unheard-of, chronicling some rich elder mythology, almost incomprehensible. A fairyland orgy, a fantasy of otherworldly gods, bestial and profane. How the builders contrived to chip and carve those disquieting, larger than life bas-reliefs, Dereas could hardly fathom.

They came to witness other evidence of marvel, proto-human culture too, lost in those mists of past ages. Tall beings of stone, thin and brutish, not unlike the squat winged hominids that guarded the tunnels earlier. They seemed to be scattered everywhere in this desolate world—some straddling the pathway, forcing them to skirt it with awkward hops; others up the wall at shoulder height; others huddled below the ledge. Presumably these statues were the work of ancient peoples who worshiped winged gods, avatars, or some form of demons with characteristics of hybrid man and bird, both squat and tall. Perhaps they were of the same stock? Albeit disparate races that supported mutant threads of evolution? The genealogy was unclear and Dereas's mind grew befuddled with such conjectures.

Cautiously they swerved round a sharp bend and ran nose to nose with a pair of mammoth statues—nay a single eldritch monument. Dereas saw they were carved of serpentine jade that guarded an ancient ropeway spanning the dusky, blue-shadowed chasm below. The monument also guarded the entrance to a massive gate, one branch which led back into the mountain—a dark, silent tunnel, hauntingly eerie that raised hairs on Dereas's neck. Directly opposite, stood another which gave way curiously to an intricately twined bridge which sagged heavily on frayed cord over the daunting chasm to gain a similar vantage on the opposite cliff.

At this the wanderers gaped in awe, for it was of such sight to belie common understanding. The gateworks consisted of two, huge, megalithic statues clinging in ghastly symbiosis to each other, both poised on a sinister stoneworks of thick flat slabs. Squinting in the gloom, Dereas saw similar statue-works in the dusky distance brooding across the chasm. They guarded the black tunnel at the other end of that frayed, faraway rope way.

Dereas saw cords as wide as a man's leg run in places across the bridge—brown and rotted things hung with many thick tattered threads knotting together slats of wood. The disturbing guardians watched sternly, entrance and exit to the gate, things of perverse origin and configuration.

He craned his neck, strove to take in the hideous stoneworks in a glance. The ropes hung danglingly from the raised palms of one of the statues—a tall, thin, winged man, perhaps thirty feet high. The cheerless effigy hung from its toes, gray-green wings tucked back in miserable supplication, dangling upside down from a giant stone gibbet suspended in the curved beak of a colossal bird, larger than the man, but with hoary wings outstretched and beak slightly ajar, perched on a rude, dark mantle of solid jade. The bird's eyes glowed with prehistoric force—they were fierce, individual, invasive orbs, and omniscient, while the bestial face of the man was curled in an oppressed rictus of utter woe.

The whole panoply set Dereas's nerves a-tingle. He gripped his lizard blade with new fervor. The image lent such monstrous insinuations as to sicken his soul and to provoke such inquiry as to why any race would sculpt such grotesque monsters or dare to step one foot on that bridge. Who were these morbid builders to fabricate such infernal architecture? Were the grim sentinels markers of some passage of rite of death? To the nether world across the chasm to the other side?

None would never know. Those strange mortals who had lived and died eons before him, had taken their dark secrets with them.

Dereas scratched his chin with wonder. Beings such as those might have worshiped beasts akin to the Eakors—beasts that may have been privy to even more monstrous doings than their present day cousins.

Muffled tumult suddenly boomed below—a large creature crashing on stone?—the snake's head perhaps? It appeared to issue from a cave carved scores of feet down in the side of the mysterious underground cliff. The noise echoed and the tumult rose nearer and Dereas felt a quickening of blood and panic. The mountain had a limited ceiling as he observed now, hazy outlines of a gray-black rock slitted with daylight peeking through vents too far up to discern. On this evil oasis they were now trapped, with the snake toiling below them in fury, on this inner mountain of doom. A predicament, Dereas mused gloomily—as doomed as any which had assailed them thus far.

The rope bridge would perhaps be their only recourse, he thought. The snake could not navigate the structure, surely? Its weight would crumple any man-made construction. The old ropes would snap, if it followed?

He rapped Rusfaer hard on the shoulder, directing his attention toward the bridge.

"What are you insinuating?" snarled the warrior. He regarded the bridge with impatient eyes and quirked his lips in a grimace of contempt.

Before the New Wolves' chief could spout his criticism, Dereas caught a faint blur of movement—a whisper of smoky gray far down in the chasm, the stir of a great dim shape.

Dereas shrank back from the edge.

At the same moment some cavernous, gurgling croak as of a giant tortured raven poured forth from far below—and Fezoul's eyes widened in terror.

A familiar monstrous green and brown wedge-shaped face suddenly reared itself up behind them at a bend in the ledge. The hypnotic head transfixed them with dread in the shadowy nearness.

Without warning Pygra leapt. Fezoul grabbed for Dereas's legs with a whimpering sob. The beastslayer lunged with his own grunt of terror. He grasped for the open palms of the statue at the ropeway, while Rusfaer and Jhidik clawed fast on his heels.

Grunting in horror, the four had hardly clambered over the bird man's outstretched stony palms, before the beast had maneuvered her scaly hide in the space where they had last crouched. Raking her slithering tongue across the crisscrossing of ropes, she lunged. With a tremendous surge of strength, the creature sprang in a vicious 's'-shape, nearly ripping Jhidik's and the mountain king's legs from underneath them. Its hideous mouth gaped and a wash of putrid vapors poured forth at their backs like a septic sea of ancient filth.

Gasping, they picked themselves up, running, tripping down the ropeway as the ancient ropes swayed back and forth but the ladder bridge held where Rusfaer and Dereas struggled ahead, scrabbling on in horror and confusion.

Cords shredded. In a nightmare of dismay, Dereas reeled back, felt the bridge lurch under his feet. The snake was on the bridge. He watched as cords severed from under him, and the snake behind blew fetid vapors from her flaring nostrils. The serpent dug disgusting fangs into the toughest wood of the bridge and held on. Like a pendulum, the fragile ropeway began falling, drifting, a dreamlike lifeline through space. With breakneck speed it whistled toward the opposite cliff while the four hung on with claw-like grips in utter despair.

The bridge was a renegade sail now full of a thousand holes with no wind to stop it; ghost-like, it fell across the gaping chasm.

The descent was everlasting and Dereas felt as if his heart leapt into his mouth. His eyes rolled upward. For a lunatic second the roar of wind rushed by his ears, and he felt his life pass before him, for the rope was overlong.

The snake thrashed and hissed now mere inches from his ear. Time stood still. Death stalked openly. Splatter by impact seemed imminent, for the fast approaching cliff teetered into view and the gray bestial faces carved in the sheer rock loomed ominously, hurtling nearer by the second.

From the gulfs below came a strange winged shape, emerging like a ghastly phantom like nothing ever before witnessed in this unholy mountain. And with a breath of underworld gods, drifted an otherworldly wind-like flapping, churning a dank breeze.

The tangle of ropes was no more than fifty feet from smashing into the cliff wall. The titanic winged thing swooped, lifted the writhing serpent in its claws.

The shape rose, bearing the body of man and the wings of a great bat, lifting the ophidian terror with the supreme power of titans while the flapping of its gray-skinned wings pounded like a scourge on the tomb-like air. The crippling burden on the ropeway suddenly lifted.

Dereas's jaw hung open even as he swung in limbo. The upswing of forces and the play of thrusts of inconceivable magnitude careened in the opposite direction. It stopped the terrible momentum of the bridge. The ancient ropeway lightly crashed against the stone wall, sparing them an impact which would have crushed every bone in their bodies.

Dereas bowed to fate. Rusfaer, Jhidik and the mountain king hung like fish in the tangled rigging, gasping, heaving, sucking in great breaths of air. The mangled ropes spun in midair, banging and twisting against the cliff wall uneventfully.

Dereas looked up the sheer face. It was a hundred feet up to where a gigantic jade statue, not dissimilar to the one they had just left, hung in macabre, inverted poise. Below spread an ancient ledge, similar to the one they had vacated.

Rusfaer hung possum-like in the twines above his brother's head. His rippling thews worked to climb those straining ropes and gain the ledge, the place where the gigantic bird-statue loomed.

Jhidik twirled slowly below in a tangled mass of shredded ropes. Directly above him, Dereas grimaced. He strove to gain another few feet up the twines of that impossible ladder. One hand was hooked into the mountain king's robe, another gripped the straining ropes. He pulled the moaning monarch up to a stable perch where he could grab the jiggling cords himself. The mountain king did not fall to his doom as was fated, prey to the shadowy abyss below.

In morbid curiosity Dereas's eyes strayed to the struggle across the gulf between winged creature and serpent—an eerie battle between inner mountain and sky. As a man in a dream, the beastslayer watched hypnotized as the tall, winged man-shape made play with talon-like feet—to clasp Pygra tighter and croak out a terrible, ravenish rasp. Swiftly it beat its ribbed, condor-long wings to keep the two of them aloft.

Dereas skin crawled. What was it? Bat? Gryphon? Man?—it was

not evident. The strange being had secured its prize and now traced slow wide circles down to the place where it had come from—the place it had slept, the sleep of death, for an eon with the patience of a martyr.

Squinting, Dereas perceived that the creature's torso looked human, but the breadth of its eccentric body was altogether avian—and completely ghastly. The feet depending from the barrel torso housed claws, which had gouged rivulets into the snake's hide, at roughly its middle section. Bat-like ears crowned a face with a crow's beak. It drew greenish blood dripping in frothy streams down into the fissure. In this grip the snake writhed—if torment was any word for it, an emotion that Pygra could feel—that caused the bird-man to sway drunkenly in its meandering flight. The beast circled down, down slower and slower in broad loops.

But Pygra was not one to know defeat. She whipped her tail up and over the man-bird's head. How, was a mystery only the gods could know. She was graced with a dexterity that Dereas could only marvel at. He saw that her body whipped faster than the strike of a cobra, and that she coiled gummy loops around the winged beast's chest, faster and faster, pinning wing and constricting the thing's lungs. The defense, a miracle in itself.

The bird-man arched in ghastly anguish and with a raucous roar lashed out its curved beak to snap at the slimy loops that plagued its flight. The dance of death caused the creature to jerk in midflight, but as it did, even its wretched lurching could not penetrate Pygra's log-thick, steel-sprung coils. While she wound and wound, tighter and tighter, hissing fiendishly, a gurgling cry rasped from its throaty beak and its ribs splintered, bone by bone, vertebra by vertebra, spine snapped like a rotten twig.

Across the chasm, the fiendish roars and hisses caught the clinging companions broadside and they grimaced upon hearing its agony trumpeted as it died. The eldritch thing fell like a stone, but on an angle that was nearly diagonal, straight for the opposite cliffs. There it smashed headlong, cracking its skull open on a ledge, a few hundred feet from the place they had traversed.

Pygra quickly unfurled her coils and sprang from the lifeless corpse. She latched herself onto a stone projection abutting the ledge. Part of her glistening body was still wrapped around the thing's neck, and while the mass slid down the sheer slope, the bird thing's own weight ripped the grisly crown from its frame in a stringy spray of gristle and hanging tendons.

The great serpent widened her flexible mouth and fed on the gory head even as torso and wings slithered down into the abyss. In one rocking, swallowing motion she upended the head, and with massive throat muscles rippling and digesting fresh meat, the gory clump was gone, as if it were no more than scraps left out for the dogs to chew. The small bulge grew smaller as it travelled down her bulbous gullet and into the swelling coils as had Draba, Hafta and countless other beings...

Pygra turned and arched her ophidean head upward. Nostrils flared, she flickered tongue up at those who clung hundreds of feet across the gulf, sensing from that vast distance that their desperate crawl up the frayed ropes would do little to escape her. Her dead eyes fluttered, caught the dusky light twice and projected an interest and a sinister intelligence.

10: The Hall of Beasts

Each beast was worshiped in blood,
As a champion of ages,
Throughout time,
In cloud-wreathed Tutraken...

—'The Rites of Passage of Vharad'

Even as Dereas stretched corded muscles to pull and heave his way up the tangled rigging, Rusfaer struggled for the ledge, his boot heels hitting Dereas full in the face, causing him a grunt of anguish. As he clawed angrily after his brother, a thousand questions poured through his wracked mind. Had Balael seen to their survival? What was this strange, sad creature that had died back in the abyss, crushed in Pygra's coils? Something akin to the hideous bird thing carved at the steps leading up to the landing? What were its motives? The questions ran deep in Dereas's brain, and he quailed.

The pain and shock of the impact still throbbed in his joints. He wondered if yet there were more of these somber, misshapen beasts slithering down in that abyss.

The thought made his blood curdle. He sent eyes scouring the frowning gray shadows for movement. But he could detect no sign, no hostility, nor hear any answering flap of barbaric, cruel wings come to sweep them away.

The creature seemed hauntingly similar to the one that hung upside down from the gibbet, but at the same time, different. Much broader of face and squatter of frame, and more gruesome than the thinner, smaller-winged, man-like version teetering in the dimness above. But then, who had dared craft these perverse effigies? Perhaps the carven creatures had evolved to their present day grisly renditions?

Slowly the companions heaved themselves closer to the statues, inch by lung-bursting inch. The cord-twined ropeway had turned ladder.

Dereas looked up aghast through the wreath of webs, into the stone-carved face of a bestial hawk-like vulture not a dozen feet up. Which evil was worse?—that or the real thing that had crumpled in a mangled heap somewhere below?

For an interminable instant Dereas's senses refused to believe that the monster guardian looming above was not real but just some stone facsimile of the thing on the other side of the chasm. In any case, an inverted visage peered into his own.

The black-jade crow with bald crown hung upside down, with twined talons suspended from a familiar, ghastly gibbet. The hangman's brace was held aloft in the arms of a tall, thin-winged man, somber and imposing, straddling the entrance gate carved into the cliff face. Whatever sinister symbolism the inverted poises held was lost on him.

He pushed aside thoughts of the anthropomorphic horrors and struggled up the dangling vines of cords, likewise did Rusfaer, who heaved his figure erect, rolling onto the outstretched bird's claws holding the ropeway. With instinctive skill, he wrapped his thick thighs round a projecting buttress, laid himself flat on his belly, and with a warrior's strength, lowered his arm to help his brother up, grunting a wordless note of encouragement. For an instant, Dereas and Rusfaer were natural allies, arm clasped in arm with something of camaraderie, and the beastslayer glimpsed a penitent cloud fall over his brother's bronzed, harsh face.

Fezoul, clinging to Dereas's leg, trembled dizzily as he flopped over the side, panting like a sheep, clucking like a frightened hen. Dereas afforded him a croaking grunt. He patted him on the shoulder while he hauled Jhidik up, his face darkened with grief, for the Pirean's face was a grimace of agony, wincing with the effort it took him to stand on his throbbing leg and lean on his friend's shoulder. No broken bones at least and Dereas studied the ring of grim, sweat-stained faces around him. Not without solemn reflection and a fierce sense of appreciation. These men had survived beyond the hope of survival.

In silent awe, the company watched the snake slither its way down the opposite ledge. With a sinister flick of her supple tail, she disappeared into the bends of darkness.

A shudder raced up all their spines, for they saw she moved with an uncanny stealth and a confidence, despite her lack of sight and her fresh wounds.

Dereas felt a sick horror in his stomach. Part of him still refused to believe the snake had actually tracked them this far. How could she have? Was she from another world? They were truly lost in this dim world of forgotten time. What horrors had these people known? Certainly they must have had many, denizens of an age that one could hardly imagine. Was the winged man haunting the chasm part of an extinct race, the last of its kind? To be snuffed out by Pygra at last?

Dereas could not help but feel a shiver of emptiness raise the hairs on his neck and a sense of futility for humankind's primitive idolatry. The beings who worshiped the winged creature, had been inspired enough to carve an effigy of similar, dismal grandeur, consumed as they were with a fiendish fascination with death, cruelty and darkness. The power of terror that the beasts had over them was as palpable as the sepulchral air around them. Such a power permitted these beasts to rule over their lost race in a cesspool of evolution, within caverns of nightmare over the eons. Did they derive a warped sense of identity from the subservience?

Dereas struggled with the concept. What was there to gain from worshiping these horrors? The idolatry and tragic falseness of it all brought such a queasiness to his gut that he felt the urge to retch.

Draba was dead; so was Hafta, no less Amexi.

Why all the futile, senseless deaths? To what end did those senseless sacrifices serve?

He staggered back limply into the bat-haunted gloom that stretched back into the cliff, braving the lower tunnel that yawned past the gate between the winged man's legs. It was a tunnel choked with shadows and sinister wafts of chill and chiseled from the oldest rock of Vharad. The tunnel wound up like a witch's loom, ceiling rising twice as high as a man, perfectly bare. Sometimes a rank pool filled with black water would block their passage as they groped their way along. They would have to skirt it, wincing with puckered mouths and grimacing frowns, for fear of disturbing whatever eerie thing might dwell there.

A trickle of blue-green water streamed down the tunnel and offered some dim luminescence, but little to combat the near blackness. Bestial faces, carved from the primal rock, crowded the flanks of the tunnel and leered out at them like phantoms out of time: snouts of ibexes, horns of bulls, the hairy ears of bats, the ribbed wings of condors, and the demoniac, leering, pug faces of apes, boars, crocodiles. The greenish pall distorted reality and painted the leering faces and the tusks and horns in otherworldly clouds of godless lunacy. Dereas could not help but feel ghosts of shivers crawl down his back. It was a complete menacing menagerie of every possible kind: animal, demon, incubus—ever to walk Darfala. They were tiered in endless synchrony, end on end.

By no means were these human, nor were there remotely human characteristics among them—almost a deliberate omission, as if to discount the very existence of humans in this world, the ultimate degradation of humankind...

The exception were the skulls that lined the rank floors on either side of the idol-cursed tunnel. Such skulls numbered in the hundreds, sitting meekly subservient to the towering gods above.

The eye sockets of the skulls faced outwards toward the center of the tunnel, eyes pools of darkness, as if peering inward to the dead souls of the men within. Some were corroded with age, bleached or blackened beyond recognition. Back-sloping brows and jutting forejaws were pitted with age and of such primitive construction as to indicate that they were the kith of long-lost proto-man. The symmetry of the arrangement suggested order and precision, the workings of a possibly philosophical and ordered race, though fatalistically and primevally backward in their bestial demon-worship.

Dereas's speculations rang in his skull. Why was this odd tunnel different from all the rest? Was it one that marked the rite of passage to beasthood? To manhood?

The beastslayer's mind rose and fell to strange, disquieting conjectures: he imagined scores of acolytes or would-be warriors traversing the tragic corridor, after doubling back across the ropeway, inundated in heady incense, smoke and aromatic herbs. Perhaps a sentenced or doomed man might make a horror-filled journey to the agonized spirit of the hanged man that was poised gruesomely on the other side of the chasm.

The beastslayer's head swam. He thrust all the possibilities aside, for such speculation bred madness and it was *Saeth's* work. His nerves quivered. The crashing impact of the ropeway had left his head dizzy and the resulting vertigo still cavorted among his senses, leaving random stars prickling before his eyes.

A thunderous rumble suddenly echoed back down the winding way they had come. The companions crouched tensely alert. Lizards? Pygra's mischief and her shuddering aftereffects? Dereas felt the rock shake under his feet again. Then a rattling and slithering of nightmarish proportions receding behind him. A chill crawled up his spine. He ran cold fingers through his tousled hair, now helmless since the lizard realm. The disturbance passed. He knew as the others did, that they faced beasts whose wrath exceeded every threshold of imagination.

He and Jhidik forged onward up the hallowed tunnel in a hollow trance, Rusfaer and Fezoul following. Their chests heaved to gusty breaths; their eyes roved in their sockets, searching for some side tunnel, some crevice or cranny that would admit no snake and would get them as far as the end of Vharad.

But there unfolded only the endless dimness of the passage, with its leering, bestial faces and endless rows of macabre skulls lining the way.

"Black Balael!" fell Dereas's urgent hiss upon the gloomy passage. "Is there no end to these idols? Look—rows of them! And no side tunnels. Balael have mercy! Must we claw our way out of this ghoul's tomb with our bare fingernails?"

Rusfaer grunted, "Balael aside, batslayer. We will break our nails scratching at doom's door either way." His blade traced mock circles in the air.

"'Tis a dead end." Jhidik muttered at last. His roving eyes, keener than the rest, had scanned deep into the darkness, and blinked now in resentment, as if seeing only dead empty air and failure. "All this— effort, for naught. It must certainly be Pygra on our tail."

"What else would it be?"

"You heard!" Fezoul moaned. "He said 'tis a dead end. We are all doomed! There is no way out!"

"Shut your mouth, you worthless rabbit turd," growled Rusfaer.

And true to Jhidik's prediction, they all stumbled upon a sheer rock face. They halted, panting before the impasse. The rough wall hosted a ghastly stone snake's head mounted in its center with wolfish ears perked on its scaled crown. A steady stream of water seeped from the open mouth to slap on the smooth stone below, trickling at their feet like a marsh's ooze. It was like some parody out of an accursed ghoul's temple. Dereas mused: not unlike Pygra this stone beast was, minus the ears, perhaps an imaginative artist's embellishment to endorse the monster's insatiable appetite.

Lesser deities were arrayed around the snake at respectful distances—two raptors, a jackal, and three hideous crab faces with pindrops for eyes and stalks stemming from their scalloped crowns.

Dereas felt his knees buckle. Rusfaer surged forward and struck blade at the ophidian face in sheer blood-fury. He sent blue sparks skidding off metal and stone, smiting left and right at snout and ears, notching his blade.

Dereas pulled him away, sour mutters on his breath, "Save your steel and strength, you fool."

The sounds of distant muffled rustling issued behind them. All eyes turned restlessly and Rusfaer stopped his hewing and blinked in uneasy wrath.

Fezoul murmured in a hypnotic monotone, "'Twas said that the Old One Snake guards the treasures of the 'Soul'. From its mouth flowed the Waters of Eternity—upon which the salvation of the Chosen depends." He narrowed his eyes on the devilish snake head with a studied intensity which gave the others no comfort. "Only the most penitent can reach the place to seize the boon and become victorious over the body and bodily death!"

"Enough of your maundering!" snarled Jhidik. "Your priestly homilies are for the dogs. We face bare rock, nothing more. Tis no soulful treasure here—" and in a fury of frustration, he jammed his sword up into the snake's mouth.

The dwarf's eyes bulged in warning. "No, 'tis true—Mymar, our elder, was adamant, he told us that—"

"I'll jam good steel into *Mymar's* gullet. Cease!" The Pirean's lips boiled froth and he jammed his four foot blade further into the beast's mouth which ran with blueish water.

There was a metallic clink as something caught on the Pirean's blade. Jhidik slid it back after only a short penetration before it jammed again.

He pulled the weapon free with force and frowned, sheathing his sword. In a blind rage, he plunged his hand up into the bubbling orifice.

His intent was perhaps impulsive. Dereas guessed he hoped to grab at the bauble or whatever ancient object caught in its stony throat. But the Pirean found his fingers only arching around a slight bend in the throat before he winced. He retracted his hand, as if a stinging pressure had smitten it. "Kizoi's fiends!" he cried, gasping.

There was a sudden whir of activity behind the rock face. Then, the startled company jumped back. The slabs parted in two, splitting the idol down the middle where a near invisible crack had run down the center. It widened, swinging inwards with freakish synchrony to reveal a secret chamber and a gloomy tunnel that wound up the back.

Many musty odors poured forth and they gaped in awe at the black yawning passage that greeted them, one that had not likely seen the gaze of human eyes for eons.

Dereas saw a small rough ramp of stone that directed the trickle of water from a higher point, now retracted. Water sprayed full out on the smooth flags, sending sloshing echoes around the chamber. Their eyes traced furtive circles around the periphery.

Jhidik shook out his wrist and looked closely at his right hand. A cross-marked bite blossomed in a red angry welt, not unlike that of a serpent's. His face twisted in agony, conjuring up all the superstitious fears of the past. Jhidik tried to shake out his hand with an unconcerned laugh.

"The mark of the snake!" shrieked Fezoul, veering close to study Jhidik's wound. "'Tis a curse!"

"Would you shut it!" Rusfaer lumbered forward to shoo him out of the way, but the dwarf scrambled back.

Dereas's dark eyes scanned uneasily about the chamber. If this tunnel were a rite of passage, then only the most worthy—or desperate acolyte or warrior, would have the impulsive foresight to thrust a hand in the snake's mouth, as had Jhidik.

Dereas took tentative steps into the cloying blackness; skulls glared up at him in owlish vacancy, a double row of twisted shapes, where in the previous tunnel there was only one.

He stared in dislike at the massive intricate stone hinges that controlled the sliding portal and found that the barring flanks of stone had completely disappeared, merging into the surrounding chamber's stone, as if it had never been. If any of them squinted narrowly, they could discern the vague outlines of primitive gears or pulleys floating somewhere in the cobwebbed murk near the ceiling. "Balael—'" Dereas's whispered hiss faded to a murmur in an eerie echo. He wondered at the minds that had created such fiendish contraptions.

Search as they might, they discovered no catch, lever or serpent head that would slam the door closed once again.

Rusfaer finally blew out a curse and motioned them up the tunnel. "'Tis a fool's errand to search for logic in this evil place. Let us be away!"

The beastslayer grunted in agreement. The others grumblingly acceded. With determined strides they sought the innermost tunnel. And yet, as Dereas straggled back, he struggled to thrust the incident from his mind, for ever was the fact that they could not close the door a detail that gnawed at the back of his skull, for he had an uneasy feeling that some terrible consequence would come of it.

With a fateful curse he joined the others and they lurched up the chamber in grim huddles. The passage became a tunnel of girth wider than the last, oddly bearing smoother walls and more intricate carvings—of bestial countenances and dead things and forgotten glyphs, yet draped heavily with the weight of ancient sorrow.

Rusfaer strode along with long strides. There was a noticeable spring in his step, as if some vague belief had washed over him with the discovery of the hidden tunnel that the snake had no chance of pursuing and crossing the chasm. Dereas wondered too if there was any way the slimy horror could negotiate the tons of rock and hundreds of tunnels, many of them twisted and small, that might connect to this dim, out-of-way place.

Dereas searched the mountain king's face for any clue as to what chances they had of exiting the mountain, but found no encouraging sign. Nor of escaping the snake. Only a reflection of sheer hopelessness, and ahead a mounting grade.

Dereas made a wry face. What a dour fellow, this mountain king...But then again, who wouldn't be after all the carnage they had witnessed? The beastslayer refused, however, to believe in any god of fatality. Balael was not of that nature. They were lost, true, and he forced himself to believe there must be a way out of this tomblike prison. He slammed a fist into his sweaty palm, muttering to himself, as if he were not with other men who mumbled similar thoughts as dark as his own.

Rusfaer chuckled in sinister mirth. "Of course there is, brother.

It's called faith. Look at what it did for those primitive monkeys who worshiped blindly their outworn gods."

Dereas could not tell if his brother was jesting or dropping a lurid hint to the quandary that faced them. They had crossed that barrier of transparency where men's lives are threatened to a degree that no matter what the shared animosities were, they would band together in the interests of survival.

Jhidik waved a dismissive hand, refusing to dignify Rusfaer's cynical remarks and dark humor.

Flights of crooked stairs carried them higher and higher, worn smooth with the pad of a thousand thousand feet. The passage was distinctly older here and more primitive than any of Vharad's ghoulishness thus far. Each step they took with the rigor of pilgrims, until their ears were finally popping with the altitude and their lungs bursting with the effort of climbing so high.

Dereas mentally counted the skulls they had passed. Thousands? Perhaps these all were the proto-humans, or perhaps monkeys or apes that Pygra, or some other similar creature, had devoured in its bloodthirsty reign, excreting out the skulls when the beast was done. The ghastly thought brought a clammy sweat to his body.

They reached a place where four men could walk abreast. On either wall, panes of unpolished glass rose smooth to the touch and held back a depthless cube of water. Strange fish swam behind those panes, Dereas saw to his marvel—some with square fins, others with bellies like blowfish. Others had no eyes or teeth and looked more like mutated eels or snakes than fish. Their twin tubular bodies were intertwined. Water leaked around the edges of the walls. It was a curious aquarium, crafted of crystalline glass, where it imperfectly joined the stone and dribbled into the Vitrin stream at their feet— thus watering the throats of the skulls that crouched there like forgotten apes from a haunted past.

The weary men grabbed handfuls of *arizoi* that grew between the cracks of the glass and rock, and past these sights they moved chewing the leaves with shivering disfavor. Their brains were too full of past horrors to quail much at this time. Fezoul jumped back when a loathsome fish-like shape darted toward the glass as if to peer forth and inspect him, which it did with sightless eyes. Others gave the tank wide berth, reminded of the restless reptiles that echoed faintly behind them and the deep low reverberations that shook the rock under the mountain. The glass shivered and threatened to crack under dull thuds. Whether the lizard king's monsters caused such disturbance or whether it was the aftermath of Pygra's uncanny violence on the walls, was anyone's guess.

As to what strange sustenance the aquatic mutants fed on, none knew, or considered, except Dereas, who guessed that the waters behind the glass stretched to underground streams teeming with newts and other forms of fish food.

Up the trail they climbed.

A sudden fresh booming came to their ears. Dereas jerked around in white-eyed alertness.

It could have been the dim resonance of pounding deep in the stone tunnels below.

Pygra? Lizards?

Fezoul's body shriveled with such fears. He stumbled on wildly, lurched into a shallow pool, causing Rusfaer to stare, leaning on his sword, blinking with indifference.

Could the reptiles have penetrated thus far? Dereas hooked his mouth in a scowl and pulled the clumsy king out of the water. It was not impossible. The hour of the *Saeth* was upon them—sooner or later the mountain would run them to the ground. When they ran out of dips and turns, what then—?

Dereas's worst fears were confirmed, for in the murky distance they spied a barrier and heard the echoing purl of water lapping on stone. Nothing to surprise them, but—

The winding stairs took them to a T-junction and they gazed up into the eyes of a giant bull skull with curled horns hanging on the opposite wall. The stern face leered at them like a fateful demonic avatar of stony yesteryear. A trickle of greenish water issued from its snout, similar to the serpentish portal with the fox-eared serpent. A dozen skulls and grisly carvings were arranged below and beside, cunningly crafted as to appear part of the rock itself. Big bold characters carved out by a giant's chisel stood out like the runes of distant lands, speaking some forgotten language which Fezoul identified as an arcane rite of passage in an older, ruder tongue.

The passage to the right gaped down a wide, tall tunnel, black as pitch, endlessly yawning into gloom, with no Vitrin stream to light it. Cold drafts issued forth, reeking of must and molder and the most unpleasant dampness; also the sounds of dim thuds came from frightful distances down. Dereas could not help but feel a cloying chill, for that passage was large—large enough to host creatures like Pygra and the Rgnadon, and it did not give him much confidence in their safety. To the left, a drier tunnel wound, though no less spacious, in a direction upward.

Rusfaer mumbled resentfully.

They took the leftmost passage. Into a dim alcove they crept, eyes adjusting to the gloom. They stood blinking before a flight of age-cracked stone steps that wound up into near darkness, lit only by a thin trickle of Vitrin.

They swung heavy legs up. At the landing's top loomed a massive door, forbidding for its size, half open. On ancient hinges it hung and comprised the first traces of iron since they had left the lizard realm. A peek beyond showed an even wider tunnel, opening up to admit twenty men abreast. Into the corridor they tottered and Dereas wheeled to grasp the portal's gem-encrusted edge. The stumbling wanderers managed to swing the stony braces creaking shut. With a grunting gasp of triumph, they slid back the bolt. Whether the rusty bar would gain them some real protection against a blooded foe would remain to be seen.

The chamber was mightily domed, edged with thousands of crystals on its lofty ceiling. Thousands of amethysts and rose quartz and carnelian glistened from heights above and in crannies to the sides.

Dereas's aquiline eyes swept about the cavern in awe-struck wonder.

For a time his breath caught, for there was fresh, colder air here; also the first breath of natural light smarted his eyes in a frisson of brilliant color.

A low waterfall ran from the back of the cavern like a curtain of white foam to fall into a jade-green pool covering a third of the length of the hall. It spilled out through an opening that admitted shafts of pale light from the open air beyond. All along the stone gallery at the pool's edge ringed a mighty pantheon of gigantic carved birds, beasts and reptiles: fishes, crocodiles, lions, wild cats, monster scorpions, serpents, lizards, and iguanas. About their feet ranged chains. They ringed in a wide half moon about the pool, some twice as tall as a man, others squatted like frogs. At one time they had been colored with exotic pigments, but now they were faded, colorless and gray with age.

On wary feet the four wandered about, taking in their surroundings with the bright wonder of pilgrims.

The artisans' skill however, did not end there. Dereas was quick to see that the rendering of claws, eyes, snouts, legs, wings or talons half lifted in flight or dramatic stealth, was shiveringly real. The figures crouched in aspects of almost magical surrealism.

The four intruders squatted uneasily on their knees at the pool's edge to sip the cool mountain water—so cold it was that it stung the temples. The rippling wake carried tiny gray-green chunks of melting ice and Dereas's eyes rounded. They had climbed so high that they were likely near the source of the mountain stream itself.

Dereas staggered up as close as he dared to a place along the brim of the pool from where the mountain water spilled—likely from the melting snow peaks, now a noisy small river as it gained momentum to plunge out over the cliff and down into thin air. Despite the fear of the threat at hand, Dereas felt light-headed...and surprisingly, a sense of relief. At last, they had reached some form of their destination, some vague place of protection. It was hardly anywhere near the base of the mountain, but at least miles away from the dreaded lizard kingdom.

At last they had found the sun! Dereas caught a glimpse of the blazing sky out there, past the outflow that streamed down a towering waterfall to spill out into a pool far below; also the ragged, puffed edge of real white clouds, the copper haze of distant ridges and the yellow-ocher of baking desert plains. He blinked his eyes in joyful contemplation and craned his neck to see farther. He saw the sheer cliff drop in an ice-fed waterfall that fell many feet to a foaming green pool below, shaded by wide-leaved balboa trees. Not a pleasant drop, he mused; no way to easily skirt that raging water and foot a path down to the pool below. Jhidik had discovered a side tunnel hidden in dusky shadows on the far end of the cavern seeking shelter...to this place Dereas now crept.

The others huddled in reverie and Dereas grimaced in awe as he staggered by, noting the beast-sculptures faced each other in a rough oval, as if they were pitted in some final ritual battleground. Dereas frowned, for he saw that the huge chains coiled to the sides of each massive statue were buried in inches of must and molder, prompting any number of sinister speculations. He could not help but surmise who or what had forged those iron shackles or what they had restrained in the racing shadows of time's mysteries. The terrible, ferocious epic struggles that had occurred in this dim, sepulchral world of yesteryear, were unimaginable.

His mind traveled to an age earlier when beasts might have mastered beasts and worshiped their own gods and held their own rituals in honor of them—creatures hidden in caves from the world of men for eons in their private sanctuaries...In the same way as men held their own games to the west in the amphitheaters of the bustling markets of Belramus and Toringol.

Back in the dimness flush to the edge of the waterfall, Dereas saw the tunnel was blocked with stone, admitting only a crawlspace barely large enough for a man to squeeze through. Yet beside the tunnel was a rusted grill, melded in the stone, so twisted and corroded that looked as if it would crumble at the merest touch.

He took slow, careful steps toward it, his bootfalls no more than a bare whisper in the hall of dusty, smooth-worn stone...noticing some of the animals had jagged cracks running up their middle. Here, a buffalo body had lost its horned head which lay in crumbling ruin at the beast's hooves, there, a forlorn condor had lost a wing...

The companions passed eyes over the inscriptions and ancient symbolism etched on walls and statues in solemn silence, and not without apprehension. Of all of them, Rusfaer's face remained the most inscrutable.

Perhaps the most imposing statue of all—was the half lizard and frog whose legs straddled the place where the water gushed out of the mountain. It was a creature not dissimilar to the sorrowful winged man that had died in Tutraken. And its face was a fanged oval peeled back into a mocking snarl—a hideous expression of rapture and horror that the companions cringed back from in grimacing abhorrence...for the lizard-frog wore a crown!

The second last in the ring was a special coiled snake with a python's beak encircling the torso of a horned man, and the serpent's tongue licked the unfortunate man's cheek with fanged mouth ready to strike!

Dereas crawled back in revulsion. The attitude of that ghastly pose was all too real, and familiar. On the upper tiers of the cavern, dark shrines were cut into the rock—cubbyholed sanctuaries, each with its own bestial statue—teetering shapes with slab-sided faces, jackalish snouts and weird renditions of tongue and ear.

Fezoul wandered around the amphitheater, blank-eyed, looking humbled with the realization that his kingdom was puny under the shadow of the colossal, bestial grandeur here. Dereas could see lines of doubt carved on his strangely aged face. As if he too had dwelled too long under the mountain, a lifetime in his own individual world, wearing the crown of a people now dead.

In hurried silence they searched the place, Jhidik poking his sword about the hooves of a basalt belamyl, looking for tools or weapons or anything useful in its litter of dust and rubble to help them survive. Dereas came beside him and his eyes stared in awe at the statue's perfect form, its hunched shaggy back, and its thousands of carved hairs, a master feat of craftsmanship of its own. The Pirean looked small in the midst of these exalted, omnipotent effigies, which were perfectly and flawlessly hewn. Rusfaer seemed oblivious to the lost grandeur and remained almost contemptuous of the sinister forces of idolatry lurking about that had somehow seeded this realm and given birth to nightmare.

The first metallic booms came smashing at the portal in ear-deafening peals, reverberating about the stone, blocking out hope and reason. Dereas crouched on his haunches, staring grimly. Every muscle quivered in tense expectation. The access tunnel was too large for his tastes and could admit any number of violent beasts or terrors. There was the rusty grille too, and yet—

Dust billowed under the cracks of the portal. The bolts shivered. A reptilian snout smashed through, wrenching them from their sockets.

The fugitives' bleary, bloodshot eyes widened in lunatic unison.

Jhidik swallowed hard—and ran.

Rusfaer, gripping hilt, glared incredulously. The wracked door was beyond reach, not an option. Eyes darted to the cavern's rear. Escape by the moldering grille toward which Dereas was gliding, seemed a fool's venture. Rusfaer swept strides about the chamber, verily dancing from foot to foot in indecision. Here was a desperate man facing a dead end with foes at his back.

"Quickly, laggards!" he shouted. "This may be our last chance. We are dead unless we find some way out of here."

"But how?" croaked Jhidik. "Shall we fly on wings like those mutant, filthy—"

"Shut up! Do what you must!" Rusfaer yelled. He scrambled vigorously over to seize the rusty bars and try to rip them out of their sockets.

No luck.

When the snake did come bursting through that bolted door, the company was completely unprepared.

The stone and protruding iron buckled in on itself, and a slimy, wedge-shaped head with slab-skinned eyes slid past the jagged hole. It inspected them with incalculable loathing.

Her immense bulk pushed forward, scattering stone and metal as if they were chaff. Then, she was in the chamber, all vast, glistening glory of her.

Dereas knew horror, for like Draba, they were on open ground, pitted against a ruthless fiend. Fezoul, his body a mass of loose-running jelly, grovelled on his knees.

In the dim light the serpent's head lifted, swayed in anticipation of the gluttonous feasting to come. Her mutilated tongue flickered between triple fangs as she assessed her prey with her inborn sense of smell. They were defenseless, puny things, easy fodder in the wake of her might. Her slanted crown was flayed and scarred from previous bashings as grievous as men could imagine, partly in encountering those sword-wielders who stood before her, but mostly from crashing her head against rock to force her way through the myriad, impassible tunnels. Her once-good eye sagged in a bloody ruin, her body caked with dried blood and coiled calmly, looking more like a gigantic, prehistoric predator than a snake of the present world, shimmering in the greenish gloom. One of the elder beasts, Dereas thought, in meditative contemplation of his impending death, and the other men within that domed chamber blanched upon seeing that mythical snake for the first time in all her stark reality—trapped as they were, alone, in a truly exposed arena—and they shuddered under the breadth and size of her.

Realizing her prey had no escape, the beast slithered calmly toward their brace-legged numbers.

Tumult drifted past the hanging doorway, which the snake ignored. Dereas, rooted firmly, raised frozen sword in a killing grip. He knew he would get only one chance before the monster snapped him up in those strangling coils and upended him into her cavernous jowl. One sweep!—and then, victory—or oblivion. From the booming sounds echoing without, there was more hell to come. The broken door smashed inward and from it flooded the disturbing pad of flat feet on stone, a chittering of unspeakable magnitude. Then the gnashing of countless abominable lizards and monstrous howls and baying of something larger still—something more violent. If the snake did not finish them, it would be the lizard king, and his horde of scaly brutes fast approaching.

Flesh crawling, Dereas began to dimly understand what had happened. Pygra had been stalking them from the very beginning, unwittingly leading the wretched lizards here. The lizard king had vowed to track them down, and that much he had done, as hissed in his last scalding speech. The lizards merely had to follow the spoor of the snake and her trail of carnage to find their quarry—which they had.

Pygra heeded none of this. She hovered there like a brooding phantom, a courtly length from the ancient doorway, a vast bulk of coiled, human nightmare. She sensed them through hideous flaps of her sightless eyes, but all the time, she smelled their man-scent and fresh blood. Her repulsive notched tongue slicked oddly from her maw after its encounter with Dereas's blade.

Rusfaer scuttled toward his brother. Jhidik swayed at their side. Fezoul quivered on their heels. Frantically the four backed away, for to confront the snake on open ground was suicide. Instinct drove them to shelter behind the line of statues by the arching pool. Pygra slithered sideways—a keen shape eager to cut Rusfaer off from his swordslinging comrades, the particular one who at a time before had cut her so badly. It was clear the sharp instinct of her reptilian smell-sense preferred to single out her prey, rather than chance all to band together in a united attack and pincushion her with sword pricks. Painfully she had endured the merciless and cunning slashings from those two wolfish savages, strokes she did not want to repeat.

With a raging cry, Rusfaer swung good steel a looping feint at the serpent's toad-warted head. He lured the monster closer to the pool, and Dereas saw his plan—to slash at her midsection and bait her into a vulnerable lunge, then make a break for the open door or the rusty grille. But his hope was dashed—for the snake was too fast and she whipped her brutal tail to batter him sideways and send him smacking against the opposite wall. He fell like a downed ox at the base of the horned ibex.

Rusfaer looked up in dazed confusion, a look expecting his own death, only to discover the open portal dangling on its hinges and from there issued a distant echo of a lumbering creature more menacing than Pygra...

Jhidik rushed to the Wolfrunner's aid, thundering the battle cry of the Pireans, and he slashed a whole section of the snake's hide where her trunk joined the back of her neck. Dereas realized the Pirean's assault was effective only while she was focused on Rusfaer. Warily Jhidik half shuffled back to his place of safety behind the antlered ibex. The serpent, blood-mad at this point, slithered forth with fangs outstretched, but her face met with solid stone and she succeeded only in bashing her slab-shaped head on Jhidik's protection.

The beast came at him again, hitting hard, rocking the statue's frame, and Jhidik hunched back, grimacing behind that adamantine bulwark, swearing luridly, his face a whitened mask of fear and hate and his lungs heaving.

The antlers of the statue cracked, smashed at his feet, then a hind leg splintered and now it was Dereas's turn to rush in, charging in a shrieking rush. He raised his gleaming tulwar high and slashed a ruinous line across Pygra's midsection, laying open flesh and a fetid gash of liquid meat to spew out on the stone.

The snake screamed, writhed, hissed and curled her ravaged body, whipping snout back and forth to deal with the skulking attacker. Dereas ran lightfooted to pull his dazed brother to his feet and they both scrambled in behind the fanged, serpent statue.

Pygra smashed her battered head up against the stony effigy in an attempt to send them reeling to their deaths, but they formed a ring around her, dodging left and right while she lunged at them. It was a game of cat and mouse, miss and strike. Such was the snake's frenzy that she became more demon-like than reptile, infused with the memory of fresh feasts on her mind. She bore the vicious, terrible punishment with stoic barbarism. The cuts and gashes grew like stitches on her face and trunk. She did not relish this heavy dragging of her sizely bulk around that statue to the amusement of those mousy vermin. It only registered in her consciousness that she had feasted a lot of late, with the dozens of tender lizards and the great big man-bat head fresh in her stomach.

Rusfaer and Dereas had developed enough confidence to bait the snake. They slashed and retreated behind another statue when she got too close. Legs squared, they held great blades two-handed, carving chunks in fiery triumph. They leapt back, while one teased the snake, and the other would cleave and rend its hide from the side. The snake switched to the other attacker, and the other brother would hew her gleefully. Jhidik snuck in to jab and thrust from the side.

In such baiting the play continued and Pygra's wounds grew in that bestial, tomb-like hall, with the brothers fighting shoulder to shoulder, racking up revenge on the monster that had caused them so much grief. Dereas caught a glimpse of the brimming wrath burning on his brother's face and he felt a kinship stronger than ever before—even in their young escapades running wild on the steppes.

Rusfaer bellowed: "This is for Hafta!" and he slashed right and left at the snake. "And Draba!" He rained blows off the snake's scaly hide like a blacksmith's hammer.

On went the twisted game of lunge and slice, and hack and dodge.

Pygra became tired of such mousy sport. Her features knotted in recollection of the recent past, how she had outwitted such pretenders and tricksters who had been too stubborn to die. In a moment of cold reptilian calculation, she reared up, hovering like some vast quivering tower, surveyed them with primal malevolence. She waited her turn. With a swift striking instinct, she thrust beak in a feint to Rusfaer's sword-right, drawing his attention wide and swiveled her body hard to knock him flying, his weapon clattering uselessly on the stones. Quick as an adder, she lashed coils around his husky frame before the startled warrior could scramble to safety. Slimy coils looped tighter in a tongue-flickering hiss of gratification. Grimaces blossomed on Rusfaer's face; his scarred features purpled, the tip of her tail curled like an iron-shod belamyl-shoe around his chin in ultimate mockery....

Dereas gave a gasp of horror. He could see in his brother's eyes such agony as he had never before.

In moments of hysteria bordering on lunacy, Dereas unleashed a savage flurry of strikes upon the beast that held no equal, too fast for the eye to follow. He thrust and cut double-handed with wild abandon. Splattered in blood from head to foot, he rained berserk blow after berserk blow.

Frothing cries roared from his throat. How his blade skipped and plunged!—darting in and out, raking flesh and scales, ringing off the crusty hide in leaping bounds, notching its keen edge on her toughest parts. In a dancing fury of death, he crouched on the balls of his feet, avoiding the snake's lethal fangs by inches and the play of reeking tongue and coils that would furl around his chest in a moment's passing while he laid into the slime-streaked hide with a vengeance that was commensurate with the hateful fate she deserved. But for her grip on Rusfaer, the beastslayer would have been crushed to death in those unforgiving coils.

Jhidik had skipped out from behind the crumbling statue and joined in the fray, but was surprised by a sudden murderous slap of Pygra's tail. The whipping flesh was too fast for his failing wits and he was sent flying between the serpent and lynx statue, and on into the pool. Thrashing and gasping, the Pirean broke surface. He flailed in ice cold water. But helplessly he was pulled along by a current too merciless for his tired limbs to combat and the icy water numbed him, his mail dragging him down, and he rolled head over toe, out over and between the legs of the frightful toad-lizard squatting like a barbaric gargoyle, grinning savagely, guarding the gateway of Hell, the Hall of Beasts, and down, down the soulless cliff.

Dereas gave a croak of dismay. But he could not help him.

The snake had lessened her ruthless grip on Rusfaer, momentarily checked by the beastslayer's assault, and Rusfaer managed to wriggle free of her unfurling coils to crawl gasping on the stone behind the serpent idol. He staggered to his knees. A supernatural resilience sparked his blood, as if providence had given him chance once again to embrace his beloved Pameel, and fulfill his life mission.

He stumbled on weak legs over to the pool's edge where he grasped his sword. Gasping in the reek of the snake's filth all over him, he turned to face the monster, but this time with grim acceptance, and the last look of tragic understanding that he could not stand against the snake. One stroke he had before her ugly mouth closed on his body.

The monster's tail swished forward. It passed near Fezoul's crouching place and the mountain king, feeling somewhat useless in the fray, stabbed out his blade deep into scaly hide.

The snake jerked. Momentarily distracted, she turned her full attention to where the figure with the small blade had struck. She bypassed the staggering warrior and whipped out a loop of tail around the astounded king before he had taken his next breath.

The mountain king's eyes bulged in shock. A short, sharp shriek stuck on his lips.

Dereas watched dumbfounded as the diminutive king was lifted in that rippling coil and the dwarf's features contorted in a grisly resignation of a fate destined from the day he was born. The dwarf's lips puckered in a ghastly gurgle. "Aaaaaggh! I curse you, Pygraaa," he croaked.

Dereas surged forward and hacked at the glistening coil. A terrible unreasoning rage burned in him at sight of the defenseless king locked in a monstrous loop. Pygra's grisly trunk sprouted blood. Rusfaer, tottering at his side, grabbed at the king and pulled him to safety, free from the slackening, suffocating grip of the blood-maddened snake.

Pygra hissed. She thrashed and writhed, her tail a whip of spasmodic rage.

Dereas threw himself headlong toward the reptilian jaws of death. His brain and every cell of his wracked body was overcome with a giddy sense of nothing to lose. His blood burned with the revived daring and recklessness of his youth—that fearlessness that had earned him the name 'Beastslayer'. A wild, unheeding battle lust came over his soul. He gripped his sword two-handed and rained thunderous stroke upon thunderous stroke on the snake. The arched midsection of the great Pygra knotted and looped and whipped with terrific anguish. Sword dripped red, as Rusfaer stumbled in again for another thrust. The mountain king, supine, began to roll in a heap, but somehow mustered some resolve. He rose up, eyes wild and fierce, glaring at the snake and cursing demoniacally with smoldering vengeance. This was not the Fezoul whom Dereas knew, but in those transformed features Dereas saw a regal figure standing up to his full height, his heart filled with hate for this ghastly snake. Fezoul staggered forward on small but determined feet, stripped clean of fanatical bond and tie to his hallowed deity, and he hacked and stabbed the snake's hide without care or consequence for his actions.

The serpent came rearing back to smite him and the little warrior sagged, but Rusfaer, coughing and staggering, snatched up the king once more and dragged him away from that hissing wall of death before the fang-forked mouth could swallow him in one gulp.

With the loss of her sight it took a split second for Pygra to use her smell and questing tongue to scope out the new situation.

The same glinting fangs now aimed at Dereas...

Dereas blinked, jerked back to avoid her bared fangs. He raised a gleaming blade and with a flying leap and a wild ululation of his people on his lips, fled across the snake's line of smell and sense, smiting and laying a wicked, slicing arc which parted Pygra's beaked nostril in twain. Her battered beak parted in a painful gush, and her coils knotted and whipped along the moldering pavestones. The strange silent statues bore witness to Pygra's pain and agony. A stray loop flailed and Rusfaer and the mountain king were knocked sideways, inches from the pool's lapping edge.

The end was near for them, for the snake was invincible, and could seemingly forebear any human punishment. No human strikes could fell that immortal thing! He panted for breath, his elbows on his knees, sword hanging slack, and he murmured an appeal to Balael one last time...

But creeping weirdly from the open portal came a cadaverous shadow, a chill larger than even Pygra, larger than life. And from the shadow emerged a hostile dark shape hewing past the dangling hinges of the shredded door, smashing and crumbling rock that held it. The shape snorted steam through a set of flared nostrils.

Xabren's mother-lizard!

In the thick of battle, they had missed the thuds and roars of wrathful lizards.

Pygra halted to assess the new danger.

It was the female saurian, who had clawed her restless body into the cavern, driven by the smell of serpent, a spoor for which she hankered and had been tracking for days now. On her hind legs she stood, bellowing like an ox, the volume of a hundred war horns, torn by her loathing for her most hated enemy of her race—the snake.

Greta's plated ribs rose and fell in a chest heaving to lusty pleasure, still drunk with rapture at her recent release from the cage. Her front legs wind-milled, her crusted barrel body jacked on hind legs. She might have been mad for snake flesh, however winded or fatigued she was from her long chase through the miles of caves carved in the haunted mountain. But she had pushed and squeezed through small places and her hide and forelegs were scored and bloody and notched and rubbed raw in places.

Dereas's knees sagged. It was a well known fact that lizard and serpent have been mortal enemies—since the beginning of time, and when Pygra sensed that giant shape swaggering in like a stuffed sow, she abandoned Rusfaer and Dereas and the tiny straw puppet that comprised the mountain king, and she slid with relish to meet the gnashing, roaring lizard that threatened to undermine her domain and snatch away her well-earned prey.

11: The Time of the Lizard

The ages drift, and men's dreams with it,
And time's wheel rolls from Snake to Lizard,
On a day when Darfala weeps tears of blood!

—Skald's cry...anonymous

Greta perhaps did not see the threat in the snake at first. Her newfound freedom to hunt had given her a reckless confidence and clouded her better sense. The serpent's scent was thick in her nostrils, enough to drive her mad. Caged for so long in her rank pen, she was not thinking right. Pygra was an aged snake, one of the first, primordial creatures of her time, a proto-serpent of ancient cunning, whose primitive hunting instincts had been passed down from generation to generation. Twisted genes carried echoes of gore and slaughter, which had evolved since her ancestors had first dropped into the slimes of faraway swamps—from the time of the primordial egg at the beginning of everything. She had developed a deviousness which far exceeded her ugliness and her small brain capacity and she lured her prey into slippery, death-dealing coils with instinctive skill, without pretense. Stalking was her craft; she was a master at it. She dreamed of hunting her prey in idle moments in the darkest places below Vharad. And yet, if she had any fault, it was insatiable gluttony. It prompted her to eat and eat for slaughter's sake. After consuming thrice her weight, she could consume a barrow-load more—no different a habit than the tusked dogs of the northern steppes, beasts that tear flesh and rend hide for the pure sport of gorging meat.

Not surprising then, when the great serpent lunged, the mother lizard fell.

Greta fell on all fours as Pygra propelled her massive body forward and struck with terrific strength and agility. Greta snapped out her horrific jaws, but quicker still was Pygra, who dodged, faster than the strike of any Eakor. Green teeth aimed for her iridescent trunk only grazed her. Now the serpent ducked once under the plated underbelly and wrapped thrice about the bloated abdomen that carried fresh young.

Greta rolled thrashing with claws unfurled and snapped with her curved neck trying to throw Pygra off and stop that accursed, constricting death. But the snake had wrapped a dozen loops about her midsection before she could do anything, and she felt the wind wheeze out of her ravaged lungs like an arrow-torn sail. Greta's spine was breaking, her ribs cracking under pressures of muscles too sinewy to claw through. Her bones were being crushed. She lay wheezing in pain. The crafty serpent loosened her grip for a brief instant to bend her snout close. As fast as the coils had furled, the fanged mouth spread wide and grabbed hold of the crusty, hooded, lolling head and gulped the female saurian down, spasm by spasm, ingesting that still, warm flesh with ghoulish delight. Each convulsion of that repulsive, wedge-shaped head brought the lizard disappearing further and further inside the swollen tubular body, foot by everlasting foot.

Such was Greta's demise—and Pygra's obsession for living flesh. The snake did not flinch or think about the consequences.

Dereas gulped back his horror—shrinking away, witness to one of nature's grisliest acts. Out of the corner of his eye he noticed that the water pulsing out of the waterfall had turned a bleaker hue, a pale amber, after the snake had ingested Greta.

Fezoul rocked back on his heels, his lips bleating out a fateful warning, "Death in the tunnels! The shadow of death to all!" And his voice rose like the stroke of a gong.

How it happened that the green water turned to amber, Dereas did not know; only that mystic forces still lived in Vharad, and were at play in this devilish place on top of the world.

The bulge that was Greta slowly traversed down the curling

swath of Pygra's body as Dereas and the others watched the ghastly feeding with a horror that knew no bounds. But for only a few seconds. Jerking to attention, they willed their feet toward the exit. But escape from the shattered doorway was thwarted. Another terror was coming. A monstrous shadow darkened the threshold of the ancient doorway. A dark head poked through the gap, sent them back reeling.

The male lizard had sniffed twice, forging its way into that vile chamber, and knew that tragedy had hit the moment it stepped foot within. Kruger was not as naive as Greta who had died horribly and without requital, and it sensed the power of the snake whose body glistened with preternatural vitality and whose maimed eyes stared sullenly—but also it had the advantage of fresh wits, something that the cretinish serpent who skulked sinuously before it did not, so laden and dulled with fresh kill. Pygra was not acting as shrewdly as she normally would. The enormous, cursed lizard she had swallowed was a foul weight in her coiled bulk and the terrible claw-edged monster that lumbered into the chamber now, head moving back and forth like a bear, had its razor teeth pressed in a dangerous snarl.

Pygra seemed detached, sensing the new presence with perplexity. Then she bristled with excitement and bared fangs. The prospect of so much fresh meat in her belly made her tongue tremble to the scent of fresh flesh. A bounty was hers on which to gorge! Too many dark years had passed of scant feasting on only rats and vermin and the odd careless lizard. She had grown grasping, willful, covetous. Already she had a giant lizard inside her and would have more! How she swished her tail in anticipation of such feasting! And in her excitement, her mallet-like head reared high, smacked the lower ceiling, flaking chunks of rock from the walls and sending boulders falling into the pool with splashes and thuds. She slithered sideways down the cavern in serpentish glee. Her notched tongue flicked and her salivating maw yawned in a mounting hiss of celebration and obscene jubilation.

Without warning, Kruger went berserk, rushing forth with the knowledge that its dead mate was inside that gluttonous thing. Pygra was perhaps overconfident in her abilities. Her record of kills was formidable and she rose bristling with looped coils to greet the bellowing menace. Grunting with primordial savagery, Kruger lashed out with gnawing teeth and hewed the snake sorely with its barbed claws, laying bare huge patches of her skin and flesh. Pygra sprang, coiled about its neck, but she was so bloated from her fresh kill that she did not have the strength to quickly despatch the saurian, as normally she would do.

In one swift movement, the vengeful lizard dipped its head, sank on its hindquarters, raked its front paws across her hide and broke free of her murderous clutch, only to sink teeth into her bare fleshy neck. The serpent slashed about in a perfect circle, her loops still writhing about the big lizard's body, and muscles still squeezing slow life out of it, but weaker now.

The fugitives fled out from behind the statues as Kruger toppled sideways, crashing upon salamander and crab effigies. The two monsters beat their tails in frenzy and lay there in a dizzy tangle of limbs and blood-splattered hides and coils, thrashing feebly. Only moments before they had been bent on killing each other. Now the reptiles wheezed out their failing breaths and Kruger's jaws still clamped on the serpent's neck, as it bled out on the rocks. The serpent's snout parted in a rasping gurgle.

Rusfaer watched in a kind of dazed fascination. Dereas saw his brother crawl to his feet, wobbling on shaky limbs. Their torsos were bloodied and blood-spattered weapons rose in nerveless arms. Pygra, the aged snake, still twitched and flailed, but not nearly as forcibly as before. Nonetheless, she rose with awful strength, one of her fangs now snapped and slanted inward on an angle. She swayed her head back and forth, assessing movements around her. She was a gargantuan tower of supple vigor. Even as the blood pulsed out of her glistening hide in a dozen places, she gained her resolve. Leaving behind the dead Kruger, she slowly moved toward the figures she sensed nearby.

Fezoul held his hands over his eyes, shaking like a torn leaf, cowering behind the safety of the bat statue. Yet moments ago, he had come to Rusfaer's aid, during his hour of recognition of the horror that was Pygra, stabbing at the serpent's tail when it swept by his hiding place. Now he efforted to block out the sordid reality of his own death.

A new threat riveted Dereas's attention. At the shadow of the entranceway he heard the familiar pounding of clawed feet and the rattle of a hundred tulwars and rustling mail shirts. A sea of menacing faces milled behind a rising shape, pushed in from the back, groping for human flesh—a desperate mob keen for retaliation or whatever deranged cause their king had given their brainwashed skulls.

Rusfaer and Dereas struggled toward the pool, ready to jump in if need be. A mounted figure and a set of watery eyes rose over the crest of the twitching bodies, a fervid glint in the darkness—the lizard king riding on the shoulders of the Rgnadon. His eyes were bloodshot and glowering with triumph. Somehow, during the long journey up the tunnel, he had managed to tame and ride the beast again.

Dereas had fought dozens of battles in his life, but this was certainly his most tasking and bizarre. And yet, he was wise enough to know that numbers were not everything and that discipline offered as much as tactics and strength.

On came the Rgnadon and the pompous, demented lizard king riding upon its plated back. The lizard folk streamed after like lemmings through the mangled doorway, gnashing and brandishing their weapons, driving and dragging small battering rams on wheels and jury-rigged barrows and baskets of weapons, muttering in low, garbled, weird voices.

Dereas scrambled back behind the stone tortoise statue, his eyes desperately questing for some means of escape. The grille was blocked access.

Seeing no easy solution, he gripped his dripping weapon, struggling to fathom why the lizard king would drive his subjects like cattle all through this hopeless zigzag of tunnels, transporting all those weapons—crates of them, and strange siege engines to boot. Did they use them to carve or blast their way through the tunnels, and provide a way for their obscene reptiles to squeeze through? Another testament of his cruel insanity?

Dereas furrowed his brow and willed himself to comprehend the scope of the lizard king's demented mind—this sinister renegade who was once a dwarfed man with the name of Xabren.

He grimaced with disgust, realizing the ultimate reckoning had come. None could stand against the Rgnadon. Perhaps the time had truly passed from Snake to Lizard...

The lizard king flourished his arms in a frenzy. "Seize them, you fools!" He pointed a jeweled finger. "They must be punished, suffer ritual abasement and incubation in eggs!"

Dereas hissed in Rusfaer's ear: "What I wouldn't give for a bow and quiver to put an arrow through that miserable wretch's heart."

Rusfaer mumbled agreement, a toothy scowl on his face.

Dereas held his notched blade ready to fight; Rusfaer grimly planted his bulk at his side. The two swaggered forth, crouched in fighter's stance, balancing on the balls of their feet. Fezoul pulled himself together and set his toes clambering at their heels, moved by their courage. His poniard was raised and gripped tremulously in his hands.

The Rgnadon had other plans for the fugitives. Contrary to its master's wishes, the beast lumbered into the cavern's center and studied the lump in Pygra's middle. It cocked its head to the side, seeing the mass bulbed like a rotten tumor, heavy as stone. Even in its slanted skull, a dim intelligence began to register and a sequence of monstrous connections fired, that Greta had been eaten alive. Its eyes gleamed malignantly; its bestial jowl parted redly and teeth dripped with slavering effluvia as it tossed its head back and threw the lizard king several feet behind on its turreted back. The lizard king, drunk with power, clawed his way back up, hung on the barbs of the long neck, laughing and howling. He was imbued with a reckless confidence, not entirely sane. A monarch he was, but a wild rider he was not. He flirted with death as the beast reared toward the eternal foe, the primordial Pygra.

With a feral roar, the monster attacked the languid, recumbent snake. The Rgnadon bolted straight for her jugular, ripped green-gummed teeth into the snake's back. The growing swarm of lizard-folk halted and quaked, enthusiasm suddenly dulled upon sight of the snake and the bloody mass that was Kruger.

Pygra indeed had come back to life. Baring fangs and hissing, she rose in murky afterlife, and Dereas saw in fascinated horror the force of will that she had. He shrank under the shadow of that demonic reptile. The snake's coils rippled to ripe life again and Dereas's mouth hung slack. *She must be possessed*, he mumbled to himself. The giant lizard smashed its heavy skull into the snake's crown just behind the ear, grinding sidewise into flesh and sinew. Pygra was stunned, but not daunted. She rocked her massive body sideways and hissed and looped her trunk slithering in a writhing offensive, sidewinding under the Rgnadon's kneecaps.

The lizard king was thrown clear, flung to the stone with a resounding thwack to land in a dazed heap before Dereas and Rusfaer. Pygra began to encircle the Rgnadon's legs, twining her coils and binding him with crushing force. Heedless of the epic violence at play, the lizard king advanced on the warriors, stabbing with his scepter.

Dereas parried, stepped inside the lizard king's instep, struck and elbowed him in the fleshy part of his midsection, hearing a rib crack.

The king bellowed in pain, swept out again with his jeweled scepter. The two glared eye to eye. Dereas knocked the ineffectual weapon aside, his quivering blade egging for reprisal, but resisted the urge to run him through. Rather, he used him as a shield, instead of cleaving him scalp to sternum, as Pygra, whose dim brain now realized the significance of this person, loosed her hold on the gasping Rgnadon and reared up like a cobra and whipped hard to wedge a head down to pitch fangs into the exposed king.

Recovering from the assault, the Rgnadon thrust a knotted foreleg forth and blocked the strike that would snap the king's head off. It thrust its saw-toothed teeth into the snake's neck.

Perhaps it was one wound too many for Pygra. The snake, weakened with the blood-spilling and still heavy with fresh kill, jerked like a kite in the wind. She swayed out of reach of the death-giving teeth. Amid her fluting hisses and the roars of the Rgnadon, the lizard king clambered back up on the spine of his saurian, tilting back his own head, despite his wounds, flinging a maniacal cry to the crystal-laced ceiling.

"Kill all!" he shrilled, white foam spuming from his mouth. And the lizards moved forward, sling-darts aimed, ready to pincushion Pygra. But most swayed back, giving grunts of uncertainty, with the belief that they would pierce their god instead. Some iron bolts found their mark in Pygra's trunk. But many missed their mark and thunked into the hide of their god instead, at which the creature bellowed in wrath.

Pygra for the first time, shrank in the face of that awful shadow of the Rgnadon. Despite her atrocious wounds, she tried to slither away, but the hideous weight of Greta anchored her like ball and chain.

For her there was no escape. The Rgnadon snapped like a rabid wolf at the snake's retreating, uncoiling body, grabbing at a place here, a place there, behind the neck, at the base of the trunk, whipping the snake back and forth as a hound the unfortunate rodent or rabbit.

The writhing snake flew through the air and landed in a thudding heap amid the circle of ravaged beast statues. There would be no mercy. A hundred years of ghoulish feasting was coming to an end, and the Rgnadon, enraged beyond measure, rent the serpent ear to ear. The beast knew the foul snake had eaten the mother lizard and killed its male kin. It held her down with its webbed, clawed forefeet and disemboweled her without compunction, while tearing chunks out of her hide and face, ripping the carcass where the great bulge lay, half way down her tubular mass.

The battered snake squealed a last cry of mournful, desolate agony. Then it thrashed and twitched, and tried to wrap her blood-gummed coils about that merciless foe for one last time, as she had done so many thousand times to hapless victims. But she could find no hold in the slippery blood streaming off her failing muscles and knew that she was at an end.

Dereas shuddered to think of the succession of carcasses amassed in that grotesque body. For now in the cavern's ethereal light, the mother lizard's corpse was exposed, but not the same lizard that had entered Pygra's noisome gullet. The acid from the snake's digestive tract had already eaten away at Greta's skin, turning it from a dark green to a horrid milky white, making it barely recognizable.

Dereas recoiled at the sight—that repugnant, mucilaginous mass that was once green-backed Greta. He wanted to vomit. Rusfaer and the mountain king both doubled over nauseous, as other nondescript grizzled shapes and egg-shaped lumps poured out with the Rgnadon's snuffling and clawing into its innards—shapes that might or might not have been Hafta or Draba or any other of the countless lizards that the monster had wolfed down in her grisly gluttony of late.

The Rgnadon dragged the mother lizard out of the snake carcass whole, teeth bared, slavering, dripping, and snuffling in grief. It bellowed and whimpered, assessed the grizzled skin with tilted head, blinking its blazing yellow eyes. Dereas entertained little doubt that the ruin of the Rgnadon's sister-kin was imprinted on its lizard mind forever. The beast hopped back in surprise, as the dead, floppy thing that was the mother lizard, suddenly jerked in a death spasm and sighed out a last stream of slimy pus. The egg she had been holding popped out of her genitals—and was the last act the reptile managed, as it loosed a slobbering sigh.

The warriors stared in glassy-eyed revulsion, bearing silent witness to what they had survived. Dereas did not doubt that the serpent would have killed them all, if her gluttony had not been so overpowering.

The terrible vitality of the snake was even now chilling to witness. Chopped and maimed, turned inside out by the Rgnadon's teeth and webbed feet, still the lambent eye flickered and the muscles of her invincible body twitched.

Could she still be alive? Dereas's mind balked at the concept.

From aloft the lizard king gave a sudden shriek, "Get them, you fools!" He thrust his staff at his dawdling, sloe-eyed subjects who had stood mesmerized, moon-faced throughout the battle lust. His sceptre rapped hysterically on the Rgnadon's skull and lanced in the direction of the two, blood-stained warriors who stood bare of arms and gaping with mirthless fatality at the miniature authority who had been the force behind a long series of horrors.

The lizard king rasped with triumphant awe. "Dawcocks! Did we creep blindly through the murk to avoid the snake and the crab and other dire enemies to stand here like zombies? Attack!"

But the throng shifted restlessly from foot to foot, staring at each other, an indecisive rustle rising in their ranks.

"Fools!" raved the king. "Did we let the serpent guide us to these rude, backward cretins, so you could cringe and mewl? Stand up! Do not gad about! Capture the offenders. Or I will loose our god among you." And with a low murmur he goaded the Rgnadon to motion and a shrill cry rose over the stunned gathering. "Defy me, if you dare!"

Dereas and Rusfaer grimaced with contempt and shifted defensively behind the larger, bull statue. The lizard king spumed froth. He spurred his heels into the back of his reptilian charger, prompting the Rgnadon to jerk forward and peel back its fleshy jowl and send a terrible roar to the roof that rocked the cavern.

But the throng shrank back, stunned in the jumble of terrible carnage, so great was their fear of the twitching snake that still knotted in unnatural agony. Some semblance of grisly vitality still showed in that glistening mass of loops. The ghost-gremlin light that glared in the dead eye was a nightmare that would haunt the lizards' souls and be a reminder to all of what had tainted their realm for so long, but yet still smoldered, bright and alive.

"Cowards! I will have you flayed! Get them!" The lizard king's raving voice rose in a lunatic howl. "The Time of the Lizard is now! Now, I say!"

Resolve sprang into the limbs of the lizard people. In a teeming rush they charged the companions, hefting glinting curved blades and sling-darts and screaming as one mad mob.

"Gnador, Gnador!" The mob chanted, a rising, lurid echo which built in volume, becoming a dim thrum of chaos. It reached a crescendo that shook the cavern as much as the Rgnadon's baleful roar, and they acted as one again.

Dereas and Rusfaer snapped out of their dumbstruck trance, considered their few options.

The Rgnadon sprang forward on a signal from the lizard king, head-butting the big bull statue sideways behind which the companions had ducked. The horned statue fell, split in twain, a few yards from their stubborn crouch. The Rgnadon violently swept the pieces into the pool with its forefeet.

Without protection, the three slunk back in terror. Dereas and Rusfaer held their swords, prepared to fight and die, taking many goodly numbers of the lizard king's minions with them. But now a blur of motion and an enemy lizard's excited cry gave the mob pause. The gleaming egg that Greta had laid started to shake.

Others halted, bobbed and swayed in superstitious awe as if the birthing of a lizard on a battlefield were an omen. A tiny claw punched its way through the glistening top, while a section of the cap flipped off and sent a wet liquid and a slick snout poking through. The hole grew, admitting a glistening neck and a set of bright round, blinking eyes.

A hushed murmur rumbled from the gathering. Dereas and Rusfaer stared with wonder. How could any creature survive such a compromised birth?

The egg cracked, and a slick wet thing, some new being of nightmare, rolled out on the stone beside the pool, wearing its birthing liquids still.

A being like no other! On superficial examination, the newborn was similar to the other lizards, more white-skinned than greenish-black, a premature entity, cursed with a lizardish head and a man-shaped body and man-limbs, except for lizard-clawed feet and deformed forefeet.

With ghastly repugnance, Dereas saw that the body of the mother lizard had protected what was once Amexi from the acid of the snake's digestive tract.

Several of the lizards scampered out to collect the newly-birthed citizen. As bewildered as he was, the lizard that was Amexi, twitched and crawled in his own slime, and allowed them to herd him back to their huddled throng—a place of comfort and safety, not understanding that the blood and twisted body parts lolling gruesomely around this beastly place of horror, had been his place of entry into the world. His childlike expression eclipsed Draba's in the seconds of rebirth and the rank setting shattered all illusion of a gentle, halcyon world.

A growl of anguish burst from Dereas's throat. Both he and Rusfaer nursed emotions of unfathomable disgust and loathing at the grisly birthing. Dereas felt cheated of justice, being witness to their warrior-comrade taken in by that lizard horde and nursemaided beneath slimy feet. His heart fell when the lizard's pale misty-gray eyes scanned briefly at their trio and registered no familiarity at all. He struggled forth, cursing and calling on Balael, arching blade, ready to lay sword to end that mutant life, but had no chance. In the teeming wall of gnashing foes that confronted him, the lizards left no crack or file wide enough for him to plunge through. Thin bolts of sharp iron flew wide in close quarters. Dereas dodged the missiles. In a throat-choked frenzy, he slashed hard at the wall of long-snouted, knob-kneed lizards that pushed him back. Dozens died under his scythe-like strokes; others rained tulwars on his mail. His blade bit hard into helm and skull, others went shrieking sideways, crashing to their knees, faces crimson mashes of teeth and brains.

But that was as far as Dereas got.

Sparked by the birth of a new citizen, the lizard king took matters in his own hands and spurred the Rgnadon on, surging through the teeming throng, trampling some of his own subjects.

"Gnador, Gnador!" The crowd parted and started up the chant again until it grew to a hysterical fervor. So was birthed in the perverse chaos a man-lizard, seeded from Amexi and a squirming newt—as a man more than lizard.

With ever more revulsion, Dereas and Rusfaer fought and slashed and hewed while their flesh crawled.

The two crabbed back, letting blind instinct and whistling swords protect their flanks, their brains blocking out the sight they had just witnessed. Now the Rgnadon's evil attention turned on them in force, with red eyes blinking with wrath. The grunting hordes darted between its legs, bobbing and pressing forward in numbers with insidious zeal.

The lizard king rode his steed with a joy approaching rapture. He stood tall in his saddle, gloating with delight. "Disbelievers! Since you will not join us, prepare to die! The Time of the Lizard is now!"

Before the Rgnadon could smite them, Dereas and Rusfaer rolled back closer to the pool, dodging missiles aimed for their vitals. The rush of cascading water rang loud in their ears only feet away. Pushed desperately toward the icy water, they glimpsed a towering mass of foam that dropped on high, where the raging stream rushed out of the mouth of the mountain in between the twin horns. The daylight streamed in, stinging their eyes.

A giant mouth snapped down at them.

They ducked. The grisly incisors flew wide and while Dereas and Rusfaer beat back the attackers, Fezoul, shaken by the rebirth, eyes staring wildly, leaped among the throng in a savage blur, hacking at lizards left, right and center, his compact blade gleaming and rising and falling. Up and down it plunged, a tiny whirling flame, while Rusfaer joined in, making mockery of the snarling, shambling shapes which threw up scaly limbs in defense and fell in twitching heaps, having underestimated the timid king and his ruthless, sword-slashing companions.

Dereas marveled. It was almost as if something had snapped inside Fezoul, having faced his worst fear in the coils of Pygra's wrath. Now he was a seething foe, all the timidity burnt out of him.

Rusfaer and Dereas laughed in maniacal unison; they tore a red path through that motley mix of lizards, shredding reptilian hide with zeal, sending shrieking lizards and their captains lolling headless to their knees or in bloody ruins into the pool, swept away in the icy waters.

The brothers' mail was shredded, their swords notched, and bodies dressed in red and awful cuts. But their faces shone alight in the afterglow of slaughter and mayhem.

The numbers were too great and they were being pushed back in a crushing wall of lizard hide. The blades felt heavy in their hands. They stumbled back against the last standing statues and the lapping edge of the pool. They crouched and darts thumped against the stone. The lizard king made a dramatic motion; the Rgnadon bulled its way forth, cued by its rider's imperial sweep of arm. It roared and crushed a dozen lizards in its wake. Its great mottled head swung low.

Dereas held his ground. He slashed mighty strokes across the beast's raging snout, slitting a dripping nostril as he had Pygra's tongue. With the Rgnadon's mighty roar in their ears, they scrambled into the shadow of protection of the sinister serpent statue whose feet touched the pool's edge. Darts ripped into the stony coils inches from where they had last been. It was a hop and skip from doom.

The creature violently ripped the hated effigy from its stony roots, and hurled it end over end to land splashing into the pool. It then came lunging at them for the kill, its nauseous snout a rank, bloody battering ram, snuffling, snorting, blowing hot air and rancid breath into their faces while the lizard king rocked like a grinning cherub in his saddle, screeching and hollering at the top of his lungs till he was pink in the face. The cat and mouse game was over. While lizard blades wheeled and foes circled from all directions, Rusfaer, in a growl of hatred and dismay, pushed the two of them roughly into the water as he jumped himself, before the Rgnadon's feet could stomp them to pulp.

Backwards they fell into the icy waters, rolling swiftly, passing under the massive stone toad's squatting underbelly and out into the open air. Dereas felt ice chunks rake his numbed body. The water was so cold—colder than hell's winter—and it sent burning shivers up his spine. His head broke the surface, the first hint of exposure taking its toll, and he gasped, shivering, and was swept over the edge...

Eyes swimming with stars, Dereas felt a certain weightlessness, a tumbling, dreamland rush. Natural forces gripped him, in a free fall of spinning horror and nightmare. Faster and faster his body spun, with the roar of falling water in his ears, while white foam and spume sprayed everywhere. His descent was broken by snatches of blue sky, as azure as the day it was ever breathed into being by whatever dream god was responsible for the whole of existence. The desert plains lay choked with an unwholesome brown, and boulders reeled and rocks thrust cliffborn. The sky was one minute his horizon, the next, a raging wash of crushing liquid. Then, the foaming water was spent, and he tumbled into a maelstrom.

Splash! Down into a murk-haunted, greenish pool. In water cold as ice. Dereas's lungs cried for air, his muscles screamed. But all three rebels tumbled like rocks, rolling in greenish-white froth. Over the rim of the world they peered, down another cascade and a rolling spray, at least eighty feet down...

Dereas and Rusfaer's shredded mail was light enough to keep them from getting hopelessly dragged under the roiling spray; luckily, the current swept them to shallower water and closer to a bank where they could wallow without drowning.

They looked to the cliff above, in between the rough rises and dunks through the spume of the cataract, and Dereas thought to see a slick, scaled head of a beast peering down malevolently over them between the two fangs of rock where the waterfall cleaved. The ogreish face glistened in the saffron light more than a hundred feet above and the creature was terrible and gleaming to behold in its hour of glory and victory. It was mightily flanked by gargantuan statues carved in the cliff itself: one, a raging serpent, grim twined about an ornate throne, the other a hideous lizard rearing on its hind legs and roaring at the sky. Dereas recalled these statues while clutched in the talons of the Eakors, though now he could see both statues faced each other as timeless, eternal enemies. The twain flanked the place where the water fell and where the Rgnadon stood with the lizard king and his staring hordes.

Sputtering and choking, Dereas paddled toward shore, wading through lizard corpses that had fallen with their heads split or throats cut.

Shaking a quaking fist upward, he lolled finally chest deep in a tranquil lee of the pool. "Behold," he croaked, "the end of your kingdom, you fiend." His mind surged with the pleasant reassurance that the mother lizard had finally died in the belly of Pygra and could birth no more vile eggs.

But this bitter summation was not entirely accurate.

There would be other queens to crown.

And still the Rgnadon lived...

The creature ducked its stone-battered hide back into that black-mouthed gap and bashed about, smashing its armored snout repeatedly against the cavern walls.

Dereas stared in dull wonder. What could it possibly be doing? He shuddered as a section of rock face slid free and a massive rib of the mountain collapsed in a crumbling heap—capsizing the great leering serpent statue to the left, sending it and whole scree-sloped arms of the mountain crashing down the cliffside. Trees and bushes crushed like wheat, and a rubble-strewn path cleared a way for the lumbering beast and its chattering horde to scramble down the cliff.

No, it was not possible! Dereas crowed madly. He shook the fog out of his brain and grunted with torment, as he struggled still for shore, but his frozen limbs hardly obeyed him. The gargantuan lizard did not go away, nor did the chanting, gnashing horde that came streaming out of the gap, down the steep ramp of fallen rock and shattered trees that marked the place very close to their own forlorn landing.

The water slowed in a series of foaming eddies, and lungs bursting for air and limbs numbed to the bone, Dereas lifted his aching arms in an attempt to dog paddle near to Rusfaer and the mountain king whom he saw floated spent, also catching their breath, wallowing near the shore. Almost half drowned, the fugitives clawed their way to shore and lay in ravaged, pallid heaps, trying to slap the warmth back into their ice-numbed bodies.

The time was midday. A pale light streamed down from the sky and stung their eyes. No broken bones reigned among the company. Large shapes hovered in the air, Eakors, roving in dark circles amid the sheer flanks of the impassive mountain. Not far enough away for Dereas's comfort.

Black Balael! Could the day turn any worse?

Dereas swept his blinking eyes among the low sagging palms clinging to the ragged slope and scoured the irregular shores of the pools that bulged outward from the main rush of water. The rough tumble continued zigzagging down the mountain side, in a distant white froth that hugged the avalanche-wracked landscape and the boulders and blasted flints that trailed like shattered bones down the slope, before it met the hard-baked desert plains far, far down at the mountain's foot.

There was no sign of Jhidik in those bleak vistas and Dereas's heart lurched with a sudden strange, panged distress.

Maybe the blood-spattered warrior had been swept farther downstream? Perhaps he lived still?

The hope seemed dim, judging from the rough cascades tumbling down the white surge and the hostility of the terrain blossoming up like fungal growth. Either his friend had drowned or been torn away by the mighty stream—or, as he thought grimly now, hauled away by the unspeakable Eakors hovering greedily amid the cloud-cloaked cliffs.

The idea was hideous, and Dereas directed his morose thoughts to other possibilities.

Rusfaer stumbled to his side, leaning rough hand unsteadily on his shoulder. "If he is dead, then I'm sorry for him. He was a valiant warrior. I regret not complimenting his courage while I had the chance." He had divined his brother's thoughts and Dereas was appreciative of the acknowledgment. Genuine remorse shone in Rusfaer's expression and Dereas felt a quiver of comradeship upon realizing how far his brother had progressed since that grim skirmish before entering Vharad.

"Perhaps he lives still," muttered Dereas defiantly. "He could still be hiding in the brush somewhere."

Rusfaer shook his head. "The Pirean would have called out. If he was alive and near here, he would have."

Dereas choked on the fact and the truth of it. He hung his head in limp, silent resignation.

Biting back his sorrow, he turned away and Fezoul likewise dipped his head in mumbling tribute to Jhidik who had fought many battles bravely throughout the trials in the haunted mountain and had saved all their skins many a time over.

Dereas accepted these disclosures with lips furled. He moved grudgingly away, treading a path through the low prickly cactus and weedy vegetation that followed the pebbly shore of the stream. He hoped there was something they had missed...

A scrap of Jhidik's blooded cloak they found in the mud and sand washed up on shore farther down. One of the short blades that comprised the splint Dereas had fabricated for him lay glinting dully in the pale sunshine not a few yards away. What did this imply? That his weapon was not abandoned here too, could mean many things. Dereas ran his eyes savagely about the terrain, but in the dark shapes in the sky he saw the only truth.

The mountain king moved a step closer. "Recall, your friend was stung with the mark of the serpent." He narrowed his eyes in cryptic anguish. "The serpent always demands a sacrifice—like it or not."

Dereas rounded on him in angry denial. "What do you mean, 'mark of the serpent'?" But Fezoul withdrew, shrinking under Dereas's gaze. As conveyed by all Fezoul's prophetic words, the 'mark' was hint of the blood prices to be paid. When Jhidik had willingly thrust his hand in the stone serpent's mouth, he had struck a bargain with the dark gods of Vharad themselves, and it did not bode well for him.

At that moment, a raucous sound drifted from above and forced them scrambling back into the shelter of a patch of withered bushes, pre-empting any more search for Jhidik.

They sought shelter on stumbling feet, or any means of escape from the swarm of lizards that were scudding down the slope. They hunched, bent-kneed among the tall, willowy weeds and the blasted boulders and flints. The purl of distant waterfall rushed to their ears—it rose above the sigh of the wind and the croaking of scavenging Eakors. With a sad acknowledgment they stared forlornly at the dominant cliff, gripped with the sudden awareness that their weapons were useless—swords had tumbled free of scabbards in the roil of water and only their dirks strapped tightly at their hips remained.

Jhidik would have to wait for another day, Dereas sighed, if Balael wished it.

He frowned, assessed his wounds. Blood seeped from a mess of gashes on his breast, shoulder, arms and legs. Rusfaer was bleeding from a score of old and fresh wounds. The mountain king remained remarkably unscathed, escaping any serious injury, only minor cuts, and luckily, no wrenched joints.

Dereas's mind wandered upon a phrase he had read in a distant place, a recollection of a childish fable of the past: "*And terrible beasts shall wander the world.*"

A queer tingle shuddered up his spine. An old memory jogged in his head, a series of surreal but vivid images. He remembered now of old, while wandering lost in the shalelands of Zim—in an ancient land full of dark secrets and ruined edifices of an elder age, that he had stumbled on one of those cursed temples of Amor-Amon-Reth, the Telamon King, where thousands were butchered in dark sacrifices to nameless gods. It was a place of earth, stone, filth and fire. He had blanched, swallowing hard, blinking back the curse of ages seen in those carven glyphs in a tumble of fallen masonry. They were sculpted on a toppled entablature, a ghoulish script of soul-disturbing warning—*Of terrible beasts, clawing their way down from the top of mountain, to rule Darfala...*

A gurgle escaped Dereas's throat and at the same time, the naked truth lay bared...as the roar of a feverish beast interrupted his ghastly reverie.

He shook his head, gripped his lizard dirk in torment. What had he loosed? Would he be remembered as the black pariah who had helped slay the 'great worm-serpent', only to release the ultimate scourge that broke Darfala? No, it couldn't be, not his legacy!

And yet, the terrible hints were in plain sight. He could no more stop the hands of fate and the lizardish march as fly to Zim's bloody, sacrificial-soaked altars on a winged stallion.

Fezoul's voice, whether from delirium or prophetic insight, came as a sibilant murmur. He whispered, "One day the lizards will come forth and overrun the world. When that day comes, the creatures of Darfala and her innocent peoples should fear—aye, fear, beastslayer—fear for their souls..." And with that prediction, he closed his eyes and fell in a swoon.

Rusfaer recoiled and crossed himself in the old tradition of the Huughite warrior warding off a curse. Dereas accepted the king's bleak finality. Some part of his primitive spirit knew that the gods had spoken through this mountain king, that a spoke had broken in the wheel of fate and that time had shifted.

With the destruction of Pygra, the yoke on the depraved lizards had been lifted and now there was nothing to stop them from their lusty assault abroad.

Ever were the lizard king's cries a darkling imprint on the natural environment and tree, leaf and rock cringed at the jubilant shouts that polluted the ravine. The lizard man's direful commands rose on the eastern wind, soaring like the mock cries of hellion gulls over the sea.

"Now onward to Tuyokton!" his shrieking wails caromed. "I rally you forth on a mission of the Rgnadon!" Rising in his seat, he launched his subjects on his twisted, perverse crusade.

Rank upon rank of the fiends marched down from that dark slab of the mountain, threading their way like black-green flies.

The throng switched-backed down the precarious defile flanking the waterfall, like teams of ants—hordes of them, great green-black gleaming things, jabbering in filthy tongues, with a hive-mind mentality, lapping at the heels of their mad leader on the back of the Rgnadon. The creature swung its plated bulk like that of an ancient ogre, its head swinging back and forth like a lumbering belamyl, a rambling beast on the prowl for dominion.

Crashing through the dwarfed, shredded trees, it snapped boughs and trunks like twigs; it kicked and batted boulders with its immense snout, making waste of the landscape and anything in its path. So the beast advanced, and the lizard king slapped his knees and bobbed like a pompous, yellow-eyed peacock.

The mad king thrust out his scepter and called out in a belligerent voice. "If you can hear me, unbelievers, then be dismayed! You must know by now this age of yours has come to an end! You rabble skulk close in the brush somewhere. I can smell you, like a batch of cock beetles and dung mites!"

And the king's throng's chants rose in a gusty crescendo of reptilian fervor.

"We will carve out an empire!" the monarch gusted and his screech rose over the roar of the falls and his voice seemed to gather weight in the tide of his maniacal crusade. His followers' screeches echoed dimly down the side of Vharad. "Perhaps it is providence that you prematurely hatched my pet, the Rgnadon!" he called out fiercely. "Come out, come out, wherever you are, skulking dogs!—become one with the Lizard! I can make you great yet! You cannot persist in these parched wastes. Become a lizard, while you can!" And down into the ravine his saurian beast sauntered, crunching great strides through the broad-leaved trees and rocks and prickly brush, until there was a long line of lizards flooding in his wake, tramping the wild goat paths and the hidden landings not far from where Dereas and his weary gang huddled in strange, shivering defeat.

"I would have waited another hundred years in my caution!" he boomed, chuckling in his jaunty humour. "The time is on us now. The Time of the Lizard!"

And they were a thousand strong, that frenzied host. For as far as the eye could see, lizards shambled out of the blasted cliff and came padding with their instruments of war to smash Tuyokton, and other cities, Dereas guessed. A march to the plains, ready to take on mighty kingdoms—even Yismin, the olive-river kingdom of the far south, with bone tulwars in their hands, like a skeleton brood of renegade mercenaries from a dark distant land of nightmare.

The Eakors, circling in expectant hordes, caught sight of the lizard vanguard and flew down in savage, hungry knots in a flurry of anticipation. They picked off marchers one by one, pulling them into the air like green locusts, and tore green limbs from their sockets or carved grisly hunks from their backs or scaled limbs.

Undaunted, the lizards bore baskets of darts with them, weapons formed of Tyrannus bones. These darts they had amassed, the same Dereas had caught glimpses of earlier.

The lizards fitted them to their slingshots and trained them up at the diving birds and shot them out of the sky.

The Rgnadon whipped back his wattled neck and snapped low-fliers out of the air, cleaving their skulls whole and spitting out the bones in clumps of filth into the bushes.

Dereas grit his teeth. He had hoped the Eakors would win this fight against the lizards that advanced on Tuyokton, that ancient city whose king had precipitated the mountain people's exile centuries ago.

The first ranks of the lizard army had come level with the companions' position at two-hundred yards, where they stared from behind a knot of fallen boulders and gillhorse bushes. Dereas tore off a segment of his ragged cloak to wrap a gaping wound on his left shin. He loped away, crouching for cover, and urged the wheezing mountain king to keep up with his hobbling trot. Rusfaer, wax faced, still in shock from narrowly escaping the snake's coils, followed on Dereas's heels. The trio left the chanting hordes behind to pick their way through scree and boulders and bushes like scavengers themselves, while the fervid lizards pushed onward down, ever down toward the plains where they might fulfill their accursed mission.

The ragged fugitives did not crane their necks over their shoulders or pause to watch that marching horde any further. They slunk away from that vulnerable position and blended into the foliage, sliding on a zigzagging path down through patches of wild scree, using all the protection of low-lying bushes and stranglewood hedges. To be spotted by Xabren and his throng at this time would be a grievous error. Down in the boulder-choked ravines and clumps of forked cacti, streams of lizards had poured from some hidden exit near the base of the mountain, wheeling and maneuvering rams and catapults. Thousands strong, they advanced, raising weapons in one wild rush in salute for their king whose very appearance proved he had emerged victorious over the snake.

Dereas did not know what to think of this new development. Numbed and shaken, he led Fezoul and Rusfaer away from that grim place. Shelter they found at last near a small brook overlooking a grove of palm trees, fed from the falls they had left behind.

The smack of webbed feet and the roar of beast and birds and lunatic king faded in the whine of the wind and Rusfaer, after drinking his fill of water, fell into a dazed heap in the downy weeds by the creek.

Dereas watched his brother, all muscled, sweat-soaked, mail-torn iron mass of him. Rusfaer slid painfully on his side, groaning, and slept the dream of exhaustion. From time to time the corners of his lips would twitch or he would roll over on his weedy pallet, snatch at his blood-tatted beard and call out in his sleep. Dereas did not relish this aimless flight of his brother's slumber. Who knew what roving horrors flitted back and forth in his brother's mind's eye under the dark veil of Vharad?

Dereas, too, sagged to a supine heap beside his brother, envying the rising and falling of his soft breathing, still stunned by the combined lizard advance and the king's ambition. He curled his knees up and took long drafts of air himself, let his eyes flutter, and the ache of endless anguish to wash away from his wracked limbs. He clutched at his beard and heard the silken words of the mountain king in his ear after a time:

"I never expected to leave Yarim-Id. I am indebted to you. The witcher's spell is lifted. Pygra is dead."

Dereas rolled restlessly on his side, gritting his teeth as he listened to Fezoul with half an ear.

"For saving my life, I pass on to you this charm of good fortune." And the mountain king pulled the amulet of his ancestors from around his grimy neck and snapped the shiny chain. "Good that Xabren let me keep it in the end. 'Tis the most significant thing I can give you, beastslayer."

Dereas graciously but sleepily accepted the talisman in a limp palm. He mumbled a thanks in his daze of exhaustion, feeling a stir of emotion. Without the guidance of the mountain king, he and his company never could have survived the mountain's horrors. As gray and nebulous as the dwarf's directions may have been, his cryptic words had rung true and in the end, he had proven himself a hero.

Drifting to sleep, Dereas thought he saw the slick, scaled beast peering once more down between the two fangs of rock where the waterfall fell glistening in the ruby light—but that was only a nightmarish dream.

The last fateful image would haunt Dereas's waking life for the rest of his days, the Rgnadon looking down that grim, daunting cliff with impassive superiority. To either side hung a hundred doomed souls, Xabren's children, Children of the Lizard people, overshadowed by the statues of the lizard and the snake of a dead realm...He felt, even in his dream that he was caught in a dream within a dream, that he had been only a figure in a great god's consciousness, as he walked a path that was not destined to be. A chill raced up his spine.

While a kingdom had brooded and festered in the bowels of the mountain, the world had lain unaware—of the reptilian storm that would take it one day, as prophesized in the grisly texts of Amor-Amon-Reth...

Rusfaer nudged and kicked the beastslayer awake some unknown time later with a rough boot toe.

Cursing and grunting, Dereas hauled himself to his feet, wiping the rheum out of his eyes. He saw to his horror that a wan light now trickled from a low hanging sun in a sky cracked with a thousand wispy clouds. How many hours had passed?

With grunting curses, Dereas tagged after Rusfaer, a sour taste in his mouth. The mountain king dogged at their side. They left Yarim-Id behind with all its dark secrets. Dereas felt some dark amusement in knowing that he had left his mark on the abhorrent Rgnadon, whose face was scarred for life, as had the snake been delivered her just desserts...Doubtless the lizard folk would crown a new queen among their lizard beasts before long, to spawn their loathsome eggs.

A mirthless grunt escaped his throat. He gave his head an angry shake. It was a joyless victory. Rubbing his temples, he wiped away the awful memories.

Aches, hunger, privation...the three gnawed at his senses. What now?

The fugitives foraged among the sun-baked bushes, poking blades here and there, searching for food, while the fading light of the afternoon dwindled. A sudden fleeting thought gripped Dereas—lost, hungry, exhausted, physically and emotionally battered, what purpose lay in that journey to the haunted peak? Why the struggle, terror and death? Seasoned warriors reduced to hunted animals? He shook his head. For the life of him, he could think of no reason, outside of the uncanny series of events that had brought him and his brother together in a fierce, fiery, fragile union.

The Eakors spread wings, still circling above, high enough to not be a threat. Such scavengers had turned their attention east, toward the lizard king and his demented horde who roved farther abroad with the malign beast. Doubtless the birds smelled the trio's blood below, but they could not or cared not to pinpoint their diminutive prey amid the scattered boulders and ragged bushes. At night, they would sneak away, Dereas considered, out of sight of the mountain and the predators that prowled the sky and take to the desert plains north—back to the steppes.

Rusfaer made a hoarse cry. He pointed to a fresh find of birds' eggs that had fallen from a nest in a scrawny balebollow tree. Starving as he was, somewhere after the experience of the lizard folk and their cursed, ghastly eggs, Dereas could not suck the life juice out of an egg, especially raw.

Good men had died. Only three had survived, while Jhidik's fate remained uncertain.

The beastslayer looked to the west, in the direction of Ahrion and Pameel, and in his heart leaped a fierce impulse, knowing what he must do...

CURSE OF THE KRAKEN

I : Lore of the Ancients

In the year 712, three shrewd mages, Anamog, Dranmog and Thanmog, became the elite *Magi Consules* to King Pyrmog at Mog palace. Anamog, wise, thoughtful, experienced, was the maven, the unspoken leader, who founded the group, and was wary of the power of the dark arts. Dranmog, edgier, was prone to a degree of risk-taking while Thanmog resided somewhere in the middle. The latter maintained a special skill of the taming of the beasts, this hooded monkish figure. Whereas Anamog guarded an aristocratic face, rich with somber features and a cultured tongue known to articulate wise and careful phrases, Dranmog was wily, with cat eyes of the softest amber, and graced with a darting expression of certain penetrating compass. He was forthright with chuckles that often irked listeners who did not realize what he found so amusing. It was more precise to say that of all in the realm, these three were the intellectual force behind the kingdom's functioning, creating policies that king Pyrmog would be a fool not to heed.

It had been nine hundred years after the third great ice age that the north-dwelling gnomes had migrated down from their blue-glittering ice caves and founded the fortress of Elsmaere on the bleak mound at Mog. They had come to be the forerunners of the Mogel race—a short, burly, dark-complexioned people with skin like leather, wide, tough heads and uncannily deep olive-green eyes. These gnomes were squat, no more than four feet tall, and enjoyed two main loves in life: sacred magic and the crafting of stonework, which included the finely-wrought structures of vaulted archways, adorning pillars, buttressed gothic stairwells, and graceful scrollwork, reminiscent of the Mogel famous palace, which had its beginnings in the earliest of times as a single turreted keep.

One day in the fall of 729 the three mages embarked on a pilgrimage. The 'quest', as it was called—which was surprisingly much against the will of Anamog. He could sense ill coming of the venture, but through one means or another, acceded to the cause anyway. It was Dranmog's idea, the youngest of the three, who with great ardency urged the others to comply and search out the krakens' treasure. It was reckoned past the fabled snow downs into the haunted land of the ice crags. This was the place of their heritage and interested Anamog at least for its mystery. For two moons Dranmog had been digging through moldering chests in the cellars and crypts filled with tattered remains of the Sisenian Scrolls. Here were writ hints of ancient treasure among the lost antiques of the five lands. The Scrolls, whose origin was shrouded in myth, were quilled by the long line of scribes, a doughty folk who had recorded events since the times before the Great Pillaging. Dranmog had read more than most, and one eerie reference to a fabled beast, or beasts—*krakens*, which were reputed to live in holes in the hills in the frosty fastness where the ice gleams an aquamarine blue and the snow sparkles silver. Krakens learned to 'collect' shiny things, so it was told, most beautiful and pleasing to eyes. The beasts flew hither to the southlands to acquire glittering items of beauty and resplendence. Terrible and ferocious was their means of locomotion: forty-foot wings that edged the sky with thorn-tipped spikes, flapping hideously like mechanical crocodiles. Gory-pointed snouts mantled razor-sharp teeth; bony-finned backs glinted gold and hooked claws dangled. With wicked gleaming magenta eyes, the creatures swooped, waving their hammer-pronged tails, and with one fell sweep crumbled the mightiest towers of the Valkorian people along the eastern shores of the Emerald Sea and lay low the strongest outposts of Kusse and Neanz farther away in the realm of the plains where dwelled the giants. Hungrily, the krakens would savor the spoils. The flesh of men and ogres they would eat, but the jewels, shiny and twinkling, they licked up with relish with their horrid black tongues, regardless of the scintillating sword hafts and shining blades clenched between their teeth. The treasure chests piled high with necklaces, diadems, scepters, pendants and lolled at the back of their throats. The beating of their wings was like the creak of castle gates as they tore across the sundered sky, whilst the denizens of Valkoria and Ogredur, who had been raped of their treasures, would whip out their pikes and curse the krakens while sadly picking up the pieces, repairing the damage wrought upon their citadels.

Dranmog translated a curious riddle from the Scrolls.

"Caves of old where krakens and gold,
Lie in darkness and dream, so it's been told,
In moldering depths an intrepid one finds,
The unnameable things which always bind,
That which is more precious than treasures bold,
Glinting brighter than silver, brighter than gold,
A vessel guarding secrets never been told—"

"I say there may exist a chance that this enchanted plunder remains," he cried.

"And what of these beasts—these krakens?" argued Thanmog.

"I've heard nothing but similar horror about their lot," attested Anamog.

"How do you propose we contend with the like of these hellions, when and if we find these mythical caves?" demanded Thanmog.

"Do not be pessimistic!" Dranmog muttered. "For long seasons we have fine-tuned our magic. Surely we can make a go of it? No creature is immortal. All the monsters can't have survived."

Thanmog tugged at his beard.

"It has been an age since the beasts have come down to ruin and pillage," Dranmog went on in his conniving voice. "Surely krakens must die sometime? Why do we not investigate the truth of the riddle? The guardians are likely piles of dust now—and yes, Anamog, I agree, the enchanted brooch of Olion may still exist in the plunder."

Dranmog and Thanmog turned to face their leader, awaiting his ruling, for his decision would be final. Eldest of the lot, Anamog stood pensive, frowning, with eyes narrowed and big black brows twitching, the weight of ages on his shoulders.

"We shall go, brother Dranmog," he sighed, "—as you suggest. But I sense no good to come of it." His voice betrayed his qualms. "It is a long and difficult trek to the Fiasma Hills. We will need a few moons to get there and back."

"That we shall," responded Dranmog promptly, and with more enthusiasm than his usual. "But there may be other items of interest for the finding. You heard the riddle: *That which is more precious than gold.* Is this not a glaringly obvious lure worth the chance?"

"Perhaps."

Dranmog scoffed. "What would we be as mages if we did not pursue our dreams?" His voice had gathered an echo of passion in its momentum as he edged closer to the old mage.

Anamog, who had grown wiser and more cautious in his years, demurred. He saw only too well his fellow's flawed plan. "Adventure is all good in moderate doses, Dranmog, but not on ill-planned impulse. In haste, a venture as this could be watchword for disaster." He looked deeply into his fellow mage's eyes; they were so full of hope, and an unbending striving he had seen far too often in others. Anamog hesitated. He saw a miniature version of himself from the past. In distant days he was Dranmog's mentor and had often wondered whether his pupil had chosen the right path . . . Ah, well, so was life. Dranmog, stripling acolyte who had shown great promise in the early thaumaturgical arts, was not grounded in restraint . . .

"Fate be it that your eyes wandered over that excerpt, Dranmog," he acceded wistfully. "Still, after all these seasons, it baffles me what strange paths our deeds lead us on to. The king shall not be pleased with our news."

"Bother the king!" laughed Dranmog. "Our monarch too often depends on us for strength. We are *Mages*—not petty politicians. Is it not time that dear old Pyrmog learned to rule on his own?"

"Calm your tongue," warned Anamog. He paused, considering. Clearly, he was assailed with some doubt. "Yet perhaps . . ." he mused. His mind was wandering in other regions. Why the sudden change in Dranmog? The mage was eager for discovery and plunder, no doubt— but what had infected his already zealous overconfidence these days?

The old mage chose his words with care, "For the nonce, we must help rule Mog—to keep peace and prosperity in the hands of the people. It is our duty—not the royalty's. Without us, the wisest of kings or queens would have turned to mischief and war as we have all seen many times. More than just mages we are—we are statesmen . . ."

Dranmog stared dumbly at his master. He had spoken with haste— yet he resented Anamog's sanctimony. Ambition was one thing, but he was no fool. Plans for future glory occupied his churning mind. He was a ship caught between two boiling waters. Anamog would be passing into his dotage . . . *yet he was still young.* And who would supersede the old master?

II : Ice Cave

Within the next moon, the last one of Harpy's fall, the three set off north—wrapped in billowy capes, skull caps and wolfskins. They were somber-faced, determined Mogels, trudging through the lands of the Never-ending Graves, and the ruins of Bosolnith, to the rugged ice crags at the far ends of the Oldenland. Over the bleak landscape they trudged, sleeping by day in quiet burrows or in crannies atop the high ridges. They traveled by night when the silver moon stained the lands with long lonely shadows of ghostly pallor. There were less things of evil in this territory, professed Anamog, yet it was his counsel that the three should travel undetected by folk or beast under mantle of wind and star. Thanmog and Dranmog could only agree, for they followed dutifully at Anamog's heels.

When the three had journeyed far north after a moon of trekking, they approached the legendary ice crags of Tormallon. By evening they saw a valley, pale, blue and dreamy with ice, where a frozen river lay, once running and gurgling free, now covered cold with ice and snow and strangely silent.

Dranmog gasped, pointing a quarter way up the hills. "There are holes up there! . . . caves, crevices—home of the krakens!"

"Indeed, there are," whispered Anamog under his frosty breath. "Do not be so eager to name them."

The three struggled along a faded line of snow drifts and surmounted the nearest of the hills. Here, abounded several curious, jagged openings into the ice and rock-crystal that they had spied from afar.

Quickly the explorers moved into the last of the twilight for it was getting cold, and already a chill wind bit their faces as a quarter moon bent its pale face in the sky, giving the valley an eerie luminescence.

The mages came at last to a great gaping hole thrice their combined heights. They guessed it was carved haphazardly into the mountainside by the wicked art of kraken talons. They peered cautiously inside and could see nothing but cinder black—not a glimmer of candlelight or a shimmer sparkling in their eyes.

Anamog flared up his torch, by means of his will and he stepped down into the dark, while his friends stepped after with less sureness and a glum wariness. The three peered into what seemed an endless, vaulting cave. Amazed at the sight, they craned necks, saw a high ceiling sparkling with green and blue jewels. The gems licked up Anamog's torchlight and seemed to effervesce stars.

A muffled cry escaped Dranmog's lips, "Only an unheard of magic could have carved this chamber!"

"Or an unheard of beast," said Thanmog.

Anamog muttered, "I don't doubt that there are still wary ears to detect our words. Sh!"

Dranmog rallied forward, in his characteristic haste.

Anamog touched his shoulder. "Careful, brother, we are in unknown territory. Do not forget the High Teachings."

Dranmog did not reply, nor did he lessen his pace.

Thanmog hissed: *"Careless fool! Let him race to his doom, not I."*

Anamog silenced his pettishness.

Many strange standing stones reeled drunkenly in the midst of the mysterious cavern. Anamog's torch flickered over them like a magic wand. Rows of rocks stood like menhirs, and they could see that they were blackened and scored as if a great battle had taken place here. In the murk-haunted distances, frayed ropes dangled from rocky overhangs on the walls. Cable bridges seemed long burnt. The shadows of pathways could be seen switch-backing crudely up the sheer cliffs, no doubt footpaths that linked the upper reaches with those below.

An ancient home of the great clan of ice gnomes? Dranmog was not convinced. He knew they lived almost ten thousand years ago, and it had once been a beautiful rock-ice palace with painted ceiling that rose richly with rare and precious gems quarried from the deep ways under the mountain. Pillars rose like towers up to greet the roof;

walkways and tunnels connected the frescoed antechambers and vaulted halls. Until the coming of the krakens, the cavern had likely deserved all its splendor, yet the krakens could smell the like of jewels and beautiful things hid from leagues away. It did not likely take long for a particularly cruel monster to discover that treasures under the ice were worth pillaging, while passing overhead.

"Look," Thanmog cried eagerly, "there are writings on these rocks." He knelt down, gesticulating, examined the intelligible script that ran down the side of one of the still-standing monuments.

Dranmog peered on and kicked at the charred rubble at his feet. "The standing stones look like ruined towers."

Anamog joined the two at a particularly large stone that was tilted on a steep angle. He struggled to decipher the writing. The petroglyphs were not so cryptic here that they eluded the old master's knowledge. His bloodless lips worked as he read. After a time, his face paled and he muttered in a low voice, bowing his skullish head, as he traced the line of ancient characters with his gnarled forefinger. "These are runes, yet . . ." His eyes widened in disquiet. "They are all too familiar."

"Speak!" cried Dranmog. "What is it?"

Anamog shook his head. "*Our heritage—our brothers.* The messages inscribed here were writ by our ancient brethren—the Fronza Ice Gnomes. I never imagined that their realm was so vast . . ." He trailed off, fixing eyes on the ceiling, letting them become one with the faraway shadows.

"What does it say?" cried Thanmog, exasperated.

"It recounts the old times, the changing times—when 'our kin were smitten and forced to move on'. A wind—an evil gale—rages from the sky in the form of a *demon.* It terrorizes our blood! We look to the heavens with hope—but instead we find only blue fire, ruin and death."

The old mage would read no further. A snuffle and a rasping gasp came from below like a long-crumpled bass horn.

The three scrambled to their feet, hearts beating like hammers. Clutching at their talismans, all heard a dreadful sliding fill their ears, an infernal creaking as if some iron snake were dragging its coils from a pit across the cavern ruins. The sound was soul-disturbing, old—reminiscent of a rusty memory. A monstrous shape had emerged from a shiny black archway and hung over them like a shadow of death. Thick pungent breath pinned the three to their places, exposing the intruders there like flags before a wind.

Their lips worked with spells too forced to combat the menace that now stalked toward them.

"Well, well!" came a rasping roar that seemed to rock the very chamber. "At long last—*fresh fodder!*"

The voice was hideous, booming. The mages looked up. Horror chilled their hearts as they spied a purplish mass duck under the darkness of the archway. It held a crocodile-snout, a hoary array of dirty teeth and a thousand membranous gums. The spine was curved, flecked outward like a dinosaur's, but the body was bloated like a bullsow's. Dranmog winced. In the distance he discerned a huge tail swirling in the darkness and disappearing into the cold murk like some sea-serpent. The member thrashed to and fro, kicking over standing stones like leaves in a storm. The boom of the rocks deafened their ears.

Thanmog wheezed out an oath.

"K-kraken!" Dranmog bayed.

The creature bellowed, "*Correct!* But what of it? I see that you are not accustomed to one such as I."

Anamog was astounded by the presence. That the beast could manage the common tongue was indeed a surprise. A sinking feeling welled in the pit of his stomach. He would not have guessed that one of the elder-beasts would still be living so close to the surface.

He cursed his raw foolishness to have ventured to this forsaken place. He gulped back his despair. To allow himself to be inveigled into this risky mission . . . It was pure foolishness!

"From whence have you come?" thundered the beast. "Why do you gape so rudely and stand like slack lilies?"

The mages did not reply.

At once the creature reared up indignantly on its hind legs. "Come! Do not be afraid of loosing your tongues—Mogels, you are, if I might guess. I alone reside here in this great hall under the Moon! The insect folk who toiled carving this place came to a hasty end—an end which I personally oversaw. The creatures were extremely tasty! And my appetite has increased over the ages—in ever larger masses."

"You have guessed correctly," Anamog conceded with as much calm as possible. "We are Mogels. You have a crisp memory, fair one, for one as old as yourself."

"Old?" The monster's voice grew baleful as it advanced a step closer to the old mage and he could feel its weight of ancient breath brush his face. "You do not know the meaning of old, little scarecrow! I have lived for three hundred centuries! I have seen and heard all that there is in this world. I was here when the Sea Lords rocked the oceans, when the fools divided the kingdoms into four. I was here when the faithless Valkorians came over the Emerald Sea and sought adventure and found only ruin—I was here when peace was upon the ocean and Queen Natalius had been crowned in her palace beneath emerald Aluntia. I was here when the burrower peoples fled and gave up their ice empire to their new master—*me!*" The kraken's gaze shone wickedly behind its sapphire eyes. Like the monster she was, she rose and flapped four beaten, writhen wings—however useless with the weight of the passing eons.

"Marvelous!" cried Anamog, clapping his hands in amazement. "Perhaps you could answer some questions then about gaps in my memory."

"Silence!" the creature bawled. "'Tis I who shall ask the questions. Now which one of you is to be the first?"

Dranmog grunted displeasure. "First for what?"

"Do not be so impious. To be eaten, of course!" the beast snapped.

Thanmog moaned, "Dear one, we only—"

"Before we are to die," interrupted Dranmog impulsively, "grant us one last wish! Show us the extent of the treasure of our ancestors."

The monster opened her maw in mirth and anger. All saw blue fangs and diamonds wedged in those fleshy gums. The chamber began to glow with an insidious eye-shine.

"Wishes! Wishes! Indeed I've heard them all," she snorted, "—as many as there are stars in the sky. What may your name be, overweening one?" The kraken thrust a massive head closer to Dranmog. Now she could get a better look at his features. "Know it that you address *Ucyglion*, Queen under the Ice. I am Queen where rivers run dead and things are turned to living stone!"

The monster's eerie lamplit eyes rained down harshly on the mage, exposing them all like beggars in a cruel prison. Yet her eyes were for Dranmog and Dranmog alone.

"I am high Mage of Mog," asserted Dranmog. "With my colleagues we tackled the wastes from Mog nigh two moons, only ready to explore the caves for treasure."

"Treasure?" mocked the monster. "Well, you are sated then, pilgrim." She drew in a sardonic breath and snorted out a waft of yellow steam from her crusty lidded nostrils. "Three mages, is it? Indeed this is a surprise. Three Mages of Mog. Never has the like ventured into my halls since an age and age, the time before the great quake."

"Nor would we expect it," replied Anamog adamantly. "Queen under the Snowy Lands, I am rather peeved that Dranmog would divulge so much of our habits as it is."

"You!" she bellowed, raising a thorny paw at Anamog, "shall call me Ucyglion—'Ucyglion the Terrible', as I was named by my ancestors. And as for your peevish colleague, the same—and why should I not comply with his last request? You see for yourself what my living quarters have become: rubbles of ruin and debris scorched by fiery storm. Come!—and foist no tricks. You have not yet seen all. There are many side passages in this warren that lead down under the mountain to many places that are dismal beyond imagination."

With the creak of her crusty bones, the creature slithered among the rubble and back deeper from where she had come.

The mages followed dutifully, keeping a goodly distance from the spiny barbs and hooks on the creature's dorsal. Anamog flashed his comrades a warning glance to oblige the beast, and attempt no arguments or sudden movements. To their astonishment they saw that the great hammer wrought at the tail's end was hardened black and tough as hide—no doubt the wicked weapon had received much use over the ages . . . but now . . . ?

Ucyglion came down out of the rubble and descended like a worm into the hollow of a passage where it was very cold and drafty. The mages followed, with Anamog leading with his torch. Rank airs came to their noses from side vaults: the acrid smells of rat dung and kraken, as if this were truly the dungeon-lair of some depraved beast.

How long had the creature resided in these quarters? Dranmog had no answer. He saw that the tunnel was carved of jagged rock and scored with countless holes of purposeful creation where blue ice had dripped down to crack the rock. Water had once oozed freely from the fissures and trickled into the pools below, but that had completely frozen over, and now grim torchlight caught the transparent ice and cast a sapphire glow. Up ahead the violet shine of the creature's eyes paved the way, through dim and distant corridors, and it seemed that the creature's attention was only for the mages.

Up in the narrow reaches, stalactites had been shorn by the creature's hide. Now the shards lay on the ground amid the parched bones of unfortunate creatures, crushed by hoofed paws. The party trod over them with wincing dismay. The tunnel had taken on many twists and turns and weaved past numerous side tunnels that led always down. No idea did the three have where they were going, or how they would find their way back.

Suddenly the group saw before them a vaulted arch with a smoothly polished mantle. A golden light poured out. The beast lifted its snout: "Here is my *hoard!*"

Many carvings of runes and pictographs were inscribed on an enclosure of pillars marching high up into the darkness. A dome painted of towers and carved stars greeted them: of lightning bolts and battlements; rows of script which they could not understand.

Above they could hear a flutter of birds or bats or more dreadful things. But most conspicuous of all was the treasure that lay heaped at the far end past a row of massive pillars. The jewels blazed like fire. The cold, ghastly closeness of this dreadful pit was sundered under the mountain.

The beast turned and sank onto its bed of treasure with a sigh of satisfaction. "Here I sleep—and here I have the dreams of empresses!" A great cloud of sulfur billowed from her nostrils, creating a whistling stench.

Dranmog flinched. There were no torches here; no need for it. The treasure shone like a rainbow, illuminating the creature in its entirety: huge, hideous, warted, with a bloated belly, under which lay a priceless treasure: every item imaginable: diamonds, rings, golden scepters, lamps, swords, bracelets, necklaces, helms, statues and figurines.

Thanmog uttered a gasp. "What a trove you have here, Ucyglion! You were not so truthful when you described your riches. Dranmog, the riddle speaks the truth."

The kraken snorted pridefully. "No riddle here! Behold the plunder of ages! The ransom of kings. You will naught see its like anywhere. From below the murky Gray Sea, from the islands where the giants' outposts lie on the wave-torn waters of the Emerald Sea. I flew over mountain and meadow with glowing eyes that would shame the royal gyrfalcons back to their eyries. I spied the most secret and hidden towers, which I hewed with my tail and ransomed their treasures. The proud folk soon learned why I was called *Sky Scather*. Far and wide I flew, feared by all, and sung about in hymns and poems with trepidation on their lips."

Anamog whispered in pretended awe, "So, you are even more powerful than I ever imagined, Ucyglion. There are verses written of 'Sky Scather', a leviathan, sung to this day by the Argosian knights, which delight courtiers and children alike."

"Children?" By this time Ucyglion the Terrible was growing tall in her skin indeed. Her memory dove back to the year 214 in Gwonalan when the world was young and she had pillaged Hunusped, the Valkorian town of Three Rivers, and watched in triumph as terror throbbed in the eyes of the townspeople.

She drew herself erect, rearing on her monstrous legs as if to let her horrid jowl bob up to the top of the cavern and boom out her familiar decree of dominion.

Dranmog who cared not for gold or diamonds had fixed his attention on things other than kraken trinkets. He was searching for talismans, and his eyes grew interested in anything that resembled a magic item. It did not take his Moglish eyes long to spy something moldered and forgotten lying in a tattered heap at the end of Ucyglion's unseemly mound. There was something special about the item, even from this distance, Dranmog saw. A sudden urge to snatch up the item gripped him. Why? He wanted to glut his eyes of its mysteries, its secrets!

"I say there, Ucyglion," he called out jauntily, "What's this book you are hiding?" He feared the object would be crushed under the beast's malodorous tail.

The monster hitched herself forward, dragging the volume into sight with a clumsy sweep of tail. She let loose a childish snort. "For a Mogel you have good eyes. I have been meaning to throw this wretched eyesore away. Only pretty things do I covet! Not things of antiquated must—like this book. Things of color and marvelous shape! By accident I snatched this curio up with a handful of jewels in a vault from the simpleton folk of Hunusped with their feeble forts by the seashore." She chuckled but quickly grew somber again. "What interest would you have in it—such a half-decayed tome?"

Anamog spoke quickly, hoping to deflect a perilous confrontation. "Dranmog speaks on whim only. See here, Ucyglion, I was thinking that this cavern, so wonderfully wrought, may have been the brainchild of a sorcerer I once read about."

Dranmog cared nothing for the like of caverns or old gnomish sorcerers and sought to steer the conversation back to the book. "What compelled you to keep this thing?"

She swung her eyes on him. "Why do you ask, you grinning ant? You're a cocksure one, aren't you? But I do remember the incident well: the Lord of that land at the time—was a certain Vascor of Valkoria—

sorely vexed at having his kingdom pillaged under my direction. He was like one of those sullen brats who had his favorite toy taken away from him. Nevertheless, I only wished to irritate him by taking it."

At the rustle of Thanmog's wolfskin, Ucyglion grew much incensed. "You'll have to do better than that, little mouse!" She let out a warning roar. "Tricks like sneaking up on me shall not work. You are in the presence of an artisan of stealth!"

Thanmog shrank back. Secretly, he'd been making signs under his coat, an attempt at rubbing his silver pendant with the warmth of an open palm, while muttering incantations under his breath.

Thanmog gulped back his terror. He had not banked on Ucyglion being so observant. Sibilances that would normally have tamed an ox or lulled a bloodhound into submission had no effect on Ucyglion. His enchantments were annoying at best to the kraken, and he blanched.

"I read your puny thoughts like raindrops in the sky, little tick! You bore me with them, you who thinks to lull me to sleep with a paltry spell invoked by a rubbing of silver! You have no love for silver or gold! The very idea appalls you. Come closer where I can see you."

Ucyglion curled up a withered fore-paw and leveled a scarred nail at Thanmog.

Thanmog backed away, frightened and empty of spell-weaving. His retreat only served to irk the beast. Quick as an adder she thrust out her fetid jowl and gobbled the stunned mage whole without even stopping to chew.

Anamog was wracked with sudden horror. The murder of his fellow was a shock too much to bear. Already his fellow was half mangled in the creature's maw and he raised a hand in a fit of anger. A gray powder he threw into the air. The kraken stopped its licking. The mage cried out a freakish incantation and a magical star-shimmering form suddenly burst in the chamber. Red fire singed the hairs on the beast's crown.

For a moment the monster was struck dumb. Ucyglion fell back roaring with wrath, shaking the cobwebs out of her crocodilish head and thrashing ineffectually at the loss of sight of her pain-ridden eyes.

All too well Anamog realized that the unpredictable evil of this creature would be his doom.

Now or never—they must all escape!

Dranmog did not turn to dart out of the kraken lair with Anamog as expected. He stumbled forth, stooping to grab the book while the beast was impaired, and he gazed at it with expectant rapture.

"Flee, you silly fool!" cried Anamog.

Dranmog did not leave the chamber right away. He tucked the object deep inside his cloak and Ucyglion gave a horrid scream and steam burst through her nostrils. The whole room was filled with clouds of churning gas. The floors cracked. The pillars toppled. Rocks smashed to the ground before thrashes of bone-hard tail. A horrible hammer tail slewed about, devastating both treasure and stone.

The behemoth was momentarily bested by the puny creatures, with her eyes temporarily blind. Searing fumes blasted out of her flaring nostrils. Just moments ago, she had mocked their titles and underestimated their guile, and now they seemed to have gained the upper hand. But her fury grew to crimson wrath, so deep to snap boulders deep beneath the cavern. A rumbling cascaded like mighty engines tumbling out of control. A deep fissure opened beneath the creature's feet. And it caught her off guard. The mighty kraken screeched, an angry tail windmilling . . .

But her ungainly bulk slipped and fell. And ever wider did the earth gape and yaw, and desperately she tried to claw her way up out of the widening pit, but she failed. Flapping withered wings . . . she tried to rise above the crumbling floor, but those wings were useless at this late hour and her forepaws only slipped another notch. The fissure spread like a pair of giant jaws.

The kraken was swallowed whole. Ucyglion fell, with a shrieking bellow, into the nethermost depths.

All the mages stood silent. They could hear the beast's last gasp. "*A curse on you, trespassers! On all your descendants and all your meddling magic. In this life and thereafter shall I curse you forever!*"

Whether or not old Ucyglion met her doom, was not known. For the mages fled back through the disintegrating tunnel. Anamog clutched his torch while Dranmog gripped his costly book like a zealous acolyte. Through the great cavern they stumbled and scrambled while rock crashed all around them with the furious abandon of a thousand harpies. Among the falling boulders they weaved like weasels, aiming themselves toward the far glimmer at the entrance portal. The dreadful crack of stones deafened their ears. But they forged on and managed to jump out of sight under the madness of that melee just in time to see the cavern pitching forward in a crazy rain of tumbling stone. The whole mountain seemed to be collapsing in a ton of ice and snow.

The two would have surely been buried alive if it had not been for Anamog's foresight. He had grabbed a chunk of ice at the last second. Ensorcelling it into the guise of a makeshift sled, they used it to grant passage down the snow-crusted valley.

The two fled on a sled of frozen crystal, down the side of the ice-slicked mountain whilst the snow and ice raged about them. Their momentum carried them up the other side and safely past the valley where they watched the old kraken mountain crumble to dust. The long lost civilization was no more.

III : The Book

In the long days that followed, Dranmog and Anamog plodded wearily back to Mog in the early moons of winter. They were cold and dispirited, bitten by fierce winds and lamenting the loss of their comrade, Thanmog.

Ever long shadows rolled drearily over the snowscape as they trekked on legs of wood.

Anamog spoke crisply to Dranmog, "Let us have a look at this wretched volume you thieved from the kraken's lair. An ill token to trade for Thanmog's life. Foolish of you to snatch it." Peering at its front cover, the old mage became instantly distraught and astounded to learn that the tome harbored no title and that its pages were faded and completely blank.

"What's this?"

Briefly, he flipped through the pages. He stared hard at the book, frowning from time to time. The blankness of the sheets disturbed him in a way that nothing could. For an instant he caught a brief glimpse of a picture . . . but only a flicker of imagination. The mage blinked. He scowled at Dranmog before handing back the book.

"Tricks, illusion! It seems you have a dud here. So! This is our token of trade for Thanmog's life?"

The words made Dranmog quiver. The thought of his peer sitting mulched in the belly of the kraken under a thousand tons of rock repulsed him. He bore the guilt stoically and dared not look at the old mage's eyes on the long march back.

* * *

A moon and some days passed. They arrived safely back in Mog where royal guards herded the two to the court. News was presented to the king who, curious of their quest, became aghast at the discovery of Thanmog's terrible demise. "Taelmere's Hells! The existence of the legendary kraken troubles me in the extreme!" He stood up from his gilded throne. "How many other horrid beasts are free now to roam the lands north of this kingdom?!"

"I cannot say, O king," replied Anamog gravely, "though Ucyglion claimed she was the last, but—"

"That is good to know—and that you brought this foul creature to justice! Who knows when such a monster will fly down again and raze our city?"

"Sire, it has not been for an age that one has come down from the ice wastes to discommode us," reassured Hanumog, the king's advisor.

A matron of the upper caste spoke ever wisely, "Nor should they, Hanumog! We were lucky enough that these meddling mages did not anger the creature to the point that it flew down to kill us all!" A series of excited expostulations flew from the mouths of the courtiers. Disdainful glances brushed the two Mages with shame and heat.

"Perhaps there are more beasts then," commented the king idly. "Who would rout out these wicked monsters?"

"Not us!" growled Dranmog. "We are mages—not kraken hunters."

"Silence your tongue, and speak not in such brazen tone to your king!" warned the king's advisor.

The king gestured indulgently. "Enough, Hanumog. We shall overlook this misdemeanor and speak more on this topic later. For now, why did you not bring back any of this 'royal treasure' that you claimed to have witnessed under the kraken's belly?"

Dranmog's eyes glowed and Anamog swiftly gave him a cautionary glance. "Sire, we were not in any situation to collect trinkets while our kraken was playing us for fools. We had only our lives to guard and our wits to aid us."

"Not even a bauble?" the king crowed in disbelief. "What of the recovery of the gold and silver? Was this not your primary goal?" Pyrmog's eyes narrowed.

"Of that there is no possibility, unless you fancy digging under a hundred tons of rock," responded Anamog airily.

Hanumog was not convinced of the mage's account and his mind grew ever suspicious of the too-convenient explanation. "Such a minatory beast must have an enormous hall, brother Anamog! Surely huge beyond reckoning, if the kraken lore was as prodigious as you claim? Why would the creature reside in such a small burrow skulking about, rather than live in the Great Hall of our ancestors?"

"Who is to know the ways of the krakens?" Anamog remarked frostily, and for the rest, he remained tight-lipped.

"Perhaps you could have located and secured this treasure for your own—a hoard that rightfully belongs to the kingdom and her citizens! You then concocted a yarn to cover up the fact!" accused Pyrmog. "Many times in the past it has been known for the mages to dissemble the truth and reveal only what is best to their advantage." Passion flew in the king's words and his conviction surfaced with clarity.

Dranmog's reply came as spiteful. "Why, O clever one, would we have foolishly bothered to mention the existence of any treasure then to disbelievers as yourselves?!"

Astonished cries rang through the court. It was unheard of for the king to be addressed in such an insolent tone. Had the king not raised his voice for royal order, bloodshed would have ensued. "Silence! Good Hanumog and brother Dranmog will arrest their arguments! We shall not abide squabbles in this court. Dranmog, you are out of order, yet you have my leave. Rest assured that you and your 'mentor' have both enacted a noble deed, though unconventional. You shall be rewarded for these services rendered and recognized as loyal subjects. But do not test me." Here his voice grew grave. "Pray for brother Thanmog that he might find peace in his resting place."

Gloomily, Anamog and Dranmog departed the hall and returned to their respective towers in the East Court to rest from their long trials. Both passed serious periods contemplating krakens and the lore of the elder beasts and the mysterious constructions of their past ancestors.

* * *

Another moon had passed and the mages held private council in Anamog's tower at the pinnacle of his obsidian keep. Only by articulating the proper spells could one gain passage to his study, which was further riddled with false entrances. Anamog vowed to keep the Book's existence secret from all, a burden that the old Master revealed grudgingly, and which caused his face to look worn and weary, something unlike him. The old mage warned his colleague to exercise caution with the Book, for it was an agent of woe. He had been reading up on kraken lore and was not thrilled with what he had discovered. *Krakens commanded powerful curses.*

During the long nights that followed, Dranmog and his master spoke rich words and brewed complex potions and talked of matters that they had not spoken of for years, such as when Dranmog was an apprentice learning the arts.

The days passed and the topics of krakens were slowly forgotten. The court settled into its regular routine: daily quibbles and politics.

No routine existed for Dranmog however. He spent many sleepless nights wandering up top his tower absorbed in disturbing thoughts. He had visions: of an undead Ucyglion roaming the depths of the earth until she could break free from her chasm and take revenge on those who had cast her into a nether-world.

Even he, in his blithe insouciance, shivered. A fortnight of such evil-tinged visions went on before Dranmog gathered enough mettle to face the Book again. It was not an effortless task, for he could not just open the pages and take lightly what he saw there. Swirling images he saw, of himself, in faraway places, faces also from a time long past—or was it the future? The young mage was not sure. It was like facing his worst fears, his most subtle demons, and his most vivid nightmares.

A serious obsession grew to a demanding addiction. Dranmog dug up all the lore he could find in the castle archives, but it told him little. The power of prophecy had been lost for generations. Why did he think the Book was a tome of magical riddles in the form of suggestive magic? Surely such a plain ordinary item with nothing of legible interest contained no secrets in its binding?

Well, he begged to differ. He could only attest to a fabulous hunch. On each of its pages, he saw faces continually changing. Why? At first glance, he saw only an old historical book, from cover to seam, but if he stared long enough, he began to discern bits of script so faded as to include the most fleeting truths. Something intelligible should be scrawled on its parchment—a line, a piece of text, a picture, a character—should it not?

Lengthy hours Dranmog passed, staring blearily at the pages. Finally something took form—something so indistinct as to be nonsensical, and yet shapes that had no order or symmetry: symbols of power, archetypes, fires, destruction, woe. The more Dranmog focused, the less he discerned, and the more frustrated he became. Finally, the pages became blurs of nothing. Dranmog, wincing, threw down the book in a fit of disgust.

He was forced to turn his attention to other mysteries. Why was the Book amid the treasures of the ancient kraken in the first place? He had been determined to pick it up even in the face of death. Why? It seemed to be his destiny. Musings like this blazed in his mind and gave him no peace.

Time wore on. Dranmog began to stare at the Book's ancient pages with red-eyed obsession—his vision was filled with strange images. He beheld a beach on fire, a gray grove, a darksome gloom of cloud and pale-yellow smoke. Another vision: a city, possessed of demons, possibly his own, cheated of a king and a crown and plunged into anarchy and despair.

The images caused Dranmog despair. Ridiculous! How could he—?—yet how could it—how was it possible to ignore such visions?

Sinister spells Dranmog caught glimpses of—conjurations of terror which he would have never conceived of himself. But then they vanished as quickly as they had appeared. Tantalizing snatches of thaumaturgy, more than enough to convince him that the Book was powerful, and that he was a pawn in a game of unguessable proportions. Until now his tests and researches had been fraught with disappointment. He had come to a dead end in deciphering the riddles.

Late one night a curious reference caught his eye: a passage written by a Moglish philosopher of the 2nd century. It was more a fairy tale than a riddle. Ah, poor fool, this dear Fehlmog. Perhaps it was a nonsensical extract. Yet he was ever obsessed with it and read it over hundreds of times:

> *"Two tomes, taken by the Lords of the Seas,*
> *Two kept in crystal towers,*
> *One was destined to pass into the world, shape it as it would,*
> *Promising neither right nor wrong, good nor evil,*
> *darkness nor light,*
> *But promise it had, for those who would look into its pages,*
> *And believe! . . ."*

Dranmog grew very excited by Fehlmog's excerpt, but at the same time, very frustrated. Nowhere could he proceed with this researches unless he cracked these riddles. The reference seemed to speak of profound things, but it was too vague to offer any clue as to the Book's secrets. The last line frightened Dranmog, for a reason he was all too chilled to admit.

Why was it that he could feel his heart ache, or feel a tremor of fear run through his bones when he gazed into the graying pages? Did he not wish to 'believe'?

Dranmog scoffed. Believe what? He tried to gaze at the book's pages for longer periods but his vision swam.

He decided to consult with brother Anamog and crept to the latter's forecourt. He became suddenly leery of the idea. His wish to accomplish things that Anamog had not, glared at him. He wanted to better his mentor—to succeed where the old man had failed. He was quite convinced that he was his superior—that this was his last chance!

Dranmog came finally to the foot of his master's tower and halted. For from high up in the observatory Anamog uttered a spell of unbinding and the gleaming portal admitted Dranmog into the misty interior.

In a candelabra-lit chamber the two discussed the Book. Each tried to understand its hidden power, but Dranmog, who had read up on lore of its making, was convinced that the secret lay in the last line of the stanza-riddle: *"Promise it had for those who would look into its pages and believe—"*

Anamog saw the obsession on his disciple's face and knew that the Book was no common ornament, or minor talisman. He very casually suggested that Dranmog entrust the Book into his keeping.

A look of horror passed over the young mage's face. He refused to even think of such an idea and almost violently yanked the book off the table. It was only the deepest degree of malice and spite for his senior that he exuded.

"Dranmog, listen to me!" cried Anamog passionately. "We must not use the Book for curiosity sake or look into its pages! We will become tainted—cursed by its fiendish power, made more potent by Ucyglion's last words!"

Dranmog sneered at the concept. "You, who would have left it in the dust, tell me to let it go? I risked my life to regain it, while you would have let it languish into ruin."

Anamog sighed. He realized it was not the Dranmog he knew speaking, but rather some caricature that had taken control of him.

The old mage remained silent. He let his eyes rover over his peer like soft beacons. "Dranmog, you are a great Mage, you know it, and and I know it. You have the potential to be an even greater one, but I ask you—what know you of the curse of the krakens?"

Dranmog grimaced contemptuously. "Curse of the krakens? What is this nonsense?"

"Ucyglion has corrupted us! Look! We are bickering like children. We are not even safeguarding the lands any more. We neither attend Pyrmog's court nor give counsel to the Mogels who are the ones who need us most. Ever since have returned from that accursed mountain our minds have not been our own. Recall! I have been laboring for some time on a counter-spell to Ucyglion's malediction, but I have found none. I know the taint is a curse, a hex stronger than we know. It shall devour us if we are not wise. It will grind us to dust if we are not steadfast! Do you hear me? Hand over the accursed thing! Right now!"

Dranmog almost committed an outrageous deed. The sneer forming on his face began to fade as a clear picture opened in his mind of what was to come. Was it the Book, or was it Anamog's blessing of compassion? Perhaps the latter. As the old Mage focused his will on the other's mind, slowly Dranmog's madness began to fade away. His angry grip loosened on the Book. With trembling hands, he gave it to the old Mogel, who jerked it slightly with a final tug, out of Dranmog's white-knuckled fingers.

All should have been well—but as the adage goes, once evil has worked its way into one's mind, there is no return.

So started the rift between Dranmog and Anamog. When Dranmog returned to his tower, his mind churned, and he could not easily dismiss the loss of the Book. It haunted his dreams! It filled his world with temptation. The thing's essence would not give him peace, until he discovered its secrets. Even worse, a growing resentment festered in his heart for his old master, the one who had taught him his first lessons on the lore of the great winds and the mystic rhythms of nature. 'Twas Dranmog who had found the Book! Why should the old man be its guardian, and learn of its secrets and not him? The old goat was full of hubris, locking it in his tower away from him like that, all the while unfolding its power in secret . . .

Such were Dranmog's spiteful meanderings—ungrateful, ruthless and agitated. One evening in Midsourn, he lurched up in his pallet and began to conjure means by which he would break into Anamog's tower and fuddle the gate's binding spell. He could elude the thief-traps and beguile certain ethereal watchers if he were clever enough. For a fact he meant to breach Anamog's stronghold and claim what was rightfully his. The treachery went deep enough that even Anamog failed to foresee the fateful consequences . . .

In his precaution, Anamog had hidden the book in his enchanted strongbox with a sense that the grief it had wrought upon Dranmog would percolate to others. He would not touch the tome himself until he had further researched the fact that it was marred, and seen Dranmog back to his normal self. The mage's probings only confirmed to him that the Book was not evil in itself, but rather a prophetic accessory—a vehicle for the kraken's curse, which had coincidentally tainted it.

On the night of the new moon Dranmog snuck down from his turret, armed with spells of unbinding, and he spake them upon Anamog's door. With a groaning shriek, the brass bound portal hurled itself ajar on its hinges. Up crept Dranmog, mounting the stairs like a stealthy panther, traversing the wide corridors with a murderer's tread, through darkness and crescents of cool moonlight playing from the small oval windows above.

He was before his master's chambers, holding his breath like a ferret. Then, he lit a small candle and approached Anamog's inner sanctum where the old mage was sleeping soundly on a pallet in a shadowy corner across from a notched, oaken table.

The Book was nowhere in sight. No great chance would he have of finding it.

Dranmog began moving about silently in search of his prize. But Anamog's ears were keener than Dranmog thought. He awoke—in the midst of a dream, imagining that a presence had come to rob him of the cursed ornament: which at the instant, was true—

"What are you doing?" the old mage snapped at Dranmog. He jerked up from his pallet, peering intently across the table. "'Tis not like you to come uninvited into my chamber." His tone was cross, as if he were speaking to a child.

"I wished to see that it was—*safe*," stammered the young mage.

"It is," growled Anamog. "So begone."

Dranmog did not budge. Anamog urged him with smiling calm: "You should go, Dranmog, but you needn't explain yourself—it is written all over your guilty, scheming face. Would you like to see it?"

"Yes!" Dranmog's eyes lit up.

"Then!" The old Mage stepped over to his magic cabinet and lifted the latch. His heart beat quicker for he knew that Dranmog's condition was far worse than he imagined. A dread that Ucyglion's curse had incubated, crossed the barrier from spectral to reality, frightened the old mage. Never would Dranmog have attempted such a breach of entry if it had not become this strong. "I believe this is what you desire, brother. But you cannot have it."

The words stung Dranmog like needles.

"You are clever to have bypassed my holding spell," remarked Anamog. "I'll give you that. Indeed, you have grown much in your training, but remember! You are still a fledgling—and I am the master."

Dranmog's eyes were now alight with loathing. For a time neither spoke and Dranmog barely contained his resentment. His hopes vanished at recovering his Book tonight, but he did not reveal his desires. "You are right, brother." A last glimmer of reason seemed to shine through the cloud of disappointment fogging his brain. "I hope you have forgiven my intrusion."

Anamog grunted. "This deed shall not go unpunished. Now go. As penance, you shall not come to my tower until the moon has thrice turned full. Any attempt will result in the wrath of my ethereal watchers!—which you had better not meet."

Dranmog bowed and left. He lay on his pallet, seething with animosity, plotting to undermine Anamog's mulish edicts.

Meanwhile the old mage lay on his own bed, thinking hard on Dranmog's transgressive act. A decision finally dawned. With a weary croak, he alighted and rallied his sire at dawn. "Pyrmog, you are a wise and just ruler. Understand that I must leave you for a time, and take this obsessive thing out of Dranmog's reach, where he will not find it. You may think me eccentric, but I fear for the safety of our kingdom."

The king sighed. "Never have I doubted your counsel, Anamog. Do what you must."

Promptly the mage fled with the Book, to where none knew—but with the intent to hide it from the world. Even as he took flight through the Graslian forests and the Sispli fens on bareback, he used his best magic to conceal him, biting back his misgiving, for he could sense awful things in motion.

When Dranmog discovered that Anamog had disappeared, he was fearfully enraged. He knew the talisman had gone with him and stormed to the king's chambers and demanded to know where his associate had vanished, but of his whereabouts Pyrmog would say naught. It irked Dranmog to be kept in the dark. He believed Anamog to have taken the Book to discover its power for his own in some secret place. Jealousy burned in his heart like a hornet's sting.

As the days crawled by, darker plots began to brew in Dranmog's head. If he could have seen himself—full of hate and loathing for his former teacher—he would have been shamed. Once he had loved Anamog like a father. He had forgotten the ominous visions in the Book, the smoking forest, the pale yellow gloom at the edge of the placid sea—all the Moglish soldiers marching on their own keep, sacking the city and riding with him eastward, southward, and eastward again.

Still, Dranmog may have saved himself had he been a more gifted visionary; but he wasn't.

The cocky mage was completely out of control, drowned under the spell of Ucyglion's curse. His eyes glazed over, glistening with outrage, his face burned a wraithlike mask of insect fury. The better part of him did not want to continue along this path of destruction, but he could not save himself. His lower lip quivered; his fingers hooked like claws.

He concocted spells from the Dryunian Tomes like one possessed—the same that Anamog had forbidden him or any ever to read.

He would hunt down his old master and slay him! Yes, there was no other way. He brewed an elixir which would blind the eyes, make one who sniffed its vapors believe the unreal. Upon the changing of the palace guard he crept unawares, ensorcelling the night watchmen with his brew. He repeated such skulduggery until he had acquired a miniature army at his disposal. As for the king, pah! What could that fop do? If he would not help him, he would give him doom. Through arts of trickery, Dranmog won the hearts of abundant Moglish warriors who were pliable; he convinced them that Pyrmog was mad, an ailing fool whose rule was a threat to their safety. With a cloud of darkness hovering over their shoulders, the Mogel host stalked the palace, grim-faced, bearing maces, axes, swords. The king raised his bodyguard, eighty strong, and there ensued a clash of such terrible arms and raging sprites and sorcerous elementals that Dranmog employed from the nether realms, that the very stone and pillars shook with grief. They overthrew Pyrmog and his retinue and laid ruin to Mog citadel. When the dreadful deed was over, they rode out of the city with a pale orange glow at their backs against a backdrop of smoke and ruin. So it was, that the first part of Dranmog's vision as seen through the pages of the Book had came to pass.

Over heath and hillock Dranmog pursued Anamog with his newfound allies. It was summer and only pale fingers of snow fringed the forests and plains. By fortuitous chance he tracked him down: far east, between the gray forest of the Wildtrack and the lonely strip of beach flanking the vast green sea. Fifty knights sat high on their wild-eyed mounts, pikes lowered upon a certain foe—a lonely Mogel clutching a book, who, back turned to the ensorcelled host, looked sadly upon the headland. It was leagues south where glittered the ancient jeweled spires of old Valkoria.

The dry leaves rustled and crackled underfoot. Leaves blown from glades which gleamed coolly under stars hidden on moonlit eves. So it was written that the final strife between the mages of Mog on the known edge of the world was to come to pass.

Dranmog flicked a livid finger. The Book was seized out of Anamog's hands by a ragged condor wheeling nearby, employed into Dranmog's dark service. The bird swooped low over the young mage's head and he snatched the prize out of the beast's talons.

"Give back the book, Dranmog!" cried Anamog hoarsely. He struggled up from the beach. The knights drew back in trepidation, fearing the old mage's spells.

"Dranmog, together we must learn its secrets," croaked Anamog. "Together! Without our combined efforts, the magic will fail—our race will perish. Do you wish that? I beg of you to reconsider!" His face burned with the glow of a thousand worried creases, his eyes were bleak, bloodshot and red, and he looked twenty years older.

Dranmog chortled. "And have you drunk its delights—siphoned its mysteries and magical sublimity? No, I think not, *master*!" His tone was derogatory. Anamog's teachings were pushed aside—as a cloud covers sunshine and splashes only lightning down on unsuspecting lands below.

"There will be folly to come of this ere the moon has risen!" bawled Anamog. "Fool! You know not what you do!"

"Listen to yourself, you old charlatan!" jeered Dranmog. He alighted from his unicorned mount and flapped an insolent hand. "Are you now one to play 'master' with me, second best your pupil? I wield the book now! 'Tis I who has 'The Sight'." He let its pages flip wantonly in the breeze.

"You are wrong, Dranmog! You have not completed *The Path*; you are not a High Mage. If you continue with this farce, you will be the worse for it and destroy all we have worked for!"

Dranmog raised his chin with cackling mirth. "What are you but an old geriatric, floundering with the same old antiquated slogans and spells? Bah! The days of herbs and healings are gone, old man! Now is the age of foresight, where power is rife, to be channeled and mastered by one as daring as me."

"Fool! You know not how to use such power—or have even an inkling how to control its nature. Do this, Dranmog, and you are dead. Power breeds evil if it is not carefully controlled. Was that not the first lesson I taught you from the Sisenian scrolls when you were but a novice? You have forgotten the power that blinds the eyes and steals discrimination! Come to your senses! You will regret your acts. In the end, the Book's magic only corrupts!"

Dranmog only snarled and thrust open a page of the book. "Look for yourself!"

At first Anamog didn't want to, but then the two both looked together—upon the Book's wondrous pages—and believed . . . They saw a crafty kraken gliding insolently through a cloud-capped sky, then tumbling down, through an abyss, black beyond black. Then they saw a once king, strangled, bloodied, torn, doom-ridden. Followed by a palace on fire . . .

For a second Dranmog hesitated as if remembering the strange doomed visions from months ago. Did he cause all that? He was suddenly smitten with odd remorse. He was fourteen seasons old and Anamog was patiently teaching him his letters, correcting his half-formed spells, ever patient, ever forbearing, when he would mispronounce a cantrap or allow his attention to innocently waver. A tear came to his eyes.

The memory abruptly vanished, and the sneer returned. Dranmog remounted his unicorn, shook the reins, turned to depart, leaving Anamog and his pleas foundering in the breeze.

"Very well," muttered Anamog gravely. "So it must be." He raised his arms over his head and closed his eyes. He uttered an unheard of spell under his breath. A horrible smoke began to brew in the forests. The immaculate snowy-white sand on the beach was covered with a loathsome rain of black cinder. Sparks flew about; the trees were caught in grinning flames of banshee fury and leaves crisped.

Dranmog's host halted before the blaze most uncertainly, hissing and trembling. The woods shuddered. Dranmog looked back with a dreamlike awe as the Book jolted out of his grasp and floated harmlessly through the haze back into Anamog's ageless hands. What spell was this? Had he not just placed a protection spell on the tome?

The old mage shut his eyes. He wiped his brow and gave the book a mighty toss. The thing rode on magical wings, dropping a mile out to sea.

Dranmog's cry was like the blare of a horn. He summoned his warriors to fetch the sinking talisman, but they could not, for their feet were half glued to the earth. The cruel truth was, that the host drowned then and there under the deadly weight of their armored costumes when he forced them by threat of his magic to plunge after the fabled book into the Emerald Sea.

Dranmog's rage knew no limits. The Book was out of his reach. His stallion reared and he rode it balefully down upon Anamog. Fingers crooked like stag's antlers; Dranmog smote his nemesis with forces unrecognizable.

Forbidden magic ripped through the air, forces that he had only recently secured, and Anamog stood dumbfounded, hardly believing that his pupil could command such demonic terror. But he summoned blue-order protections, guarding himself against Dranmog's onslaught, precautions that he hadn't taken in years. Even as he did so, he was seized by a great sadness that tore him shreds. He could barely fight—against one he had loved so much.

The two hacked and hewed at each other; spells and necromancy too terrible to name—green fire, romping discs, disembodied ghouls, chained sprites, sorcerous winds, demonic storms, circling bombs. In the swath of that hateful battle, the mages set the beach ablaze in crimson, so too did the peaceful trees of the Wildtrack's fringes catch in fire. Eventually the seashore's waters began to boil and Anamog and Dranmog destroyed each other completely. Ucyglion's curse was complete . . .

* * *

The Book sank to the bottom of the Emerald Sea. It caught in the jaws of a porpoise which conveyed the volume to an underwater cave on the buttressing shelf of a mysterious island called Quefar. Three leagues off the Valkorian coast, the Book lay silent in the plum-colored darkness for an age, protected from sun, wind and the grasping fingers of gnomes, giants and men.

The three mages of Mog passed out of memory, and then to dust, as of time out of mind.

As for the Book, it remained in the humble care of the Dolphins of Quefar Isle, that is, until the coming of the storm of *Asapan*... but that is another story...

ABOUT THE AUTHOR

Chris is a prolific author of fantasy, adventure, and science fiction. His writing spans many genres: heroic fantasy, sword and sorcery and speculative fiction.

OTHER SWORD AND SORCERY BOOKS
BY CHRIS TURNER:

ICARUS
WARLOCK
FLAME OF EROS
VALLEY OF THE GODS
LAND OF MAJA
DRAGONCLAW
THE RELIC HUNTER
FANTASTIC REALMS

https://innersky.ca/books/home

www.ingramcontent.com/pod-product-compliance
Lightning Source LLC
Chambersburg PA
CBHW020240030726
47499CB00001B/4